The Balance of Power
Trilogy

BRIAN RATHBONE

ISBN: 1-945465-07-7
ISBN-13: 978-1-945465-07-9

DEDICATION

For my family.

The
Godfist
N
W
E
S
Barrier reef
Pinook Valley
Marshlands
Plateau
Chinawpa Valley
Arghast Desert
Master House
Cold Caves
Harborton
Volker Farm
Old Lumber Mill
Pinook Harbor
Barrier reef

REGENT

<u>**Chapter 1**</u>

Wisdom is the reward for surviving our own stupidity.
--Wendel Volker

* * *

Run!

Instinct and compulsion drove Sinjin's lean, teenage body to greater speed, his shoulder-length, auburn hair streaming behind him. Running was the one thing he did well, and the landscape slid by in a blur punctuated by moments of perfect focus. Leaping over a protruding tree root, his eyes locked on another dark-robed figure moving within the trees. Startled, Sinjin lost his step and nearly went down, but through strength of will, he heeded his father's command and ran.

Faster. Run, Sinjin, run!

Ahead the trail turned sharply upward on a direct course to the top of a steep incline. An unfamiliar pain stabbed Sinjin's side, and he placed a hand over it, hoping it would make the cramp go away. It didn't. The Wood Run was designed to challenge even the best runners, and it succeeded in that, but Sinjin gritted his teeth and persevered. Sweat stung his eyes by the time he crested the steep hill. He wanted to stop and rest, to slow his labored breathing, but knew he could not; something was wrong. There should be no one in these woods, especially not shadowy figures in black hooded robes, and his father's mental commands reinforced his fears. It was unusual for Prios to speak with Sinjin over such distance, and Sinjin knew it must have required a great deal of energy and effort. It was equally unusual for Sinjin to be competing in the Spring Challenges, something that had been expressly forbidden.

Stop!

It took a moment for Sinjin to react to the abrupt command, and his momentum carried him forward. The air sang a sharp note, and a dark flash crossed the trail only a hand's width in front of Sinjin's unprotected abdomen. Thrown from his balance, he lost control of his limbs, and a loose rock turned his ankle. Using his next off-kilter step to hurl himself upward, he tucked and rolled, just as Uncle Chase had taught him. The air sang once again, and a slender bolt struck a nearby tree, giving Sinjin a clear view of the deadly implement. It was not like the thick, stubby bolts used to hunt game; this was delicate and precise and seemed a much more frightening weapon.

Cut the course! Turn left ahead!

More shadowy figures moved within the trees. Sinjin started to turn but caught sight of the next ribbon on his right. Tied around the trunk of an elm, it was the last of seven ribbons he needed to collect. Each was signed by Master Edling, and all were required as proof of staying on the Wood Run course. The thought of facing Master Edling and his father made Sinjin want to quit the race and get home, but he could win this race; he knew it. He'd allowed Durin to talk him into it because he'd secretly desired it. Things were not going to go well for him when he got home--if he got home--and he knew this might be his only chance to win. It wasn't the prize he sought; it was the chance to prove that he was good at something--the best, even. Youthful desire overwhelmed sense and his father's command, and Sinjin turned sharply to the right.

Barely slowing, he grabbed the long end of the slipknot and charged toward the clearing, but just as the lush grasses of the Challenge fields came into view, a dark-robed figure stepped onto the trail and raised his arms before him. Sinjin could not see what weapons threatened from within the folds of the overlong sleeves, but he felt the danger.

His blood froze and he nearly ran headlong into death's embrace, but his training was not so far from his mind. Without slowing, he ran up the trunk of a nearby oak and flipped himself backward over the stunned assassin. Using the longest stride he'd ever attempted, Sinjin propelled himself into the clearing. A roar erupted from the gathered crowd, and Sinjin knew he must be running a faster time than Hester had. All he had to do was finish the race to defeat a living legend. Bolstered by this thought and the sight of the exuberant crowd, Sinjin ran. His shoulders itched, almost expecting a bolt to strike and demanding he at least turn his head and look back, but the pain never came.

Durin stood at the head of the crowd, jumping, shouting, and pointing at the sand clocks.

Sinjin suppressed a smile. Then he lowered his head and poured all the energy he had left into a final sprint. At the finish line, he stuffed his seven ribbons into Master Edling's hands. The crowd erupted. Edling, who normally wore a haughty and sour look, could not keep the surprise from his face.

Get home. Now!

Sinjin barely heard his father's voice in his mind, and that worried him more than anything else. Durin's dumbstruck gaze followed Sinjin as he ran past, not even bothering to accept his prize. Sinjin just placed a hand on his aching side and kept moving.

Durin ran up alongside. "What are you doing? You won! You beat Hester's record! You have to stop and accept your prize. You're supposed to get a wreath of vespa and a kiss from Alissa. I can't wait until Kendra hears about this."

"My dad already knows," Sinjin said between sucking in breaths. He couldn't even think about Kendra; she was an unsolvable problem.

Durin's look was apologetic, as it often was, his expressive face and liquid-brown eyes almost comical. "I didn't think he would find out--at least not this soon. Sorry."

"And there are people trying to kill me."

"What? Really?" Durin asked, stumbling as he tried to keep up.

Sinjin just grunted and jogged north toward his home, and for once, Durin matched his pace.

* * *

By the varying light of five herald globes, Catrin hunched over a crumbling scroll, trying to unlock its secrets before time rendered it back into dust. Her translucent hair fell to one side, a constant reminder of the consequences of power. Four more herald globes rested in small iron pedestals, which currently held down the corners of the ancient vellum. Each globe cast its unique glow over the surface of the scroll accompanied by muted reflections from the polished stone table on which they rested. Catrin didn't notice the white and blue filaments that arched from her delicate fingers to the table.

She sighed and closed her eyes. Vast amounts of knowledge had been uncovered in the past decade, much as a result of the ancient cache Catrin herself had found at Ohmahold, but little had been deciphered and even less truly understood. So many of the things they found seemed meaningless and out of context. Each discovery brought more mystery than certainty. The scroll that currently held Catrin's interest discussed the principles and behaviors of energy. It had been found deep within Dragonhold.

That name still made Catrin shiver. She had proposed Volkerhold as the name of her keep, but the instant Chase had suggested Dragonhold, people latched on to it. Leave it to her cousin to come up with a name irresistible to most yet made Catrin very uncomfortable. She'd seen the true majesty of dragons, and it seemed an impossible name to live up to, especially since her relationship with Kyrien was in question. He was a free beast, and nothing bound him to her. After the war with the Zjhon, he had come to her once every year for eight years straight. For the past two years, though, he'd been absent.

For months Catrin had been trying to make contact with him, but he was distant, and what little communication they managed was garbled and only served to worry and confuse her. It disgusted her that deep down she also wanted more dragon ore. Kyrien was far more to her than just a source of the precious stone, but she was suffering without it. Working the stone into herald globes, though tedious, calmed her nerves and filled the hold's coffers. Truly, a visit from her dragon would do her good. With another sigh, she pushed the scroll aside, unable to achieve the level of focus needed for translation, and a sloppy translation would do her no good at all.

Other papers and scrolls awaited her attention, but she returned to one she'd read a dozen times before. It was from her cousin's husband--a man she had nearly married, a man who might have wished he'd married her instead of her acerbic cousin Lissa. While the letter was polite enough and the words themselves gave no real reason for alarm, the letter's presence alone was cause for concern, and Catrin couldn't help feeling that there was a cry for help hidden beneath the bare words. The messenger had refused to tell exactly how he had come into possession of the letter, but he had said that it hadn't come directly from Wolfhold or Ravenhold, and he had no way to guarantee its providence.

Once again, Catrin's thoughts wandered to Thorakis the Builder, the man said to have saved the Greatland from starvation by building massive fisheries. Much of Jharmin's letter told of Thorakis's achievements, including a huge network of man-made rivers within walls of stone. It was almost too much to believe, and though Jharmin spoke well of Thorakis, there was something else, but Millie's sudden arrival and the worried look on her face brought Catrin to her feet.

"Come quick," Millie said as she pulled Catrin from the room, her breathing heavy. "It's Prios, m'lady, he's taken ill."

"Where?"

"In the viewing chamber, m'lady."

Catrin charged ahead, her lithe form moving easily, leaving Millie to shuffle along behind her, the older and heavier woman's joints allowing for only so much speed.

Though Prios was Catrin's first concern, she also worried that this would cause undo anxiety over the safety of the as of yet untested viewing chambers. Catrin knew the perils of improper astral travel, but she also knew the chambers would be safe. Still, she felt like less of a person for having those thoughts. Any right-minded person would be thinking of her spouse.

When Catrin turned the corner, she found Prios supine on the rough stone floor of the first viewing chamber, his head in Brother Vaughn's lap. Though he was breathing, his pale complexion and trembling hands troubled Catrin. Even in his current state, he looked beautiful to her. The kindness in his eyes offset the hard lines of his regal visage. Even staring into empty air, his expression was locked into a look of compassion.

Seeing her dragon ore carving, Koe, lying beside him, chalky and depleted, Catrin was shocked. Even in its most inert state, the carving had an imposing feline form. Koe had been fully charged, glossy and slick, and had been resting in their bedchamber. Prios would not have taken the carving without very good reason; he knew how important it was to her.

She'd never been able to carve another like piece; no other dragon ore had ever revealed its true form to her. A sick feeling clutched Catrin's gut, and she asked, "Where's Sinjin?"

Brother Vaughn, his long gray hair pulled back into a braid, looked up with an apology in his eyes. "Prios charged in here, saying he had a bad feeling about Sinjin and that he needed to use the viewing chamber. I tried to stop him, but he just stared out the opening and fell to the floor. He'll be back. I just know it. He's strong."

Catrin slapped Prios hard across the face. Millie sucked air through her teeth, but Catrin knew he would feel only the most intense sensations while out of his body. Shouting in his ear, just as Mother Gwendolin had once done for her, Catrin told him he was going to die. She scanned the painful memories, hoping to recall something that would help save Prios. Without the grounding effect provided by the chairs of stone and metal, he would have nothing to guide him back to his body. He would be lost.

Lost.

Whether the thought came from Prios or from Catrin's subconscious, the effect was the same, and it drove Catrin to reckless action. Without the aid of the stone chairs to anchor her or the monks' chanting to shake loose her spirit, Catrin gazed out of the viewing portal, pulled deeply on the energy around her, and wrenched her soul free from its mortal trappings. Though she left most of her physical senses behind, she did not miss Millie gasping, "By the Gods! She's gone too. It's like they're trying to kill me!"

Unlike Catrin's previous experiences with astral travel, movement was anything but effortless. Just staying whole required most of her concentration. The world seemed to pull at her spirit from a thousand directions, slowly tearing her apart. What movement she did manage was clumsy and out of control, but her son's life and that of her husband were at stake, and nothing would deter her. Driven by a mother's instinct, her spirit flowed down the Pinook Valley, over Edling's Wall, and into the lands that had once been her home. An almost irresistible urge to visit what had been her family's farm tugged at her. Painful memories rose unbidden, the dull ache of loss all too familiar. With extreme mental effort, she focused her energy and thrust those feelings aside. Nothing mattered more than finding Sinjin and Prios.

The world moved wildly beneath her, bucking and lurching as she cast out her senses, searching for familiar patterns of energy.

Go back.

Catrin barely heard Prios in her mind, but his words struck like thunder. She could feel his pain and the effort it had taken to communicate with her. His essence was nearly depleted, and someone interfered with his attempts to return to his body. Feeling helpless, Catrin reeled with fury. Never before had she tried to influence the world around her when traveling outside her body; always before she had been but an observer. Now though, she sensed an enemy approaching her son and another slowly killing her husband.

Dark energies swirled around her as Sinjin and Durin half limped and half jogged into view. The pain in Sinjin's eyes made it clear that he was in no condition to outrun anyone. The darkness coalesced into two figures that materialized as if made from nothing but shadow.

Durin saw them first and shouted, "Run!"

"I can't," Sinjin said, but he picked up his pace as much as he could. It would do no good. Both assassins raised their arms and aimed at Sinjin.

Though they could not hear her, Catrin screamed and thrust herself into the face of one of the men, feeling for his eyes with her energy. A sound like a sizzling pop split the air, and the assassin fell to the ground, screaming and clutching his still-hooded face. The second assassin seemed frozen in time, yet Catrin watched in silent horror as a slender bolt sliced the air on its way to Sinjin's heart. Leaves rustled as what felt like a tornadic wind rushed past Catrin, and she recognized Prios's spirit. Emotion overwhelmed her as she watched him alter the flight path of the bolt so it soared harmlessly over Sinjin's shoulder. A moment later a wall of malicious intent slammed into her like a wave of fire and nausea. Catrin struggled to hold herself together as her unidentified adversary tried to help the world tear her spirit apart. Everything turned a shade darker, and Catrin knew she would soon succumb. As the assassin aimed once again, she made one last desperate attempt to communicate with Sinjin: *"Run!"*

* * *

Never before had Sinjin heard his mother's voice in his mind, and the sound of it terrified him. It felt as if those words might be her last. Screaming, he ducked under the next bolt loosed by the assassin. Behind him he heard a wet *thunk* and a grunt. Turning to look, he saw Durin drop to one knee, his face pale and drawn. Anger welled up in Sinjin and would not be denied. Howling, he turned and ran toward the assassin, who seemed surprised and momentarily stunned. Using what Uncle Chase had taught him, Sinjin coiled his muscles and focused his core strength to launch his attack. He struck with more force than he could naturally muster, and he felt tingling hands assisting him and reinforcing his strike. The assassin went down and did not rise.

With a lump in his throat, Sinjin turned to Durin, who was now on his side, one leg trapped beneath his body at an awkward angle. It looked to Sinjin as if he were already dead. Tears filled his eyes, but he forced them back. When he pulled Durin from the ground and wrestled his limp body over one shoulder, the boy moaned and Sinjin risked a moment of hope--it was a brief moment. The assassin, too, moaned, and Sinjin moved off as fast as he could while carrying Durin. Once again his shoulders itched, waiting for the next deadly bolt to strike. He nearly dropped Durin at the sound of a snapping branch, but it was Uncle Chase and five of his best men who approached.

Chase rushed forward when he saw the boys and charged past them, looking for their assailants, his soldier's body rippling with intent. Sinjin turned to watch his uncle go, terrified by Chase's deadly charge but also by the thought of losing him. The valley behind was now empty, though, and nothing of the two assassins remained. It was as if they had been taken by the wind. Only the still form of Durin and the deadly bolt protruding from his shoulder gave evidence that they had ever existed.

"What happened?" Chase asked. "Never mind. It doesn't matter. We need to get you back to Dragonhold. Bradley, Simms, you carry Durin. Jorge and Morif, grab Sinjin." Words of protest were cut short as Sinjin suddenly found himself slung over the shoulders of two men who immediately began to run. The desire to run on his own two legs was nearly overwhelming, despite knowing his energy was already spent.

Chapter 2

The power of words, used with artfulness and skill, can be immeasurable.
--Surry the Minstrel

* * *

"You should all be ashamed of yourselves," Millie said as she walked among the beds in the now overfull infirmary. The tears that gathered in her eyes seemed to anger her further. "When you are all well enough to hear me, you can be certain I'll tell you what I *really* think. I most certainly will. Selfish and thoughtless, not to mention plain stupid. Did I mention stupid? No respect for a fragile, old heart such as mine."

Her footsteps echoed off the cold stone walls.

Sinjin waited until Millie thundered from the room before raising his head. He alone was unscathed after the events of the previous day. Fault was his alone to bear, yet those he loved had paid the price for his impetuous and selfish decisions. Millie was right; he truly was detestable. Tears threatened to fall from his eyes as well, and his chin quivered. Durin groaned, causing Sinjin to leap; it was the first Durin had stirred since Brother Vaughn had administered a series of poultices. Each one had seemed to pull some of the poison from the boy's body, but no one knew if it would be enough.

"Durin," Sinjin whispered. "Can you hear me? Wake up. Don't make me beat you into consciousness."

Durin's eyes did not open, but one side of his mouth twitched and turned upward. It lasted only a moment; then he was gone again. Sinjin's parents were faring no better, and the room began to close in on him, forcing him to accept the guilt and responsibility. Part of him wanted to run until he could run no more, to escape from the horror of having killed his parents and his best friend. What kind of monster would do such a thing? He'd risked everything on a silly race. He'd won the race and lost everything else.

Returning in a rustle of skirts, Millie entered the room looking pale, and she leaned on the rough-hewn walls. "Master Edling is within Dragonhold," she gasped between breaths.

Sinjin's head snapped up. Master Edling had never entered Dragonhold, and not since the erection of the wall bearing his name had he come north of it. It wasn't until recently that anyone could cross the wall. As a result of the Pinook Treaty, a gate had been built and limited trade established. Looking at the still forms of his parents, a chill clutched his bowels. This was no time to show weakness. Sinjin was not weak minded or completely unprepared. "Tell him my parents are involved in matters that cannot wait and will occupy them until after nightfall."

"Edling and his gaggle of fools are not here to see your parents," Millie said with a look that Sinjin knew all too well. "They're here looking for another fool, one that seems to have won a race, I believe."

* * *

Standing as rigid as stone, Sinjin allowed Millie to dab powder around his eyes.

"We can't have them thinking you've been crying," she said. "Now look at me. Your eyes are as red as roses. But I can't fix that."

That did little to bolster Sinjin's failing confidence as he walked to Dragonhold's main entrance. What had once been a jagged gash in the stone wall had been carved into a broad entranceway. The inner gates, which had been constructed using whole tree trunks, stood open, showing the cloudless sky beyond. Within stood Master Edling and his party, which was dwarfed by the massive scale of the ancient hall. Delicately curved pillars the size of greatoaks extended high into the darkness, leaving the ceiling of the chamber hidden from view. Some said the place was named Dragonhold because dragons could fly within the hold; others said an ancient dragon lived in the darkest depths of the mountain fortress. Sinjin knew he could use the majesty of his home to his advantage.

"Master Edling," he said with a bow that was little more than a nod. He could almost feel Millie's pride as he had shown just enough respect to offset the insult. Again, he could sense Millie's approval as he let the silence hang between them. Someone less trained might have launched into apologies or explanations or excuses, but Sinjin knew better; Millie and Uncle Chase had seen to that.

"Lord Volker," Master Edling said after an uncomfortable silence. "I had hoped your parents would accompany you. I was so looking forward to congratulating them on raising such a fine and strong young man--not to mention fast. Hester was none too pleased that you broke his record, I can assure you that! I don't believe I'd buy any butter or cheese from Hester if I were you," Edling finished with a condescending smile and a too-deep bow.

Sinjin, again, said nothing. Those behind Master Edling shuffled their feet and fidgeted, perhaps uncomfortable on Edling's behalf.

Master Edling coughed. "Yes . . . as I was saying . . . you left without claiming your prize. The Spring Challenges and Summer Games are based on tradition, and some traditions simply must not be broken, for the sake of continuity. It is for that reason that we have come to you. I present you this wreath as a sign of your victory. Let your countrymen know that your right to the title Champion has been duly earned and cannot be taken away."

Sinjin accepted the wreath, knowing Edling had other, less honorable reasons for coming to Dragonhold, such as assessing his enemies' hold in person.

Alissa stepped forward and Sinjin was utterly unprepared for her kiss. He had expected a quick peck, but she grabbed the back of his neck and kissed him deeply. Sinjin took a step back, and she moved with him, as if she'd forgotten anyone else was present. When finally she allowed Sinjin to pull free, there was a look in her eyes that made Sinjin feel like a doe before a mountain cat. His skin flushed and his face reddened nearly as deeply as Alissa's father's as the man ushered her to the back of Edling's party.

Sinjin flushed even further when he looked into the gathered crowd to see Kendra Ironfist looking like a storm cloud--her face flushed, her eyes afire. Despite it all, Sinjin had to admit that she was beautiful, though he'd never admit it to her. Too many times she'd caused him trouble. Still, her long brown hair softened the scowl on her face, and there was a certain twinkle in her glare. Sinjin's current circumstances once again demanded his attention as another strained silence hung over the hall.

"Thank you all for coming here to present me with this prize," Sinjin finally said. His face still burned and a tremble crept into his voice, but he kept from showing his fear. "If you will excuse me, there are matters that require my attention."

"I had hoped for at least a brief tour," Master Edling said. His eyes took in the details as he scanned the great hall. The tile mosaic floor had been returned to its original glory, and the ancient suits of armor that lined the walls gleamed under a patina ages in the making. Ornate entranceways led to halls shrouded in shadow, and Sinjin guessed that Master Edling must dearly wish to know what lay beyond.

"Perhaps another time, Master Edling."

A long silence allowed the tension to rise as Master Edling attempted to silently compel Sinjin.

"Perhaps you could have your steward contact me, and we can arrange for a proper tour," Millie said from behind Sinjin, who gave no indication that he would speak again.

"Uh, yes. I suppose that would be best."

Sinjin knew it would be a long climb back down the wooden stairs that led to the valley floor below and that it would most likely be dark by the time Master Edling's party reached the bottom. Insulting Master Edling was a risky thing to do, and Sinjin was in no mood for taking more risks, but he definitely didn't want Master Edling to know that his parents were incapacitated. If Edling wanted to launch an attack on Dragonhold, this would certainly be the time to do it.

Edling left without another word, his party hurrying in his wake.

"If I weren't so angry with you, I do believe I'd be right proud about now," Millie said.

Sinjin turned to see her smiling, and the weight on his soul was just a little lighter. "Thanks, Millie. I'm sorry about all the trouble I caused."

"I don't suppose you'll be making that mistake again, now will you?"

"No, ma'am."

"It wasn't all your fault, now. There're darker forces at work here, and you've just got to be more careful. If they were to have killed you . . . why, I don't know what I'd have done." There was a catch in her voice.

"Yes, ma'am."

"Now you run to the kitchens and get something in your belly. Can't have you falling over too."

Sinjin's stomach agreed with Millie, and he jogged toward the kitchens. Leaving the cool air behind, he descended to the great forge. Rhythmic ringing echoed through the tunnels of stone, and the heat of the central fire radiated from the heart of Dragonhold. Here, all those who needed fire could do their work. Sinjin glanced into the smithy on his way by and could see Strom's muscular form glistening in the orange glow of hot metal. He was not a lumbering brute of a man, but he was lean and powerful, the cut of his muscles making him look like a living sculpture. His hammer blows set the cadence for the chorus of the forge. In the adjacent chamber, Osbourne and Milo worked glass into wondrous forms. As he peered in, he could see them putting the final touches on a glass dragon made in Kyrien's image, an image that was becoming ever more popular despite his long absence--or perhaps because of it. Sinjin pulled his gaze away as thoughts of Kyrien led to thoughts of his mother and father.

The smell of baking bread overtook the earthy fragrance of the smithy and smelting room, and more savory aromas drifted in from the kitchens. Sinjin charged past the bakery and slowed to a respectful speed when he reached the main kitchen. He couldn't count the number of times Miss Mariss had told him to slow down in her kitchens, and as he'd gotten older, he'd begun listening to her--most of the time. Several smacks on the back of the head with a wooden spoon had helped motivate him.

When he entered, an unnatural silence greeted him. The kitchens were a place of noise and constant activity, but everyone in the keep knew what had happened the day before, and the cooks silently waited to see what he would say.

Miss Mariss had been fanning herself near one of the precious few ventilation shafts, seeming reluctant to come talk to Sinjin. "I'll never get used to this heat," she complained, as she had many times before. "The kitchen in my inn is always hot, but you can walk outside and escape it for a bit. Here you just cook along with the meat! Do those men really need that much heat to forge metal and make glass?"

Sinjin walked alongside Miss Mariss as she talked. Absently she grabbed a wooden bowl and a slate. Into the bowl went red sausage, smoked bacon, salt-cured ham, eggs, and walnuts, Sinjin's and Prios's favorite breakfast. Onto the slate went a small loaf of dark bread that had been cut open and stuffed with soft cheese and honey.

"Go," Miss Mariss said, not giving herself or anyone else the chance to ask him questions she knew he did not want to answer.

Sinjin left without looking anyone else in the eye, but when he turned the corner, he literally ran into the last person in the world he wanted to see. Kendra looked down at the honey that now stained her smock, which was snug and seemed to demand that Sinjin stare at it, and she cast Sinjin one of her least pleasant looks. "You oaf!"

"Kendra! You apologize this instant!" ordered Kendra's mother, Khenna.

"It was my fault. I wasn't looking," Sinjin said, and he tried to slide by both of them, but Khenna blocked his path.

"This won't do. Kendra, say you're sorry."

"I won't because I'm not sorry. He thinks he's better than everyone else and he's not!"

"Forgive her, Lord Volker," Khenna said, causing a flush of a different sort to run over Sinjin's face. He hated to be called "Lord Volker," especially now. And Kendra was the last person he wanted to hear someone call him that.

"If he's a lord, then I'm a horse's--"

Kendra's words were cut short, and Sinjin did not look back. The less he did to provoke Kendra, the better. It was not that he feared her, but a battle with her was one he could not win; this he knew from experience. Khenna was a trained fighter, and Kendra had proven a quick study. She challenged his authority at every opportunity, and one time he let his temper get the better of him. "Go back to your momma's skirts," he'd told her. It was a stupid thing to say. She hadn't even waited for him to finish the sentence before spinning on one leg and landing a kick on his jaw. That was all it had taken. After he'd regained consciousness, his mother had scolded him for fighting with girls. Confrontation with Kendra was best avoided.

"Some champion," Kendra said as Sinjin retreated.

Watching his food grow colder, Sinjin quickened his step. It was then that he realized there was nowhere he wanted to eat. Normally he would eat with Durin's family since his mother usually ate in her workroom and his father often ate by walking through the kitchens and grabbing whatever attracted him--a habit that drove Miss Mariss to distraction. Sinjin remembered the pain in Durin's parents' eyes when the news of his friend's condition had been delivered, and he could not face that pain again, especially not when it was his fault. As he neared the barracks, he considered eating with the guards, but the heated shouts from within the barracks caused him to keep going. It seemed the entire hold was in turmoil as a result of his thoughtlessness. As he neared the halls where he and Durin had played as children, he remembered a nearly dark alcove where they used to hide; perhaps he'd not completely outgrown the spot.

Behind the statue of some ancient king, Sinjin crouched. Beside him a glowing rune chased the darkness. Carved into the stone were delicate yet cavernous sigils. The narrow, fine lines cut deep enough to allow light from the central fire to shine through. The sigils had caused quite a stir after the lighting of the great hearth. When they began to glow, people feared some ancient magic had awakened. Sinjin thought that perhaps it had.

Putting his slate over the rune, Sinjin let the warm air reheat his now cold food. Most now agreed that the runes were the ancients' way of distributing warmth to the entire hold from the central fire, but some still held on to the belief that the runes were magical.

"Haven't seen him," a voice said in the distance, and Sinjin heard footsteps approaching. He pulled his knees to his chest and waited for them to pass. The pain in his chest had become unbearable, and he did not want to be found. He was afraid he would be unable to find his voice.

"How are they?"

"Not good," Sinjin's uncle Chase said, and Sinjin pulled his knees tighter, trying to will himself out of existence. It was all his fault.

"Do you know what happened?" the voice Sinjin could not quite place asked quietly.

"No, not really." Chase hesitated. "Our best guess is that someone is interfering with their return. They've both traveled before, and I think they would have found their way back unless someone hampered them, as Prios once did to Catrin."

Sinjin's heart beat fast. He was sure they would hear his quickened breathing. How would he explain his eavesdropping, especially now that they were discussing things that were normally kept hidden from him? Their family history was not entirely unknown to him, but certain details were never discussed in his presence.

"What can we do to help?"

"Keep your eyes open for Sinjin and hope for the best, I suppose," Chase said. The pain in his voice brought Sinjin to tears. Guilt stabbed at him, but he remained silent.

"Our prayers are with you."

The footsteps faded into the distance, and Sinjin knew he needed to get back to the infirmary. A whiff of his now warm food made his stomach growl, but he froze in fear as a shadow detached itself from a nearby alcove and moved along the hallway slowly as if afraid to be seen. Sinjin willed his stomach to silence as the figure melted back into the shadows. Afraid to move, Sinjin waited in terrified silence.

* * *

Chase paced the polished granite floors of the war room, waiting for the rest to arrive. With consensus unachievable, the tension at these meetings had been growing for months, and the present crisis stood only to exacerbate the situation. With a deep sigh, he looked up. Around a table hewn from the very rock that surrounded him, oppressing him, sat three of the five people he expected. Two chairs would remain empty, a fact that haunted all of them. The chairs had been a gift from Jharmin Kyte, the husband of Catrin's cousin. It was said that Lady Lissa broke every vase within Wolfhold when she found out. The chairs themselves were a marvel. Carvings of dragons wrapped around the arms and legs. Gilded threads woven by the hands of a master graced stiff cushions, which Chase thought were far nicer to look at than to sit upon.

Strom sat, tracing the designs on the outer edge of the table with his fingertips. The construction of this place had baffled him from the first time he'd entered it, and Chase could see his mind working, trying to figure out just how the ancients had done it.

Brother Vaughn and his wife, Mirta, huddled in quiet conversation, discussing the condition of Catrin and Prios. Chase couldn't keep from listening, and he did his best not to despair. When Martik and Miss Mariss arrived, he nearly snapped at them, but the platters of food they carried greatly improved his mood.

"If Catrin were here," Miss Mariss said, "she'd grumble that none of this food was grown within Dragonhold, so I'll do it for her. 'We need to grow more food within the hold. We must be self-sufficient, or all we've done will be for naught.' Now eat up." There was a catch in her voice, and the food was consumed in relative silence.

When the trays were empty, the silence remained. Finally, Chase cleared his throat. "I know we all wish Catrin and Prios were here, so let's just get on with the usual business, and then we can talk about what, if anything, can be done to help them. Agreed?"

All those assembled nodded.

"The guards are in order and are on high alert. I have men looking for Sinjin, and once we find him, we'll be keeping a closer watch on him. I shouldn't have let him out of my sight, and I won't make that mistake again. As for the finances, things are as grim as ever. I'm not sure how much longer we can keep paying the number of men required to protect us. That's my report."

"The smithy is fully operational, but we need more ore. As I've said before, we either need to start new mines or reopen some of the old mines. All the good mines are south of the wall, and Edling will just raise the prices and drain our coffers. If we create new mines as extensions of the keep, then we might be able to create additional open areas for some sort of agriculture."

"With the number of herald globes it would take to provide enough light to grow anything," Brother Vaughn said, "we could sell the globes and import our food supplies."

"There's still the possibility of growing mushrooms in the dark," Miss Mariss interrupted. "Then we only need light to harvest them."

"Even if we can grow enough mushrooms to feed the hold, we can't live off mushrooms alone," Martik added.

"Can we at least agree that we should invest more time working on mushroom farming methods?" Chase asked with an edge to his voice.

The others nodded.

"On a positive note," Mirta interjected, "our herb- and flower-drying efforts have provided enough medicinal herbs and spices to last at least three winters. Our stockpiles of nuts and dried fruits are also enough to last several seasons with proper rationing."

Chase tried not to frown, knowing even that success would not satisfy Catrin. If the hold were ever to be truly self-sufficient, they would need to find ways to satisfy all of their needs from within the hold. While Chase understood her motivations, every passing day made it more difficult to convince people that the hold needed to be self-sufficient. A warming weather trend had brought bountiful harvests, and the populations north and south of the wall were growing rapidly. The darkness of Catrin's visions seemed worlds away, and there were few people who believed they would ever need the protection Catrin so desperately sought to prepare. These thoughts weren't new, and he'd yet to find a solution, so Chase set his jaw and committed himself to simply making forward progress.

"The fishery remains healthy, and we've found a kind of pond moss that grows well in low light. Berman Ross found it in a cave down south, and since we've introduced it to the waters, it has flourished. We may be able to create a sustainable fishery yet."

This effort at least was one that everyone was behind. If the subterranean lake now known as the God's Eye could prove a reliable source for food and fresh water, then it truly would be a gift from the gods.

"How about your efforts, Brother Vaughn?" Chase asked. "Have you found anything new?"

"Not much, I'm afraid. I've found more references that confirm the keep once had fresh water running throughout, but I can find nothing to indicate the source. The basins and channels throughout the hold make it obvious that water once flowed, but what needs to be done to make it flow once again is a complete mystery. This whole keep is enough to relieve a man of his wits. Hidden chambers, hallways that go nowhere, strange runes that seem impossible to re-create--truly the ancients knew a great many things we do not."

"Perhaps we should consider sending another envoy to meet with Thorakis," Miss Mariss said.

"We've already sent two envoys, and neither has returned. I think we've already received our answer," Chase said then took a deep breath, preparing himself for Miss Mariss's reaction to that statement.

"I wish I knew what happened to those men!" she blurted, surprising Chase, who suddenly found himself coughing. "If they're on the Greatland getting fat and leaving us to our fate, why I'll . . ." Miss Mariss continued under her breath, but her words were not meant or fit for the ears of others.

Chase shared her frustration. Since the end of what was now called the Herald War, it seemed every bit of news from the Greatland was tied in some way to a man most called Thorakis the Builder. Some called him Thorakis the Savior, but that name was less popular here on the Godfist. Regardless, the man's accomplishments were undeniable, and already people around the world, including present company, were trying to figure out how to duplicate some of his feats. The establishment of an enormous fishery had been his initial achievement. Feeding the masses gave him the ability to effect great change. Every achievement brought more people to his cause, and those people further increased his ability to achieve the otherwise unachievable.

"Whatever the cause," Brother Vaughn finally said. "I don't think we can expect any help from the Greatland any time soon. I suggest we continue as we have been, and we are bound to discover new things over time."

His statement was greeted by silence. It sounded all too familiar, and since most of their meetings ended on a similar note, it did not inspire confidence.

"On Catrin's behalf," Chase said, "I'll note that we still have approximately a thousand herald globes. With no sign of Kyrien, we don't expect to have more any time soon. I suggest we hold on to them. If we can't produce more, then we'll need to get more for the ones we have. We've orders for ten times the amount we have, so it won't take long before the offering prices start to go up. I also know that Catrin wants several hundred to remain within the hold at all times, so there really are very few that remain to be sold."

"We'll have to keep an even closer watch on those we have," Brother Vaughn said. "I know those within the hold are trustworthy, but greed can make people do things they normally would not."

"Agreed," Chase said. "Based on Prios's last report, there are no places available within the academy, but people continue to arrive on every ship in from the Greatland and the Falcon Isles. Now we even have ships coming from Garaway and Foss. We need to figure out what to do with these people."

It was an increasingly troubling problem. Most of those who came seeking entrance to the Herald's Academy were turned away, and the majority had no way to return home. The fact was that most of them were misfits and outcasts, sent to the Godfist by their families with the anticipation that they would not return. In the absence of any quantifiable method of judging each person's potential, the academy had simply accepted all those who came until there were more than Prios and his staff could handle. After that, everyone was turned away with few exceptions. Generally only those who had manifested powerful abilities on their own were admitted. In some cases students of less potential had to be excused. It was a difficult and disconcerting process.

"We also need to figure out who will maintain order until Prios can return to his duties," Chase added, and again silence filled the hall. "And most importantly, we need to figure out a way to help Catrin and Prios. There must be something we can do, and Brother Vaughn, I think you are the man to figure out exactly what that is. Unfortunately I also think you are the man to run the academy in Prios's absence."

"I'll do everything I can to achieve both, but I'm going to need some help."

"We'll do what we can to get you what you need," Chase said.

"I've an idea," Mirta said. "I know I'm no expert, but I remember the tale of Catrin's astral travel to find the Firstland. She had no stone and metal throne, as she had at Ohmahold, and she became lost. Was it not the dragons who assisted her return? Did she not say that they aided her?"

The rest of the group seemed dubious, but it was Brother Vaughn who gave their concerns a voice. "While our memories agree, I don't see how that will help us at this particular time. Catrin has been calling out to Kyrien for years, and he has not returned."

"But we could try," Mirta interrupted. "Perhaps this is something the academy could help with. Maybe they can call out to the dragons and ask for help. What harm can it cause?"

Brother Vaughn nodded slowly, his deep brown eyes thoughtful. "I don't suppose I see any harm in it, and it might help the people to feel they are doing something productive. We must, of course, continue to keep Catrin and Prios's actual condition secret. Perhaps we could just tell everyone that we need them to call the dragons here so we can obtain more dragon ore."

"Maybe you should just throw the dragons a party," Martik added with a smirk.

"I hadn't thought of that!" Mirta exclaimed.

Martik rolled his eyes.

Chapter 3

Light blinds as readily as shadow.
--Hurakin the Assassin

* * *

Black sails crowded the horizon beneath a roiling mass of darkness. Unlike any storm clouds Pelivor had ever seen, towering formations curled in on themselves and emanated malevolence, as if the clouds themselves wished to destroy him and everyone else aboard the *Slippery Eel*. Even if the storm were simply a storm, the fleet of black ships drew ever closer, and Pelivor could feel their intent. It made his knees tremble.

"You just need to believe you can do it," Kenward repeated, as if those words could somehow convince Pelivor that he could do something that only the most powerful person on all of Godsland could do. Though he considered Catrin a friend, she was the Herald of Istra, and he was nothing compared to her. Though he'd shown the slightest spark of talent with Istra's powers, it had been only that, literally, a spark.

"I'm trying," Pelivor said, doing his best not to let his annoyance put an edge on his voice. Though Kenward was the captain of the *Slippery Eel*, he was also a friend. Cold air pressed his loose-fitting silks to him, and his normally tight and deeply tanned skin drew even tighter, making him look as if he were carved from stone.

"I know, but--"

He didn't have to finish the statement; both could see the darkness closing in on them. The towering clouds looked as if they would swallow the world, and sudden bursts of lightning illuminated them from within, dark silhouettes standing out against the temporarily lit backdrop. Pelivor took a deep breath and tried to calm himself with no success. Lives depended on him, and he had no reason to believe he would succeed. All he had to go by were Kenward's descriptions of what Catrin had done, and those were decidedly vague. Perhaps if she were here, she could teach him, but she wasn't here. He also didn't have her dragon ore figurine or staff to draw energy from; the only power within his grasp was what he could draw from the air around him. He could feel it, smell it, and even taste it, but he had no idea how to gather it or focus it. He might as well try to gather fog with a bucket.

Walking back to the bow, Pelivor couldn't help feeling like a charlatan as he spread his arms wide. The crew remained silent, watching him, willing him to succeed, knowing another failure would likely mean death for them all. That thought made Pelivor ill. When Grubb approached with a mug of aromatic broth, it was all Pelivor could do to force it down.

"It'll cure what ails ya," the ship's cook said, his voice steady and a half smile on his face. Pelivor wished he shared the man's confidence, and it must have shown. "Don't worry. That man's been trying to kill me for years, and he ain't succeeded yet," he said, jerking a thumb in Kenward's direction.

Handing the empty mug back to Grubb, Pelivor hoped this day would not change that. Ever since they'd left the Greatland bound for the Godfist, loaded with precious cargo, he'd had a bad feeling in his gut, and since the appearance of the black fleet, his fears had only grown.

* * *

Kenward paced from bow to stern and tried to avoid making eye contact with Pelivor, knowing the man was near his breaking point and there was nothing he could say to ease the burden. For years the *Slippery Eel* had been among the fastest ships on the water and had evaded even the most determined pursuers, but she was weighed down, and the ships behind them moved faster than any he'd seen before. He wondered again if the unnatural storm drove them to such great speed or if some new design allowed them to cut the waves faster than ships that had come before. Using his looking glass, he could see nothing that distinguished those ships from any other, and he came, once again, to the conclusion that some malevolent force drove them forward. The sense of impending evil was the most telling factor, and Kenward felt a rare wave of fear overtake him. Despite his efforts to hide the fear from his crew, he knew they could sense it, and that alone was enough to put them all on edge.

Watching Pelivor from behind, he prayed the gods had not lost patience with him, and after tossing another gold coin into the waves, he hoped it was enough. A dim glow pulsed around Pelivor's hands, and Kenward dared to hope, but nothing happened. Soon after, the glow faltered and the sailor lowered his hands, his frustration clear in his posture. Again Kenward ran through his options, and again he came to the conclusion that nothing he could do would save them. Catrin's stonework thrones, cut from the mines deep below Ohmahold, were too heavy for his men to move without rope, pulleys, and substantial frameworks--none of which would be available until they reached the Godfist. He'd known the risk and accepted it, but now their precious cargo became their biggest liability, and jettisoning the other heavy cargo would destabilize the ship, only making the problem worse. Pelivor was their only hope, and that hope was as thin as gossamer.

"They're gonna catch us soon," came the voice of Bryn, the bosun, and Kenward turned to him with an annoyed glare for stating the obvious. "I know we can't unload the thrones, but if we just keep going as we are, we'll have to fight them on their terms."

"What are you suggesting?"

"Do something they won't be expecting," Bryn said with a wink, the freckles standing out on his reddened skin, which never seemed to tan, and his blue eyes twinkled.

Kenward grinned, a plan forming in his mind.

* * *

Pelivor watched in horror as the darkness swallowed the blue skies above them. Soon the black ships would overtake them, and all of them would die because he had failed them. His friends would die because he was feeble and weak minded. *No.* He would not give up. Catrin would not have given up, and he let the memory of her drive him. He remembered how she had fought to make him think more of himself and how he had grown to love her. Even if he could never have her, he would always have her in his heart.

With a shuddering breath, he set his jaw and let his fears melt away. Catrin had believed in him, and he let that belief become his own. Opening himself to the energy around him, he pulled it to him as best he could and let it fill him, slowly and steadily. Before he had let his impatience and fear drive him, but now he tried something different, filling himself with more energy than he'd ever held before. It felt as if he would catch fire or simply explode, but he continued to gather energy and hold it within him. It was like holding his breath, and his body began to burn with need, every instinct telling him to release it before it was too late, but still he held on, knowing that failure meant death.

The world around him ceased to exist, and he felt as if he might pass out, but he held the image of Catrin in his mind. She became his focal point, and by concentrating on her, his body's urgings became more distant and less poignant, as if he were but an observer of his own form. With her translucent hair blown back by the wind in his mind, Catrin's face held the strength of nations; her eyes, the fire of the sun; and her body, the might of the world. Though she was slender and slight, she looked as if she could pull the moon from the sky and cast it into the seas. When she looked at him, he felt her warmth wash over him, and he smelled her fragrance. In that moment he remembered their kiss, knowing it would be the only one they would ever share, yet it was enough to sustain him and hold him in thrall. Always before he'd let the guilt prevent him from reliving the memory, knowing that she'd given her heart to Prios, but this time was different. She loved him too--he knew it--and something told him that just this once, Prios would not object. Pelivor did not wish to steal her; he only wished to take strength and solace from her love and friendship. She had urged him to believe in himself, and for once he allowed himself to do just that.

In the next moment, though, everything changed. The deck beneath his feet lurched, pulling Pelivor from his meditation as the *Slippery Eel* executed a sharp turn. Crewmembers armed themselves and prepared for battle. To his surprise, Farsy and Nimsy held one of the light anchors they used in rocky areas where they were likely to lose the anchor. Angular and pointed, this anchor was nothing like the heavy, rounded anchor used in deep water with sandy or muddy bottom.

Now charging straight toward the approaching fleet, the *Slippery Eel* cut through the waves, seemingly pulled closer by a strange inflow, as if the storm itself were sucking them in. Pelivor despaired, his chance lost, and now all he could do was arm himself for the inevitable battle. No more could he hope to save his shipmates or himself; all he could do was hope to die fighting. It was a sickening feeling, yet there was a release in it. A strange and unfamiliar calm came over him as he watched his death approach. Those around him stood silent and stoic as they, too, accepted their fates with honor and grace.

The ships before them began to separate and turn, only two holding their course. As they drew closer, Pelivor expected to see men on those greasy black decks, but what he saw caused his fear to return. There were men but beside them were reptilian creatures in crude armor covering skin that looked nearly as tough as the armor. These demons watched with cold eyes as the *Slippery Eel* approached, and when the two ships flanked the *Eel,* they began leaping across the distance that separated the ships. Their strength and speed far exceeded that of their human counterparts, who could never have made such a leap.

Given no more time to contemplate this new enemy, Pelivor found himself facing a towering demon with golden eyes and elongated pupils like those of a snake; the pupils narrowed as the monster eyed its prey. Opening its mouth in what Pelivor could only guess was the equivalent of a smile, it bared its black gums and curved, yellow teeth. The stench of death reached out first, followed by a whistling mace that nearly took Pelivor's head from his shoulders. Taking a step backward, Pelivor wanted to run and hide, his courage fleeing in the face of such evil, but there was nowhere to run. Even jumping overboard would only lead to his death, and he did what he would not have thought himself capable of: he planted his feet and faced the demon.

Drawing energy as quickly as he could, having lost hold of his previous store, he extended his hand and lashed out with all the power he could muster, hoping it would be enough. A thread-thin line of blue light reached between his outstretched hand and the chest of the hulking demon, and a loud crack split the air, but the attack had no other effect. The demon tilted its head back and issued a barking laugh before raising its mace. Pelivor waited for the killing blow, but the demon suddenly stiffened and dropped to the deck, accompanied by a loud clang and a sinister sizzle. Behind where the beast had stood was Grubb, smoking skillet in hand. He offered Pelivor the briefest smile before both braced themselves.

"Hold on!" Kenward shouted. "Now!"

Pelivor watched as Farsy threw the anchor at one of the passing ships. It landed on the deck and skidded across the oily planks, looking as if it would simply slide back into the sea, but the sharp tips caught on something and bit deeply. Nimsy released the coiled rope as it raced away from him.

"Brace!" Kenward shouted.

A moment later the *Slippery Eel* slowed sharply, and water rushed over the rails as it spun around. Timbers groaned as the cleat holding the anchor rope strained against the tremendous force. The black ship also turned, and its stern dipped low in the waves, sending water rushing along its deck, causing it to dip even lower in the water.

The creaking of timbers accompanied the sounds of battle as the demons tried to bring down Kenward's crew. The sight of their ship rapidly sinking beneath the waves drove them to reckless action. As the ship sank, though, it threatened to take the *Slippery Eel* with it, and Kenward ordered the rope cut, but the demons charged in and protected the straining rope, seemingly intent on making sure the *Slippery Eel* joined their ship on the ocean floor. Splinters of wood filled the air as the rope cut through the railing, and the ship began to list badly, its prow pointing toward the depths. Just before it seemed they would be pulled under, the rope caught on a sharp edge and snapped, recoiling with massive force and taking pieces out of the demons that had been guarding it. As they reeled from the stinging lashes, Kenward's crew forced them through the gap in the railing to join their sunken ship.

The other ship they had passed was now executing a full turn, and the *Slippery Eel* headed straight for it. Howling in what sounded like maddened glee, Kenward ordered all sails unfurled, and the *Slippery Eel* reached ramming speed, its secret weapon hiding just below the surface.

* * *

"What've you got?" demanded the gate guard, whose dour face presided over the Kraken crest emblazoned on his armor.

"Vinegar," Kevlin Weil responded, thinking the man looked as if he'd never smiled.

"Who wants a whole wagon load of vinegar?"

"Grimwell," Kevlin replied, knowing that uttering the name of Thorakis's wizard was considered taboo. The people feared he would hear them and visit his dark powers on them. Kevlin didn't believe in wizards, but the people saw more of Grimwell these days than they did of Thorakis. It was difficult not to smile when the guard took an involuntary step back. Kevlin had apprehensions of his own about meeting Grimwell, but the wizard had sent out a request for all of the vinegar and spoiled wine that could be had. He didn't even want the spoiled wine cultured; it was ludicrous. But times such as these didn't afford a man the luxury of picking and choosing his customers, and Thorakis's coffers seemed almost bottomless. With more people flocking to his protection every day, Kevlin knew whom he would serve for at least a time, and this was an opportunity to distinguish himself and establish a more regular trade relationship. Kevlin would wager that Thorakis was ill and that Grimwell was planning to succeed him. Given the way most people felt about Grimwell, Kevlin didn't think it likely the wizard would rule for long. Being a realist, Kevlin thought it best to earn whatever coin he could now before the hard times returned. He'd heard others come to similar conclusions, and it seemed the tide was turning. The wise prepared for such things.

"Get this stinking mess away from my gate," the guard said after a brief inspection.

Kevlin chirruped and smacked his mare, Hera, on the rump with the lines, and his wagon slowly rolled a wobbling track toward the gates of Riverhold, the largest construction project in known history. The keep was a marvel, and Kevlin was approaching one of the first magics, as the people had come to call them. Before him waited a wall of granite, unadorned and seemingly singular and whole, but as Hera stepped onto what seemed like a loose bit of cobblestone, she snorted and sidestepped. Kevlin held on as a hissing sound echoed around him. Hera turned her head, and he could see the white in her eyes; he was beginning to have serious thoughts of turning around and abandoning the idea of selling to Thorakis.

Beneath the hissing sound came a low, deep rumble that had Hera backing up as fast as she could. Kevlin jumped from the wagon and grabbed her by the bridle before she turned the wagon over. Before them, the granite wall split not cleanly down the center, but in a complex geometric pattern that allowed the two stones to come together as a mesh. The massive gates rumbled open. Though Kevlin was uncertain how much actual 'magic' was involved, he could not argue that the term was fitting. Never before had he seen such power and majesty. Knowing Hera would not walk through those gates willingly, he calmed her enough that he could retrieve a cloth sack from under the seat of his wagon. Using the sack, he blindfolded Hera and walked her slowly through what now looked to Kevlin like the jaws of a monster. Beyond lay the second magics.

Riverhold was unlike any other hold. It straddled the mighty Yan River as part bridge, part keep, and part dam. From a distance, the spans looked delicate and too thin to support the weight of the keep, like the legs of an overly fat spider. Up close, the spans looked much more substantial, but the white and swirling water that flowed underneath, just before plunging over a thousand-foot waterfall, made it seem as if every step might be his last. While leading Hera over the span, he almost envied her. Traders made this journey every day, but that did not stop his mind from replaying the image of his and Hera's plunging into the water and over the falls.

At the foot of the span waited a pair of guardhouses that sat before what appeared to be another wall of solid stone. The guards waved him past, and he walked Hera forward. The stone beneath him gave under his weight and sank lower and lower. It was a sickening feeling, and Hera began to tremble. He put his hand on her neck and spoke soothingly, but she broke into a sweat and refused to stand still. The stone walkway before them continued to sink until it became a downhill entrance that ran under the massive walls of the keep proper. The moment they were within the awaiting courtyard, the stone moved back up without a sound and seemingly unbidden. It made the hair on Kevlin's neck stand on end, and all he wanted was to make his trade and get out of this place. Even the most practical man could see that there were unnatural forces at work here.

Other traders waited in the courtyard, and Kevlin removed the blindfold from Hera. The sight of other horses relaxing nearby helped to calm her, but she was still skittish.

"Kevlin Weil!" shouted a young and shrill voice. "Kevlin Weil!"

"Over here!" Kevlin said, waving.

"You're t'come with me right away, sir. You're late, sir, and hisself is proper angry, he is."

Kevlin didn't bother to explain why he was late, as the young man turned and trotted back toward the inner keep, which towered above him.

"Are you coming?"

"C'mon, Hera old girl," Kevlin said. "Just a bit farther, and we'll be there."

Hera moved forward but it was obviously not fast enough for the young man's liking based on the looks he shot over his shoulder.

Kevlin cast his gaze left and right, trying to take it all in. To his left, the roar of rushing water was accompanied by a low, grinding sound, and enormous pillars rotated as if turned by the arms of some lumbering hulk. To his right were the now legendary hammers of Riverhold. These stone hammers, big enough to crush a house, beat relentlessly on softer rocks to grind them into powder. Kevlin assumed the rotating columns were part of the mill. Though he knew the river provided the power to run these massive machines, it still seemed as if it were more than any man should be able to accomplish. Thorakis had mastered the Yan River, and Kevlin was humbled.

The keep proper moved like the inner workings of the most elaborate wooden toy, and it was difficult to conceive that this was worked in stone. Shafts of light poured through the room at strategic angles so that even the shadows seemed alive. Ahead waited a pair of immense stone soldiers, looking ready to strike.

As if this place needed to be more frightening, Kevlin thought.

When Hera passed through one of the light beams, she jumped at the sound of stone moving. Had he not heard stories, Kevlin would have turned and run; instead he stood on trembling knees and watched the mighty statues bend down and look at him, their stone blades poised to run him through. In truth, the swords were so large that they would more likely crush him and Hera than pierce them. As he led Hera between the statues, both heads turned smoothly and almost silently to follow Kevlin's every movement. They were so detailed, even their expressions changed as they moved. Their cold and baleful glares held him in thrall. For the briefest moment, Kevlin considered stopping and backing up to see if the statues would notice, but he thought better of it. Ahead, his guide stopped, put his hands on his hips, and let out an annoyed sigh.

Kevlin kept Hera moving as quickly as he could, more to get away from the scrutiny of the stone guards than to appease his guide. Wondering if he would see the leaping elk or the stone eagle or any of the other wonders he'd heard about, Kevlin prayed he wouldn't encounter Thorakis's dragon. It was said that no one had ever seen it and lived to tell the tale. He was relieved and just a little disappointed when his guide led him to a nondescript hall.

"Wait here."

A moment later, Kevlin held his breath.

"If you can't get me what I need on time," the unmistakable voice of Grimwell echoed in the halls, "I might as well toss you into the hammer mill."

Dressed in a heavy, wool jacket so black, it seemed to suck in the light, Grimwell looked every bit the part of a wizard. Silver tipped the corners of his lapels and the tassels that hung down on the sides. Spiderwebs of lightning stood out on the black sleeves in glossy black thread; the subtlety of it drew the eye. The man's black hair was cut short and formed jagged peaks that framed his face. He wore no mustache, but his beard was trimmed into thin lines that ran alongside his mouth and into a point on his chin. All that dark coloring made the wizard's pale skin look almost translucent in comparison. There was no warmth in his black eyes and no trace of humor. Kevlin prayed this encounter would be over quickly.

"Open them, you fool," Grimwell said, and Kevlin started to move, but a look from the page stilled him. Grimwell had not even looked at Kevlin, and it was not Kevlin he addressed. The page moved to open the earthenware jugs resting on a bed of straw in the wagon. Grimwell inspected them and merely grunted, "Unload them."

Kevlin watched as the page made a number of trips to unload the wagon. He would have offered to help, but it was clear his aid was neither required nor wanted. When the last of the jugs were gone, Kevlin waited. Time slipped past, how much Kevlin could not guess. The place had a timelessness that could not be denied, but Hera's fidgeting agreed with Kevlin's feeling that it had been too long. Just as he began to wonder if the page would return, the sound of boots coming from the direction Grimwell and the page had gone made him straighten.

When Grimwell appeared, he made eye contact with Kevlin for the first time, and Kevlin wished he hadn't. Being the target of the wizard's icy stare made Kevlin wish he could become invisible. Perhaps he should just leave without getting paid. The coin no longer seemed worth it.

"Why are you still here?" Grimwell demanded.

Kevlin flushed and could not seem to find his tongue.

"Are you deaf or mute?"

Still Kevlin remained frozen.

"I suppose you wish payment for your insignificant contribution to the betterment of man?"

Kevlin tried to shake his head no, but even that ability seemed to have left him.

Grimwell sneered at him. "Here, take this, then."

Kevlin suddenly found himself able to move once again, and he caught the two silver coins Grimwell tossed to him. The wizard moved past and never looked back. Kevlin was left to find his own way out of the keep. The coins clinked in his palm, and he retreated as fast as he could lead a blindfolded Hera.

* * *

Thorakis the Builder waited near the fire, resting in his wheeled chair. Pages waited behind him, on either side, ready to satisfy any need their patron might have. Thorakis looked older than his years would warrant, and his hands trembled when he pointed. His voice, though, remained strong and clear. "Take me to Grimwell."

The pages moved quickly but smoothly, certain not to jar the ailing genius. They had come to him with their families after the Herald War, seeking food, shelter, and protection from bandits and raiders. Though the Zjhon had ruled the Greatland in an unforgiving manner, they had at least ruled. Their downfall had left the Greatland in chaos. Some of the old families had regained their power, but most had been lost. The once safe countryside had become a place of smoke and death. Either page would give his life for Thorakis and do so knowing his family would remain safe.

When they reached Grimwell's study, which more resembled a laboratory, the right-hand page, Yoric, shouldered the heavy wooden door open. He knew better than to knock or announce himself. As the arm of Thorakis, to do so would belittle his patron. Grimwell bent over a basin filled with a murky yet glittering solution. The acrid smell of vinegar charged the air along with a coppery tang. A fortune in the orange metal had been worked into heavy wire. The copper reached from the basin to each of the earthenware jars, making the basin look like the body of a giant spider.

"Wait outside," Grimwell said. Thorakis's eyes narrowed.

The pages moved without a sound and closed the door as they left. They would wait just far enough away so as not to hear the conversation inside. They knew their place. Others before them hadn't been so wise.

"You'd best be able to explain yourself, *wizard*."

Grimwell finally looked up and acknowledged Thorakis. "Yes, m'lord. Of course."

"We've precious little gold left, and I'm told you've taken it along with most of the silver and copper. Where is it? You're not drinking again, are you? I heard you were buying large quantities of wine."

"Spoiled wine, m'lord."

Thorakis harrumphed. "I see what you've done with my copper. Where's my coin?"

Grimwell flushed. "The silver coin is here, sir." After ducking beneath the web of copper wire, he opened his strong box and showed Thorakis the silver coins, knowing his lord was very proud of the casting that bore his likeness. Destroying or defacing his likeness was listed among the highest crimes and was enough to land a person in the hammer mill.

"Where is my gold?" Thorakis asked, leaning forward with an unpleasant gleam in his eye.

"It's not . . . I mean, I don't have--" The look on Thorakis's face made him reconsider his words. "I've had our most trusted men grind the gold coins to powder."

Thorakis went rigid and his face flushed.

"Please, m'lord--" Grimwell stopped when his door rang with a loud knock, which could only be his men. The wizard breathed a mighty sigh of relief when the men carried in the sacks of gold powder. "You asked me to find a way to bring in more gold, m'lord. Please allow me to demonstrate." Grimwell knew the next few moments would bring him either glory or death; there would be no in between. Holding his breath, he carefully poured gold powder into the basin, trying not to react to Thorakis's sharp hiss. After agitating the solution, he pulled a silver coin from his pocket and connected it to a length of copper that had a notch in its end specifically designed to hold a coin by its edge. With trembling hands, he lowered the coin into the solution and prayed Istra and Vestra would not let him down.

Thorakis leaned forward, almost sitting on the edge of his rolling throne, and his eyes went wide as the silver coin began to gradually change from silver to gold. Thorakis did something he rarely did: he smiled. "You continue to impress me, Grimwell. I fear I may one day have to have you pulped for your insolence, but for today, you are forgiven."

Grimwell smiled but held his silence, savoring his victory for what it was, despite the threat.

"What of our ambassadors? Have they properly greeted the old families?"

Grimwell winced. "Some have, m'lord. Others may have as well, but I am awaiting word of their success. I assure you, m'lord, we'll achieve your will. The extra gold will ensure our success as I can now send additional ambassadors."

"Do not gloat, *wizard*."

"Forgive me, m'lord."

"Yoric!" Thorakis barked, and his pages soon wheeled him from the room.

Grimwell smiled.

Chapter 4

Fate is most unkind to those who fail to prepare for the worst of circumstances.
--Edmoor Reese, scribe

* * *

Anxious tension polluted the air around Brother Vaughn. His ability to sense what others were feeling was normally something he considered a gift, but when in a crowd, it could become overwhelming. Without the ability to filter out the feelings of others, he often found himself taking on the emotions projected at him. Thus, he found himself excited yet skeptical and cautious. The people would not turn down an opportunity for revelry, but no one seemed convinced that an impromptu party for the dragons could be as simple and innocent as Mirta and the others portrayed. The people of Upperton and Lowerton and those who lived in the keep all knew that dragon ore provided most of Catrin's wealth, and the thought of Kyrien bringing her more dragon ore seemed to supply enough motivation to stifle any uncomfortable lines of questioning.

Catrin's absence from the festivities was certainly not easily explained, yet no one asked. Most were content to let the Herald of Istra do whatever it was she did without the need for details. She was an enigma and probably best left that way.

The sound of a man clearing his throat brought Brother Vaughn out of his contemplation. "I'm sorry to disturb you, Brother Vaughn, but I've come to ask something of you," Cattleman Gerard said.

The timbre of his voice made Brother Vaughn look up. The man's anxiety drowned out that of the crowd. Brother Vaughn's eyes drifted lower, and his breath caught in his throat. Staring up at him was a girl as slight as the wind, pale and thin, with piercing, black eyes that spoke of more wisdom that her wispy form would belie.

"Does her father know she's here?" Brother Vaughn asked, already knowing the answer was no. This girl was Trinda Hollis, daughter of the man who'd murdered Catrin's mother and aunt and who had tried to kill Catrin and her father. She was a puzzle, to be sure. Though she was not responsible for any of it, her safety had been the motivating factor behind the crimes. The Kytes, the age-old enemy of Catrin's mother's family, had tortured Trinda to coerce Baker Hollis to poison the Volkers. The Volkers had somehow made peace with the Kytes and found forgiveness for Baker Hollis, but his name was never spoken within Dragonhold, and the sight of Trinda could bring only pain. "This could start a war," Brother Vaughn whispered. "You know that, don't you?"

"I do," Cattleman Gerard replied, his eyes downcast. "But I cannot turn away a child who's come to me for help. I just can't." Tears ran down the big man's cheeks, and Brother Vaughn could not help but respect the man's heart, even if he seriously questioned his judgment.

Though of an age with Catrin, Trinda was tiny and her manner childlike. Perhaps the trauma of her childhood had stunted her development, he thought. Trinda waited patiently, but when Brother Vaughn met her eyes, he was captivated. She radiated calm, yet there was a desperate plea in her eyes, one that pulled at every thread of his humanity. In her hands she gripped a folded parchment. She held it out to him.

My little girl needs help. Do not blame her for my crimes. Be kind to her, please.

No name, no seal, nothing that could directly link the note to Baker Hollis. Brother Vaughn refolded the parchment and handed it back, trying not to meet Trinda's eyes. "For now, take her to the Watering Hole. I'll see what I can do," his lips said, but his eyes told Cattleman Gerard that he was not at all optimistic.

At that moment, Mirta climbed atop a makeshift stage. The crowd grew quiet.

"Thank you to all of you for coming to honor our friend Kyrien, dragon to the Lady Catrin, he who has provided for all of us. Tonight we thank him or his service and we call for him to come back to us--with dragon ore or without. He is what is most precious to us, and I'm hoping you will help me express that to him through our thoughts and songs."

The crowd responded with what seemed almost genuine enthusiasm, though Brother Vaughn still sensed an undercurrent of trepidation. Yet when he looked down at Trinda, he felt a sudden and overwhelming sense of hope. Her eyes glistened and she looked as if she might actually smile.

"You want to help thank Kyrien?" Brother Vaughn asked, but Trinda just shook her head. Brother Vaughn thought for a moment. "You want to help ask Kyrien to come here?" This brought the most enthusiasm from Trinda that either man had ever seen. She nodded briskly, tears streaming down her face. Her little hands trembled, and Brother Vaughn could now better understand Cattleman Gerard's dilemma. He took her tiny hand in his and walked her over to where Mirta stood.

Mirta saw him coming and cast him a quizzical glance but continued as she had been. "I know we don't have any songs to sing specifically for Kyrien, but harvest songs are full of gratitude, so I thought we could start out by singing "The Piemaker's Dirge." Do you all know that one?" Enough people in the crowd clapped their hands that Mirta began to sing. Her voice shook with emotion, very clear as she started the song alone. Then slowly the crowd began to join in. Brother Vaughn cringed at the sound and thought the song might better serve to chase things away. He instantly thought less of himself for even thinking it and added his steady baritone to the mix.

Trinda pulled free from his grip and ran to Mirta, pulling on her skirts and shaking her head. Mirta looked down in surprise and stopped singing. The crowd trailed off, all eyes resting on Trinda. She took Mirta's hand and quite simply began to sing. Her voice was truly magical; it cast even the birds into silence and held those who heard it within her spell. Mirta, joined in, somehow knowing where the simple tune would go next, playing near-perfect harmony to Trinda. A woman in the crowd stepped forward and began to sing along, as the melody repeated and became recognizable.

Brother Vaughn held his breath as Trinda demonstrated more ability and control than any student of the academy had shown since its inception. A dim light shone around her and Mirta, and the crowd swayed in unison, following her movements like a field of grain blown by the wind. Time seemed to shift and move. Brother Vaughn didn't know how long they had been singing, though it seemed longer than he could reconcile. When he spotted something unbelievable soaring through the valley, his heart nearly stopped.

Frozen in place, Brother Vaughn was entranced by the gorgeous beast that winged its way through the valley toward the awaiting crowd, yet it filled him with fear. This beast looked nothing like Kyrien, and its gaze made Brother Vaughn feel more like prey than an ally.

Trinda seemed lost in a trance, and her voice alone continued to sing. The rest were trying to decide if they were excited or terrified; soon most opted for the latter. The glistening black dragon shone blue for an instant as it turned into the sun, but then it trimmed its wings and dived straight for Trinda. Like an arrow, it sliced the air.

Movement surged through the crowd as one person leaped, flipped, and twisted her way to where Trinda sang. In the instant before the dragon would take her, Kendra shoved Trinda to the side. Brother Vaughn's heart jumped into his throat as the fearsome dragon grabbed Kendra in its claws. With three flaps of its mighty wings, it sent everyone below sprawling and thrust itself higher into the air. Kendra appeared to be trying to wriggle free, but the great beast soared up to the top of the ridgeline. Once over the ridge, it could disappear into the Chinawpa Valley or even into the Arghast Desert. Brother Vaughn knew the girl would be lost.

The crowd regained its feet and froze, watching the dragon fly away. Then the people gave a collective gasp as another, larger dragon slammed into the first, sending Kendra tumbling out onto the rocky ridgeline. She landed hard and began to roll, loose bits of rock sliding around her. It looked as if she would be tossed over a steep cliff, but she slammed into a scraggly tree that held her fast.

Dark shadows raced along the valley, and those brave enough to look up became awash in primal fear. At least a dozen feral dragons had heard Trinda's call, and now they seemed to be looking for a free meal. Screams filled the air as people tried to find shelter, but the valley floor was all too vulnerable. The wooden buildings there were no match for the might of a full-grown dragon, and the steep climb to the main entrance of Dragonhold would leave them exposed for far too long.

Swallowing hard, Brother Vaughn realized there was no place safe to hide. Once again, he looked up and saw something his mind had difficulty grasping. From the top of the ridgeline, men were jumping onto the backs of dragons as they passed. Convinced he was losing his mind, Brother Vaughn did what he could to shepherd people into what little shelter could be found. The modest protection of the buildings was far better than standing on open ground, waiting to be eaten.

With Trinda over his shoulder, Brother Vaughn ran as fast as he could, the dragon's breath, hot, moist, and smelling of death, buffeted him from behind. Ahead the doors of the Watering Hole stood open. Miss Helen stood within, ready to pull the heavy doors shut, for all the good it would do them. He could see her screaming but heard no words. He could feel Trinda shifting and stretching, as if she were reaching out to the dragon instead of fleeing from it. It was the girl the dragon wanted, this Brother Vaughn knew, but he would not allow her to be sacrificed. Thus, he risked himself and everyone within the Watering Hole in an attempt to save her. The waiting inn seemed impossibly far away, and dust and debris flew around them. Brother Vaughn could feel the changes in air pressure as the leviathan approached, and he knew he was not going to be fast enough.

After a life of dreaming about giant, flying creatures, Brother Vaughn now knew just how terrifying such creatures could be. The deadly strike did not come, and Brother Vaughn fell into the Watering Hole, into waiting arms that supported and somehow turned him around just in time to see the door shut. Through the ever-narrowing gap, he saw that the dragon, which had been pursuing him, was also busy contending with one of the Arghast. The man stood atop the root of the beast's neck, which seemed to be the one spot where neither claws nor fangs could reach. In the last instant before the door closed, the dragon slammed itself against the canyon wall, trying to crush its unwanted rider.

Miss Helen pulled Trinda away from him and tended to her scrapes and bruises. Brother Vaughn and everyone else in the inn did their best to keep quiet. Constructed from multiple sections of a greatoak, the Watering Hole could withstand high winds and tremors, but a hungry flight of dragons might be too much for it. Cries rang out as the common room suddenly lurched sideways. Driven to his knees by the impact, Brother Vaughn noted that the dragons did not need to get them out to kill them; just turning the building upside down and giving it a shake would do the job just fine.

Bowls, mugs, and even knives flew from shelves and cupboards as the Watering Hole shook. The highly polished bar cracked with an ear-crushing snap. It seemed the end was near.

* * *

Within the humble hall he called home, Chase paced the floor, biting his lip and trying to come up with a plan. Without a plan, his efforts felt fragmented and ineffectual. If he could only set his mind on some obtainable goal, he would be free to commit himself to that effort, but in the challenges they currently faced, he was powerless. He could do nothing to bring Catrin and Prios back, and it seemed he could not even find his own nephew within the hold. If anything happened to Sinjin . . .

"Sir!" came a shout in the hall, and Chase turned sharply, recognizing the voice of his second in command, Morif. The old veteran could address Chase on equal terms, but he seemed to pride himself on knowing his place in the chain of command. What worried Chase was a hint of panic in Morif's voice, which Chase had never heard before. "We found him, sir. Come quick. It's not good sir. Not good."

"Where?" Chase barked as he rushed from the room.

"Infirmary," Morif replied, and Chase took off at a run. This couldn't be happening.

Chase charged through the halls, a pain in his chest making it difficult to breathe. He stood to lose almost everything that was important to him. Catrin and Prios lay helpless, slowly dying, and now Sinjin. Suppressed rage made his face twitch, and he silently vowed to find whoever was responsible and wring the life from him or her with his bare hands. As he approached the infirmary, he heard a haunting melody echoing through the hold, distant yet clear. It pulled at him, but he shrugged it off and ran. Morif matched his pace; his one eye focused on the sloping hall ahead. Nothing was certain these days, and the seasoned warrior seemed ready to face anything, even the wrath of Millie. Though he was no longer charged with guarding her, everyone knew it was a position he could not fully relinquish.

"All of you, get out of here this instant!" came Millie's voice from within, and Chase had to wait for a line of people to stream out before he could force his way in. Millie cast him a glaring look that softened when she saw who it was. "It's not as bad as it looks. He's got a gash on his head, and it's a bleeder. I'll get him cleaned up and some fluids in him, and he'll be good as new."

Sinjin lay still on the feather-stuffed mattress, his eyes open just slightly. The bluish pallor to his skin made him look already dead. Only the steady rise and fall of his chest gave Chase any reassurance.

"General Chase, sir!" came a shout in the hall. "I must find General Chase. It's urgent!"

"Easy there, young man, breathe," Chase called into the hall. "It's all right. I'm here and I know Sinjin has been found. You may return to your duties." Chase turned back to watch Sinjin breathe.

"I'm sorry, sir," the young guard said, still breathing heavily and clearly uncomfortable with the position in which he found himself. "There is another problem, sir. The tribes of Arghast have gathered near the entrance to the God's Eye and they want to speak to Lady Catrin."

"What?"

The young guard looked as if he might faint. Chase stood silently for a moment, trying to decide what to do. The Arghast were renowned for their horsemanship and their fiercely insular culture. Relations between Catrin and the Arghast were generally good, despite the fact that their very nature made the tribes volatile and unpredictable.

Morif spoke softly, "Catrin generally offers them water, wine, and meat, sir."

"Get someone working on it."

"Yes, sir," Morif said, offering the wink of a one-eyed man that unnerved most but assured Chase that the job would be done properly.

With a last glance at those who meant the most to him, Chase wondered if any of them would ever be returned to him. With nothing more he could do, he left them in Millie's capable hands. For a moment he wondered where Mirta was since she was almost always near the infirmary, but then he heard the melody from outside again, and he recalled the party she was holding for the dragons. As insane as it seemed, he wished her luck. Maybe Kyrien really could help Catrin and Prios. That thought froze in his blood as the haunting melody shifted and was suddenly drowned out by cheers, which almost instantly turned to screams.

Chase ran.

When he reached the front entrance of Dragonhold, he gazed into the valley below, horrified by what he saw. Dragons. Not the color-changing regent dragons that had befriended Catrin, but those that seemed carved from pure darkness. Feral dragons, Chase realized, having heard the ancient descriptions. Verdant dragons had been said to be the largest and most plentiful during the last age of power; feral dragons, the most dangerous; and regent dragons, the most rare. As Chase watched, a man dressed in Arghast garb soared through the air and landed on top of a dragon that was swooping down on the still milling crowd. To his amazement, the man held on and even managed to secure a leather line around the beast's head. Soon, though, that dragon flew beyond Chase's view. Another took its place and soared straight for Chase, who took a few steps back then turned and ran. "We're under attack!" he yelled as the hold's wooden fortifications exploded.

* * *

Halmsa of the Wind clan clenched his teeth and held on as best he could, his clan's namesake buffeting him. The dragon beneath him certainly knew he was there and had been trying to dislodge him for some time, but Halmsa was strong and fast and clever. Even when the beast had slammed itself into the canyon wall, he'd been quick enough to slide around to the underside of the dragon's neck, just barely avoiding being crushed. Other dragons had nearly knocked him free as well. It didn't seem as if they were trying to protect their brethren. The beasts were just adept at flying within very close proximity to one another, at times glancing off each other or rubbing together in midair, yet they managed to do it without knocking themselves from the sky.

The sensation of flying overwhelmed Halmsa's senses for a time, and he simply enjoyed it. An instant later, the dragon dived steeply and aimed for a patch of tall trees. Branches rushed toward Halmsa at impossible speed, the first struck him like thunder. His world nearly went black, but he willed himself to stay conscious. The dragon, now desperate to be rid of him, had taken too great a risk and misjudged the trees. Halmsa held on to his leather lines alone, having lost his footing, and he was tossed wildly as the mighty feral dragon slammed into the treetops.

Despite the intense desire to fly once again, Halmsa climbed down, knowing this dragon would fly no more. Blood warmed his scalp and caked around his ear, but Halmsa's grin was huge. He'd flown a dragon! His people had waited many lifetimes for this day, and he was among the first. Pride filled his chest and motivated Halmsa more than ever. There was much work to be done, but the first step had been taken. Riding a dragon was not at all like riding a horse, and they all had quite a lot to learn.

Limping and bleeding, he climbed along the ridge, watching the skies. The dying dragon thrashed in the trees, crying out its anguish. Halmsa fled but stopped as the skies above him filled with writhing black shapes dancing through the clouds. Like a practiced dance, they dived in near unison. Halmsa felt his courage tested as the dragons fell on their own, ending the dragon's suffering. Feeling exposed and vulnerable, he limped along the crest of the ridgeline toward the remains of Dragonhold's front entrance. He could see the wooden stairs swinging away from their moorings; the mass of people seeking refuge within the hold had no choice but to climb through the shattered timbers to reach the safety of solid stone.

* * *

Flames and dark smoke leaped from makeshift torches attached to metal-tipped spears. Guards stood at intervals on the stairs, guarding the line of refugees from the dragons, which patrolled the skies, waiting for a chance to grab an easy meal. Chase watched as Martik and his crew worked to repair the fortifications and entryway that had been reduced to splinters in a single devastating strike. In one day, the world had changed, and Chase knew they were not ready. *Boil Nat Dersinger and his visions.* Chase knew that Nat's visions couldn't have actually caused these events, but he needed to aim his anger and frustration somewhere. The dragons were wild creatures, and he could not expect them to show kindness or listen to reason. How could he fight such an enemy when so grossly overmatched? *Hide.* The thought made him sick, but the process was already under way.

He also knew that he could not blame Trinda for calling the dragons to them, though that hadn't stopped others in the hold from casting curses at the girl. How could he blame them; the girl's father had tried to kill Catrin when she was but a babe and had succeeded in killing Catrin's mother and Chase's mother. Chase was somewhat surprised that when he saw her, he'd felt no malice or revulsion. She still looked like a child, and her deep-set eyes contained the sadness of ages. Truly this girl deserved respite.

"She'll stay with us," Mirta had insisted, and Chase was grateful for it. Mirta had a heart full of kindness, and not for the first time, Chase congratulated Brother Vaughn on landing the ideal wife for him.

The great hall now looked more like a shantytown as people did what they could to claim their own space. The disorder seemed out of place amid the towering grace of the pillars and the worn but nonetheless mighty bas-reliefs.

"Out of my way, fool!" came Miss Mariss's voice across the great hall, cutting through the rising din.

Chase turned to see her marching directly toward him. He sighed.

"This whelp is trying to tell me that I can't take the grain and salt I'll need to feed all these people. It's going to take a mountain of food and an army in the kitchens to keep up with so many. The Herald was right all along, may her name be blessed! Now you listen to me--"

Chase raised a hand to stave off the rest of the tongue-lashing. "I hear you, Miss Mariss. I do. My men have standing orders, and you're going to have to work with them on this. I haven't yet had the chance to brief everyone on these new circumstances, and they are just trying to do their jobs."

"Do I look like I would steal all of our grain?"

"I know, I know." He turned to a soldier standing off to his right.

"Jerrick, please allow Miss Mariss access to any supplies she needs. Get me an inventory of all our stores, and start working on a rationing plan that will stretch what we have for at least a year."

The young man looked up with fear and anxiety in his eyes.

"It's just a precaution. Don't panic and don't get everyone else any more wound up than they already are. Everything is going to be fine."

As if to disprove his words, shouts and screams rose outside, and Chase turned in time to see a huge black shape blot out the entranceway. The guards' battle cry filled the air, followed by cries of pure anguish.

"Go!" Chase said as the entering mass of refugees surged ahead, driven by fear. It was everything Chase's men could do to keep anyone from being trampled. Miss Mariss and Jerrick retreated, now fully aware that their squabble was the least of Chase's concerns. It was impossible for him to cut through the throng, and all he could do was listen to the cries of men and dragon.

"They got one!" a woman shouted as she entered. "The guards stuck one of them demons, and they brought it down, they did!"

"How many are there?" someone asked.

"Too many," the woman said. "Too boilin' many."

Chase gathered all the guards nearby and sent runners to get more. The men donned leather armor and readied every spear and pole in the hold. Most dipped the tips of their weapons in pitch and lit them from nearby fire pots.

"To one side!" Chase barked as he led his men out onto the wooden bridge and stairs, which swayed under the weight, the damage from the first attack still nowhere near fixed. The makeshift repairs that still held were strained, and it seemed that the entire staircase could collapse at any moment. Below, dozens of people still climbed, desperately trying to reach the safety of stone. Only two guards could be seen, and those were unable to prevent the dragons from plucking people from the stairs before turning on a wingtip and soaring away. The cries of the dying now echoed through the valley.

Abandoning caution, Chase charged down the stairs and was almost immediately engaged by a swooping dragon. Claws extended, it dived in close, reaching for a young man who was helping an old woman climb. Chase nearly went over the railing as he lashed out with his spear, which now seemed far too heavy and short. Still, the dragon shied away from the flames and turned his attention to Chase. When it struck, Chase was ready and jabbed the point of his spear at the beast's eye. Though he didn't manage to blind it, he did smear pitch around the dragon's eye, and it screamed as it flew back toward the coast.

Two more dragons were wounded, and too many people were lost before darkness obscured the battlefield. With the setting of the sun, the dragons retreated, and Chase watched them go, trying to figure out where they were going, but the beasts scattered, melting into the darkening skies. He and his men retreated, helping the wounded and the elderly finish the climb.

When everyone was finally inside, Chase ordered the shattered fortifications rebuilt. "Don't bother trying to repair the gates. Just fill that hole as best you can. For now, we just need to keep everything out."

Exhausted, Chase dropped to the floor. His arms ached from hours of overextended spear thrusts, and his stomach muscles felt as if they were all torn. Even breathing had become difficult, and he allowed himself to rest. Where were Catrin and Prios when he needed them most? he asked himself. Many of those Chase turned to for advice were gone. Benjin and Fasha had sailed with his father and uncle some six years back, their only guide a madman's map, and no one knew when or if they would return.

Just as the largest timbers were being rolled into place, there came shouts from outside. Chase turned to look as Mirta charged forward. A man in bloodied desert garb stumbled into the great hall, in his arms, Kendra. Men stepped forward to aid him, but he shouldered away their efforts. Mirta spoke to him in soothing tones, and when he reached a place where some blankets had been stacked, he laid her down.

"Help her," he said, his accent thick.

Mirta looked Kendra over, and her apprentice Loriana approached the Arghast, a damp cloth in her hand. He stepped back at first, but Loriana grabbed him by the arm and looked him in the eye. She guided him to the floor and tended his wounds. Slowly he relaxed.

"Catrin," he said with fervor.

"First we must get your wounds clean," Loriana said in a calm and even tone.

"Need Catrin," he urged, but as Loriana tended his wounds, he slowly eased back and fell to sleep. Loriana tensed when she heard him mutter in his sleep, "She will teach us to fly."

Chapter 5

Even the most supple rose must sometimes face the frost.
--Hadda Mick, farmer

* * *

Sinjin had never realized that light could hurt so badly; it felt as if it were trying to burrow its way into his brain. His vision swam until he took a deep breath, then he slowly began to see. His ears, however, worked just fine.

"You tell me this instant what happened to you!"

Millie's voice cut into Sinjin's consciousness like an axe, and it took him a moment before he could respond. "I don't know. I don't remember."

"What's the last thing you remember?" she asked, no less intent on getting an answer.

"Um . . . I . . . uh . . ." Sinjin stammered, ashamed that the last thing he remembered was hiding in an alcove and eavesdropping. "I don't know."

"How can you not know?" Millie asked, her glare suspicious. "What's your name?"

"Sinjin Volker," he responded, and he heard someone snort in derision.

"And what's my name, then?"

"Why, you're Millicent, former maid to the Lady Mangst and current keeper of the aforementioned Sinjin Volker."

"Your memory and attitude appear whole. If only you could tell me what you were doing when you sustained this injury!" Not waiting to see if he would say any more, Millie walked away, seemingly having trouble keeping from throttling Sinjin.

"This is all your fault," he heard Kendra say, and he almost had the sense to duck before her fist landed on his cheekbone.

"Kendra! Never hit anyone in the infirmary! How could you?" Khenna said, her mouth agape.

"It's all his fault."

"Are you all right, Sinjin?" Khenna asked.

Sinjin just moaned and levered himself out of the cot.

"Look at that eye!" came another familiar voice, and Sinjin's heart felt a bit lighter as he turned to see Durin grinning back at him.

"It sure is good to see you," Sinjin said.

"You look worse than I do now but not as bad as Kendra; she looks *terrible.* I'm betting most of those cuts and scrapes are going to leave scars. Hideous."

"If you two boys feel well enough to pick on this poor girl while she's a-healin'," Mirta quipped, "then you just get your butts out of here. There are more sick and wounded in this place than we have beds for. And go easy for once, the both of you! I don't want to see you back here 'cept for visitin'. Now git!"

Sinjin narrowly avoided Kendra as he stood to leave, his legs only vaguely responding to his commands, which he supposed were now more like requests. Durin was not so lucky or so quick, and the remainder of her salted fish slapped him in the side of the head.

"You just wait . . ." they heard Kendra say as they left.

"Things are a mess," Sinjin said once they were out of the infirmary and out of Kendra's range.

"You don't know the half of it. The dragons attacked while you were out."

Sinjin nearly choked and could find no words to respond.

"The Arghast showed up just before the dragons attacked, and now we know that they came looking for your mom because the dragons had been tormenting them."

"Why are the dragons attacking? Is it Kyrien?"

"No, no," Durin said. "It's not Kyrien. These dragons are nothing like him. They're as black as night and shiny, like a snake, and they're meaner than a cornered bear."

"And the Arghast want my mom to make the dragons go away?"

"Nope. Guess again. Get this: they want your mom to teach them how to catch and tame the dragons so they can fly."

"Now you're just telling tales," Sinjin said. He turned his head as he noticed a low din slowly growing louder.

"Am not. You'll see. Oh, and those people who shot me weren't assassins. Morif told Millie that if they had been trying to kill you, I'd be dead. What do you think of that?"

Just then they walked into the great hall, and Sinjin stopped, dumbfounded by what he saw and heard. A tent village had sprung up in the hall, and it seemed everyone had something to say at the same time. The noise was difficult to describe, and the great hall's acoustics only added to the effect.

"Told you."

Sinjin grew more anxious with every step, suddenly feeling cramped and crowded, wondering if anyone among the gathered masses wanted him dead. For once, seeing Morif shadowing him and Durin did not anger him. He felt safer knowing Morif was about. He'd taught Sinjin much of what he knew about fighting and about defending himself. Fighting was not one of Sinjin's strong points, which had been proven on just about every one of his encounters with Kendra.

"No one goes out in the daylight now," Durin added as if it were exciting news. "We have to harvest at night. Brother Vaughn says that given ample food supply, the dragons will multiply. He said something about their gentryfication period being short, and that meant there could be a lot more dragons by spring."

"Gestation period," Sinjin said.

"Whatever. The point is that what your mom said was gonna happen actually happened, and now all these people are stuck in here. And let me tell you, stay away from the kitchens if you can. Sheesh, you'd think the world had already come to its end. It's like a kicked anthill down there, and Miss Mariss is in rare form. Last time I went down there for a snack, I came back soaked and covered in flour, and I can't do as much as I used to. That nearly dying stuff takes it out of you."

"I suppose that rules out some food, then," Sinjin said, his hand on his aching stomach.

"Are you kidding? Sometimes you just have to take your chances, and I need food," Durin said. Besides, with the old man following us, it's not like we can hide."

Sinjin noticed a tremble in his friend's hands that had never been there before. Guilt stabbed at him. *"All this is your fault,"* echoed in his mind. "Do you think my parents will live? I mean, do you think they will come back?" Sinjin tried to keep the hitch from his voice, but it betrayed him, as did the tears that gathered in his eyes.

"Of course they'll come back. Soon. I promise."

Sinjin wished Durin wouldn't make promises he couldn't keep.

"This is not a good place for you boys to be spendin' time. How 'bout we head to the kitchens and get some food? I'll keep Miss Mariss occupied while you make your escape." Sinjin looked up at Morif in surprise. The weathered warrior smiled back. "I may be missing one eye, but my ears work just fine for an old man."

Durin winced. "Uh. Sorry."

Morif gave him a light smack on the back of the head. "Let's go."

What Durin had said about the kitchens was not as much of an exaggeration as Sinjin had thought, and the two ducked into the guard hall while Morif shouldered his way into the kitchens. The guard hall was eerily quiet; normally one of the more boisterous rooms in the hold, it stood nearly empty. Never before had so many guards been needed on duty at one time.

Durin and Sinjin sat at one of the long tables, feeling silly with so much table all to themselves. Morif returned sooner than either of them would have thought possible given the mass of people around the kitchens, but Sinjin supposed if there was anyone who could command the attention of so many, it was Morif. The man seemed to be afraid of nothing, and Sinjin had always looked up to him. He'd also gotten to see the other side of Morif--the side that loved to play pranks and to make Millie's face turn red.

"This is the best I could do at the moment," Morif said as he sat down across from them. Before him was a pile of food that would have lasted Sinjin three days. "Too bad there wasn't enough for you two."

Durin and Sinjin both laughed and grabbed some food. It was good to have his friend back, and Sinjin drew strength from that, but chilling fears still haunted him.

"There are a whole lot of people trying to figure out how to best help your mom and dad," Morif said, perhaps reading Sinjin's mind or perhaps he'd simply overheard the question earlier. "I think they'll be all right. When your mom traveled astrally from Ohmahold, she was gone for at least twice as long as your parents have been gone for. Worrying won't do you or them any good, so try to stay positive. A little work always helps keep my mind from worry, and Miss Mariss did say something about needing more flour."

Durin rolled his eyes.

* * *

Catrin's spirit floated in the half light, drifting on the breeze, feeling so weary. All she wanted to do was rest. Nearby, Prios lacked substance, becoming diffuse and wavering like smoke in the wind. Only the idea of losing him kept Catrin from giving up and letting herself become part of the oneness once again. She knew that, while she may have been created, she could not be destroyed; she could only change form. The need to protect Prios became impossible to ignore, and she called out for him. He did not respond immediately, and she willed herself closer, yelling his name. His form wavered and looked as if he would be whisked away and dissolved until that which was Prios was no longer whole.

"Prios! Wait! Don't go!" Catrin willed the words to him.

Slowly he gathered himself. Then he turned to her and smiled. "Oh. There you are. I've been looking for you."

If Catrin could have cried, she would have, but in this formless state, all she could do was hurt with no tears to release the pain. Both knew they were dying, yet neither of them could do anything to prevent it. Barred from returning to their bodies by what seemed a sea of dark shadows, Catrin and Prios had retreated to a place that was, for her, familiar. The place had once been her home before she and her family had been driven north. It was not to the hearth she went but instead to the place where she had spent most of her time: the barn. This place constantly reminded her of who and what she was, and this was perhaps the only thing that had saved them thus far. Prios seemed unable to anchor himself as firmly, and Catrin exhausted herself watching over him, protecting him, and finding him when he searched for her.

"I think we should go back," Prios said, and Catrin noticed once again that his energetic form was whole and his spirit spoke to her with its lips and mouth. It had been disconcerting at first since her husband normally spoke only in her mind. The loss of his tongue at the hands of Archmaster Belegra had prevented normal speech. "We'll die if we stay here."

"We've tried," Catrin said. "They are out there, waiting to tear us apart. I can feel them. I've nothing left to fight them with. If we leave, we die." Though the air reeked of power, her spirit was weak and insubstantial. Outside waited darkness that seemed to feed on the light of the many comets that now crowded the skies. It frightened her how quickly her world had changed.

"I could go out alone and lead them away," Prios said. "Maybe then you could get back. The world needs you. Sinjin needs you."

"The world and Sinjin need us both."

Weariness once again set in, just the act of talking depleting what little willpower Catrin still possessed. She turned back to Prios, expecting him to say something, but his form was fading, his eyes fixed on a point far away, and Catrin once again doubted either of them would survive.

* * *

Clouds hung low in the sky, and the light of a dozen herald globes lit the way as Chase and his men escorted farmers to their lands. The livestock were gone, much of Lowerton destroyed, but Chase was determined to get all the food, oil, salt, spices, and other goods they could into the hold. In fortnight since the dragons had arrived, the hold's stores dwindled far too rapidly. Crops continued to ripen under the eyes of the dragons during the day, and it seemed one male in particular had claimed this area as his territory. The people called him Reaver. Venturing out in the daylight meant risking being eaten.

Bats flew overhead, attracted by the moths that gathered around the herald globes. Chase and his men were armed with spears, but it was truly little defense against a dragon attack. Only the darkness kept the monsters at bay. Many within Dragonhold would no longer use the hold's name, and Chase felt guilty for having come up with the name in the first place, as it now seemed grossly inappropriate. He couldn't have known things would work out this way, but that didn't stop him from tormenting himself about it.

Climbing along the terraces that lined the valley was treacherous in daylight, and the group moved slowly. A yawn slipped past Chase's defenses; the guards on duty pretended not to notice. Double shifts had become the norm, and the number of people caught sleeping on duty was embarrassing, but they were all overtaxed and trying to adjust. This new life they lived was far less forgiving than what they had known for most of their lives, and the people of the Godfist were a hearty folk who knew their share of hard times. What lay ahead looked grim, and everyone knew it. Even Master Edling seemed to see the need for unity, in his own haughty way. Messengers had been arriving nightly since the dragons first arrived, requesting refuge for a large number of citizens from south of the Wall. Chase knew it was a game of resources; that much he had learned from the Zjhon invasion, if nothing else. Every additional body in the hold was an additional body to feed.

"Knowing Edling," Morif had said to Chase, "he'll send us every person with a sniffle, cough, or rash in hopes that disease will wipe us out for him. Then he can just take Dragonhold for himself. He seems already to think it belongs to him." All his talk about Dragonhold belonging to the people of the Godfist sickened him.

Such cold realizations made Chase feel ill. These were his countrymen, in many cases people he grew up with or attended lessons with, and he felt as if he were abandoning them. In truth, he knew the Masterhouse could hold a large number of people, as could the cold caves. What he didn't know was how well or poorly the Masterhouse and cold caves had been restocked with supplies after the siege. If Master Edling and the council had been lax in their planning, then turning people away could be sentencing them to starvation. Of course, accepting too many could assign the same fate. Chase sighed.

The group had moved on, and he was no longer at his post. He hurried to catch up, and again the other guards pretended not to notice. Chase was their leader, their strength, and they all knew that double shifts for them meant triple shifts for him. Sleep had become something grabbed in the moments between crises, and tonight was little more than shepherding farmers with no signs of any threat. For Chase, it was an opportunity to survey the land and crops for himself, and if nothing else, escape from within that oppressive rock for a time. He'd never known himself to fear confinement, but living beneath a mountain of rock weighed upon his soul, and he longed for the freedom he'd once had.

Ahead, the terrace walls had been damaged, and great care was required to climb past the broken section. The earthen works looked as if they might slide into the valley under the group's weight, but they held. Beyond lay a section of ripe corn, essentially cut off by the damage on one end and a sheer face on the other. Chase felt trapped with the treacherous section as their only means of escape. He cursed himself for a coward, and when the clouds parted, he felt a bit better. At least with the light of the near-full moon and the comets, the trek back would be less of an issue. The herald globes provided consistent light, but they cast shadows, making climbing dangerous.

As a strong wind drifted down from the north, Chase looked to the skies. Dozens of comets cast their twinkling light across the sky, blotting out the stars so only the moon and comets could be seen. It was a strange sight to behold. For most of his life, in fact for thousands of years, there had been no comets in the skies. The prophecies had said they would come, and so they had. They also said Catrin would destroy the Zjhon and, in a way, she had, but what the prophecies said would come next made Chase quail. He had hoped it all to be fantasy, but the situation just kept getting worse with no signs things would improve any time soon. Perhaps he needed to accept the fact that it would get far worse before it got better--far worse indeed.

The farmers had gotten ahead of him again, and Chase was about to close the distance when he noticed something strange in the corner of his vision: light, then darkness, then light. As he looked back to the sky, he saw a pattern as something large blotted out the comets, and whatever it was grew larger with every passing moment.

"Get down," Chase said in a half whisper, half shout. A brief moment of pride filled him as the entire crew ducked down without another word. Many met his eyes, and he motioned to the sky, making his hands into the shape of flapping wings, now known as the sign for dragons above. When he turned his attention back to the sky, it was nearly too late. A blast of air pelted them as the massive wingtips came close to taking Chase's head off. He fell to his stomach and waited for the debris-filled wind to pass. When he stood, he braced himself and readied his spear. His men did the same without the need for command, and they waited for the attack to come. Instead what they heard was the snapping of trees and timbers followed by a mighty exhale.

"The beast has gone down on his own, sir. Should we move in and finish it off?"

"Bradley and Simms, with me. The rest of you, wait here."

The sound of labored breathing echoed on the wind, and Chase knew the beast still had the potential to be very dangerous. A wounded dragon could be worlds more deadly than a hungry dragon. More cracks and snaps echoed through the valley as the beast thrashed, accompanied by mighty roars that ended as grunts.

"We might be best off letting this one die on its own, sir. I'm no coward but I can't see risking lives if the beast truly is mortally wounded, sir," Bradley said.

"I agree," Chase said, "but I want to get a closer look at what we're facing."

Shouts from above rang out, and Chase looked up to see Morif leading a group of men down the stairs. There was no mistaking the towering presence that was Morif, and it brought a smile to Chase's face. There might be a bit of gray in the old soldier's beard, but he'd certainly lost none of his warrior spirit. As he rounded a bend and got his first glimpse of the downed dragon, he got an impression of size but little else, as most of the creature was engulfed in shadow. It was the size of a large male, and Chase's knew that even a swipe of its tail could be an end to anyone caught in its path. The valley was still, and the wounded dragon had gone quiet.

"Stay where you are!" Chase shouted across the valley to Morif and his men. "I'm going in for a look. You stay here," he told Bradley and Simms. The men seemed uneasy about his order but didn't argue with him. Descending into the darkness, Chase tried not to think about what it would feel like to be crushed to death. When he reached an area where the terraces ran near a rooftop, he leaped across and shimmied down the side of the building, which had been constructed of whole tree trunks and offered a variety of hand- and footholds. When he peeked around the corner, he found himself face-to-face with a very alive dragon. His heart nearly stopped.

It took his brain a moment to register that this was no feral dragon. The head was wider, and the eyes were more on the sides of the head. Color was hard to guess, but this dragon was clearly not the shiny black of a feral. Those huge eyes, flecked with green and gold, held Chase in thrall, and he knew. It was not like what Catrin had described when Kyrien showed pictures in her mind. Chase simply knew: this was no ordinary dragon; this was Kyrien, Catrin's dragon.

* * *

Catrin sat up so suddenly that Millie fell out of the chair she'd been leaning back in.

"By god and goddess!" Millie shouted while gathering her skirts. "Lady Catrin!"

That brought new shouts from down the hall, and Mirta soon charged through the door. Millie poured a mug of water and handed it to Catrin, who had yet to speak or acknowledge anyone else. Her hands trembled but managed to grasp the mug, and after a few moments, Catrin drank. When she looked around, she had eyes for only one: Prios. His still body was the color of ash.

"Back to the viewing chamber," Catrin said in a raw voice that left her coughing.

"You're in no condition to be up and walking," Mirta insisted, but Catrin would not be deterred.

"I'll carry him there myself if I have to," Catrin said as she stood on unsteady feet.

Millie wrapped an arm around her. "Do as she says! Guards! Help Mirta carry Prios back to the viewing chamber."

Men rushed into the chamber and carried both Prios and Catrin down the hall. Another man helped Millie, who was breathing heavily enough that she was having trouble complaining that she didn't need help.

"Get Brother Vaughn," Catrin gasped. "Tell him we need the chanting. He will understand."

"He tried for a time, m'lady, but when it had no effect after days, he finally gave it up," Millie said. "I'm sorry, m'lady."

Weariness washed over Catrin, and she hadn't the energy to respond. Instead, she just concentrated on breathing. Her body felt weak and disconnected, which was not unexpected. She'd been through this before, but this felt worse, as if troughs had been carved deep in her mind, and she doubted she would ever be whole again. For the moment only Prios mattered. Every second increased the chances he would simply fade away.

"Hold him in front of the left portal. I'll stand in front of the right," Catrin said. In truth, she leaned on the two young men flanking her only slightly less than Prios's unconscious form did. This was not entirely a bad thing as she uttered, "Hold on to me tight."

"Don't you dare leave me again!" Millie shouted, but it was too late, Catrin was already gone. Soon the air was filled with rhythmic chanting as Millie wept.

Chapter 6

Faith is belief in the absence of reason.
--Barabas the druid

* * *

Demons held the darkness, which surrounded Catrin's spirit and tried to smother her, but she conjured a herald globe that shone brightly, like those that lived only short lives. It was something she had learned while her spirit had been trapped at the farm. The things she was adept at creating in the physical world she could conjure on the astral plane. She used the globe to pierce the darkness and find Prios. She found him cowering in the corner of the barn; somehow he'd made it back. Memories of their battle would forever haunt her. Kyrien had spoken to her, and he had seemed so close, but the darkness was too strong. Weakened by prolonged separation from their bodies, the two had been in no shape for a fight.

Again, the demons closed in around the farm, leaving them to rot inside. Catrin often wondered why they didn't attack, but she supposed it didn't matter; death would come either way.

Prios whimpered and pulled his knees to his chin.

"I'm here. I came back for you," Catrin said, but he did not seem to hear. Rocking back and forth, he seemed to have left this reality for another, and Catrin shouted for him to wake. Still he didn't respond. Movement caught Catrin's attention, and her spirit froze. Slipping in from the blackness came the demons, seemingly no longer willing to wait. The sound of movement behind her alerted her to more danger, and Catrin prepared herself for one final effort. She would carry Prios and simply make a run for it. It seemed like suicide since they would both be defenseless, but Catrin could find no other solution. At least they would die *doing* something.

Reaching down, she gathered Prios's energy, which had weight and mass and was more difficult for her to carry than she had imagined; she would not give up, though. Pulling energy from the night air, she conjured four herald globes, each taxing her but intended to drive the demons back. It didn't work.

Pain seared her soul as Catrin moved past the first of the demons. She spun slowly, awkwardly, and half fell out of the barn and into the night. Demons poured down the valley walls like a flood of evil. Shadow dragons flew overhead, ridden by men with twisted faces. Only Catrin's conjured herald globes cast any light, and she moved like a candle afloat on a raging river. Roiling clouds of deep black obscured the night skies. Her beams of light illuminated the fog, casting rays of color around her and Prios, but the darkness pressed in close, causing the sphere of color to shrink. Claws and slavering jaws broke through the light. Gibbering madness drove searing knives through Catrin's mind and she screamed.

Prios flung his limbs outward, seemingly awakened by Catrin's anguish, and he sent balls of lightning into the demons. Catrin screamed as burning embers branded her soul. With a cry of rage, she rose up and cast flames in a wide arc, knowing it was the last of her reserves. Any more and she would simply dry up and blow away.

Light parted the darkness. Like a knife of fire it raced from the skies and cast demons spinning as it came. Awestruck, Catrin saw Kyrien in the form of flame and lightning. He was even more beautiful than in the physical world, and he proved as deadly as well.

We have done this before.

Catrin wondered if she heard a bit of sarcasm or perhaps even a bit of reprimand in Kyrien's thoughts, which came to her in images and impressions. The fire dragon swooped down low and grabbed Catrin in his mighty claws. Demons leaped and snapped at them, but Catrin cast beams of light, scorching them with their brilliance. She gave herself to the effort, unconsciously drawing energy from Kyrien, and only his urgings moved her toward restraint. In a moment of exhilaration and fear, Kyrien caught the wind and soared higher, aiming at two holes in a rock face. An instant later, he slammed into it with a force that should have left a crater in its wake. Instead, it left Catrin's spirit once again in her body, gasping for air and waiting for the feeling to return to her limbs. Beside her, Prios lay nearly as still as death, his breathing slow and shallow. With the world spinning before her, she said, "Take me to Kyrien."

"But, Catrin," Millie said, so beside herself that she slipped; she almost never used Catrin's name in public. "You must rest and drink and eat and recuperate yourself. You're in no condition to go anywhere. And I'm sorry but Kyrien hasn't been here in years."

"He's here," Catrin said.

* * *

"Get more men down here!" Chase shouted as he watched his nightmares spring to life around him. Dark beasts loped down the ridgeline while others howled their way down the center of the valley. These creatures were different from anything he'd ever seen, but when one turned and howled, Chase saw traces of Gholgi, the fabled enemies of mankind he and Catrin had faced on the Firstland. These monsters were even more terrifying. There was intelligence in their piercing eyes accompanied by chilling savagery. They wore crude armor and wielded jagged weapons. Sounds barked among them sounded like a canine language. When a dark shape soared over them, the demons moved almost as one. In tight formation, demons created a mesh with their crude and varying shields. They approached Kyrien, who lay thrashing on the valley floor, his eyes focused on something no one else there could see. Behind the shield bearers came hulking beasts. Chase knew he was helpless, and the numbers he saw coming were more than his men could fend off, but Kyrien had saved Catrin's life more than once, and Chase would not let him die if he could help it.

"Find a good place to brace your spears," Morif shouted. "When they come, let them fight the Godfist itself instead of the strength of your arms. Let them impale themselves!"

Chase appreciated Morif's enthusiasm, knowing his men would need every boost in morale they could get just to keep them from turning and running. It was all Chase could do to face this new enemy--such malice!

Dust and dirt leaped from the ground, blinding and scouring, as the first of the dragons attacked. Morif stood facing the beast, watching it come, his spear lying on the ground before him. Just before the dragon reached him, he knelt down and raised the tip of his spear. The butt he jammed into a saddle of rock. The dragon was ready, though, and managed to make it only a glancing blow. Before it passed over, however, it knocked Morif and a dozen other men from their feet with a lash of its tail. Some did not rise again. More dragons circled and Chase knew it was only a matter of time.

Demons slipped past the downed guards and hacked at Kyrien's sides, trying to get to his soft underbelly but so far were stymied by his thick scales. One grabbed the spear from a downed guard and ran at Kyrien's eye.

Chase cried out, willing his body to move faster than he knew was possible. He was supposed to protect Kyrien. How would he ever tell Catrin that he'd let them kill her dragon? "No!" he shouted just before the demon was engulfed in liquid fire. It pulsed like lightning and blasted the air, sending Chase and others sprawling. Landing on his back, the breath knocked from him, Chase nonetheless found his soul lightened; Catrin stood atop the stair with lightning pulsing around her outstretched hands, lashing out at feral dragons and demons simultaneously.

"For Catrin!" Chase roared, and those around him rallied, many smoking and limping as they pulled themselves from the ground. The darkness was undeterred, and a flood of demons clogged the valley, the dragons protecting their flanks. More people streamed down the stairs with Catrin among them, warding off attacks from the air. She could not guard the people and Kyrien at the same time, which left Chase and his men vulnerable. The sight of Morif leaning on Kyrien with a spear in his hand did much to bolster Chase's morale; at least his old friend was not dead.

Thunder rolled through the valley, though no rain fell, and the skies were now clear. Webs of light arced overhead, and Chase could not look up for fear of losing what night vision he possessed. If he had looked up, he would have seen the massive black dragon bearing down on him. Instead, he was caught completely by surprise when what looked like a tree trunk slammed into him. The air rushed from his chest in a whoosh, and he flew backward. For a time he watched the battle rush away from him, but then his feet struck something.

The world spun wildly.

Darkness.

* * *

Catrin watched a dragon tuck its wings and dive, aiming for Chase, and she screamed, lashing out with more energy than she could control. Lightning struck the dragon and caused it to veer and land only a glancing blow on Chase. Still, her cousin's body tumbled through the air. The out-of-control blast also struck people around her, and just as Catrin hastily released the energy, it recoiled. The concussion sent those around her sprawling, and she fell to her knees, no longer in full control of her limbs. Before her was the most frightening thing she'd ever seen: the eyes of a feral dragon rising over a ledge. The beast clung to the rock and seemed to sense an opportunity. Gathering herself and trying to stand, Catrin prepared for the strike. One snap of its massive jaws, and she would be dead. At least it would be fast, she thought.

A high-pitched battle cry echoed sharply, and Khenna leaped across the gap. The fighter landed between the beast's eyes and sent a kick at one eye. The dragon blinked just in time, and its thick skin rendered the attack ineffectual, but then Khenna did something that stole Catrin's breath. Before the dragon could spring into the air, the woman took a coil of leather from her belt, held one end in each hand, and looped it over the dragon's snout. Had it made it under the lower jaw, Khenna might have been saved, but instead the leather strap only cleared the top jaw. The dragon bit down hard and leaped into the air. It turned and dived toward the valley floor. For a moment, Khenna stood tall, the wind whipping her hair and clothes. Catrin thought she might be able to stay upright, but then the dragon bit down again, and the strap snapped, one side breaking free and the other wedged between massive incisors. Khenna tried to catch her balance atop the head of a flying dragon, and for a moment she did, but in the next breath, she was tossed in the wind, still tethered to the dragon by the strap that was now twisted around her ankle. As Catrin watched in horror, they disappeared into the darkness.

There was no time to mourn Khenna as more dragons entered the fray. Far too many landed blows on Kyrien's still form. Catrin reached out to him, lending him energy she did not possess. Guilt washed over her as she pulled energy from those around her, making her nothing more than a leech.

Disgusted, she nearly vomited, but then Kyrien flooded her mind.

They give their energy freely. They try in vain to aid me. You are simply focusing what they are unable to give. Do not run them dry, and you will have done no harm. Do what you must; just do not do too much. This is more important than you know.

At that moment she could not imagine anything more important than saving Kyrien and her people, but his thoughts left her weighted with responsibility. Though she knew not exactly what hung in the balance, she knew that it was partly hers to protect. Breathing deeply, she drew the energy and lashed out. Demon and dragon alike felt the fury of her wrath, and the darkness receded like twilight chased by the dawn. Slowly, gradually, they faded until only the cries of the dying filled the air.

When Catrin finally made it to the bottom of the stair, she fell to one side, unable to stand on her own without the aid of the railing. A man she didn't recognize caught her.

His eyes went wide, and she thought he might faint, but he stammered, "Are you . . . I mean . . . are you all right, Lady Catrin?"

"Almost," she said as another wave of dizziness overwhelmed her.

The man tightened his grip and kept her upright. "I need some help here! Need help for the Herald," he called out, and even in the chaos, people rushed to her aid.

From above came Millie's voice. "You're not going to die on me today, no you're not! Get some blankets around her before she freezes 'death."

Men scrambled to find something, and finally a man wrapped Catrin in a warm coat. In truth the cool air felt refreshing, but Catrin could not seem to find her voice. Her body trembled and her legs refused to support her. She continued to lean on the man whose name she did not know.

"You there," Millie instructed, "get some men and prepare a litter for Lady Catrin."

"That won't be necessary, Millie," Catrin said. "I'll be staying here with Kyrien."

Millie looked as if she would balk. A moment later she sighed. "Get up there and bring back blankets, tents, cots, everything we'll need for an infirmary. Tell Mirta we need all the bandages, stitching thread, and needles."

Wobbling, Catrin was grateful for Millie's efforts. She needed a place to sit down, but there were far more important tasks at hand, not the least of which was tending to the wounded. From the southern part of the valley, the silhouette of a man shambled toward them. A shout arose from men closer to that area, and Catrin felt an incredible sense of relief when someone said it was Chase. It was clear that he was injured, but she knew he was strong.

As the sun rose, the carnage became apparent, and guards were assigned the grisly duty of burying the dead and burning the bodies of the demons.

When Catrin looked upon the demons, she found herself reminded of the Gholgi, yet these creatures were very different from what she remembered. Instead of lumbering brutes, these demons possessed delicate fingers and crude armor. The beasts she had encountered years before had seemed much more like wild animals. Bile rose in her throat as the wind shifted and the smell of death drifted around her.

Though her body screamed out for rest, she made herself stay awake. "Take me closer to Kyrien," she said.

"Are you certain that's wise, m'lady?"

"Wise or not, please do as I say," Catrin said, driven by need; everything she loved was at stake.

"Yes, m'lady."

"What's your name?"

"I'm Zander, m'lady."

"You may call me Catrin, Zander, and I'm sorry I didn't recognize you."

"Yes, m-- uh, Catrin."

"You make toys, do you not?"

"I do."

"Sinjin loves your puzzles. Thank you, Zander," she said, laying her hand on his shoulder.

The man looked thunderstruck and did not respond. Catrin urged him toward Kyrien. With the exception of his breathing, which was short and shallow, the dragon appeared to be dead, and Catrin worried about him and Prios. When she placed her hands on him, she was transported to the astral plane, assisted by some natural ability inherent in regent dragons. She rode a dragon of flame and lightning, gouts of fire ready to be hurled at their enemies. While the battle in the physical plane had ended, there was still fighting on the astral plane, and it was worse than what Catrin had left behind.

Prios stood within a ring of the Gholgi-like creatures, defending himself with a sword of fire. He looked so handsome yet so very much in danger. Her heart leaped and longed for him. Kyrien roared and dived, dipping to fly directly over Prios, then went sideways. Pure darkness slammed into them, liquid eyes focused for a deadly strike. In a single heartbeat, it drew back and struck at Kyrien's flaming throat. Monstrous spherical sparks leaped into the air and scorched whatever they touched. Something akin to pain cut deep into Catrin's soul, and Kyrien reeled from the massive strike, but he flapped his mighty wings, turned, and dived. In the next moment he climbed sharply, and Catrin looked up to see the pale gray underbelly of the hulking wyrm.

Striking as quickly as she could, she sent only a small burst of fire, but it struck just under the beast's right wing. To Catrin's astonishment, the shadow dragon rolled over and crashed to the ground, crushing demons beneath. A writhing mass seethed around the spirit of Prios, and black blades with gleaming edges leaped from the battle seemingly at random. She could not imagine how he had found such strength, but then she considered the possibility that it was the same place she found her own strength: the love of her spouse and son. This brought a battle cry to Catrin's lips, and she rolled from Kyrien's back. As she plummeted toward the battlefield, her vision focused on one of the beings at the fore. It was bigger than the others, its weapon poised to strike. Tucking her knees as she flew, Catrin drove her heels into the creature's chest. The throng parted. The big one fell, and the black tide flowed back in as if the big one had never been.

Catrin wondered if she existed, and a familiar numbing feeling crept over her, soaking her slowly then accelerating. Dark hands grabbed her, and blades bit into her aura, yet she barely felt it. Once again the mass parted, and when Catrin forced her head up to see what had happened, her eyes landed on Prios. He looked horrible, his energy looking to have been sliced to bits, but the determination in his eyes drove the darkness back. He opened his mouth to roar, and though no noise came out, Catrin watched the demons retreat from his silent cry. Catrin drew on the energy around her, and painful tingling rushed in to drive away the numbness. Catrin told herself the pain was better even as she cried out.

Prios knelt down and brushed her hair away from her face. With extreme effort, she turned her eyes to meet his. He smiled back and winked. In the next breath, he was spinning and roaring at the Gholgi. The dragons retreated and Kyrien helped drive off the last of the demons.

* * *

Zander stood holding Catrin's limp body, his legs trembling and his heart skipping. How had he found himself here, holding the Herald of Istra next to her dragon and watching other dragons drop from the sky? It was the most surreal and bizarre thing he had ever experienced, and he wasn't certain he could handle it. His back ached and his legs shook. "Help," he said far too low to be heard over the cries of the wounded and those trying to help them. "Um, I think I need some help here," he said a little louder.

He steeled himself when Morif turned. The old warrior was fearsome to look upon, and everything about him made Zander uncomfortable, his long hair and beard, metal rings braided into them, just highlighted the sunken place where his left eye had once been. Truly, Morif could look a man into the grave.

When he saw Catrin, the look on the grizzled face softened as much as Zander had ever witnessed. "We must get her back to the infirmary."

"No!" Zander said involuntarily, and he nearly dropped Catrin as he choked.

"What is it?" Morif asked, his face no longer anything but hard. "Speak up, man."

"I . . . don't know . . . I don't know why, but I just know she needs to stay with Kyrien. She asked me to hold her, but I can't do it any longer."

Morif stepped forward to take Catrin from Zander's quivering arms, and Zander saw something he would never forget: Morif turned as pale as a whitefish, and his eye went wide. Zander saw it for only the briefest instant, as Catrin suddenly went rigid in his arms. Doing his best to hold on to her and not fall, Zander took two steps backward and bumped into Kyrien's side. As he looked up, a pair of massive eyes glared back at him, and it was more than he could stand. Zander fainted.

* * *

Holding his ribs, Chase took one step at a time. As he turned a corner, he found his way blocked by what had been the Upperton Apothecary, now a large pile of firewood partially obscured by the body of a dragon. Fear overcame Chase, even knowing the beast was dead. This was a super-predator, a killing machine. He would need to learn as much as he could about these feral dragons as fast as he could. Climbing over the dragon's tail was terrifying and painful. He didn't think anything was broken, but he was severely battered.

Beyond, he saw a very alive Kyrien supporting Catrin with his maw as another man fell to the ground. The bodies of dragons, men, and demons littered the valley floor. Amid the chaos, Morif brought order. Already the wounded were being loaded onto litters and carried up to the hold. Chase's second in command stepped in to support Catrin, who was now standing on her own. Chase moved faster despite the pain, tears gathering in his eyes.

"We need help over here," Morif shouted and Chase almost laughed; leave it to a one-eyed man to see him first. Morif always found a way to surprise him, and this day was no different. "Are you all right, sir?"

"Sort of," Chase said. "I think I'll live."

Morif grinned. "A little pain is a good thing. It reminds us not to be reckless."

Chase had often uttered the maxim himself, and he couldn't deny the truth of it.

"It took you long enough," he said when he reached Catrin.

She almost smiled.

"Prios is back!" came Millie's shout from above, and Catrin did smile briefly. The destruction around them defied optimism.

"You have that look on your face," Chase said to Catrin. "What is it?"

"Kyrien is injured," Catrin said. "We've got to figure out a way to protect him. If the ferals come back, he'll be defenseless."

"They will come back. There's a big one that has claimed this as his territory. We're not sure where he sleeps, but during the day, he keeps a constant watch on this valley. The people call him Reaver."

"All the more reason I need every able person down here now. We need to build fortifications around Kyrien to protect him."

"There are no fortifications we can build that will keep them out, Cat."

"Well, we have to do something!"

"The only things that've worked so far are spears and fire. I'll get people working weapons and training. In the meantime, we need to get you back in the hold. You look horrible."

"You're not looking your best either," Catrin replied. "And I'm staying here. Kyrien needs my protection." Chase looked Catrin in the eye and knew that arguing would do no good. Then he saw a look of pain and guilt flash across her face. "Sinjin?"

"He's fine," Chase said. He saw relief in Catrin's eyes, but the guilt was still there. "And Durin as well."

"That ornery rascal could survive just about anything, I do believe."

"Get back in here. I don't care who you are. You need rest!" Millie's shouts drifted down to those below.

"I believe that would be your husband coming now."

Chapter 7

Followers are like leaves before a strong wind. Leaders are the wind.
--Morif, soldier

* * *

Nearly a fortnight passed, and the darkness pressed them no further, though the dragons kept constant daylight vigil. It seemed they were waiting for something, or someone. The thoughts haunted Catrin. Prios was busy running a hold in turmoil and under siege, though the times she saw him, there was tenderness in his eyes. As they passed in the hall, he would reach out to her, their hands caressing each other, ever so briefly. Sometimes she'd see Sinjin trailing her husband, watching everything he did. Catrin had seen less of Sinjin, and it pained her. There was guilt in his eyes, and she couldn't seem to convince him that she would forgive him for whatever it was. Something haunted his eyes, and that troubled her more than anything else. Knowing she needed to concentrate, Catrin quieted her mind.

Squinting, she winced at the pain of pushing her needle through the supple but thick leather once again. She could have given this task to the seamstresses, but it would have been impossible to convey to them the image in her mind. She often wished for Kyrien's skill at communicating in images and feelings. Catrin could see every detail from any angle, as if he had implanted the memory of this object directly into her head. A saddle! Catrin could hardly believe it. She was working on a saddle for Kyrien, and it was unlike any saddle Catrin had ever known. Certainly the seat, cantle, pommel, and horn were similar, but there were no stirrups. Instead there were multiple cups of leather and iron on the flaps that could be used in a similar fashion to stirrups.

So many details had flowed into Catrin's mind. A collection of girths made with thick strands of wound cotton waited in a corner, but none of Catrin's many straps were complete. First she needed metal rings with a flat edge on one side, which only Strom could provide. Her childhood friend was far too busy, yet he refused to take on an apprentice, saying he was still an apprentice himself, though none would argue his skill with metal and fire. He had mastered the art of bringing things to life from only a picture in his mind. Wielding his hammer like a paintbrush, he created works of art. Now, though, much of his time was spent making pot stands, candleholders, and anything else needed by the hundreds if not thousands of refugees now forced to live in the great hall.

After draping a roughspun sheet over the saddle, Catrin left her workshop, pulling the rawhide curtain to cover the doorway, not wanting rumors to spread. She also didn't want to worry Sinjin, unable to imagine how he would feel about his mother riding Kyrien with the ferals and demons guarding the valleys.

The cool air turned warm as Catrin walked toward the forge, and with every step, the heat became more oppressive. Sweat ran into Catrin's eyes well before she reached the smithy. Within stood Strom and a man Catrin knew she should recognize, but she could not recall a single detail about him. Hoping he would not engage her, she stepped into the smithy. She needn't have worried. Though people seemed to fear Catrin less these days, she rarely had to wait for anything. Those in her path leaped to get out of her way, and it sometimes frightened her. What had she become?

"If one more person asks me when their commission will be done, I'll throttle 'em," Strom said by way of greeting.

Catrin smiled. "I'm sorry you have to make everyone else wait so that my requests are fulfilled." She turned her head so he would see her grin. "I know that must be terribly difficult for you."

"What makes you think I've made anyone wait on your account?"

"Well," Catrin said, knowing she was risking not getting the parts she needed anytime soon. "I figured there must be some reason everyone was asking when their commissions would be ready. Something must be slowing you down. I figured it must be me."

Strom's dark skin glistened as he breathed heavily, and Catrin saw his face darken even more as he flushed. "You've no idea how much time it takes to do what I do! The next person who questions how long it takes to do things can forge their own cook pots! Ungrateful lot. To the fires with all of you!"

Catrin could no longer hold back her laughter, which only seemed to fuel Strom's anger.

"And you just stuff a melon in it. I've heard about enough out of you. Why, I ought to melt these down and put you to the back of the line!" He stuffed a heavy bag into her hands, and she could hear the sound of rings and buckle pieces clinking against one another.

"Thank you, Strom."

"Get out of here before I change my mind! If not for the fact that it would just make more work for me, I'd do it. Now git!"

"I still need a sword, Strom."

"Don't make swords."

"Strom."

"The only thing swords are good for is killin' people. Don't make swords," Strom said and turned his back to Catrin, returning to his anvil and a rod of metal glowing red and white in the forge.

"Swords can protect as well. You know I don't want to kill anyone. I just need to be able to defend myself."

"Why not retrieve that staff of yours? It seemed to serve you quite well."

"I can't," Catrin said. "It's . . . alive now. I can't just yank it up, cut away the growth, and walk off with it, now can I?"

"I'll make you a new staff, then."

Catrin sighed. They'd had this argument before, and never had she won. "Not even one as talented as you could re-create that staff. It lay dormant for thousands of years and then bloomed when I planted its heel in stone. No. Not even you can replace the Staff of Life." Part of her knew she was being unreasonable.

"I never said I'd create you another Staff of Life. You must have rocks in your ears, and perhaps between them as well. I said I'd make you a *new* staff."

"But a staff is not what I need. Now I need a sword."

"Did the voices in your head tell you that?" Strom asked, not looking at her.

"It's not like that. I just know I need a sword. That's all."

Strom waved a hand and grabbed his tongs. There would be no more words spoken about it today, and she left him to his work, knowing she'd been partly correct about her requests causing him grief from his other customers. If it weren't so important, she would have waited her turn, but this meant everything. She didn't know exactly why; she just knew. With Kyrien so close by, she'd begun to wonder which thoughts were her own and which belonged to her dragon. Though many of these strange, new thoughts surprised her, she always seemed to agree with the course of action Kyrien desired. It didn't seem to matter.

Strom's comment about her staff had been well aimed. Part of her wanted nothing more than to rest her hands in the grooves left by her own fingers. The memory of her grip biting into the flesh of the staff was one she'd rather not relive, but that event had linked her to the Staff of Life forever. By some magic, she'd planted the Staff of Life within the Grove of the Elders, at the center of the destruction she herself had wrought. The staff had given her the greatest gift of all. It had taken root and bloomed. Twenty-four acorns it had yielded, just enough to replant the mighty trees she had destroyed.

"I hope the day has greeted you well," Brother Vaughn said as he appeared from around the bend in the hall.

"It has, and for you as well."

"How are your hands today? They were so red yesterday, I wanted to make you stop sewing, or at least let someone help you."

Catrin almost didn't want to bring her hands out of the pockets of her robes. Her knuckles and thumbs were inflamed and swollen, her skin shiny and slick in places. Knowing Brother Vaughn as she did--his persistence was legendary--she pulled her hands out slowly.

He didn't say anything at first. He just sucked air in through his teeth.

"Come with me, young lady. I have something for you."

Catrin wanted to say no, wanted to get back to her work, but she also knew the pain would hinder her progress. Experience told her it was best to let Brother Vaughn help when he offered. It was difficult to believe any single mind could contain so much knowledge, and he seemed to learn more each day.

"When I came across this, I didn't believe it would work, and there seemed no place where I could test it, but there is a shelf of rock just outside the viewing chambers where the air is always moving, always in the same direction. It's a puzzle I haven't yet worked out, but that is beside the point. What's important now is that it works."

"What works?" Catrin asked, knowing it would do no good. No one loved surprising people with his findings as much as Brother Vaughn. He enjoyed seeing the looks on people's faces as much as he enjoyed solving monumental problems.

"You'll see," he said.

When they reached the viewing chamber, Brother Vaughn shot her a look of concern.

"I'm not going anywhere," she said with a sigh. Perhaps if Kenward had returned with the metal-rich thrones, she might have ventured back onto the astral plane.

"Young man, come here," Brother Vaughn said, and a teenage boy wearing the livery of Dragonhold rushed to do as the elder statesmen asked. "You're more limber than I. Reach into that hole and stretch your arm as far as you can to the right. You'll feel a gourd bowl covered with sticks. Don't spill it! Just gently retrieve it for me. Keep it right side up! You hear me?"

"Yes, sir. I'll try, sir."

"Don't try. Just do."

"Yes, sir."

Catrin watched the boy reach out. She was worried that no matter how steady his arm was, his trembling knees would defy his efforts. It took some time for him to stretch far enough and find the bowl with his fingers. Brother Vaughn stood in tense anticipation. A look of extreme relief washed over the teen's face when he handed the bowl to Brother Vaughn, its covering of sticks intact. Catrin watched in silence, curious but trying to be patient.

"The constant breeze causes the water to evaporate," Brother Vaughn said. "And once I found the right level of airflow using different configurations of twigs, I was able to produce this." He removed the twigs from the top of the gourd bowl and extended it to Catrin. "Wrap this in cloth and rest it on top of your hands until it's melted."

In the gourd was a nearly solid block of ice. Ice in the warmer months was something they had all lived without since they no longer had the luxury of storing it in the cold caves. The loss of that resource was among the things Catrin most regretted. At times the thought of taking back the lands in the south had become almost appealing enough to warrant the violence, but Catrin abhorred war, and she had no wish to see her own people killed. That point chafed. Her people had divided themselves and taken what was rightfully hers. Only the luck of the gods had provided sufficient shelter for everyone. The discovery of Dragonhold remained one of the things Catrin was most thankful for. Another was Kyrien's recovery. His wounds had been many, and some had required the efforts of every healer within the hold, and Catrin was proud of what everyone had done.

The feral dragon attacks created fear of dragons, and Catrin had worried the people would turn on Kyrien, but instead they seemed to have hung their hopes on him. Not all dragons were evil killers, and many hoped Kyrien's kind would be their saviors. Catrin wondered the same, especially given her compulsion to create the saddle, riding clothes, and even the large, leather flaps whose purpose Catrin had yet to fathom. In truth, there were parts of the saddle and riding clothes she didn't understand, but she knew enough to create what she saw in her vision, a vision that showed little but her astride Kyrien. Only fog surrounded them, and Catrin could not glean a single hint as to what the future would hold.

"Keep them dry and that should help," Brother Vaughn said and Catrin came back to herself.

"Thank you, Brother Vaughn. You constantly amaze me."

The older man flushed. "I do what I can."

"I must get back to work on the saddle. Thank you again," Catrin said, and when she turned to pick up the bag from Strom, she knocked it over. Two rings and a buckle slid out. On top of them rested a thimble.

Brother Vaughn smiled. "I knew Strom would take good care of you."

"He always does," she agreed.

There was a thrumming of life within the hold now, far different than it had been before the ferals and demons came. Though the uniting of their purpose was something Catrin had always hoped for, it would have been far better had it happened before the need was so great; now they found themselves grossly unprepared. All the work Catrin and her followers had done for nearly a decade now seemed insignificant in the face of their current circumstances. Unless something changed, they would eventually starve and be forced out of the hold, which was the only thing protecting them from the darkness.

Going out of her way, Catrin made certain to pass by the main entrance, where she could momentarily catch a glimpse of Kyrien, who rested below, still mending from his wounds. Around him had sprung up a bristling compound. Men wielding spears surrounded him, and walls of sharpened spikes had been erected around a wide perimeter, leaving enough room for Kyrien to move. It had been a rude awakening after the first fortifications had been raised and Kyrien turning himself had brought it all crashing down. Within the new fortifications rested four massive ballistae, designed to resemble the ones the Zjhon had mounted on their ships. Catrin remembered the fear they had instilled in her, and she hoped it had the same effect on the ferals. Already the dragons knew the feel of their bite, and the bones of the unlucky littered the valley floor.

No one liked eating dragon, but almost every part of the dragon carcasses had been claimed for some purpose. Many of the men guarding Kyrien wore shields made from massive scales, and the teeth had become highly valued as spear tips--far more effective than their iron counterparts. Kyrien seemed ready to climb his way out of the valley. Catrin could feel his impatient desire as if it were her own; in many ways it was. The visions of her riding Kyrien had brought with them an intense desire to fly, to see the world from above. Part of her knew it was crazy and that flying meant facing the ferals. The monsters seemed to be multiplying, and every passing day, the danger they presented became greater.

With conscious effort, Catrin pulled herself back into the hold, back to her workshop. It seemed strange now to be working on the saddle when there was dragon ore once again within the hold. Guilt stabbed at her whenever she looked at it. Kyrien had given so much of himself to be here for her and to protect her, and as if that were not enough, he also managed to bring her more of the precious stone. Now Catrin had no desire to create herald globes, and no more trade would fill their coffers. The dragons and demons effectively prevented that, even if they didn't stop the steady stream of refugees who came from the south in the night. Though Catrin loved her people as a whole, those who had opposed her in good times and now sought her help in bad times angered her. She was tempted to turn them away, to send them back, but she simply could not.

Every new body that entered the hold presented new challenges and changed the rationing requirements. There were those who vehemently objected to allowing the refugees in, but Catrin had had the final word so far. She knew there would come a time when she would need to change her stance, but for the moment she put those thoughts aside. Again the desire to finish her saddle came to the fore. Though she considered returning straight to work, she took the time to make good use of Brother Vaughn's gift and iced her aching hands.

* * *

With sweat soaking his clothes, Sinjin followed Durin, who walked at a terribly slow pace. "Hurry up. The sooner we get this done, the sooner we can go do something else."

"That's just the problem," Durin said without turning. "As soon as we finish this, they'll have something else needin' done. You watch."

Sinjin didn't argue. Durin was right, yet Sinjin didn't mind as much. The work helped him feel as if he were contributing something. So often he felt helpless and useless, but at least he could achieve menial tasks. The hard work and sweat also helped him regain his strength and even grow stronger. He could feel the power in his newly toned muscles, and he liked it. The past moon had been the most difficult any of them could remember. In many ways, Sinjin and Durin were but spectators watching a most terrible drama play out.

Sinjin curled the mostly full water buckets he carried, switching between right and left. He found he could alternate along with his stride and establish a rhythm; that was if Durin would keep moving.

"No more draggin' your butts through these halls, now; especially not the *champion* runner," Miss Mariss said when they finally returned to the kitchens. "I needed that water long before now, and you've thrown off the entire kitchen. Now tell everyone you're sorry. Listen up, everyone! These two sluggards have something they want to say to you." With a steel eye, she turned to Durin. "Well, boy, what do you have to say for yourself?"

"I'm sorry," Durin blurted, his eyes cast to the side. If he'd been looking her in the eye, he might have seen it coming; instead, he was caught completely by surprise when she smacked him on the back of the head.

"And what about you?"

Sinjin looked up. "I'm sorry we took so long. It won't happen again."

"Your boilin' right it won't. Now empty the wastewater buckets and bring more clean water back with you."

"Yes, ma'am," the boys said in unison, neither with a great deal of enthusiasm. Bringing fresh water was difficult, but taking out the wastewater could be most unpleasant. Miss Mariss saved this task for those who irked her the most, which meant Durin was first in line with Sinjin running a close second.

"Why do I get lectured and smacked on the head and you just get lectured? I'm tellin' ya, you can get away with anything," Durin said in a nasally voice, trying not to breathe through his nose. Sinjin understood the wisdom of that decision since it was often better to never know how bad the water smelled; for some reason, the worse it smelled, the more likely it was to get spilled. Doing the laundry and scrubbing the passageway floors was worse than the carrying. Sinjin would prefer to just get the task done, but Durin slowed once again.

"There's gotta be a better way," Durin said, glaring at one of the many basins throughout the hold, all of which were dry. The one he glared at now held some dried flowers. Everyone speculated that the hold had once had water flowing through it. Durin couldn't imagine how such a thing could have been achieved, and he often wondered if everyone else weren't wrong. Perhaps the basins had served a completely different purpose altogether. He'd often been tempted to pour the wastewater down one of the basins, but the idea of trying to get rid of the smell if it didn't work stood in his way. Of course, sometimes that was the only thing that stood in his way, especially when his shoulders and his chest ached.

"I don't want to get yelled at again," Sinjin said. "Let's go."

Durin set down the buckets and turned. "I need to rest."

Sinjin was about to make a sarcastic remark, but he noticed how slowly Durin straightened after lowering the buckets to the stone.

He turned to Sinjin with eyes filled with tears. "I'm not as strong as I used to be. Sometimes I need to catch my breath."

Familiar guilt engulfed Sinjin. His friend was only weak because he'd been hit by a weapon intended for Sinjin. "I'm sorry."

"Don't be. It wasn't *all* your fault."

Sinjin started to protest, but Durin just laughed, which turned to a cough. After a couple more steadying breaths, he hoisted the buckets and started moving once again along the hall. Sinjin shuffled silently behind him, his mind consumed with problems for which he had no solutions.

It seemed to take all afternoon to reach the God's Eye. There, small barges waited to carry waste products across the subterranean lake where they could be taken into the Chinawpa Valley and buried or otherwise disposed of. It was a tedious process that took more time and resources than anyone would care to admit.

Simms and Bradley manned the poles of the nearest barge, and they grinned at the boys as they approached. "More wastewater, eh?" Simms said. "Don't ya ever git tired of carryin' wastewater? Ya always stink by the time ya git down here."

Sinjin just stepped onto the greasy timbers of the barge. Though small, the barges could carry an amazing amount of weight, far more than Sinjin and Durin ever came with. Simms detested putting out so much effort for such small loads, but Sinjin and Durin had no choice in the matter; their instructions were quite clear, as were Simms's, but that didn't stop the older boy from complaining loudly.

"Don't have nothin' t'say?"

"Mind your tongue," Bradley said. "You don't want the Herald coming down here and lecturing us again, do you?"

Sinjin flushed at the memory and wished, once again, that his mother would learn that sticking up for him was not in his best interest; it only made things worse. The rest of the trip passed in tense silence, and Sinjin watched the cavern walls slide by. Archways along the walls marked tunnels that had been blocked by the ancients. No one quite understood how it had been done. While some tunnels had been blocked with only loose stone and mortar, most of those leading away from the God's Eye were blocked by similar obstructions for a short distance before the tunnels dead-ended in solid granite. Once three tunnels had been excavated with the same results, all efforts to explore the remaining tunnels had been abandoned. Still, Sinjin tried to imagine what wonders could lie beyond and what magic the ancients used to conceal and secure them.

"Hurry up," Simms said. "I'm not waitin' all day."

Sinjin grunted when lifting his buckets, and Durin looked unsteady on his feet.

"I'll help you with that," Bradley said, earning a glare from Simms.

Late-afternoon light streamed in from outside, casting a ruddy glow over the pocked stone floor. Guards flanked the entranceway, ready to close multiple sets of gates should the hold come under attack again. Thus far, their fortifications had repelled the ferals and demons, but many feared the enemy had merely been testing their defenses in preparation for a major assault.

"Hold," came the guard's command.

"It's just us," Durin said, clearly annoyed.

"State your business."

"We brought you supper," Durin said.

"Wastewater," Sinjin said, glaring at Durin. "Was that so hard?"

"Every time it's the same thing. 'State your business.' We're carrying water buckets, for Kyrien's sake."

Bradley laughed and shook his head as he led them through the ancient hall, which opened onto the more recently built timber fortifications, stairs, and lift mechanism. Men worked nearby, all guarded by soldiers with spears, and all seemed ready to retreat at the first sign of trouble. Sinjin couldn't blame them.

"Wastewater to the right," the overseer barked.

"Wastewater to the right," Durin mimicked, causing Bradley to chuckle.

It felt good to be outside and breathing fresh air, and this brief moment was one of the reasons Sinjin didn't mind the task. The air near the freshly dug latrines was rarely pleasant, and the three dumped the buckets and retreated as quickly as they could.

A low murmur suddenly flowed across the valley floor followed by a dark shadow. Sinjin, Durin, and Bradley ducked down and stayed still. The dragon did not return, and people continued their work, anxious and on constant alert. It was exhausting and those who worked outside could do so for only short periods of time. Too many were overcome with fatigue and became careless; that was all it took these days to get dead.

Instinctively walking hunched over, as close to the ground as possible, the three did their best to get back to the cavern in silence. Sinjin looked over the beds of herald globes charging in the remaining sunlight, and he worried over their safety, but if they didn't charge in the sun, they wouldn't glow during the following nights. Sinjin had always found it amazing that one day of charging in the sun was enough to make a herald globe glow for nearly a fortnight. So many of the things his mother was said to have done seemed far away, as if they were but fairy tales, but these brought those stories closer to his heart. This was something only his mother could make, and they were among the world's greatest wonders.

Torches and candles were still used by most with only the most affluent able to afford the luxury of herald globes, and only those with jobs that could not be done otherwise were allowed to make use of the hold's inventory. Many globes were used to light the common halls and work areas, but there were still many parts of the hold left permanently in the dark. Sinjin had not expected such darkness when he returned to the cavern, but the torches on Simms's barge were almost lost in the distance.

"One of these days, I'm gonna leave that moron in the middle of this lake," Bradley said to Sinjin and Durin.

Chapter 8

The might of kings soars on leathery wings.
--Fedicus Illiani, historian

* * *

Heavy wisps of black smoke curled from whale-oil lamps as Thorakis turned the herald globe in his hand. Such a small thing. The most powerful person in the world had been working for more than a decade, and this was the best she had come up with. It was sad, really. Thorakis had achieved so much more without using a lick of Istra's power. His might had come from foresight and wit. His power rested in water, wood, and stone. All this he did on his own, his intellect his most powerful tool. He wondered at times what he could accomplish if he ever tapped his other talents. A deep sensation of cold ran through him, leaving him nauseated and unsettled, a cold sweat forming on his brow.

No one could know, he reminded himself. His power and will must come from his natural abilities alone. He renewed his vow, all the while stroking Seethe's head. The mighty serpent had grown quickly and now curled around Thorakis's throne, his bulk spilling onto the dais, his head resting in Thorakis's lap.

"I beg of you, sire," Grimwell said, kneeling before Thorakis and Seethe. "Address the troops. It is you they follow, not I. Please. Lead them."

Thorakis nearly dismissed Grimwell again, having heard this plea before and not liking the idea any more than he had the last time. He did not wish to leave Seethe alone, and the troops were not ready to meet his dragon yet. The feral dragon was still young and needed Thorakis to protect him. The thoughts came readily; he'd been through this before. "Proceed with construction of the aqueducts as I have requested. Be certain my specifications are met exactly!"

"Will you not speak to them, sire?"

"You try my patience, wizard!" Thorakis began with a wild gleam in his eye. Seethe shifted in Thorakis's lap, and Grimwell's eyes grew wide. A vision overwhelmed Thorakis as he saw himself delivering an oration like none ever achieved before. He could feel the energy radiating from the crowd as they cheered his name, and with every breath, he was filled with it. When he looked back at Grimwell, the wizard shrank away. "Yes. I will speak to them, wizard. Gather them and prepare them. I am ready."

Grimwell retreated backward from the hall, his eyes locked with Seethe's, and it was everything he could do not to run. Had he seen those who stepped from the shadows after his departure, he would have.

* * *

Within the modest room he called home, Brother Vaughn sat facing Trinda. "Please tell me about the dragons. How did you call to them?"

Trinda shrugged. "I sang."

"Had you sung before?"

"Yes."

"When and how often?" Brother Vaughn asked, hoping she wouldn't make him pull every detail from her.

"Just sometimes."

"And what happens when you sing. Please, tell me."

"When I sing, I think about things, and they come to me."

Brother Vaughn let that statement sink in. "What things have come to you?"

"Butterflies once. And birds once. And one time fish. And now dragons, I guess."

"Fish," Brother Vaughn said and Trinda nodded. "Will you show me?" She nodded again.

From the three-pronged stand that Strom had made him, Brother Vaughn grabbed his herald globe and a ball of string. Trinda looked interested but said nothing more. As they walked, he noticed how much Trinda shied away from anyone they passed and, in more than a few cases, how the people they encountered reacted to Trinda. It was a small hold, and Brother Vaughn hoped he could find a way to keep the girl safe. Many associated Trinda with the death of Catrin's and Chase's mothers, and no matter how hard they tried, some simply could not accept her presence in the hold.

As they passed through the dark halls, only the glow of his herald globe lit the way, and Trinda huddled within its light. Those they passed had their own business and paid little mind. At the dock, no barges waited, the area eerily quiet. Trinda drew a deep breath when she beheld the God's Eye, and Brother Vaughn couldn't blame her. No one seemed prepared for the sight of a natural vaulted chamber of such size and capacity to hold what could only be called a lake. This end of the lake received the least light and had no algae growing in it, which meant that the fish usually stayed at the far end of the lake, where food was more plentiful.

Using his string, Brother Vaughn created a cradle for his herald globe and showed it to Trinda, who looked dubious. He lowered the herald globe into the water, not really knowing what to expect. To his surprise, the light became brighter and cast distorted beams through the water, but it also did an excellent job illuminating the steep slope that dropped away from the cavern entrance. No fish could be seen.

"Would you sing now for me? And think about fish? Just the ones in this lake, mind you," he added, suddenly envisioning fish leaving the sea to find her. Trinda hesitated and Brother Vaughn said nothing, not wanting to coerce her. She closed her eyes for a moment, and Brother Vaughn thought she might not be ready, but then she nodded and began to sing a soft, wordless tune that pulled at his heart. Brother Vaughn lost track of time while he listened, and he forgot the reason they had come, forgot what he had asked her to sing for. When he looked down and saw the glowing water filled with writhing bodies, all aligned and pointing at Trinda, he jumped and lost his grip on the string.

Trinda stopped singing and tried to grab the string as it slipped beneath the water. The globe looked as if it might come to rest on a shelf of rock, but the shifting water pulled it out and sent it tumbling into the depths. Brother Vaughn watched in morbid fascination; the light grew brighter as it moved deeper. He could see the smoothness of the slope; there was nothing to impede his herald globe, which had left the string behind. Both of them gasped when the shape of a shipwreck appeared from the darkness and was then lost again in shadow. Just as suddenly, the light stopped moving, apparently stuck on a rock formation of some sort.

"You dropped it," Trinda said.

Brother Vaughn couldn't contain his excitement. "Did you see that? That was amazing! You called the fish to you, and that was wonderful, and then, like the great oaf I am, I dropped the globe, but even that brought discovery. Did you see that ship? It must have been built *inside* this cavern. Can you imagine that?"

"By the gods!" came Simms's shout. His barge was over where the herald globe had come to rest. "Would you look at that!"

Bradley, on another barge, quickly poled his way to where Simms waited, seemingly too stunned to move. Bradley looked down and, cursing, poled his way back to the dock. Simms remained where he was as if paralyzed.

"What is it, man?" Brother Vaughn asked.

"Get on," Bradley said. "You just have to see it."

Brother Vaughn hesitated a moment, unsure how Trinda would do on the water, but she stepped behind Bradley and onto the barge so fast, all he could do was follow. Bradley poled them back to where Simms was now issuing a steady stream of curses with occasional prayers interjected.

Below them lay an unmistakable form, or at least part of it. What looked back from below was a gleaming feral dragon, its menacing maw clear in the light. The globe had landed quite close to the eye of the giant serpent, which seemed to be made of enormous crystalline structures, as if the gems had naturally formed into the shape of a mountain-sized dragon. The beast's body faded into the darkness, but Brother Vaughn imagined it stretching to the far shore. The dragon's glare inspired awe and fear, and seeing the fish now gathering around the dragon's eye, attracted by the light, was among the most vivid images Brother Vaughn had ever seen.

"Are there any divers within the hold?" Brother Vaughn wondered aloud.

"There's Logan the spear fisherman," Bradley said. "That guy can hold his breath for a really long time. I bet he could get it back."

"Could you go find him for me?"

Bradley seemed hesitant to leave his post. Though he was working as a bargeman, he was officially part of the guard, and abandoning one's post was a serious crime.

"This is important. Let's go see your commander. I have something to ask of him as well," Brother Vaughn said.

Bradley followed. Simms looked as if he didn't care, but Bradley wore his concern openly.

"Don't worry. I'll take care of this."

"Yes, sir," Bradley said, looking no less uneasy.

Brother Vaughn could understand his worry and uncertainty. So many things were new in Dragonhold, and so few people knew with absolute confidence what they should do and to whom they should listen without question.

It came as a bit of a shock when it was Morif Bradley sought out. It would appear that Bradley ranked higher than one might think, and Brother Vaughn suspected Morif was keeping a special eye on the hold's entrances.

"What's all this about?" Morif said as they entered his home.

"Sir, I'm sorry, sir," Bradley began, and Morif held him in a steady, one-eyed gaze.

"I pulled him away from his post," Brother Vaughn interjected, and Morif turned his imposing stare.

"I've made a discovery! Well, several, actually, and I need a diver to get my herald globe back from the bottom of the God's Eye. And you should see what's down there!"

"Why did he bring you up here?" Morif asked Bradley.

"He wanted me to find Logan so he could dive for the herald globe Brother Vaughn dropped in the water."

"Then go get him," Morif said.

Bradley left in a hurry.

Morif nodded. "That's a good man."

Brother Vaughn nodded his agreement. Trinda tried to remain unseen. Millie was one of the people who couldn't stand the thought of her being in the hold, and Morif was conditioned to look after her interests. Somehow Trinda must have sensed that she was not welcome.

"And I suppose there must be something else, or I suspect you'd already be gone." He didn't look at Trinda, but he didn't have to.

"I need to borrow your herald globe," Brother Vaughn said.

"Why?"

"I just need to borrow it for a little while, and then I'll bring it back. I promise."

Morif harrumphed and pulled his globe from its stand. "Let's go see what we've got here."

He led the way back toward the God's Eye, never actually giving Brother Vaughn the herald globe.

At the docks, they waited for Simms to return. He'd been floating over the sunken herald globe when they arrived, and seeing Morif on the shoreline had him moving in a hurry. Morif didn't say anything, and it was clear by the look on Simms's face that he didn't need to. "Get me out there so I can see what all this fuss is about."

"Yes, sir."

Brother Vaughn and Trinda followed Morif onto the barge, and he felt the same sense of fascination this time when the mighty serpent came into view. He found entirely new details that he had missed before. The herald globe continued to glow brightly, though only an occasional fish now played in the light.

Morif said nothing; he just stood, stroking his beard. Brass adornments braided into the beard made a soft noise that seemed to soothe the old warrior. Brother Vaughn knew better than to try to get something out of Morif. The man would speak when he was ready.

Bradley returned with a man Brother Vaughn assumed was Logan. He was thin as a sapling with skin still sun darkened, something that was becoming increasingly rare. Bradley poled his barge to a stop not far away, and Logan spared not a word. He simply slipped into the water and swam toward the light. He moved like a seal as he swam, and Brother Vaughn worried he would drown. Even once the man had grabbed the globe, he appeared to rise to the surface far too slowly, but Logan broke the surface and seemed only moderately winded. He swam to Brother Vaughn and handed him the glowing orb.

Turning the herald globe in his hand, he watched as it dimmed to a softer glow. "May I see your globe?" he asked Morif.

The wizened veteran grunted and handed it to him.

"Was that the deepest you could dive?" Brother Vaughn asked Logan.

"No, sir. I can go deeper than that."

"Don't even think about it," Morif said, but Brother Vaughn was already moving, and before Morif could stop him, he'd thrown both globes back into the water.

Brother Vaughn hoped Morif didn't lose patience with him, and he wore an apology on his face for only an instant. Then he watched in fascination as the two globes cast slightly overlapping rings of light, and the first sailed down close to where the ancient shipwreck lay. The second soared beyond the dragon's eye and gave only the slightest glimpse of something else resting on the coils of the dragon.

"Do you think you can dive for those?" Morif asked Logan.

"I think so, sir. I just need a bit of time to breathe."

"Simms, get your butt back to the docks. There're people waiting." He turned back to the monk. "With all due respect, *Vaughn,* don't do that again."

"Yes. Um. Yes, of course," Brother Vaughn said, secretly hoping someone else would annoy Morif and take the focus off him. The barge was feeling rather small and more than a little crowded. A moment later, though, Logan disappeared under the water and moved into the light. First he went to the globe near the sunken ship, and Brother Vaughn nearly fell in as he leaned over to watch. Logan had the globe in one hand yet didn't start back up immediately. Instead, he glided along the side of the sunken ship and spent what seemed an eternity sifting through the wreckage. Brother Vaughn suddenly remembered to breathe, only then realizing that he'd been holding his breath as though he were underwater with the diver.

Even Morif rushed to see what it was that Logan brought back up. He handed the globe back to Brother Vaughn, and he seemed less enthusiastic about handing the object in his other hand over, but then he seemed to have a change of heart. "Here," he said.

Morif and Brother Vaughn both reached out at the same time, and it nearly sent Morif into the water. Brother Vaughn tried not to think about how that would've turned out but was distracted by the sight of a small, gold-trimmed box made of jade and wood inlay. The perfectly preserved artifact rested easily in Morif's hands. There seemed no apparent way of opening the box, and he handed it to Brother Vaughn.

"If that thing happens to entitle the bearer to wine, whiskey, and women, you'll give it back, right?" Logan asked.

"Deal," Brother Vaughn said. "Even if it's just two out of three."

"Fair enough."

Logan's dive for the second globe was as excruciatingly slow as the first, and it seemed he was having trouble dislodging the globe from where it had come to rest. Morif cast Brother Vaughn an accusatory glance, which Brother Vaughn did his best to pretend he didn't notice. After a few tense moments, Logan freed the globe and made his way slowly back to the surface.

"I don't know how you do that," Brother Vaughn said, "but it makes me breathe heavy just watching you." Though Logan's ascent had provided no new detail of what else waited on the lake floor, Brother Vaughn was thrilled by what he had learned. "Thank you all for your help! This is wonderful!"

Morif snatched both herald globes out of Brother Vaughn's hands. "You'll get yours back when we get to shore."

* * *

Chase shook his head. Before him stood Catrin in the craziest outfit he'd ever seen. She'd taken supple leather and created a tight but flexible body suit covered with straps, rings, and zippers. Her ears were covered, and over her eyes she wore clear lenses mounted in leather-wrapped iron rings, which were attached to a second pair of rings with flaps that tapered into a strap and buckle. "You look like Strom attacked an otter."

Catrin grinned back at him and turned around. Then she climbed up onto the saddle. Chase continued to shake his head as he watched her draw the straps and buckle herself to the saddle. The largest straps secured her at the waist, and other smaller straps formed an interplay. Cinching tight on one strap gave slack to another, and because of the clever design, Catrin could move around on the massive saddle while still being firmly tethered. It was brilliant and insane.

Hunching down as if she were in mid flight, Catrin moved her feet to an upper set of toeholds and wedged herself under the two massive shield flaps, which were lightly armored and apparently padded inside. "You see," came Catrin's muffled voice. "There's enough room for me and a few things."

"Even if we could make a thousand of these, we don't have a thousand dragons. We have one and we're not certain he'll fly again."

"Don't you say that," Catrin said, looking imposing despite her ridiculous garb. "Kyrien could fly now if he wanted to, but *we* are not ready. *We* are unprepared. And why are *we* unprepared? Because *we* did not listen to *me*."

Chase let out a brief sigh, which was cut off by another sharp look from Catrin. How anyone could expect to be taken seriously with those goggles on was beyond him, yet somehow she pulled it off. The pair of knives holstered on each leg did help, he supposed. "Yes. You're right. Let's not have that argument again. My point is that I don't think this saddle provides a solution to our immediate problems."

"What's your solution?"

Chase searched for words, but he could find none that hadn't already been said by Catrin herself years before.

"Then don't look down your nose on what might be part of the solution."

"Perhaps it will help to mollify the Arghast as well," Chase admitted. "They're quite unhappy that you've not taught them to fly yet."

"Don't start with that either. How am I supposed to teach someone how to do something I don't know how to do?" Catrin asked in futility. "At least not without a ship, that is," she admitted. "That doesn't change the fact that I haven't ridden a dragon . . . yet."

"The problem is this: If we take that saddle down there and put it on Kyrien, the people are going to expect you to fly. The Arghast will expect you to fly. And we both know it isn't even close to safe for Kyrien to fly with Reaver patrolling the skies and demons on the ground. What makes you think the ferals won't immediately gang up on Kyrien?"

"I don't intend to fly yet. There will come a time, yes, but not yet. For now we will just need to explain to everyone that it is simply a test to satisfy my curiosity and that we will not be flying."

"You know how much turmoil this will cause."

"I do and I cannot fix that. People are going to have to come to grips with the fact that the world has changed. We ourselves must either change or die. Deal with it."

It was clear to Chase that he would not win this argument. The truth was that he partially agreed with her. Still, he did not look forward to the uproar it would cause. "When?"

"Now."

* * *

With little besides hard breads coming out of the kitchens, Durin did his best to avoid them altogether. Since Miss Mariss now refused to let anyone take more than one portion of food, no one could bring him food, and hunger eventually won out. If Sinjin were around, it wouldn't be so bad, but Brother Vaughn had sequestered him away with only Trinda for company. Durin felt for his friend; carrying water buckets wasn't nearly as bad. Trinda was the least happy person Durin had ever met, and she always managed to dampen his mood. When he took the family history into account, he worried even more about Sinjin's safety.

Worrying made Durin hungry. With a sigh, he made his way deeper into the hold, where the heat was nearly unbearable. Durin wondered how people managed to breathe the hot air for so long. It suffocated him. Strom's hammer rang an angry tone, and Durin stepped quickly by the smithy entrance. Taking his place in line, Durin waited, trying to be invisible. A line of guards approached; far more than usual, Durin noted with dismay. The guards would get fed first, and that meant a long wait and the chance that there would be nothing left by the time he got there. It had been happening more and more lately. Even with many in the hold cooking their own meals, the kitchens simply could not keep up with the demand for food--cooked or rationed. The stress it placed on Miss Mariss was obvious, and Durin felt guilty for hiding.

Just as he was considering asking Miss Mariss what he could do to help, though, the man next to him decided he didn't have time to wait for the guards, and he suddenly turned and left. Never one to miss anything in her kitchen, Miss Mariss immediately spotted Durin.

"You see that wad of guards come in, and you hide in line? I ought to make you carry buckets until your lazy little legs fall off!"

Durin considered telling her he was about to ask what he could do, but even he would not have believed it. Instead, he just walked to where the buckets of dirty water waited and grabbed two. Miss Mariss simply glared at him. As he made his way toward the kitchen exit, a guard charged through the door and bumped Durin, which sent dirty water into the air, most of which landed on Durin.

"If you're gonna spill it, then clean it up," Miss Mariss said with the closest thing to a smile that Durin had seen on her face in weeks. At least his misery served some purpose, he thought.

"Sorry, mate," the guard said. "I'd help you clean it up, but they want all of us--uh . . . we have something important to do."

Durin just put down his buckets and caught the clean rags Miss Mariss threw at him. He'd been breathing through his mouth, hoping not to smell how bad the water was, but it became tedious and he breathed in through his nose. To his surprise, the water did not smell bad at all. After cleaning up the spill, he tucked one of the remaining dry rags into his belt; the rest went into the laundry pile, which he suspected he would have to carry next.

What he really wanted to do was go see why all the guards were needed. With Sinjin closeted away and double the guards on duty, there had to be something afoot. When he reached the alcove where he and Sinjin used to hide, he stopped. Too many guards cast him glances as they passed, making it clear he'd get nowhere near the excitement. Already his back ached, and a short rest was too difficult to resist. He would find out what was going on soon enough. Not wanting anyone to know, he brought the buckets back into the shadows. Within moments, he was asleep.

Chapter 9

Forgotten are those who fail to achieve. Doomed are those afraid to fail.
--Brother Vaughn, Cathuran monk

* * *

Blue skies filled with nothing but towering cloud formations, white and fluffy, appeared nonthreatening, yet most watched the skies in tense anticipation. Reaver had yet to make an appearance, but his presence was almost palpable. Few other dragons ventured in close to Kyrien, or the Pinook Valley at all for that matter, but Reaver seemed determined to root out the humans and especially Kyrien. He exuded frustration every time he attacked despite the scars he bore from previous attempts.

Chase's people learned from every encounter, and between Morif and Martik, they found either tactical or mechanical solutions to their weaknesses. Crews were now adept at loading, aiming, and firing ballistae, and stacks of sharpened tree trunks waited near each of the six super weapons. Each one had its own personality, and crews had to learn the quirks of their specific weapon. Misfires and mistakes had been costly, and those who still lived were determined not to suffer the same fates as their lost brethren. The visions of Reaver flying off with friends and comrades burned in their memories.

Kyrien moved among them, his every step causing men to scramble, and many walked a thin line between protecting Kyrien and being unintentionally killed by him. The saddle was nearly down the stairs, and Kyrien looked more alive than he had in weeks. Stretching his wings, he reminded everyone in the valley of his true size. From the stair, Catrin beamed down at him, trying to contain her impatience. Bringing the massive saddle down the stairs was a slow and arduous process.

Swiveling his head on his long, slender neck, Kyrien watched their progress and let out an echoing call when finally they approached. Catrin wished he, too, could contain his enthusiasm. No doubt Reaver heard his call and would come to investigate. Those guarding Kyrien reached the same conclusion and scanned the skies for any sign of the massive feral dragon. The men carrying the saddle also quickened their pace beyond what might have been considered prudent. In times such as these, safety was a relative thing.

Kyrien met Catrin's eyes, and the world ceased to exist. His gaze captivated her, and excitement filled the air between them. *Hurry.*

Alongside the final landing, Kyrien positioned himself, extending one wing so his girth was fully exposed. It was an awkward position, and it left him vulnerable, but it made it much easier on those who were trying to get the saddle in place.

"You'll never be able to clear the gap!" Martik said as he pushed his way toward those handling the saddle. It was clear the men were already spent. "I need some fresh bodies up here! Fetch a block and tackle, and find me an anchor point on the east face. And rope! We need at least three coils of rope."

No one waited long to obey. Though Martik held no title or military power, his genius was undeniable, and the people had come to trust his judgment. Trust, it seemed, was a better motivator than political power as people obeyed him with confidence. After securing the pulleys and ropes, Martik positioned people around the saddle and orchestrated their movements like a symphony, constantly reacting as conditions changed. Even with his skills and the peoples' trust of him, it was a dangerous task. Swinging wildly at times, blown by gusts of wind, the saddle struck at random, sending one man over the railing. Kyrien managed to catch the man on his side, preventing what might have been a serious injury.

"Bring me slack!" Martik shouted at the two men closest to him. "Steady. Steady."

The saddle dropped into place more quickly than Martik had intended, and Kyrien let out a *woof* when it landed, but then he shifted and squirmed until the saddle fell into place, looking as if it had been designed exactly to fit him, which it had, but Catrin was still amazed by how good a fit it was since it had been based on mental imagery alone.

Raising his body up on his two powerful legs, Kyrien provided enough room for the girths to be run under his belly. Catrin watched a young man slide under Kyrien, risking his life for her, knowing that he would be crushed if Kyrien chose to lower himself at the wrong time. Kyrien watched the young man and made sure he was well clear before the mighty regent dragon raised himself up higher, bringing the seat near to where Catrin watched. Using a loop in the rope lift, Catrin stepped up and allowed Martik and his men to raise her up and maneuver her over the saddle.

"This time bring me slack *slowly* and *evenly!*" Martik demanded.

The men holding the ropes did the best they could, but Catrin still landed hard. She didn't care. She was on Kyrien's back, just as she'd seen in her visions, though perhaps the next time she mounted, she thought, she would simply climb up. After pulling the girths snug and securing the breast collar, Catrin strapped herself into the saddle. Stiff leather resisted going into the keepers, and hooks resisted sliding through awl-punched holes, but she was eventually satisfied that she had constructed the saddle correctly. When she raised her hands in victory, a small cheer went up from the crowd, which Catrin noticed contained more than a few Arghast. Halmsa watched her with unwavering attention, seemingly absorbing every detail so he could relay the information to his tribesman.

What Catrin had not expected to see was Strom descending the stairs carrying a blanket-wrapped bundle. Noting the storm cloud he had in place of his face, Catrin wondered what could be afoot. When he reached the landing, the crowd parted and let him pass though he'd said not a word. The look on his face made it clear he would part rock if he had to. "Here!" was all he said to Catrin before he unwrapped the package and thrust a weapon, shielded pommel first, across the gap to Catrin. Martik stepped in behind him to make sure he didn't fall into the valley below.

Catrin opened her mouth to speak, but Strom immediately withdrew and walked to where Kyrien could easily see him. Strom glared at the dragon, who regarded him with what looked like mild amusement.

"There! Are you happy now?" Strom shouted up at Kyrien, bringing a shocked roar that ran through those assembled. Kyrien simply closed his eyes for a moment and bowed his head to Strom. "Good. Now stay out of my head!" When Strom turned away, the crowd parted even more quickly, not wanting to impede a man with the courage to browbeat a dragon.

Even Catrin found herself speechless as she watched Strom climb the stairs, leaving without another word. In her hand she held a blade like none she'd ever seen or imagined, yet it fit her perfectly. The pommel was contained within a shielded sleeve that allowed her to swing it without keeping a tight grip, and she guessed it would protect her wrist should she strike something unforgiving. The blade forked at the end into two blades, each tip shaped like an indented triangle that tapered to a deadly point. Though not covered in scrollwork, there was a subtle design that seemed to hide under the glossy shine, and Catrin could not imagine how the delicate image could have been created. Truly Strom had become a master of the anvil and forge, quite possibly with help from Kyrien, whether Strom liked it or not. After his outburst, Catrin guessed not.

Even the sheath had been designed to work with the harness that secured Catrin. Kyrien had been accurate in every detail. Catrin moved from side to side, her feet jumping from toehold to toehold, and she felt secure at all times without feeling trapped in place. If ever it did come to a midair fight, Catrin felt she would be able to take evasive and perhaps even offensive action without fear of plummeting from the sky.

Looking up, she found the eyes of all the Arghast who remained at Dragonhold regarding her with wonder. "Fly!" one shouted, and the others took up the chant, despite those who tried to quiet them.

Almost instantly someone else shouted, "Reaver to the north!"

"Demons to the south!"

"Fly!" demanded the Arghast.

Catrin froze, certainty beyond her grasp. Indecision held her fast, and Kyrien turned to look at her. In his eyes she saw acceptance of death and something more, something indefinable and magical. This was his only communication to her as their enemies approached. A furor had erupted around them as people sought to arm themselves or flee. There was no time for Catrin to unstrap herself. Morif ran forward with his long knife bared. He had two straps cut before Catrin forced him back. "No!"

"Now is not the time to risk everything, Catrin. You must get inside to safety. Cut yourself free and I'll get you there. I promise you. Let the guards defend Kyrien as they've done before."

"Demons to the north! By the gods, they're everywhere!"

This attack was unlike those that had come before. This was no feint meant to harass them and test their strength. This was a full-on assault. Among the demons walked giants in chains. Catrin felt her courage flee. These beasts were like something straight from a nightmare. Towering over the demons, they looked like the massive statues in the Valley of the Victors come to life. Every muscle in their upper torsos stood out, pronounced and defined, giving them a hard and angular look. Short, coarse hair covered their legs and whiplike tails. Thick fingers and toes made appendages look more like battering rams.

Reaver swooped low from the north and skimmed over what were obviously *his* troops. Even the giants cowered in the shadow of Reaver, whose size made his aerobatics seem impossible. The twang of a ballista split the air, and a tree trunk soared over Reaver's right wing. The dragon dipped below it with ease and picked up speed.

"Hold your bolts! Wait for it," Morif shouted as he left Catrin's side. "Wait for my command!"

Catrin looked down at the straps that had been cut away, knowing she could not cut her way out of the saddle in time to retreat, she tried to think of a way to repair them, but then the world turned upside down.

* * *

Durin woke to the sound of footsteps rushing through the halls of Dragonhold. Shouts echoed from a distance, and a cold feeling washed over him. His muscles were stiff, attesting to how long he'd slept.

"Catrin has saddled Kyrien," someone whispered as he and a companion passed the alcove.

Durin shuddered. There had been hints and rumors that the Herald had been building a saddle and that she would use it to teach the Arghast to fly dragons, but he'd never really believed it. Catrin had always been a part of his life, and though she occasionally did things he couldn't explain, she didn't seem as powerful as the tales would imply. Excitement charged in and he wondered if she really could be saddling Kyrien. In that moment, he wanted nothing more than to get to the front gate and see what was really going on. He was tired of hearing about the battles and excitement that had taken place while he was carrying water, and he wanted to finally witness something for himself.

The distant shouts took on an alarming note, and it became clear that something was wrong. Knowing Miss Mariss would have his hide if he took too long to return with fresh water, he came up with a plan. The only way he could save time would be to run to the God's Eye, which he couldn't do with full buckets. Turning his eyes on the glowing rune that waited in the darkness, Durin smiled.

Slowly he emptied the first bucket into the rune. The glowing chasm seemed bottomless, and Durin grinned, knowing he'd just come up with a brilliant solution to some of his problems. A bit of steam rose from the rune, but Durin didn't hesitate and poured the second bucket in as well. Now he could jog to the God's Eye with empty buckets after taking a quick peek at what was happening in the great hall. Before he left the alcove, though, more steam rose from the rune and a high-pitched whistle sounded.

Durin considered running, but he had to find out what would happen next. The stone beneath his feet trembled, and a deep, bone-chilling rumble gained intensity. An enormous gout of steam rose from the rune, driving Durin back. The whistling grew higher and higher in pitch until it and the steam suddenly stopped. For a moment, there was silence.

Then Dragonhold moved.

Chapter 10

In a war with the mindless, there is no room for surrender or mercy.
--Enoch Giest

* * *

Straps pulled tight as Catrin fell back in the saddle, driven far into the seat by the force of Kyrien's launching himself into the air, colliding with Reaver, and ending up locked together with the massive feral dragon. Catrin found herself hanging, upside down, and flying over an army of demons that approached from the south, the air pressing her goggles back into her face. Spears flew at her, and she dodged them as best she could. Her left side remained firmly strapped in, but with every move, the right side of her harness loosened.

Reaver forced Kyrien low over the trees, and branches assaulted her. A stand of ancient pine rose above the canopy, and Reaver drove them toward it. Kyrien roared and Catrin felt his muscles bunching. Just before she struck the trees, Kyrien flexed and rolled, turning Reaver over and driving him into the trees. A terrible snapping resounded through the valley, and Catrin felt Reaver let go of Kyrien. Again she was driven into her seat as Kyrien climbed sharply. After cinching up the right side of the harness as best she could, she gripped the severed ends of the straps. It seemed a futile effort, but it was the only thing she could think of.

As Kyrien turned on a wingtip, Catrin caught sight of Reaver righting himself and slowly gaining altitude, as he did, he let out a terrifying roar that Catrin felt as much as heard. With little more than a quick mental warning, Kyrien tucked his wings and dived at Reaver, who roared again. Dropping like a stone, Catrin felt as if she would lose her stomach. Then she moved into the upper toeholds and gripped the horn with straining hands.

Brace!

Almost too late, Catrin prepared herself. With a terrible impact, Kyrien struck Reaver, who had rolled over and extended his claws just prior to the collision. The terrible sound of three sets of lungs being emptied of air echoed in the canyon. The world darkened as they plummeted from the sky, tangled together. In a haunting moment, Catrin wondered if she were dreaming. All around them flew dragons, which dived in close only to retreat. Just before she thought she would succumb to unconsciousness, Catrin lurched sideways, seeing another feral dragon reach in and pull Kyrien and Reaver apart. Immediately both dragons righted themselves, and still branches raked them before they could regain the air.

Kyrien stayed low and sped south of Lowerton. Edling's Wall marred the landscape, a brown and gray line that divided her homeland. The new gate was progress, but Catrin would prefer the Wall ceased to exist. Following the river as it broadened, Kyrien flew low over a waterfall that poured into a familiar lake. Catrin had no time to reminisce as Kyrien dived straight toward the lake surface, pulling up only when they were within the cloud of spray. One dark shape rose just above them and nearly clipped them; another climbed too late and struck the water at full speed, driving a wall of water before it. The backsplash sent water high enough to soak Catrin and Kyrien. Fortunately, Kyrien used his speed to get them clear.

In the reflection of the lake, Catrin saw dragons diving at them, and she looked up to see dozens ready to strike. Kyrien seemed to sense them, and just before the strikes came, he took sudden evasive action. Catrin thought she would be sick. His sudden moves unsettled her equilibrium. A loud crack sounded as another dragon struck the water, this one cartwheeling across the surface of the lake then landing flat and motionless in the shallows.

Dark columns of smoke choked the air, and Catrin cried out when she saw her old family farm burning to the ground. Everywhere was the same: smoke, fire, and nothing alive but demons. Kyrien suddenly climbed as the sound of ballistae firing rang out. Catrin tried to figure out how the demons could have so quickly replicated the weapons used against them, but as they moved toward Harborton, it became clear that the demons and dragons were not working alone. Greasy, black ships clogged the harbor, and men in equally dark armor laid siege to the Masterhouse. All of Harborton burned. This was not as much an invasion as it was extermination.

The taste of bile filled Catrin's mouth as Kyrien turned sharply again but not fast enough. A massive ballista bolt struck Catrin's saddle and smacked into her side before she knocked it away. The air pressure around her changed, and Catrin turned to see the jaws of a feral dragon about to close around her. She could feel the heat of its breath as it soared ever closer. Once again the sound of a ballista firing filled the air. Kyrien turned, dived, and pulled up sharply, using his head and neck to drive the other dragon into the path of the approaching bolt. It struck with a wet *thunk*, and Kyrien peeled away before the other could entangle him in its death fall.

Seeing the armada that choked the harbor, including ships armed with ballistae and other weapons Catrin didn't recognize, she urged Kyrien to go back north toward Dragonhold. It had all happened so fast that Catrin could hardly believe it. Even the return north was faster than she would have imagined as Kyrien used every trick he knew to gain speed. Always behind them came darkness on wings. Not far from Dragonhold, Kyrien climbed and gave Catrin a view of the Pinook and Chinawpa Valleys, her home contained within the range of mountains that divided the two. She almost cried when she saw Lowerton being utterly destroyed. The demons climbed the stair while their giants held a barrier of lashed tree trunks over their heads, protecting them.

In the Chinawpa Valley, hordes of demons built an assault ramp leading toward the back entrance of Dragonhold. Catrin let out a cheer when she saw those within the hold fighting back. With a tremendous noise, the mighty, wooden stair and framework pulled free from the mountainside, using the failsafe mechanism Martik had designed. It was terrifying to see something that had seemed so permanent suddenly come tumbling down, taking the demons and giants with it. Elation turned to horror when Kyrien climbed toward an unnatural-looking cloud that hung over Dragonhold. Below, gaping holes in the landscape looked as if a god had been trying to tear the mountain apart. Enormous holes plunged to unknowable depths where Catrin was certain there had been solid rock only a short while ago.

Light glinted from newly exposed fields of massive crystals that jutted up through rifts in the rock and soil. She caught only a brief glimpse before a huge shape burst from the dust cloud and slammed into them. Another dragon struck them from behind, and again Catrin experienced the terrifying feeling of falling.

Kyrien managed to break himself free of Death's grasp, and Catrin was whipped side to side then pressed deep into the creaking saddle as they climbed. Kyrien's flight wobbled and Catrin could see gashes on his neck and upper breast. From her vantage point, she could not see his belly or hindquarters, but she suspected he had injuries there as well. Gaining altitude, Kyrien dived in and out of the clouds, more than a dozen ferals giving chase. Their serpentine movements belied flight, and they appeared to be swimming in the air rather than flying through it.

It became very apparent that ferals were not mindless creatures and that they were not acting independently. Something was orchestrating their movements, and Catrin shivered at the thought. Not since Archmaster Belegra had she faced the power of slavery and coercion, and that was what the dragons' actions seemed like: the result of coercion. She could feel their anger and hatred; it did not seem directed at her and Kyrien, but that did little to keep them from taking it out on them.

Dark shapes moved within the clouds, never really giving Catrin a clear view until an entire formation of ferals suddenly dropped through the clouds at the same time, creating what was effectively a giant net that forced Kyrien down and into the open once again. Tucking his wings, he dived, and Catrin watched the mountains disappear behind them. The Arghast Desert lay ahead. There, she knew, would be massive thermals rising from the desert sands, and Kyrien could use those to gain altitude once again, but he continued to dive.

Soon Catrin saw what he was aiming for; near the head of the Pinook Valley, a small fire blazed, and around it stood more than a dozen men in black robes. Hatred rolled from them like rippling waves of heat, and Catrin recoiled. Kyrien extended his wings just a little, causing a rushing sound as he pulled up and reached out for one of the robed figures. Amorphous gouts of darkness leaped from the hands of the assassins, as Catrin knew they were. These monsters were here to kill her and everyone she loved. Using her sword as a focal point, she cast a violent burst of energy into their midst, hoping it would incinerate them all, only a small and lightning-quick feral dived into the narrow space between Catrin and the assassins and took the brunt of the blow. With a sickening crack, the dragon fell, struck stone, and would rise no more. It was but one of many, and malevolent force concussed the sky, like explosions of pure night.

Leaning heavily to one side, Catrin recovered from another thunderous concussion that erupted not far from her head. Kyrien tucked and dipped down to soar low over the sands, stirring a roiling dust cloud in his wake and pulling up only when Catrin saw riders approaching from deep in the desert. A sizable group of Arghast tribesmen approached, and their battle calls lifted Catrin's spirits if only for an instant.

The tribesman launched their spears into the air. Catrin turned in the saddle to see a few spears hit their marks, but the ferals shrugged them off as if they were little more than bug bites. It was then that the dragons turned their anger on the Arghast. Catrin cried out for them to retreat, but Kyrien left her no time to see what happened next. Pumping his powerful wings and riding on the overheated air, he thrust them back into the clouds.

Whether by luck or by Kyrien's design--Catrin wasn't certain--for a brief time, they dipped beneath the clouds. Below them, amid towering peaks, lay a lush, green oasis, the air above it alive with birds. When Catrin had struck the well, this was what she had hoped would happen, but actually seeing it exceeded her expectations. It was beautiful. That vision sustained her during what seemed an endless flight. Despite her urgings, Kyrien would not respond to her. His flight was direct, his path unerring, yet she had no idea where they were going or how long the journey would take. Her heart yearned for her husband and son, but they were lost to her. The pain was almost more than she could bear.

Catrin let the straps hold her in place as her mind wandered aimlessly without direction or reason. She was exhausted and allowed herself to doze off in the saddle. Some time later, Catrin woke, soaked and freezing. The gray mist that surrounded them was an ever-changing landscape. Where the air became thicker, Kyrien would suddenly rise higher, and where it thinned, he would drop. It was an uneasy feeling. Catrin had done what she could to shore up the weakness. When the air tossed Kyrien in a certain way, she was sure she would be torn from his back, but the straps held firm despite the two that had been cut. It was during those times that she came back to herself, drifting out of the half sleep long enough to try to communicate with Kyrien. His continued silence worried Catrin as much as anything else, though she had worry aplenty.

The fate of those within Dragonhold weighed heavily on her mind along with the fate of the Arghast and even that of those south of Edling's wall. Despite their disagreements, she wished them no ill, especially not the likes of which was now taking place. There was little doubt that Master Edling wanted Catrin dead, but she did not reciprocate. While she wanted to see him fall from power and be forced to live like those he oppressed, she did not wish him dead.

The sight of the assassins had raised her fury like nothing else. Those people had tried to kill Sinjin twice already, and they had nearly killed Durin in the process. Someone was behind this evil, and Catrin burned to know who and why. For most of her life, she'd been misunderstood, thought to be a mighty hero or the basest devil, but she was neither of those things. She was just a wife and mother who happened to have access to Istra's power. Certainly she had abilities that no other could claim, but those powers did not make her invincible, nor did they make her wise; they simply gave her the ability to do things that could not be undone, and with that came tremendous responsibility. Most of the time, it seemed the wisest thing to do with her power was nothing. For years she had concentrated on preparing Dragonhold, and she had failed; those within were doomed. She tried not to think about it. It was simply too painful to imagine.

Now when the greatest need she'd ever known had arisen, she was mostly powerless against the forces that sought to wipe her people out. Even the attacks she could launch lacked real power and accuracy. The darkness the assassins controlled was devastating, and Catrin knew she would need to learn a great deal in a hurry. The problem was that she had tried before and had made absolutely no progress. Her dragon ore carving had given her access to more power, but Koe was back within Dragonhold. The Staff of Life rested in the Grove of the Elders, possibly already in the hands of the demons. She'd been such a fool.

Cupping her hands, she collected moisture from the surrounding air until she had enough to quench her thirst. It amazed her that she could be so wet and still be so thirsty. It didn't quite make sense, but her mind was addled. Bright sunlight assaulted her eyes as the clouds suddenly dissipated. Desperately Catrin searched the skies around her for ferals, but she saw nothing but clear skies and occasional fluffy white clouds. The comets, though hidden, flooded the air with energy, and Catrin reveled in being beneath the open sky. She didn't know how long she and Kyrien had been flying, but she had the hunger of days without food, and she thought she might pass out.

On the horizon rose a smudge of darkness. Catrin quailed at first, but then she recognized the shape of a volcano protruding from the sea. Clouds gathered around its peak, but no smoke or lava could be seen. Kyrien glided closer and, as if reading Catrin's mind, landed on the black beaches south of the volcano, where a string of tiny islands waited. From the air, Catrin had seen whales and other large marine creatures. There should be plenty of food to be found, she thought, though by the size of some of the shadowy forms in the water, she would need to be careful not to end up food for something else.

Desperation and grief made the sunny day seem disrespectful. The sudden shock of icy cold water brought her fully alert, and she panicked, afraid she would drown while still attached to Kyrien by harness and saddle. Kyrien, though he did not communicate with her, obviously knew this and moved to the black sands. After unbuckling straps that were now cinched tightly took longer than Catrin would have thought, but she eventually wriggled free.

Light surf caressed the shoreline with more of a murmur than the roar Catrin recalled from the coast of the Godfist. A warm wind blew from the far side of the island, and the smell of brine was heavy in the air, its saltiness somehow refreshing despite its tang. Orange crabs with white bellies skittered along the black sands, holding their one massive claw up high, their pointed legs leaving scroll marks in the sand.

Along the horizon nothing could be seen but occasional whitecaps, and Catrin had no idea where they were. When she looked inland, Catrin saw steam rising from what looked like a giant wound in the landscape. Like claw marks, a series of glowing gashes marred the otherwise seamless black stone. The air above them shimmered, and jets of steam issued forth at regular intervals. Catrin backed away, unable to bear the waves of heat that radiated from the massive claw marks. Memories of an erupting volcano and the nagging feeling the gashes had been created by a giant monster made Catrin look over her shoulder more than once.

She found Kyrien sunning himself in a field of stone that looked almost liquid with its ridges and swirls. Catrin feared it would sink under her boots, but it proved solid. With his wings extended, Kyrien's many wounds were exposed. Seeing his flesh rent repeatedly and places where scales were missing brought tears to Catrin's eyes. Many new gashes ran alongside old scars, and some crisscrossed, making his hide look like old leather with only patches of scales.

Ignoring her own needs, Catrin laid her hands on Kyrien, hoping to ease his pain. The energy here felt pure and uncluttered, and Catrin drew deeply. Her vision swam, her legs trembled, and her knees buckled. She would have struck the stone hard had it not been for Kyrien, whose muzzle supported her. Many would have been terrified to be so close to his daggerlike, curved teeth, but Catrin knew he would never hurt her. He had once carried her in those jaws and had been as gentle as if she were his child. She had no fear of him, despite his looking like a giant snake made of moss-covered stone. His membranous wings and stout legs capped with claws that looked like they had been carved of solid marble added to his formidable appearance. His green-flecked gold eyes seemed incapable of conveying warmth, yet she could feel how much he cared for her.

Eat.

Kyrien's communication was clearly a command, and for some reason, it infuriated Catrin. "You haven't spoken to me in hours, and now all you can say is *eat?* What is it? What are you hiding? What don't you want me to know?" Her voice carried with it all her frustration, anger, and worry, and she instantly regretted her tone.

They can hear us.

That thought drove all suspicion from Catrin's mind and left guilt in its place. Of course there had been a reason. Someday she would learn to trust those around her, she reminded herself. It was not an easy thing to do when there were those who really were trying to kill her, her family, and her countrymen. Kyrien, though, was above such suspicion, and Catrin vowed to trust him from now on, no matter how strange his actions might be.

To speak to you I must speak loudly. They are coming. Eat.

"Will we go back?" Catrin persisted. "Will we save the people of the Godfist? Can we save them?"

Though Catrin sensed impatience from Kyrien, he raised his eyes to meet hers, and visions flowed across her consciousness, making it feel as if she were being drowned in a river of thought. What she saw made her want to weep. Such darkness and loss was overwhelming. Catrin knew now that much more than the fate of the Godfist was at stake. Even if she didn't know how the future would unfold, those terrifying glimpses were enough.

Eat. Rest. Prepare.

His words and emotion drove her back to the beach. There were no trees or vegetation to speak of, and Catrin knew that creating a fire would be impossible. She considered using Istra's energy to cook, but the thought nearly made her retch. Doing so would require more energy than the food would provide, and Catrin was weak enough. Along a rough section of the shoreline, she found a piece of black rock that had broken away from the rest of the flow. A deep ridge ran down the center of the slab, and it held a bit of water.

After chasing a few of the crabs, Catrin decided they were not worth the effort since she had worn herself out and not caught a single one. Instead she concentrated on the shellfish that clung to the rocks in pools. These at least could not run from her, though dislodging them was not always easy, she soon had enough for a decent meal.

Piling the dark-shelled muscles onto the indented slab, she carried them to the glowing gashes. After placing them near the edge of the gaping orifice, she backed away from the heat and waited for the shells to open. When they did, she rushed in and tried to pull the slab away, but it had become too hot for her to touch, even with her leather gloves on. Instead she used one of her knives to slide the muscles from the steaming slab.

Not waiting for them to cool, Catrin pulled the fleshy meal from within the delicate shells and was surprised by how good the muscles tasted. Soon all that remained was a pile of discarded shells. Part of Catrin wanted to go get more, but her eyes became heavy, and before she could form another thought, she slept.

Chapter 11

Adversity is often accompanied by opportunity.
--Medlin Reese, healer

* * *

Sinjin kicked at the still dirty floors in the hall known as the "false hall" since it went nowhere and seemed to serve no purpose. A few paces away, Brother Vaughn explained the mystery of the hall to Trinda, who seemed intrigued. Sinjin had heard it all before and knew that the mystery had very little to do with why they were there. Brother Vaughn had become convinced that forming a bond of friendship between Sinjin and Trinda was the way to mend the animosity between their families. At least he had not proposed they marry, Sinjin thought--at least not yet. He knew how these things worked, and he had no desire to find himself bound to the least pleasant person he'd ever met.

It wasn't that Trinda was mean or spiteful; that would have been easier to deal with since Sinjin could at least strike back. Instead she was almost always sad, her deep-set eyes seeming to hold the pain of ages, and any enthusiasm in the face of such anguish seemed trite at best. Though he had tried on several occasions to hold a conversation with Trinda, the most he ever received in return was a single-word response and most times just a nod.

"Look here," Brother Vaughn insisted. "Look at this corner, and tell me what you see."

Sinjin continued to drag the toe of his boot in the dust, knowing what it was Brother Vaughn wanted her to see. At times he wondered about the aging monk's sanity, for the strangest things would hold his attention.

"A seam," came Trinda's hollow response.

"A seam, indeed!" Brother Vaughn said with a triumphant look at Sinjin. "You see, m'boy. I told you this girl has an eye and ear for mysteries!"

Sinjin kept his eyes downcast, not really caring. All he really wanted was to get this over with so he could return to his normal life, not that many things were normal these days. He'd heard the whispered rumors that his mother would saddle Kyrien, and he'd even sneaked a few peeks at the saddle. Normally his mother shared all of her projects with him, and he'd spent much of his life in her workshop, but she wanted to keep the saddle from Sinjin. It seemed too surreal to be true, yet he had seen it with his own eyes, despite his mother's efforts to keep it concealed. Brother Vaughn wasn't convinced that Kyrien would ever fly again, and the presence of Reaver and the other dragons also reduced the likelihood of his ever leaving the valley. Without the protection of the guards stationed around him, he would be easy prey for the ferals.

Sinjin tried not to think about them, yet the images came to his mind unbidden--images of ferals clouding the skies and ruling the world from above. He would never look at the skies the same way again, and he found himself grateful for the stone that hung above him. Even if it did press down on his spirit, threatening to crush it, at least it protected him from the death that waited under the skies. Never again would he be able to walk in the moonlight without wondering if something was about to swoop down and devour him.

"Tell me: How do you think the ancients did this? And what do you think their purpose was?" Brother Vaughn asked, and he grabbed Sinjin by the shoulder and pulled him closer, a not-so-subtle reminder of why they were there.

"Maybe they wanted to give you something to think about," Sinjin suggested, and Brother Vaughn gave him a disapproving look. When Sinjin looked over to Trinda with a grin forming on his lips, he saw disapproval on her face as well, and he resigned himself to the fact that they would never find anything to bring them closer. This girl was simply no fun at all.

"Magic," Trinda said with a firm nod.

Brother Vaughn was clearly taken aback by that answer. The word *magic* seemed to bother the Cathurans a great deal. Sinjin recalled his mother telling the tale of how Mother Gwendolin had reacted to her use of the word, and it seemed Brother Vaughn wanted to scoff as well, but he resisted. Sinjin respected his restraint but didn't possess its equal. "A magical riddle, then. Perhaps all you need to do is wave a wand and speak the magic words."

Trinda glared at him, and Sinjin thought Brother Vaughn might scold him, but Trinda caught them both by surprise when she turned back to the barely detectable seam in the corner. "Open," she said as she ran her finger along the seam.

Sinjin nearly laughed out loud, but then the stone beneath his feet trembled. Before anyone could say another word, movement at the other end of the hall drew their undivided attention. Slowly a wall of stone moved across the opening that was their only egress. Though ponderously slow, the stone would close off their exit long before they could reach it.

With only the glow of Brother Vaughn's herald globe to illuminate what now seemed more like a tomb than anything else, Sinjin turned to Trinda. "I don't know how you did that, but I think you had better undo it, and fast."

Trinda wore a shocked expression, and Sinjin could see the fear in her eyes. In a moment that forever changed him, he reached out and put a hand on her shoulder. "Just try."

Running her finger along what was now an almost identical seam, which had only recently been an open hallway, Trinda repeated her command, "Open."

Nothing happened.

The silence that followed was the kind that could only be experienced when encased in solid stone.

* * *

Monsters approached. With a scream of primal fury, Chase charged to Martik's side. "Fall back!"

"Help me!" Martik shouted as he cut at the massive sap- and tar-soaked ropes that bound the stair to anchors in the stone of the mountain itself.

"There's no time!" Chase shouted. Grabbing Martik by the shoulder, he pulled the engineer back away from the approaching hoard. What rushed toward them went beyond the natural order and had been somehow perverted, twisted, and manipulated. Slavering beasts climbed with no concern for their own safety, as if all sense of self-preservation had been stripped from them. Chase could see it in their eyes: no fear, only hatred and death. This was not an enemy that could be reasoned with. It was a river of gibbering madness intent on their destruction.

Morif and a handful of guards stood before the onslaught, about to be engulfed.

"Retreat!" Chase shouted, but either none heard or none obeyed.

Beneath a shield made of bound tree trunks came the giants, and the demons crowded around them, protecting the giants with their lives, throwing themselves in front of any attack intended to bring down the lumbering monstrosities. Still, some attacks pierced the defenses. One giant opened its mouth to issue a gargling bellow, revealing its haphazardly arranged teeth stained brown and furrowed by deep ridges. The giant next to it responded by shrugging off the tree shield, sending it crashing down the rock face, where it struck the lower stair, crushing dozens of demons and cutting off the rest of those waiting in the valley below.

This seemed a small victory as the giants slowly picked up speed, roaring as they came, striking fear into all who heard their terrifying calls. Chase watched in horror as Morif charged to meet them, somehow fighting through the attacks of encroaching demons as though they were nothing, though Chase knew some of those attacks had landed squarely. The old veteran somehow kept his legs under himself. One giant raised its boulderlike fist into the air and sent it crashing down toward Morif's head. With more speed than Chase knew he possessed, Morif leaped aside and narrowly avoided a blow that severed massive timbers and sent splinters of wood into the air.

Men gathered behind Chase, waiting for his command, but his mind went blank. All the years he'd trained could not have prepared him for anything like this. Only the claws of a swooping dragon drove him back to action. After diving out of the winged monster's path, Chase made up his mind: he would not let Morif and his men die alone. "Ready your weapons! Form up in ranks!"

Those around him moved without question. Martik leaped at the command too, though Chase could practically hear the wheels turning in the engineer's head. He now realized the flaw in his failsafe release mechanism: in order to be strong enough to hold the stair, he had made it too difficult to release. His mighty trigger more resembled a lock.

"To Morif!" Chase shouted, and those at his back raised a chilling cry that split the air.

Even the giants took notice as the small fighting force poured onto the now swaying stair. A strangled scream rang out, and Chase watched one of his men tumble over the railing. Another went down under a dark blade, but the demons took losses as well, and with those below forced to climb the sheer rock face, it seemed the battle might be one they could win. That was until Chase looked back up to the ridgeline, where hundreds more demons poured over the crest, half running, half falling toward them. Giant claws snatched the man closest to Chase, and before anyone could do anything, the beast tucked its wings and veered away. Before it moved out of Chase's vision, he saw the dragon turn and close its jaws on the flailing guard.

The dark tide washed over them, and Chase knew that he and Morif had both made a mistake. There was no way they could win this battle, and the loss of them would only weaken those within the hold. He could almost hear Catrin scolding him for letting his battle lust overwhelm his good sense. A cold feeling of guilt washed over him and filled him with the greatest need. Catrin was counting on him, and he couldn't let her down. Since the death of their mothers, that had been his role, and beyond anything else, that drove him to remain alive.

As he struck one demon down, another climbed atop the first and leaped directly into Chase's chest, driving him backward into the railing, which struck him in the low back. Pinned between the rough bark and the leathery skin of the demon, Chase struggled with every bit of energy he possessed. The cords in his neck stood taught, and sweat blinded him, leaving only a reddish haze, but the bright flashes made him avert his eyes. The demon was suddenly ripped from atop him, and Chase wiped a torn sleeve over his eyes to clear his vision. On the stair stood Prios, alternating between casting lightning into those that assaulted Morif and the few guards still surrounding him and using fire to incinerate the demons advancing on Chase and his dwindling force. For a brief instant, the distance between them was clear, and Chase let out a hoarse battle cry.

Morif, covered in blood, returned the cry, and the two groups became one, slowly fighting their way back into the hold. All thoughts of victory had long since fled, and those left alive now concentrated on staying that way. As the last guard, a woman who had fought as valiantly as any of the men around her, got her boots on solid stone, Prios unleashed his fury on the ropes that Martik had failed to cut. For a time the ropes continued to hold. Demons and a single giant forced their way inside Dragonhold. The stairs looked surreal as the landing moved away from the mountain, gaining momentum. Creaks and groans gave way to snaps and screams, and much of the wooden stairs crashed into the valley below.

"Retreat to the God's Eye!" Chase cried out, his voice now high pitched and strained.

"The way is blocked, sir."

"Fall back to the forge!"

"The forge is blocked as well, sir!"

Nearly howling in frustration, Chase knew they were in trouble. The great hall was filled with refugees unprepared to defend themselves, and the guards who still lived were barely hanging on. Prios was their only hope, and as a mass of black bodies sought to surround the man who now looked as if his entire body were afire, Chase used the last of his strength to raise his sword and charge.

* * *

Jets of dust, stone, and debris clogged the air around Durin as he retreated. Shouts and screams pounded against his hearing while the deep bass of grinding stone made his bones tremble. What little natural light that reached this area was soon extinguished. Seeking fresh air, Durin moved deeper and deeper into the hold, back toward the kitchens and forge. Little fresh air was to be found.

Within the kitchens, what was usually orderly chaos was now true chaos. Fire clogged the air with smoke. Normally the kitchens where completely isolated from the great fire; the stone of the ovens formed the outer wall of the great hearth and were thus heated. Durin watched as people tried to guide the wounded around burning sacks of flour, overturned tables, and slippery puddles marking where canisters had broken. Of course, they were unlikely to find safety in the halls. The cooler air of the halls drew the smoke and fed the flames.

"Stay low!" Miss Mariss shouted above the terrible clamor. "Don't breathe the smoke! Get Millie out of here, and get me more water!"

Despite the fact that the dust had chased him deeper into the keep, Durin turned to go back, knowing the best thing he could do was listen to Miss Mariss. Staying low, below the growing layer of smoke that rolled along the tunnel ceiling, he moved as quickly as he could. From the darkness came Bradley, covered in dirt and grime, only his eyes clear of debris. "Go back," he coughed.

"But Miss Mariss needs water."

"Can't get there anymore. The way's block and the air is clogged with dust."

Durin heeded Bradley's warning; the young guard had always looked after Durin's and Sinjin's best interests. Seeing Bradley's distress, Durin grabbed his arm and draped it over his shoulder. "Come on. I'll help you." The fact that Bradley did not protest told Durin much, and he didn't like it one bit.

"Smother the fire with your cloaks!" Bradley shouted into the kitchens.

"I'm trying, you derned fool! Now help me! And where is that water?"

"The halls are blocked, ma'am. We've no access to water."

Had the kitchens not been burning, his statement might have brought some reaction, but instead people simply worked harder at putting out the flames. Osbourne and Brother Milo appeared moments later with buckets of water from the glass smithy. Osbourne was bleeding from a dozen places, and Brother Milo looked as if he'd been on fire. Again. Durin often wondered if the man's robes were made of tinder.

A terrible howling came from above, breaking through all the other clatter and sending terror through the hold. There were monsters within Dragonhold.

As people moved the wounded to the smithy, where the smoke had dissipated, Durin found himself wanting to do something, anything to help. His heart yearned to relieve some of the pain he saw around him or chase away the fear that permeated the hold. Demonic howls still resounded within the halls, and the sounds of battle were but distorted echoes made more frightening by their ambiguity. No one here could know what horrors were taking place within the rest of the hold.

Once again, Durin drummed up the courage to speak. "Strom, I need to tell you something."

The well-muscled smith ignored him. "Bradley, come with me. The rest of you, stay here and guard the wounded." Hammers swinging from metal rings on his belt, the smith moved with purpose.

"But, Strom!" Durin did his best to interrupt.

"Durin, keep your mouth shut and follow me. We might need your help."

Swallowing hard, Durin just nodded and did as he was told. It was a strange feeling. He'd worked up the nerve to tell Strom what he'd done, but following the smith into battle against the demons was an entirely different thing. He envied Bradley, who, armed only with a short sword and a dragon scale shield, seemed to find confidence having Strom at his side, and the two looked like great heroes to Durin. The continued echoes of battle made his guts go watery, and he wanted nothing more than to hide.

Near the great hall, Strom pulled a herald globe from the pocket of his leather vest. Ahead lay a mass of stone and rubble that blocked the hall. The ceiling had collapsed.

"We need to get this cleared. Step back. I'm going to pull some of these large stones down."

"Won't this make those around the hearth more vulnerable?" Bradley asked.

Durin agreed with his assessment.

"I'm going up there, but neither of you have to. Just help me clear a hole so I can get through. Then you two can fill the hole back up once I'm through."

Durin suspected Bradley would have said something in response, but Strom didn't give him the chance. Instead he started digging his way through the shifting pile of stone. Bradley and Durin did what they could to keep the area behind Strom clear, so he had an open space to deposit the rocks he freed. Several times rocks tumbled into an open space he'd just cleared, and Bradley had to pull him out. With every stone that came free, the sounds of battle drew closer, and terror nearly paralyzed Durin, but something made him move, made him help Strom.

Though he'd expected some sort of speech or announcement, Strom simply disappeared through the hole as soon as it was large enough. The big man was gone. Bradley did not look back to Durin or hesitate in any way; he followed Strom through the hole without a sound. A new battle cry filled the air beyond, and Durin's legs trembled. In that moment, though, his life changed forever. For once, he would not let fear hold him back from his true potential. Still, as he climbed through the hole, he asked himself, "What am I doing? This is crazy! What in the name of all that's good and right am I doing?" The last part became a scream as he tumbled down the loose rocks and directly into battle.

Strom hadn't gotten far before two demons pushed him backward. Bradley charged forward and leveled a kick at one, but the heavily armored demon shrugged the blow aside, which sent Bradley stumbling toward more demons and a pair of giants. Durin could see that more were pouring into the hold, a small band of guards all that slowed their progress. From within that group came fire and lightning, and Durin hoped Catrin and Prios would save them all. With no more time for thought, he ran forward and did the only thing he could think of. He fell onto all fours and slid between Strom and his attackers. Strom continued to fall back, and the two demons' legs tangled when they tripped over Durin. It was all the break Strom needed, and he used his hammers to finish off the dark hulks.

He looked terrifying to Durin as he rose and charged toward where

Bradley was going down under a rain of blows. Again his battle cry filled the air, and this time, it was answered not only by the guards but also by Durin. Grabbing a gnarled, black staff from one of the dead demons, he charged behind Strom and landed blows on anything that moved. None of his strikes brought demons down, but they did distract, and that helped keep them off Strom. The smith's strength became apparent as he landed devastating blows with his hammers. Even when demons tried to grapple with him, he used his might and the skills Chase had taught him to send them tumbling into their brethren.

There was a shift in the battle, as lightning crept closer and closer to where Strom, Bradley, and Durin fought. Blood ran down Bradley's face, but Strom pulled the young man behind him and took the brunt of the oncoming attacks. Bradley did not cower and hide, though. With another cry, he lashed out at any demons that came too close. Wielding his staff, Durin landed a solid blow on the kneecap of a nearby demon.

Movement brought Durin to full attention. For the first time, a demon looked him in the eye. It grinned at him, showing black gums and holes where teeth were missing. Nothing had ever frightened Durin more than that grin. The smell of the demon's breath alone was enough to send a man running.

Durin swung his staff, but the demon easily stepped aside. Raising its angular mace, it looked one direction but stepped the other, catching Durin by surprise. Were it not for Bradley's dragon scale shield raised in his defense, Durin would have been dead. As it was, Bradley's defense was off balance, and both shield and mace struck Durin in the head, knocking him to the ground.

Strom seemed to realize how futile this fight was, and he started to push Durin and Bradley back toward the great hearth, but then he stopped. The guards were now accompanied by a hoard of people wielding anything they could find. Young and old, as ineffectual as they may be, they charged at the dark beasts. The demons seemed stunned when the people attacked; such ferocity was not to be expected from mothers and grandmothers and children, which made it all the more effective. The fact that Arghast warriors were dispersed throughout the crowd did not hurt either. Durin let out a cheer when he saw his own mother smack a demon in the face with a skillet. The victory was short lived as more demons rushed in, and he almost cried out as he saw people he knew go down. Durin could not bear to see his mother overrun, and he ran faster than he ever had before. Strom and Bradley matched his stride, and they bowled over the enemy.

When the three met up with the mass of humanity, Durin went straight to his mother, who was bleeding from a cut on her brow.

"Don't fuss over me," she insisted. "Teach those beasts some manners!"

As if responding to her command, Prios let loose a series of thunderous blasts that shook the mighty pillars supporting the great hall.

"From where did you come?" Morif shouted.

"From the great hearth! The way is still mostly blocked, but we can get through given time."

Durin guessed that Morif would try to direct them back toward the partially blocked hall, but for the moment, he called for a full retreat.

With four demons holding the chains around each of their necks, a pair of giants lumbered to the fore, and no one could stand before them. Those who tried were tossed aside or crushed underfoot. Durin's mother had recovered enough to stand, and she launched her skillet at the nearest giant. It struck the hulking beast in the shin, and it let out a terrible bellow. It shook the hall, dancing on one foot for a moment. Then the giant looked down at the petite woman and charged. Defiant, the tiny woman shook her fist at him. Durin tried to get to her, but someone else grabbed her and pulled her back before the giant could retaliate.

Prios launched balls of shimmering air at the giants' heads, and they exploded with thunderous claps. The giants raised chained arms to cover their ears, dragging the demons holding the chains into the air. Again Prios attacked. Seemingly driven to madness by the massive thunderclaps, the giants turned on their captors. Using the chains that had bound them more in spirit than in body, they swept the demons aside in their attempt to escape Prios.

"Now! To the hearth!" Morif yelled.

Chase, Strom, Morif, and Bradley ushered the crowd toward the halls. Demons still attacked, but they were far less organized, and the group made progress across the giant mosaic that covered the floor of the great hall. Durin found his mother, supported her, and helped her through.

"One at a time!" he shouted after helping his mother. "I'll help you. Just don't push and shove!"

"Do as he says!" Morif barked, and Durin felt a rare moment of pride. It didn't last. The rocks beneath him shifted and moved, and he went tumbling, smacking his head as he fell. Determined, he climbed back up and did what he could to help people through. It was a time-consuming process, which left Prios, Chase, Strom, Morif, and a few others to hold off the demons. From the sounds of the fighting, the demons had regained their strength and were attacking once again in full force, though Durin did not see any giants.

When the last helpless person was through, Durin turned back to those who stood and fought. "They're all through! How are we going to get the rest of you through?"

"Go!" Morif ordered.

Durin hesitated. He could not leave these brave men to die, and he knew they would not be able to get through without someone protecting them. Then Prios turned, his face bloodied and bruised, and with a finger, he issued a single silent command: *Go!* Durin did as he said, though he lost his balance and slid through to the other side when the booming started. Like the beat of an enormous drum, the thunder rattled Dragonhold to its core. Scrambling, Durin did his best to get clear as more men followed him through.

With each new face, he looked for Chase or Morif or Prios, but only the faces of guards came through. When Kendra and her mother emerged, Durin took a step backward and lowered his eyes, not wanting a confrontation with Kendra. He stopped for a moment and looked again, his gut telling him something was not as it should be. He had no more time to think about it as Chase fell through the hole, and Durin joined the men who moved to pull him free. Morif came moments later, but Prios did not come. The thunder continued and grew more intense. Rocks slid as the vibration caused them to settle into gaps.

Morif would not let the guards pull him free. Instead he climbed back up and stuck his head through the hole. "Now, Prios! Make a run for it! I'll pull you through!"

In the next instant, the thunder stopped, and in its place came the most terrible battle cry Durin had ever heard. Morif jerked upright as he pulled, but then he was thrust forward and began to disappear back into the hole. Durin tried to get to him, but a mass of guards rushed in to grab Morif by the ankles. The guards suddenly flew backward, and Morif came sliding through, bouncing roughly across the stones. "Let go!" he cried. "Let me go!"

The guards released his legs and he climbed, but a single thunderclap, far louder than all that had come before it, sent everyone tumbling backward again. Morif immediately pulled himself up and charged back through the hole. Moments later he reappeared, dragging the still form of Prios. For a moment it seemed they were safe until dark forms filled the gap and the silence shattered.

Chapter 12

The most dangerous mistakes are those you don't realize you've made.
--Enoch Giest

* * *

Hot stones. That was what it had finally taken to keep the demons from pulling down the barrier of rubble that stood between them and the only survivors in Dragonhold, at least as far as any of them knew. When Durin returned to the smithy for another shovel load of hot stones, he saw Strom standing to one side, silently watching those who worked in what was usually his smithy.

Seeing his opportunity, Durin approached and spoke before he lost his nerve. "I'm the reason the hold moved."

"What?" Strom asked, looking confused.

Durin saw a couple more adults stop and wait to hear his response. "I didn't want to carry a bucket of almost clean water all the way to the God's Eye, so I dumped it into the glowing rune behind one of the statues. It started steaming and whistling, and when it stopped, the hold moved."

Strom didn't say anything at first. He opened his mouth a few times as if he'd speak, but he still didn't say anything. When he finally did speak, his eyes were far away. "Something so powerful and no idea how to use it." Then his eyes returned to Durin. "Now tell me every detail. I want to know what you heard, what you felt. I want to know how it smelled. Everything. Sit. Talk."

Strom listened with so much interest that Durin's hands and voice trembled. When Martik entered the smithy, Strom called him over and made Durin repeat every word. Martik, an experienced engineer, sat back heavily and stared, open mouthed, at Durin.

"If only Brother Vaughn were here with us," Martik said. "He'd love to know those runes actually do something."

Both Strom and Durin looked away, knowing his absence did not bode well for his safety. Already, Prios had sworn to go back out after Sinjin and any other survivors, but it was uncertain if there was anyone at all still alive in other parts of the hold. And many felt it better to spend their time reinforcing the barrier and not bringing it down to fight a losing battle.

"Keep building up the barrier," Strom told Martik, and he pulled Durin from the smithy. "Brother Vaughn may have saved us without even knowing it."

* * *

Strom wrinkled his nose as he poured a foul mixture into a glowing rune. "What *is* this?"

"Wine and pickle juice," Durin responded with a shrug. "It's all that was left." But then he fell back. Wisps of steam escaped the rune, then more steam came and the whistling sound grew. An instant later, the whistling abruptly stopped, and the floor trembled. When the trembling stopped, Durin watched the truth settle onto Strom's face by the light of a shaking torch. By pouring liquid into the rune, they had done something that would have wide-reaching consequences. For Durin, it was the second time he'd had one of these realizations, and the second was no better than the first.

"By the gods," Strom said, looking down at the steaming rune then at the now open hall leading into the darkness.

"You said Brother Vaughn called that one *respite*. That should mean safety, right?" Durin asked, wanting reassurance and knowing that had been Strom's argument for selecting the rune, but screams from above drove them both to move.

"What have I done?" Strom asked aloud as they ran. "What was I thinking?"

"You said it would've taken too long for everyone to agree on what to do, so you were making the decision for them."

The screaming and shouting continued, and Strom looked like he might be sick.

"Where in the depths have you been?" Miss Mariss barked when they arrived at the forge.

Strom couldn't find words, and Durin followed his example.

"Idiots. The keep has up and moved again, and by the sound of it, some of the demons are trapped as well. They certainly don't sound happy."

"I know now why the keep moved," Strom said at last, and Miss Mariss stopped. "Durin caused it the first time, and I caused it the second time." Miss Mariss looked as if she would shift from stunned to a full-blown rage, so Strom spoke more quickly. "I wasn't sure it would work. Durin's experience could have been a coincidence, and I knew it would take too long to come to a consensus, and we needed everyone to continue working on the barrier, so I . . ."

"You acted like an irresponsible fool and could have killed us all. You should be ashamed of yourselves, both of you. Now the demons are even more determined to break down our barrier."

"Respite," Durin said, looking up at Strom.

"A new corridor has opened," Strom said. "I think Durin and I should explore it and see what new resources we have available to us."

"Or what new dangers we face. You fools. Fine. Go. Just try not to make things worse."

Durin flushed and he could see Strom wasn't faring much better. It made him feel very good that even someone as strong and skilled as Strom could still feel guilt under Miss Mariss's stare. Perhaps there was hope for him yet, Durin thought. Then again, he knew Miss Mariss had not yet realized there were pickles and wine missing.

Strom grabbed more torches and his hammers. Durin looked around for something to arm himself with but found only a rasp. Strom gave him a disapproving look. "You're gonna have a hard time filing your way out of trouble." After what looked like a moment of pure conflict, Strom reached up and grabbed something from the back of the tallest shelf in the smithy. He shoved a cold, black handle into Durin's hand. "I want that back."

"I thought you didn't make weapons?" Durin asked after drawing a gleaming, curved blade from the sheath. The handle felt good in his palm, solid and smooth but with an unusual texture that provided a sure grip. Durin looked in amazement at the finely crosshatched lines that made up the grip. Never before had he seen such precision. The blade itself was black, but the edge gleamed silver and promised blood.

"Knives are not always weapons," Strom said without looking at Durin.

"You don't expect me to believe that you made this for cutting cheese, do you?"

Strom stopped and glared.

"Right. Uh, sorry."

Not far ahead, in a room that had once been a storeroom, despite the glowing runes in the floor, now waited respite--at least Durin hoped that was what awaited them.

* * *

The silence was often worse than the hunger or thirst; still it was generally preferable to the sound of Brother Vaughn trying to get information from Trinda. The sullen girl's responses drained the energy from Sinjin, and he wondered how anyone could be so unhappy.

"It needs more," Trinda said, pointing at the herald globe, whose light was fading. Sinjin turned away, not sure how to respond to such an inane statement. It seemed unlikely they could charge the herald globe in the sun without first finding their way out of where they were trapped.

"He doesn't like me," Sinjin heard Trinda say, and he turned toward where she and Brother Vaughn sat.

"I don't think that's true," Brother Vaughn said, and he waved for Sinjin to come closer. "Now that's not true at all, is it?"

"It's not that I dislike you," Sinjin began, but his tone changed under the weight of Brother Vaughn's gaze. "It's just that you are sad a lot, and that makes me feel sad."

"You feel sad because I feel sad?"

"Yeah, that's what I said," Sinjin snapped, earning another glare from Brother Vaughn.

"You should be nice to me."

"Why's that?"

"'Cause someday you're gonna need somethin'."

"And you'll be there to help me?"

Trinda just raised her eyebrows and looked doubtful.

"Perhaps you'll both need something, and wouldn't it be nice if you were there for each other?" Brother Vaughn said.

Sinjin and Trinda both rolled their eyes at him, and in rare moment, Sinjin saw Brother Vaughn's frustration show through the cloak of calmness he usually wore. He took a breath to say something, but then the world began to move. "Hold on to me!" he shouted.

Sinjin grabbed Trinda and pulled her with him, wrapping his arms around her. She didn't struggle and though she was older than he, she seemed but a child, slight and frail, counting on him to save her. It was an odd feeling that bloomed in Sinjin's chest. Dust seeped into the air as the deep grinding reverberated through the keep. Relief flooded through Sinjin as the walls moved, and once again the way they had come in was clear. Still the keep moaned and trembled. Brother Vaughn pulled Sinjin forward, and Sinjin half carried Trinda back toward the main hall, which led between the God's Eye and the great hall. As they neared the junction, Dragonhold returned to rest, and what had become a near-deafening roar suddenly stopped. What remained was far from silence, and it chilled Sinjin's blood. Howls and grunts echoed through the halls, sounding like the cries of tortured animals, and only occasionally did he hear the shouts of people. Sometimes those calls were more frightening than those of the demons, especially when they ended in shrill and strangled cries.

Brother Vaughn stood as still as stone and listened, his head turned one way then another. "May the gods have mercy," he whispered, and he pulled Sinjin and Trinda back the way they had come.

"We can't go back that way," Sinjin said louder than he had intended.

With a sharp look, Brother Vaughn pressed a finger to his lips and pulled them with him. When they reached the part of the hall where they had been trapped, Sinjin nearly shouted in relief. The hall was now clear in both directions, and unexplored darkness lay ahead. Not even slowing, Brother Vaughn kept the group moving at as brisk a pace as the light of his fading herald globe would allow. Soon it would go dark, and they would be lost. Brother Vaughn hadn't said that, but Sinjin knew it; he could read it in the old monk's posture. Still, moving into unexplored parts of the keep piqued his sense of adventure--if only their light would hold.

"So foolish of me not to bring a fully charged herald globe or some other source of light," Brother Vaughn said as their progress continually slowed while the unnatural sounds filling the keep grew louder. Then he drew a sharp breath. Sinjin followed the small circle of light that surrounded the herald globe as Brother Vaughn slowly moved it over bold runes that covered a tile floor.

"It needs more," Trinda complained.

Brother Vaughn ignored her, and Sinjin nearly clamped his hand down over her mouth to keep her quiet. The sound of demons continued to grow. Looking over each rune and mumbling to himself, Brother Vaughn cursed. Holding the herald globe out, he cast soft shadows over doorways cut into an elaborate, multifaceted room, shaped almost as if someone had cut a gemstone away and left this cavity. Stepping forward, he cast out the light to the far doorways, and he stopped suddenly when the tile beneath his boot sank down with a grinding sound followed by a sharp snap. Sinjin looked up as dust fell from above, and it sounded as if the ceiling were collapsing. Indeed the stone above them was moving, but before they could do anything, it stopped.

"This room is a trap," Brother Vaughn said.

"What kind of trap?" Sinjin asked, wondering if they would be crushed.

"I think it's a riddle, but I can't see all of the runes, and I'm not quite sure."

"It needs more," Trinda observed. Sinjin opened his mouth, but she didn't give him a chance to make his snide remark, instead, she snatched the herald globe from Brother Vaughn's hands. "Let me have it. I have some."

Trinda closed her eyes. To Sinjin's amazement, the globe began to glow more brightly through her fingers.

"That's enough," Brother Vaughn urged in a low voice.

Trinda's eyes opened. At first she appeared calm, but then her eyes slowly went wide, the light growing brighter all the while. Brother Vaughn reached for the globe, and power leaped across the open air with a crack. He jerked his hand back. Moments later, Trinda made a popping noise with her lips. She turned and handed Brother Vaughn the now glaring orb. Holding out his hand to shield the light, he accepted it.

Trinda turned to Sinjin, locked eyes with him, and shrugged. "I don't have any more." Then her eyes rolled up into her head, and she collapsed into his arms. Unprepared, he barely caught her and was trying to hoist her onto his shoulder when he heard a low growl--this one not distant. Brother Vaughn turned toward the sound, and the light drove the demon backward, but the growling continued from the shadows.

Brother Vaughn mumbled rapidly while scanning the now brightly illuminated runes. "What's lighter than a feather, worth more than gold, more precious than air, and cannot be seen?"

Silence hung between them for what seemed a long time. The riddle reminded Sinjin of how his mother had explained astral travel, how she said her spirit had flown free of her body and had moved as if it weighed nothing. "A soul," he said. After casting a surprised look, Brother Vaughn stepped onto a new tile in the floor. Nothing happened.

"Excellent," Brother Vaughn said, already scanning more tiles. "What never stops moving but is always in the same place?"

Brother Vaughn's movements had cast part of the room back into shadow, and the growling grew more intense. Turning to face the demon, Sinjin watched in horror as the beast stepped into the light, its eyes now adjusted. Its first step had no effect, but the second sent the ceiling tumbling another notch.

Brother Vaughn leaped to another tile with a wheel carved into it. Sinjin followed, Trinda still draped over his shoulder, and he nearly took a bad step onto the wrong tile, but Brother Vaughn steadied him.

"What's heavier than air and flies with no wings?"

Sinjin tried to think of an answer, but the demon leaped closer to them, stepping on two separate tiles, both of which sank down. Sinjin fell to his knees. Locking eyes with the demon, he saw panic in its eyes, but that fear turned to anger and hatred. "Just go," Sinjin said.

"I can't figure it out," Brother Vaughn said, but Sinjin pushed him, and off balance, he had to make a choice in mid step: water. The ceiling held, but Sinjin pushed again, seeing the demon preparing to attack. "But I don't even know what the riddle is," Brother Vaughn said in a high voice when Sinjin pushed again.

Neither was prepared when the demon lunged.

Flying sideways, Sinjin realized that he'd been hit by the demon. Clinging to Trinda, he waited for impact, knowing they would eventually hit something solid. What they slammed into was Brother Vaughn, who cried out and tried to guess which tiles to step on as he was thrust forward. The grinding sound of stone on stone resounded again, and clouds of dust fell from overhead. Screaming, Sinjin thrust Trinda ahead of him and jumped with all the power he could muster. Feeling the stone closing in on them, he landed roughly and had poor footing when he made his final push. The stone slammed down and caught the toe of his boot, which he struggled to pull free. It was then that he saw the other demons glaring at him over the rubble. The falling stone had only partly obstructed the hall, and the demons were already clearing the way.

Trinda climbed to her feet and cast him an accusing glare. "You hurt me."

"I was trying to keep you alive," Sinjin said, but it didn't look as if Trinda believed him. At that moment, he didn't care. Brother Vaughn helped him stand, and with the herald globe wrapped in his robes, they moved deeper into the unknown at a near run, the light still seeming overly bright, especially with the howls coming from behind. Nothing more was said about the incident. Trinda seemed embarrassed and retreated even further within herself. Sinjin watched her closely, not wanting her to suffer. Though she annoyed him at times, Sinjin realized that all he really wanted was for her to be happy, and the fact that he could not bring her that happiness was what really made him uncomfortable. After a while they slowed.

Once he caught his breath, Sinjin said, "My mom had trouble the first few times she accessed Istra's power, and I'm not sure if she has ever become truly comfortable with it, except for the things she says just come natural. I think maybe that's how your singing works."

Brother Vaughn raised an eyebrow when Sinjin met his eyes, but then he just smiled, nodded, and said nothing more. Trinda looked at him sideways and shrugged. Sinjin had no more time to speak before the light revealed a chasm whose jagged edge made it appear as if the earth waited to swallow them. Brother Vaughn unwrapped the herald globe. The light danced from dainty, crystalline structures that looked like flowers with glass daggers as petals. They dotted the walls of the ravine. The dark rock they clung to drank in the light rather than reflecting it, which made the brilliance of the crystals stand out in greater contrast. Before them lay a bridge of sorts that formed a pathway across the chasm, but the closer Sinjin looked, the less he liked what he saw. The drop down to the top of the span was farther than he was comfortable jumping, and he wasn't sure they would be able to climb back up--here or on the other side. No solid surface topped the span. It was just a pile of stones that sloped downward on either side and into the darkness.

Brother Vaughn held the herald globe over the ledge, and Sinjin stepped back from the dizzying height, but he was drawn back by the shadows on the distant cavern floor. A pattern emerged from the nothingness, random yet orderly. Right angles and plumb lines made what he instantly recognized as a city. Moving the herald globe to the other side, Brother Vaughn illuminated more architecture, yet on this side there were nearly no straight lines. All the buildings formed curves, arches, and other structures that seemed drawn from nature. Sinjin sucked in a breath when some of the shadows began to move. The others had seen it as well, and all three turned to run back the way they had come, driven by instinct to flee the things that creep in the darkness.

The noise of the demons grew more clear and distinct, and panic set a lump in Sinjin's throat.

"We're going across," Brother Vaughn said after a moment.

Trinda just looked at him, but Sinjin could see she was trembling. "I'll help you," he said. "It'll be fine. You'll see."

Watching Brother Vaughn climb down was little help, as it was more of a controlled fall, arms waving and body dancing as loose stone provided unsure footing.

"You're next," Sinjin said, but Trinda just shook her head, not meeting his eyes. "We need to go, Trinda. Don't worry; Brother Vaughn will be there to catch you if you fall."

Trinda raised her head and looked him in the eyes, tears falling from her own. "I can't. I'm scared. I want to go home now." The last statement was said with a quavering, high-pitched note, and the tears came more quickly.

Feeling helpless, Sinjin was torn by fear, empathy, annoyance, and helplessness. There was nothing he could do to help her, yet he could not leave her behind. With a sigh, Sinjin stood with his back to Trinda and held his arms slightly out to his sides. He didn't have to say any more. Trinda scrambled up, wrapped her arms around his neck, and clung to him. Sinjin hadn't been certain he could do it, but she was much lighter when she was conscious, and he stepped over the ledge onto the steep incline, which ended abruptly where the larger stones were piled. Brother Vaughn waited, looking concerned. For Sinjin there was no more time for thought. Once he put his weight on his forward leg, the loose stone broke free and sent him skidding downward. Trinda buried her face in his neck as they fell.

Trying to make sure he did not fall backward, Sinjin kept his weight forward, and for a moment they skidded gracefully, as if on sleigh rails moving over snow, but the smooth ride ended abruptly as one stone refused to move. Catching his toe, Sinjin pitched ahead. Tucking his legs and throwing his weight forward, they rotated in the air, and Sinjin landed slightly forward on his feet, which sent him sprinting straight into Brother Vaughn, who gave a great *woof* as the air rushed from his lungs. The three went down in a heap, and larger stones rolled away, clattering down the steep sides of the pile. It took a moment for them to determine that no one had been hurt, but the need for escape kept the inspection brief.

With the herald globe wrapped tightly, Brother Vaughn led them into a landscape that consisted of only a pile of rubble and darkness. Distorted echoes made it sound as if enemies approached from every direction, a mourning wail mixing with the grunts, barks, and growls. As the demons drew closer, one gave out a deep roar that sounded like thunder. Moments later came the clatter of stones down the slopes, and Sinjin knew the demons were on the pile of rock and gaining on them.

"We've got to move," Brother Vaughn said.

Sinjin stepped in front of Trinda and again raised his arms out to his sides. She wasted no time in climbing up onto his back once more. It looked as if Brother Vaughn would offer to carry her, but when he met Trinda's eyes, she just buried her face in Sinjin's neck. Half running and half falling, Brother Vaughn and Sinjin made their way across the loose and shifting stone, all of it the same deep black. Nothing new emerged from the scenery, just ubiquitous stone leading off into the darkness. Always expecting to see the other side suddenly materialize became exhausting. Outside of the stone on which they tread, they could see nothing above or ahead. It was as if they had left the real world behind. Perhaps they were already dead, Sinjin thought, but then a chill ran over his skin, and a rumbling boom echoed for what seemed an eternity. Brother Vaughn stumbled when lightning split the air and showed a frightening landscape. The pile of stone continued for what looked like a day's walk, and on the other end, above where the stone pile met with a towering wall of rock, waited a city that dwarfed those in the valleys below.

"What kind of place has lightning inside?" Trinda asked.

Sinjin wondered if they had not somehow come out of the mountain to open air, but it did not feel that way. He could feel the land pressing down on him, its weight always a reminder that the world could come crashing in at any moment. Trinda weighed on him in more than one way. Her whispered questions deserved answers, but he had none; all he could do was run. When the world lit up behind him, Sinjin spun around in time to see a giant demon, its treelike arm raised in the air, blazing like the sun, a thread of lightning throbbing and pulsing as it poured energy from the roiling clouds above into a single point. The shape of it stayed in Sinjin's vision long after the lightning vanished. The giant rolled to the side and took what sounded like a dozen smaller demons with it. The darkness closed back in and left him blind for a moment.

"Our bodies form the highest point," Brother Vaughn said. "Get down, Sinjin. Get down now!"

Feeling the hair rise on the back of his neck and Trinda choking him as she clung to him for dear life, Sinjin got low as fast as he could. Lightning struck the demons again, and when it did, they could see the rest still moving toward them. Sinjin prayed for the lightning to continue, but the darkness remained. Only a pattering rhythm filled the void. The first drops of rain struck with such surreal randomness that Sinjin could hardly believe it, but the patter became a roar, and a deluge rushed in.

"We've got to move," Brother Vaughn said, and Sinjin did not argue.

Now slick and glossy, the stone provided even worse footing, and they moved slowly. It seemed as if they weren't moving at all against the persistent, rain-filled wind. He blinked when he saw the stones ahead move in the deep shadows cast by the lightning. He couldn't believe it, but soon they found out why as the stones were crawling with crabs. Sinjin remained still as the crabs gathered closely around his feet; their powerful claws ready to tear through the leather of his boots. Taking a deep breath, he was about to ask Brother Vaughn what to do when Trinda began to sing.

Sinjin wasn't certain if it was just the rain that drew the crabs or Trinda's singing, but they came in such numbers that he could only assume they heard her call. Either way, they did hamper the demons, even if only for a brief time. Cries and howls had come as the demons walked along the writhing blanket of crabs, and Sinjin assumed that he'd been right about the claws being both strong and sharp. The crabs had drawn around them first but then had moved toward the demons. Still more were coming, and the way before them remained clear, making it certain these creatures were under Trinda's control. The rain, however, continued to pelt them.

Shouldering his way forward, Sinjin set his mind to taking one step at a time, each one difficult, but his runner's training kept him from faltering; he could work through the pain. Brother Vaughn struggled alongside him, not having a much easier time of it, despite the fact Sinjin carried Trinda. She remained quiet for a time after she stopped singing, and Sinjin suspected it had drained her, just like his mother's activities often did to her. There always was a price to be paid.

When the rain subsided, Sinjin almost wished it hadn't as it had at least given them a meager bit of cover. Now all that stood between them, the demons, and the giants was an open expanse of rock. The distance between them was difficult to gauge, but it was shrinking. The demons seemed tireless, and Sinjin felt as if he had jellyfish instead of legs. The light of the overcharged herald globe still shone brightly, and there was no hiding. The awaiting city still looked to be hours away.

"Never before has my will been so tested," Brother Vaughn said. "It would be so much easier to just give up."

Sinjin simply grunted in response, unable to form the words. Seeing someone he admired as much as Brother Vaughn falter was enough to shake Sinjin's confidence to the core.

"Please don't let the dark things get me," Trinda said, and her words spurred them both on. "Let me down. You need rest. I can walk as fast as you are carrying me."

Sinjin couldn't deny it; his pace had slowed, and not just because of how slowly Brother Vaughn was moving. He was exhausted, his will nearly spent. He lowered Trinda to the stones and put his arm around Brother Vaughn. Trinda, the better rested of the three, led the way, the gleaming herald globe in the palms of her tiny hands.

Brother Vaughn stumbled and Sinjin could not keep them both from falling. Neither was hurt, but neither attempted to rise. Each breathing rapidly, they took an involuntary moment to rest. Trinda watched with a worried eye and urged them to hurry, but it was too much to ask. Even when Sinjin did manage to regain his feet, he could not get Brother Vaughn from the stones. The older monk tried to stand but lacked the strength. The time was costly. By the time Brother Vaughn regained his feet, the demons were within bow range. Sinjin did not see any bowmen, but he was looking at the situation based on his training, and he knew they were perilously close.

Trinda was crying now, and with every step, she urged them to hurry. She knew as well as Sinjin that they would not make it to the city ahead. It was a goal beyond their grasp. Once, he'd tried to imagine what would happen if they did reach the city, but it had become a nightmare, and he tried to keep his mind within the confines of the current problem. To each side stood a possible route of escape, but Sinjin did not know what awaited them in the darkness below. All of them had seen movement down there, and he didn't think crabs were the only things living within the darkness. For a moment Sinjin wondered how anything could live in here at all. Then a fading rumble of thunder reminded them of the rain.

The sound of demons running, their crude armor creaking and their booted feet striking the stones, was the only warning they had that the attack had begun. Sinjin had somehow expected them to slowly catch up, but the demons had been keeping a burst of speed in reserve, and now they rushed forward. Acting on instinct, Sinjin reached out to the energy around him, energy that he knew existed and that his parents could access. He, too, should be able to access it, he presumed. Trying to remember to breathe, he reached out with his fingers and tried to grab on to it with his mind, as his mother had always said. It had been a long time since he had tried to access Istra's powers, but never had he tried when his life depended on it. That was how his mother had come into her powers, and perhaps that was what it would take for his abilities to manifest. Given his encounter with the assassins, it seemed unlikely, but there was nothing else he could do but try.

Crying out and thrusting his arms forward, Sinjin released the accumulated charge. A small spark leaped between his outstretched fingers, and there was a light crackling sound, but his efforts yielded no other effect.

Trinda just stared at him and said nothing.

His face flushed and his pride deeply bruised, Sinjin turned to her. "Is there anything you can do? I'm sorry. I failed."

"You tried," Trinda said with a shrug. "I have a little more now. I'll try too."

Before Sinjin or Brother Vaughn could say another word, Trinda cupped the herald globe, and it grew steadily brighter until it shone like a star, and she threw it as hard and as far as she could. The herald globe sailed high, higher than a girl of Trinda's size should have been able to throw, and Sinjin understood that Trinda's powers continued to manifest, even if his own did not.

Shielding his eyes, Sinjin supposed it would buy them a moment when the demons would be blinded, but without a light to guide them, he wasn't certain how much good it would do them. He didn't have to think about it long. The herald globe ended its flight, and even from a distance, it seemed as if the globe exploded before it ever struck the glossy black stone. A massive burst of energy radiated from it, leveling the demons and sending a wash of angry air over Sinjin, Trinda, and Brother Vaughn.

"By the gods," Brother Vaughn said. "What did you just do?" Then he seemed to recall himself. "Never you mind that question, dear. You saved us. That's what you did." Still, when Brother Vaughn found a still-slightly glowing and perfectly preserved herald globe at the center of an area where even much of the black rock had been blasted away, he retrieved it with cautious awe. "Come. We must leave this place. Quickly."

Chapter 13

The true measure of a person can be seen in the way they treat those less powerful than themselves.
--The Pauper King

* * *

For Sinjin, reaching the end of the stone bridge was like waking from a bad dream only to find himself in a new nightmare. More howls came from behind, and he grunted with exertion as he did his best to give Brother Vaughn a boost. His strength was fading, and Brother Vaughn had to find what toeholds he could to complete the climb. Trinda was much easier to lift, and Brother Vaughn was there to reach down and grab her, but that left Sinjin standing alone at the bottom of a nearly shear face. Down low, the face was smoother and devoid of toeholds. Brother Vaughn took off his outer robe and held it down to Sinjin. With a running start, Sinjin jumped without a great deal of confidence, but fear and adrenaline brought him close to success. With his second jump, he got a grip on the robe. The sound of tearing cloth was nearly as frightening as the sight of Brother Vaughn nearly going over the edge, but the robe held and Brother Vaughn regained his balance.

Even with the robe to hold on to, it was a difficult climb. When Sinjin finally reached the top, he slid down into a heaving and quivering mass.

"I'd let you rest, m'boy, but we've got to go," Brother Vaughn said, and Trinda showed her agreement by pulling on Sinjin's shirt, her eyes pleading.

Sinjin knew they were right; he could hear more demons coming, and he knew they needed to move, but he could not get his body to respond. He felt Brother Vaughn grab his jacket between the shoulders, and he tried to stand, but he leaned heavily on the already abused monk. Trinda eyed them both with doubt, as if she expected them to collapse at any moment. Sinjin did his best to prove her wrong and, after a few minutes, was able to walk on his own, though he and Brother Vaughn stayed side by side in case either needed help. Trinda walked ahead of them without complaint. The herald globe glowed brightly, as if it had been charged in the sunlight, though not as brightly as it had been when Trinda had fed it her energy.

"Did you give it more?" Sinjin asked Trinda when his strength began to return.

"A little." She shrugged.

"And was it easy to give it just a little and not everything you had?" Sinjin asked, and Brother Vaughn looked up, awaiting her answer.

Trinda just gave him an annoyed look. "I didn't have very much." Her look made it clear she wanted no more questions about that.

Sinjin sighed and wondered if he would ever understand the ways of those with power. It seemed so foreign to him, even though he was part of the most powerful family on Godsland. He'd seen things no one else had, yet he could explain none of it, could feel none of it, and that terrified him. It was a fear he'd carried most of his life, and these days seemed no more likely to bring an answer or solace.

The sights around him would have been met with awe under any other circumstances, but Sinjin barely noticed the carvings and reliefs or the repeating scrollwork along the walls of the gracefully arching halls. Feeling like prey chased into someone else's territory, Sinjin forced himself to move faster, and he found himself offering support to Brother Vaughn, not knowing where he had found the strength.

Walking in a daze, he almost didn't notice the change. It had been gradual, but the light continued to grow until they no longer needed the herald globe to light their way. Brother Vaughn looked as if he wanted the globe back from Trinda, but she put it in the pocket of her dress, and the elder monk said nothing. Hues of amber cast a warm glow on the otherwise cold stone, and Sinjin felt a weight lift from his soul. Even though he could not access Istra's power, he missed the warm radiance of sunlight and, he supposed, the light of the comets as well. His mother always said that the comets were the most beautiful things she had ever seen and that they had not been in the sky when she was young, but for Sinjin, the comets had always been there. Even though there were more than when he was younger, he couldn't imagine a time without them. They were so commonplace to him, they did not seem so beautiful. Also detracting from their majesty in his eyes was that they seemed more like the force that divided him from his family and had caused most of the bad things that had happened to his mother. If not for Istra's powers, would the Zjhon have ever invaded his homeland?

The beauty of what lay ahead tore Sinjin from his melancholy thoughts. First came the sound of moving water over the rush of a distant fall, then the smell of lush grasses and apple blossoms. Before them waited an underground world that was full of life and wonder. White birds glided in the air over trees that were far wider than they were tall. Though the mighty cavern could have held greatoaks, it seemed most of the vegetation remained closer to the ground. Looking up, Sinjin's breath caught in his chest. A latticework of giant amber crystals formed a vaulted ceiling for the chamber, and these crystals acted as lenses, gathering and intensifying the light from above.

A herd of small deer gathered near a shallow pool for a drink. At first they looked like fauns to Sinjin, so slight were their forms, but several bore small but fully developed racks of antlers. Sinjin wondered what other strange creatures roamed the caverns and how they had come to be there.

Then he looked at the waterfall, which cast rainbows about the cavern, and he knew that the river would bring life, though he still wondered about the deer and birds and whatever else might be alive in this place. The land and trees appeared almost manicured. Shadows occasionally moved within the trees. Sinjin did not know if it was merely his imagination, but as they moved closer to the water, his anxiety grew. Still the chance to get a drink of cool, clean water was too good to resist. Mostly ripe apples waited on a nearby tree, and Sinjin picked three, feeling like a thief. As he did, he noticed no apples on the ground nor stray leaves or sticks.

Trinda eyed the apple Sinjin handed her with suspicion and waited for Sinjin to take a few bites of his before she ate it. He couldn't blame her. There was something curious about trees growing inside of a mountain. He wasn't sure what apples grown in such conditions would be like, yet they tasted delicious. When they had finished the apples, Sinjin wondered what to do with the core. Brother Vaughn looked to be having a similar quandary, but Trinda just finished off her apple and threw the core on the grass. Sinjin and Brother Vaughn eyed it as if they might be punished for their disrespect of this place.

Trinda just put a hand on her hip. "Don't be silly. The deer will eat it."

* * *

Not knowing how long she'd slept, Catrin felt thick and groggy when she woke. The cries of gulls filled the air as they feasted in the shallows during low tide. Her skin felt coated in salt, and her hair lay in ropelike clumps. Black sand clung to her leathers and her exposed skin, and she wiped it away, trying to clear the fog from her sleep-addled mind. The sight of the endless horizon brought fear and anxiety, as if she were the only person left on Godsland. Looking around for Kyrien, she found nothing but empty beaches and bare fields of black stone. If not for the gulls, she would have been truly alone.

Tears gathered in her eyes as she felt the guilt of leaving her son and her husband and all of her people to their fates. Though she knew Prios would protect Sinjin and that Chase and Morif would do their best to protect them, she knew what was to come; she'd seen it in visions she prayed would never come to pass. Standing on a lump of rock in the middle of an ocean, she could not have felt more useless. Forcing her tears aside, she climbed to the highest point of the dormant volcano, the only sign of volcanic activity the still glowing gashes in the field of stone and an occasional burst of steam from the far shore. Standing at the edge of the crater, she scanned the horizon and still saw nothing. Within the crater itself, grasses grew, and Catrin was surprised to find berries and leafy greens growing among porous rock.

While she ate, Catrin began to sense the land pulsing with life beneath her feet, and in some ways, she felt closer to the land than she ever had before. Similar to the feeling she had when standing in the Grove of the Elders, it was as if she could reach into Godsland itself and draw upon its power. She let the land guide her to a place near the center of the crater, a place where moss carpeted rounded stones. Here she rested. Composed and calmed, she moved with the pulse of the land, swaying and breathing deeply.

Using the technique Benjin had once taught her, Catrin focused on her center, which rested within the Grove of the Elders as it existed in her memory: a mighty field of black stone surrounded by twenty-four towering greatoaks. At the very center stood the Staff of Life, still blooming in the place where Catrin had planted it more than a decade before. At no time in history had the grove ever looked exactly as Catrin pictured it, at least not all at one time, but Catrin remembered this place the way she wanted it to be: a place of ancient power untouched by the mistakes of a young girl. Old guilt shrouded her heart despite the fact that she had done everything she could to rebuild the grove. Now only time would return it to its previous glory. The crater reminded her a bit of the grove in the way that the power of the land seemed more acute here. It also reminded her that the Staff of Life rested in lands now occupied by dark forces.

Anxiety poured unbidden from the depths of her soul, fears so dark and personal that she could not face them. In her most terrifying visions, she'd seen herself become the face of death, a wielder of such weapons that all would cower before her, and she had fought to become something else ever since. When making the herald globes, she'd been a creator, yet it seemed as if her true destiny was to be the destroyer. Perhaps in that the old prophecies had been right. Perhaps she had no choice but to become an avatar of death.

Is a sword only used to kill?

The thought echoed from Catrin's subconscious, distant and faint but nonetheless poignant. Catrin had used that very argument to convince Strom to make her a weapon: the sword that lay in her lap, gleaming in the preternatural light of Catrin's meditation. It was a tool--a deadly and dangerous tool. It terrified her. Always she had questioned her right to end the life of another, always she wondered what made her life more valuable than the other's, and always she felt unworthy of those who had died so she could live.

Your work is not yet done.

That thought came from a memory of the druid Barabas and his farewell to her. He'd given his life to save hers, and his parting words frightened her more than anything else. She had yet to earn that sacrifice. Her greatest challenges lay before her, which meant there was the chance she would fail, that she would dishonor those who had made the greatest sacrifice. Fear that she would fail all those who were counting on her came to the fore and threatened to smother her, but Catrin was no longer a little girl, and she would not let fear rule her. Something had happened to her when she became a mother; her own well-being had become somehow secondary to the needs of Sinjin, and as long as he lived, she would have everything she needed to overcome her fear.

Thoughts of Sinjin drew Catrin out of the grove, and her consciousness soared. In the past she had astrally traveled and had visions, but what happened next seemed more like a mixture of the two. Unlike past visions, she could exert control over where she was, but unlike astral travel, she felt uncertain of *when* she was. Something about what she saw made it seem unreal. It rippled and shifted as in dreams, and her thoughts influenced all that she saw. Her heart was drawn to the Godfist, and she soared over the seas faster than the swiftest bird. The Godfist rushed toward her, accompanied by a heavy feeling in Catrin's chest. Smoke rose over parts of the island--her home--and armies of demons and giants clogged the valleys, some even spilling out into the Arghast Desert. Black ships filled the harbors, and the entrances to Dragonhold were infected with darkness. To the south, everything burned; when she soared over the landscape, nothing moved. Then she saw them: feral dragons sunning themselves along a ridgeline, looking almost serene. Catrin knew better.

Desperate need pulled her back to Dragonhold, deep into the stone. There she felt a pulse of life, and it spoke to her, "Mother! Please help!"

Every ounce of Catrin's energy became focused on finding Sinjin and helping him. Nothing mattered more than being there when he needed her most, yet she could not prevent the present from pulling her back, from making her experience the now. When Catrin's eyes opened, she had no idea how long she'd been gone, but the sun was already dipping into the water.

A sudden, pounding thought from Kyrien forced all else aside.

Prepare yourself!

What Catrin saw on the horizon shocked her to her core, something she'd never thought to see, at least not from this vantage point: a flying ship! And it was not just any ship. Like a lover come home after far too long, Catrin recognized the *Slippery Eel,* her normally submerged battering ram now cutting the wind. This alone was enough to rock Catrin back on her heels, but the air around the *Eel* was filled with dragons, lightning, and fire. To add to her horror, the backs of the ferals bore riders who reeked of power. It was these men who cast lightning and fire at will.

Kyrien crashed into ferals, his saddle no longer on his back. He was not alone, though, and Catrin nearly shouted in triumph when she saw the other regent dragons coming to Kyrien's aid. She'd not seen another regent dragon since her flight from the Firstland many years before, but their beauty was unmistakable, even from afar. The ferals had their own fierce splendor, but the regents nearly glowed and shifted colors in the changing light.

Catrin drew a deep breath and prepared to face her destiny. Opening herself to Istra's power, she focused on becoming the sword Strom had made for her: sharp and dangerous but finely tuned to work for good. She found the sword in her hand and raised it high, issuing a battle cry from the core of her being. From the deepest part of her gut, she released all her frustration and channeled it into deadly intent. Energy crawled over her body as she waited, knowing Kyrien would guide them to her.

Soon Catrin could see the crew of the *Slippery Eel*, and she smiled at the thought of fighting alongside Kenward and his shipmates. Tempted to swim out to meet them, it was all Catrin could do to make herself wait.

"There!" came Kenward's shout across the water, and Catrin waved her arms. "I told you! None of you believed me, but I told you she'd be there, didn't I? Ha ha! I told you all her dragon spoke to me, and you didn't believe me! Now who's the crazy one?"

For a brief moment, Catrin grinned, knowing Kenward's crew would not hear the end of this anytime soon. Her grin vanished, though, when the ship slowed and lowered from the skies into the dark waters. Ferals dived at the ship, and only the maddened defense of the regents kept the ferals from tearing the *Slippery Eel* to pieces. Unable to contain her energy any longer, Catrin aimed her sword at the nearest feral and unleashed a torrent of energy that crackled with life. It struck the beast in the chest and knocked it from the sky. The seas around the *Slippery Eel* roiled as dragons continued to strike the surface, some dying, some fending off attacks. Only a few regained the skies and even fewer with riders still in place. Having seen her strike, the regents raised a call that stirred Catrin's blood. They recognized her!

A boat dropped from the side of the *Slippery Eel*, looking tiny and vulnerable in the frothing waves. Catrin feared it would capsize, but the men aboard knew their business and somehow managed to brave the dragons and the surf to make their way to shore. Catrin recognized Bryn and Farsy. The former was as red faced and freckled as ever. Farsy looked as rugged as the sea, his leathery skin hatched with lines and his graying hair pulled back into a braid. Even his tattoos were faded, but his smile shone brightly.

Racing ahead, Catrin looked for the best place for them to land, a place with more sand than rock, and they made for the same place. As they approached, a rippling wave followed them, a monstrous head rearing from the water. Bryn smacked it with an oar and was knocked backward when Catrin's attack struck the beast under the chin, snapping shut its massive jaws. Moments later a regent struck the mostly submerged feral dragon from above, and Catrin had to concentrate on getting into the boat, hoping no more ferals waited beneath the frothing waves.

The ride back to the *Slippery Eel* would haunt her dreams.

Chapter 14

We can reach our full potential only if we are willing to learn, which means we must occasionally admit we are wrong.
--Master Jarvis, teacher

* * *

Kenward grinned as he grabbed Catrin by the arm, pulling her onto deck. "Welcome back to the *Slippery Eel!* I told you all she was here, now didn't I? None of them believed me." In a quieter voice he said, "It's a good thing you're here; I was starting to wonder if I'd gone as mad as Nat Dersinger." Kenward's wink brought back mostly fond memories, but now was not the time for reminiscing, though seeing Bryn and Farsy brought joy to her heart in spite of the darkness that surrounded them.

"How did you do it?" Catrin asked as soon as her boots hit the deck. "How did you make her fly?"

"I thought you might ask that," Kenward said, his grin not fading. "I present you with my flight master."

From the prow approached a lithe man dressed in loose-fitting silks that shimmered as he moved, giving hints and glimpses of his taut form. It was his face that shocked Catrin, for she recognized him.

"Pelivor? Is that really you? By the gods, look at you!"

Stepping forward, he lifted Catrin into an embrace. "I knew we would find each other again. I've learned so much from you, though I've had to do it from afar. Now perhaps you will teach me in person."

"Right now the two of you need to get us out of here," Kenward said, and his words were reinforced by the thrumming of the ship. The *Slippery Eel* had come in perilously close to the rocks, and it would take only one strike from a feral to send them onto the jagged formations.

"Would you like the honor?" Pelivor asked. "I'd love to study your technique."

"Actually I've only done it a few times, and that was years ago. Please, show me what you've learned."

Pelivor nodded and Catrin noticed how much more confident he'd become. Not arrogant or vain, he was simply comfortable being who he was and secure in his knowledge and skills. He'd taught Catrin to speak Zjhonlander and how to read High Script, and there was no doubt he was among the most educated men she knew. Seeing him spread his arms and open himself to Istra's power made Catrin beam with pride. In that, too, he exerted calm control.

"You should have seen him the first time," Kenward said, seemingly reading her mind. "He nearly sunk us."

Pelivor turned his head and raised an eyebrow, and Kenward went silent, save a quiet chuckle.

The *Slippery Eel* gracefully left the water and turned on Pelivor's will, gliding just above the water's surface. Catrin watched him, wide eyed. When she'd first discovered the ability to make a ship fly, Catrin had been able to achieve little more than raising the ship up and riding the wind. What Pelivor did was much more impressive as he seemed to command the wind. Even as ferals continued to swoop and dive, he maneuvered the ship as easily as if he held the wheel but with more agility than any ship's captain could ever have hoped for. It did not seem that Pelivor had access to even a fraction of the amount of energy Catrin could pull from the air around her, yet he exerted such fine control that he did not need as much power to accomplish the task at hand. Catrin felt clumsy and inefficient after watching his precise control.

Standing beside Pelivor, she took his hand. There was no lurch, as Catrin remembered from when she'd been interrupted. Truly Pelivor had found mastery where she was inexpert and required the use of brute force. Slowly she opened her energy to him, and he turned to her, his eyes now wide. "You have so much!"

"And you need so little," Catrin said. "You amaze me."

Slowly Catrin began to see the intricacies of what he did, the way he created a latticework of energy that was equally strong yet required much less effort than Catrin's wing formations had. She considered lending him more energy, but he did not need it. Instead she concentrated on what she could do to make the ship go faster. Her efforts sent cargo shifting, and Kenward held on to the railing.

"Here we go again," Bryn said, and Kenward grinned.

Pelivor observed for a while. Then he interrupted her. "Everything you do is so . . . big. Let me show you something. I can't do it for long, but I think perhaps you could. He took her to the stern, where a strange apparatus had been erected. Resting on a pedestal of iron-reinforced timber, a hollow tube of wood looked to have been carved from a single tree trunk. There was nothing else, no moving parts and no ornamentation, just a strangely shaped tube of wood with a flare in the fore opening and a smaller opening in the aft.

Catrin watched closely as Pelivor took a long breath and drew as deeply as he could. Dividing his attention had a negative impact on the amount of lift his latticework structures provided, and the ship seemed more like it was bouncing across the waves, like a flat stone skipping over still water. When he applied his will to the air in front of the flare, things changed. Air clung to air, and as he forced it through the chamber, more came of its own volition, allowing him to compound the amount of force generated.

The effort came at a price, and Pelivor soon had to stop. The *Slippery Eel* slowed abruptly as the hull once again found the water, and Pelivor dropped to the deck. "Do you see?"

"I do," Catrin said. "I'm sorry I did not help you. Are you well?"

"I'll be fine in a moment. For some reason, I can't seem to do two things at once. Perhaps with more practice."

"You did very well. Already I'm learning from you."

Pelivor smiled.

Kenward watched the skies. "That burst of speed gave us a bit of time, but the dragons are gaining on us."

Catrin turned to see a writhing mass of darkness rolling in and out of the clouds, some attacking and others defending. It was aerial chaos, and the thought of being on dragonback during such a battle made her stomach hurt. Perhaps that was why Kyrien had brought the ship to her instead.

Grubb, the ship's cook, brought Catrin and Pelivor some of his restorative broth, which they accepted eagerly. It was always wise to take what Grubb offered; his skills in the galley were legendary, and Catrin was not disappointed. Though little more than a light soup, the meal warmed her belly and brought clarity to her thoughts.

In a short time, the broth was gone, and Pelivor turned to Catrin. "I suppose I should get us back in the air. If you want to try working the aft, just let me know, and I'll do my best to maintain control."

Seeing Kenward and the crew looking equal parts excited and terrified, Catrin grinned. "Let's do it!" Those words sent everyone into motion. Anything loose was secured, and the crew found places where they could hold on.

"I've waited a long time to say this." Kenward raised his voice and said, "Catrin, Pelivor, let's fly!"

Pelivor exerted his will with the same level of quiet confidence, and Catrin did what she could to emulate his control. Slowly she gathered air and forced it through the narrow chamber. A low howling sound grew in volume and pitch as the stream intensified. Soon it was accompanied by another sound that matched its intensity.

"Woo hoo!" Kenward bellowed as the ship moved forward faster than anyone could have imagined. The sails exceeded the speed of the wind and slowed the ship rather than speed it along, and Kenward shouted for the crew to trim them.

"You're doing it!" Pelivor shouted, sounding triumphant. "I knew it would work!"

Catrin looked back from the stern, watching as a spray of water rolled behind them, curling in on itself, racing into the space that had held the ship only a moment before. Dragons still filled the skies behind them, but the battle was breaking up; feral and regent dragons alike retreated to the clouds. The sun sank below the horizon, clouds obscured the moon and comets, and darkness enshrouded them. Knowing it would be foolish to fly blind, Catrin eased their speed, and soon Pelivor lowered them back into the water.

"The landings are the hardest part," he said as his shoulders heaved from the effort.

Though she knew she should rest, Catrin's body throbbed with excitement and anxiety. It was a heady mixture that she knew would prevent sleep.

"The seas only know how good it is to see you, Catrin," Kenward said as he wrapped her in a warm blanket. He and Bryn guided Catrin and Pelivor into the galley, and Grubb appeared with food more substantial than the broth they had earlier. Catrin was grateful since flying ships, or even propelling them, gave her a mighty hunger, and hearty fish steaks were just what she needed. From the wonderful taste, she knew Grubb had not gone light on the herbs and seasoning.

"How did you learn to fly the ship?" Catrin asked Pelivor when he'd finished his meal. For the first time since she'd arrived, Catrin saw him flush, and he seemed slightly embarrassed.

"It took quite a bit of time and many tries, but Kenward kept explaining to me what you had done, at least to the best of his ability. Finally I started building models of the ship and I played with them in the wind." This statement seemed to embarrass him, but Catrin admired his creativity. "One day I found something that worked, and after countless failures, I found some success. Kenward, of course, wanted more, and I began practicing every day. Each time, I got a little better. And now . . ." He shrugged.

"You've become a master," Catrin finished for him.

"He doesn't drop us from the sky as often as he used to," Kenward corrected. "I almost had to throw him overboard for trying to fly us into low-lying clouds. Who knows what flying through clouds would be like? We'd be blind and we might even drown!"

Pelivor flushed and would not meet Catrin's eyes.

"It's wet, true, and very difficult to see, but you can breathe just fine," Catrin said.

Kenward involuntarily spit out the wine he'd been drinking and broke into a fit of coughing. When he'd recovered, he said, "When will I ever learn not to try to match wits or questionable behavior with you, m'lady?"

Catrin shook her head. Coming from him, that was no compliment.

"Did you really fly through the clouds?" Pelivor asked.

Catrin told the tale of her and Kyrien's flight from the Godfist. It was difficult to get through without crying, but she managed--just.

"We nearly made it to the Godfist," Kenward said, "but Bryn spotted dragons--the nasty-looking black ones--and we turned back. The devils gave chase, and it took everything Pelivor had to keep us in one piece. The greenish ones like Kyrien came not a day too soon. That was when I started dreaming about you being stuck on an island."

"I'm glad you came," Catrin said.

"None of this lot believed me," Kenward said for what seemed the twelfth time, and Pelivor rolled his eyes. "So why are we going back to the Firstland?"

"What?" she said, standing up.

"Well, every time I dreamed about you being on that island--sometimes even when I was wide awake, mind you--I'd always see us sailing back to the Firstland. I figured you'd know why."

Catrin said nothing for a time, every part of her conflicted. Nothing mattered to her more than getting back to Sinjin and Prios, but she had no idea what had become of those within Dragonhold or even if the defenses had withstood the assault. If they still lived--Catrin's chest ached at that thought--her chances of getting inside were dismal. Letting their defenses down to admit her and Kyrien would open the doors for the hoard of demons, and Catrin did not want to put her loved ones in greater peril, yet staying away went against every instinct she possessed. She clenched the top rail of her chair and stared down at the table.

"Do you want to go back to the Godfist?" Kenward asked.

"Yes," Catrin said.

Kenward sucked in a deep breath. "I'm not sure we should do that."

"Then why did you ask?" Catrin snapped. "If you're just going to sail to the Firstland regardless, then don't bother asking me."

"I'm sorry, Catrin. I just wanted to know what you desired while still advising you on the dangers--"

"I know, Kenward. I'm sorry. It's just . . . Sinjin. How do I abandon my son? My husband? My people?"

"I don't know," he said, her pain reflected in his eyes.

Not able to look at her companions, Catrin gripped her chair and looked down at its seat.

"I'll take you home if that is your wish, Catrin," Kenward said.

Silence hung between them for a time. Catrin made no move to respond, and Kenward started to stand up from the table.

"I can't leave them behind," she said. "Even if it takes me to my death, I must go back."

Kenward swallowed. "I understand."

"I don't want you to take me, though. I'll call for Kyrien, and he can take me home."

"But how will you fly if you no longer have your saddle? You said that was the only thing that kept you on his back."

"I don't know. We'll just have to find a way."

"I don't know either, Cat, but I've seen dragons fight, and I don't think you want to be anywhere near when that happens. Maybe you should let me sail you home."

Again silence.

A feeling crept over Catrin, but she pushed it away, not wanting to let anything alter her course. She was a mother; nothing could stand in her way, but that feeling, which fostered doubt, would not be ignored. Gripping the chair so hard that she thought she might snap it, a thought occurred to Catrin. "Kenward, what is your cargo?"

"Spices, seeds, a variety of things for homesick Greatlanders living on the Godfist, and a pair of boilin' heavy stone thrones for your highness."

"That's it. I can use one of the thrones to travel back to the Godfist."

"Oh, no," Kenward said. "I'm not going through that again. The last time you tried that, you nearly died. And how do you think I'd feel with your dead carcass on my deck? No, sir. Not me. Nope. Besides, you can't get to those thrones. They're acting as ballasts and are underneath the rest of the cargo."

"Surely we can manage to get one of them on deck," Catrin said.

"No. It took ten men and a hoist to get them where they are, and even if we could move one up here, I wouldn't. That would make us top heavy, and we'd likely capsize. I'm sorry. No."

* * *

"You owe me," Kenward said hours later, looking more agitated than Catrin had ever seen him.

Shifting, she tried to find a way to get comfortable on the cold, hard stone. She reminded herself that the throne was designed not for comfort but to act as an anchor to her physical form, which would guide her back to her body.

"I can't believe I let you talk me into this. What was I thinking?"

Looking out at clear, blue sky, Catrin knew better than to smile. The hastily cut hole in Kenward's deck provided just enough of a view for her purposes. Bales of herbs had been stacked as strategically as possible to provide the proper acoustics and the separation of the two individual chants. Many of Kenward's crew, including Kenward himself, knew both sides of the chant from their harrowing voyage to the Firstland in search of Archmaster Belegra. Those memories brought fear and mourning, and Catrin tried to put that out of her mind as she concentrated.

Before her, Pelivor knelt, looking up into her eyes. "I'll attend you. Just as I did all those years ago."

Catrin smiled. "I know I can count on you." She also nearly laughed when she heard Kenward complaining that he should just start keeping drums on his ships so he would not have to constantly make them from whatever was in his hold.

Voices rose slowly on either side, each with their own cadence and melody that uncannily merged into seamless harmony. When the drums did start, Catrin was impressed by the amount of vibration she felt. The crew had done well. Those vibrations allowed her to slip beyond her mortal shield, and Catrin flew free in a rush of exaltation. The open sky welcomed her, and she soared through it. Behind her, a silvery thread ran back to her waiting form. She, Prios, and Brother Vaughn had been right; it was indeed the mixture of metal and stone that created the anchor effect. Had the thrones ever reached the Godfist, everything could have been different. Catrin and Prios would have had the ability to safely travel astrally anywhere they wished; they could have been so much better prepared. Instead, she and Prios had nearly been killed just trying to travel a short distance to save their son. Catrin did not blame Kenward for the horrors they faced, but she did shiver at the memory of them and wished again that Kenward could have come sooner.

Instinct guided her as she sailed straight toward Sinjin, her course direct and unerring. The waves raced beneath her, a feeling of bliss nearly overcoming her as she flew. Such freedom! Twisting and spinning, she reveled in the glory of being naught but energy, free of burden and driven by pure purpose. Only the nature of that purpose brought Catrin out of her revelry. The thought of the demons that ravaged her homeland brought with it a dangerous odor, and the wind cried afoul. Those who stood against her overwhelmed Catrin's senses; single-minded hatred engulfed her, and it was that obsession that frightened her the most. It was not as if each of them hated her for his own reason. The hatred was homogeneous and felt as if it came from a single, dominating source. An oily and cloying feeling encroached on Catrin, and she felt insignificant and small. Every sense told her that she would be dead already if not for something surrounding her, protecting her.

No! her spirit cried as she sensed the falseness of the will that was trying to subvert her, and she recoiled, but it pursued her with relentless vigor. Only when another energy came close did the oppression wane, and Catrin could feel Kyrien as he reminded her what it felt like to be truly protected.

You should not go back . . . yet.

Catrin wanted to scream at him, to accuse and blame him. Lacking the form to utter the words, she cast angry energy at him, and still he remained unwavering.

We are not ready to face them . . . yet.

I cannot abandon them, Catrin wanted to scream.

The world spun as Kyrien overwhelmed Catrin's senses with a vision, a projection of his thoughts that felt as if they were her own. She experienced not some memory of Kyrien's past; she lived his fears as if they were her own. He bared his soul, showing her the things he knew were to come, as surely as if he were a prophet. The future horrified her, but it was not enough to dissuade her. No one and nothing could convince her to leave Sinjin to his fate. She had to see him. She could sense his fear. He needed her.

I must go, she thought with all her might.

Kyrien relented but stayed by her side. When the attack came, he thrust himself in front of her. Catrin screamed as his energy was torn apart.

Her spirit shouting a reverberating battle cry, Catrin gathered her energy and attacked. The silvery thread that trailed behind her blazed furiously, and energy raced along the thread to devastating effect. Dark forms gathered in the air around her, each twisted and deformed, as if nature itself had been subverted. Such single-minded rage and malevolence was difficult to face, but Catrin's web of lightning knifed through the air, seemingly random in its path, the tendrils were well-defined and tightly wound, which was a product of what Pelivor had taught her. Now she could create larger, more powerful, structures using less energy. When the beams of liquid light struck, they severed the bonds between the demons' spirits and their mortal forms. She could feel them as they were freed from compulsion, freed from a life of torture, and returned to the well from which they'd been sprung. More came, and Catrin attacked, again and again, relentlessly, feeling no pain and no weariness.

Voices called to her, but she ignored them. She was winning! She could defeat this enemy and find Sinjin and Prios. She was going to *win!* Kyrien's spirit overwhelmed her as his energy embraced her.

You must go back now.

No! I'm winning!

The cost is too great. You will die. The darkness is drawing you in and can strike at any time. You must turn back now!

Catrin didn't care if she died. It was not her life that mattered, but the thought of Sinjin growing up without his mother made her soul ache. A sparkling cloud of threatening energy gathered around the Godfist as she approached, and she could feel the pent-up charge waiting for release. What she'd seen so far had been but a feint; what awaited her now was a full assault. The enemy had tested her defenses and knew her weaknesses. Soon she realized that Kyrien had been right, but it was too late, the attack was swift, without further warning, and deadly. Catrin felt something akin to all the air being sucked out of a room, and the darkness reached out all at once, hurtling toward her with the most foul intent. The hatred battered her senses.

Catrin opened herself to all the energy she could pull across her lifeline, which now resembled a bolt of lightning racing toward her. When it struck, Catrin felt herself become the conductor. She felt as if she, too, were illuminated from the inside out and that she shone like the sun. The brightness fought the haggard darkness that reached out to her with lethal force. Without thought or reason, Catrin released the energy in a single pulse that sent a wave of light radiating out from her like a massive wall of water. The darkness was tossed before it, and lost in the wave, it dissipated and vanished. It was a small dent in the massive cloud of darkness, but it gave Catrin heart.

Kyrien soared around her, keeping her safe as she gathered energy for another attack, ready to give all she had left to annihilate this threat to all she loved. The air behind her began to sing, and Catrin turned to see what new threat she faced. A howling form flew straight toward her, and it took her a moment to recognize Pelivor. His speed was terrifying, and had she been in her physical form, Catrin would have taken a step backward. As it was, Pelivor's scream grew louder and louder, and Catrin realized it was not a battle cry, but a warning to get out of the way. Pelivor was out of control.

As he screamed past, Catrin felt a wash of energy douse her, and she could see the fire racing along a glowing cord attached to Pelivor's spirit. Just before he struck the cloud of darkness, he lit up from within and, flailing wildly, sent gouts of fire and something that looked like boiling air into the darkness before him.

Without another thought, Catrin followed him and, using what energy she could muster, blasted a trail before her. Still, the darkness clawed at her, its grip madness, its odor cloying and sweet. Issuing her own scream filled with horror and fear, Catrin felt the darkness close in behind her. No feeling could compare to being cut off from the light, to lose touch with all that is sane, and to be immersed in chaos. Before her, only the vision of Pelivor gave her something to hold on to, and she tried to get to him.

His screams slashed the air, cutting into Catrin's soul, but she could not reach him. The same darkness surrounding Pelivor and falling on him like a pack of starving dogs on a fresh kill also assaulted her. She barely felt the attacks. Twice, bursts of light drove back the darkness, and Catrin ignored the demonic forces and the voices demanding she come back. The only thing that mattered in that moment was Pelivor. Each pulse of light he sent out gave Catrin a chance to get closer to him, and she felt as if she could stretch out and touch him, yet he was just beyond her spirit's fingertips. Screaming violently with effort, Pelivor reached out to Catrin wildly and savagely, lacking the control of experience. When he and Catrin did connect, there was a flash far brighter than any of those that had come before. In the next instant, Catrin opened her eyes, back in her body.

Standing above her was the most hideous visage she had ever seen. Gray and twisted, the face of the demon spoke of a slow and painful death. A curved blade gleamed in the light, and with a warrior's precision, the demon reversed its blade while raising it for a devastating strike. Something dark slammed into the side of Catrin and the demon. The demon's blade threw sparks into the air as it struck only stone, and Catrin realized it was Kenward who had saved her by tackling the demon.

Trying to regain control of her body after the astral travel, Catrin was dismayed to find that she could barely move. Her arms trembled with fatigue, and a glance to her left showed that Pelivor was not faring much better. The demon, though, was struggling to get Kenward off its back, and Kenward looked small and weak against the massive beast. Reaching over to Pelivor, Catrin grasped his hand in hers. He looked up at her, met her eyes, and nodded, knowing what was to come. The demon was overpowering Kenward, and Catrin released all caution. She drew as deeply as she could on her own energy and what she could get from Pelivor. His eyes went wide, and the air between them sang a high-pitched note before light arced between Catrin and the demon with a crack that sent Kenward stumbling backward. Nimsy arrived a moment later and finished the demon off while it was still stunned.

"Are you hurt?" Catrin asked, not knowing exactly whom she was asking.

Pelivor shook his head but could not or would not speak.

"I'm fine," Nimsy said, but he grew quiet as Kenward straightened suddenly.

"What was I *thinking?*" Kenward asked. "It would be great to sail with Catrin again!" he continued, mocking himself. "Nothing bad ever happens when Catrin's aboard."

For a moment the comment stung, but Catrin remained silent, letting her old friend vent his anger and frustration. When she looked up and saw two jagged holes in his deck and down to see a dead demon in the bilge, it occurred to her that he was probably right.

"We'll just cut a hole in the deck! How could I ever have gone along with that, I ask you? And now look. *Two holes in my deck!* And you darn near took Pelivor with you! And why is it that as soon as you two trip off to play in the skies, we get attacked by demons straight from the depths?"

"Black sails on the horizon, sir!" came a shout from above. Catrin recognized Farsy's voice, and he sounded shaken. "An' that black cloud is back on the horizon. 'Cept it's bigger. And the wind has died."

Kenward stood with his arms out to his sides and his mouth wide open, but no sound came out. Turning to Catrin and Pelivor, he raised his palms. "Can you make her fly?" The look in his eyes made it clear that he really hadn't wanted to ask the question.

"I don't know," Catrin said.

"By the gods, does it always hurt this much?" Pelivor asked, his hands over his ears.

"Should I take that as a no?" Kenward asked.

"I can try," Pelivor said and Catrin nodded.

Kenward softened then and blushed. "Are you certain? Nimsy, Farsy! Help these two up on deck."

He hadn't really waited for Catrin to answer, but she just clamped her jaw and got ready to climb to the deck. Unsteady on her feet and feeling only loosely attached to her body, she was grateful for Nimsy's help. Pelivor's head lolled from side to side, and Catrin doubted he was up to the task; he looked barely conscious.

As the sun melted into the sea, the largest and brightest comets showed themselves in a wash of color that ranged from gold to deep violet. It was strikingly beautiful, and that alone brought Catrin hope and refreshment.

"Where are we going?" Kenward asked.

Taking a deep breath, Catrin stood on trembling legs. She'd seen the darkness laying siege to the Godfist, and she knew that the odds of any of them surviving were terrifyingly slim. Then she felt a comforting presence and heard the crew shout out. She saw Kyrien circling low over the ship.

Everything before her faded away, and Kyrien sent her a vision of darkness and loss that made her soul tremble. Then he flashed a vision of Catrin and Kyrien standing as the last defense of man and dragon alike. The vision replayed, and each time they made different choices. Over and over again the vision played in her mind, but every time one or both species were lost. For one waited a hollow victory; for the other, extinction. Catrin reeled at the implications and tried to control her reaction to the horror they faced. This decision--her decision--would affect all that happened from here on out, and she could only hope that she chose wisely.

Despite the visions, Catrin was determined to save them all or die trying. "We go to the Firstland."

"I knew it," she heard Kenward say, and she received a rather shocked look from Pelivor, who was slowly recovering.

"Let's see if we can get this ship into the air," Kenward said.

Pelivor smiled then winced. "I'll give it my best."

Catrin remained by his side as they tried to get the ship out of the water, but the still air made it impossible.

"You're going to have to propel us," Pelivor said.

"Are you sure you'll be able to get us out of the water?" Catrin asked.

"Are you sure you can propel us?" Pelivor asked Catrin.

"Not really," she admitted.

"Then we're even."

Walking to the back of the ship under her own power was an accomplishment, but it seemed insignificant in comparison to what she was about to attempt. Standing beside the massive, wooden tube that was bolted to the deck of the *Slippery Eel,* Catrin knew that getting the boat moving would be her greatest challenge. Forcing air into the tube had been relatively easy with air already rushing toward them, but grabbing still air and forcing it through was a great deal more difficult. Progress was painfully slow, and Pelivor offered to come back and help her get them started, but Catrin did not want him to exhaust himself by helping her. He would be responsible for keeping them airborne, a task they could not afford to have unfulfilled. Catrin waved him off and applied her will, feeling as if her head might split into two. At first the wooden tube emitted a low moan, and the ship sank lower in the water, but the ship did move forward, albeit in painfully slow fashion; still every bit of speed forced more air into the tube and helped drive them faster.

"Ships approaching from all sides, sir!"

An instant later, Kyrien turned, rolled, and dived into the waves off their port side. Hushed cries from the crew pulled at Catrin's senses.

Kenward's every attention centered on Catrin. "You can do it," he whispered.

Nimsy had remained by Catrin's side, and she leaned on him for support, knowing her task was impossible. Even with her greatest effort, the ship had not gained enough speed to sustain the reaction, instead requiring more and more energy from her. An instant before she released the energy flow, the ship thrummed and surged forward, as if they had been struck from the stern. And in fact, they had. Kyrien proved his swimming prowess by driving the ship forward. His serpentine body and tail propelled him through the water, showing the efficiency of his form. With no time to revel in the marvels of dragons, Catrin redoubled her efforts, and the air came to her more easily, partly because of Kyrien's efforts and partly because the winds had picked up.

"Did you see that?" came a shout from on deck, and Catrin risked losing her concentration to look around. Black ships approached from every direction, dark clouds following those from the west. Lightning danced in the charged air amid the rigging of the dark ships. Catrin felt more than saw the presence of someone using Istra's powers. She could smell the discharge in the air, and she felt the hairs on her neck rise. Again she regained her focus and applied as much energy as she could to increasing their speed.

Pelivor gave no warning, and Catrin heard men hitting the deck as the ship suddenly left the water at a steep angle and just as suddenly slowed when it struck the next wave. Three more times they skipped across the waves, and the crew barely held on. After the third, Pelivor gave out a roar, and the ship gained the air, catching the growing tailwind.

Catrin worked to shape the air as it entered the tube, and in doing so realized that the design was flawed. If she could change the shape of the inner chamber, it would be far more efficient, but she had no time for that. As the ship's speed picked up, so did their altitude, and she could only hope that Pelivor did not drop them from the sky.

Catrin returned her attention to the approaching ships, which were now far too close. The *Slippery Eel* was airborne but was by no means high enough to clear the approaching ships with their spiring masts and inky black sails. Once again they would need to rely on speed and agility. With Catrin and Pelivor not at their best, she wasn't sure how nimble their movements would be, so she kept her focus on speed. The adverse side effect was that the ships ahead drew closer at an alarming rate. A moment later Catrin's heart fell into her stomach as the ships before them crested a large wave. Racing down the trailing edge of the wave, each left the water at the exact same moment. Lightning flared and created a web between the three flying ships.

Pelivor turned and looked back to Catrin, and the ship dropped sharply. Pelivor never got to see the panicked expression on Catrin's face, as he needed every ounce of concentration to get more altitude. A cold feeling washed over Catrin as the realization sank in: all their advantages were gone, and they no longer had any way to defend themselves from the darkness that approached. Perhaps they could take out one or two of the ships if they had enough speed. She looked over to Kenward, who seemed to have come to the same conclusions. He just nodded to her and gave the order. "Arm yourselves and prepare for ramming speed!"

Chapter 15

Our greatest limitations are often self-imposed.
--Dirk Burunda, mountain climber

* * *

Durin had known Prios his entire life and knew he was a nice man with Durin's best interest at heart, but he couldn't stop the fear from stirring in his belly. A tongueless man with such power was in itself somehow frightening, but it was the need in Prios's battle-weary eyes that terrified Durin. It made him accept that his actions may have resulted in Sinjin's death. That thought haunted him, and he wanted nothing more than to believe that this tunnel would lead him to Sinjin, Brother Vaughn, and even Trinda, but so far this new section of Dragonhold had proven to be little more than empty rooms and halls. The deep rumbles that came from the heart of the mountain had been the most interesting part of their journey thus far, that was, until Prios had arrived.

Durin and Strom had been walking at a brisk pace while they explored the halls, but some three hours into the journey, Durin had turned around to find Prios stalking him. His shriek had given Strom a start, but then they had seen the look in Prios's eyes. He needed to know if this was the way to where Sinjin was. No words were required. And of those who had come with Prios, none spoke. When Durin spotted Kendra and Khenna, he looked away, still troubled by their presence. Prios, though, had pushed them on, his herald globe brightly charged and shining the way.

Since then, they had been searching through an area that must have once held more people than currently lived on the Godfist. Durin found it depressing. Why would anyone choose to live in darkness, in a place of cold stone that seemed to suck the joy from the air? At least that was how it felt to Durin. Perhaps it was only the product of his current mood, but the tense silence seemed to indicate that the others felt the same. The inherent sense of order in the place also bothered Durin. Here rested an abandoned city, yet the halls were clear, and not a bit of refuse could be found. The chambers they did explore were bare as well, adding to the mystery. It was as if the city had been built as a precaution and had never actually been occupied.

Rumbling echoes continued to break the silence at seemingly random intervals, and each time Prios listened intently. It seemed impossible to tell where the sounds were actually coming from, but Prios continued to lead them with what appeared to be confidence. Strom walked by his side, not questioning Prios's judgment. More meticulously carved entranceways lined rough-hewn corridors, but it came as a shock when they reached an imposing hall, the corridor turning left and right around the perimeter of the hall, and the most elaborate entrance yet stood directly before them, ready to welcome them or devour them--Durin couldn't tell which. Mighty creatures, from dragons to giant cats, had been carved around the entranceway, and their beauty was eclipsed by only the fear they generated. Prios gave them but a single glance. Only Strom's sideways look and his subsequent checks over his shoulder made Durin feel any better.

Every footfall sent echoes cascading through the halls, and Durin knew that if there was anything alive in this place, it surely knew they were there. The place must have been designed to carry sound from the dais to the audience, and it did its job well. Prios's sharp hiss reverberated throughout the hall, and Durin fought the urge to hide.

Before them lay the remains of what had once been a finely dressed man. His clothing had been almost perfectly preserved, though his body was a desiccated hull that somehow still clung to his bones. Most shocking was the simple dagger wedged between two ribs and leaving no doubt that this man, whomever he was, had been murdered. The thought made Durin look over his shoulder, though it was obvious this crime had taken place in the distant past. After listening intently to the faraway thumps and rumbles, Prios led them from the amphitheater, and Durin couldn't help looking over his shoulder, wondering if the murderer were lurking in the shadows.

* * *

The sound of creaking timbers and a low buzz filled the air as the dark ships encroached. Catrin turned to Kenward. "Do you remember the drills we ran when we were lost trying to find the Firstland?"

"We weren't exactly lost; we just didn't know how to get where we were going," Kenward said, but he stumbled when he saw Catrin's exasperated look. "Yes, I remember."

"Can we do something like we did that time you turned to the side at the last moment?"

"I don't know that it would work," Kenward said. "Much of that technique relied on the water, and empty air would not provide the same effect. That would just put our weakest side forward."

"What do you plan to do, then?"

"We'll slip between two ships, turn, and ram one of them in the belly."

"Slip between the ships that have lightning flowing between them?" Pelivor asked, his voice high pitched and strained.

"I didn't say it was a perfect plan. What do you suggest?"

"I suggest we try to gain more altitude. That's the only thing that will give us room to move."

Catrin swallowed hard, knowing she'd already given her best effort, and she assumed that Pelivor had as well. This last effort might be in vain, but she had to try. Working at the wooden tube, turbulent air fought her, demanding its freedom and refusing to do her bidding. Still, she managed to gain a bit more speed, and Pelivor, his outstretched hands crawling with energy, lifted the ship higher. The dark ships stayed just above the water, and from the *Eel*'s current height, they would slam into the masts and rigging of the approaching ships. Pelivor cried out as his arms trembled, and the veins stood out on his neck as he tried, without success, to get them high enough to clear the other ships.

"Get ready to board the ship to port!" Kenward shouted, and Catrin nearly lost her concentration. She could not bear the thought of the *Slippery Eel*'s crew going to their deaths. She could see the demons on the other ships now and with them, men. Dressed in black armor and looking as if they bathed in ashes, men worked alongside demons. It was a terrifying sight. Some wore the mark of the hammer, which was Thorakis's sigil, but Catrin could still not figure out why Thorakis would do such things and align himself with evil. It made no sense.

"One more try," Pelivor shouted as the ships moved close enough for lightning to reach out to the *Slippery Eel*'s rigging. Catrin let out a cry of her own as she reached for the comets, begging for the energy she needed, pleading with the goddess for more power. If only she'd had Koe or her staff, but she had none of that. All she would wield would be the sword Strom had made for her against his own will. It was a beautiful blade with a magic of its own, but Catrin was uncertain how much use that magic would be under these circumstances. Nonetheless, the feeling of the pommel in her hand steadied her, and she held the blade high.

Just as impact was imminent, the hull thrummed, and the ship lurched upward. Knees bent, Catrin absorbed the upward thrust and did her best to take advantage of the gained height. Pelivor shouted with what sounded like a mixture of terror and relief as they soared above the towering masts.

A momentary slowing and the sound of snapping rigging gave everyone pause as it seemed they had not gotten away clean after all. Catrin moved to the rail and looked down to see wings--not structures of energy but real wings, Kyrien's wings. Even as he helped to lift them into the air, he was taking the opportunity to attack the rigging of the ships below. Once he let go, he and the *Slippery Eel* turned on the wind and soared back low over the water, now well clear of the ships. The dark cloud that had been approaching was nearly upon them. It overflowed with energy and malicious intent, and Catrin did not want to be anywhere near it. To the east, another bank of clouds threatened. It, too, reeked of energy, but its charge, at least, was that of a natural storm. What approached from the west wanted her dead; she could feel it.

The dive back to low altitude had gained them speed, and Catrin shaped the wind to give it the most efficient flow. The air sang and, as the rigging began to vibrate, Kyrien thrust them upward and into the approaching storm. Screaming gouts of fire clogged the air, leaving behind trails of oily black smoke. One struck the deck, and immediately fire spread. With most of the crew holding on for their lives, the fire got a chance to establish itself. By the time the crew had tied a rope around Farsy's waist so he could let go and fight the fire, the flames were spreading. With Kyrien's unpredictable movements, there was not much Farsy could do to protect himself, and Catrin hoped that slim line of rope would be enough to save him from going overboard.

Another flaming projectile struck the mainsail, which was soon awash with fire. Catrin had to remind herself to breathe as Bryn climbed the rigging without a rope to secure him. Kyrien banked a sharp turn as another screaming ball of flames arched over the bow. Bryn hung by his arms alone, and he nearly swung in a complete circle as the ship banked, creaking and groaning against Kyrien's back, but when the ship righted itself, he landed deftly.

Catrin's efforts continued to lend them speed, and Pelivor kept most of the weight off Kyrien. It was only when they needed to climb or change direction that Kyrien would take more of the weight onto his back. It must be painful, Catrin thought, but she could sense Kyrien laughing.

I am stronger than you might believe.

Catrin smiled.

"I'm not so sure about this," Kenward said as they neared the leading edge of the towering storm cloud, its structures larger and more imposing than any fortress ever built. The *Slippery Eel* was about to disappear into it, even as lightning continued to illuminate it from within. "I didn't agree to this!"

Still, Kyrien drove them upward and directly into the storm. Almost instantly it became clear that the air currents within the storm were more unpredictable than Kyrien's movements, and the ship along with Kyrien flew erratically, sometimes dropping through pockets of air as if they would crash to the sea. Light flashed around them, and Catrin felt the ship building up a charge. It reminded her of when she'd been struck by lightning in Pinook Harbor. Her skin crawled with energy, and a coppery taste filled her mouth. The structures Pelivor used to provide lift seemed to gather the charge as they sliced through the excited air around them, and balls of floating lightning danced along the deck and through the solid walls of the deckhouse. The curses that poured from the galley made it clear that the lightning continued to the other side of the walls.

"I should have listened to my mother," Kenward said after having to duck ball lightning and nearly being thrown overboard by turbulent air.

"Now there's a first," Catrin said, unable to resist.

"Really?" Kenward said in mock horror. "You're going to hold that over me now? While we're flying through a storm I wouldn't sail through and being chased by balls of light and fire, if we're not tossed into the open air first. I'm not certain which death I prefer, but I'm pretty sure I don't want one of those balls of light catching up to me."

"Get low and stay away from the mainmast!" Catrin said.

"Oh, I don't like the sound of that at all," Kenward said. "Why do I even let you on my ship?"

Catrin got no chance to respond as the storm chose that instant to relieve the ship of its charge. She had expected it to hit the masts, but she had not considered that they were inside the cloud instead of below it. In a surreal moment that would forever be burned into Catrin's memory, she saw a fine, silvery web of energy form, and in the space of a breath, it grew to blindingly bright light that crawled over every part of the ship and its crew. In the next moment, darkness engulfed them and rain whipped around them, but the most terrifying part was the feeling of falling. Even stunned and confused, the crew managed to hang on to the now plummeting ship. Pelivor remained where he'd been clinging to the railing, but he appeared to be having trouble hanging on. Catrin couldn't blame him; neither of them had been prepared for this, and she did not know how much more she'd be able to endure, but for the moment, she knew she needed to get control of the ship.

Standing up and supporting herself against the deckhouse, Catrin tied herself to the steerage, having flashbacks of nearly drowning as a result of the same idea, but she forced herself to do it as the prow dipped. The ship dived straight down into the clear skies below the storm clouds, and the seas rushed up at them with incredible speed. More turbulence caused the ship to twist, and Catrin drew a sharp breath when she caught sight of Kyrien below them, falling in a flat spin, as if he were already dead. Catrin cried out across the distance and tried to communicate with his spirit, but she got no response, and his body continued to spin out of control. Knowing everyone aboard would suffer Kyrien's fate if she did not do something, Catrin gathered her will. She created structures more like those Pelivor used than the ones she had created in the past, and she found them easier to maintain, except the speed of the air coming at them was so intense that it tried to tear the structures apart.

"I knew this was a bad idea!" Kenward shouted, even as the angle of their descent lessened.

The speed made the rigging sing, and Catrin wanted to look down and see what had become of Kyrien, but the ship was far from under control. Backlit by a flash of lightning, a giant shape filled the air near them. One could not confuse a regent dragon with a feral dragon, and this was definitely a feral. Its black scales glistened in the rain, and it matched their dive. Using all her might, Catrin changed the angle of her wings, scrubbed off some speed, and sent them back into as steep a climb as she could maintain.

"Hold on!" she shouted.

"Now you tell us to hold on? How can it get any worse?"

Catrin didn't bother to answer Kenward. She let the port-side wing dissolve into nothingness, just as the feral attacked, which sent the ship rolling aside. A mighty crash resounded and sent the ship careening as the dragon planted its claws on the hull and thrust itself away from the *Eel*. Catrin tried to reestablish the port wing, but the spinning of the ship made it difficult to do anything but hold on. After several tries, she managed to right the ship. Soon after, Pelivor joined her and did his best to secure himself in a similar fashion. With his help, the ship regained stable flight.

"Watch for the feral!" Catrin shouted.

It wasn't long until someone cried out, "Here it comes!"

The information wasn't all that helpful in the sense that Catrin had no idea from what direction the attack would come, only that it would come soon. With a sharp turn to starboard, Catrin hoped she'd guessed correctly.

A muffled roar that sounded like a snake moving over rawhide, only a thousand times louder, shook the *Slippery Eel*, but the ship maintained stable flight. Momentarily allowing her concentration to waver, Catrin looked around, trying to figure out what was going on in the air around them, but once again, clouds had engulfed them, and she could see almost nothing. Even sound was dampened by the wet air, and the cries that rang out seemed distant.

Grubb brought a thick soup that sat heavily in Catrin's stomach and made her eyelids feel as if they weighed as much as a pair of hams. Nimsy braced her and took more of her weight as she swayed on her feet. It was simply too much to ask of her exhausted body. She needed rest more than anything. Vaguely she thought she heard someone calling her name. Wanting to tell the person to go away and just give her a little more time to sleep, Catrin realized she was falling; everything was falling.

Trying desperately to clear the sleep from her mind, Catrin lent energy to Pelivor, who looked as if he, too, would drop at any moment.

"We need to get the ship back in the water," Catrin managed to say between gasps.

Pelivor just nodded without fully lifting his head.

Darkness crowded Catrin's vision, and she remained conscious only by the sheer force of her will. Nothing mattered in that instant except getting the *Eel* back in the water. If it killed her, then so be it. None of this seemed worth it anymore. How could anything be worth the pain and suffering she endured? How could anything make up for the anguish of loss or the frustration of failure? Catrin howled in spite of it and guided the ship lower.

"First we need to get clear of that!" Kenward shouted as the feral soared straight toward the prow of the ship at incredible speed. At the last instant, the dragon reached out and grabbed a crewman as it passed. The man's screams pounded against Catrin's resolve, trying to convince her that she could not win; they would not survive.

Buffeted by the wind, the ship angled toward the waves, and Catrin stood, trembling, ready to release the energy and collapse the instant they hit the waves. Farsy's support appeared to be the only thing keeping Pelivor upright, and she knew he felt the same.

"Get down!" someone shouted.

Catrin saw it then, approaching for another pass, its eyes gleaming with hatred and purpose. Like a giant snake, it undulated in the air, as if swimming through the clouds. Folding its wings, it raced toward the *Slippery Eel,* aiming for Kenward. Catrin could not allow it to take him from the deck--not Kenward or any other member of the crew.

"I'm sorry!" Catrin cried out, not having time to warn anyone or ask permission. Instead she did something she wished she didn't know how to do. Reaching out to all those aboard, she borrowed their energy. None could resist and had no chance to avoid her embrace. As quick as lightning, her power locked on to them all, and they were hers to do with as she pleased. With the flick of her wrist, she could drain them all. It was so beautiful, and Catrin wanted more. How could she not? It was the most glorious thing she'd ever experienced, yet she knew the consequences, and it took only an instant to regain her composure.

Pelivor stared at her with the widest eyes she'd ever seen, and Catrin loosed a single, white-hot bolt of energy that left the air crackling and smelling of charcoal. The crew, still locked in a frozen rictus, was illuminated in morbid detail as the bolt flashed over the deck. Then they were lost in a conflagration that burned into Catrin's soul. She felt the dragon reaching for her spirit even as it died, as if its energy stretched beyond its mortal shell and sought to burn Catrin alive with its last reserve. Releasing the crew as quickly as she could, Catrin threw her arms up before her. There was no time to use the energy to shield herself, and she was suddenly awash with flame and lightning. It lasted only an instant; then it was gone.

Singed and in some cases still smoking, the crew moved as if they were drunk, and Catrin hoped she hadn't taken too much from them. Aware that she could kill a person by drawing too much energy, she worried what would happen if she drew *almost* too much energy from them, and she feared permanent damage. The thought was yanked away as she was suddenly thrown forward against the ropes that bound her. Icy water surged over the bow, drenching her and everyone else on deck. Pelivor appeared dead as he floated toward the rail on the receding wave, his body limp and almost liquid in its movements.

Everyone aboard was silent, and Catrin watched in mute awe as crewman regained their feet and began checking the rigging. It was not long before shouts came from below. "We're taking on water, sir!"

Darkness once again crowded Catrin's vision, and she could no longer fight it. She felt like an empty and desiccated husk that would never be whole again. With a heavy sigh of resignation, she slumped toward the deck, only the ropes holding her upright. As the darkness claimed her, she heard Kenward shout, "Man the bilges and buckets!"

"It's too much, sir!" came the response from belowdecks. "We're sinking!"

* * *

Even complete exhaustion could not overcome the shouting of the crew and the complaints of the rigging. Her vision blurry at first, Catrin awoke barely able to make out the dark shapes that ambled past, seemingly standing at the wrong angle. It was then that she realized the ship was listing heavily to port and the water was creeping ever closer, ready to claim them in its cold embrace. Kenward's orders contained a note of panic she'd never heard from him before. Of all the trouble they'd been through, this was the worst. Kenward's voice and the efforts of the crew who were no less exhausted than she, especially after her abuse of them, motivated Catrin and drove her back to her feet.

Water streaked down her face after a wave broke over the deck. The surf was growing, and the sight of the endless crests and troughs, now white tipped and blowing in the wind, made Catrin's skin crawl. Hanging at her side, Catrin's left arm was numb and unresponsive. Her right arm trembled as she steadied herself against the rail, the angle of the deck making it difficult to stand.

"The bilge handles are submerged, Captain. We've got to get ahead of this or we're sunk!"

"More men to the bilges!" Kenward ordered in a shrill voice. "I'll bail the hold by myself if I have to. This ship *will not sink!*"

Catrin reached his side and used her right arm to take a full bucket from Kenward. Without a word, Kenward dipped back down for another. Pelivor appeared a moment later, holding his head and mumbling something too low for anyone to hear over the furor. As the waves grew, the work became more and more difficult, and Catrin was thrown to the deck when they crested a large wave. It was as if the deck had jumped out from underneath her only to come crashing back up with explosive force. The taste of blood filled her mouth, and when she put her weight on her left arm, it was too much. She collapsed back to the deck with a whimper.

Strong hands grabbed her by the buckles on her leather pants, pulled her upright, and left her standing there. The world moved in unexpected ways, even more than the high seas would account for, and Catrin took deep breaths while she searched for balance and calm. Death was close now. It would take only a little more time and all of them would be lost forever. Sinjin would be left without a mother, and Prios would be a widower. The thoughts made her weep, but still she helped bail, Pelivor now lending her strength. Where he had found his reserve, she did not know, but she loved him for it.

When Kenward met her eyes next, she could see the defeat in his visage. Even giving everything they had left would not be enough. The *Slippery Eel* had taken too much damage, and there was no way she could be mended on rough seas and nearly full of water. Catrin wasn't even sure what was keeping them afloat. To everyone's surprise, they began to make some progress, the water dropping back below the bilge arms. Catrin suspected a regent dragon was helping them, but her suspicion was based on feelings alone. Nonetheless, this sudden improvement gave Kenward pause.

"We're not going to be able to keep this up," Farsy shouted from belowdecks. "Even if we can get the bilge emptied, I'm not sure we can plug a hole that big. Not in the water at least, and we might as well be a lifetime from dry dock."

Kenward scowled. "Do you all want to face my mother in the afterlife when I tell her you gave up?" His words got them moving a little faster. "Would you prefer to face my sister? Or maybe you'd like to answer to Prios?" The words seemed aimed at himself, rather than the crew, but the effect was the same. "There, see? We can do this!"

The water level dropped enough that one could straddle the hole in the ship and still have his head above water.

"Bring me oakum and planks! Use the shelves if you have to! Farsy! You're a lanky sprite. Use your feet to get some oakum around the front of the hole and then get a board across it. Bryn, you can hold your breath a long time. Swim down there and secure the planks. Just make the hole smaller. That's all I'm askin'. Just make it smaller."

By some unknown force, the water continued to drop lower, and Bryn was able to work with his head above the water line. Still, water surged sporadically through the remainder of the hole, the high pressure making it even more difficult to patch. Then even that flow lessened. There came a strange thump on the hull, and the timbers creaked. The deck rolled back to being almost level.

"What's happening?" someone asked.

"I don't care what's happening!" Kenward answered. "Get that hole fixed! We might live yet!"

There was a sound of relief in Kenward's voice, but Catrin knew his hope had the potential to be false. The damage to the *Eel*'s hull was extensive. By her guess, the result of giant claws and the collision with a rough, scaled hide. Looking over the side of the ship, she could see nothing in the failing light.

A towering wave brought them high above the trough, and as they were about to race down the trailing edge, the timbers creaked again, only this time much louder. Shouts came from belowdecks as the ship took to the air. Catrin turned to Pelivor, who looked as shocked as she. Both knew there was no time to waste if they were going to capitalize on their good fortune. With practiced precision, Pelivor built his structures of energy, and the ship remained in the air, just barely clearing the whitecaps.

"You've done it!" Kenward shouted. "You've given us a fighting chance. Keep us in the air for another couple hours, and we might just be seaworthy again."

A couple hours--it might as well have been an eternity. Catrin knew they had no more than a few minutes. The world shifted between full color and a dull gray haze. Faraway voices called to her, and strong hands held her steady. In her dreams they flew across the desert, nightmarish creatures attacking from every side, and nowhere was safe. Dust curled up behind them as they flew, and Catrin could feel that this dream was different. This was a dream, yet it was real, and all of her senses were engaged. The battlefield was a maelstrom of aggression and pent-up rage, and all she could do was fly.

Chapter 16

Some of the most beautiful things in this world will kill you quick as death.
--Farsy, sailor

* * *

Black sands rose from the sea, and the Firstland looked much different to Catrin. The land had healed itself from the devastation of the tsunami, and now Catrin could see the lush forests in their true glory. Chillingly beautiful was this unforgiving land of her ancestors, with the blacks and browns of the shoreline opposite fertile greenery that blanketed the land like moss on a giant stone.

All on board kept their gazes skyward, watching for ferals, and in Catrin's case, for Kyrien. She knew he lived, knew he had helped get them airborne, yet she had not seen him, and until she saw him, the reality of his survival would not be assured to her.

The fact that the Firstland looked like a beatific and idyllic setting and all around them was still and peaceful only served to unnerve the crew further. All of them knew they had come here for a reason and they might never leave. The placid beauty seemed almost inappropriate and garish in the face of their impending doom.

It didn't help that Kenward was not speaking to Catrin. At first she'd thought him simply angry, but he had attempted to speak to her and had failed. Each time he had opened his mouth, nothing came out. Eventually he raised his arms in defeat and walked away, mumbling to himself about flying through Catrin's nightmares and holes in his deck. Catrin knew she couldn't control her dreams, especially when she was beyond exhaustion, but still she felt guilty for having traumatized Kenward and the crew. The thought of flying the ship while sleeping haunted her.

"I'm amazed you could do it at all," Pelivor had said. "How did you do it? No, wait. Don't answer that. I don't want to know."

Perhaps it was best that Catrin could not have explained it if she had tried. Somehow she had transitioned from waking to sleep without letting go of the power. She'd done it once before, in Pinook Harbor, but that was nothing as complex as keeping a ship in the air. And that seemed to be the rub. In her altered state, Catrin's mind had somehow overlaid reality with her dreams, and as she had been dodging monsters and attacks of power and fire, the *Slippery Eel* had been under her command. Kenward had insisted that Catrin and Pelivor sleep for at least two full nights before they attempted to fly the ship again, and even now they moved through the waves under the power of the wind alone.

Catrin knew she would need her strength for the battle ahead. Kyrien had brought her here for a reason. He'd shown her visions of pain and death, and she knew the calm would not remain. Not knowing when the darkness would come made Catrin want to climb out of her own skin, and not knowing Kyrien's true fate gnawed at her.

"You need to eat something," Pelivor insisted.

The acid in Catrin's stomach stole what appetite she had, and she shook her head. Even the smell of Grubb's fish stew did little to attract her. Kenward stood behind Pelivor, and though he still said nothing, she knew he was coming around. With his arms folded over his chest, he raised an eyebrow and tapped his foot.

Sighing, Catrin accepted the mug, thinking she would just sip it to satisfy Kenward. After a few tastes, though, her appetite returned enough to finish the mug.

"You know I love you," Kenward finally said. "But I have to admit that I'll be glad when you're off my ship. You're nothing but the worst kind of trouble, and you seem determined to kill me and sink my ship."

"It took you all this time to come up with that? You're no poet, Kenward, but I can understand you feeling that way. Still, I think you're just jealous because I've managed to endanger your crew more than you have."

Those words drove Kenward back into silence that was finally broken by Grubb's laughter. "I say we keep her on board just to shut him up!"

A look from Kenward silenced him, but his shoulders shook as he walked back to the galley.

Kenward just shook his head. "I suppose you'll want me to take you up the river toward Ri? You know, the place where the Gholgi nearly sank us the last time we were here?"

The memory was burned into Catrin's mind. She could recall every sight, smell, and sensation of that day. It was also the first time she'd been rescued by dragons.

"Yes. I suppose that is what I want. I had hoped for guidance from Kyrien, some sign as to what he needed from me, but no matter how I try, he will not respond. He's alive--I know it--but I think he is waiting for a reason, and until he's ready, we're on our own."

"It seems we face the same dilemma once again," Kenward said. "I don't have enough men to send with you and still be able to defend the ship."

"This time will be different," Catrin said. "This time I will go alone."

"But you could be facing dangers far worse than those in the past."

"True," Catrin said. "I am not as well prepared as I would have liked, but I have done everything within my power to get ready for this, and now I must simply let the bones fall where they may." Instantly Catrin regretted her choice of words. No one else seemed willing to speak in the silence that followed. "Please. Just take me to the place where you dropped me last time. I'll either be fine or I won't, but staying aboard this ship will not accomplish whatever it is I'm here to do. Now I just need to get on with it."

Members of the crew approached her one at a time, each in his or her own way and only when ready. Catrin had known them since she was a teenager; she loved them like family, and to many of them, she was an adopted daughter. To have their love and respect meant the world to Catrin, and their words bolstered her confidence. If these brave and talented men and women believed in her, then surely she could believe in herself, even if she did face an impossible task: win a battle that would take place at a time and place beyond her knowing. Her only choice was to surrender to fate and hope that her knowledge and power would sustain her. It must have shown in her eyes, given the respect she got from the crew. Even those who had nearly died for her cause in the past looked at her with new eyes, as if they only now saw her true potential and sacrifice.

It was good that these things propped up Catrin's confidence as the next moment brought pure chaos.

Like a flock of birds launched from a shaken tree, dragons appeared all at once and, within moments, filled the air around the ship. Battle centered on the *Slippery Eel*. Ferals dived in to attack, and regents flew in defense. It was impossible to believe the ferocity and power of their attacks; even one strike would likely kill the entire crew of the *Slippery Eel*. If not for the regent dragons, their greenish scales glinting in the sunlight, the *Eel* would have been lost.

Kyrien was nowhere to be seen. Catrin would have been able to pick him out of the chaos with her eyes closed, and she longed to find him and communicate with him, but her calls remained unanswered.

Crouching and shying away from another monstrous collision, Catrin thought the sound of dragons fighting might be the most frightening part of all. Not only did their growls make the air tremble and their screams inflict physical pain, the sound of their armored bodies slamming together was something Catrin thought no creature should ever have to hear.

"Full sail!" Kenward shouted. "Get this ship out of the water! We need to get out of here."

No one hesitated or questioned Kenward's words. His command gave them purpose and something to distract them from the horror that was taking place around them.

"Look out!" was all the warning anyone got before a pair of twined dragons struck the ship. Locked in a battle to the death, the two flailed and rolled, taking part of the rigging into the sea with them before disappearing under the waves. Had it not been a glancing blow, they'd already be sunk. Kenward was right; they needed to move.

Raising her arms to the sky, Catrin reached for the comets, and to her absolute shock, they felt a thousand years away, as if they had suddenly been flung back into the darkness. One look at Pelivor showed that he was experiencing a similar horror. Looking up, Catrin saw an unnaturally dark cloud blocking their views of the heavens. Like a stain on the sky, it roiled above them, sometimes lit from within by webs of lightning. The hair on Catrin's neck stood as she realized there was a filament of energy extending from her head and the ship and reaching up to the clouds above. Time was running out.

Denied direct access to the comets, Catrin reached to the air around her. Pelivor did the same and was soon trying to generate enough lift to get them out of the water. Catrin did her best to focus on providing thrust. Farsy watched from nearby with a glint in his eye, and Catrin smiled at him despite their peril. Under her direction, he had modified the tube of wood, changing the shape of the inner surface so it opened more at the entrance and remained more constricted midway along its length. The changes reduced the strength and stability of the wood, and Catrin could now feel it trembling as she forced air through. A low whistle began, and as they moved faster, it grew in volume and pitch. Over a steeper wave, the hull left the water, lurching suddenly to one side as a feral came at them unblocked until the very last moment.

The whistling continued to grow louder, and Catrin applied as much energy as she thought was safe. Again the crew had to trim the sails as their speed increased. Before they were even finished, the rigging began to vibrate, and the wind tore at the crew. Staying low to the water, they skimmed along as fast as they were able. Above, the skies were far too dangerous, and the *Slippery Eel,* even with Catrin and Pelivor in control, was no match for a feral dragon in open air.

"At least the water makes it hurt really bad when they miss," Kenward said. "We need to get through the harbor and into the river valley. Then there won't be room for many of these beasts in the air above us."

"Sails ahead, sir-- What the--? *Sir!*"

It didn't take long for Catrin to see what the lookout had seen or for Kenward to start cursing. Thorakis's sailors seemed to be learning new things at an alarming rate. Hovering above the water came a formation of ships linked together by blood red lightning. The ships appeared equidistant from one another and flew as a single unit. Standing at the prow of the lead ship was a tall man in long robes, his arms cast out to the sides, lightning flowing from his hands and into the deck itself. Dark paint made him look like the demons that wandered his decks. Again these Gholgi-like abominations would haunt Catrin, and she watched in horror as similarly dressed men emerged on the prow of every ship in the array. When they raised their hands, a new web of power sprang into the air, joining over the lead ship, focusing, and splitting the air toward the *Slippery Eel.*

Catrin banked the ship to the right, accelerated, then slowed. White heat seared the air but went wide.

"Higher!" Kenward ordered.

Catrin and Pelivor did as he said. No sooner had they gained open air than a feral locked on to them. A pair of regents gave chase, but this feral was bigger and faster than most of the others. Closing the gap to the *Slippery Eel* and leaving the regents behind, the feral made it clear it wasn't going to give up easily. Dividing her attention, Catrin reached back out to the comets, and as the *Eel* moved out from under the dread cloud, the comets answered, flooding her with energy. The ship whistled as she pushed for more speed, but she wasn't certain the *Eel* could take much more. Instead she focused part of her mind on building up a charge and sending a finger of lightning back at the charging feral. The lightning connected, and in that instant, she felt small and insignificant. The will of the feral washed over her. None of what was going on around her seemed to exist; all that mattered was avoiding the wrath of the lord of the night.

Lost in his rapidly approaching eyes, Catrin watched, entranced.

"Why are we slowing?"

The voices were distant and meaningless. Nothing could be more important than what she was doing, of that she was certain.

"Catrin! Wake up!" Kenward shouted as he shook her.

It took Catrin a moment to realize where she was and what was happening, but then it all rushed back at once and nearly caused her to swoon. In the meantime the feral had drawn closer, and the sight of him sent Catrin scrambling to get them moving fast again. What lead they had was now lost, and the dragon would almost certainly catch them. The regents in pursuit flew in what looked like desperation as they climbed higher and higher. Watching as they disappeared into the clouds, Catrin's hope faded.

At the fastest speed she felt the ship could handle, the feral continued to gain on them. Twice more she attacked, and twice more it seemed only to infuriate the beast. Standing near the stern became a liability as the dragon overtook them. It came all at once, as if it had been holding back and only making them think it had been at maximum speed. The sudden attack caught Catrin off her guard, and she scrambled to cast out energy in hopes of warding off certain death. Behind the feral Catrin noticed two dark shapes diving toward the surface at unbelievable speed. Then those shapes extended their wings and pulled up to skim over the waves, sending spray circling in the roiling wind behind them. They hit the feral hard and fast, knocking him off course and away from the ship. It was a costly victory, though, and Catrin cried out when the feral struck like a snake and sent one of the regents into a lifeless spin until it crashed into the water with a series of sickening pops and snaps. Afraid of going much higher, again in the shadow of the unnatural cloud, Catrin guided them closer to the harbor. Approaching the tall ring of stone that surrounded much of the harbor,

Catrin looked up almost expecting to see a Zjhon warship still nestled among the peaks, but it was gone, lost to the ravages of time and weather, she guessed.

When she lowered her gaze, she let out a gasp, which was immediately followed by shouts from the crew. Another formation of ships was leaving the harbor, just clearing the massive semicircle of stone peaks. The base of the passage was far wider than the top, and Kenward cursed when Catrin took them higher and turned sharply so the ship entered the narrow opening at an angle. In trying to match the angle of the rock face that would likely snap off the mainmast, Catrin pitched the ship onto its side, nearly losing Farsy. The wind whispered over the rocks as they passed, and an instant later, they emerged into the massive harbor. Instead of the giant sea and land creatures she'd been expecting, Catrin saw a waiting navy. A mass of ships clogged the waters, and enough land had been cleared to build fortifications. Smoke billowed from stacks on ships and from buildings.

The air above was no safer than that above the open seas. In fact, the rock faces made it even more dangerous to navigate. Bringing the ship down low, Catrin saw dark shapes in the water and knew that the large sea creatures may not be fully visible, but they were still there.

"If we set down," Kenward said, "they'll attack from underneath, just as they did the last time we were here. If we stay here, the dragons'll get us, and who knows what's waiting in that river valley. I don't recall it being a pleasant trip. And we had to turn back at those boiling statues."

"Do you have a better idea?" Catrin asked.

"No," he admitted.

"Then hold on."

"Get ready!" Kenward shouted to the crew. "This is gonna be a bumpy ride."

The whistle of the ship echoed off the canyon walls, and Catrin brought them higher, even as approaching formations of ships readied themselves to attack. These groups were smaller, some consisting of only three ships, but they moved with nimble grace and seemed capable of greater speed.

"This is insane!" Kenward shouted as they whisked over the first formation of ships, which remained just above the surface of the water. The air around them shimmered, and the smell of smoke polluted the air. "They're setting us on fire! Put us down! Put us down!"

Not wanting to lose speed, Catrin tried to only bounce the ship along the surface of the narrowing and shallow waters at the mouth of the approaching river. She'd envisioned the ship skipping like a stone, but the drag was far greater than she had anticipated. Everyone and everything aboard was thrown toward the prow. A jet of oily fire spewing black smoke struck the waves before them and set the water itself afire.

"Up! Up!" Kenward shouted.

Catrin would have obeyed his orders if she could, but it was simply too much to ask, and the ship struck the flames, which left the *Eel* covered in burning pitch. The crew watched helplessly as smoke streamed up through the railing. Realizing that even the water would not extinguish this fire, Catrin concentrated on getting the ship back into the air. Though it seemed like the worst possible thing to do, Catrin had a plan. Pelivor cried out as he exerted himself, the cut of his muscles standing out as the wind plastered his silks against him.

Just before they reached the next cluster of approaching ships, they left the water and banked to port, this time greeted by a series of thumps that slammed into the hull. No one knew how much damage they had taken, but crewmen were shouting from below, and some had to evacuate the deckhouse due to smoke.

"She's gonna burn up!" Kenward shouted.

Left with no other options, Catrin pushed the ship for more speed, even as the valley walls closed in on them. This time the carved figures that adorned the hillsides were even more intimidating simply because they might slam into one of them at any moment. Catrin soon found herself soaring through a narrow and twisting canyon, mere inches above the waterline and with far too much speed, yet the fires still burned.

No ships pursued them up the river, but a shadow passed over them and raced along the valley just ahead of them, as if the dragon were just biding its time, waiting for the best moment to strike its prey--prey that had nowhere to go and no place to hide. Feeling naked and exposed, Catrin tried to resist the fear that ferals seemed designed to create, but it was difficult to do. Crewmen wept on deck, and Kenward looked more frightened than Catrin had ever seen, but that may have had more to do with the way she was flying his ship. When he looked at her, he wore a looked of unabashed horror, as if she might truly be a monster.

It was no use. Catrin knew that almost every path would lead to their deaths, and even if her actions left them stranded on the Firstland, then it would be better than all of them perishing in the sea or the air above it. Staying low had its own dangers, proven by a protruding rock face that had remained hidden until the last moment, protected by a natural illusion. It smacked into the hull and sent them flying sideways. The dragon picked that moment to attack, and Catrin tried to split her attention between guiding the ship, providing thrust, and sending a defensive strike against the approaching dragon. She never got the chance to release that strike as Kyrien soared in between them and sent the much larger dragon careening away from the ship.

"No!" Catrin cried out, knowing that Kyrien was no match for a dragon more than twice his size.

Fly.

It was the only response she got from him before he collided again with the feral. Catrin could not watch, not only because it was too painful to see, but because the valley continued to narrow and every instant was critically dangerous to the ship.

"The fires are out, but there are holes in the hull, sir! Big ones! We're not seaworthy."

Kenward looked stricken but Catrin was not surprised. Still, it didn't matter to her; all it did was reinforce her decision. Ahead lay the Eternal Guardians, watching over the Valley of the Victors. The name seemed ironic to Catrin since all the images were of men, yet they had not ruled here for thousands of years.

"Catrin!"

"Hold on, Kenward!"

"Catrin!"

The panic in his voice made Catrin regret what she was about to do, but he said he had no better ideas, and she did what she could to save all of them, even if it pained her to do so. Though she'd seen them before, the Eternal Guardians formed a daunting barrier. Both figures crouched over waters that swirled around the stone they had sprung from. The one closest to them was worn to the extent that its visage was lost to time, which made it look all the more imposing. The other had only half its face remaining, but even that cast them a baleful glare. The feral grew larger in the skies before them and would pass above the Guardians about the same time they would reach the massive monument. No going over the monuments, then. "Hold on and stay clear of the masts!"

Splinters of wood filled the air along with a series of gut-wrenching snaps. The mainmast tore up the foredecks and slammed into the deckhouse before launching into the air behind them.

"Catrin!"

The word was now a high-pitched scream, like the sound of a man losing a limb. It was not a sound Catrin ever wanted to hear again, but fate had other ideas. Just beyond the Eternal Guardians, she urged the ship higher, scanning the landscape, looking for something she knew would be there but not really believing she would find it. With the feral gaining on them and Kyrien nowhere to be seen, Catrin urged the ship for more speed, the tube of wood singing a howling tune, vibrating and flexing as the pressurized air rushed through. The speed would not be enough, and Catrin forced more air in, but it was too much. With a suddenness that sent Catrin sprawling, the cylinder cracked, split, and exploded. Splinters dug into Catrin's flesh, a large chunk flying by and barely missing her face.

She turned back with tears of frustration and loss in her eyes. But then she saw a field of deep, rich grass strewn with megalithic granite boulders, as if they'd been tossed like dice by the gods. A smile came to Catrin's face, and she hoped that once again she would find solace in this idyllic location, despite the pure chaos that surrounded them.

The tops of trees slammed against the hull as they made their approach, and only the sound of Kenward's screams rose above the cacophony.

"Brace!" Catrin shouted and an instant later, she was vaulted forward, the ropes that held her digging into her flesh. The pain and sensation of being crushed was overwhelming, and she could not believe how hard they hit when they landed. The initial blow had jarred Catrin and Pelivor enough to make them both lose control over the power they wielded.

In the moments that followed, dragons unfolded themselves and Kenward wept.

Chapter 17

The most courageous acts are often committed by those who believe themselves already dead.
--Merchill Valon, soldier

* * *

The *Slippery Eel* lay on her side, groaning as if in her death throes, filling the silence left by what her captain was not saying. He looked at Catrin with horror in his eyes, and she wondered if this would be the end of the friendship they had developed. The loss of the *Slippery Eel* was bad enough, but the thought of losing Kenward as a friend brought tears to Catrin's eyes. It was only a single moment in time, but it was burned into Catrin's consciousness. Immediately after, time rushed forward and there were wounded to tend.

Though there were many cuts, scrapes, and bruises, the worst wounds had been Catrin's to bear. She winced as Pelivor removed the splinters of wood from her right side. Large and small, they dug into her flesh and made every movement painful. No one left the ship, as if they feared they would drown in the lush grasses. More likely it was the dragons surrounding the ship they feared. They looked like Kyrien, only larger, older, and far less friendly. They waited, though not patiently. Their eyes urged her forward, and their hearts tugged at her. She could feel them calling to her, calling to all of them.

Eventually Pelivor had removed most of the larger splinters from Catrin's side, and both of them stepped onto the grasses and toward the largest of the dragons. He brought his head down low and swayed back and forth in a rhythmic movement. The beautiful dance captivated them. Soon the entire crew of the *Slippery Eel* joined them.

"I'm sorry we crashed into your lovely valley," Catrin said.

If a dragon could smile, this one did, and there was a glint in its eye. *You are ignorant, child, but that is among your strengths. This valley has been waiting for you. It was made . . . for you.*

Those gathered heard the words in their minds, felt the mirth and the warmth in the dragon's communication. It instantly put them all at ease, despite the fact that they had been, up until that moment, fighting for their lives. Here, in this valley, under the protection of these dragons, they were safe.

I must ask you once again to save him. You must save Kyrien.

The compelling energy, though leaving room for free will, nearly sent them all scrambling toward the sound of distant wailing. Catrin's breath caught in her throat when she heard it.

It has begun. It cannot be stopped. You must save him.

Kyrien's call was the same as when she had first heard it, all those years ago. Trapped in a cell of stone, fed and made to grow too large to get out of the entrance, he would have been left to die a horrible death had Catrin not defeated Archmaster Belegra and set Kyrien free. The memories brought physical pain, and that's when Catrin realized the large dragon was now looking her in the eye, its head hovering only a hand's width before her face. She felt the sensation of something pulling on her skin followed by wet clicks, and Catrin looked down to see splinters on her boot and the grasses around it. The pain in her body dissipated. Moving its head back and forth, the dragon captured Catrin in its gaze once again.

Be strong. You must not fail. The future of us all rests in your hands. Do not let fear stop you. Not your fear or that of another. Know that dragons and humans are not so different. We, too, are gifted and flawed. Not all of us agree about what the future holds, and Kyrien is suffering for that. Go. Save him.

Nodding, Catrin could formulate no thought beyond the need to save Kyrien, his wails once again punctuating the silence.

Go. Now.

Catrin turned and walked to the northern end of the valley with a determined stride, her purpose clear; all that was left was to find him. If his wailing continued, that would not be difficult. Only when she left the soft grasses and climbed onto the uneven granite did she realize she was alone. The rest of the crew of the *Slippery Eel* stood entranced, and Catrin wondered if they would ever forgive her. It was better this way, better that she go alone. At least that way she would not be responsible for their deaths. She couldn't save them, but perhaps the dragons could.

Climbing with a mixture of sadness and grim satisfaction, Catrin moved toward Kyrien. The ascent was not difficult, and for much of the way, she followed a natural ridgeline that cut through two peaks. It wasn't long until Catrin saw things she recognized, and soon the hollow mountain emerged from the fog, its zigzagging stairs clinging to it like mighty serpents, crawling out of the archways that decorated the massive rock face. It had been in one of those halls that Catrin had faced Archmaster Belegra and only barely won. Now that mountain seemed entirely abandoned, only spirits roaming the dark halls.

Kyrien's wails echoed from the valley walls, and Catrin could not pinpoint the direction from which they came. Just past the hollow mountain, she turned north, hoping she was right. She listened, straining, and in the distance, she thought she heard someone calling her name. It was faint but persistent, and as she listened closely for Kyrien, she couldn't help but hear them calling for her. The voice was Kenward's, she was almost certain. And he sounded no more calm than the last time she'd heard him. She'd hoped the dragons would keep them in the valley and guard them while she went off to help Kyrien, but it seemed fate had other plans.

Torn and wanting to go back for them, Catrin forced herself to continue, though she cried at having to choose. If she was abandoning them, it was only for their own good. She doubted any of them would see it that way, but she persevered nonetheless.

Cold wind drifted to her, and beyond the valley lay the sea. Rising out of the surf, a megalithic beast climbed into the skies. Dark shapes filled the air around it, and its surface seethed like a kicked anthill. Demons scaled the rock face in unbelievable numbers, making it look as if the mountain were breathing. Ships crowded the shoreline, and formations patrolled the waters beyond. This was a well-organized, massive, lethal attack.

Diving and attacking anything that reached the higher parts of the mountain, Kyrien fought as if he wished to die. Her heart breaking, Catrin cried out to him, but all she got back was a wash of panicked energy filled with despair.

This is not how it is supposed to be. This must not be. I cannot take you to her, or her visions will come true. I must stop this!

Catrin wanted to stop it for him, and she vowed to try, but she knew her power would be insignificant before such massive forces. The demons and giants outnumbered her by tens of thousands to one. How could she possibly hope to make any difference? She was worthless and small. Nothing she could do would stave off the inevitable. It would be far better to die in as quick a fashion as possible; that at least would end the pain, end the suffering.

The thoughts themselves were the only warning she had, but Catrin knew the thoughts were not hers, and she turned to find a small feral dragon stalking her. Low to the ground, it remained still for an instant, as if hoping Catrin wouldn't see it, but as soon as Catrin raised her hands, it lunged. Lightning crackled between them just before they collided, and both were sent sprawling. Catrin wasn't exactly certain she had attacked, and she wondered if the dragon had struck her with lightning. It seemed unlikely, since the dragon could just as easily have snapped her up in its jaws. Deep down, Catrin was relieved; feral dragons with the ability to wield Istra's power would be truly terrifying things.

Even without power, the beast hunting Catrin seemed made of fear. A single look from it caused Catrin to tremble, and its every movement forced Catrin to envision her own death. None could stand before such a dark and menacing visage and not quail. Catrin did the only thing she could think of, foolish or not: she ran.

The dragon moved in slow pursuit, seemingly unworried by Catrin's sudden flight. What looked like a tree branch swung out into the air before her, but it was no branch, and it moved to intercept her neck.

The pole arm cut the air with a sound that promised death. Only narrowly avoiding the strike, Catrin ducked low and let her momentum carry her forward, which proved to be a mistake. She'd have had a better chance facing the dragon. At least a dozen demons were clawing their way toward her, and behind them came the giants. Each one was a walking exaggeration; everything frightening about the demons only made larger. And now Catrin was tumbling into their midst. Without much thought, she compressed the air around her and released it all at once. The blast sent demons tumbling, and even the giants took a step back. The smell of ozone assaulted Catrin's nostrils, and a quickly evaporating mist hung in the air around her. The air was cool and moist, and for some reason, that meant something to Catrin, though she didn't know exactly what.

Lumbering past their fallen and disorganized comrades, the giants continued forward, single file, unable to move two abreast in the narrow valley. Taking two steps back, Catrin turned and froze. The feral dragon rose up to its full height. Even if it was a small feral dragon, it still managed to be terrifying, and Catrin considered trying her luck against the giants. When they saw the dragon, the hulking brutes stopped, seemingly ready to assault her if she tried to pass but nothing more.

Cocking its head to the side, the dragon approached, low to the ground, its head now level and weaving in a hypnotic motion. It took one more step forward then stopped, looking up. A moment later, it was backing up the ravine as quickly as it could before turning and launching back into the sky. Catrin did not want to raise her head to see, but instinct made her look, and she nearly fell down in fear. Staring back was the face of the largest feral she'd seen, one she recognized from when it chased the *Slippery Eel*. This massive beast radiated terror, and Catrin raised trembling hands. The dragon struck, quick as lightning, and again Kyrien intervened. Dropping from the sky and flying between Catrin and the feral, Kyrien intercepted the strike with his side, and the regent dragon cried out in pain when the feral bit down.

Unleashing all the energy she could muster, Catrin sent fire and lightning at the feral's eyes. It arched back and released Kyrien from its deadly grasp, and Kyrien rolled away. Sensing movement behind her, Catrin lashed out at the giants, again going for the eyes. One managed to block the attack with a massive wrist guard, but another was struck full in the face and went down, leaving the third stuck behind its corpse.

Raising her arms for another attack, Catrin felt the air leave her lungs as Kyrien snatched her from the ground in his powerful claws.

This should not be! What have I done!

Catrin could almost feel the tears in his words, and she wept for her friend and for the fact that she was somehow the cause of his anguish.

* * *

Moving through the darkened halls within Dragonhold, Halmsa of the Wind clan was determined to learn as much as he could from Catrin, even if he could not learn it in person. Nothing in the prophecies ever said that she had to be there to teach them how to fly dragons. It seemed strange that something that had seemed so far away when he was a child was now here before him. There had always been a silent disbelief in the back of his mind that the things foretold would come to be, and now he was humbled. He had ridden a dragon, and now he was ready to try flying one. *These ferals are feisty,* he thought. It seemed like a challenge worthy of the Arghast.

Feeling like a thief within the hold, Halmsa searched for a room that he knew existed, yet he had few clues to its whereabouts. He knew that holes in its walls faced open air and that it must be along the outer walls of the keep, but still it eluded him.

A deep growl sounded nearby, and even its echo challenged Halmsa's courage. He reminded himself that brave men felt fear, but they did not let it make their decisions. Keeping to the shadows, he waited until the demon passed, this one sniffing the air as it went. Halmsa moved back toward the God's Eye, a thing he would not believe existed had he not seen it himself. Moving deeper into the mountain was contrary to his mission, but there were also more places to hide. He'd found nothing leading from the great hall, and this seemed a logical next step. The fact that it moved him away from those growls reinforced the decision.

His eyes had nearly adjusted to the darkness when a dim light appeared at the end of a descending hall. Quickly he moved closer, and when he reached a junction, he found another descending hallway bathed in a ruddy glow. Halmsa nearly shouted for joy, but he wisely kept his mouth shut. Moving toward the light, he found a room with two head-sized holes in the wall and beyond, open sky. Halmsa smiled despite his fear. He could not fail at this. This was the foretold time; he was certain of it. One of them had to step forward; one of them had to prove himself worthy of the title dragonrider, and Halmsa was determined to be that person.

In spite of the inherent danger of leaving his body completely unprotected in a part of the hold occupied by demons, in one of the few rooms that gets any natural light, he prayed for release from his prison of flesh. It seemed an unwise thing to hope for, but Halmsa wished with all of his heart as he stared out into the open sky. Reviewing the tales in his head, trying to remember exactly how Catrin had described astral travel, he tried not to despair. He had no access to the Cathuran chant or drums, and he chose to take another wild risk and hum a tune. Catrin had said it was the vibration that helped her and not the melody. Perhaps, he thought, the melody was there only to entertain those who must chant for hours at a time.

Humming, Halmsa stared out at the sky and strained his eyes, trying to look himself into the open air. A trickle of fear ran down his spine when he wondered if he would ever be able to return to his body should he break free of this mortal shroud.

Still humming, he closed his eyes and envisioned himself soaring through the skies, a dragon beneath him. When he opened his eyes, nothing happened. Frustrated, he sighed and sat back. That was when he remembered that Catrin had done the same; only she had smacked her head on the stone chair. Halmsa wondered if it had to be by accident and come as a surprise and exactly how hard he would have to hit his head. He was not afraid of the pain or a coward, but no man would slam his head against stone any harder than he might have to.

With his eyes open, he moved his head backward until it struck the stone lightly. Nothing happened. Doubtful but determined, he threw his head back and it hit with a solid *thunk*. He had been concerned he would have given away his position, cursing from the pain, but he barely felt it as he soared through the skies. Halmsa of the Wind clan could fly.

* * *

Faint sounds melded with the rush of the waterfall and the calls of birds carried on the light breeze. This place seemed impossible, yet it remained very real. The aroma of grasses mixed with mosses near the falls. The smell of moist soil and supple grasses painted the air. Sinjin even found ripe strawberries scattered throughout the grasses where the light was the brightest. The afternoon was drawing on, and the light changed to a deeper hue, making the place seem even more surreal.

With the shadows growing long and the light playing tricks with their eyes, Brother Vaughn suddenly pulled Sinjin and Trinda back behind a squat tree. Holding a finger to his lips, he slid on his belly until he could see the rolling hills beyond. "By the gods! Come out quick!"

Hesitating for only a moment, Sinjin followed Brother Vaughn and helped Trinda back to her feet. Looking annoyed, she brushed herself off, and Sinjin didn't bother to tell her that there was nothing to be brushed off. All thoughts of sarcasm left him when he spotted movement back near where they had entered the cavern. In an instant he recognized his father and Strom and Durin! He wasn't quite as pleased to see Kendra, but it mattered little. A huge grin crossed Sinjin's face, but it instantly vanished.

Hissing balls of flame leaped from the shadows and exploded, casting flaming pitch over anything nearby. Waves of what looked like gelatinous air rushed forth from another portal, and Prios's company was quickly pushed into a full retreat.

"I'm here, Dad!" Sinjin cried out, and Brother Vaughn looked as if he would scold Sinjin, but they both saw Prios look up.

Issuing a wordless roar, Prios ran toward them.

Sinjin could not stop himself. He had to get to his father, had to have his forgiveness. All of this was his fault, and he could no longer stand the guilt. Tears stung his eyes as he did what he did best.

He ran.

Stunted trees flew by in a blur. Tiny chipmunks scurried to get out of his path. And for an instant, his eyes met those of a hunting cat, which crouched in the lush grass. Every moment in time became images burned into his memory. It was as if he were in a dream. Surely none of this could be real, he thought as the demons poured onto the field like a dark stain spreading across the precious landscape. Birds filled the air, driven from the trees by the malevolent forces charging into their midst with a cloud of angry energy raging around them. Sinjin could feel the contempt if not the energy itself.

Moving out of the darkness and into the fading light came demons holding weapons of wood and iron, smoking and glowing. It took two demons to carry the barrel-like portion and another two to carry a smoking pot attached via a length of articulated wood and steel hose. Truly this enemy was evolving quickly, and Sinjin had no idea how to defend against such things. Seeing the barrel belch fire and blackness made his courage flee. Already flames threatened to claim the trees and the grasses smoldered. This alone raised Sinjin's anger, and his fury was perhaps the only thing that could conquer his fear and guilt. That these abominations would destroy a thing of such beauty was what allowed him to know that he was right, that his rage could be righteous and holy.

Watching his father cast out his energy to shield those in the line of fire gave Sinjin great pride, and he wanted nothing more than to be by his father's side, but there was still distance between them, and as the light mingled with darkness, more demons came--these like a knife between father and son. Sinjin could almost hear Brother Vaughn shouting for him to come back, and he could barely hear Trinda crying out his name, but he could not simply turn around when at a full run. It took time for him to slow himself from his fastest sprint to a speed where he could execute his turn, and by the time he did, the flames had grown far too close. He could see the eyes of the demons that wanted him dead, yet when they had him in their firing line, the flames did not come. Sinjin had expected to be engulfed in a conflagration, and instead something large and black flew at his head. Ducking, he felt only the slightest bump as something heavy but soft whizzed past.

A flash of light and fire ripped through the line of demons, and Sinjin saw his father for a moment. The look on his face terrified Sinjin, and he never wanted to see such a look again. Such pain, anguish, and desperation should be inflicted on no one. There was no more time for thought as a melon-sized fist landed on Sinjin's jaw, tossing him backward. Trinda's voice took on a shrill note. The demon grabbed him by his ankle and started pulling him back to their lines.

"No," Sinjin heard a high-pitched but firm voice say. Part of him knew it was Trinda, but she sounded different. She didn't sound afraid; she sounded angry. Sinjin's head continued to bounce along on the soft grass. "I said *no!*"

Trinda's command froze the battle as quickly as if the entire cavern had suddenly been filled with ice. Sinjin willed his body to move, but it seemed to care more about what Trinda wanted than what he wanted. When Trinda turned her gaze to him, he found he could move again and crawled free of the demon's grip. When he saw the demon, frozen in place, he landed a kick square on its rear and sent it toppling forward. Looking back to Trinda, he froze again. In her hands was Brother Vaughn's herald globe; it shone like the brightest comet, and Trinda's eyes were wide, her face locked in a look of shock. When she made a popping sound with her lips, Sinjin knew what was coming, and he stepped forward to catch her.

"I don't have any more," she said, and she handed Sinjin the blazing herald globe before collapsing into his arms. A moment later the demons stirred, and Sinjin took the chance to look for his father, but he couldn't find him. Then he saw Strom crouching over a body, and his heart leaped. In the next instant, he was running with Trinda over his shoulder.

Chapter 18

In the most critical of times, decisions made in an instant can affect the rest of history. To experience such power is my greatest hope and deepest fear. If it comes to pass, I pray I choose wisely.

--Archmaster Belegra

* * *

Even clutched in Kyrien's claw, Catrin could see the demons below on their inexorable climb toward the top of the hollow mountain. The holes in the side of this mountain were larger, and it was apparent that these were not man-made halls. There were no decorated arches, straight lines, or right angles. The way this mountain had been hollowed out spoke of claws and jaws doing the work, and Catrin shivered at the thought of jaws powerful enough to crush stone and claws sharp enough to part granite. Kyrien's firm but gentle grip on Catrin was a marvel. Surely he could crush her without even exerting himself. She knew she was safe in his grasp, but the fact made her feel small and powerless.

I cannot make the decision. I simply cannot. You saved my life!

Catrin was unsure what he meant, but he either did not hear her or chose not to respond to her questions. It seemed he was so overwhelmed by his inner conflict that Catrin had almost ceased to exist. This would have been all right if his anxiety were not causing him to tighten his grip on Catrin a little bit more with each passing moment. As Catrin's mental shouts became screams, he realized what was happening and relaxed his grip. In his effort to let her breathe, the startled dragon overcompensated and loosened his grip too much.

In a gust of wind and the blink of an eye, Catrin went from catching her breath in Kyrien's claws to free-falling. She'd have screamed if there had been enough air in her lungs, but it was all she could do to breathe. Kyrien caught her before she took her next breath, and the impact took what air she had. It was thus that she found herself suddenly thrust into the uppermost hall, barely able to breathe and completely unprepared to face an enormous and unfriendly dragon.

I'm sorry. I could not choose. Now you must. I'm so sorry.

Kyrien wept in her mind, and Catrin reeled at the possibilities, trying to understand what he meant.

Coward! came a new voice in Catrin's mind, and it pounded until she thought her head would crack open. *Traitor! Failure!*

The words came from what Catrin now knew was the queen of the regents--the *only* queen of the regents. How she knew this, Catrin was unsure, but she knew it like she knew the sun would shine. Still she had no idea what choice she had to make. She knew it was important, but she didn't know why, and she had no idea what to do about it. Standing in front of the largest regent dragon she'd ever seen, Catrin desperately tried to catch her breath. The dragon looked down on her with a clear lack of patience, but Catrin had no choice but to take time to compose herself.

Cowed by the queen's words to Kyrien, Catrin quavered and wondered what he had done to deserve such an indictment. He'd fought so hard to save Catrin. How could the queen talk to him in that way? The more she thought about it, the angrier Catrin became. Soon she snarled at the regent queen, power flowing through her.

Moving like a giant snake, the queen made an aggressive move that brought her closer to Catrin. The huge regent looked down her snout at Catrin, poised and ready to snatch her up in her jaws.

I should just kill you myself. I should do what Kyrien failed to do.

Given the greeting she'd received, Catrin was not surprised by the communication. "Then perhaps I should kill you now and finish off what the demons are taking so long to do."

Catrin could almost feel the dragon laughing, but there was no humor in that laughter, only derision and something Catrin sensed beneath it, something she was shocked to find: fear. This magnificent and powerful dragon, queen of her kind, was just as afraid of Catrin as the human was of the dragon. It was difficult to believe, but she reminded herself that she was perhaps the most powerful person in all of Godsland, and perhaps this queen of dragons had good reason for fear.

You should not be here. This should not be happening.

"I don't want to hurt you or the other regent dragons. I don't understand why you hate me and why I shouldn't be here. If you want my help, then you are going to have to tell me what is going on!"

You cannot help me unless you cease to exist.

Catrin gaped. "Surely you can't mean that."

The bones have been cast. The choice is not mine; never has it been. The choice, instead, lies upon you, and may you have more wisdom than any other of your kind. May you find the dragon's wisdom in this pivotal time. The rest of this age rests upon you.

Never had another creature held Catrin's attention so completely, and yet the effect faded and Catrin sensed things around her, powerful things-- *very* powerful things.

I have seen the future where the humans survive, and I've seen the future where the dragons survive. It is one or the other, you see. There can be no coexistence. Kyrien knew this and still he brought you here. He left the choice to you. In doing so he betrayed and most likely doomed his kind, unless, of course, I can convince you to take a nice jump from this ledge?

Catrin did not move. The words made no sense.

Kyrien is every bit the traitor and fool I say he is. He could have let you die, could have killed you himself, yet he'd rather doom his entire species, and for what? Love?

"Then kill me."

I cannot.

"Why not?"

The dragon managed to look exasperated, as if speaking to a dense child, *I cannot kill you because I have seen that future as well, and the only thing worse than a future without dragons is a future without dragons and humans. Now there is no other way. You must choose. I have seen the future if you live, and mankind will not stop until the entire planet is consumed. Is that what you want? The future without you is far less creative, but the world will continue to flourish, and balance will be maintained. Don't you see why it must be you that dies and not the regent dragons? Do you not love Kyrien? Do you not wish to save his life and let his kind flourish? Are you so selfish that you could let him die, just so that you may live? Is there no charity in your heart? Did your mother not teach you what it is to be selfless?*

The questions pounded against Catrin's resolve, and she took a step back. The last question, however, raised her hackles and put her on the attack. "Don't you dare bring my mother into this or I'll turn you inside out, right here, right now. You got that? You might think you can threaten and intimidate me, but I'm not afraid of you. At least I'm not so afraid of you that I won't fight you if I have to. And who says both of us can't survive? Maybe if we worked together, we could defeat the demons and the ferals. Then what would that future look like?"

That is the same path that leads to the death of us all. The chances are too great. There is no room for uncertainty when the fate of the world is at stake.

"No," Catrin said. "When you are unwilling to face the risk, you take away the chance for hope. Let's fly away from here now--"

Before she could finish, the dragon queen shifted and her pupils narrowed.

You either have no eyes or you wish to mock me. Which is it?

Involuntarily taking a step backward, Catrin took a good look at the rest of the dragon queen. Long and thick, her body was bloated and her wings small. A cold feeling washed over Catrin. The queen couldn't fly. When the demons arrived, she would be mostly defenseless, forced to hold her ground against the massive horde. There was no way she would survive such an attack.

Looking over the interior of the cavern, Catrin saw it was lit by only small holes that dotted the walls and outer edges of the ceiling. Most of the lair was smooth floor and nothing else, but here and there were neatly organized piles of massive stones. Some were little more than vertical columns, but others seemed to form something like a sleeping platform. Besides barricading themselves in, there was not a great deal to work with. It was only a matter of time before the demons reached this level.

Fool! You waste time when it is the most precious thing we have. You must choose.

Now!

The thought of condemning the dragons to extinction made Catrin physically ill, and she couldn't keep from thinking there was some way they could all survive. Still she remained silent, and still more time passed.

Kyrien was a wretched fool to bring you here.

* * *

Farsy and Bryn by his side, Kenward watched with grim determination as their deaths became increasingly likely. An insurmountable army of demons and dragons was slowly swallowing a mountain, the same mountain where he believed Catrin to be. There had been a battle; that he knew. He'd seen Catrin fight from afar before, and he recognized the light and the sound of it. The sensations were burned into his memory from one of the most dangerous times in his life. A sick feeling clung to him, and when he looked to Bryn and Farsy, he almost wished he hadn't brought them with him, so dour were their faces.

Only the presence of the regent dragons gave them any measure of safety, and Kenward wondered about that. Already the numbers had thinned as two dragons would leave, and only one would return. Of the last pair that had gone on patrol, based on Kenward's assumptions, neither had returned, and he knew they needed to face a future without the dragons' protection. But Catrin had put them in an impossible situation. She had been his friend for a very long time; she'd saved his life multiple times and put it in great danger just as many. He knew she did not leave him in this way out of malice, and he knew the world was at war and nowhere was safe, but none of that prevented him from being angry with Catrin. Seeing one's death rapidly approaching, it can be difficult to think it is all one's own fault. Far better to place blame on someone else, he thought, than to go to your grave feeling guilty.

"What are we gonna do?" Bryn asked. "How do we even survive this? They're gonna come up here in larger numbers sooner or later, and then what do we do?"

Farsy turned back to where he saw Pelivor pacing. "Maybe the boy can get us out of here on the *Eel*."

"No wind in that valley," Kenward said.

"I know but--" Farsy continued. Kenward cut him off with a look. Still, Farsy had sailed with Kenward most of his life, and he knew when not to keep his mouth shut. "We got dragons, sir. Surely one o' them could get us in the air."

"The dragons don't seem to care what I say," Kenward said. "They only seem to listen to Catrin, and I'm not sure they actually listen to her. Seems to me they're the ones doing the talking. The more I think about this whole situation, the less I like it. We can't get to Catrin, and it doesn't look like she's going to get back to us. For now, we need to proceed as if we're on our own."

Bryn nodded sadly and a tear streaked his face. "Blessings to my friend, Catrin," he said softly, not meant for anyone else's ears, but by some trick of the wind, Kenward heard him nonetheless. "Keep her safe."

Kenward bowed his head and echoed the prayer. Farsy sniffed and wiped his eye. Then they headed back toward the peaceful vale, to a place that seemed trapped in time, unaffected by the war that raged so very nearby. Six dragons watched over them.

* * *

Go!

Catrin felt the queen's compulsion acutely, and it shocked her how close to the ferals the regent queen would stoop.

Fight them. Protect me with your life. Die with honor. You will be martyred, and your name will live on forever.

"Even if human beings cease to exist? No. I don't care for your bargain. I will, however, stay here with you and protect you until my dying breath. No species will cease to exist because of a decision I make."

Fool! the queen boomed. *Even the choice to not make a decision is a decision, and that choice will have consequences beyond your worst fear.*

Screams echoed into the chamber as dragons and demons clashed around the openings that led to this vacuous hall. When the dragon queen faced Catrin again, there was real fear in her eyes and what looked like the recognition of one of her visions, as if she now saw the future and what she saw terrified her.

You've condemned us all! You think to protect us, but no one as daft as you could possibly save us now. If there were any other way, I'd not give this to you, but now I must leave the fate of the world in your hands, and though I despise you, I love this world more than life itself. Go, fool. Prove me wrong if you can. The bones have been tossed, and my fate is sealed, but I will do my best to buy you time.

A sound like leather on stone accompanied by rhythmic clicks announced demons in the hall, and Catrin knew time had indeed run out; now she could only act on instinct. The regent queen swung her massive body around to face the threat, and her tail smashed into a stack of stones against the outer wall of the cavern, which sent the rock flying into the demons. Bones snapped as the stone crushed rows of dark beasts. More rock collected near the entrance, constricting the demons to a narrow channel.

Catrin watched as the queen erected defenses on top of the bodies of demons, using the fallen monsters as building materials. She would have aided the queen, but the mighty serpent swung her head around to meet Catrin's eyes. *Go!*

This time Catrin allowed the compulsion since it only told her to turn and look. Her eyes found a huge, irregularly shaped hall that wound away from the main cavern. Glittering light danced on the floor and walls of the hall beyond, beckoning to Catrin with its beauty.

You will find what you need in there, Destroyer. Know that you have received gifts due to only the most noble, Dragon Slayer. Know that your actions will be remembered by all or by none based on your choices, World Render. May your fool of a dragon, the betrayer of his own kind, find solace in the emptiness that awaits him. You two are perfect together. Now, go!

Coerced as much by the darkness in her heart as the dragon queen's compulsion, Catrin retreated into the glittering hall. As she turned the corner, she saw things she would never have dreamed existed. There was a saddle, like the one she'd made, only hers was the crudest representation of this masterpiece. Every inch glittered in what Catrin knew was dragon ore; she could feel the energy radiating from it. Looking up, Catrin saw that enormous crystals made up the ceiling, and beyond lay open sky. Light poured in from the multifaceted crystals as they somehow gathered, focused, and amplified the light. The feeling of it was overwhelming for Catrin; never before had she felt so alive, so powerful. The sounds from the great hall kept her from falling into a trance, and she quickly turned to see what other wonders awaited. She could feel complex energies around her, energies more organized and structured than anything she'd experienced before.

From her left, she felt a pull that was elegant and poised, yet there was a potency to its touch that promised wondrous power. Catrin's eyes fell on something that looked like a herald globe, only a thousand times more evolved. It was beautiful. Reaching out her hand, Catrin moved toward the clear glass that housed what looked like a spider, its red and black body perfectly preserved in what had almost certainly once been molten glass. Catrin could not imagine how such a thing was created, and she hesitated before touching it, nervous caution temporarily stifling her desperate need to feel it. Another crash from the great hall and a bellow from the regent queen got Catrin moving again. Her hand closed around the globe, and pulses of power coursed over her body, enshrouding her in a latticework of power that undulated and moved like liquid.

Knowing the saddle would be of no use with the flightless queen, Catrin drew her sword and held the spider globe high as she charged back into the main hall, determined to save the queen of the regents.

* * *

Only one dragon remained to guard the vale, and Kenward knew that they would soon be completely unprotected. The regent dragons were losing; that much was clear. There was nothing he or anyone else could do about it. His ship was grounded high in the mountains, and even if they could get her into the air or water, she was neither sea- nor airworthy. It would take weeks to repair her. Kenward shook his head, cursing his own foolishness. Why worry about fixing a ship that would never sail again? He should be thinking of how to dismantle the ship and reassemble a smaller ship along the water. The thought nearly brought him to tears. Never before had he been faced with the prospect of dismantling his ship, and it was like thinking of taking his mother apart piece by piece and trying to reassemble her somewhere else. He knew he couldn't do it. If he were to build another ship, it would have to be built from what existed here on the Firstland.

In truth, there were plenty of raw materials on the Firstland; what Kenward lacked were the skilled hands of shipbuilders and the leisure to employ them. As it was, he had only the hands of sailors. There was not a safe place to be found except where they stood, and with only a single dragon remaining, he wondered how long this place would remain safe. Thunderclaps split the air, and the screams of demons followed. Everyone in the vale scrambled to high ground, peering into the war-torn valley beyond and trying to catch a glimpse of what was going on. Most already realized that what they heard was Catrin, and if she was still fighting, then there was still hope.

Lightning and fire coursed in and out of the top of the nearby mountain, as if the mountain itself were breathing fire. Dark bodies were tossed into the air and fell back down into the clogged valley below, their bodies acting as weapons as they tore through the rest of the demons trying to reach the top of the mountain. A gasp from behind made Kenward turn, and he saw what had frightened Farsy. Pelivor stood with his arms raised, and power pulsed around his hands like liquid light. A stream of it stretched across the empty air, reaching for Catrin, but what was even more amazing and terrifying was the white hot line that extended from the mountaintop toward Pelivor, as if Catrin were trying to connect with him.

When the two streams of energy were still some distance apart, the air between them filled with a humming line of plasma, and once the two flows were connected, a thundering crack split the air and knocked everyone except Pelivor back. He stood rooted in place, engulfed in a raging torrent of energy. There was no fear in his face, though, only a look of awe and sudden understanding. Then he started to move like a machine, his fists pumping in and out, and each movement released a swirling conflagration that he hurled at the demons and giants.

Kenward knew this could be the savior of them all, but it also meant that the demons would know exactly where they were and would surely send forces here to deal with them. The last remaining regent dragon looked down at Pelivor and gave a cry. Kenward tried to discern what the cry meant, but it soon did not matter as the dragon leaped from its perch of stone and disappeared into the air beyond.

"So much for the loyalty of dragons," Kenward said.

Chapter 19

Sanity is but a temporary state.
--Nat Dersinger, prophet

* * *

Feeling like the wind itself, Catrin attacked. Everywhere she turned, demons flew like leaves in the wind. Her sword high and the spider globe sending light streaming out through the gaps in her clenched fist, Catrin roared a primal battle cry. Twice she pumped her fist, and thunder shook the mountain. Wild energy reached out from her and licked the walls. Her hair rustled in a preternatural wind that gusted within the charged field around her.

The regent queen turned to look at her. *You should be gone. Call him to you. Use the saddle and lance. Become your destiny and leave me to my fate.*

"I don't want you to die." It was the most honest thing Catrin could say.

You are a credit to your race that you would still feel that way given my treatment of you. I'm afraid it is too late to save me, and in attempting to do so, you are endangering your kind's future. We are lost but I'll not allow you to be lost as well. Now go! Kyrien! To me!

The last might not have been intended for Catrin to hear, but the powerful call must have been heard on the other side of the world. Catrin reeled with the power of it, but she knew now the best thing she could do was get Kyrien saddled and fight the enemy from the air. She could save the regent queen yet.

But Kyrien did not come. No one could have resisted that call, and Catrin's heart climbed into her throat. The world moved unexpectedly as darkness crowded her vision. The thought of Kyrien lost, all of his kind dead or dying, nearly brought Catrin to her knees. Needing strength, she reached out for something familiar and comforting. Like the swiftest arrow, power extended from her outstretched hands toward Pelivor. The essence of him slammed into her an instant later, and lightning cleaved the air between them.

Catrin staggered back to her feet, feeling the texture of the energy Pelivor lent her and, in doing so, learning all he knew about controlling the power and building efficient structures with energy. His mind amazed her in its precision and logic, the way he moved through problems by breaking them into smaller pieces and tackling each piece individually. Another energy responded to her call, and Catrin was shocked to see Kyrien land within the great hall. Blood dripped from what seemed a thousand wounds, and his nostrils flared with his rapid breathing. Frothy foam gathered around his legs, which trembled as he stood, panting. Never before had

Catrin seen a creature that had given so much of itself. Kyrien looked as if he would drop over dead at any instant, and Catrin ran to him, her energy already caressing him, bolstering him, healing him.

No! his voice rang in her mind. *Save your energy for the fight. I will survive.*

Catrin wanted to argue, wanted to take the time to tend his wounds and give him time to recover, but he pushed her before him, his muzzle driving her toward the saddle.

If this must be done, then let us do it. I can no longer take the guilt. Let this be at an end.

Catrin moved as if in a dream, her mind unable to cope with the consequences of this day. Never before had she seen a species wiped from existence, and she prayed she'd never witness it again. When she sat astride Kyrien, goggles on and strapped in, she could barely remember how she had come to be there, and she marveled at the beauty of the saddle. In her hand waited the greatest shock: a lance of gleaming filigree extending from the sword Strom had made for her, as if the two had been made to fit together. When Catrin's memories began to return, she realized that the sword had been made to Kyrien's specifications, yet she could not reconcile why Kyrien would have done that if this were not supposed to happen. Taking a deep breath, Catrin had no choice but to return her attention to the present. Atop the saddle, Catrin felt secure; the many buckles on her leather flight pants allowed her to strap in. Again she was amazed at the foresight of her dragon.

Kyrien, though seeming only slightly recovered from battle, tucked his wings and charged back into the great hall. An unbidden battle cry issued from Catrin's lips, and it turned to a scream as Kyrien leaped from the heights without ever opening his wings. Demons clogged the entrances and flew into the open air before Kyrien's maddened charge. With a trail of energy leading back to Pelivor and the wind trying to tear her apart, they fell like a stone. There were lurches and bumps in their descent that Catrin eventually realized were the times Kyrien attacked. They dived along the mountain face, Kyrien extending his wings in only small amounts to make adjustments to their flight path. Catrin would have launched attacks of her own, but she could not get her body to respond; the forces acting on it were simply too intense. Even her scream was choked away.

Then the saddle pressed into her hard, and Kyrien extended his wings. Catrin saw the army of demons, giants, and men in orderly formations, waiting to fill the void when their comrades fell. Finally Catrin was able to control herself, and she reached out for energy. She nearly swooned. The saddle responded with alacrity. The charge of millennia leaped to her call. The fiery link with Pelivor surged, and the energy of the comets resonated in a way she'd never felt before.

You're burning up!

Only then did Catrin realize that she rode amid a maelstrom of fire, her body a conflagration. Without hesitation, she launched a dozen attacks at once. Pelivor's control combined with the saddle's energy and Catrin's will caused the world to explode. Ranks of the enemy, formerly so orderly and geometric from above, now looked as if they had been tossed by a giant wave. Trails of smoke filled the air as balls of fire streamed into those who scaled the rock face. Lightning reached out to anything close to the great hall, but in the back of Catrin's consciousness, she knew that she needed to be careful not to hit the regent queen. Determination filled her as Kyrien brought them around for a pass along those closest to the queen, and Catrin almost smiled as a cloud of demons filled the air before them, thrown from the great hall by a very alive regent queen.

"We can save her!" Catrin shouted.

Kyrien made no response.

The air around them suddenly filled with teeth and claws, reaching for Catrin and tearing at Kyrien's already tender hide. Nothing could have prepared Catrin for the maneuvers Kyrien undertook to keep them both safe. It seemed impossible that they were still alive. A sizzling, crackling sound followed by a loud boom made her wonder how much longer that would remain true. Light exploded around her, and Catrin felt the shock of it, even though Kyrien took the brunt of the attack. His flight became erratic, and Catrin scanned the skies, ready to protect the stunned dragon from any new attacks. Kyrien regained stable flight, but Catrin knew he was not fully recovered. Ferals came in close, and Kyrien's reactions seemed delayed. For a brief instant, Catrin's mind registered the fact that the dragons were all riderless. She wasn't certain what it meant, but she was certain it meant something. It was not something she could ponder long.

When the buzzing, crackling sound filled the air around them again, Catrin searched the clouds and seas, trying to find its source. It was coming from the ships, which were now moving in formation once again.

Catrin opened her mouth to tell Kyrien, but he was already turning to dive for the attacking formation of ships. Just when Catrin thought the lightning would strike, the air exploded with fire, but she felt no pain, only the radiated heat. Alongside them, a feral dragon was engulfed in a web of charged air. It folded up like a swatted moth, dropping beside them. When Kyrien pulled up, the dragon continued falling and struck a warship on the prow, driving it underwater in a shower of exploding timber and sending its masts crashing into the ship adjacent to it.

Missed me.

Catrin almost laughed--almost.

No dragons had gotten close enough for Catrin to use her lance, but it felt good in her hand, far lighter than she would have believed from looking at it. Even as thin and delicate looking as the gold wire comprising it would seem, it felt solid and gave her confidence. When she pointed it at the next ship she could hone in on, she applied her will, and the lance responded. The delicate wires hummed and shone, light dancing across them in rolling waves with shape and texture. Like mist over the world at daybreak, it flitted along the surface and even over the empty areas between the wires. Erupting from the tip of the lance like liquid smoke, it roared through the air toward the ship. When the beam of energy struck amidships, the warship did something Catrin had never seen before: it imploded. It started slowly then accelerated, essentially folding the ship in half and sending it to rest at the bottom of the shallows.

Kyrien banked away from another feral attack, and Catrin could hear the cries of man and demon from below. There was panic in many of those cries, and as unlikely as it was, Catrin felt as if the battle were turning in her favor. The ships had no way of avoiding her attacks, and it was just a matter of time before she took all of them out, stranding them, just as she'd done to the Zjhon when they had invaded the Godfist. Sending waves of devastation into the midst of every formation of ships she could see, Catrin did her best to cripple them. Only the ferals were able to disrupt her attacks. Kyrien's evasive maneuvers made taking aim exceedingly difficult, and many of her attacks missed their marks. Those that landed, though, were equally as destructive as the first.

Doing their best to stay above or behind Catrin and Kyrien, the ferals made for elusive targets. They knew how dangerous she was, and they had no intention of giving her a clear shot. Instead, they tried to hide in Kyrien's blind spot and attack Catrin from above. It was an extremely uncomfortable feeling knowing she was being hunted from behind, let alone from above and behind. Somehow Kyrien seemed able to sense them and managed to keep Catrin outside the reach of their attacks. Twice he was able to cause ferals to collide with one another. The first pair had simply flown off in separate directions, but the second pair collided with a sickening crack. Though the impact had killed only one of the beasts, the two became hopelessly tangled, and both plunged into dark water. Neither rose again.

The problem was that all of this was but a distraction from their true purpose, which was to defend the regent queen. It seemed only an instant had passed, but when Catrin looked back to the top of the mountain, waves of demons were swarming into the great hall, and no more flew from the entrances. Panicked, Catrin shouted to Kyrien, but her voice could not be heard over the rush of the wind. Still, Kyrien made straight for the great hall, his own anxiety radiating from him. Both seemed to realize that their attacks on the ships and ferals may have come at the ultimate cost. Catrin's skin felt clammy, a prickly feeling making her shift in the saddle. Hurling vortices of air before them, Catrin knocked the demons clear, making a place for Kyrien to land. Even as he glided in, Catrin pumped her left fist, and from her right hand issued pulses of power that traveled down the lance, intensified, and pounded back the demon horde.

Quickly scanning the area, Catrin could not, at first, locate the regent queen. Then her eyes landed on a swarming, black mass roughly the shape of the dragon queen. The taste of bile filled Catrin's mouth, and she did not hesitate in blasting away the demons using nothing but air, trying to be careful even in her haste. The giant dragon's great maw turned to them, demons still clinging to her face, trying to blind her. Catrin used targeted blasts of air to dislodge them, Pelivor's precision aiding her greatly. The thought of Pelivor caused Catrin to panic anew. The gleaming trail of energy still extended back to the sailor, but she could no longer sense him. Immediately she released the link, and all she could do was pray that she had not inadvertently killed her dear friend.

So many consequences rendered Catrin numb. No matter what she did, people and dragons were going to die. This realization made her choices a great deal easier to make. *Just act,* she thought. With remarkable speed, Catrin removed the buckles that held her in the saddle and leaped to the cold stone floor of the great hall. Demons flew like kindling before her, and more of the regent queen was once again exposed to the light. The mighty dragon showed wounds, but none seemed mortal. A spark of hope shone in Catrin's consciousness. *The future is not written in stone,* Catrin said to herself, and she leaped into the air, engaging any demons she found still standing.

The regent queen turned and looked at Kyrien. For the first time, Catrin saw something other than anger and hurt in the queen's eyes.

You should not be here, Kyrien. I do not want you to see this. No one should have to see such a thing. Now take the human and go. Please, Kyrien--for your own good--go.

Catrin could feel the emotion, and tears came to her eyes. Kyrien's feelings mingled with her own, and such grief was more than anyone should ever have to bear. Desperate, Catrin continued to drive away the demons. Rearing back, the regent queen reached a towering and imposing height. The demons fell back of their own volition, and even Catrin felt fear in the face of such tremendous power.

You are worthy. Protect him.

The words reached Catrin with a wave of compassion, and she could feel the honesty and sincerity as the regent queen looked her in the eyes. The air was sucked from her lungs in shock when she saw a single demon charging through the masses. When it broke into the open, Catrin was terrified to see it wielded a lance similar to her own, save this one looked as if it were made of black glass instead of gold wire. Streaks of light danced over the glossy surface of the lance, and without slowing, the demon thrust the lance into the regent queen's exposed breast. There was a wet sound accompanied by a terrible sigh. Not satisfied with simply running her through, the demon twisted the blade then yanked. Only instead of pulling the blade back out, it yanked it sideways. The lance shattered into thousands of daggerlike shards. With a final wheezing grunt, the queen rolled to one side and collapsed.

In that moment, Catrin realized just how perilous her situation really was. With the regent queen dead, the demons could concentrate on killing her and Kyrien, and she wasn't even mounted. Running back to Kyrien, she leaped onto his back. His pain was palpable and unbearable. It tore at Catrin's resolve, soaking her in guilt and remorse and regret.

"We must live!" Catrin shouted. "You and I are not done--not even close. If we die now, then she died for nothing."

The last words drove Kyrien to reckless action, his anger a force that polluted the air around them. Demons drew closer, their ranks thickening until they blocked the light, which seemed to be moving farther away. It was a maddening view.

Be ready.

Catrin didn't need to ask what for; instead, she drew deeply from the stones in the saddle and the spider globe. When Kyrien started moving, Catrin unloaded a barrage of attacks that turned the great hall into pure chaos. None were safe from her fury, and the air around the openings was once again filled with flailing demons. A rare few managed to remain in the hall, and only one of those managed to stand. Catrin decided to blast those farther ahead since Kyrien could easily handle a single demon, but the beast reached down and, from behind a fallen body, produced another of the glass lances. Catrin thought her heart might just burst.

Planting its feet, the demon was in a perfect position to strike. All it had to do was let Kyrien's momentum carry him forward and he would impale himself. The shock of it stunned Catrin and slowed her reaction. The demon smiled a dark, wet smile as Kyrien approached, even though it must know its own death came just as surely. As the lance was about to pierce Kyrien's breast, Catrin acted out of pure instinct; she cast a wave of vibrating air that sang a high-pitched note. Part of her brain registered that Pelivor knew how to break glass with sound. Glass struck dragon scale, and for a moment the lance held its form, but then it fractured in a thousand places, just as it had been designed to do, only it did so before entering Kyrien's flesh. The look of triumph on the demon's face turned to utter terror as Kyrien ran him down.

Again, Catrin had to concentrate on the demons that blocked their escape. Kyrien needed speed to get them clear of the rock face. His trembling form gave evidence to her concern. Catrin, in contrast, felt as if she could sunder the world, and she feared she would go too far. When she lashed out again, she did so with as much restraint and control as she could. Using a delicate web of energy whose vibration was extremely high and resonance packed a nasty sting, Catrin went for the enemy's eyes. Though she doubted it did any permanent damage, the result was nonetheless astonishing as every demon in the great hall reeled in agony and disorientation.

Pushing stunned demons out of their way, Kyrien gave a heroic effort, trying to take advantage of Catrin's attack, but the effort slowed them. Some demons recovered their vision and moved to block their path. Catrin lashed out with short, precise strikes that pierced the demons and dropped them, the sounds of their deaths lost in the screams of the still blinded.

Holding her breath, Catrin gripped the saddle horn and squeezed with her legs, some of her straps still not secured. When Kyrien launched himself into the air, Catrin bent her knees and braced herself. Though they dropped sharply, they did not quite clear the rocky crags below the entranceway. Based on the abrupt jolt that felt like it broke every bone in Catrin's body, she wondered how Kyrien could endure, but he extended his wings and caught a favorable wind that sent them soaring into the valley.

The air below them hummed with arrows and bolts, and Kyrien turned aside. Only a few shafts managed to strike him, and his scales deflected those. Both he and Catrin remembered the last time she had removed an arrow from a wing joint, and Kyrien still complained that it ached before the rain. Using their speed, Kyrien climbed higher and out of bow range. A pocket of less dense air sent them downward, and Kyrien used it to turn them back toward the mountain. The view that waited would haunt them both. Accompanied by a victorious roar that frightened Catrin more than anything she'd ever heard, the head of the dead regent queen reached the entranceway and was sent tumbling down the rock face. It was an exceedingly stupid manner of celebration, as the rock face was crowded with demons, and the huge dragon head took out scores of them.

For a long moment, Catrin held her breath without realizing it then inhaled sharply when the ferals filled the air around them. In an instant, Catrin readied herself, but the attack never came. Instead the ferals attacked the remains of the regent queen. Kyrien's outrage flowed through the bond, but Catrin convinced him that the queen was already gone and that this could give them time to escape.

Though she no longer maintained the link to Pelivor, she knew that he was still in the dragon's vale--her vale. Kyrien raced along the valley toward the vale unbidden, and Catrin could only hope that her friends were still alive. Guilt and remorse stabbed at her as she second-guessed her decision to leave them. Had she truly been protecting them, or had she simply placed them in even greater danger. The thoughts made her want to cry, but she waited to see what reality truly existed.

She saw Kenward first; he was pointing at her and shouting, but she couldn't hear his words. Blood pounded in her ears, and she could hear nothing over the roar of it; not even the rumble of the wind pierced it. As

Kyrien dipped low, Catrin sensed a presence above and behind her, and it was then she turned and saw the giant feral bearing down on them, claws extended and jaws agape. It was a terrifying sight that made Catrin's nightmares seem warm and safe. Nothing can be compared to the feeling of knowing you're about to be torn apart, and Catrin's body trembled.

With unsteady hands, she unbuckled herself as quickly as she could. Kyrien dipped low, allowing her to roll unharmed from the saddle onto the rushing grasses. Tumbling, she hoped she could stop herself before she struck rock. A moment later she found herself lying faceup on the grass, watching a pair of claws only just miss grabbing her, Kyrien having done his best to keep her safe.

Kenward ran toward her. Then Pelivor was there, helping her stand. The rest were huddled within the remains of the *Slippery Eel.* Pelivor led her back to the ship, and she could barely meet the eyes of those who waited. She had brought them all here, endangered their lives, then abandoned them. And after all of that, after betraying her friends for the sake of the dragons, she had failed. Now they would all die--her friends, her son, her husband, her people--all would die because of her folly. It hurt so badly that she thought she might crumble under the weight of it. The thing that made her feel worst of all, though, was the fact that instead of wanting to protect her friends, all she wanted to do was abandon them again.

Familiar hands pulled her into the hold, and tears came to Catrin's downcast eyes.

"Thank the gods you're back!" Farsy said, and Catrin felt wholly unworthy of his enthusiasm.

"I'm sorry," was all Catrin could manage to say.

A long silence hung between them, but the cries of dragon and demon filled the space.

She turned to Pelivor. "I know I can ask no more of you, but I will. Pelivor, you must protect us," she said as she handed him the spider globe.

He looked intrigued at first when he saw the globe, but when it dropped into his palm, there was an audible click and a small spark. His eyes went wide, but a smile crossed his lips. The smile faded when she handed him the lance, his hand sliding into the guard and closing over the handle of her sword. "The rest of you, please get the drums."

"Oh, no," came Kenward's voice from behind. "You're not leaving us again."

"I can go with or without your help, Kenward, but I am far more likely to return if you help me."

Kenward stepped backward, as if Catrin had struck him, but he knew the stakes. This was no time for hurt feelings. He could get her back for those later, provided they survived. The captain looked critically at Pelivor. "Can you protect us?"

Pelivor responded by smiling and holding his hands out to his sides. Preternatural breezes stirred the silks he wore, and light danced around him. When he spoke, it was not to Kenward. "Death awaits those who would do us harm!" The words rang through the vale, the deep bass of his voice amplified by the power flowing through him. The spider globe sent beams of light from within his clenched fist as he held it high. In his other hand, he held Catrin's lance, and he leveled it at an oncoming feral. He did not wait for the dragon to get close. He used the lance to focus his attack into a narrow beam of boiling liquid fire that seared the air with a roar.

Catrin turned to Kenward. "Drums!"

Chapter 20

Only a fool stands between mother and cub.
--Wendel Volker

* * *

The journey to the Godfist took only the span of a thought, but Catrin's spirit slowed before actually reaching her homeland. Had she been able to, she would have traveled directly to Sinjin's side, but the air grew thick with energy and malicious intent. Hatred washed over her, and it made her want to scream. It was like being covered in fire ants.

Dark with malevolence, an unnatural storm, seemingly ready to swallow the world, dominated the horizon. Vast networks of lightning jumped across its surface, and the thunder was nearly continuous. Smaller patches of darkness coalesced and gathered into formations--dragons of black fire with riders of pure night.

Never before had Catrin witnessed such utter wrongness, such warping of nature, and she felt naked against the storm. Twisted darkness, launched from the fingertips of the black dragon riders, streaked toward Catrin. She prepared for the assault, casting out defensive energy. As he had in the past, Kyrien took the brunt of the attack, having seemingly appeared from nowhere, his energetic form of lightning and fire pulsing with light. He was a jewel amid the horror.

More attacks came and Kyrien could not absorb them all. Doing so would likely kill him, and Catrin cried out for him to stop. There were simply too many attacks coming at once. Catrin and Kyrien were alone against thousands, and their numbers seemed to grow continually. Weariness overwhelmed her and a sense of resignation took hold. This was a battle she could not win. When she saw Thorakis, the feeling of utter defeat solidified.

Shining like a black sun, he rode atop a gleaming feral dragon. Even at a distance, recognition caught in Catrin's throat. In one hand, Thorakis held a staff; in the other, a carving. A cry escaped Catrin when she realized he held the Staff of Life and Koe. Both were precious to her and held great power. Each had been shaped by her hand, in their own way, and she could not imagine standing against their combined might. Ever since she had carved Koe, she had not wanted to know what it would feel like to be faced with his aggressive stance, and now she knew; it was terrifying. There was only one consolation, and that was Thorakis did not rest his fingers in the grooves left by Catrin's grip. For some reason that made her feel better; the thought if his touching those places made her feel ill.

Thorakis gave her little time to contemplate his presence before he lashed out. Torrents of power slammed into Catrin, and it felt like being caught in the surf before a storm. Energy pounded against her with relentless force, and she felt as if she were being torn apart. In the next instant, she could almost hear Kenward shouting. His words had no meaning, though they did serve as the slightest warning before power surged through her. It was a source she recognized: the queen's saddle. The instant she felt one of the straps hit her physical hand, she sensed the saddle and Kyrien. Looking down, she saw his fiery form now under her, and together they felt more powerful. Their energies mingled and where she was weak, he was strong, and she felt she brought something to him as well. He was not incomplete without her, but together they were stronger. That thought comforted her, as did the momentary clarity with which she heard Kenward say, "Go get 'em, Cat!"

Emotion threatened to overwhelm her, but she kept it in check, using it instead to fuel her rage and fury against the darkness that sought to despoil all she loved. From Kyrien she sensed the burning desire for revenge, not so much out of spite, but out of the need to absolve his guilt. He had let the regent queen die. He had betrayed his own kind, and no knowledge could be so damning. Catrin could not completely understand his inner struggle; she could not grasp his relationship with the queen nor truly understand how he had betrayed his kind. It was very clear, however, that Kyrien believed he had done just that. Though Catrin had shown love to the regent queen, she hated her for that last bit of spite with which she inflicted this guilt on Kyrien. But the regent queen was dead.

Emitting a roar that would make a lion quail, Catrin unleashed a wave of furious attacks, the line of energy extending back to her physical form now blazing like a new star. Deep troughs tore through the darkness, but like the deepest ocean, more flooded into the void, making it look as if her attack had done no damage at all. Twice more she cast out weblike attacks, trying to break the darkness into smaller chunks, but again it flowed back together. Then there was no more time for attacks.

From every direction came a massive assault that dwarfed all those before it. It felt to Catrin as if her universe was collapsing in on itself, and she was at the very center of that crushing weight. Despite her power, despite her will, and even in the face of her closest ally, Kyrien, this attack made them seem insignificant. Nothing could withstand so much hatred. None could endure so many wishing they had never existed. It was the most terrible thing Catrin had ever experienced, being made to think that she was worse than useless; her very existence was harmful to everything else around her.

Seethe. Kyrien uttered a single word in Catrin's mind, and instantly she knew that Thorakis was not the true threat. The real threat was Seethe, the dragon Thorakis rode. Seethe was not Thorakis's dragon; Thorakis was one of Seethe's many humans. This realization struck Catrin like a thunderbolt, and she looked into the feral dragon's eyes, trying to understand the true threat.

You are worthless. Give yourself to me, and you will be part of something much stronger. How can you hope to stand against this?

The thunderous voice in her mind was accompanied by a wave of compulsion that made what Archmaster Belegra had done look like friendly persuasion. This voice sought to obliterate all thought but its own, and it hammered at her as the collective will of tens of thousands joined in. Then something occurred to Catrin: If the feral dragons were so powerful, why did they need humans?

This thought must have been betrayed to Seethe as Catrin heard pounding laughter in her head. *You are but tools to me, implements designed to achieve my will. I wouldn't bother keeping you around at all, but you do have such delicate fingers. But if you prove too troublesome, you are something we can certainly do without.* Seethe then flooded Catrin's mind with the vision of the death of mankind. Perhaps he'd meant to frighten her, but she'd seen it before.

You underestimate the power of a single will, Catrin thought with all her might, and despite the singularity of her statement, she felt the wills of others backing her. The world around her was suddenly filled with light; flaming dragons surrounded her and reinforced her will. One in particular caught Catrin's attention as it bore a rider, and Catrin nearly shouted in glee when she recognized Halmsa of the Wind clan, who looked as if he would burst with pride, but moreover he looked ready to die for Catrin. Somehow he thought that Catrin had fulfilled her promise to him and taught him to fly dragons, though she knew not how she had done any such thing. Still, she could feel his gratitude as he sent it toward her; it bolstered her soul.

It was a proud and brief moment. Then the world exploded. Both sides released the full extent of their might and fury, holding nothing back. The heavens shook and the pillars of Godsland trembled. Catrin felt the energy of the planet surging through mighty keystones--six of them. One of which was within the Grove of the Elders, another at the great shallows. Catrin did not know exactly where the others were, only that they existed. Anyone who controlled them would control the world. Catrin tried to bury that thought lest the dragons find out--that is, if they did not already know.

The vision of the Grove of the Elders persisted in Catrin's consciousness, like spots left by the sun. There she saw the mighty greatoaks as they had once been, and at the center of the grove stood the Staff of Life, blooming. It was an anachronistic vision, true, but it felt real to Catrin, who had planted the staff there. She'd been a fool to leave it there. Chase must have been right when he'd said the staff had given her acorns to replenish the grove and no more; it must have fulfilled its purpose. He'd begged her to bring the staff back to Dragonhold rather than leaving it in lands controlled by Master Edling. Now the staff rested in the hands of Thorakis, a once great man now subverted by Seethe. Thus, it rested within the feral's grasp--all that power, his to command. It was a frightening thought, and it was painful to feel its bite.

Koe reached out to her and left claw marks through her psyche. A creature of her own creation, she was defenseless against it, and Catrin cried out to Kyrien to retreat. Instead, the regents responded, throwing themselves onto Thorakis's attacks, and by their sheer numbers, they broke through and sent Thorakis tumbling into the darkness. Seethe bellowed and exacted a costly price for the victory, and Catrin felt the light dimming around her. Despite their heroic efforts, the darkness was still winning.

Though despair threatened, Catrin looked around her and found that she was far closer to the Godfist than she had been at the start of the battle. They had taken great losses, but their progress was more than the ferals would have them believe. Much of their power was in deception, and Catrin was now fully aware of this.

Seethe's voice was now quieter in her mind. *Your son is about to die.*

* * *

Doing what he did best, Sinjin ran. Slowly the demons recovered themselves, and Sinjin dodged their sluggish movements as he wove his way toward where he'd last seen Strom. The scene ahead was a blur, and when he broke free of the demons and into the open, he saw them: his father, Strom, and Durin, all laid out on the grass. Sinjin's knees went weak, and he thought he might fall; only the need to keep Trinda safe kept him from giving in. Kendra and Khenna were among the few still standing, and Sinjin realized how hopeless his situation was. He had left Brother Vaughn behind, something he now regretted deeply. The demons outnumbered them hundreds to one, and they were quickly thawing. Trinda clung to him. He knew she was already overexerted, and he didn't expect much help from her.

Seeing Brother Vaughn standing alone, between them a mass of angry demons, Sinjin abandoned fear. "Dad!" he shouted as he ran, and his thoughts turned momentarily to his mother. "Mother! Please help!"

Kendra came into view, and Sinjin angled away from her. Khenna stood nearby, looking ready to defend Strom, Prios, and Durin, all of whom remained unconscious. Sinjin had no time to check on their conditions as the demons resumed their attack. He wanted to drag his father and friends to safety, but he was left with no choice but to defend their unmoving bodies. After quickly putting Trinda down next to his father, Sinjin turned to face the demons with fury and desperation in his eyes. With the herald globe gleaming before him, Sinjin thought he saw another bright light. Not knowing its source, he threw the herald globe into the midst of the demons. Before the globe struck, he saw Brother Vaughn trapped on the shoreline of the turbulent river waters. A flash of light drove the demons back, and Brother Vaughn dived into the depths. Sinjin would have cried out, but an instant before the herald globe erupted, something slammed into the back of his skull, and the world went dark.

* * *

Breaking free from Thorakis, Catrin's spirit raced toward where she sensed her son and husband; their life forces dim yet calling to her. Below her, fields of amber crystal beckoned, and she burst through like rays of sunlight, only a thousand times brighter. Immediately she was faced with an amazing yet terrifying sight. The underground cavern was beyond images from even her wildest fantasy. Never before had she considered that an entire ecosystem might have survived underground for ages undisturbed. The stain of darkness and evil despoiled the view.

Catrin first saw Brother Vaughn alone, trapped by demons on one side and dangerous-looking waters on the other. Not knowing what else to do, Catrin cast her light into the demons. Somehow amplified by the crystals and with an amber tint, her beams sent demons tumbling backward. Others moved in to replace those, but Brother Vaughn took control of his own destiny and slipped into the churning water. Catrin could only pray that he would survive. After losing sight of him, she knew she could no longer protect him, and she began looking for Sinjin and Prios.

Her soul cried out when she found them, both laid out on the lush grasses along with Strom, Durin, and others. Khenna and Kendra alone remained standing, and they appeared to be fighting. Catrin did not understand what could possibly be happening. Confusion and anxiety overwhelmed her as she moved closer. Kendra looked angrier than Catrin had ever seen her, and she moved in to swipe her own mother's knees. Khenna, though older and not as nimble, had a great deal more experience and anticipated the move. With a simple sidestep, she gained the advantage on her now off-balance daughter. A single punch sent Kendra to the turf.

"Get her out of here," Khenna shouted, and a demon lifted Kendra's limp form in its arms. Catrin nearly retched. Then the woman turned back to Catrin's husband and son. "That boy comes with us. Kill the rest."

Roaring, Catrin attacked. Fire, smoke, and lightning raced toward Khenna but were deflected at the last instant and sent racing back toward Catrin. It was something she had once done to Archmaster Belegra, and she quailed, knowing she was about to feel the bite of her own power. Over the roar of the fire and the crackling of energy, Catrin could hear Thorakis laughing, a high-pitched and maniacal sound that turned into the roar of a mighty feral dragon now bearing down on her. Pain erupted all over Catrin as her very essence was scoured and eroded. Every instant, she lost something of herself, and she could hear the dragon calling to her, its voice assuring her that it could make the pain stop; all she had to do was surrender. Then her son, husband, and all those she loved would be spared. All she had to do was join them. The future was already written, and she could not change that which was recorded in stone. The thoughts battered her senses, and it was so tempting to simply give in, but the sight of her son in the arms of a demon shook her from the feral's delusion, and she launched another attack, aiming for the legs of the demon carrying Sinjin's limp form.

Again, pain erupted. Thorakis and Seethe attacked with overwhelming force and ferocity that exceeded anything Catrin had ever seen in nature. She knew the role of predators, but nothing she'd ever seen compared to the overwhelming desire to destroy--not to kill and eat, but to abolish from existence. This kind of evil would consume the world, and Catrin knew she was among the few things stopping that gruesome future from coming to pass.

"The future is not already written!" her spirit screamed as she blocked an attack and launched another of her own. Demons now stood over Prios, Strom, Durin, and Trinda--only the wisp of a girl alert and able to fight. Again Catrin thought it strange that she thought of Trinda as a child when the girl was actually her elder. And that frailty gave Catrin no confidence that she would be any use at all in a fight.

In that instant, Catrin had to make a choice: prevent the demons from escaping into the darkness with her son or save the lives of her husband and friends. Trinda's eyes looked up to her, pleading for mercy, and though Catrin had never really liked her, she rushed in to save them all, flames searing the air before her. Demons flew from her path, even as others carried her baby boy back into the depths of the hold.

Turning to race after them before it was too late, Catrin felt fiery claws rake her soul, and they bit deep. Thorakis used Koe to flay her, and the familiarity of the attacking energy made it all the more difficult to defend against. Even as Catrin was reeling from Koe's attack, feeling as if she were gulping for air even if not in her physical form, there was no way she could defend herself from the Staff of Life. Its ancient power slammed into her with unrelenting force; it knew her weaknesses and exploited every one. In the next instant, Catrin was back in her body, trying to suck in enough air to scream, then wanting nothing more than to cry as she looked out at what she knew was the last of the regent dragons.

Kyrien wept.

Epilogue

* * *

Crying as he ran, Durin couldn't believe how things had turned out. His best friend was gone, and there was nothing he could do about it. Brother Vaughn had either escaped or drowned, and there was no way for him to know which. His entire family's fate was unknown to him, and he doubted he would ever see any of them again. It seemed the end of the world had come, and he could see no possible future that included happiness or family. It was the kind of realization that could drive the weak to their knees, but through all of this, Durin had learned one thing: he was not as weak as he had once believed. Now he realized that he had not been lazy as much as he had been afraid to apply himself since that left him open to failure. Now he realized that failure was necessary for success, something that seemed far too philosophical for his usual thoughts. Durin, though, had left childhood behind in recent days, and there was no time for such thoughts.

Running alongside him was Strom, who carried a still unconscious Prios over his shoulder. Trinda ran with them, having difficulty keeping up. Durin thought she might want him to carry her, but he was not Sinjin, and even if he had grown up quickly, some of his childhood prejudices remained. Trinda would have to stand on her own two legs if she wished to survive. Even as he had the thought, he knew he would not leave her to die, but that didn't mean he had to like saving her. What was even more difficult was for him to admit that she had saved him. Strom had been the only thing defending them when Durin had come to, and Durin had been little help, even armed with Strom's wicked blade. Only when Trinda had stepped up and chastised the demons did the battle turn in their favor. It still seemed unreal to Durin that Trinda could do such a thing.

"Bad demons!" was all she had said, and it was as if she had struck them all with just her words. No matter what Durin believed, that moment had been the key to their escape, and only by moving deeper into darkened halls did they manage to gain any measure of safety. Again, Durin had to admit that Trinda had saved them since she had retrieved the herald globe, and to Durin's amazement, she had somehow recharged it. This girl was really starting to irritate him.

"We're completely lost," Strom whispered. "But maybe that's a good thing." Groaning as he shifted Prios on his shoulder, he looked as if he might not make it much farther, and Prios gave no indication of stirring.

"I want to go outside," Trinda said.

"I'd like to fly too," Durin said, not expecting a response.

"It's this way."

Given no other direction, Strom followed Trinda, the light of the herald globe drifting away as Durin remained where he was. The darkness closed in all too quickly, and Durin raced to catch up.

"Are you sure you know where you're going?" Durin asked after a number of turns down seemingly random halls. They passed halls that were still filled with items, but Trinda did not waver in her course, and Durin's imagination was left to run wild as he caught only glimpses of the treasures that waited within. He'd heard the stories about the artifacts Catrin had found at Ohmahold, and he imagined them stumbling on a similar cache of wondrous things. The thoughts helped to keep him from thinking about the fate of everyone else.

When Trinda walked into a circular hall and stopped, it took Durin and Strom by complete surprise. Without a word, she just stared at the markings on the floor of the chamber. Immediately Durin knew this room was special and the carved tiles were more than mere decoration.

"Step on the one that looks like mountains," Trinda said, looking at Durin.

Examining the tiles, Durin spotted one in the third row of tiles away from him, farther away than he guessed Trinda could jump. Even for Durin, he had to take a running leap to make it, and in mid air he heard Trinda suck in a breath. Perhaps she had not expected him to do as she asked; Durin wasn't quite sure why he had. When he landed, the stone sank beneath his weight, and he had a sick feeling in his gut.

"Not that one, silly," Trinda said.

Durin's sick feeling intensified as a low grinding noise filled the halls and the stone beneath their feet trembled.

FERAL

<u>Chapter 1</u>

Permanence is an illusion.
--Nat Dersinger, prophet

* * *

Shades of darkness crowded close, creaking and rocking in the muffled silence. Unable to move, Sinjin Volker struggled against his bonds without effect, always expecting something to come hurling at him from the darkness; it had happened before. With the ship rolling beneath him, he imagined finding his end at the bottom of some nameless ocean. Those on this ship bore no love or humor, and though they kept him alive, he wondered how much longer they would do so. Even after days aboard the ship, his guts churned. His mother had loved sailing. It was a painful memory. Sinjin almost smiled at the memory of his father, who had secretly admitted that he hated sailing and hoped never to step foot on a ship ever again, especially one captained by Kenward Trell. Though this memory was a fond one, it did little to raise Sinjin's spirits or calm his stomach. He did not share his mother's love of sailing. Had she traveled in the belly of a foul-smelling ship while trussed up like a spring pig, he guessed she would feel the same.

Without warning, a beam of light poured in and brought searing pain. Sinjin averted his eyes, able to discern only a silhouette. Once again, he tested bonds that held him fast. Nothing had ever terrified him more than being helpless in the hands of his enemies. The light retreated as quickly as it had come. The hatch slid silently closed.

Sinjin sucked in a ragged breath. Delicate hands removed the gag and immediately clamped down on his mouth.

"Do not speak," came a whisper. Sinjin could not identify the voice, but his addled mind knew it was familiar. "I didn't know," the voice continued. "I would never have gone along with this. Now you listen to me and listen to me good. If you want to get out of this alive, you're going to have to trust me. When I take away my hand, I only want to hear a quiet, one-word answer. Do you understand?"

Sinjin nodded his head, and she slowly took her hand from his face.

"Do you trust me?"

Cool air rushed in, and Sinjin breathed deeply, not caring about the stench at that moment. His memory fuzzy, Sinjin tried to understand what was going on, but he just found himself confused and frightened. "Yes," he said after an overlong pause.

"Meaning, no. You're still an idiot."

"Where are they taking me?" Sinjin asked, his mind starting to warm up.

"Somewhere you do not want to go," she said. "Somewhere I don't want to go," she added in a soft whisper.

The pain in her voice was clear, but Sinjin could think of nothing to say.

The darkness was silent for a time, but the sounds of boots on the deck soon sent Kendra scrambling back out of the hatch. For a brief moment, he saw her face, frightened and tense, yet he still could not claim to fully believe her. There had been no kindness between them in the past, and he could see no reason for it to start now. Still, he was surrounded by enemies, and no one else was extending a hand in friendship.

The sound of boots still approaching drove the thoughts from his mind as he realized that his gag hung below his chin. In a split second, he managed to grab a piece of the gag in his teeth and pull it mostly back into place. The rough-looking man who dropped into the hold barely spared him a glance as he retrieved a wooden crate from the stacks of supplies. Another man reached down from above, and Sinjin prayed they would leave him alone this time. After the case was lifted from the hold, the man climbed out without a word, and Sinjin was plunged back into darkness.

* * *

Those gathered in Catrin's Vale had not yet recovered from the shock of the loss of the regent dragons--Kyrien now being the last of his kind. It seemed too impossible to be true, but that fact hung over every moment, especially since Kyrien rested among them, looking as if he might follow his brethren to the afterlife at any moment. The *Slippery Eel* lay on her side, a constant reminder that most of them would be stranded on the Firstland. There had been few words since Kyrien had last spoken in Catrin's mind.

Now I will accept your healing.

That single thought, full of pain, and the admission of weakness were the only things he'd had the strength to convey. Her voice had cracked when she told this to the others.

"Please help me get the saddle off of him," she said, her voice a little more steady, and those around her assisted wordlessly. No one else seemed willing to speak in this new world in which they found themselves. Everything had changed, and there was no chance of it ever going back. Knowing this, Catrin laid her hands on Kyrien. Pelivor swayed in the light breeze and lent his energy to Catrin and, thus, to Kyrien by proxy. To his eyes, it seemed the poor beast ought to already be dead, but there was a stubborn refusal to die that made Pelivor proud. For Kyrien, he would give of himself freely. Feeling her eyes upon him, Pelivor turned to Catrin. Her smile was sad and forced, and it was almost worse than seeing her cry. Pelivor wanted no more of that. Kyrien's aura, though, radiated remorse, and it was difficult not to take on his dangerous and black mood.

Still trying to read Catrin's expression, Pelivor found himself lost in old feelings, and he castigated himself for such treachery. Prios was his friend, and yet he found himself tempted. She was here, in front of him, wounded, her heart broken. Prios was not here. He could not comfort her. Should not Pelivor comfort her in his stead? Would his friend not want his wife to feel consolation and love? No. He had to stop himself before he gave away his feelings.

Catrin's eyes told him that he had betrayed them long before. She knew. She would not act but she knew. It was a heady thing, and he slowly pulled his energy back. The instant she sensed his desire to withdraw, Catrin released him, and the suddenness of it left him reeling. Wishing he had kept his thoughts to himself, he watched her turn away. Their energy no longer connected, she felt distant and receding as she concentrated on Kyrien. The feeling left Pelivor longing.

Looking at the last of the regent dragons, he could see no visible effect from Catrin's healing. He had felt and experienced the deep impact, though, as if it were his own essence that had been revived. Instead of healing each individual injury, Catrin fed energy to Kyrien's core being and allowed his body to heal from the inside out. The cuts and gouges in his hide still looked angry and grave, but his breathing was deeper and steadier. All the while Catrin drew on the mighty saddle that now sat alongside Kyrien. When finally the dragon forced her away and made her stop, Catrin stepped back, looking unsteady on her feet, the moon and comet light casting her in soft hues and shadow. Even drained and bedraggled, she was beautiful.

Pelivor looked to the saddle. The dragon ore stones were now cloudy despite retaining their glossy sheen, proof of how much energy Catrin had drawn from them.

Rest, came pure, raw compulsion from Kyrien, and Catrin was defenseless against it. Pelivor felt as much as heard the command, and he caught her before she fell to the ground, but only just, and he helped her back to the *Slippery Eel.*

With Catrin safe and comfortable, Pelivor returned to the vale and joined Kenward at one of the massive rock formations that provided a commanding view of the valley beyond. The memory of regent dragons perched on those rocks not so long ago was like a knife in Pelivor's chest. They had failed the dragons. Even though he hadn't been with Catrin physically during that battle, he had sent his energy to her, but they had failed. Part of him could not believe such a thing had worked, but any excitement over the accomplishment was doused by the painful reality that it hadn't been enough to save the regent dragons.

"The black devils are leaving," Kenward said in a flat voice. Moving to his side, Pelivor saw what he meant. Bathed mostly in long shadows and violet, the valley was filled with pinpricks of light from slowly moving torches. Inexorably they marched toward the coast, where tall-masted ships waited, silhouetted against the horizon.

"If the *Eel* were still in the water, she'd almost certainly be sunk," Kenward said.

Pelivor wasn't certain if this statement inspired Kenward to new hope or if it was simply a reminder of how impossible their situation really was. Pelivor chose hope. Seeing the armies of demons leaving and giants being loaded onto massive barges also made him wonder, though, where this black navy would strike next. No force the world had ever known could stand against such a foe, and the thought made him shiver. Returning to Catrin's side, he yielded to Kyrien's continued insistence that he join her in sleep.

* * *

When the sun sent isolated rays of light through a patchwork of clouds, Pelivor stirred, though part of him wished to sleep longer. Catrin was no longer beside him, and he rose to look for her. Kenward and the crew slept deeply, their snores filling the valley. When Pelivor saw the glittering saddle on Kyrien's back, he stopped short. Though the dragon's hide was crisscrossed with deep chasms and slashes, there was dark, shiny flesh now covering them.

There is no pain.

Having a dragon speak directly in his mind was not something Pelivor was entirely prepared for, and his reaction proved it as he fell backward, landing on his rear and staring up at Kyrien, agape. Catrin had obviously heard the same and more while she worked at cinching the girths.

"You're not really going to fly again so soon, are you?"

Catrin looked at him but did not smile. Her eyes carried an apology he didn't want to accept. She was leaving him. She was leaving the crew of the *Slippery Eel* on the Firstland, alone. The thought was terrifying. Even if the dark army did leave the Firstland, how would he and the others ever get off this unforgiving rock?

Continuing to strap herself into the saddle, Catrin's expression changed into something that frightened Pelivor more than the black army. Smoldering rage built in Catrin like a boiling kettle, and he could feel her drawing on the saddle, its ancient store of power still vast and mostly restored after basking in the light of the comets. It seemed to Pelivor as if Catrin had the power to tear the world apart; it was frightening and exhilarating.

Kyrien shifted beneath her, appearing to take on Catrin's mood. The fierce scowl he cast around the vale just about sent Pelivor scrambling for cover. Shining like the sun, Catrin looked like the goddess come to life. So terrifying was her beauty that Pelivor fell to his knees, the lush grasses cradling him, reminding him that this place had magic of its own. Natural or not, this place was magical, and the light radiating from Pelivor's dear friend only served to illuminate that fact.

"When the armies have gone," she said after a moment more, her voice loud and clear, "gather wood and build a fire. A ship will come for you."

Pelivor's head slumped forward.

"This is not the end," Catrin said. "You'll have to return this to me one day."

When Pelivor looked up, there was confusion in his eyes, which grew wide when Catrin handed him the spider stone.

"I couldn't--" he said.

"But you will," Catrin said, her expression distant and haunted. "You must keep them all safe, my dear friend. I never meant for this to happen, but I'm putting most of those I love in your care."

Pelivor looked up, unable to hide his emotions, and her look softened for a brief moment. "I am sorry, Pelivor, so very sorry." Those words brought Pelivor great pain, and that seemed to make Catrin even angrier than she had been. Agitated, Kyrien turned, climbed the nearby rocks, and, his tail twitching, launched himself into the air, giving Pelivor no more chance to say what was in his heart.

* * *

Though the sounds of demons within Dragonhold remained, the attacks had stopped, and Miss Mariss insisted everyone stay quiet, even though there was little doubt the demons knew they were there. Still, the kitchens were eerily quiet when the hollow echo began. Gradually it grew louder and louder and higher and higher in pitch until dust and the debris of ages began to issue forth from long-dormant channels.

"What have those fools done this time!" Miss Mariss exclaimed, earning a few glares from those she'd silenced, but that didn't deter her. "When I get my hands on those two, I'm gonna--" Her words were cut short when brackish water gushed from the opening in the wall and began to fill the basin that had been holding a store of brown rice. The rice poured over the ledge, along with the water, and ancient channels that had baffled them all since the hold's discovery were once again filled with flowing water. Despite the dust that hung in the air and the overflowing water, there was a sense of jubilation. Even if it did not solve all their problems, it was something magical and unexpected. It was as if part of the keep had come back to life, not unlike when the central fire had been lit. The water seemed to play counterpoint to the fire, and together they made Dragonhold breathe. One channel brought icy cold water, which was steadily becoming clearer, and another yielded steaming hot water. Throughout the hold, channels were blocked or had supplies and other items stacked in them. Water began to pool and spill from the channels that were clear, and Martik stood watching the situation unfold. Deep vibrations thrummed through the heels of his boots, and he could feel it in his teeth. Some of the tremors were more violent and made him wonder if the keep would collapse.

"I hadn't anticipated this," he admitted.

"Well it's not like those fools could see fit to give us a bit of warning. And since causing the hold to move is nothing to them, why not do whatever they did to cause water that hasn't flowed in a hazel's age to start flooding the hold? If I could reach 'em, I'm telling you, I'd throttle 'em."

Martik didn't argue with Miss Mariss, partly because he agreed with her. Strom was his friend, but he wasn't sure what the smith had been thinking. The thought of trying to defend Durin was laughable.

"What do we do about it?" she asked after a long silence.

"We've got to get these channels clear. Have people gather up broom handles or anything else that is long and thin . . . and rags, we'll need rags."

Miss Mariss knew good sense when she heard it and was moving before he finished the sentence.

* * *

Growling and with her teeth bared, Catrin stood in the stirrups and held on to the pommel with one hand, her lance in the other. Never before had she armed herself with the intention of attacking for no other reason than to cause the destruction of her enemy. This fight, in particular, was not about protecting what she loved; it was about avenging what she'd lost. Kyrien writhed with furious and righteous intent, ready to throw his barely healed body back into the fray for the memory of his very race, his species, and his loved ones. Such passion and rage could not be contained by their physical bodies, and their fury raced before them like a brooding storm front, dark and foreboding and promising destruction. When they struck, it was an attack like nothing Godsland had ever seen. With the might of the saddle and lance and total reprieve from all rules and boundaries, Catrin focused and released their combined rage.

Spinning and flowing, energy leaped from Catrin's lance with a thunderous clap. Plasma burned and danced across the winding surface of the lance before rings of boiling light and air thrummed toward the remains of the demon army. The bulk of the ships waited in deep water, but a dozen or so were still anchored along the coast, waiting for their turn to load.

Demons and men milled around in disorganized groups, and that was where Catrin's cones of destruction struck, tearing into the land and turning it inside out, launching everything into the air. At any other time, Catrin would have been appalled to see such destruction of the land, and surely she would never have conceived of having so much righteous rage. But fate had made it so, and Catrin vented her potent fury. Again and again, she pumped her fist, and her enemies were tossed like leaves in the wind. Great swaths of soil erupted, looking like bleeding wounds in the land. Kyrien brought them in low, and vengeance was Catrin's. Thrusting her energy before them, she tore trees from their roots and hurled them at the black army. There was no counterattack the army could launch, as Catrin literally threw the forest at them. The song of the dryads came to her loudly, and it contained a note of vengeance that salved Catrin's guilt over killing the trees. That was one of the problems with acting without thought: consequences.

On the horizon, sails climbed masts and ships moved slowly out to sea. Catrin let out a harsh and terrible laugh that rang through the valley before turning into a ululating battle cry. With grim satisfaction, Catrin changed tactics, looking for an attack that did not drain her so quickly. Rather than compress air, she evacuated it and asked the winds to part. She smiled as the vacuum reached the hold of a mighty ship before it imploded and brought the ship crashing in on itself. The sweat on her brow gave proof of the effort required for either attack. Always there was a price to be paid.

Ahead a group of ships gathered into the largest formation Catrin had seen, and as red light leaped and churned between them, they simultaneously left the water. Kyrien used his speed to come in behind the formation and hold at a short distance. With a sort of wicked of glee, Catrin constructed a series of latticework structures around the formation of ships, lifting them higher on the growing winds. Red lightning lashed out at her and Kyrien, but Catrin shrugged it off, barely feeling the sting. Eight ships were now joined together by Catrin's will alone; those aboard with power were concentrating on attacking Catrin and Kyrien with everything they had. Her howling rage made it clear that she had no intention of ceasing her attacks. Higher and higher the ships climbed, until the shouts and cries of those aboard trembled with panic. Still higher they moved, and a strong tailwind sent them hurtling toward the waiting armada. Soon anxious cries rang out across the water. In an instant, Catrin released the structures. What followed was the most terrible sound she had ever heard. They deserved it, she decided, every one of them.

Fully loaded ships dropped from the sky and landed on top of equally loaded ships, and even amid that chaos, attacks of fire, air, and lightning were launched against Catrin and Kyrien. Wood and metal struck wood and metal with thunderous force, and masts tore through hulls like knives at a feast. Screams filled the air, and final bolts of red lighting reached out for Catrin and Kyrien, some making their bite felt but not stopping the dragon and his rider.

Focusing on the remaining ships, Catrin imploded most and just blew holes in the sides of the rest as her fatigue threatened to overcome her.

Flying in behind a fleeing ship, Catrin swayed in the saddle and had no good angle for an attack but found she needed none as Kyrien came in low and grabbed the railing at the bow, their speed and inertia carrying them forward and bringing the ship with them, forcing its prow into the waves and eventually flipping the ship over forward.

When not a single ship remained, Catrin felt some sense of satisfaction, which soon turned to even greater anger. Though the men clung to flotsam or drowned, Catrin could see that the demons and giants simply swam away, like a dark current moving in the direction the ships had been headed. Unwilling to grant them this victory, Catrin attacked the seas themselves. Hurling balls of compressed air, she blasted away the water to leave the demons bare. Roaring, she sent them into the air then slammed them back down. Dark water rushed back in to fill the void, and none escaped Catrin's wrath.

Kyrien expressed nothing after the battle, but Catrin could feel the same sense of disappointment in him as she felt in herself. It hadn't helped. The vengeance had not eased her pain. But she did not regret it. This darkness had to be stopped, and if that was how she met her end, then she would die an honorable and worthwhile death. She reminded herself that she was a good-hearted person who would not willingly bring violence to those who did not deserve it. But she was cursed to know that some truly did deserve it, and for them, she would become the nightmare.

Chapter 2

Even the mighty can be laid low.
--Morif, soldier

* * *

"What did I just do?" Durin asked as deep booms rumbled and echoed through the keep, lower and different from anything that had come before. Standing within the circular room, he stared helplessly at the stone tile on which he stood; it was now depressed and activated, for good or ill.

"That one means water, silly," Trinda said. "I said to step on the mountains, not water."

"Water?" Brother Vaughn said as if to himself.

"Uh, so I suppose I should step on that one?" Durin asked, pointing at a carving similar to the one depicting water, only there was but a single set of wavy lines with sharper peaks.

Trinda gave him a look that said, *Duh!*

Strom just shrugged.

Stretching to make the long step without slipping and stepping on the wrong tile, Durin jumped. When he landed, the tile sank down, and moments later a grinding noise sounded from directly above them. Dust and dirt fell around them, and the ceiling of the chamber suddenly retreated, revealing a gaping cylindrical chasm above them. Though it retained its circular shape and soared all the way up to open air, the shaft was far from clear. The debris of ages had gathered there, including vines that looked like tree branches. This would not have been so troubling if the floor of the chamber had not begun to rise at an alarming rate. Within the space of a breath, all opportunity for escape was gone. The doorway through which they had come disappeared below them.

Strom pulled Prios's still unconscious form away from the outer edge of the cylinder as sparks flew and bits of rock were blasted away. Above them the obstructions grew ever closer, and Durin could think of no way to save them. There seemed no way to make the floor stop rising. Durin moved to every tile to see if he could make it stop, but the rapid ascent continued unabated. He looked up at the rapidly approaching debris that would kill them, and Durin felt cold wash over him--the harsh realization that he was about to die. Trinda stood next to him, looking upward, and in that last moment, he felt sorry for her.

"Sorry," he said.

Trinda just stuck her tongue out at him then thrust her hands into the air, her eyes squeezed shut and her tongue sticking out of the side of her mouth. Above them, the air shimmered, and as the debris raced in to crush them, the translucent shield blasted through, sending an ever-increasing cloud of vines and stone racing before it as the walls of the cylinder were blasted clean.

Without warning, they began to slow, leaving a strange feeling in Durin's gut. Light erupted around them, and the air above was filled with soaring debris, much of which was caught by a swift crosswind and sent crashing down the side of the mountain. Bits and pieces fell around them, but most of the big pieces had been carried by the wind.

"You can put your arms down now," Durin said with a bit of sarcasm, but then he considered for a moment that Trinda had just saved him for the third time. Gusts of wind cast stinging sand into the air, but Durin could not avert his eyes from the sight. Only a low, jagged stone wall surrounded them; nothing obscured the view of the twin valleys below and all the way to the sea on all sides. Much of the scenery was marred by the presence of the demon armies and dragons resting on the heights.

Feeling exposed and knowing how vulnerable they were to dragons while standing on the top of this mighty peak, Durin whispered, "How do we get back down?"

Trinda just shrugged, "I don't know."

Looking at the tiles again, Durin saw that the one with mountainlike shapes carved on it had risen back into place and was level with the other tiles. Knowing that dragons might come investigate the commotion at any moment, Durin stepped back onto the tile with mountains carved on it, hoping it would take them back down and slowly at that. Nothing happened, and cold fear bloomed in his gut. Taking another look at the tiles, Durin saw a symbol that looked like fire, and there was one that looked like water, but he didn't think those were what they needed. He was just trying to figure out what the tile with a series of vertical lines meant when a dark shadow passed over them, sending more sand and dirt into the air.

Strom ran to the stone wall and looked down. After a moment, he drew a sharp intake of breath. Trinda crouched by the still form of Prios; the extent of his injuries was difficult to gauge. He'd nearly given his life to protect his son, and now his son was gone. Durin did what he could to stifle his worry and ran to where Strom stood. Looking down from the dizzying height stole Durin's breath.

Strom shouted, "Look out, Brother Vaughn! *Dragon!*"

Durin hadn't seen him at first, but then he saw the robed man running. He was both thankful that Brother Vaughn was alive and terrified that he wouldn't be for very much longer. Looking tiny at such a distance, the man who had been Sinjin's mentor, and thus also Durin's, stood nearly halfway across an expanse of open grass. There was no way he could move fast enough to get to the cover of the trees or back to the river. Sound carried well in the valley, and they saw Brother Vaughn look up. Durin could only imagine his puzzlement at hearing their voices from the top of the mountain. Then he saw the dragon and turned to run. Durin could see that he would not be fast enough, his death a near certainty. In desperation, Durin threw rocks at the swooping dragon, but the beast was far beyond his reach.

The thought of seeing Brother Vaughn taken made Durin nearly ill, but then he heard something that chilled his blood. Trinda sang. The dragon, fixated on its target, did not react at first, but the longer Trinda sang, the less intent the feral remained on Brother Vaughn. Durin realized that this might save Brother Vaughn, for which he was truly grateful, but he also realized that it made their own situation far more dangerous. The dragons would come. The sight of it was more terrifying than anything Durin had ever seen. Mottled black and gray feral dragons came from every direction. Knifing through the air with economy of motion and awe-inspiring speed, they nipped at each other, issuing deep, guttural growls that sounded like rolling drums, flying with what seemed pure aggression. With one last glance, he saw that Brother Vaughn was near halfway to the trees. Durin looked back up at Strom, who appeared as worried as he was.

Looking again at the carved flames, Durin realized that what he'd thought represented fire also resembled the formations of rock that hung down in the God's Eye. Stepping across, knowing there was no time for discussion, Durin's heart leaped when the stone started sinking beneath his weight, but it stopped sooner than the others had, and nothing happened. It was stuck. The dragons were near, and waves of primal fear washed over Durin and paralyzed him. Strom stepped closer, landing on a tile with a circle carved into it. Nothing happened. The stone Durin stood upon still didn't move, except as part of a tremor that seemed to shake the entire mountain. An instant later, Reaver peered over the jagged stones, his gleaming teeth dwarfing even Strom while promising a knife's edge. Hot breath buffeted them like storm winds, and the eyes of the enormous feral narrowed, seemingly more concerned with understanding how the humans had come to be at the top of a mountain he was guarding rather than looking for a meal, which to Durin was far more frightening. The beast looked as if it had been in a fight every day of its existence. One dark, back-turned horn was sheared off, leaving a jagged stump, and deep crevices ran across its face, making its scales look like a macabre mosaic. Jagged teeth lined a mouth that smelled of death, and Durin nearly retched. Black nostrils flared with each powerful breath, which knocked the shrubbery low and sent small stones tumbling into the valley below.

Nearby, Strom crouched and Prios stirred. Trinda sang. Durin reached out to grab her, but she stepped out of his grasp and closer to Reaver, a feat that Durin was unable to match; deep-seated and overpowering fear rooted his boots in stone. What looked him in the eye was the worst possible nightmare. Trinda took another step; then her pale and delicate hand landed on glossy black scales and deep scars. Reaver remained still for the briefest instant, but then he snorted and drew back his angular and monstrous head. The force of his breath sent Trinda stumbling backward right into Durin's arms. Their combined weight on the jammed tile resulted in a loud snap. Reaver roared a deafening call filled with malice and intent, and the stone beneath Durin dropped.

* * *

The echoing call from above spurred Brother Vaughn to reckless speed. He'd known that trying to cover open ground would be risky, but dragons had been coming to drink at the river's edge, and it would only have been a matter of time until one of them had found him. As it was, he'd been cold and wet and not thinking clearly. Then the top of the mountain exploded. Brother Vaughn had looked up but saw little besides a cloud of debris and quickly continued his trek, knowing Reaver would come to investigate. Now he stood amid grasses not tall enough to hide him and Reaver bearing down on him. Breathing hard, he pushed his body for all the speed it could produce, knowing it would not be enough. The trees were too far away, and the shadow of the beast closed in behind him. It felt as if all was lost when a familiar and wordless tune rang through the valley like a seductive bell, and Brother Vaughn could only hope the dragon would be drawn away by the singing of the little girl. He could not figure out how she could have gotten to the top of the mountain, but that girl was turning out to be a worthy ally. The instant he had the thought, he regretted it as the realization came that Trinda was at the top of the mountain singing for the dragons.

Darkness rushed up on him, and driven by instinct, Brother Vaughn dived to the ground. An ill wind rustled his robes, and an enormous pair of claws tore trenches in the grass only a hand's width from where Brother Vaughn now lay. Looking up, he saw Reaver extend his mighty wings and soar up to the top of the mountain, where he came to a crashing halt, his claws digging into the stone and his massive head peering down at Trinda.

Jumping up and down, Brother Vaughn tried to get Reaver's attention, but then he realized exactly what he was doing, and he started, once again, to run, hoping to make it to the trees before any other dragons saw him. Like in nightmares, the black devils arrived just as he thought of them, and he wasn't certain what he was seeing was real. The only thing that kept the horror from overcoming him was the fact that the dragons were not looking for him; they were looking for Trinda. That thought made him feel no better. Shouts and singing continued to echo from above, and he couldn't help but look up when he heard Reaver snort. A moment later it looked as if the top of the mountain had exploded again. Dust and debris filled the air. Reaver reared back and lunged at the top of the mountain three times as quickly as a striking snake but with stone-shattering force. With a frustrated and angry cry, Reaver leaped back into the air.

Brother Vaughn could only hope that Trinda had found some way to escape. At that moment, though, all he could do was run.

To his astonishment, the world above him erupted again only moments later, and Godsland trembled.

* * *

Catrin and Kyrien rested in the Terhilian Keys for only one night, and she worried over his fitness for battle. His wounds had healed with her assistance, but still she worried.

I am designed for flight, and I can rest while flying. Granted, it is easier to rest on the ground or in water, but I am well rested nonetheless.

His annoyance at her worrying over his well-being was clear, but she could not help it. She cared about him deeply, and their fates were forever bound together. In many ways their desires and intentions had become one, as had their guilt. It was something that only the two of them could share, as no one else alive could claim the guilt of having caused the loss of an entire species. Kyrien's guilt was all the worse since it was his species, but Catrin's pain was as close as anyone alive could get. There had been time for thought and deep reflection, for tears and rage. There had been time to see changes in herself that could not be undone.

As the Godfist materialized from the rising mists, a sick feeling crowded Catrin's gut, and she could feel Kyrien's apprehension as well, but that anxiety soon fanned the banked coals of her anger. This was her homeland, and she would purge it of these wretched devils. Her son was gone, and she wanted to scream. She had let him down when he'd needed her. She had abandoned him for an unsuccessful quest to save the dragons, and now she had lost them both. Miserable over her failure, the pain of it nearly made her burst. Only the presence of her husband's spirit and those of loved ones still shining from within the hold, waiting for her to save them from this menace, gave her strength and hope.

Black ships at the northern harbor came into view first. They would receive no warning and be afforded no mercy. These invaders of her homeland would pay for their arrogance, and Kyrien soared low over the waves, aiming for the ships. A rumbling echo reached them, and a dark cloud rose up from an inland mountain peak. Her uncertainty of the cause became secondary to the realization that the air around that peak was now filled with feral dragons. All of them were in one spot.

It took the sum of her will to resist attacking the ships but she managed. Soaring in low, Kyrien wound through the twisting valleys; Catrin held on and tried to anticipate his next shift based on the approaching terrain. Together they found a rhythm and moved almost as one. Cries occasionally rose up from beneath them, but no warning bells or other alarms rang out, and Catrin watched for signs of trouble. Black armies crowded the valleys, but they were marching out in orderly retreat, leaving behind an obliterated valley. What had been a thriving community was now little more than ash and stone and mud.

Another shout rose from beneath them as they passed, and Kyrien soared higher as the alarm bells rang. The ferals, it seemed, had recovered from their fixation and were in the process of dispersing. The alarms, though, had them all coming toward that sound. The sky ahead became aerial chaos; only instinct kept the dragons from colliding as all of them turned at once to intercept Kyrien.

Catrin launched no early attack and waited for as many of them as possible to get close. Trying to appear wounded and weak, she delayed, her true power kept hidden. She knew these cowardly beasts, and she wanted them to believe that the odds were overwhelmingly in their favor. Instead of worrying about how dangerous their prey was, she wanted them to worry over getting their share of the meal.

Reaver soared closer, an avatar of madness at the head of this storm of violence. Waiting was terrifying, but she had to let them get closer. Reaver alone instilled debilitating fear, but the raging horde was indescribable. Such fear should not exist, for it is almost more than the mind can bear. What approached was madness. She could feel the will of Reaver trying to crush her, trying to subjugate her will, trying to find a way to shatter it completely. Like water through sand, Catrin felt her energy draining away, and every breath became less her own. The gnarled beast had synchronized its breathing with hers, matched its heartbeat with hers; it felt her fear and knew her pain and Catrin screamed.

Kyrien was there.

Unaffected by Reaver's psychic attacks, Kyrien did something that Catrin had never imagined: he took control of her body. Using Catrin, the saddle, and the lance, he leveled an attack on Reaver. Though it felt as if the attack had been wrenched from her gut, it struck Reaver so hard, he looked like a swatted fly.

Two other ferals were injured in the first strike, but Catrin struggled against Kyrien's will. "Neither of you can control me!" she screamed, and Kyrien immediately released the compulsion.

There was no time for anything more. Dragons flew in close; others landed nearby where crowds of men parted.

Catrin launched a series of attacks that would have made Prios proud. Short bursts of thunderous energy cleaved the air and struck dragons, sending ripples through their bodies as the force of the blows spread. At least a dozen dropped from the skies after a single strike and did not rise again; others regained the heights. Aerial chaos reached a new zenith, and only Kyrien could predict where they would be in the next instant.

When Kyrien leveled off for an instant, he gave Catrin the chance to launch another round of attacks. Using the air itself as a weapon, Catrin created a massive concussion. After what had felt like tearing the winds apart, they soared through a cloud of dragons in a variety of states. Some were stunned, others retreating, and a handful were in free fall, quite possible already dead. Kyrien did what he could to evade the attacks of dragons still in the fight, but there was no avoiding some impacts, and Catrin did her best to move away from where the next contact would be.

The air before them once again cleared. Blue skies showed no hint of the danger behind them. But the battle was far from won.

Looking back, Catrin set her jaw. Along the valley floor raced a dozen smaller dragons, now with black-robed men atop their backs. Catrin wasn't certain if Reaver was dead or incapacitated since she could find no sign of his body. For the moment, these riders presented an even greater threat, and she could not let them escape. Turning away from the riderless ferals, Kyrien and Catrin soared over the Pinook Valley, gaining on the mounted formation. Edling's Wall rose up before them. It took a moment for Catrin to understand what she saw. The massive trade gates along with much of the surrounding wall had been blasted away. Almost too late Catrin saw the black scales that waited just beyond the open gate.

Rising to his full height, Reaver extended his mighty wings and roared in triumph. His roar was cut short as Catrin leveled an especially deadly attack at his exposed chest. Reaver's flesh moved like water as it waved away from the impact. Fingers of plasma rolled over the screaming dragon, and the force drove the massive creature backward.

Kyrien landed, his claws on the mighty black dragon's neck. Pushing off as hard as he could, he thrust Reaver the rest of the way over backward and sent himself and Catrin back into the air, which began exploding around them.

Chapter 3

Creation is the act of being unwilling to allow something not to exist.
--Aleese Berunda, artist

* * *

Catrin had often wondered what it would feel like to be hit by one of her attacks, and now she knew. The energy felt as if it would rip her apart from the inside out, and the pain could not be compared to anything she'd ever experienced. Each time the pain from one excruciating attack eased, another slammed her from a different angle, and she was tossed from side to side by the force. These men on dragonback were potent and fearsome adversaries; she could feel their hatred of her. She would have screamed if she could have gathered any air into her chest; this attack would surely suffocate her if it continued. In the next instant, though, she was sucking air into her lungs as they had turned upside-down and the attacks simultaneously ceased. Feeling as if her ribs were broken and with blood on her lips, Catrin could do little more than breathe, and that was difficult.

Turbulent air buffeted them, and Kyrien's flight path wobbled. Through their bond she could sense his pain, but she could not form a cohesive thought required for action. With growing horror, she watched Kyrien's head jerked side to side, absorbing the attacks. With a thunderous crack, a mighty blow caught Kyrien under the chin, snapping his head back toward Catrin. In the next instant, they were plummeting toward a rocky death. Knowing Kyrien was unconscious and would be unable to save them, Catrin quickly, almost instinctively, mimicked what she'd done when flying the *Slippery Eel*. The knowledge that the ship would never sail or fly again haunted Catrin, but she had no time for those thoughts. Flying an unconscious dragon was nothing like flying a ship, and Catrin nearly crashed them into the trees. The dark riders had turned and were gaining on her, their dragons looking fresh and ready for a fight.

Getting low in the saddle, Catrin connected with it and the lance she held, her body humming with power, the vibration singing in her ears. Air shimmering around her, she focused on the approaching formation, which was tight and orderly. Reaching out from them with deadly intent, red lightning tested Catrin's formidable defenses. She waited until they were so close that they could not turn away before she launched a single, concentrated attack. A craterous implosion again turned the skies themselves into a potent weapon. Ferals folded like dried husks and dropped from the sky--all, that was, save two.

With a suddenness that made it seem surreal to Catrin, a dragon and rider appeared beneath. The rider's hood was blown back, and his mottled gray flesh could be seen within. His madness was complete, and he hurled insanity at her. There was no pain, no fire, no iron; there was only disorienting madness. Where was she again? What was she supposed to be doing?

The questions took only an instant to cross her mind, but that instant was all the time the feral needed to close the gap between them. The feral sailed toward Kyrien's exposed belly, knowing it would have no trouble killing an unconscious dragon.

Power pulsed along the lance Catrin held, and she hoped her control of their flight was sufficient. Doing as she had done so many years before on the *Slippery Eel,* Catrin created a wing structure that slowed them. By applying this to only one wing, she caused them to suddenly spiral downward and directly into the feral's path. There was no time for dragon or rider to avoid the collision, and Catrin thrust out with the lance. The gleaming weapon danced with energy, and power leaped from its tip before it touched the breast of that mighty feral dragon. Momentum carried both dragons forward, and the lance's impact pressed Catrin backward until the back of her head touched Kyrien's scales. Feeling as if her legs might break, Catrin watched the wild-eyed feral impale itself.

The deeper the lance sank, the more slowly the feral approached, until the beast reversed direction and started to fall. Catrin was nearly pulled from the saddle by her grip on the lance. Remembering the demon with the glass lance that had killed the regent queen, Catrin gave the handle a twist. The lance did not shatter as the glass one's had, and the pommel was wrenched from her hands. Along with the dying dragon and its doomed rider, Catrin's lance fell.

Reeling from the release, Catrin lost sight of the remaining dragon and rider, and she decided it would be best to let that one go. Her vision swam, and Kyrien had only begun to stir. His wings were doing more of the work, but Catrin knew they would fall from the sky if she did not keep them stabilized. She could think of only one place safe for them to land, and she guided them north and east, an odd feeling in her gut, as if none of this were real.

When the sands of the Arghast Desert came into view, warm air greeted them. Before Catrin could figure out how to safely land, Kyrien returned to full, if tenuous, consciousness and instinctively used the thermals to gain altitude. After taking a few moments to compose himself and convey to Catrin that he would live, Kyrien used the altitude to gain momentum. Soon they were skimming over the desert sand. Catrin's head spun with the sensation of speed as the sands flowed beneath them, broken by plains of rock, some with openings visible in vertical rock faces.

On the horizon came what Catrin had been looking for: tall peaks surrounding a mostly hidden valley visible from only a specific angle. There waited soft sands and cool water and the tribes of Arghast. Catrin could only hope that they remained loyal to her and would welcome her and Kyrien and protect them. It was, again, more than she wanted to ask of the Arghast, who had already given more than her conscience could bear.

Lush grasses surrounded emerald green water, and thick-maned horses grazed amid the rich pastures. With a single roar, Kyrien announced their coming, which brought something akin to controlled panic to the valley.

From what Catrin could see, most of the Arghast within the valley were running to their horses. One horse had broken free from the lines and was subdued only when a fleet-footed man blindfolded the animal with a blanket. From outside of the valley, riders sent long trails of dust into the air as they raced toward the valley entrance.

Kyrien was sluggish and Catrin knew she would have to guide him in. The peaks surrounding the oasis were so tall that Catrin dreaded the thought of having to descend into the narrow valley from such a great height; it would have been a terrifying experience with Kyrien under complete control. As it was, they were both just barely conscious.

Men on horseback gathered near the valley entrance, and they pointed wildly into the skies behind her and Kyrien. The meaning was clear from their frantic movements, and when the attack struck, it at least did not come as a complete surprise. Pain exploded all over Catrin's body as every one of her muscles contracted as hard as they could. Red lightning flowed around her, and she lost her grip, only the saddle straps keeping her on Kyrien's back. The shouting from below grew louder, and the Arghast did their best to attack the feral and rider that were bearing down on Catrin and Kyrien. The sound of metal striking dragon scales rang out and echoed within the valley.

With the smell of burning hair heavy in her nostrils, Catrin did her best to catch her breath. The mountains rushed toward them with what seemed impossible speed, and Catrin prepared herself for impact. They were moving too fast to land outside the oasis, as Catrin had expected they would. Suddenly Catrin's guts moved to her ears as Kyrien executed a drastic maneuver.

Throwing himself up onto his left wing, he put Catrin in the awkward position of staring sideways at rock formations that were hurtling toward her. Despite her trust in Kyrien, she screamed. Below, his left wingtip nearly touched the valley floor and a trail of dust rose up in its wake. Above, his other wing twitched and flexed as he avoided jagged edges. Ducking as low to the saddle as she could, Catrin prayed Kyrien would find a way to squeeze them both through. In an instant it was over, and Kyrien just as suddenly righted himself.

Whipped from side to side by the unexpected move, Catrin barely had time to regain her handholds and brace herself before they slammed into cold, green water. At first Kyrien dragged his claws in the water, slowing them, but then he gave a mighty grunt, and they dropped into the lake with the full force of his weight. A tremendous roar filled the air, and a wave of white water flew before them. Still their speed carried them forward, and the air was forced from Catrin's lungs in a whoosh as they slowed.

Ahead, the water grew shallow before ending at a narrow beach, which opened into a slim pasture of grassland. The pasture was relatively small given the confines of the valley, and horses crowded, trembling against the valley wall. Kyrien skimmed across the water and pitched forward when his chest struck sand. His mighty head stretched into the grassland, and his jaw snapped shut when it struck the ground, most of his body still in the water. The horses beyond were soaked by the wave that preceded the dragon, and they stood trembling and drenched. Kyrien simply gave a great sigh and closed his eyes. If Catrin hadn't been strapped in, she would have fallen from the saddle in a heap.

The noise level in the valley continued to rise, and Catrin felt every hair on her body stand. Turning to look behind her, she saw the feral and rider break through the narrow valley entrance. Even as they righted themselves, Catrin could feel this man gathering energy and focusing his will. This attack would do more than singe her hair. Drawing a deep breath, Catrin prepared to defend herself, but the tribes of Arghast came to her aid.

They did not take kindly to those who trespassed on their lands, and this valley was among their most sacred places. Without the benefit of even a saddle, a tribesman rode atop a shining black stallion whose mane and foretop flowed like the sea at night. Long spear in his hand, he slowly but steadily stood on the horse's back, which was nearly level and steady despite the full gallop at which they traveled.

As the feral approached, its rider stood in his saddle, which gave Catrin a good view of the dark leather that encased his lower torso. It gripped the man in a way that kept him secure while allowing for a limited range of motion, just as Catrin's saddle did for her, yet accomplished in a completely different manner. She had only an instant to make this observation as the charging tribesman leaped from atop his horse. In a single, fluid motion, the man flipped in the air directly in front of the feral dragon, which snapped its jaws at him. Just before the dark rider released his attack, the Arghast used both arms to throw the spear with all his might. Red plasma reached out to Catrin in what she knew was the precursor to red lightning, but then the spear struck the dark rider full in the chest. The man's torso appeared to implode from the impact, and only the saddle kept him in place. Still the feral came. The Arghast warrior, rotating in mid air, was about to hit the sand when the feral's tail whipped to the side and struck him like a stone sledge.

The man who'd saved Catrin's life now lay unmoving in the sand. Overwhelming sadness and responsibility welled up in Catrin, and she nearly swooned. Kyrien, who had not moved a muscle since their landing must have been saving his energy for one last attack. His tail flicked upward and struck the feral an equally devastating blow. The mighty, winged beast reeled. Carrying too much speed, it careened across the valley. With two great flaps of its wings, the feral tried to gain altitude, but it was too late. The dragon slammed into the valley walls with enough force to break a section of stone free from where it had rested for eons.

The Arghast and their horses retreated from the area, and no one was hurt when the stone and dragon plummeted to the grassland below. Arghast warriors rushed in to make sure the feral dragon was dead.

For a time, only the nickering of nervous horses filled the air, and Catrin tried to focus her thoughts. Slowly she started to unbuckle herself, but a crowd of Arghast elders erupted into cries begging her to stop. It took a moment for Catrin to understand, but then she stopped. This seemed to appease the men, and they approached slowly, their hoods pulled back to reveal their faces, and their heads bowed to Kyrien, who was oblivious to their homage.

"May we look at saddle?" a man asked, and Catrin thought she recognized him, but she could not recall his name.

The only thing she could manage was a lopsided nod.

The men were quick about their business. They unbuckled Catrin's straps, noting how they worked as they did so. Her head now lolled from side to side, and she was only vaguely aware of the commotion around her. There was a rushing, pounding sound in her ears, and the world took on an amber hue. Catrin slid from the saddle as soon as the straps were loosed, her limbs not responding, and she was glad the men were there to catch her. Younger men and women reached up to her from the water, and she was gently carried to shore, where she was placed in a tent of the finest Arghast silk. Strange faces looked down at her and murmured their concern. Wet cloths were used to wipe away blood and grime. Within moments, Catrin succumbed to sleep.

* * *

Durin wasn't sure which was worse, traveling upward on what he now called "the rock of death" or hurtling downward. When at last the stone beneath their feet began to slow its unreasonably fast descent, Durin prepared himself, not certain where they would end up. At least, he thought, it had gotten them out of the reach of Reaver, though bits of rock had rained down on them from his attacks on the mountain itself. Soon, though, Durin was rewarded with a most remarkable view. Before him were mighty fingers of rock reaching down toward the glistening surface of a subterranean lake. The rock of death had delivered them to the God's Eye.

211

Having been directly below where he was currently standing hundreds of times, he knew that there was no indication from below that this place even existed, yet a finely carved stone railing stood before him, giving him a commanding view of the God's Eye. Seeing the barges drifting in the water with no one on them gave Durin a terrible feeling in his gut. Something else nagged at his senses, but he couldn't place what it was; still, it bothered him deeply.

"We need to get Prios to Millie and Mirta," Strom said, "and they are in the kitchens. It looks like there's a hidden stair leading down from here to the keep-side entrance of the God's Eye. The way to the kitchens is most likely still blocked. As much as I hate to say it, I think we are going to have to go back down, and return the way we came."

"That way is longer," Trinda said.

Durin turned and gave her a look that clearly said he thought she was daft then began looking at the stones again. "Do you think the one with the straight lines will take us back where we started?"

The fact that Trinda was the only one likely to have a good answer was less than comforting. She refused to answer, though, and just turned away with a huff. In that moment, there came a splashing sound from below. A chill crept into Durin's blood, and he moved slowly to look over the ledge, doing his best to remain concealed. Strom and Trinda crept to the edge as well. What Durin saw brought him no comfort and confirmed their decision. Several black masses moved through the water then disappeared beneath the surface, leaving only a few ripples to give evidence that they ever existed.

Strom caught Durin's eye and motioned back to the cylindrical platform. Though he doubted the demons would hear them under water, Durin and the others remained silent. Trying to decide which stone to jump on, Durin considered the one with three concentric circles on it, and one with what looked like a fish on it. Strom looked at Durin and shrugged then made as if he were tossing coin. Going with his gut, Durin waited until Trinda was fully on the circular platform and stepped onto the stone with the straight lines on it. There was no hesitation this time, and it felt as if the stone moved with almost no resistance and would simply keep on falling. When it finally stopped, Durin stumbled from the suddenness of it. Then the entire cylinder began to slowly descend. This, Durin could deal with; he never again wanted to experience anything like their trips to the top of the mountain and down to the God's Eye. His guts still felt as if they had been tied in knots. When the platform slowed and stopped again, they stood in complete darkness. Light poured, then, from the herald globe that Trinda held. The way it lit her face made her look like a living sculpture, dainty and smooth.

Looking around, Trinda rolled her eyes at Durin. Dark halls stretched away for a short distance in two directions, but both passages had collapsed long ago and were completely blocked.

"Try again. We need to go back down and return the way we came," Strom said, and Prios stirred at his feet. "That is the only way that should be open to the kitchens."

"Open," Durin said, "because of us. The demons can get to everyone because of us. We should never have left them."

Strom nodded. "I know."

Trinda just looked at them both as if they were idiots then stepped on the stone tile that had what looked like snakes carved on it. Durin had never even considered stepping on that one for obvious reasons. The platform descended much more slowly before depositing them smoothly and gently in the room where they had started. With her arms over her chest, Trinda wore a smug look.

Prios moaned and put his hand on his head. His eyes came slowly open.

"Can you stand?" Strom asked.

Prios nodded, slowly, cautiously. He made a motion that let Strom know he needed a moment longer, and Durin could see his chest expanding and contracting for a series of deep breaths. Then he extended his hand, and Strom helped him up. Prios looked around, a question clear on his face: *Sinjin?*

Strom shook his head and laid a compassionate hand on Prios' shoulder. A tear fell from the man's eye, but then granite resolve settled over him. With a firm nod, he turned back to Strom and motioned for them to get moving.

Durin walked forward without a word, Trinda at his side. Neither spoke. Uncomfortable silence stretched as Trinda's instincts led the way. Prios looked at the girl on occasion, a puzzled expression on his face, but he made no move to communicate further. Durin always marveled at Prios's ability to communicate without words, and knowing he could do so at any time made his silence all the more poignant.

A look at Strom revealed his thoughts. The big man walked with his shoulders hunched and his head down. Durin felt bad for him, knowing that all of this was really his fault and that he had just dragged Strom into it. If he'd never told anyone about making the keep move, they wouldn't be in this mess. Then there was the fact that he'd made the keep move in the first place. Durin guessed that his silence was pretty easy for the others to figure out. It pained him that his loved ones were endangered because of him. His first mistake may have been the result of laziness, but the second truly was the result of his desire to help everyone.

Now he'd just gone and made everything worse. He wasn't really certain how he could have made things any worse until they had traveled beyond the underground river and plain and were nearing the halls that would take them back to the kitchens. There they met a peculiar sight: water flowed out of the halls. Water, Durin thought. One of those tiles had had water on it. A cold feeling grew in his gut until they reached the room where he and Strom had poured wine and pickle juice into the glowing rune, which had caused the hold to move and the passage behind them to open. Once there, he could clearly hear Miss Mariss cursing the name of the person responsible for all this water.

"When those fools get back, I'll wring their necks."

Prios looked at Strom and Durin, put his hand on his forehead, and shook his head. Trinda did something he wasn't certain he'd ever seen her do before: she smiled. It was a wicked little smile, and there was no warmth in it. It was very clear that this smile was at Durin's expense. Considerable effort had been put into keeping the runes dry, but most of the water flowed to the far side of the hall. Durin suspected this was part of the ancients' design, and he marveled, once again, at what those people had accomplished. He could not imagine how they had done it all, or even for what purpose, but their mastery was clear.

Prios stepped to the front and led them to the kitchens. When Miss Mariss saw him, her face drained of color. "Get Millie," she said. "Prios is hurt, and..."

Her words fell away when she saw Durin and Strom standing behind Prios. "Which one of you is responsible for all this water?"

No one said anything, but Trinda smiled and pointed at Durin.

"Thanks," Durin said.

"I should have known," Miss Mariss said with clear exasperation. "In fact, I did know. You just confirmed it. Well, I don't care what you have to do, but you go back there and *turn it off*. Do you understand me? Don't do anything else. Don't try to save us, please, whatever you do."

Durin didn't bother to argue. Instead he just said, "Yes, ma'am."

"It wasn't the boy's fault," Strom said. Miss Mariss wheeled on him, but he held firm. "Trinda told him to jump on the tile with mountains on it, and he jumped onto the one with waves instead. It was an honest mistake."

Durin looked up, surprised by Strom's words, even if they were true. Miss Mariss just took a deep breath and sighed. "Fine. Can't say as I completely understand what that means, but I won't be angry with him for the moment, at least not for that. Fair enough? Now go."

Oddly it made Durin feel much better.

After being forced into a chair by Miss Mariss, Prios looked up to Strom. His eyes conveyed his thoughts. Sinjin was his only concern, and Strom wished he could go with Prios. Torn, Strom also needed to get Durin back to the right place to turn off the water. He wasn't even sure how they would know if they had done it or not without coming all the way back to check, but he really didn't have any other choice. He couldn't expect Durin to go alone because all of this was partially his fault.

Moving his head and his eyes to one side, Prios might as well have said, "Go."

Only a nod was exchanged between them after that; everything was understood. Strom hoped they would meet again.

* * *

Familiar smells invaded Catrin's slumber. She'd been here before, all this had happened before, only this time was different. Again, there were Arghast outside her tent, waiting to serve her, but this time they needed no proof of who she was. Catrin was different this time; she, too, no longer needed proof of who she was. She was the most powerful person in the world, and it no longer terrified her; instead it filled her with resolve. She knew what must be done, and she steeled herself to the necessity of it.

Her stomach growling, Catrin could no longer resist the smell of food, and she pulled aside the tent flap. The muted hush turned to absolute silence, save the occasional rattle of harness. The last time she'd stood before the Arghast, there had been more of them. Catrin had asked them then to protect her and her people. She couldn't help but feel that her request was the reason there were now fewer Arghast. Part of her knew that some were probably still within Dragonhold, but that did not account for the stark contrast in their numbers, and Catrin's mood would not allow for justification. She must choose her words wisely, or the regent dragons might not be the only ones to fade from existence.

The Arghast, since they had become convinced of her power, had been the staunchest of allies and had risked everything for her. They came close to worshipping her. Though she wanted nothing of the sort, she had never tried to discourage it since doing so would inherently reduce her influence over them. Kyrien, too, they worshipped, and in some ways, they showed him even greater respect, which suited Catrin fine. Even as the assembled crowd gathered before her, a host of Arghast were hard at work scrubbing Kyrien's scales and claws. Her concern for him lessened when he spoke in her mind.

This is not at all unpleasant.

If not for the assembled throng, Catrin would have laughed, but she suppressed her mirth, knowing the Arghast did not always understand her. "Thank you, mighty tribes of Arghast. You have once again come to my aid, and I am grateful. And my most noble steed and companion, Kyrien, is also in your debt." These words rolled over the Arghast like wildfire, and the assemblage hooted and raised a hearty cry. It seemed the Arghast did not want the Herald of Istra to have to ask for food, as she had so many years ago. Men and women rushed forward and offered her a dazzling variety of food, many of which Catrin remembered and had even dreamed of. She reached first, almost involuntarily, to a cake made of roasted nuts, honey, and partially dried fruit. It tasted even more wonderful than she remembered. When someone brought her a leather of desert mist, Catrin thought of Mika, and she sent blessings to the spirit of her old friend. He had been instrumental in her negotiations with the tribes. They were a difficult people to understand. At times they groveled before her, and at other times it seemed they made impossible demands of her, demands beyond her ability to satisfy.

"We have cared for you and your dragon," the man Catrin now recognized as Malluke of the Horse clan said. "Is there anything more that you require of us?"

It seemed an innocent enough question, but Catrin knew better. There would be a price. They would ask her to teach them to fly.

"Do you have any straw?"

The question caught Malluke by surprise. After a moment, he nodded.

"Do you have enough to make a stack as big around as Kyrien? And enough rope to tie it into a bundle?"

The man's eyes went wide, and a broad smile crossed his face. "Yes. We have that much straw. And we will stack it as you have said. Thank you, most honored Herald of Istra."

Catrin simply smiled and nodded. Malluke excitedly issued orders to his people, and it wasn't long before they scrambled to comply. Word of the straw dragon traveled fast.

Again, though, Catrin's eyes were drawn to where Kyrien rested, his wings extended in the sun, and people scrubbing, polishing, and oiling his hide. Still she knew he chafed under the saddle, and it was plain that the Arghast would not touch that mystical saddle without her permission.

Malluke followed her as she walked. "I will need assistance removing his saddle," Catrin said without a hint of emotion, though she could sense Malluke's anticipation building. "We must have somewhere to secure the saddle while Kyrien is not wearing it, and we should make sure it is very secure. It is a very precious saddle."

Malluke bowed down before her. "You honor us."

Catrin did not comment; instead, she walked to Kyrien's head. A teenage girl was stroking his closed eyelids, and he was practically purring. Laying her hands on him, she sent him energy.

No.

Kyrien's statement was not compulsion, but it also left no room for argument.

You need to heal as well. The tribes will take great pride in restoring my well-being, and I want them to have earned it. It's important.

Though she wasn't quite certain why it was important, Catrin smiled and asked, "Anything else?"

The saddle is restricting me... and it itches.

"Anything else?"

Be ready. We are being watched.

Before Catrin could turn to look, Kyrien showed her the image of a small feral dragon and its rider concealed on an overhang high above them. As if it had heard the entire exchange, the feral moved and sent rocks tumbling into the valley. Catrin and the Arghast all turned to where the sound had originated. Alarm cries rang out. Within moments, dozens of men wielded long spears, looking to have been made for the sole purpose of fighting dragons. Catrin admired the Arghast for their preparedness.

"The dark one knows it has lost the advantage of stealth," Catrin said, "and now it must wonder how deeply the tribes of Arghast will bite. It would appear they have very sharp teeth."

Malluke grinned at her, though most of the Arghast remained on high alert. Malluke quickly assigned rotating watches and instructed all spearman to remain on standby. In truth, few could take their eyes from the spot where the dragon and rider were now poorly concealed.

Still, the Arghast were dedicated and determined. Men and women carried and bound straw until they had constructed something roughly the same shape as Kyrien's torso. With the gathered now turned to face Catrin, waiting for their next instructions, Catrin took a moment to inspect their work. She made a point of checking the ropes that tied the bales and the larger ones that joined multiple bales together.

Then she turned to the Arghast. "This will suffice. Thank you." She knew she was risking their wrath, but she couldn't have them think her a pushover, no matter how powerful they knew her to be. This was, at its heart, a negotiation, and she intended to bargain from a place of power. She had come to these people a prisoner once, but now they must acknowledge her as a leader.

"Come," she said. "Let us remove the saddle from Kyrien and make him more comfortable." Another thing Catrin knew was that Kyrien was her greatest source of power over the Arghast, even if she hated to think of things in that way. Some of her closest companions had been Arghast, and the memory of their loss shamed her. Still, she needed these people, and they were not easily swayed. Using every opportunity, Catrin demonstrated that she knew Kyrien's mind and heart and that her communication with this most revered of steeds was complete. This, she knew, would be the way to earn their ultimate respect for her. If there was one thing that the Arghast respected, it was the bond between rider and steed. The fact that her steed had wings didn't hurt.

"Kyrien will now retract his wings and hold them up, so they are clear of the saddle. Then we can loosen the girths." The hush that fell over the tribes when Kyrien did as Catrin had said was broken only by the excited murmur over the saddle and its multiple girths, each one set at its own angle and with subtle stitches in the supple leather that helped the saddle conform to Kyrien's body.

For a moment, the air grew tense and the murmur angry when someone asked who would be allowed to touch the saddle first. Catrin had seen the Arghast negotiate before, and they didn't have time to staunch bleeding noses, so she held up her hand and the tribes fell silent. Sweeping her eyes across those assembled, Catrin's gaze landed on a young girl who was soaking wet and covered in sand from her efforts to scrub Kyrien's scales. Without hesitation, Catrin pointed to her. "This girl has earned the honor."

Given the unpredictability of the Arghast, Catrin didn't know how they would react, and it took a moment for the group to decide its mood. Slowly, though, the eldest of them turned to the young girl and bowed deeply. They did not grovel or supplicate, but they acknowledged the girl with great respect. The girl looked as if she might faint, and Catrin moved to her side, taking her arm to steady her. A collective gasp rolled over the Arghast.

Kyrien, too, had turned his head to gaze at the girl, and he nodded to her with closed eyes. *You chose well.*

Catrin smiled, and she held on tightly to the girl, who it seemed also heard Kyrien since her knees buckled when he spoke. "You've done well," Catrin said to her. "Things are going to change for you, but they will be good changes. Are you ready?"

The girl nodded unconvincingly.

"Can you tell me your name?"

"I am Mikala, most honored Herald of Istra."

"You can call me Catrin, Mikala."

"You honor me, Lady Catrin, just as you honored my grandfather."

"What was your grandfather's name?" Catrin asked, happy to see the girl's confidence growing. "And it's just Catrin, please."

"Yes, Lad--, uh, Catrin. The people called him Aged Goat."

Catrin didn't let her finish, "But his name was Mika, wasn't it?"

"Yes, Catrin," Mikala said with tears forming in her eyes. "You do him a great honor by remembering him."

"Your grandfather was a good man. I miss him."

Those words seemed to seal Mikala to Catrin, and the girl squeezed her hand. "What do you want me to do?" she asked.

"Place your hand on his side and convey your intentions to him through your physical bond."

"Just as I would with a horse," Mikala said in little more than a whisper. The girl closed her eyes, and a look of serene calm came over her face. She laughed. "He's funny."

A smile came to Catrin's face. She'd not gotten to see this side of Kyrien often enough, and it was a very nice change. For a moment, she felt the stress ease, and though she was still driven to get back to her family and to know that everyone was all right, she allowed herself this brief pleasure.

"Start with the outermost girth," Catrin said. "Then work your way in."

Mikala did as she was told, and Kyrien grunted with each girth that was loosened. When she finished, she turned back to Catrin with a questioning gaze.

"We're going to need some help to get the saddle the rest of the way off and moved over to the straw. Would you please gather six strong, young people and some rope?"

A giggle escaped Mikala's lips, and she smiled a shy smile. "He says he wants me to scratch first. May I? Please?"

"Of course," Catrin said.

Kyrien groaned and stretched out his neck, his top lip moving back and forth and a faraway look in his eyes. After ample scratching, Mikala brought a group of well-built young men and one young woman, along with coils of soft rope. The ancient saddle was lighter than the one Catrin had created and by a good margin, but it was still large and unwieldy. In truth, Kyrien could have wriggled out from under it now that the girths were unstrapped, but Catrin wanted the Arghast to have a chance to work with Kyrien and the saddle. They did, after all, expect her to teach them to fly dragons.

The young people Mikala had selected seemed uncertain if they were worthy of the honor. Watching the reactions of the elders, Catrin was proud to see them accepting the girl's decision, rather than taking Catrin's and Mikala's selections as an affront or an attempt to diminish their authority. This moment had, in its own way, been foreordained, and Catrin knew that the Arghast would tell tales of this day for generations to come.

The saddle came free easily in the strong hands of the young people, and it was only the size and complexity of the saddle that made it difficult for them to carry it. When they reached the bales of straw, great care was taken to treat the saddle with the utmost respect. Catrin was unsure if any of them could sense its power, but its beauty alone was enough to create a sense of awe. And of course, to the Arghast, saddles were sacred, especially the one that would help them fulfill what they believed was their destiny: to become dragon riders.

The energy in the valley was almost too much for Catrin, and it made her head swim. She sat down hard and put her head in her hands. Waves of excitement and anxiety washed over her from all around. The rush of blood in her ears drowned out the alarmed cries from the Arghast. Mikala was there, keeping her upright and speaking directly into Catrin's ear.

"Please, Lady Catrin, tell me what I can do."

"Call me Catrin," were the last words spoken before the world went dark.

* * *

In the darkness there was nothing but the smell of salt water and the creaking of cargo; it never stopped. The ship moved at the mercy of the waves, and so did Sinjin, his bindings secure. Cramped and chafed, he wanted to scream, but he saved his energy, knowing no good would come of it. After trying unsuccessfully to do as his mother had taught him and find his center, he remained frustrated and unsuccessful. In the end, though, he had nothing but time to consider the many questions in his mind and eventually found himself thinking these thoughts in a field of lush grass with blue skies and warm sunlight on his face. Only the smell of salt water ruined the illusion, that and the sound of boot steps on deck.

The sound of the hatch made Sinjin shy away from the coming light. He never knew what to expect when someone came through the hatch. Most of the crew ignored him or treated him with indifference, but there were a few who liked to take their frustrations out on him, and he squinted, waiting to get some sign of what was coming. Instead of blazing light, Sinjin saw Kendra silhouetted against churning black clouds in relative darkness. The girl slipped in as quietly as she could, but it still sounded thunderous in Sinjin's ears. He tensed when she came near and closed his eyes when she put her lips up to his ear. "A storm's coming," Kendra said without preamble. "If you want off this ship, this is your chance. The boats stand at the ready, and with the storm to provide cover, I think we can launch one without anyone seeing us."

"Us?" Sinjin asked after she pulled his gag free.

"Of course, us. You don't think I want to stay on a ship with these monsters, do you?"

"I don't know," Sinjin said.

"Oh, shut up and listen to me," Kendra said. "When I come back for you, you have to be ready. I'll cut you loose, and then you'll follow me up the ladder and keep low once up on deck. Just follow me and be ready to pull hard on the ropes when I tell you. Got it?"

"That's a terrible plan," Sinjin said.

"Do you have a better one?"

Sinjin had to admit that he didn't, so he remained silent.

"Then be ready when I come back for you. And eat all of this. You're going to need your strength. Into his hands she pressed smoked beef and dried orange slices. His bonds allowed for some movement, and he managed to get a bite of the smoked beef; it was hard and salty, and the smoky flavor emerged as he chewed. From within her jacket, Kendra produced a flask of water and a partially eaten loaf of bread. It took a moment to identify the items by feel, but Sinjin accepted them greedily. The water soothed his throat but made him cough as he tried to drink too much, too fast. It seemed to echo within the hold, and the sounds of boots above were getting closer. Kendra retreated again and was gone, the hatch slamming shut behind her.

Moments later, Sinjin could hear conversation from above. He couldn't make out the words, but he didn't like the sound of it. Even if Kendra's plan was crazy, he had to admit that it was better than no plan, which was what he had. For some reason, he still wasn't ready to show Kendra that he trusted her. It might be that he still wasn't certain he did trust her, yet he could find nothing for her to gain from plotting with him, except maybe to gain his trust. His thoughts traveled in a vicious circle that left him frustrated and angry. Only the increased action of the waves distracted him. What had been graceful rocking before had now become moments of being suspended in air before dropping off a cliff, only to rebound and do it again. It was making Sinjin's stomach churn.

Occasionally he heard shouting from above, but the hatch never moved. He began to wonder if someone had found out about Kendra's plan or if she had only been toying with him by getting his hopes up only to dash them. He had to accept the fact that Kendra might not be coming back for him. This led to the deeper admission that she was his only hope. He needed her. He hated to admit these things, even if only to himself, but without her in this situation, there would be nothing but darkness and no hope that he would ever escape from these monstrous captors. The ship leaned farther and farther away from the wind, and he considered the possibility that the waves would save the demons the trouble of killing him.

When the hatch slid open, Sinjin jumped and almost exclaimed but managed to keep his mouth shut. By the looks of the horizontal rain and the spiderwebs of lightning, it wouldn't have mattered if he had screamed his loudest. Kendra was quick and continually looked over her shoulder while she worked to free Sinjin. Trying to cut Sinjin free in the dark without cutting him was turning out to be more challenging than either of them had expected, especially with the violent roll of the ship on the growing waves. Finally Kendra cut through the last of Sinjin's bonds, and he was, for what it was worth, free.

Movement came slowly to Sinjin's body, and he winced at the pain.

"Are you all right?" Kendra asked, sounding more annoyed than concerned.

Sinjin could only nod in response. With great difficulty, Sinjin pulled himself up the ladder behind Kendra, trying to keep the grunting to a minimum.

They emerged onto the aft deck, and the wind tried to send Sinjin flying. With his feet planted on the slanting deck, he walked into the wind. Kendra was quicker about it and waited in the boat, clearly distraught with how slowly he was moving, but Sinjin was doing his very best. His head swam, his vision was blurred, and the tossing of the deck was sporadic and unpredictable. After a bad step, he fell to the deck. Kendra reached out to him from the boat as if trying to pull him in. With a burst of speed born of desperation, Sinjin levered himself up and covered the remaining distance. He managed to get into the boat without further difficulty.

Aboard, he saw salted fish and casks of water as well as the ropes that he suddenly remembered he was supposed to pull on. Looking over at Kendra, he saw she had wrapped the ropes around her hands, and he did his best to do the same. With one last glance at her, Sinjin expected to see a look of fearful excitement, but instead all he saw was her mother's boot as it landed on his face.

Chapter 4

Accountability is rarely reciprocal.
--Greggor Faulk, conscript

* * *

When Catrin woke, even the pale light was more than her eyes could bear. Every part of her body ached, and she thought her hair might shatter if the wind blew. An itch in her throat made her swallow, and her parched mouth and throat were raw. Coughing, she drew herself up and pushed the tent flap aside, hoping the Arghast would never have to care for her unconscious form again. It was a very uncomfortable feeling to wake up somewhere strange, knowing you did not get there under your own power.

Outside, night had fallen, but comets lit the skies, and the beauty of the goddess caressed the world. Moonlight from a nearly full moon in a cloudless sky added to the preternatural glow that bathed the hushed crowd.

Having regained her breath, Catrin felt compelled to silence. All faces were turned toward the saddle, where Mikala was strapped in and moving within its confines. The rest of the Arghast stood in awestruck silence. As had happened before, the gathered group had swelled while Catrin rested, and it lightened her heart to see more of the Arghast. For the moment, she didn't feel as if she would be the death of them all. It was a fleeting moment. An unmistakable sound of wings came from above, and Catrin was afraid the watching feral had finally decided to attack, but the reality was actually much worse. When Catrin looked up, she saw feral dragons alighting on the tallest peaks until they ringed the valley. Once again Catrin was trapped within the valley that now bore her name. Striking the well, all those years ago, she had created the lake, which gave birth to the lush oasis they currently enjoyed. Verdant grasses felt cool under Catrin's feet, and she felt as if she could lie down on them and sleep once again, but the nightmares above would make sure no one slept well this night.

The minds of the Arghast were so consumed with the fulfillment of their destiny that none of them had seen the additional dragons arrive. Not wanting to cause undue alarm, Catrin approached a man she did not recognize and gently laid her hand on his arm. "Pardon me," she said.

The man jumped and turned in surprise.

"I'm sorry," Catrin said. "I didn't mean to startle you."

The man's eyes went wide, and several tribesmen around him turned to see what was happening.

"I'm very thirsty," Catrin said when no one else spoke. The crowd effectively blocked her off from the water's edge.

"Yes, most honored Herald of Istra and rider of dragons!" the man said a bit too loudly, and it echoed in the otherwise silent valley. Above, dragons shifted, but still the Arghast did not see. Catrin accepted a proffered flask and drank deeply. She took a deep breath before drinking again. Her body felt as if it were made of glass and were being rung like a bell, but the desert mist restored at least some of her strength.

After handing the flask back to the awestruck man, Catrin walked toward Mikala, who had stopped what she was doing to watch Catrin's progress. Like magic, the crowd opened before her and closed behind her, leaving Catrin moving through the Arghast in a bubble of open space.

Mikala unstrapped herself and climbed down. When Catrin cleared the last of the crowd, the girl stood in front of her, weeping.

"What's wrong?" Catrin asked.

For a moment, the girl simply stood, trembling, but then she raised reddened eyes to meet Catrin's. "You honor me too much."

Confused, Catrin waited for the girl to continue, but when she didn't, Catrin said, "I don't understand."

"You chose me," Mikala said. "I am no one."

Catrin smiled a sad smile, understanding better than perhaps anyone else in the world could, "You have always been *someone;* I just helped them to see it. I'm proud of you for figuring out how the saddle works on your own."

Mikala dropped her eyes. "I did not, Catrin. Kyrien has been instructing me. I thought you knew. I'm so sorry, my lady. Please forgive me."

"There is nothing to forgive," Catrin said with a smile and a hand on Mikala's shoulder, which only seemed to further unnerve the girl. "Kyrien is a free creature with a mind of his own. If he speaks to you, then it is he that honors you, though I think you are deserving of the honor."

Tears streamed down Mikala's face, and her hands trembled. "It is too much, my lady. I mean no disrespect, but already everyone looks at me differently, and Arakhan--" Her throat constricted around the name, and tears dropped to the grass.

"Is Arakhan your betrothed?"

The girl shook her head and lowered her gaze further.

"Is he the one you wish to be your betrothed?"

The girl nodded slowly as if admitting to some terrible crime. "When he looks at me now, there is fear in his eyes... and hurt. He won't even look at me for more than a breath."

Catrin nodded knowingly. "Was he one of the young men you selected to move the saddle?"

Now the girl's shoulders shook, and her words were barely more than a whisper. "No, my lady. I did not want it to seem that I was favoring him, but instead I betrayed him."

"Can you point him out to me?"

For a moment, Mikala looked up with hope in her eyes, and she nodded, pointing to a group of young men who huddled around one who looked despondent.

It took almost no effort to convey a message to Kyrien. Catrin knew that her direct interference might only create more hurt feelings, but the Arghast would not question Kyrien; he was above reproach. Though he had been resting with his eyes closed, Kyrien now stirred. The sound turned many gazes in his direction, and the silence took on an extra note of excitement. The crowd parted like waves before a prow as Kyrien swung his massive head toward where Arakhan stood, whose eyes went wider as Kyrien drew closer. His gaze focused on Arakhan, Kyrien sent his thoughts loudly enough for Catrin to hear.

You must protect them both.

The words sent Arakhan stumbling backward, and he landed on his rear. As he did, his eyes shot upward, and he saw then that the mountains writhed with dragons, like angry hornets ready to protect their nest. He looked as if he wanted to scream but his lungs could not find enough air.

You must act now.

If the words had not been enough to spur Arakhan into action, then the sudden change in air pressure was. Dragons rained from above, impossibly close to one another in the confined valley. Kyrien thrust himself back into the water. One instant, a mighty dragon stood along the shores of the Herald's Lake, and in the next, only *V*-shaped ripples gave any evidence that he'd been there.

"Defend the Herald and Mikala!" Arakhan cried when he finally found his voice, and chaos erupted within the valley.

* * *

There were few things Sinjin regretted more than their escape attempt. Now he was back where he started, except he was pretty sure he had a broken nose. His bonds were tighter, and he couldn't reach to scratch his face. This might not have been that great of a problem if not for the fact that Kendra was now bound right next to him, and her long, brown hair that he had once found so attractive tickled his face incessantly.

"This is all your fault," Kendra said from beside him. She, too, was cut and bruised.

"I don't see how," Sinjin replied, wishing he had the freedom to kick her.

"You were slow getting up the ladder, then you were slow getting across the deck, and then you fell down, and then--"

"And then I got kicked in the face. By my guess, it was someone who knew what you were planning all along."

"That's ridiculous," Kendra said. "I told no one."

"Where did you get the supplies?"

Silence.

"I appreciated the thought, to tell the truth, but this is a pretty small ship, and that much stolen food won't go unnoticed."

"I still say it's because you were too slow," Kendra added.

Sinjin considered saying a few other things, but then he did perhaps the wisest thing and kept his mouth shut. The creaking of the cargo filled the silence.

Chapter 5

Intent cannot alter physics.
--Brother Vaughn, Cathuran monk

* * *

Darkness enveloped the valley as wings blotted out the sky. Catrin remembered seeing the valley from the sky and could not imagine a single dragon trying to enter from above, let alone what looked like dozens.

If I fight now, I die.

Guilt and fear echoed in Kyrien's words. Catrin knew he was right. There were too many feral dragons falling on them, and there was nowhere for Catrin and the Arghast to hide. Still, she knew that escape from the valley on Kyrien would be nearly impossible, and she decided what Kyrien had done was best. Taking a deep breath and doing her best to center herself, Catrin gathered her might and allowed the waves of raw energy to flood her senses. When open to the energy, she could taste it and smell it, and it was the most intoxicating thing she'd ever experienced. The darkness would not allow her to enjoy the sensations for more than the briefest instant, but she felt as if she were achieving her life's purpose when she released the energy. It left her in a rush that she directed upward. The valley trembled with her might, and it rained stone and flesh. For the Arghast, there was nowhere to run; it was as if the mountains themselves lunged down at them, mouths full of daggers to make certain they all died.

Cries filled the air. Dragons swooped in low and sent crowds of Arghast tumbling before their outstretched claws. Horses charged through the valley, broken free from the lines and panic showing in their eyes, but Arghast horses weren't like most horses. Gleaming in what comet- and moonlight still shone through the dust and dragons that clogged the air, they defended the people around them; these horses were trained to fight. As Catrin drew sharp breaths between attacks, she saw a chestnut stallion with a thick white blaze galloping along the waterline, headed toward a group of young women who stood with their backs to one another in defensive position. Black wings sent a massive moon shadow across the water's edge, steadily catching up with the horse. The girls changed to a straight-line formation and prepared as best they could to face the dragon. They were not armed with spears, and Catrin knew that a knife or staff was no defense against a dragon.

Another group of older men faced a similar fate, and Catrin was torn. There was only enough time to launch a single attack, and any time she spent deciding made it less likely that her attack would save any of those in dire jeopardy. With a cry of anguish, she turned back to the girls, only to see the feral bear down on the chestnut stallion. The valiant animal threw its weight forward and launched its iron-shod hooves at the flying beast. Both hooves connected with the dragon's lower jaw and snapped its mouth shut. Without another thought, Catrin launched her attack on the dragon attacking the older men. Her attack came an instant too late. Mighty claws raked through the men and sent them flying, and Catrin's attack slammed into the dragon from behind, driving the dragon forward like a hurricane wind. Unable to stop, the feral struck the stone with so much force, the valley trembled, and it rolled unceremoniously to the valley floor.

It quickly became apparent that even a dead dragon was dangerous when it fell from the sky, especially in such a tight valley.

Catrin was forced to not only attack the dragons, but then bend the air to hurl their bodies to where there were no people. With the valley consumed in utter chaos, it was a nearly impossible task. There were too many Arghast for her to protect and too many dragons attacking them. Picking and choosing whom to save was among the most painful things Catrin had ever done, and tears streamed down her face as she saw a group of men fall to a swooping dragon. Some of the Arghast were armed with long spears, and those men rallied, doing their best to inflict harm on any feral that came close. A loud snap split the air as one of those men impaled a swooping feral, and the spear dug into the rich, black soil then snapped off from the force of the dragon's inertia.

Feeling guilty for doing so, Catrin looked for Mikala and Arakhan, but it didn't take her long to locate them. Catrin's heart nearly burst in pride when she saw the girl carrying a spear and doing her best to rally her people. Arakhan approached from behind her, riding a roan mare bareback. Two dragons swooped down at him and Mikala screamed. Arakhan turned in the saddle and watched the dragons' final approach with defiance. He raised his spear and yelled out a furious battle cry. With only one spear against two dragons, there was no doubt Arakhan would die, and he faced death with no fear.

There came another battle cry, this one higher in pitch but no less terrifying. Mikala ran toward Arakhan and his mount with all the speed she could find with her long legs. Even her mighty strides would do no good, save to allow Mikala and her love to die together, each with honor.

Drawing a deep breath, Catrin took a step back with one foot to catch her balance as vertigo threatened to take her from the fight. Her eyes landed once again on Mikala, not wanting to see her die but unable to look away. It was then that she saw something she'd never thought to see. Mikala reached Arakhan's side. He lowered his gaze from the dragons, lowered his spear, and reached out to Mikala, pulling her up behind him in a single smooth motion. While Mikala was still in mid air, the dragons struck. Crying out, Catrin gathered what energy she could, but before she could unleash her desperate attack, Mikala exploded; at least that was what it looked like. A pulse of energy raced away from the girl in all directions, a living thing with mass and form, filled with patterns amid the light that seemed like things Catrin recognized. The energy struck the dragons with a force even Catrin had difficulty achieving. Both dragons folded up and were crushed against the valley walls. Arakhan, his mount, and other Arghast nearby were mostly untouched. Mikala, though, slammed into the side of Arakhan's mount, unconscious, and she slid to the ground.

The light had grown brighter with most of the dragons down or fled. Though there was no wind where Catrin stood, winds twisted within the tall peaks, and she watched as one dragon nearly escaped the valley but was dashed against the rocks by violent winds, and she did her best to keep its falling corpse from landing on anyone. Exhausted, Catrin fell to her knees, her body tingling and glistening with sweat.

Arakhan was nearby, and Catrin could hear him shouting for Mikala to wake up. Despite the edge of desperation in his voice, Catrin could not get her body to move; all she could do was breathe. The bodies of feral dragons littered the valley floor, and some protruded from the water. Taking one last deep breath before trying to move again, Catrin heard the sound of wings billowing like the sails of a ship. Most of her body still failed to respond, but her eyes did open, and she saw a large feral swooping back in for an unexpected attack.

The energy from this beast assaulted Catrin and everyone else in the valley. No one moved and the dragon could pick its targets. It aimed for Catrin and, following its course, would also take out Mikala and Arakhan. Blinking slowly, Catrin tried to clear her mind as well as her vision, but she was spent. All she managed to do was raise an arm up to protect herself. Like death on wings, it sped toward her, focused solely on her, and it never saw the bulging wave that raced toward it. Just before the beast snapped up Catrin in its jaws, Kyrien burst from the water and struck it in the side of the head. It was a massive collision, and a hail of soil and wind sent Catrin tumbling. The feral's tail slammed the ground not far from where she lay, a parting shot that nearly succeeded. Kyrien took advantage of the distraction and wrapped his tail around the feral's wing. All at once, he contracted his tail and squeezed hard, which caused the feral to make a very sudden turn and dive. Adding his weight, Kyrien used the momentum to drive the feral's head into the sand in the shallows. Water filled the giant beast's nostrils, and after it finally slammed to a stop with a sickening crunch, the feral did not stir.

This time, when Catrin tried to stand, she succeeded. Though far from steady on her feet, Catrin made her way to where Mikala lay. Arakhan shook her then slapped her face.

"Stop," Catrin said.

Arakhan looked up, his hand poised to strike her again and tears streaming down his cheeks.

"She'll be fine. What she needs is rest and quiet. And when she wakes up, she'll have a terrible headache. Give her cool water and a bit of humrus root."

His face flushed, Arakhan laid Mikala's head gently back to the sand with exaggerated care. "How do you know this?" Arakhan asked, doing his best to be polite.

Catrin understood his anxiety. "I saw what happened," she said. "That is how it started for me, I think. It looked different from a distance, but it felt much the same."

Arakhan looked startled at first, but then a look of pride came to his face and his chest stuck out a bit farther. "Thank you, most honored Herald of Istra."

Catrin accepted the title and did not try to dissuade him. In this instance, the title served her well. It would not hurt Mikala if she was seen to be tied to Catrin in some way, and now that was done in more than one way.

Nearby, Kyrien rested. Catrin walked to his side and laid a hand on his shoulder. She did not lend him energy since she had nothing she could safely give at that moment, but she did send her love, respect, and friendship into the bond they shared. It was a small thing, but it helped to get him to sleep, and rest was what he needed most at that moment.

At Catrin's request, a tent was erected next to Kyrien, and Catrin slept by his side, knowing the Arghast would watch over her.

* * *

Crouched behind a bush, Brother Vaughn watched a pack of demons move through the valley. It appeared that most of the enemy forces had retreated to their ships and fled, but these roving packs were proof that the dangers of the black army remained on the Godfist. He was no match for even one of these creatures, and if he were spotted by one of these packs, he would almost surely be lost. So many things had happened, and now he had so few choices, and he did not like any of them.

He could try to make for the main entrance of Dragonhold, where the primary assault had been, and he already saw that it would be a mistake. Too many of the demons had decided not to make the return trip. Perhaps it was by design, but at that moment, the cause did not matter. The back entrance of Dragonhold was guarded by the God's Eye, and Dragonhold was another place he would likely encounter the demons. The only other option he considered was to go south, over Edling's Wall and into Harborton, but he knew there would be little help to be found. Even if he could get some of the people behind him, he would need the council's approval to take a force of any size north of the Wall. He'd met Master

Edling on a couple of occasions, and the man did not make a very good impression. A bit of study on the history of the man's rule, and Brother Vaughn had more than enough information to know that Edling would never cooperate unless there was a way for him to gain power as a result. His price would be too high.

The demons sniffed the air and scanned the tree line, and Brother Vaughn froze. The luxury of time was no longer his. For tense moments, he stood, his heart beating fast, waiting until the demons finally turned and continued south. Even standing still, he risked being discovered. The biggest concern he had was crossing open ground. The Pinock Valley was wider and had more open grasslands than the Chinawpa Valley. He would still have to figure out how to get across the God's Eye and back to the kitchens, but the back entrance appeared to be a far more likely route to salvation. It seemed an impossible task at first, but he kept moving, never losing hold of the hope that there was a chance he would make it, a chance that Mirta would be waiting for him, unharmed and well. Those were the thoughts that kept him moving when the larger part of him just wanted to hide.

Signs of the demons were everywhere. Grasses and roots lay crushed against the ground. Tree trunks marked with their claws made it look as if there were hundreds of them wandering around. It made the hair on his neck stand, and he couldn't help but wonder if any of the giants remained on the Godfist. He very much regretted having had that thought, especially when he heard a thump that sounded like muted thunder then another and another. Farther south in the valley, farther than Brother Vaughn would have guessed based on how loud the steps were, a giant walked. That just confirmed how monstrous these creatures were and that they were wandering loose on the Godfist. This one still had chains hanging from the collar around its throat, each one sheared off at a different length. When the beast stood and turned suddenly, the chains whipped through the air and cut through the treetops, sending them tumbling to the valley floor. Brother Vaughn felt as if he'd been transported to another, far more frightening world. He had lived here for years and had hiked in these forests dozens of times, but now these woods were filled with monsters, and his mind was having difficulty reconciling that fact. So many of the things he saw that normally would have caught his interest or sparked his imagination now only reminded him of how everything had changed and that he was not safe.

After seeing Trinda and Strom and Durin at the top of the mountain, Brother Vaughn had begun to question his mental health, and then he'd seen Catrin riding Kyrien with a saddle that shone like the comets above. Now he was trying to figure out how to climb over a dead feral dragon. Part of him wasn't certain the dragon was really dead, and he was just waiting for it to turn and snap him up in its jaws. It would have been easiest to climb over the beast's head, but the thought of seeing those eyes open while he was on top of its head drove him to the more difficult task of climbing over the shoulders since the rest of the body was surrounded by thick brush.

Pausing a moment to say a prayer, he prepared for the arduous climb, hoping there was nothing waiting for him on the other side. When he reached the top, he had a commanding view of the rear entrance to Dragonhold. It appeared to be completely deserted. Brother Vaughn watched for some time just to be certain there was no one about, waiting in ambush. After a few deep breaths and another prayer, Brother Vaughn rushed away from the dead dragon and covered the mostly open ground between himself and the entrance. Birds flew before him, flushed from the bushes by his determined stride. He did not run, but he did not dally either. A nearby tree's branches rattled, and Brother Vaughn stepped as quickly as he could up to the wooden stairs, which he took two at a time. When he reached the lake shore, Brother Vaughn was panting and trembling, feeling more terrified than ever. Never before had he felt so alone and so afraid he would die alone. The thoughts shamed him, but he accepted them. They were a part of him. The mantra was comforting. He had almost returned his breathing to normal when the waters before him parted and a large, dark shape moved straight toward him.

* * *

Acrid smoke filled the air within the valley, and Catrin wanted to retreat from it. There was guilt in that smoke. No matter how much she felt justified in her fury, she hated to kill other creatures, especially in large numbers. Most of the dragons had been pulled from the valley and were being burned in a single, massive pyre. There were three that were too large to be moved from where they had died, and they were burned in place. In the end, all that was left were scales, teeth, and claws, all of which were highly prized, and a number of scuffles had already broken out. The Arghast were a fiery people, and these were treasures both practical and sacred.

Despite all the work it had taken to burn the dragons, the Arghast had somehow found enough talent and manpower to create a very close replica of Catrin's saddle, minus the dragon ore of course. The original and the replica sat atop mounds of straw bound with rope, and neither was empty for very long. All the Arghast wanted their turn in the saddle while they had the chance, and Catrin was about to take that chance away from some of them. She didn't have time to stay and help the Arghast; she had to go after Sinjin. Kyrien had already told her that he was ready to fly. There was no more time to waste.

Mikala and Arakhan oversaw the projects together, and it was clear that the events had elevated the two to new positions of power. Catrin felt she'd chosen well. Kyrien seemed to think so, but there was always doubt. Catrin had no desire to ruin people's lives by forcing power on them that they weren't prepared for and didn't know how to properly use. That was a fate she understood more than any other.

"Thank you, mighty tribes of Arghast," Catrin said when everyone stopped to watch her approach. "You have once again proven to be strong, capable, and wise. I wish I could stay longer, but I must go after the people who took my son." A wave of anxiety rolled over the crowd and was reflected back at Catrin, who felt overwhelmed by it but suppressed the feelings. "Would you please help me put the saddle back on Kyrien?"

It came as little shock that the Arghast were honored to have the opportunity to saddle a dragon. This was as close as Catrin had ever come to fulfilling the prophecy that said she would teach the Arghast to fly dragons. She doubted very much she would ever get any further toward really teaching them to fly. It was a burden she carried, and it had never felt heavier.

Mikala and Arakhan nominated people, and there was a sense of approval tinged with disappointment from those who had not been selected. Soon, though, there was no time for hard feelings as the saddle was on the move. Like people cheering at the Summer Games or the Spring Challenges, fathers cheered their sons, and mothers cheered their daughters, shouting advice from what the tribes collectively determined was a respectful distance. For a group who often fought among themselves, Catrin was amazed at how well the tribes worked when their purpose was united.

Kyrien watched those saddling him with a critical eye, and Catrin thought he might be laying it on a bit thick for the Arghast, but she also knew that they would take to it like water from the sky, as the old Arghast saying went. When the saddle had been secured to his approval, Kyrien bowed his head to those who had been so honored.

No one seemed to know exactly what to do, except get out of Catrin's way as she walked to Kyrien. Before she mounted, Catrin turned and said, "Thank you again, my friends, noble tribes of Arghast. You are truly worthy allies. I'll never forget those who've given their lives to protect mine. I'll never forget Irvil of the Sun clan--"

A cheer went up from a group of those gathered, though most remained silent.

"I'll never forget Vertook of the Viper clan--"

Another cheer rose from a different group.

"And I'll never forget Mika, whose clan I do not know, for he came to me with no pretense and no desire to do anything but serve his people."

The entire valley erupted in cheers.

Catrin mounted. Those who had lifted the saddle into place scrambled up and secured her with speed and skill. The Arghast now knew a great deal more about her saddle than she did. Perhaps she really had taught them something after all.

"I'll never forget Halmsa of the Wind clan," Catrin said. "May he find his way home soon."

Unlike her previous declarations, this brought no cheer from the assembled, and Catrin wondered if perhaps the Wind clan was not represented. Their clan leader had, after all, been within Dragonhold the last time Catrin had seen him. Regardless of the cause, Catrin decided she'd said enough. Kyrien bowed his head to the Arghast one last time then leaped into the air. With only a few flaps of his wings, he and Catrin were skimming across the water. As they flew, Catrin couldn't help but wonder what the place would look like the next time she came here, given how much her first visit to this valley had altered it. Even when she had struck the well, she could not have imagined just how much it would change. Her gut told her that this visit might have an even greater impact, yet she couldn't say why.

The Arghast raised cries of encouragement when Kyrien gained speed and altitude and turned to enter the narrow valley mouth sideways, hugging the terrain and trying his best to make certain there was enough clearance to protect Catrin. It was a nearly impossible task, and Catrin had to duck to avoid a number of jutting rock formations that approached at unbelievable speed.

As soon as they were free of the mountains, the desert before them was mostly unremarkable, save the fires. Kyrien avoided the pyres and seemed to not want to look at the bodies of the ferals being burned. Catrin couldn't blame him. The carnage was horrific. Part of her felt great joy at the death of the evil creatures, but another part of her hated to see so much death. The best she could do was to remind herself that these creatures were the reason Sinjin was gone. So many friends and countrymen had given their lives to protect her from the attacks of these monsters. Only when she was able to think of them as monsters could she reconcile her heart and her actions. Only then did the world make any sense.

Kyrien took them higher, and Catrin scanned the skies, not knowing if any ferals remained. The battle in the valley was blurred in her memory, and she couldn't remember if any of the dragons escaped. She also considered the possibility that some of the dragons may have remained in the Pinook and Chinawpa Valleys to keep watch on Dragonhold and what remained of Harborton. That thought pained Catrin as well. Though her countrymen in the south had long since been aligned with Master Edling, who was among Catrin's greatest adversaries, she hated that so much of their history was being lost. The academy where she had studied had been beautifully constructed and had contained the accumulated wisdom of her forefathers. The last time she had seen the academy, it was aflame and being overrun by demons. This was something she would never have wished for, something she had never desired. Even if a part of her had been angry and had felt scorned and abandoned by those who had once been her friends, she would never have wished them harm.

Catrin's guts tightened when the mountains materialized from the shimmering haze before her. Visions of what might await her within Dragonhold haunted her. Guilt stabbed at her, and tears filled her eyes. She had asked these people to trust her, to forward her goals, to move underground, inside of a mountain range. And when danger had approached and laid siege to the hold, Catrin and Kyrien had abandoned them. Kyrien's shame mixed with her own, and the two flew with heavy hearts. Despite the fact that they had left only in an effort to save both their species from extinction, that didn't seem to matter now that she had to return and face the consequences of her decision. She knew already that the dark forces had taken her son, and she would soon be going after him. She also knew her people had suffered losses during this conflict, and those losses were her responsibility. Still, she didn't know what she was going to do about any of it. Part of her wanted to turn around and fly away from all of this, but it was a small part, and they continued on a direct course for Dragonhold.

Chapter 6

Few things are respected as much as an indomitable spirit.
--The Pauper King

* * *

Dark water rippled and parted even as Brother Vaughn took several steps backward, trying to escape whatever death emerged from the water. With primal fear driving his heels, he spun around to flee. As his head turned, though, he caught one last glimpse of the form in the water. It took him four more steps before he could convince his body to stop running. He had recognized the man coming out of the water. When Brother Vaughn turned back around, there he stood, with a piece of hollow reed in his hand.

"I'm sorry," Halmsa of the Wind clan said. "You must be ready to hide. They come back."

Brother Vaughn did not need to ask who "they" were. He looked around but saw no signs of any more reeds, and he bowed his head in appreciation when Halmsa snapped his reed in half and handed a piece to Brother Vaughn. It was a gesture that Brother Vaughn knew could save his life or endanger them both. Without the additional length, Halmsa would have to stay closer to the surface to breathe, and that would make him easier to spot in the water. Brother Vaughn felt a lump in his throat when he understood the level of sacrifice this man had just made on his behalf. "Thank you," he said.

Halmsa just held a finger up to his lips and looked about. Then he pointed to the water and made a swimming motion with his hands. Brother Vaughn shook his head. He was not an unaccomplished swimmer, but the entrance to the hold proper was farther than he thought he could swim. Part of him admitted that the thought of what might be in that water frightened him. He'd already seen the enormous feral dragon that had been constructed at the bottom of this lake. Who knew what other dark and perhaps living things lurked beneath the deceivingly placid surface?

The sound of approaching footfalls stifled any argument that Brother Vaughn might have raised. The demons had returned for him, and now there was nowhere else for him to hide. The only tool he had at his disposal was a piece of reed, and it seemed a slim defense against creatures that he knew were amphibious and could probably see just fine under water. This ruse would conceal them only if the demons remained on the shore and did not enter the water. This seemed unlikely to Brother Vaughn. Why else would they come back in here but to cross over to the main keep? The barges were drifting in the middle of the lake, and there would be no other way to get there than to swim. That meant that they would be caught in the water with amphibious creatures that could probably fight better in water than on land. That thought almost kept Brother Vaughn standing where he was, but Halmsa pulled him into the water.

Fear threatened to paralyze Brother Vaughn as the water closed in around him. He had never tried to breathe from under water before, and he accidentally inhaled through his nose when only his mouth was closed around the reed. Doing his best not to panic, he took in slow, purposeful breaths through his mouth while holding his nose closed with his other hand. At first, he did all of this with his eyes squeezed shut. Then slowly and deliberately, he opened his eyes and could see multiple large, inhuman forms silhouetted against the light of the cavern entrance.

His heart racing, Brother Vaughn watched his death approach. The demons, five of them, moved toward the water. Halmsa placed a hand on Brother Vaughn's shoulder, and he nearly bolted upright. When the first demon entered the water, it felt as if all hope had gone. But then a new silhouette graced the entranceway, followed by a hulking shape that blotted out the light and plunged them all into darkness. The sound of scales on stone drowned out any other sounds. For a moment, nothing happened. Then all at once, the demons turned and moved back toward the entrance at a run. Brother Vaughn felt as if his chest would explode, and he tried to regain his calm while breathing through the reed. An instant later, a blue radiance lit the cavern in a way it never had been before. Waves of blue fire poured over the edges of the demons, and they retreated to the water, which steamed and squealed in protest to the heat.

A mighty boom shook the surface of the water, and Brother Vaughn considered raising his head above the surface for long enough to see what was happening, but Halmsa kept a hand on his shoulder and helped convince him to stay down. Brother Vaughn couldn't help it, though. He wanted to know who was attacking the demons. He could think of only one who would come with a giant beast, and he feared Catrin needed his help. Discarding caution, Brother Vaughn stood and let his head break the surface.

What he saw would remain distinct in his memory for the rest of his days. Catrin stood with her arms to her sides, her hands blazing like twin stars. A nimbus of blue surrounded her and illuminated the cavern; behind her, Kyrien was poised like a snake ready to strike. Never had he seen such a display of raw power and intimidation. Catrin saw him then, and she turned her blazing hands toward him, her eyes wild and fire leaping at her will. Terrified, Brother Vaughn watched her uncoil like a striking snake, and energy leaped toward Brother Vaughn.

* * *

Scars marred the landscape, and each was like a knife in Catrin's spirit.

She had allowed this to happen; she had failed to protect her family, her hold, and her homeland. And it had been despoiled. Tears threatened to fall from her eyes no matter how hard she tried to suppress them. One thing kept her moving toward Dragonhold: Prios. He was still within the hold. Her sense of him was vague and troubling, but she knew he was alive and waiting for her.

Though the main entrance to Dragonhold would have been more expeditious, it was also likely to be more heavily guarded. As they soared over the upper Pinook Valley, columns of smoke could still be seen, but all signs of the black armies were gone. Only the stains they left on the land remained to give evidence that they'd ever been there. Then Catrin saw movement farther ahead in the valley, near the rear entrance to Dragonhold. Kyrien skimmed low over the trees, coming in fast and silent. The dark forms climbed the stair and moved into the darkness.

"Wait for me out here," Catrin said when Kyrien alighted on the massive wooden stair.

No.

Catrin climbed from the saddle and looked Kyrien in the eye. He just nudged her toward the entrance with his rocklike jaw. Rather than question him, Catrin moved into the chamber that held the God's Eye. The demons must have heard their approach, as they were frozen on the stone shore of the lake, listening. Then they were moving into the water. Not wanting them to escape, Catrin stepped onto the shore and breathed in deeply, drawing on the power. Blue light sprang from her hands, and she felt it course through her. Like a candlewick, she felt as if she conveyed the energy and was mostly untouched by it, but over time, it wore away at her until she felt that she might evaporate or crumble.

Once the power had come to her only through great effort; now, though, things had changed. Catrin felt as if she had far too much power. The currents of it threatened to sweep her away, and only the strength of her will kept her from tumbling into madness. Still, there was a beauty and sensation that could not be described. It felt as if she could burn very brightly if she chose but only for a short time.

The demons ran toward her then, and time seemed to progress once again. Catrin cast flames into the faces of those who had invaded her homeland and fouled the very air she breathed. The demons sickened her; they were twisted perversions of nature, something that never should have been. These beasts had been created as killing machines, and Catrin could feel no mercy for them as she did what was in her nature. She, too, was a killing machine, and she knew it, but what she did was for a purpose, for the greater good, and for all those she loved.

Just as she was about to release a massive killing strike, something in the water moved. A new threat registered in her battle-ready mind. Without time for another thought, reflex brought her about to face this new foe, and her concentrated attack leaped from her, eager to split the air between her and the enemy, ready to light it up from the inside out. Somehow intellect overruled instinct as Catrin recognized the face of Brother Vaughn. Twisting back toward the demons, she did her best to redirect the attack. It struck several demons and was accompanied by a loud scraping sound, but despite her efforts, it still reached out for Brother Vaughn. The demons retreated to the water, their reptilian hides smoking and hissing as they hit the surface.

Catrin realized then that Brother Vaughn would be in great danger if the beasts managed to get themselves under water. Without another thought, she pulled the air to her breast and flung it toward the demons, hurtling them far out into the water. Kyrien uncoiled and struck two that had escaped Catrin's attack and sent them nearly as far as she had.

Halmsa of the Wind clan emerged from the water next to Brother Vaughn and cast him a very disapproving look.

"Are you all right?" Catrin asked as she stepped forward and helped Brother Vaughn from the water.

"I'll live," he said. "I'm so glad you recognized me. If you hadn't redirected your attack, I'm certain I'd be dead."

The words brought Catrin little comfort. She'd nearly killed her dear friend and mentor. Even after she'd recognized him, her power had been out of control and struck him anyway. The fact that he smelled strongly of burned hair did little to ease her conscience. Halmsa had stayed under water and appeared to be uninjured, though he looked at the singed upper portion of his hollow reed and seemed to be wondering just how safe he had actually been.

"Are you all right as well?" Catrin asked Halmsa, but the man was distracted by Kyrien's saddle. As soon as he laid eyes on it, Catrin might as well have ceased to exist. Halmsa approached Kyrien, bowing with his hands pressed together before his face. Kyrien gave him a respectful nod. Catrin knew that Kyrien remembered Halmsa as well; there was something between the two of them that Catrin could not quite understand. Kyrien seemed to want it that way and would express nothing more about it.

"It's so beautiful," Halmsa said.

"I agree," Brother Vaughn said after a moment.

"It was a gift," Catrin said, her voice thick with emotion.

Neither pressed her further about the saddle.

"I'm so glad to see you well, Brother Vaughn," Catrin said. 'When I last saw you, you were jumping into the river to escape the demons."

"You were there?" he asked, incredulous.

"I was there in spirit," Catrin replied.

Brother Vaughn looked as if he were trying to decide exactly what her meaning of "in spirit" was. Catrin knew it was certainly more than in the traditional meaning of the phrase.

"Do either of you know what the state of the hold is?" Catrin asked.

"Parts of it are closed," Halmsa said. "And sometimes it moves."

Catrin wasn't certain she'd heard him correctly.

"I don't know," Brother Vaughn admitted. "Sinjin, Trinda, and I became trapped when the hold moved the first time. And the second time--"

"Dragonhold moved?" Catrin's question cut him short. Both men just nodded, and Catrin took a moment to let that sink in.

"The walls moved and blocked us in the first time, and then they opened, and the mysterious hall to nowhere opened up to parts of the hold that have been locked away for only the gods know how long," Brother Vaughn continued. "We were trying to find our way back when we found the underground river. You say you saw the demons take that place?"

"Yes," Catrin said. "You did the best you could."

Brother Vaughn looked at the ground. "I tried to keep them safe. I know Trinda lived because I saw her, but I didn't see Sinjin with her. I did see Strom and Durin, though. I'm so sorry."

"They've taken Sinjin," Catrin managed to say, though the emotion constricted her throat.

"By the gods," Brother Vaughn said.

Halmsa looked furious. "We will make them regret this," he said.

Catrin could find no more words to say on the subject, and she was reminded that she had no time to waste. "I need to find Prios."

"The last I saw him," Brother Vaughn said, "he was by the underground river. I can take you there."

Catrin was torn. Her sense of Prios was weak, and he had not responded to her calls for him. She was worried. "How far is it from here?"

"Half a day's walk," Brother Vaughn said.

It was difficult to imagine such distances, all completely underground. The scale of Dragonhold increased dramatically in Catrin's mind. Truly the ancients created the most wonderful things. "How far is it from the river to the kitchens? Do you know?"

"I don't know," Brother Vaughn said. "I believe that is where Prios and the others came from when they came to the river. But I can't be certain."

"We can make it directly to the kitchens in less than an hour," Catrin said. "We should check there first. And then we can find out how to get to the river from there."

"Kitchen's blocked," Halmsa said.

"Blocked how?" Brother Vaughn asked.

Halmsa just shrugged. "Rocks."

"Lots of rocks, correct?" Brother Vaughn asked.

Halmsa nodded.

Catrin cast Brother Vaughn a quizzical glance.

"When we were trapped in the hall to nowhere, it was not fallen rock that trapped us, it was enormous sections of granite that moved across the doorway to form a new, nearly seamless wall. That, I don't know how we could get through, but I think we can clear away enough loose stone to get through as long as there are none of the black devils there."

"I think most of them have left," Catrin said, knowing they had gotten what they came for. "I'll take care of any that remain. The primary challenge remaining is to cross the God's Eye."

"I'm not a very good swimmer," Brother Vaughn admitted.

"We won't have to swim," Catrin said. "Kyrien managed to squeeze himself into the cavern, and he says he will take us to the other side."

"We're not going to fly in the cavern, are we?" Brother Vaughn asked, looking torn between being excited and terrified.

"No. Kyrien says that while you may not be a good swimmer, he can swim just fine."

Brother Vaughn actually looked disappointed, yet she could sense that he was relieved. Kyrien moved closer to the water and extended his wing so Catrin and the others could climb up. Catrin went first since neither man made any move to get closer to Kyrien. Once up in the saddle, Catrin extended her hand to Brother Vaughn.

He came slowly, reverently. He knew Kyrien but this would be the first time he would ever have done anything close to flying. Sitting on this beautiful saddle atop this gorgeous creature appeared to overwhelm him more than a little bit. Halmsa looked much the same when he climbed up. His eyes took in everything, and he spent most of his time inspecting the saddle. Catrin moved to one side and offered the main seat to Halmsa. He took it in awed silence, and Catrin strapped him in. As Kyrien slipped into the water, Halmsa grinned. He moved within the range of the harness and seemed overjoyed by the design of the saddle and the maneuverability it afforded him. Brother Vaughn watched in fascinated silence.

Kyrien's speed in the water was surprising, and he moved almost effortlessly, though the saddle moved from side to side with his serpentine movements, which was a little unsettling. When they reached the middle of the lake, they came upon the barges. Floating aimlessly, they were an eerie reminder that all was not as it should be. Kyrien didn't spare them even a glance. At one point, Kyrien stuck his head under water.

"I wonder what he's looking at," Catrin said.

"There's a crystal dragon down there," Brother Vaughn said.

"A *what?*"

"It's not alive," Brother Vaughn said in response to Catrin's alarm. "I mean, it's like a sculpture of a feral dragon made out of crystal on the bottom of the lake."

"How did you find that?" Catrin asked.

"I accidentally dropped my herald globe in the water. It got really bright, and we could see the dragon. Logan, the spear fisherman, got it back for me."

So much had happened in such a short amount of time that Catrin knew she was missing things, but her mind was overwhelmed with details. For the rest of the ride, they were silent, and Kyrien was able to get close enough to the docks for each of them to simply walk from the saddle onto the dock. Before she even left the saddle, Catrin noticed something strange: water poured into the God's Eye from the hall. The others saw it as well, but no one offered an explanation.

As soon as Catrin's boots were on stone, Kyrien slipped beneath the water and disappeared.

"I don't know about you, but seeing something that big disappear into the God's Eye makes me want to stay away from the water."

Even knowing Kyrien was on their side, Catrin couldn't argue with Brother Vaughn. Before they walked away, however, there was a terrible noise from the lake. Kyrien's head burst from the water, his head and neck thrust into the air. In his jaws was a demon. Kyrien gave the thing a couple of good shakes then spit it out. Catrin felt better knowing that Kyrien would free the waters of demons, but she grimaced at the thought of what they must taste like. Suddenly she was very glad not to be a dragon. Kyrien was very close to her thoughts at that moment, and he did not appreciate her sentiment.

Catrin led the way, the light that radiated from her being the only illumination they had. Brother Vaughn walked alongside her, and Halmsa kept a watchful eye as he followed. When they reached the great hall, Catrin moved more slowly. The shadows seemed to dance and move. The sound of water spilling onto the floor was persistent and seemed to be filled with other noises and often voices. Everyone was on edge as they crept along the inner wall, staying well clear of the shattered entranceway, not knowing if dragons still lurked outside.

Other noises started to emerge over the sound of water, and Catrin thought she recognized the thudding of rocks being moved. Her sense of Prios had been growing stronger, and she was now confident that she had found him. When they reached the area that was blocked with fallen stone, there were already hands reaching through and pulling away the last few stones they would need to create a hole big enough for a person to slip through.

The first person through was Prios. Tears came to Catrin's eyes instantly upon seeing him, and she rushed forward to take him in her arms. He looked weak and seemed to be in pain. Her concern for him suddenly blotted out the rest of the world, and she began looking him over with her eyes, hands, other senses.

I'll be fine.

"You're hurt," Catrin said.

I'm not hurt badly. We must go after Sinjin. I'll heal on the way.

Catrin wanted to argue, wanted to say no and force him to get into a bed and recuperate, but the greater part of her knew that he was right. It would take both of them to bring Sinjin home safely. She reminded herself that Sinjin was no good to anyone dead. Thorakis would keep him alive as a way to manipulate Catrin. He had done this out of fear, and now his worst fears would be visited upon him. Catrin knew this situation well; it had happened before.

"What's with all the water?" Brother Vaughn finally asked.

Durin, Prios said in Catrin's mind, and for a moment, she smiled through the tears.

More of the barrier blocking the kitchens was being cleared away, and Morif made his way through. A broad smile crossed his face when he saw Catrin. "It's good to see you back," he said.

Catrin gave him a sad smile and hugged him as he moved close.

"We're going to need some supplies for traveling," she said by way of greeting, and Morif just shook his head and gave her a wink.

"How many will you take with you?" he asked.

"It will just be Prios and I. I'll need enough provisions for a week."

Morif frowned and looked concerned, but he did as she asked.

Millie, Miss Mariss, and others began to stream out of the kitchens to see Catrin and, no doubt, enjoy some fresh air.

"I'm sorry I left all of you," Catrin said when the people gathered around her. "I had to try to save the regent dragons. But I failed. Kyrien is the last of his kind." None of the assembled could find any words. So much guilt pressed down on Catrin, she thought she might be crushed. "Now I plan to go after Sinjin, and I will not fail. I will not rest until this threat that faces us is no more. Miss Mariss, I charge you with managing the food, stores, and rationing. Morif, I leave you and Chase in charge of the defense of Dragonhold. Millie, I ask that you and Mirta care for the sick. Brother Vaughn can handle the day-to-day management of the hold, which means you don't really need me for anything." It felt strange to explain why she was not needed, and it was not the best feeling when she realized her arguments were sound. At least it eased her guilt about taking Prios and leaving to find Sinjin.

Stores were packed as best they could, and a few young men carried them back to the God's Eye. Prios and Catrin walked hand in hand, each leaning on the other for physical and emotional support. Brother Vaughn and others escorted them to the God's Eye, and she could feel their objections, even if they weren't voiced. She didn't want to feel these things and often wished she could block them out, but they were readily apparent to her, and there was nothing she could do to stifle that knowledge.

The hold was vulnerable, but there should be no one on the Godfist capable of launching an assault. By the time Master Edling had the people in the south rallied, Morif would have the defenses back in place. With the river and plains that had been discovered, growing food should be much easier to accomplish within the hold, and as much as she hated to fall back on it, the people could farm outside once again. Catrin hoped the recent events would convince the people that they needed to figure out how to live underground just in case the need returned. Catrin said as much to Miss Mariss before she climbed aboard Kyrien. Prios sat behind her, and they arranged the straps so they held him nearly as tightly as they secured Catrin. There were no buckles on his pants; they had to make do with what they had. Catrin made a mental note to have riding pants made for Prios and Sinjin at the first opportunity.

It was a somber and tearful good-bye as Kyrien swam away from the dock. They did get to the see the three of them twice more before they left since Morif had asked Kyrien to retrieve the barges. Once those had been delivered, though, Kyrien wasted no time getting them to the far shore.

Get off.

Catrin laughed and shook her head when she realized that she and Prios would have to unstrap themselves and dismount for Kyrien to squeeze himself out of the cavern. When they dismounted, Catrin saw deep gouges in the walls of the entranceway where there had been none before. The dragon ore must have bitten into the granite, she concluded, and it was about to do so again.

"Do you want us to take the saddle off?" Catrin asked Kyrien.

No. I want to mark our passage in and out of this hold. I want people to remember.

The result was a series of deep gashes in the entranceway walls that formed a diagonal checked pattern, which Catrin knew would be almost impossible to reproduce. This was, in as close an approximation as possible, Kyrien's signature.

Leaving Dragonhold behind, Catrin wondered if she would ever see the place again. There was a feeling of finality in their departure that had her on edge, but she knew she'd done the right thing. Prios was with her now, and together they would bring Sinjin back. Kyrien gave a triumphant roar at that thought, and Prios gave her a squeeze, as if both had been reading her mind.

Chapter 7
Let our sails scrape the sky and rake the moon.
--Aerestes, captain of the *Landfinder*

* * *

"I know you're angry, but would you please just listen to what I have to say for a moment?" The words left Jharmin Kyte like a sacrament, something uttered so many times, it had become ingrained and reflexive. Such were the arguments with his fiery wife, Lissa, intense and heated. After she stomped from the room, Jharmin ran his hand over the vase that rested nearby on a marble table supported by richly grained wood in natural shapes yet polished to a fine sheen. The vase was anything but smooth. Lines crossed its surface, and chunks of the ornate scene were missing completely. This was what had happened to every precious vase in his hold the last time Catrin had come up.

Jharmin had commissioned chairs as a gift to Catrin and Prios on the birth of their son, but he'd never told Lissa. That had turned out to be a mistake since the chair maker's wife went out of her way to thank the Lady Lissa for the generous commission. The chairs had been worthy of royalty and had fetched a kingly sum. When he thought about it now, it was almost inevitable that Lissa would find out. This was exactly why he needed her to listen to him now. He did not want to repeat that mistake. She'd slept in the atrium for nearly a month.

With a determined sigh, Jharmin went after Lissa, knowing that it was the lives of their people at stake, those around Wolfhold and those around Ravenhold. Jharmin preferred to remain within Wolfhold since it was the seat of his power, though it didn't please Lissa much. If he stayed in Ravenhold for any period of time, he knew he would appear weak, and that was something they simply could not afford. Lissa knew it as well, but she didn't want to admit it.

Anything that related to Lissa's cousin, Catrin, was likely to raise her ire, and there was nothing Jharmin could do about that. Even with his personal feelings aside, Catrin was a powerful ally, and allies were exactly what they needed most. Thorakis had gained control of much of the Greatland under the guise of a savior. He'd brought food to many people, Jharmin conceded, but at a high price. All of the men and boys had been conscripted into his armies and forced to build more aqueducts, which meant more food, more water, and more people under Thorakis's control. The man had not yet shown his dark side, but the time was coming; Jharmin could feel it.

When he found Lissa, she was in the war room and looking at the representation he'd had created of Thorakis's system of aqueducts. Depending on how you viewed these structures, they could be seen as defensive barriers to keep out brigands and thieves, which was how Thorakis described them. But Jharmin saw something far more sinister.

"You're right," Lissa said without looking up, her fingers running along the miniature aqueducts. They looked like a giant claw inexorably reaching toward Wolfhold and Ravenhold. If you looked at the aqueducts as roads, then the intent became clear. These structures could act as supply chains from a nearly unlimited food source: the fishery at Riverhold. Already they knew that the open channels were used to float barrels and other large goods outward from Riverhold. Why could they not be used to transport troops? "When Thorakis shows his true face, we're doomed."

Jharmin felt no joy in the admission, though moments such as this had been few in his marriage. Given the rumors he'd been hearing about black dragons and armies of demons, it seemed clear that Thorakis would reveal his true might sooner rather than later.

"There's no strength around us, no one else to align ourselves with, save Madra, but she has her own lands to try and hold on to. Our situation is untenable." Lissa spoke the words coldly with only brief glimpses of emotion through the cracks in her facade.

Jharmin knew Lissa possessed a kind but heavily guarded heart that had been broken too many times. Circumnavigating those defenses had taken him years, and still he caught only occasional glimpses of her true feelings. She was a challenge, his wife, but she was no fool.

"If we're right about Thorakis, then I don't see how our people will stand against him. It would seem they'd be better off to serve him than to die fighting for us."

Jharmin knew this wasn't true, and he knew she didn't believe it, but he let his wife brood. It seemed a necessary part of the process.

"I don't want her to come here," Lissa finally said, her back stiff and her eyes boring into the map, steadfastly refusing to look at Jharmin. "If she's to aid us, then she can do so by engaging Thorakis. That'll give us more time to prepare if she's defeated, and if she were to be victorious over Thorakis, then perhaps our debt will not be so great. I don't want to owe her anything, but I may have no choice."

Jharmin did as he thought was best, and he stood, listening, waiting for her to say more, his mouth firmly anchored shut.

"You may send her a message, but do not disgrace us, and offer no long-term alliance. Instead, simply make her aware of the situation, and let her decide if it's her desire to come to our aid. Ask nothing, and you will owe nothing."

Given Lissa's feelings about Catrin, Jharmin knew this was a concession not easily granted, which did not speak well of their circumstances. Lissa knew as well as he that they had failed. And only the most powerful person in the world might be able to help them, provided she was willing. In some ways, they had both known it all along, for neither was without intelligence. Each had continued family traditions of maintaining spy networks. Jharmin suspected there were overlaps between the two networks, and it was part of the game to send as much disinformation as information. Jharmin would admit only to himself that Lissa was the greater spymaster, but he did his best to keep up.

"My sources say that Catrin and her dragon abandoned those within Dragonhold. How will you get this message to her? No one knows where she has gone or why. And the poor people of the Godfist are not faring well at all in her absence, I'm afraid."

Jharmin continued his silence. It was rare for Lissa to reveal so much of her intelligence, and he was amazed by not only the quality of her information, but the timeliness of it.

"She left her husband and son behind," Lissa continued. "Which one do you think Thorakis will take?"

"You don't think he'd really do that, do you?"

"How else would you defend against *her* power?" Lissa asked, still not looking at him. "Even with Thorakis's seemingly unending supply of gold, it can buy no sufficient defense against her unnatural powers." This conversation seemed to require all the restraint she possessed. "I would take her son," she continued. "I've considered doing it in the past. It is the only thing that might keep her in check. No one should have so much capacity for wickedness and not be limited in some fashion. If she grows too powerful and the world has no recourse, then she could be the death of us all."

Jharmin tried not to push her over the edge but could not resist one more question. "How do you get your messages from the Godfist so quickly? Surely there are no birds so swift as that."

Lissa finally turned to him and smiled. "The world is changing, my husband, but the one thing that hasn't changed is the need for me to have my secrets and the need for you to have yours. That being said, if you wish for me to send the message through my network, it will undoubtedly reach its destination sooner."

Her smile didn't fade, and Jharmin smiled back. "Of course," he said, knowing full well that sending the message through her network would mean that she would know every word. In truth, she would know every word either way. Having her send the message worked to his advantage by making it clear he had nothing to hide. Still, he wished he knew how those messages traveled so fast. It seemed . . . unnatural.

* * *

Selling spoiled wine had become a lucrative business for Kevlin Weil.

He and Hera made regular trips to Riverhold, though he'd been instructed to do it under the guise of trading other goods. Those who sold him the wine believed he'd learned some recipe that allowed him to make something delicious from it, but he wouldn't tell them what it was. It was a tenuous secrecy, and he did his best to keep his growing stash away from prying eyes. It was far better for him if everyone thought he was just barely getting by. Hera wore a new halter, though, and he had a few repairs done on his wagon, but even for those, he'd haggled as if the seller were taking his last coin. The most difficult part was finding people to give him silvers and coppers for his gold. If any of those he dealt with regularly knew he had gold, their prices would double. There were a few men who would discreetly handle such things for a price. It was a hefty price, but Kevlin had no more appealing options. Still, most of his gold remained stashed away. Someday soon he would take his new wealth south and buy a farm. There, he and Hera could live out their years in peace. That was all he really wanted.

Trips to Riverhold had begun to feel almost normal; even the mighty, free-standing aqueducts that reached out from the keep like spider's legs seemed commonplace. That was when Kevlin knew the time for him to leave was rapidly approaching. Just a few more deliveries, and he could disappear. He had plenty of gold to bribe his way out of Riverhold and south with plenty left over to buy himself a comfortable future. Rarely did he deal with Grimwell these days, and rumors said Thorakis was not even within the hold, but Kevlin didn't want to become complacent. He'd been playing with hot coals for some time now; eventually he was going to get burned.

The steward inspected his cargo ever so briefly, handed two gold coins to Kevlin, and ordered the cargo unloaded. Kevlin stood and watched, his hand casually sliding the gold coins into his purse, which he then slid back into concealment. It wasn't long before he and Hera were on their way back out of Riverhold, and Kevlin found it difficult to complain. It was, in fact, the easiest work he'd ever done. Perhaps that was why he distrusted it so much. The only way to make that much money with that little work was to be dishonest, he thought, and the number of secrets he was keeping attested to the fact. Again, though, he told himself it was only temporary and he'd soon leave all this behind. Soon he'd be free to live life by his own rules instead of the rules set down by one man, a man no one ever seemed to see.

For most, the food in their bellies was enough; it was certainly better than the years after the Herald War. This seemed an improvement and a sign of progress, but Kevlin saw the price, and he was unwilling to pay. There were dark things lying under the surface, and he did not want to be around when those things reared their heads. Doing his best to appear downtrodden and beaten, Kevlin rode back into town, hoping no one noticed him. Becoming part of the scenery was among his more finely honed skills; it was something he'd learned long ago. If you look miserable enough, you won't be observed for long. This knowledge had served Kevlin well.

When at last he returned to the place he called home, he put Hera in the only stall and climbed to his quarters above it. Reaching up, he ran his fingers along the top of the beam above his bed, found the recess he was looking for, and pried the wood loose. It was a tight-fitting lid that most would assume was solid wood. Inside the hidden compartment, his fingers found his stash of gold. It felt good in his hands, and he couldn't just add the new coins to the stash; he had to feel the coins in his hands. It shamed him to know such greed, but he could not resist. Never before had he held so much precious metal in his hands. He was now richer than even the traders and business owners who had always looked down on him. The coins shifted in his hands.

Click, click, click, clack.

Clack, click, click, click.

Back and forth he moved the coins, and something bothered him more and more with every movement.

One coin did not sound like the others.

Kevlin could find no good reason for this, though along with a sinking feeling in his stomach, he could imagine some bad reasons--very bad reasons.

The more he thought about it, the more Kevlin knew the time had come for him to leave. He said no good-byes, left no notes, and did his best to slip away from Riverhold unnoticed, hoping to be far away before everything came tumbling down.

* * *

Sculpting the wind, Catrin did what she could to increase their speed. Bolstered by the power of the saddle, she and Kyrien applied their wills. Prios rested and Catrin smiled, knowing that was what he needed most. Though he wouldn't admit it, he was wounded. The more time he had to recuperate, the better. He was stubborn but he wasn't stupid, and he took advantage of the opportunity to rest. Part of her was tempted to slow their progress just so he'd have more time to rest before they entered battle once again. But she was also frightened for Sinjin, so she did her best to aid their flight. Much of the time, Kyrien also rested while he flew, his eyes hooded and only a small part of his brain still active. He seemed able to hold a course while completely asleep, which amazed Catrin and also frightened her a little. Afraid to sleep while he slept, she was unable to trust his instincts as much as he did.

When the black ships finally came into view, all three came to full awareness. Catrin's mind grew crowded as both of them communicated with her without speaking. With a thought, she silenced them and focused on the ships. She needed to identify the ship that held Sinjin, and that required complete concentration. His energy was muffled and weak, making him more difficult to locate. She wanted to see that gleaming beacon of life that was her son, but instead, what she finally found was a dull pulse, beaten, defeated. Her heart broke at the sensation of his loss, but Catrin now knew exactly where her son was.

Clouds gathered around the Falcon Isles, which materialized beyond the black fleet. It would be easier to fight them in the water, and Catrin prepared herself for battle. Silently she instructed Kyrien and Prios to do the same. Both had already begun to do so.

A cry split the relative silence, and Catrin saw one of the lookouts pointing toward them. Surprise was no longer theirs.

The air pressure change was the only warning they had before dragons attacked from above. Kyrien dived steeply, leaving Catrin and Prios holding on and still straining against the harness. It was terrifying to feel as if you were going to be hurled into the open air at any time; the harness was strong, but even that would fail given enough force. As old as this saddle was, Catrin couldn't help but wonder if it would hold up under both their weight, though it showed no outward signs of stress.

Prios, the less firmly secured of the two, was breathing heavily, and Catrin could see his tensed, white hands trembling. His panic was entirely understandable. Doing her best to breathe in deeply while she could, Catrin hoped to keep from blacking out. Huge claws raked past her face, and Kyrien banked hard into the clouds.

Even within the turbulence and dismal visibility within the clouds, the ferals continued their attack. With what seemed complete disregard for their own safety, dragons dropped through the clouds like stones, likely to kill themselves and their prey if they collided at such speed. One passed near where Kyrien flew, and Catrin's eyes met those of the dragon as it passed. Immediately, the feral unfolded itself and slowed its descent. Knowing they had been found, Kyrien gave Catrin and Prios a quick warning then tucked his wings and dived toward the ships. Attacks launched from those ships, and Catrin let the buffeting wind become their shield. Instead of working against it to make it match her vision of a shield, she asked the air to protect them, and it conformed to her intent. It took a great deal less energy, and Catrin barely felt the stings of those attacks.

With their defenses easily maintained, Catrin concentrated again on locating Sinjin. The ships had been shifting and moving, and it took her a moment to find him. His light shone brighter now, and she cried at the thought of her son having hope from her presence. He would know now that she'd come for him, and he'd know how much she loved him.

* * *

Light and sudden movement brought Sinjin awake with a start. His aching body failed to respond when a voice shouted for him to move.

"Thorakis has ordered them transferred to one of the dragons," a voice said from above.

Sinjin and Kendra both cried out as they were grabbed and pulled roughly up to the deck. Their hands remained bound, and fear made Sinjin's heart race.

"She's attacking from above!" came another shout from the steerage.

These words brought hope to Sinjin, and now his heart thundered from the thought of possible rescue. His mother had come to save him. She was here, now, and that was why they had been brought on deck; that was why they were to be taken by a dragon. Sinjin prayed his mother got there first, prayed it would be Kyrien who grabbed them in his claws.

When it happened, it happened so fast that he didn't know who had grabbed him or if Kendra had also been taken. The answer came a moment later when her heard Kendra cursing at the dragon and trying to fight her way free. The beast just squeezed tighter, and Kendra screamed one last time before going limp. Afterward she lay very still in the feral dragon's claws.

"Kendra!" Sinjin shouted, the claws tightening around him as well, and he prayed they didn't get any tighter; already he was having difficulty breathing. Kendra didn't respond. Sinjin fumed. Though he didn't trust Kendra, he knew she did not deserve to be treated in such a manner, he wasn't even certain she was still alive. Who were they to kidnap them and to kill them? His anger grew, and a plan began to form in his mind. If only Kendra were still conscious, he thought, or at least alive.

That's when the thunder began.

* * *

Watching in horror, Catrin saw Sinjin's light grow brighter. She watched as he was brought out on deck, and she could do nothing. Kyrien moved in closer to the ships, but the attacks continued. While her defenses kept the assaults from inflicting serious injury, the energy of those strikes still slowed them and altered their course. Catrin was about to start attacking the other ships when the barrage from below intensified. The enemy seemed to have figured out that they were inflicting no harm; they concentrated instead on preventing Catrin from getting close to the ship where her son was held.

Now that he was on deck and Catrin was unable to get to him, she realized that she'd put him in even greater danger. Sinjin was closer to death than ever before. He stood there, aboard an enemy ship, without even any shoes on. Kendra stood next to him, looking just as vulnerable. At any moment, both could be taken from her.

Then they were.

A great black mass blotted out the ship as it flew in between Kyrien and where Sinjin and Kendra were so woefully exposed. The mighty dragon swooped in and, in a single fluid motion, snatched Sinjin and Kendra in its claws. It felt like a knife blow to Catrin's chest, and she collapsed under the weight of it. Behind her, Prios tensed; he, too, knew their chance to rescue Sinjin from the deck of that ship was lost.

The dragon flew off as quickly as it could, and other dragons surrounded it, flying in erratic patterns that made it nearly impossible to tell which dragon had Sinjin and Kendra.

Screaming in frustration, Catrin readied herself to launch a massive attack. She communicated this to Prios and Kyrien, and they were ready to do the same. The three of them, for that brief time, were of a single mind, and when Catrin dropped their defenses, all three attacked the ships. New attacks sprang from below, and Catrin felt their bite; she knew Kyrien and Prios did as well, but each protected himself enough to prevent serious injury. Still, the pain was incentive not to take any direct hits.

With defenses erected and slowing them once again, the three prepared for another attack. Sweat streamed down Catrin's face as the effort of holding back the deluge of power taxed her will. Much of her effort went into using restraint and making sure she didn't burn up amid such potential energy. When she did release her power, she attempted to use it in ways that she could predict and control. It didn't always work out that way, even if it was her intention. Just as Catrin was about to drop the defenses again, she saw a group of ferals turn back and close in. On the backs of these dragons rode dark-robed men, and Catrin could feel their power; it polluted the air and smelled like the coming rain.

"I don't know if we're ready for this," Catrin said.

There will be a price.

Prios must have heard Kyrien as well, and they all accepted the truth. Prios squeezed Catrin's arm, and she dropped their defenses. Kyrien turned and dived then pulled up sharply to soar just above the water, their speed causing spray to leap from the water and swirl in their wake. Using the waves as a shield, Kyrien rode within the growing troughs, bringing them closer to the ships. The formation of dragons was close now; despite poor visibility, Catrin could see that there were five of them. One rider bore a long staff, and Catrin knew this was going to hurt.

Using all her energy to create a shield above them, Catrin left an opening along the waterline for Prios to attack the ships, and that was exactly what he did. Instead of trying to battle those aboard the ships, he attacked the ships themselves. This sudden change in tactic was especially effective the first time he used it. A half dozen ships were in various stages of sinking after only a single attack. Catrin should've been watching what was happening above them. When Thorakis's attack came, her shield was not enough.

His massive blow caught them off guard and slammed them into the water. Kyrien let out a giant woof when he struck the waves. At their speed, water might as well have been stone. Catrin and Prios were thrown forward by the impact, and Catrin's defenses failed completely. For an instant, they were simply floating in the water, unprotected. The dragons were coming in for another attack, and the ships were turning back to face them.

With several powerful strokes of his wings, Kyrien turned to face the wind and let it carry them upward. Koe's energy washed over Catrin, and having his potency aimed at her was more unnerving than the pain. Seeing the Staff of Life used for dark purposes made her want to vomit. It was the manifestation of life, and it should not be so polluted with wicked intent. The staff had given Catrin one of the greatest gifts in her life: absolution, the chance to make things right. Again she heard Chase in her mind, urging her to retrieve the staff from the Grove of the Elders. If only she'd listened, she might be using the staff to defend herself instead of defending herself against its awesome power. If Thorakis ever figured out how to tap its true potential, none of them would survive.

Prios regained his composure first and told Catrin to keep her defenses down until he signaled. This allowed Catrin to catch her breath, and she made no argument. Power welled up behind her, and the energy marched across her skin like ants; her mouth tasted of copper, and her teeth vibrated.

Releasing his entire store of power, Prios issued many small bursts of energy in sequence. With speed unlike any living creature Catrin had ever seen, Prios thrust his force into the enemy, though his body barely moved, the bursts of fiery plasma that issued from his hands scorched the air, roaring and hissing. When they struck Thorakis and his dragon, the plasma exploded into thousands of tiny spheres, each burning like the sun, and they clung to Thorakis's robes and Seethe's scales. With a roar of pain, the two dropped out of sight, presumably seeking water. Still Prios attacked, seeking out the remaining dragons and scorching their hides.

When the dragons fled, Prios turned his attention to the ships. Catrin had regained her breath, and she cast ropes of liquid fire into the ships beyond Prios's attack.

It seemed the battle had turned in their favor. That was until Kyrien suddenly lurched upward violently, slamming Catrin's face into the back of Kyrien's neck, nearly knocking her senseless. Prios slammed into the back of Catrin and was presumably faring no better. The ringing in her ears drowned out the sounds of battle, and it seemed like something from a dream when a dragon and rider swooped down at them, their speed difficult to believe.

Breathing in through her mouth since her nose was now filled with blood, Catrin issued a scream that she barely heard, and she launched a desperate attack. Even though she landed a direct hit, there was no stopping the momentum of the soaring beast, and its unconscious rider's limp hand struck Catrin and Prios a blow as they passed.

There was not much more that Catrin, Prios, or Kyrien could do. They were wounded and weak, and though the ferals were in much the same condition, they had to quit the fight and find some place to rest and recuperate. On this day, they would fight no more.

Chapter 8
Under Istra's light shall the nightmare be made real.
--Matteo Dersinger, mad prophet

* * *

There had been a time in Halmsa of the Wind clan's life, not so long ago, that he would have only believed in what he could touch with his hands or see with his eyes. Those days, however, were past; now Halmsa knew that he had to put at least some stock in what his mind alone could see. It had seemed foreign at first, but now it felt as natural as the wind he so revered; most times his eyes could not see that either, and though he could touch it, he could not capture it as he could sand or water.

And so it was that he departed Dragonhold in the middle of night, his guts churning. Until that night he'd been committed to staying, to waiting for Catrin to return so she could teach him to fly. The time would come, of that he was certain, but that time was not now. Catrin was gone. She was an enigma, and his head hurt from trying to understand what he should do. His people were depending on him. So many had been lost. The weight of it pressed down on him and prevented rest. His only choice was to act. For that reason, the dream had been a welcome one. It gave him immediate purpose where none had been before.

Beyond that, though, the dream vision had provided precious little direction. For a moment, he questioned himself. How could he let dreams decide his actions? It was something he would have ridiculed others for in the past. It was the dream itself that gave him resolve. Like no other dream before, it had taken him fully. He could still feel the hot wind on his face; a heavy, musky scent filled that wind and would not be denied. So strong was the smell that Halmsa could still taste it, even in his waking state. A truly powerful vision, indeed, he thought.

After climbing to the top of the ridge that divided the Pinook and Chinawpa Valleys, he gazed out over the moon- and comet-lit landscape. It looked like a different world. Taking a deep breath, he steeled himself to the uncertainty and committed himself, once again, to doing whatever it took to reach his destiny.

* * *

Under the ever-watchful eyes of Morif and Martik, the gates to the great hall were being reconstructed, only this time they were far more substantial. Brother Vaughn observed from a distance, marveling at the way these men took the theories and learning he treasured and applied them in such magnificent scale. It made him feel inadequate. He was a learned man but not necessarily an accomplished man. He chided himself for doing the very thing he advised others not to do: be his own worst enemy. There was great value in imparting knowledge to others, and he could feel a small amount of pride, having taught both Morif and Martik something in their time together.

Miss Mariss approached, looking ready to level anyone who stood in her way, though few were so unwise. There had been disagreements over rations and arguments over whether rationing was still necessary with the enemy gone. Brother Vaughn knew where Miss Mariss stood on the issue, and he stood with her: the danger was far from averted. Catrin had been right all along, and the best thing they could do was to continue as Catrin had wanted.

Trinda stood at his side, looking bored. He patted her on the shoulder and looked to see if Martik and Morif showed any signs of being ready. This meeting was being held in the great hall at their pleasure since that was the only way they could continue to monitor the construction of the defenses while meeting with the rest.

Brother Vaughn couldn't argue that the construction was of the utmost importance, but this was a most inconvenient place to meet. His back ached from standing, and he considered sitting with his back to the giant throne the ancients had cut into the wall. It had stood empty for many ages and had been left untouched out of respect.

Mirta came to the meeting in Millie's stead. "There're wounded who require constant care," she said when she arrived.

Brother Vaughn nodded his understanding. "Stay here," he said to Trinda.

She just rolled her eyes at him and crossed her arms over her chest.

It was time to get this meeting started. He approached Martik with a cautious eye on what the workmen were doing. Work of this scale was what got careless people killed. Brother Vaughn did not want to be one of those people. Martik sensed his approach and turned, his face going from stern to a frown.

"You really couldn't have picked a worse time to do this," Martik said.

"We can manage without you," Brother Vaughn said. "We know what you are working on is of the highest priority. But we need Morif. Chase is busy overseeing work at the God's Eye, and there're issues that'll require the support of the guard. Even if we can't solve all of the problems, we need to at least manage them."

Both men looked over to where Morif stood. He was pointing and shouting at the group of workmen who were moving the new gate into place.

"Just a few more minutes," Martik said, and he firmly pushed Brother Vaughn back before he charged forward, now pointing and shouting himself. A loud creaking sound filled the hall and grew louder and higher in pitch. One man leaped from where he'd been working atop the hinge. Wood screamed in protest before it split and splintered. Martik stood with his hands on his head and said nothing for a long moment. Morif issued a steady stream of curses that let the workmen, the trees, the rope, the hold, and anyone nearby know exactly what he thought of them.

"Perhaps we should have this meeting another time," Brother Vaughn suggested meekly, knowing his interference could certainly be seen as part of what caused the catastrophe.

"I don't see why we should," Martik said, and to his credit, it seemed he didn't place blame on Brother Vaughn's shoulders. "We're going to have to send the logging crew back out, and that'll give us more than enough time to remove the damaged timbers. I suppose I'll remember the virtues of grease next time. If those timbers hadn't seized going into the hinge, we would have our new front gate in place."

Morif approached, looking ready to loose his tongue on anyone who dared speak. "The fools wouldn't listen to me," he said. "I told 'em it was gonna bind up, but they didn't stop in time, and it got away from 'em. Boiling idiots."

"It was my fault," Martik said. "I shouldn't have put them in that position. It won't happen again."

Morif just glared at him, somehow his one eye making his stare even more intimidating. "I still think they should've listened to me."

Martik wisely let it go.

"Let's go have this all-important meeting," Morif said. He walked past Brother Vaughn and, with a short nod, said, "Vaughn." That was it.

Brother Vaughn just shrugged and followed him to where the others stood. It took him a moment to find Trinda, but she stood, running her hand along the rough-hewn stone walls of Dragonhold. Hoping she would behave long enough for him to participate in this meeting, he turned to Miss Mariss, who obviously had something she needed to say. Unlike most of their meetings, a crowd had gathered around to watch this one. None of them had anything to hide, but it felt uncomfortable to have the proceedings witnessed by so many. The construction of the gates had drawn the crowd initially, but this meeting now had the potential to be far more interesting.

"I don't care what any of these fools say," Miss Mariss began, drawing a wince from Brother Vaughn. "We need to continue to ration our supplies until such a time that we have sufficient supplies to replace what we currently have."

"The demons have gone!" someone shouted from the crowd.

Miss Mariss scowled and scanned those assembled, trying to identify who had spoken, but no one took responsibility for the statement. Most likely he or she was worried, and rightly so, about never getting fed from the kitchens again.

"Dangers remain," Brother Vaughn said. "Not all the demons have gone, and we need to be ready to defend ourselves or survive a siege should it come to that. These are not pleasant eventualities we must prepare for, but prepare we must, or we put the lives of all we love at risk. How many of you would've preferred to have lived outside during the invasion?" No one responded this time, and Brother Vaughn knew he'd struck the right note. "I ask that a vote be taken in affirmation of Miss Mariss's assigned duty to ration the supplies as needed to keep the hold sustained and prepared for the worst."

Among those who'd been left in charge, the vote was unanimous. Among the gathered crowd, the results were split, and Brother Vaughn recognized the danger in that. They would soon need to find ways to get more food and supplies so the people would not feel deprived. The last thing they needed was revolution. It seemed odd to even consider the possibility since all they were trying to do was to protect the people of the Godfist, but politics were rarely so straightforward.

"The guard will do its part to make certain the provisions are protected and that rationing orders are obeyed," Morif said. "But I must express my regret that it is so. Those people would better serve us by working on our defenses and gathering more provisions. Keep that in mind when next you protest."

"What of the water?" another voice shouted from the crowd.

"That is a job for everyone in the hold," Miss Mariss retorted. "Every one of us needs to help carry water or run the pumps that Brother Vaughn and Brother Milo created. Then you need to make sure that all of the water channels around your living area are free of debris and will allow water to flow through freely. In this case, Brother Vaughn and Martik have developed a method and the tools needed to clear long sections of channel that are completely encased in rock. If you want easy access to fresh water, then this is a project that should be a priority for you."

"I'd also like to ask the guard to provide an escort for an exploration party," Brother Vaughn said.

"There are only so many of us, Vaughn."

"Yes. I understand. I'm just about certain that additional sources of food exist within this hold. At the very least, there is access to the river, which should mean fish. Could you spare one good soldier?"

"Two," Morif said.

Brother Vaughn wasn't going to argue the point.

"It's my intention to install gates at the entrance to the God's Eye, to the kitchens, and to the newly opened part of the keep. These gates will be guarded at all times, and I don't want anyone giving my people any trouble.

If you do, you're going to have to stare at my face for a long time."

"The infirmary is overloaded," Mirta said when it was her turn to speak. "We need help. Millie and I can only do so much, and even those without healing skills can be of help to us. Please come and see what we are doing, and I know you'll find a way to help."

Brother Vaughn heard an annoyed sound at the mention of Millie, and he turned to see where Trinda had gone. Millie had been the strongest opponent to Trinda's being in the hold, and he suspected he knew who had made the sound. When his initial scan of the area failed to find the girl, he heard the rustle of clothing higher up, and he looked up to what should have been a vacant throne. Trinda sat on the edge, appearing impossibly small with her legs hanging over. She looked down on them as one might look down on ants, and it gave Brother Vaughn a chill. He gestured to her, indicating that she should get down, but she pretended not to see. If the others saw her, it would not go well for the girl, and Catrin was no longer here to protect her. Brother Vaughn knew his influence went only so far, and it could hardly stand up to an insult of this magnitude.

"I say we should reclaim the valley and rebuild Lowerton," another shout came from the crowd. "It won't take that much work to repair the terraces, and we can be farming again in no time." This man seemed to have no hesitation in taking credit for his statement, though Brother Vaughn didn't recognize him. He didn't know many of the farmers who had lived in the valley, so it was not surprising.

"No," Trinda said from atop the throne, and Brother Vaughn felt the blood drain from his face.

A few people looked around to see who'd spoken, but no one looked up to the throne. It was almost as if Trinda were somehow invisible, yet Brother Vaughn could see her clearly.

"I agree that we'll need to grow as much food as we can," the farmer said. "Certainly we should concentrate on ways to grow food within the hold, but in the meantime, we should take advantage of whatever is available to us."

"I said, *no!*" Trinda's voice carried over the crowd this time, and everyone looked up to where she sat.

The spell was broken, and Brother Vaughn sighed. This was not going to go well. "Come down from there," he said. "And don't interrupt the ad--"

A sharp look from Trinda reminded him that she only appeared to be a child. She was older than Catrin by a couple of years, and now the courage and resolve of those years shone in Trinda's eyes. How could he not have seen it before? How had he allowed her to come into the hold? What had he done? A very cold feeling came over him, and he waited to see what would happen next, afraid to act, afraid to make things worse. This was entirely his fault, and he could think of no excuse or justification that would absolve him of guilt. He'd felt sorry for an adult in the guise of a child, and she'd played on his sympathy with extraordinary skill.

"You come down from there this instant, you insolent little monster," Mirta said, but she, too, was cut short by a look from Trinda. There was a warning in her eyes, and Mirta, surprisingly, heeded it.

"I will not come down," Trinda said.

"If you don't come down from there, I'm going to come up there after you," Morif said, and there was no humor in his tone. He and Mirta were Millie's closest companions, and her hatred of this girl seemed to have influenced them as well.

"I said, *no!*" Trinda commanded, and she slammed her closed fist down on the stone. Radiating from the impact was an ice blue wave of energy and air that sent Morif and the others backward a step. "Your ruler has left you behind. And now you have a new ruler. If you wish to remain within Dragonhold, you'll swear fealty to me. Now. Those who do not swear fealty will be *asked* to leave."

"You don't think a little cold air is going to keep me from paddling your bottom, do you?" Morif asked as he stepped forward once again. A deadly silence hung in the air, and Morif took another step forward. Brother Vaughn prayed Morif would stand against her and end this madness.

"You may leave," Trinda said to Morif. "You and the fat woman."

This brought a flush to Morif's face, and Brother Vaughn had never seen the man so angry. In two steps, Morif would reach the base of the throne, but he managed only a single step; in the middle of the second, he was thrust backward. He could not even remain upright. Still moving backward and sliding on his rear end, Morif slammed into the unmoving gate. The workmen stopped, and everyone moved away from where Morif was now pinned to the gate.

"You there," Trinda said to Mirta. "You are forgiven because you were influenced by the fat woman. You may stay. Go back to the infirmary and send the fat woman to me. Do you understand?"

Mirta nodded and ran from the assembly, tears streaming down her face.

Moments later Millie's voice could be heard across the distance, echoing within the hall. "The little chit did what?"

Brother Vaughn tried to catch his breath and hoped Millie would cool her temper before she reached them.

It was not to be. The woman was in a red-faced rage when she approached the throne. "Well. Your *highness,* how might I be of service to your royal self?"

"You may leave," Trinda said.

"I most certainly will not."

"You will *leave.*" Again Trinda slammed down her fist, and another cold blast shook the great hall. It sent Millie falling backward, and she looked up at Trinda with undisguised hatred. "I don't like you," was all Trinda said before she sent Millie sliding across the mosaic floor to rest next to Morif, who still looked as if he were paralyzed.

"You," Trinda said, pointing to Brother Vaughn, "may stay. But you will never scold me again. Is that understood?"

He nodded.

"The gate to the great hall shall be secured and then reinforced again," Trinda said.

"It'll never open," Martik said under his breath, but his voice carried through the silence.

"I do not wish the gate to open," Trinda said. Only silence greeted that statement. "If there are any who would not swear fealty to me, move to the gate. You will not be harmed, and you will be allowed to leave before the gate is sealed. You will, however, never be allowed to return."

Brother Vaughn looked around, waiting to see who would join Millie and Morif, but no one did, and so it was that control of Dragonhold passed to Trinda Hollis, the daughter of a baker. Brother Vaughn was surprised to see Trinda reiterate most of the orders that had already been given, and only a few things changed with regard to how the hold was being run. Food would still be rationed, the water channels would be cleared, and the guard remained intact, although missing its leader. Morif had been in charge of the guard since its formation, and Chase now quietly maintained control, though everyone wondered how long it would be before Trinda realized Catrin's cousin was leading her guard. He supposed the biggest change, though, outside of Millie and Morif being exiled, was that the hold had been closed to the rest of the world. By Trinda's orders, the keep would have to function in an entirely self-sufficient manner. This was something Catrin had never been able to achieve, and it saddened Brother Vaughn that tyranny was required to accomplish the goal.

When Trinda spoke again, her forceful words made it clear to Brother Vaughn that a great many things were about to change. "Who among you will swear fealty to me and guard me with your life, step forward."

No one moved or spoke. Brother Vaughn was imagining what would happen if no one stepped forward when Bradley left the crowd and stood before Trinda. He went to one knee and bowed his head.

"What is your name?"

"Bradley, your highness."

"You are the chief of my guard. Assemble five of your best men before me."

Bradley hesitated only a moment before he called out five names. Two young men stepped forward immediately. There was a delay before two more came. Bradley scanned the crowd, looking to see if Feddy, the last he had called, was among those gathered. When the young man finally stepped forward, there was hesitation in his stride, but Bradley gave him a reassuring nod.

"I've a special task for you," Trinda said, "a task of the utmost importance. I want you to bring me every one of these that was ever made." In her hand, she held a herald globe that glowed more brightly than one fully charged in sunlight. Most would not have noticed this or understood the significance, but Brother Vaughn knew very well just how dangerous herald globes could be in the wrong hands. It definitely seemed that Trinda's hands were now the wrong hands. One herald globe in her possession was enough to worry Brother Vaughn; every herald globe in existence would give her an arsenal the likes of which the Godsland had never seen, or at least had not seen in thousands of years. When Bradley turned to his men, he caught Brother Vaughn's eye and gave an almost imperceptible nod.

"I need a messenger," Trinda said next. Brother Vaughn noted that this girl wasted little time. "Who will serve?"

A young man Brother Vaughn didn't know was shoved forward by the woman behind him, presumably the boy's mother.

"I don't need one so unsure. Are you certain you wish to serve as my messenger?"

The boy drew himself up and raised his eyes. "Yes, lady. I'm certain."

"Good," Trinda said. "Go to the Masterhouse. Tell Master Edling--and only Master Edling--that I now hold Dragonhold. Tell him to come here, with my father, at their earliest convenience. Tell them I look forward to giving them a tour of my new keep. Now repeat the words to me."

The young man repeated the words and stammered only twice, but he managed to get the words in the right order.

"Go," was all Trinda said.

* * *

Catrin knew the Falcon Isles when she saw them, and she urged Kyrien to land west of town, closer to the wilderness. She could sense his anxiety, and she shared it, but they needed rest, and the isles were the only land nearby. The ferals and the black navy had gone east, but that didn't mean they wouldn't come back. They may even have left a force behind to act as a rear guard; the thought further eroded Catrin's confidence.

When traveling between the Greatland and the Godfist, the Falcon Isles were the only significant landmass. It would make sense for their arrival to be expected.

Turning to Prios, Catrin smiled. A sad smile came to his face as well and he nodded. They would stop here to rest. Kyrien came in fast, and he overshot the beach where Catrin had asked him to land. This alone was enough to let her know that he needed rest and healing. She hadn't intended to search out the Gunata or Nat Dersinger, but she saw people in a clearing as they turned, and it was clear that they'd been seen. That would be all the signal Nat needed. Though she considered him a friend, he'd always managed to complicate her life. The thoughts were muddy and indistinct--a sign of her own fatigue. After they landed, her body still tingled from flight, and her legs were unsteady beneath her when she stood in the saddle.

For a moment, Catrin considered remaining strapped in and just sleeping in the saddle, but Prios squirmed behind her, freeing himself from the straps. It took Catrin a few moments longer to unstrap herself and climb down, and she walked with a stiff gait to where Kyrien's head rested.

"You're a valiant soul," she said.

I'm a traitor and a failure. No matter what I do, I can never make up for what I've done. I still have hope for you, but for me, time is punishment.

Catrin felt his pain deeply, and she wished there were some way to prove it all untrue. It was odd that he had hope for her and she, hope for him. Yet neither could scrape up much hope for themselves. Perhaps that was why they were together, to provide hope for each other. Prios somehow maintained a positive outlook. The pain of his childhood had prepared him well for hardship, and he seemed to deal better with that than when things were going well for him. For Catrin, he was strength and stability. Prios was always there for her and for Sinjin. He'd always been a good husband and a good father. But no one else knew him as Catrin did. No one else saw the warrior who'd fought for his freedom, who had fought with everything he had for Catrin ever since.

Catrin knew his power and fortitude, and she was grateful. Before she knew it, she'd fallen asleep, leaning on Kyrien.

* * *

A pale red hue painted the cloudless sky, and the shadows were deep when Catrin awakened. It took some time for her to realize where she was and to recognize her surroundings. When she cleared the fog from her mind, she realized they were not alone. Prios slept nearby and Kyrien was in a stupor. They were about as unprepared as they could be.

"Hello, Catrin," Nat Dersinger said. "I hope I didn't wake you. My people stand guard over you. If you need more rest, then sleep. We will be here when you wake."

Catrin should have taken his advice. Instead, she stood, walked to Nat, and gave him a hug that he did not fully return.

"It's good to see you," she said, and he did not reply. His eyes were scanning Kyrien and the beach around him.

"Where is the staff?" he asked, and there was a dangerous note in his voice.

Guilt washed over Catrin. Nat's family had cared for that staff for generations. "Lost," she said. "Stolen. Thorakis has taken it."

Nat's face grew red with rage, and his hands balled into fists. "How could you let this happen? You know the power of that staff. How could you let it fall into the hands of someone like Thorakis?"

Catrin took a step back from his unexpected anger.

"I've seen, Catrin. I've seen what happens if you have the staff . . . and what happens if you lose it. And you've lost it. May the gods have mercy on your foolhardy soul, for I will not. You, Catrin Volker, are hereby banished from the Falcon Isles. You'll find no respite here unless you return with the staff. Do not make me force you from here. Do the honorable thing and go."

Stunned, Catrin took another step back. Prios stirred on the shoreline, and Kyrien's great lidded eyes drew open just a little.

"Come," Catrin said through her tears. "We're no longer welcome here."

Chapter 9

Dragons are as easy to understand as the wind.
--Brother Vaughn, Cathuran monk

* * *

Millie walked in a daze, with Morif guiding her around obstacles and looking out for any other dangers. Even he was driven to speechlessness by the turn of events. Millie had said all along that Trinda was trouble, but even she would never have guessed just how much trouble. Catrin would not have allowed them to be cast out of Dragonhold, to be sent without so much as a biscuit and knife into country still harboring demons. Millie had disliked the girl before, but now it was personal. Now she would spend the rest of her days searching for a way to repay the kindness. She also worried about all of those who had stayed. Though it stung a bit that no one had chosen to stand with her and Morif, it was probably for the best. Morif didn't need more people to look after.

He took them north, through the Pinook Valley, heading toward where Upperton had stood. Neither knew the fate of the town, but optimism was scarce. When the first ruined structures came into view, it was clear that the obliteration of Upperton was complete. Shadows moved in the distance ahead, and Morif pulled Millie behind a fallen building. Slowly they moved from shadow to shadow. Millie could feel the presence of something else, and her blood went cold. Morif was a seasoned warrior, but he was no match for demons. Those unnatural creatures were aberrations, a twisted mockery of nature's true intention. An involuntary whimper escaped her lips.

Pulling her to speeds that she could not maintain, Morif tried to get Millie clear of the destroyed town. At every turn there were movement and shadows, and it felt as if the darkness were gathering to smother them. Daylight was fading fast, and Millie shivered at the thought of sleeping out here in the dark. Ahead, a section of roofing from a building leaned against the valley wall and formed what appeared to be a stable, dry, and defensible space. A triangular opening stood dark and foreboding.

Millie wanted nothing to do with going into that space, but she would follow Morif with her mouth closed if that was what he told her to do. For as much grief as she gave him when they weren't in danger, she knew just how close death was now, and her trust in him was complete. It brought a flush to her cheeks that blended with her already reddened and sweaty skin. It shamed her that she could not keep up, and she swore that she would make changes in her life. It actually seemed that Trinda had made that decision for her, and she didn't like that feeling one bit.

Morif moved in closer to the lean-to, and Millie's blood ran cold. She knew it was only her fear that had her convinced monsters waited in the darkness, but still that fear kept her frozen in place. Morif turned and waved for her to follow. Then the blood drained from his face. In the next instant, his powerful hands grabbed Millie by the shoulders and propelled her into the darkness.

With her hands thrust out before her, it was all she could do to keep from crying out. Some instinct stilled her tongue. Luckily for them, the space sheltered by the roof was otherwise empty, and just enough light crept in to allow Millie to find her way to a place where she could stand and remain hidden.

Morif held a finger to his lips and moved to the opposite opening. Unable to remain where she was, Millie followed him and peered out, trying to see what it was that had Morif afraid. Her knees trembled at the thought of demons and giants coming to eat them, and she cursed herself for a coward, though she knew it wasn't true. Anyone who felt no fear in the face of those horrors must already be dead, Millie thought, still unable to see anything. Then she heard something that gave her a start: weeping accompanied by hushed yet harsh conversation. Light danced across the valley floor, painting the destruction in swaying shadows.

Finally Millie saw a group of dark shapes with torches. Her breath froze in her throat as Morif tensed. When the group drew closer, wary of the darkness where Millie and Morif hid, she knew they would be found. Then a familiar voice called out, "Who's in there?"

Relief flooded through Millie and just as suddenly rushed away. From nearby came a deep growl that sounded like rolling drums. That was the only warning the approaching group had before the demons attacked. Rushing out from behind another nearby structure, they entered the fray in a state of frenzy, and to their credit, the group recovered from the surprise almost instantly. Battle was joined. A small form was thrust into the middle of the scuffle, and Millie sucked in a breath. Morif squeezed her arm and emphatically motioned for her to stay in the darkness, and before she could object, he was gone. "For Catrin!" came his shouted war cry.

Millie couldn't hide in the shadows and wait; she had to know what was happening. Otherwise, every sound and every cry created visions in her mind of Morif's death or Benjin's--she knew he was who had spoken--or Gwen, or any of the others who had sailed on the *Dragon's Wing* so long ago. When blue fire and lightning lit the entire valley in its pulsating light, Millie could see Kenward Trell and beside him a man she didn't recognize. She was certain she would remember meeting such a fine specimen of a man and the feel of his power in the air, streaming from his fingertips; it was intoxicating.

The sound of battle was otherwise terrifying, but it was the howls in the distance that raised Millie's flesh. These demons were calling out to their brethren, and the responses were drawing ever closer. Soon, she knew, this part of the valley would be overrun with demons. Why hadn't these gone with the rest? Millie asked herself in frustration. In the end, she knew the why didn't matter. What did matter was figuring out how to get all of them to safety.

The tempo of the battle slowed, and the demons drew back, seemingly content to keep them trapped until reinforcements arrived, which would be soon by Millie's reckoning.

"We need to get back to your ship," Morif shouted to Benjin and Kenward. "They'll not welcome you at Dragonhold."

No one questioned him, though there was an even cooler feel to the air. This was not a joyous homecoming, and Millie felt for them. For her, this had been real for some time, but for Benjin, the destruction of much of his homeland was fresh and new. In some ways it was new to Millie as well, and the scope of the devastation was difficult to grasp.

"We're going to knock a hole in their line," Morif said, and he waved for Millie to come out and join them. "We'll head north, back toward the cliffs. When we do, get yourselves through. We'll fall in and defend you from behind. It sounds like most of them are coming from the south. You should be all right. You understand?"

The demons knew they were planning something, and they lunged and feinted to disrupt their communication as much as possible. During one such feint, one of the demons moved between Millie and Morif. The seasoned warrior let out a howl, and the men attacked.

Gwen and Millie were shoved through a breach in the enemy line, and the charge was on. Millie wasn't really prepared for that, and she could not keep pace with Gwen, who was issuing a steady stream of curses. It seemed she felt she was old enough to fight, and to be herded off with Millie had injured her pride.

The battle was close behind Millie, and she had to push herself for speed. Her heart pounded, and her breathing was ragged, but she pressed on, hoping she wouldn't drop from the exertion. Again, she swore to get in better shape, and again, she resented Trinda. The little traitor had set all of them up and played them like lutes. Then, as soon as the opportunity presented itself, she stole Dragonhold from under them and tossed out those who would oppose her.

When Millie put her ego aside, she realized that many of those who had stayed had probably done so to get an opportunity to depose her or to just wait for Catrin's return. Still, she couldn't understand Trinda's motives. It seemed foolish to make an enemy of the most powerful person in the world. But those thoughts would have to wait for another time.

When the lifts came into view, Millie nearly tripped and fell. Only a splintered heap remained. They were trapped, unable to get down to the water from the high cliff. Fear nearly overwhelmed her again. That was when she saw it; sad and pitiful in comparison to what the lifts had been, this was little more than knotted rope forming a basket of sorts.

"Get in," Benjin ordered.

Both Millie and Gwen hesitated, but Benjin cast them a commanding glare and pointed.

"I don't even know why he let me come," Gwen said as she helped Millie into the net.

Millie's steps were hesitant, and she nearly fled, except her fear of the demons far exceeded her fear of heights. Far below, she could see dim lights reflected on the water, and she knew there were people waiting on the ship below. She wondered if it was only one ship, but that was when Benjin and a young man Millie recognized as Jessub Tillerman pulled hard on the rope that was looped over a part of the old lifts.

The net cinched up around Millie and Gwen and pressed them together. Millie felt extremely self-conscious, but Gwen made no complaint. In the next instant, they were pushed out over the cliff's edge, where they descended far more quickly than seemed safe. She couldn't blame those up above, knowing the demons would be pressing them hard. Even at that speed, the fall seemed to take forever, giving Millie too much time to think about what it was going to be like when they struck the water. Nothing could have prepared her for the impact or the cold embrace of the sea. When she regained her senses, Millie was coughing and sputtering. Gwen had an arm around her neck and pulled her free of the net, which was now racing back up to where the others would meet their fates.

Only fear of drowning kept Millie from feeling guilty; she knew it was very unlikely that all those above would escape with their lives. Gwen was a strong swimmer, and she pulled Millie to a boat launched by the nearby ship. Millie wasn't certain if she would see the *Slippery Eel* or the *Dragon's Wing* since both ships' captains were above, but her vision was so blurred at that moment, she had no idea who was in the boat with her, let alone what ships waited in the darkness.

When the boat reached the side of a ship, Millie did her best to climb the rope ladder, but Gwen had to push her from behind. Moments later, Millie lay, breathing hard, on the deck of the *Dragon's Wing*. The ship was unmistakable. Having been carved from the trunk of a greatoak, the ship was seamless. When Millie levered herself up to lean on the rail, Fasha was there to lend her support, and Grubb brought out broth. Bryn arrived shortly after with warm blankets.

"If you'll just come with me," Bryn said, "we can get you something dry to wear."

"Not yet," Millie said. "I have to know--" Her voice caught in her throat, and she could say no more.

"What are they facing up there?" Fasha asked, concern clear on her features.

"Monsters," Gwen said, her lip quivering from the cold.

"Demons," Millie agreed.

The blood drained from many faces. Again the net crashed into the water with what looked like a bone-crushing impact. The boats were there quickly, and everyone watched in tense anticipation as limp forms were pulled from the water. Millie held her breath until she saw Morif sit up in the boat. Benjin also managed to get himself upright.

The net started back up fast, but then it dropped to the water. Millie willed the net to rise again, and when it did, she gasped. The motion of the net was jerky, and it stopped at times, but steadily it moved back upward. From atop the cliffs, blue lit up the mountainsides. Muted thunder made it clear the fighting was nowhere near over. The body of a demon hurtled over the cliffs and crashed to the waves below. It did not surface.

A moment later, the net descended again, this time with Jessub Tillerman inside. That left the handsome young man all alone up there. The net descended quickly at first, but then it cut loose completely and dropped like a stone. Millie gripped the rail and held her breath again, making her feel faint. The boats moved in to rescue the young man, who was clearly in grave danger. Before they reached him, though, a pair of reptilian claws latched on to one side of the first boat. With inhuman strength, the demon pulled down sharply, causing the boat to flip. Two men managed to right the boat and climb back aboard. The third screamed just before disappearing beneath the waves.

Jessub didn't regain consciousness after being pulled in by the second boat, but both boats made their way back to the *Dragon's Wing* as quickly as the rough seas would allow.

"He's breathing," Millie heard someone say, and she started to do so again herself. She wasn't certain how much more of this day her heart could take.

Thunder from above continued for a time then stopped abruptly. A luminous form, rimmed with fire, leaped into the air and swooped down toward the ship. He did not fall or scream, despite the rapid rate of his descent. He traveled in a graceful arc toward the ship. Then he turned one hand as if to cup the wind, and he slowed, his cloak billowing behind him. His other hand clenched tightly around something that appeared afire. The wind pressed his supple clothing against his body, and Millie found herself staring. When he landed deftly at the prow, she realized her mouth was hanging open, and it shut with a pop.

"What happened?" she heard Jessub ask. The young man's voice trembled with uncertainty.

"You're gonna be all right," Benjin said. "But you pretty much took it on the chin when you hit the water."

Benjin might have said more, but his voice was drowned out by the sound of his wife giving orders. As soon as Jessub, the crew, and the boats were aboard, they would set sail.

Though Jessub could speak, it took two crewmen to get him onto the rope ladder. Just as they were hauling him up, claws once again reached from the depths. Men screamed and there was a snapping sound as rope strained beyond its abilities. The demon certainly couldn't capsize the *Dragon's Wing,* but it was trying to pull the rope ladder into the water. From the sounds of the rope and wood straining, Millie thought it might succeed.

Leaning out over the rail and trying to get a good angle, the handsome man shouted for someone to help him, to grab his ankles. When no one else moved to do as he asked, Millie did. Though she lacked his physical strength, she gripped his legs and used her body as an anchor. For once, she wished she were heavier since the man's violent and sudden movements nearly sent them both over the edge. Then she saw lightning flash around his hand, which he thrust downward. The ship rocked and a thunderous boom echoed from the bluffs.

Given respite, the crew moved quickly, not knowing how long they would have. When the demon attacked again, all were on deck, and the beast had to settle for sinking one of the boats. The other was raised with long poles capped with sturdy hooks.

It seemed surreal as they moved away from the Godfist; it soon became even more unreal.

"Are you well enough?" Gwen asked the handsome young man. She was a comely lass; her still-wet hair hung in long curls that shone in the moon- and lamplight.

"Yes," he said with a respectful nod.

"Then let's get this ship out of here before more of those devils come looking for us."

The man moved to stand near the steerage, still holding something in one palm. Gwen strode to the aft, where Millie saw something strange. She'd been on the deck of this ship years ago, and she didn't remember it having massive tubes of wood mounted side by side at the stern. The wooden structures were supported by a retrofitted platform that used what looked like shims of burlap to secure the structures while still allowing a small amount of movement.

Millie went from puzzled to amazed when Gwen walked between the cylinders of wood and placed her hands on either side. A small platform gave her a place to sit, and the girl settled in as if she had spent a considerable amount of time there.

"Flightmaster Pelivor," Fasha said. "You have the helm. Set a course for the Falcon Isles."

"Yes, Captain," Pelivor said, giving Gwen a nod.

The sound of rushing air rose up behind her, and Millie turned to see lightning crawling over Gwen's hands and onto the wooden tubes. The wind rushed into those tubes, and the ship moved forward with ever-increasing speed. When Millie dared to take her eyes from Gwen, she saw Pelivor cast his closed fists out wide, and she could feel his power on the air. The *Dragon's Wing* slipped free of the waves, and Gwen could be heard laughing as the air whined a high-pitched song. The rigging vibrated and the sails were quickly lowered.

"It's going to be fine," Pelivor said to Millie, his smile calm and confident. "You can trust us to keep you safe."

Though his words had been soothing, his actions were not. The ship angled upward, and Gwen shouted with glee as the *Dragon's Wing* outraced the clouds.

"By all the gods in the heavens!" Millie cried, and she crumbled to the deck, unable to take any more in one day.

* * *

Travel had been difficult for Kevlin Weil, and he still found himself within half a day's walk of an aqueduct. Those stone leviathans, he knew, were what he really needed to escape. Keeping from starving in the meantime was proving difficult as well. In Thorakis's lands, Thorakis provided the food, and those under his command received their rations. He could claim no ration without having to explain his absence from his designated duty. Whether these people knew it or not, they were trapped. They were entirely dependent on Thorakis, and none were likely to stick their necks out for the likes of Kevlin Weil.

Fear was a powerful thing, and Thorakis wielded it well without ever openly acknowledging it. More and more, though, there were whispers and rumors. Some said Thorakis was gone from Riverhold, that he'd flown away on a dragon and attacked the Godfist with a host of black ships. Kevlin wasn't sure how much faith to put in rumors, but there were too many whispers to completely ignore. Events of historic proportion were under way, and Kevlin couldn't shake the feeling that he would get caught under the wheels of those events.

One staple that Thorakis didn't ration was ale. For some reason, every village had an overlarge supply of ale. Still, when Kevlin made his way into a busy inn, it was filled with a crowd who looked to be drinking away their cares. The innkeeper gave him a suspicious look, and Kevlin knew he was on dangerous turf.

"Two coppers for a mug."

Kevlin had realized long before how foolish he'd been to keep all his savings in gold. The coins had been easier to carry than smaller denominations, and they had somehow served his ego better than silver or copper, but spending them made everyone look at him crosswise. Kevlin didn't care; his stomach demanded sustenance, and ale would have to do. If he was lucky, the innkeeper would have something salty to serve; that always seemed to sell more drink. Sheepishly he handed her the gold coin. The woman looked back at him with the hard eyes of one who'd seen her share of cons and thieves.

She bit down on the coin, grimaced, then slammed it on the bar. "You won't get nothin' with that."

Kevlin blinked, unsure of what to say.

"You got any more gold in your pocket?"

"Uh," Kevlin said. "No. That's everything I have." Though gold in his pocket there might be, he didn't need anyone here to know that; already people were casting him sideways glances. Some of those glances were decidedly unfriendly.

"You hadn't heard about the false coins, eh?" the innkeeper asked, the look on her face softening slightly.

Kevlin just shook his head, hoping the lie wouldn't show.

"I'll tell you what. I can melt it down and sell it for the silver." She took the coin, and Kevlin would have been grateful, but her words haunted him. It had begun.

Once the people's faith in the currency failed, Thorakis would exert military force to maintain control. Already the people were dependent on Thorakis and his fishery, but it would get worse. It would get much worse. Perhaps there was still time for Kevlin to escape to the south, but he knew time was slipping away, and the longer he remained within the reach of the aqueducts, the longer he was a prisoner of Thorakis.

When the innkeeper returned, she carried a mug of ale and three pieces of smoked fish. "I don't know what you're running from or how you came 'cross that coin, but you look like an honest man. Your hands show the signs of hard work. That's good enough for me."

"Thank you," Kevlin said. "What happened to the coins?" he asked, trying to sound pitiful.

"People are saying it's Thorakis. They always said his coffers were endless, and now we see why. Things are gonna start getting real bad, real quick. No one knows exactly how he did it, but it had to be him. Who else could do such a thing?"

Kevlin didn't answer. The innkeeper just shrugged and walked to the other end of the bar, where patrons waited. They leered at him, and Kevlin kept his eyes averted. Eye contact would only provoke them, and all Kevlin wanted was to get away as quickly as he could. In four overlarge gulps, Kevlin downed his ale and was stuffing one of the salted fish in his mouth when he pushed his way through the door at a fast walk. Voices rose from within as the door slammed shut behind him, and Kevlin knew he needed to move fast. Running as hard as he could without risking a fall, he passed by people who stopped and watched him go. He could hear little over the sound of his breathing, and he didn't stop running until he entered a thin line of trees that bordered the town.

What he saw on the other side frightened him. Somehow he'd gotten turned around and had run right into the aqueduct. Looming like a massive wall, it penned him in. Kevlin was certain that was part of its intent, and it did the job well.

His gut told him that going back could be a fatal mistake. Too many people had taken an interest in him, and Kevlin was certain he didn't want to run into any of them again. That left the aqueduct. Perhaps if he just followed it south for a time, he could slip back into the countryside unnoticed. Afternoon was fading toward evening, and he didn't see anyone else around. Hoping all the workmen had retired for the evening, Kevlin left the trees and walked along the stone structure. The land alongside it had been cleared, which left an unobstructed roadway for Kevlin.

Feeling exposed, Kevlin moved quickly and covered as much ground as he could while he still had daylight. He'd be able to walk in the light of the moon and comets, but running would be unwise. Ahead he saw a section of the aqueduct that was under repair, and he ducked into the trees. No one stirred around the work site, but Kevlin could see the exposed cross section of the aqueduct. Water dripped from a temporary structure that bridged the gap, and it was clear that the stone structure had recently collapsed. Part of that, Kevlin realized, was because the structure was hollow; something he had never before realized. Cradled within the stone was a walkway, a tunnel. Cold realizations washed over Kevlin, and he knew he'd been right about needing to get away from the aqueducts. Now, though, he knew why, and he also knew that he would have to get very far away from them indeed.

Those thoughts vanished when his attention was drawn by movement in the corner of his vision. Dark shapes left the trees not far from where Kevlin had emerged. Preceding them was a pair of hounds. Kevlin's blood ran cold when he saw the hilts of swords at the men's sides. It was difficult to see any detail, but Kevlin had seen all he needed to see. He made a snap decision then, and before he could second-guess himself, he ran across the clearing between the trees and the work site. When he reached the strip of muddy stone, he leaped with all of his might to make it into the stone tunnel in a single jump. Water rained down from the temporary construction that bridged the gap in the stone above.

Kevlin's boots left tracks on the muddy stone, but the workmen had left a myriad of tracks outside. Hoping the water would cover his scent and wipe away his tracks, Kevlin crept into the darkness. Running his hand along the cold, damp stone, he moved south.

Chapter 10

Only when the will is singular can truly great things be accomplished.
--Thorakis the Builder

* * *

The shallows came into view when a new day bathed the world in a dreamlike glow. Catrin watched the sun rise and cast its fiery light onto the lopsided volcano. She'd seen it whole once, that megalithic spire; she'd seen it breathe and move. Even the memory was terrifying. They had lost good friends that day, and only the knowledge that they had gotten some of those friends back helped temper the loss. Tears slid down her cheeks when she remembered her reunion with Benjin and Fasha amid the shallows. The place had still been recovering from the eruption when she last saw it, and it was encouraging to see new growth, new saltbark trees, and new dryads.

For years, when Catrin had lain down for sleep at night, she dreamed of the dryad she'd seen in the shallows. She had longed to embrace that lonely soul who had reached out to her, but that embrace had been impossible.

Part of Catrin was glad to be in the shallows again. Even if she somehow knew that dryad had moved on from this life, Catrin felt closer to her here. As the sun climbed higher in the sky, the blue water shone, and a shelf of land could be seen rising from the depths. It was there that giant sharks lurked, and Catrin had no desire to ever encounter them again.

Kyrien soared low over the water, sending spray up behind them. Soon his shadow raced over white sands beneath shallow water. Even at their high rate of speed, Catrin could see the diversity of life this place supported. Though she saw none of the giant rays she'd seen in the past, she saw brightly colored red, yellow, and blue fish. Impossibly long snakes moved sideways across the water or hung, coiled, from the branches of saltbark trees. The trees themselves were a marvel. Catrin could never quite get over the crystals that encased the leaves, making them look magical. What was certain was that the leaves had powerful restorative properties and were a legendary cure for a long list of ailments. Knowing the results some of those close to her had seen, she vowed to gather some.

For a while, Catrin simply basked in the beauty of the place. Prios rested comfortably behind her, and her only real worry at that moment was making sure Kyrien rested. Bad weather had harried them, and she knew he was nearly spent. If she'd been honest, she would have admitted that worry of Sinjin shaded every thought, but she did her best to stuff those feelings deep down inside until she was ready to deal with them.

Rising out of mist-covered waters ahead were stone pillars the size of greatoaks. Within the ring, Catrin knew there was a place of great power, a place where the land's energy was somehow closer and more accessible.

Kyrien cut a wide turn to bring them within the ring of pillars, all of which stood in turbulent water that frothed and foamed around them, forming whirlpools and areas where the water seemed to bulge upward. A steady wind cut through the grove of water and stone, much like the Grove of the Elders, yet very different.

The power of the place coursed through her, and Catrin knew Kyrien, too, could feel it. Perhaps that was why he'd chosen this place, or perhaps it was the constant, steady wind. With his eyes closed, Kyrien hovered in place, letting the rush of air cradle them and keep them aloft. At first Catrin worried a gust of wind might ram them into the pillars, but compensating for changes in the wind appeared to be something dragons could do in their sleep, and again she was awed by the majesty of her companion.

Prios and Kyrien slept, but the pain in Catrin's head prevented her from doing the same. Knowing she was surrounded by saltbark, Catrin decided it would be best to leave them sleeping and gather some leaves. After unstrapping herself, Catrin climbed onto Kyrien's shoulders, the wind buffeting her as she worked to keep her balance. She turned and stepped out onto the bony wing structures, hoping she wouldn't hurt Kyrien, but the wing barely moved, and she was able to walk along his bones. The thought of walking out on his wing membrane made her worry about hurting him since it looked more fragile, but she somehow knew that Kyrien found this amusing.

Near where the tip of his wing hovered, the water was shallow, though still turbulent. It was a short drop, and Catrin was soon wading toward a cluster of trees. She had wondered why Kyrien wouldn't just land, but she remembered when she looked closer that the trees were the only things above water in most of the shallows. He would've had to land on the trees themselves. Catrin was thankful he had not. This was a place deserving of respect and reverence.

The water was cold but not frigid, and the trees were not far away. When Catrin stepped out of the shadow of the pillar, she caught movement from the corner of her eye and froze. Remaining still for some time, Catrin was confident that, whatever it had been, it wasn't hostile. The first tree she came to was bursting with deep green leaves whose crystals cast rainbows around them. It was almost difficult to look upon; its leaves seemed as if they were always moving. Perhaps that was why Catrin didn't see the snake.

Brighter green than the leaves and coiled around the inner branches, the snake's head managed to sufficiently blend with its surroundings. When Catrin did see it, she recognized the wide and full head of a viper. Knowing that even moving away too quickly could cause the snake to strike, she remained frozen.

"Do not be afraid of Ellesin, heart of the land," came a high, rich voice, and Catrin could now sense the presence behind her. It appeared friendly but Catrin did not like being caught unawares. Given who she was, it could be fatal. "Ellesin is protective of the tree, yes. But a respectful hand he will not bite. And you are respectful of us. I remember you."

Catrin's breath caught in her throat, and she slowly pulled her hand away from the snake. It wasn't that she didn't believe the snake saw her as friendly; it was simply impossible for her to overcome the fear of venomous fangs sinking into her flesh. When she turned, her eyes were greeted by one of the most beautiful faces she'd ever seen. Green eyes danced with life, and vinelike hair sparkled within a coating of crystals; leaves covered most of the dryad's body, somehow making her look more appealing than the finest silk would have.

"Greetings, tree mother," Catrin said. "Were you the one I saw all those years ago?"

"No," the dryad said, a hint of sadness in her voice. "That was my cousin, but she passed down the memory of you to me--you and the man and woman who stayed here. The trees miss them, though the fish do not." She laughed at this, and her laugh was like a healing salve. It loosened Catrin's stiff muscles, relaxing her. "It is all right," the dryad said. "You're safe here and your companions are safe where they are. I've asked the land to hold you."

Catrin wasn't certain what she meant, but she did feel a great deal more calm. Tension and fear eased, and into that space rushed grief and frustration. She wanted Sinjin back. She had failed him, and she worried she would do so again. Tears again filled her eyes, and she resisted the urge to wipe them away, resisted the urge to tell herself she was weak. She needed to feel this pain. She needed to grieve for the loss of her son to the enemy so she could dedicate herself fully to getting him back.

"You have pain," the dryad said. "Let me give you a gift." Reaching out her hand, the dryad placed it under a glistening leaf. After a soft rustling sound, the leaf fell from the branch and landed soundlessly in her palm. She handed it to Catrin as if it were the greatest treasure, which Catrin knew it to be. When the dryad placed the leaf in Catrin's hand, she said, "Put this on your tongue, and let the crystals dissolve. Then chew and swallow."

Catrin was about to ask the dryad's name, but when she withdrew her hands, the dryad made contact with Catrin's hands. For an instant, Catrin saw richly painted images in her mind; memories that were not hers flowed between her and the dryad. They remained connected for some time. The experiences of entire lives entered Catrin, though she knew not how much she would retain. So much of it was like smoke in a strong wind, there one moment and gone with the next breath. When finally the flood of information stopped, the dryad broke contact, tears streaming down her face. "You've been given a gift by a dryad before."

While it was a statement, it came out sounding more like a question.

"Yes," Catrin said.

"It is so wonderful to have news from our cousins. The birds bring us bits and pieces, but they are forgetful. What you have brought us is truly a treasure!"

"I'm so glad," Catrin said, amazed to learn that she'd been carrying all that around with her for so long. She'd never noticed it or been aware of it, yet she suddenly felt as if a burden had been lifted from her, a debt paid. When she placed the leaf on her tongue, she did so with joy in her heart. The taste was difficult to describe, but the crystals seemed a mixture of salty and sweet. The meat of the leaf was tangy with a spicy bite. The instant she ate it, Catrin began to feel better. The pain in her head was mostly gone within moments, and it continued to fade. "I don't know your name."

"I am Vellatarina. You may call me Vell."

"Thank you, Vell. I'm Catrin."

Vell nodded as if she already knew this. "There are many who rely on you and expect things from you, and I do not wish to increase your burden, but I've something I must ask of you."

"Ask."

"There is something I want you to take with you. It's small but it's very important."

"What do you want me to do with it?" Catrin asked.

"You'll know when the time comes," Vell said, and she turned aside as if she needed privacy. Catrin heard soft words spoken and a catch in Vell's voice. When the dryad turned back, it was clear that she had been crying again, and in her cupped hands she held a single perfectly formed seed. It was white and tan, and each color was layered on top of the other over and over again until the seed was covered in concentric, wavy stripes that were always the exact same distance apart.

"Take this. Please. Carry it with you, and when you become inspired, please . . . think of me."

Vell's voice cracked again, and Catrin could only imagine what it would feel like to entrust your seed to another. In some ways it mirrored her own worries about how Sinjin was being treated, but Catrin knew this was something more. This was important on a completely different level, even if she couldn't quite see how or why yet. It bothered her a bit that there had been things in her head that she'd been unaware of, but that was overshadowed by the joy it clearly brought to Vell and her cousins.

When Catrin parted from Vell, she left with saltbark leaves for Prios and Kyrien. They, too, needed restoration and healing. When she reached Kyrien's wingtip, he dipped it low until it almost touched the water. Climbing back up, Catrin hoped he'd not been awake and waiting for her all this time.

I'm already feeling much better. You should rest now.

To Catrin's surprise, he accepted the five saltbark leaves she had brought for him. That left two for Prios and another for herself. Vell had been most generous with her gifts. The seed, Catrin had tucked away in her pocket, though she knew she needed a better way to store it. She knew how important it was to Vell, and she would never forgive herself if something happened to it.

Prios accepted the leaves, and Catrin placed the last one on her tongue, relishing the taste. Putting his hands on her shoulders, Prios began kneading her muscles. Despite the relief the saltbark provided, he found places where she was stiff and sore, and through some magic, he convinced her muscles to relax. Within moments, Catrin slept. Her dreams were filled with vibrating light and a warm hum that soothed her, as if it were shaking the pain loose from her body and the shadow loose from her soul.

When her eyes opened again, she saw something beyond her wildest imaginings. Near the base of each stone pillar sat a beautiful dryad, each sparkling in the light of a new morning. Between them danced intricate patterns of light that made Catrin's and Prios's power look like a child's stick drawing compared to the work of a master artist. Even given use of her saddle, staff, and Koe, Catrin doubted she'd ever be able to create such delicate and complex structures.

Even more astounding was the rotation of the water within the pillars. The dryads were feeding energy to Kyrien, Catrin, and Prios, and it seemed they did so in a circular pattern, which pulled the water along with it. So strong was the rotation that a huge spout formed, exposing the seabed below to the air. Kyrien could easily have landed in that space, but Catrin had a vision of the water suddenly crashing back in on them, and she was glad that he kept them airborne.

There was something else that tugged at Catrin's senses. Mixed in with the hum of power and the wind was a subtle and beautiful melody. The dryads were singing, Catrin realized, the old songs that Shirlafawna had spoken of so long ago. Had Catrin truly had them in her head for all these years? It seemed too strange to be true, yet the dryads practically glowed.

Prios pulled her back and kissed her cheek and Catrin smiled. Slowly the dryads decreased the level of energy, their singing grew quiet, and the waters inexorably reclaimed the seafloor, though not as quickly as Catrin would've imagined. The vibrating and buzzing feeling remained, but the dryads slowly slipped back to the trees and disappeared.

Only Vell remained sitting on the base of the column near Kyrien's wingtip. "We've given what we are able to give. Be well. I can offer no more gifts or healing, but I'll impart this one last thing to you: You must not leave here yet. Stay one more night."

It seemed a small request, but it was a great deal to ask of Catrin. Already she'd been delayed too much in the quest to get Sinjin back. Prios, too, was anxious and ready to get going. The energy imparted by the dryads had them eager to be in their way.

"Can you tell me why?" Catrin asked.

The look on Vell's face in response to the question showed disappointment, but she answered nonetheless. "There's something you need to hear. Your coming is fortuitous, and your wait will be short. Had you come on the morrow, you'd have had to wait a week."

Though Vell had still not been entirely clear, Catrin asked no more since the dryad was clearly reluctant to speak of it. With any luck, this message would arrive soon and they could be on their way.

The wind continued its steady gale, and the waters below them were back to their usual turbulence. Warm air buffeted Catrin, and she watched hummingbirds as they performed aerial acrobatics. Prios pointed out a massive sea turtle, its shell divided into golden squares separated by dark chasms. It basked in the energy below them for a time and regarded Catrin and Kyrien with curiosity. The turtle swam on, surprisingly swift as it moved deeper into the shallows. It was then that Catrin first heard a voice.

Are you there?

Startled, Catrin looked to Prios, but he just shrugged. It wasn't his voice Catrin had heard, and it wasn't Kyrien's. From behind the pillar, Vell appeared again. She held her finger to her lips, and Catrin stifled her nearly automatic response. Then she thought she heard an irritated sigh.

Must think I have all the time in the world to stand around and wait.

For tense moments, nothing happened. Catrin did her best to remain silent and even to keep her thoughts close. She wasn't certain exactly what was happening here, and she didn't want to give them away.

Are you there?

There was irritation in the voice, and again Catrin didn't answer. Now though, something was really starting to bother her. She recognized that voice.

Of course I'm here.

The response bore an equal share of irritation. And Catrin would have fallen from Kyrien's back in shock if not so firmly secured by the saddle. She recognized the second voice as well.

Get on with it, then. I've no time to spare. War is brewing, Lissa said.

It is indeed. The black navy has sailed for the Greatland, and you'll soon have more dragons than you'll know what to do with. Your beloved cousin's get is on one of those ships, so I assume Thorakis won't have much to worry about much from her, Master Edling responded.

A mistake in birth and marriage hardly makes her my cousin.

There was venom in the words, and Catrin couldn't help but feel the sting. Though she was tempted to tell Lissa exactly how she felt, she remained silent.

Your cousin and her tongueless husband ride the last of the regent dragons to retrieve their son. In your cousin's absence, Trinda Hollis, the daughter of the baker, has taken control of Dragonhold.

Again, Catrin reeled. How could Trinda have taken control of Dragonhold? Feeling suddenly foolish and used, Catrin made herself pay attention to the rest. There would be time for anger afterward.

The girl sent word asking for her father and me to visit Dragonhold, and I expect to control the Pinook and Chinawpa Valleys within weeks. The devastation from the attacks is widespread, but now we can rebuild. We will, of course, still need the supplies that you committed.

This, at least, was some consolation to Catrin. Even if the people of the Godfist were not under her rule, which she had never really asked for anyway, she wanted to know that they were well taken care of. Any supplies Lissa could send would certainly help prevent widespread starvation.

Supply ships were on their way weeks ago. You've mostly held up your end of our bargain, and I'll hold up mine. The religious artifacts you requested, however, are beyond my reach. I doubt very much that I'll ever get within sight of the objects you mentioned. Thorakis has had men scouring the land, looking for the gifted and for relics. More and more the people distrust Thorakis. His power has grown too great, and the fools are just now starting to wonder if they made a mistake putting one man in control of all the food. If Thorakis turns off the water, he turns off the food. And those aqueducts will keep the people divided.

Though she'd been born on the Godfist, Catrin felt an affinity with the people of the Greatland, the place of her mother's birth. Everything new she learned about Thorakis made her despise him more. Though Catrin tried to reserve those feelings for only the most vile, this man presented the greatest threat she'd ever known. To have the ability to starve an entire population at will was more power than any one individual should ever have.

It must have seemed so innocent to the people at first when Thorakis's laborers brought the aqueducts to a town. Water, fish, and other supplies could then easily be sent to the people there. Even when he'd asked for all able-bodied men to join his forces, it must have seemed harmless enough. Certainly it had made sense for those men to help bring the same food and supplies to other areas where people were struggling to survive. With the men had gone the horses and oxen, leaving the people without what they needed to farm without what Thorakis provided. The people had inadvertently enslaved themselves, and many of them still did not even know it. Even those would soon find out.

Master Edling continued, *It took a great deal of effort, gold, and a lot of convincing to get people to let go of the items you requested. If you cannot get me the artifacts, then I'll need pyre orchid. Or if you wish, you could simply tell me the location from which you speak. You have me at a disadvantage.*

Catrin thought that perhaps she, too, knew from where Master Edling spoke.

There have been no forest fires that I'm aware of, and even if there had been, that would be no guarantee there would be pyre orchid. It is a rare thing. I cannot grant that request. I am able to tell you where I'm standing, but I will not. You must ask for something else.

Lissa, it seemed, had not lost her charm. There was a hint of something dangerous in Master Edling's voice when he responded, as if all of this had been an elaborate gambit and it was about to come to fruition.

Perhaps, then, you will tell me of another location such as these we currently occupy. You do know of another, do you not?

There was a long pause before Lissa responded, *I do know of another such location, but I'll not tell you where it is. You ask too much. Think on it between now and our next meeting. My time has run short, and I've a long journey ahead of me.*

The annoyance returned to Master Edling's voice. *Yes, yes, of course. Please don't let me keep you from your arduous journey. I'll count the hours until we speak again. I'm certain there're more of what you want on the Godfist, especially within Dragonhold, and I will, of course, be happy to send them to you. Until next time.*

There was no response from Lissa. Catrin could not be certain what Lissa had asked for, but she had a good guess, and the thought gave her a cold feeling in her gut. It felt to her as if she had made a terrible mistake but had yet to fully realize it. It was difficult to shake, but Kyrien took them higher and executed a banking turn that took them through the columns. In that moment, Catrin wanted nothing more than to say good-bye to Vell. When she looked back, she saw the dryad waving from beside her tree, and the other dryads showed themselves as well. In silent salute, they watched as Kyrien, Catrin, and Prios flew away.

Chapter 11

It is within the subtleties of light that one finds the greatest power.
--Gemino, sorcerer and artist

* * *

Benjin Hawk stood at the prow of his ship, still amazed by what he saw. In all his days, he'd never have thought the *Dragon's Wing* would fly and at such speed. Certainly he'd known that Catrin could make a ship fly, but finding out that others could do the same had been a shocking realization. And then there were the wooden tubes. Those confused him more than anything else, partly because he couldn't grasp how they worked, but mostly because his teenage daughter seemed perfectly adapted to using these strange pieces of wood art to propel his ship faster than any ship had ever sailed. It seemed unnatural and amazing and frightening all at once.

When the Falcon Isles appeared, Benjin wanted to know, more than anything, that Catrin was there and safe. Hearing the sound of a cane on the deck, Benjin knew it was Wendel who had come to his side.

"It's been too long since I've seen my daughter," Wendel said. "I miss her."

"So do I," Benjin said. "It seems like yesterday that she wanted my help building a tree fort. Now I'm not even certain that tree still stands."

"She's a tough one, that one," Wendel said. "Like her mother."

Benjin made no response.

"And now we get to see our old friend Nat," Wendel continued.

"Perhaps I'll wait on the ship," Benjin said.

"Still holding grudges, eh?"

"I've managed to forgive him for many things, but that does not mean I've the desire to seek him out. More often than not, talking to him means trouble."

"We'll make it brief," Wendel said.

From nearby, Fasha smiled sadly, seeing that her husband was taking the worst of it.

"There could be any number of demons, turncoats, assassins, or worse on these islands," Morif said. "I suggest everyone stay on the ship and only two of us go to see the mad prophet."

"He's not mad," Millie said, but the others ignored her statement.

When the ship dropped anchor in shallow water north of the harbor, a single boat was lowered, and aboard were Wendel, Morif, and Benjin. Morif looked less pleased than usual. That alone would have put most men off, but Benjin had just shouldered his way onto the boat and refused to budge. Rowing to shore didn't take long, and they soon stood along a sandy stretch of beach. The once devastated vegetation had returned in full force.

"You don't really want to go in there, do you?" Morif asked.

Benjin scanned the tree line for some sign of a trail, some sign of where Nat Dersinger and the Gunata tribe could be found. He knew what kind of dangers lurked in those jungles, and Nat was not the least of them. He had influenced Catrin over the years, and Benjin had always disliked it. He didn't trust the man, and it pained him that Catrin did. Wendel was probably right, but Benjin still had a bad feeling that grew worse the longer he stared at the livid jungle. This wasn't a place to be trifled with. Within those leaves waited both marvels and deadly things large and small. The main problem was that he still didn't know which were which. That left them trying to avoid everything.

"Perhaps we should build a fire," Wendel said. "That would bring him to us."

"That'll bring everyone to us," Morif said, looking worried. Wendel had known the man long enough to know that he had good instincts, and if he was worried, then Wendel was worried. In the next instant, though, the choice was taken out of their hands. A booming explosion split the air. When Benjin looked out to the *Dragon's Wing*, where the sound had seemed to come from, a puff of white smoke rising into the air above the deck told the tale. Kenward stood at the rail, waving. When the wind shifted, Kenward could be heard shouting, "That should get his attention."

"Does that man ever think anything through?" Benjin asked.

"It would appear not," Morif said. "We can wait maybe an hour, no more. The only blessing is that Kenward didn't make that noise twice. To be honest, I'm still trying to figure out how he did it. Under *different* circumstances, that might actually be useful."

Time passed slowly and tension hung heavy in the air. Benjin knew someone must be coming to investigate, but thus far they had seen no one. Nat and his people were nomadic, and he knew they could be anywhere on the island. The people who filled the harbor town were potentially far closer and could be there at any time.

"We have to go," Morif said suddenly, and Benjin turned to look where the man pointed. Once again, the one-eyed man had seen what others missed. Like a stain on the horizon, a black ship moved their way. It could simply be a pirate vessel destined for the harbor, but it looked to be coming straight at them.

"I knew this was a bad idea," Benjin said.

"Always you have doubted," came a voice from the tree line, and the hair on Benjin's neck stood. "To what do I owe the honor of being summoned by the father of the Herald, the guardian of the Herald, and the servant of the Herald's mother? Given your lack of proximity to the Herald, I'd say you're not doing very well at performing your duties."

"We just need to know if you've seen Catrin," Wendel said. His tone was civil, but there was an unmistakable hint of exasperation.

"I have."

"When?" Wendel asked, his voice trembling with hope. "Where is she?"

"Several days ago," Nat said, and there was clear disdain in his voice. He stepped a couple of strides away from the trees. As he did, the trees around him moved. Bodies that had been concealed now revealed themselves. A clear message had been delivered. If only Benjin had been able to hear it. What he heard instead were Nat's next words.

"The Herald of Istra did light upon these lands with the last of the regent dragons, both seeking absolution for what they've done, but they found no respite here. The Herald failed at her duty to keep safe the Staff of Life, and she's been held accountable. Her request for healing and sanctuary was denied, and she was sent away."

"She's hurt?" Benjin asked in an angry bark.

"She and her dragon bore the wounds of battle, yes, but they should live."

"How could you turn away a wounded friend?" Benjin asked, and he moved toward Nat without waiting for an answer. "You're a monster, plain and simple. You're no better than the demons."

"Don't blame me," Nat said, his hands held out wide. "I'm not the one who let the Staff of Life fall into the hands of the darkness. My duty was done. It was the Herald who failed in hers. I've seen the future in which she loses the staff, and the blood will weigh heavily on her soul."

Nat may have had more to say, but Benjin uncoiled his anger like a striking snake, and Nat was thrown backward by the sudden blow. "How come you didn't see that coming, prophet?"

Benjin, too, was cut short. The sharp tip of a spear jammed against the tender flesh under his chin and pressed his mouth shut.

Nat approached, dabbing the blood from his nose. "That's twice, Benjin Hawk. If you ever strike me again, it will mean your death. Don't speak or nod. The spear at your throat is tipped with a very powerful poison. If even the slightest amount gets into your blood, you'll be turning black in minutes."

No one made a move until Nat nodded, and the spear was removed from Benjin's throat. At the same time, voices echoed along the beach, and a group of armed men made their way quickly toward them. The black ship had also drawn dangerously close, the wind blowing in its favor.

"We need to go. Now," Morif said.

When Benjin looked back, Nat was gone. No evidence that he and his people had ever been there remained, which was perhaps for the best.

Morif, Benjin, and Wendel got the boat back into the water and rowed against the tide and the wind to the *Dragon's Wing*. The exertion had Benjin's shoulders burning, and it looked as if the black ship would arrive about the same time as they would, if not a little sooner.

A terrifying sight emerged from the *Dragon's Wing*. Benjin had never seen anything like it before. It looked like normal air, only it distorted the light and made the things beyond it seem warped and twisted. Like tendrils from some unnatural vine, they grew and stretched, reaching toward the slow-moving boat. There was a sickening thud and a jerking sensation when the tendrils wrapped around them. Without warning, the boat surged forward and raced toward the waiting ship, toward Pelivor, who appeared to be pulling them in.

"I don't know if I'll ever get used to this," Wendel said.

Benjin had to agree.

When they reached the *Dragon's Wing*, lines were quickly dropped, and they were hoisted back up to the deck. The black ship was closing fast, and those on the beach were running back to the harbor. At the stern, Gwen stood, smiling, her hands caressing the wooden tubes. With a flick of her hair and a broad smile, she let the power flow through her, and lightning crawled from her hands and over the tubes themselves. Benjin watched again in awe.

Fasha reached his side. "It looks like it's time we leave."

Benjin nodded, still watching Gwen.

"She gets it from my side, you know," Fasha said with a grin.

The ship moved slowly at first, but then they turned to catch the growing wind. Gwen increased the air flow, causing the tubes to whine with a higher pitch. Pelivor extended his arms.

"Get us out of here," Fasha said. It was, after all, her ship, though she'd been saying an awful lot lately that there seemed to be too many captains on her ship--far, far too many. The flightmaster and thrustmaster, on the other hand, seemed to suit her just fine. Benjin couldn't argue with her. When the ship left the water and Gwen applied her will, The *Dragon's Wing* was the fastest ship on all of Godsland.

* * *

It was in the morning that she saw it, rising out of the mists that blanketed the waters, a solitary structure that defied logic. This was no lighthouse or island castle; this was a keep in the middle of an ocean, a keep that, as far as Catrin could see, had no entrance. Kyrien flew in for a closer look, and Catrin gasped when she saw a figure standing atop the towering structure. Dark and fluid, it moved with the wind, and Catrin knew that this was no natural being. The hair on her neck stood, and her breathing quickened. Kyrien must have sensed the presence as he suddenly veered away from the keep. Before he did, though, Catrin got to see the slick, black rocks that formed this megalithic structure. Relatively small chunks of the black stone made up the entire keep, and it looked as if it fit together like a giant puzzle, not loose and disorderly, but as if every stone had been molded to conform to its neighbors. The effect was unforgettable.

Catrin could not imagine how such a keep had been constructed. Erecting any structure, let alone one with masterful stonework, amid these deep waters seemed an impossible task. The place beckoned to Catrin, calling to her like the song of a dark siren. Something waited for her within that keep--somehow she knew--though she didn't think it would be pleasant. When she looked back, the figure was gone from the rooftop, but she could still feel it watching her.

For the briefest instant, she considered asking Kyrien to go back, to let her search the keep and find what it was that awaited her, but there had been too many delays already. Sinjin was all that mattered. Prios had slept through the experience, and Catrin did not want to wake him. For some reason, she did not want him to know about the dark keep. Something deep down inside told her that the place was meant for her alone. It made her feel guilty to keep it from him, but it felt as if it were for his own good, and that was all the justification she could find. It was enough.

I'll be able to find that place again, Kyrien told her. *I don't want you to go in there, but if you must, then I'll take you back there when the time comes.*

Ironically, that knowledge made Catrin feel no better. The whole thing left her with an odd mixture of excitement and foreboding. Prios stirred behind her, and she handed him a water flask and a piece of salted fish. He accepted them with a grateful nod. There was still a great deal of water to cross before they reached the Greatland and even more land to cross before they reached Riverhold. Catrin assumed that was where Sinjin would be taken, but even if it wasn't, that was the most likely place she would find Thorakis. There she would make him pay for the lives he'd taken. There she would retrieve the Staff of Life and Koe, and there she would find the information that would lead her to her son.

Prios put his arms around her, as if reading her mind. His presence was comforting, grounding. When she and Kyrien had been alone, the burden had been heavy on Catrin's shoulders, but Prios somehow knew how to lessen that weight. Perhaps by taking it upon himself, Catrin thought, and again he seemed to read her mind. He patted her on the shoulder and kissed her cheek.

With both of them awake and refreshed, Catrin began to gather her will. Prios said nothing but did the same. They had been practicing much of what Catrin had learned during the flight, especially the things that allowed Kyrien to fly farther and faster. Every minute they saved made up for some of the delays, but still it was not fast enough to suit Catrin.

* * *

Jharmin Kyte could find no solace. Wolfhold had become a prison, and being trapped here with his wife was like being trapped in a cage with a very beautiful and alluring tiger, who might purr at you while ripping your throat out. He loved Lissa but not because she made it easy for him to do so. Perhaps he loved Lissa in spite of her efforts to make him hate her, though sometimes she succeeded. There were quiet times, when she was warm and she would smile and laugh. But then there were the days when she was as dark as a storm cloud and even less friendly.

The events of her childhood had made her suspicious, and she carried the weight of her anger like a burden of pride. She had suffered more than he, and she made certain he knew it.

Today he hoped for a reprieve. Today they would have to make difficult decisions.

Lissa entered the room without a word, and Jharmin waited to see what energy she brought with her. He could sense her mood from across the room most days, but on this day, she remained shielded from him, her emotions kept close. He had no doubt she was feeling something very strongly, and he had no less doubt that she didn't want him to know what it was she was feeling. She was a difficult woman, his wife.

Neither spoke for some time, as if the first one to speak would be responsible for what was to come. "I leave for Ravenhold in an hour," Lissa finally said.

Jharmin was silent for some time. He supposed he'd known all along that she would go. But still it made him angry. "You know I can't leave Wolfhold. And you know you're safer here than at Ravenhold. You know these things."

"And I know my people need me there."

"They don't need you to be a martyr," Jharmin said.

Lissa looked up with fire in her eyes, and Jharmin knew he'd lost her. Now there was no chance she would stay. She turned to leave without another word.

"Wait," Jharmin said. "I'm sorry. I just don't want to lose you."

"If you keep your mouth shut and let me go defend my hold, then you won't," Lissa said, her voice low and angry.

She rode out on horseback with her guard an hour later, and Jharmin watched her go. The people would know she was gone soon enough. They would know that war was coming. So many were just getting their lives back in order after the last war, and now it would haunt them again. Jharmin prayed he was wrong, but his intellect suggested otherwise.

Black ships and blacker dragons were said to be on their way, and

Thorakis's endless supply of gold had finally run out. He'd seen the map, and Jharmin knew that the aqueducts were machines of war. They would be used to keep the people dependent on Thorakis, and they had clear roads on either side to allow for fast deployment of soldiers. They also made for highly defensible walls that divided communities and prevented them from joining in an uprising. If the people in one area did rise up, they could be easily put down with troops from adjacent areas. Then, once the troops were deployed to an area along the aqueducts, they would have access to a nearly unlimited supply of fish from the Riverhold fishery.

Jharmin had always suspected that Thorakis could individually control the supply of water to each section of the aqueducts and that he might use this to exert control over the people. When all these things were added up, especially considering the fact that two of the aqueducts reached toward Ravenhold and Wolfhold, respectively, one couldn't help but come to the conclusion that they were about to be attacked.

The counterfeit coins troubled Jharmin greatly since they threatened the entire monetary system. Without that stability, the Greatland's fragile and still-recovering economy would likely collapse. The best he could do was to keep himself safe, so he could provide some level of stability when all this was over. It was a thought that made him sick, but it was among the things his grandfather had taught him. The need of the people outweighed the need of his own ego or preference. It might ease his conscience to go out and fight and die what some would call an honorable death. But death, as his grandfather had always said, was death, honorable or not. And dead leaders save no lives.

Drummond, the captain of Jharmin's guard, approached. Rarely was he an effusive man, but the fact that he looked gruffer than usual gave Jharmin pause.

"I can have them all inside the keep within two days of when the order is given, sir," Drummond said without preamble. The man had never been one for small talk.

Jharmin didn't like that estimate. He needed his people inside his walls within a single day. Two days was too long, and Drummond knew it.

"If we try to prepare them, the word will spread that we're at war, and I know that's not what you want. Given the state of the villages and fields as I see them, there is no way to get them all here in any shorter amount of time."

"If Thorakis massed troops along the aqueduct, he could have an army here in less than two days."

"I know and I'm sorry, sir. I can find no solution, and I won't lie to you."

"I know, Drummond," Jharmin said. "You're a good man. I'm not displeased with you; it's the situation. I need to figure out how to protect the people and the keep without causing riots or drawing the attention of Thorakis."

"Maybe drawing Thorakis's attention is exactly what we want," Drummond said. "You know as well as I that war is coming. Anyone with any sense can see that. It may be that he hasn't attacked us yet because he isn't fully ready. Perhaps we can draw him out and force him to make his move before he can gather his full strength. And though it may sound crazy, perhaps we should strike first."

The idea seemed ludicrous at first, but Jharmin had to admit that it had some merit, though there were holes in the plan big enough to sail a ship through.

"The Cathurans certainly have seen the signs," Drummond said. "Ohmahold and Drascha Stone are sealed up tight. No one's getting in or out of those places any time soon. The rest of the world is going to figure it out soon enough. What do we gain by keeping it from the people?"

"Order," Jharmin said. "If we lose order, we lose control. It'll be better if we take the time to prepare as much as we can and hope Thorakis doesn't attack in the meantime."

Drummond clearly didn't agree, but he kept his mouth shut.

"I need some time to think and clear my head, Drummond. Find out what you can about the inventory I asked for and rationing projections. I need to know how many people we'll have in the hold and how long we'll be able to feed them. I'll come find you when I'm ready."

"Yes, sir."

Knowing Drummond would probably handle the matters better than he ever could, Jharmin walked deeper into Wolfhold, beyond his personal chambers, and into a place that only a few knew existed. When Lissa had first come here, this had been one of the few things that kept her from leaving. The atrium was the very heart of Wolfhold. A crystalline ceiling allowed natural light to flood the parklike setting. Deep green grasses, lush and cool, awaited Jharmin's now bare feet. Beyond a sweeping hill and within a circle of pillars waited a patch of marble that had been weathered by the ages. Above these pillars stood open sky. Here, he could commune with the rest of the world and not feel as if he were sealed away in a granite tomb.

When he was young, he'd come to this place to play and to see the open sky. But for much of his adult life, he had avoided the atrium, preferring instead to exercise his freedom and leave the keep altogether. It was Lissa who had reminded him about the magic of the place. Every day she had spent in the hold, she had gone to the atrium, sometimes for many hours. Jharmin knew she'd even sneaked away from their bed in the middle of the night to go there.

Now he went there because it made him feel closer to his wife. Despite everything that could have come between them over the years, Jharmin truly cared for Lissa. He'd never admit he still had feelings for her cousin, Catrin. Those feelings did nothing to reduce what he felt for Lissa, and not for the first time, he wished there were some way he could make what he felt for Catrin go away. Those feelings did not serve him, and he did his best to suppress them. Settling himself down at the center of the worn marble, Jharmin did his best to meditate. It wasn't something he'd ever really believed in, but Catrin had once told him about the benefits of meditation, and Lissa had later told him similar things. He, of course, never mentioned that the two had actually agreed on something.

Sitting with his legs crossed, he wondered how they ever managed to find peace and serenity; his mind was a cloud of anxiety and emotions that moved in a circular fashion and never left him without something to worry over. Slowly, though, he thought about each thing, and he began to chip away at that seemingly endless supply of anxiety. Inexorably, he began to drift away from the sensations of his body, floating instead in the space of his mind. The worry faded some, and his fears seemed farther away. Finally, after what felt like days, Jharmin Kyte found the silence within.

For a time, he simply reveled in the stillness, floating formless and nameless in a deep sea. Then he was yanked from his meditation in surprise. Within his mind he heard voices, still distant but approaching fast. Never would he have guessed what would happen next.

Chapter 12

To find what another man has hidden is to glimpse his soul.
--Sevellon, thief

* * *

Moving into the darkened inner halls of Dragonhold, halls that Catrin had never seen, felt surreal to Chase. It probably would have felt strange even if Catrin were there, but under Trinda's rule, everything felt strange. At first, he'd wondered why Trinda had allowed him to stay when she'd forced Millie to leave. Surely she knew Chase was loyal to Catrin and he, too, should have been asked to leave. But that wasn't what had happened. Instead, only Millie and Morif had been ejected from the hold.

He worried about them. At the time, he'd been tempted to go with them voluntarily, but something had told him to remain silent and stay where he was. Trinda had yet to acknowledge his relationship to Catrin; in fact, Catrin had never been mentioned at all since that first day. Now it was as if they had always served the child queen, as people were calling her. The girl had been cleverer than he would have imagined. She did the last thing anyone expected: she told people to keep doing what they had been doing, to continue to enact Catrin's will.

Why go to the trouble of seizing control just to have everyone do as they had been, Chase asked himself. The answer chilled him. It was to make the transition easy for the people, to allow them to serve out of habit. And once serving the child queen became habit, then she could demand anything she wanted. Chase knew she was nowhere near that point yet, but she'd made more rapid progress than most would have believed.

This was due in part to the discoveries that she and Durin and Strom had made within the hold. The water alone was enough to bring the people closer to Trinda. It was on her request that Durin had mistakenly jumped on the stone plate that controlled the water. Whether Trinda's request or Durin's mistake resulted in restoring the water was subject for debate, but nonetheless, Trinda got most of the credit. At first, of course, the water had been a nuisance due to clogged channels that prevented it from flowing freely and caused widespread flooding in the hold. Much of that had been rectified now, but Miss Mariss still had to haul water from the kitchens by the bucketful. This fact reminded Chase that Durin walked beside him. In truth, the boy walked behind him.

"Do you still think he's all right?" Durin asked when Chase looked back.

"With all my heart," Chase said.

Durin nodded and Chase could feel his pain. It was one thing to lose a friend; it was another to believe it was your fault. Chase knew that feeling all too well, and he wouldn't wish it on anyone.

"Now that most of the channels are unclogged and the water is flowing, do you think she'll let us try the other stones? I mean, they all have to do something, right? What do you think they do?"

Chase didn't know the answers to any of the boy's questions. "I don't know, Durin, but I think for now we should concentrate on what we were asked to do."

"I still think she just doesn't want us around," Durin said. "Why else would she send us looking for an underground forest? That can't really exist, can it? I mean, I know there were some trees by the river, but an entire forest?"

His questions poured out so fast that Chase had no chance to answer them, not that he had any answers to give.

"How can Trinda know all this stuff? And if she had power before Catrin, then wouldn't that make her the Herald of Istra?"

The thought hadn't occurred to Chase before, and it chilled him. But in the end, he knew it didn't matter. "The Herald of Istra is whoever people believe it to be. The belief is all that really matters. Without that, the whole prophecy falls apart."

Durin cast him a sideways glance, and Chase was pretty sure he'd lost the young man.

"Who do you think is the Herald of Istra?" he asked Durin.

"I've no idea," the boy said.

"That's probably the smartest thing I've ever heard you say."

There seemed to be nothing else to say for a very long time. They just kept walking, and Chase spent most of his time sketching a map of what they passed. The size and scope of Dragonhold was becoming apparent to Chase and Durin and a few select others. Most knew that there was more of the hold being discovered and explored, but few got the chance to experience just how massive the place was. It was as if the mountains themselves were hollow, and in many places the stone above was translucent and allowed soft amber light to wash over them.

What amazed Durin most was the number of rooms, dwellings, caves, corridors, and other structures. It seemed as if the entire population of Godsland had once lived within these mountains. It would take years to properly explore. Every hall or doorway they passed sparked Durin's desire to search for magic or treasure or who knew what mysteries that waited beyond, but Chase kept him pointed in the right direction. The only way they would find this forest was to be methodical, assuming the forest even existed. In a way, Chase wished Durin hadn't raised that doubt.

"I need another torch," Chase said as the one in his hand sputtered and looked close to going out.

Durin had already grumbled about being along only to carry torches, and he said no more when handing another to Chase. At least his load was getting lighter.

Trinda's request for the herald globes was another thing that concerned Chase. Durin had told him that Trinda somehow used a herald globe as a weapon, and a devastating one at that. In the short time that the globes had existed, Chase had become accustomed to having one with him at all times. Perhaps it was just the fact that he had been spending a great deal of time in the darkness of the hold that the globes had become such a crucial tool. Turning over his globe had been one of the most difficult parts of this entire experience. After all, what could one person do with more than a thousand herald globes? The question bothered him greatly.

Struggling to get the new torch lit, he fully realized just how revolutionary the globes really were. They represented progress, a leap ahead for all of Godsland, and now Trinda was hoarding them.

"Wait up," Durin said, and Chase realized that he'd been walking faster and faster, driven by his anger. When he lifted his head, though, his anger faded away.

"No way," Durin said from beside him. "There's absolutely no way that's real."

* * *

"Are you there?" a voice called from the emptiness above the sacred stone.

Jharmin Kyte sat very still.

"Are you there, Lady Lissa?" came the voice again.

This time the voice named his wife. All at once the realization hit him; there really was magic here. Not just the sense of magic, but real, functional magic. This magic did something important. Then the anger crept in. How had Lissa kept this from him? How many secrets did that woman have? So many questions ran through Jharmin's mind, but he knew his chance to act was fast slipping away. "My wife is not here," he said, and he actually heard the sharp intake of breath from wherever it was that the other spoke. "But I recognize your voice, and I believe you've served me longer than you've served my wife."

Stunned silence hung for a moment before the man Jharmin knew was a spy that he himself had placed within Ohmahold spoke. "I'm sorry, sir," Hand said. "I would never betray you, sir. But I could not turn your lady away, and she swore me to secrecy. I've done my best to serve you both."

The fact that Jharmin had agonized while waiting for messages from Hand to arrive by bird fueled his anger, but he drew a deep breath. "Tell me everything."

"I would, sir, but there is no time. Catrin's son will be here soon, and I must be there to greet him, or he may not be left in my charge."

"Catrin's son?" Jharmin asked, shocked. "Sinjin is coming to Ohmahold?"

"You didn't know?" Hand asked, and Jharmin flushed but didn't answer. At least Hand could not see his reaction.

"What do I need to know?"

Hand considered for a moment before speaking. "The darkness will come for you soon, and the Herald will not be able to help you. Her son will be used to draw the Herald north, where she will likely die. That will leave the armies free to take Wolfhold and Ravenhold."

"And when in blazes were you going to tell me this?" Jharmin choked.

"A bird should arrive today, sir. I'm sorry, sir."

Lissa had known and still she had chosen not to tell him. Even though her leaving was warning enough, it still galled him that his wife would keep so many secrets from him, especially those that would affect the fate of both their peoples.

"What else?"

"May the Gods be with us all," Hand said. Then he was gone.

* * *

In the blackness of night, surrounded by clouds, Sinjin knew fear. Thin air left him weak and light-headed. Whenever he woke from his fits of sleep, it didn't take him long to realize where he was. The grip of the dragon's claws added to his discomfort; it was, at least, a more relaxed grip now than it had been.

"Dragons can sleep while they fly, you know." Kendra's voice danced on the wind, making her sound distant. Sinjin hadn't known that, but he supposed it did make sense. "I think the dragon carrying us is sleeping right now."

This statement led to the sickening realization that the dragon was also holding on to them while sleeping, and if it twitched in its sleep . . . Sinjin tried to drive the thought from his mind. Rubbing his still sore wrists, he waited to see what else Kendra would say.

"I need your rope."

"What for?" Sinjin asked. Part of him wished to be rid of the rope that had once bound him. It had taken hours of painful contortions to free himself. Though the rope had caused him pain, it was also a tool, one of very few at his disposal. Part of him wanted to tie himself to one of the giant claws not so gently cradling him. That way, at least, if the dragon twitched, he would not fall.

"I need it to secure myself, so I can climb up to the dragon's head," Kendra said, sounding annoyed.

"You've lost your senses."

"Just give me the boiling rope. Or don't you want me to save your life? They probably won't kill me, you know. But you? You're a dead man."

"I appreciate your concern," Sinjin said, trying not to sound sarcastic, "I really do, but getting yourself killed isn't going to help me."

"I'm not going to get myself killed," Kendra said with exasperation. "I'm going to make the dragon alter its course. I learned everything I could about dragons from the time we left the Godfist. The walls on that ship are thin, and I could hear things I wasn't supposed to. I knew you'd be transferred to a dragon if your mother arrived."

Sinjin remained silent, made ill by the way people plotted against his mother, who had done nothing to harm any of them. His rage grew, silent and smoldering, like the coals of a banked fire, breathing and ready to erupt into flame at any instant given the right conditions.

"Something my mother taught me about pigeons gave me an idea, and it might be your last hope." From within her cloak, Kendra produced a black stone with irregular facets. The stone did not shine; instead it seemed to drink in the light.

"What is that?"

"Lodestone," Kendra said. "Now just give me the rope while the beast still sleeps. I'll explain later."

Reluctantly Sinjin attempted to do as he was asked; only it proved to be both difficult and terrifying. Kendra was clasped loosely in the dragon's other claw, and there was a sizable amount of empty space between them. Kendra stretched out toward him with her hand, the wind casting her hair out behind her like a dark flag. It shimmered and she looked beautiful, but Sinjin tried hard not to think about that, even if it was a good distraction from the fact that he could get sucked into open air at any moment. His knees trembled as he reached out to Kendra. The distance was too great.

"Throw one end to me!" Kendra shouted into the wind.

Sinjin wrapped one end of the rope around his wrist multiple times, and hoped it would be enough. If he lost his hold on the rope and Kendra didn't catch it, then it would be lost. With a tentative throw, the wind caught the rope, and it immediately stretched out behind him, at the mercy of the wind. He tried again, throwing it far in front of Kendra, hoping to compensate for the wind, but it was not enough.

"Ball up your coat and tie the rope around it," Kendra shouted. "That will give it some weight."

Sinjin did as she asked, all the while knowing he was going to regret it. The cold air bit through his loose clothing, and he shivered as he tied the rope around his wadded-up coat. Reaching out as far as his courage would allow, Sinjin threw the jacket with all his might, again aiming ahead of Kendra, and this time it worked.

Reaching out farther than seemed safe to Sinjin, Kendra caught the jacket and pulled it in to her. The rope between them was caught in the wind and went taut when Kendra held firm. This sent Sinjin moving toward open air. With a desperate lunge, he crashed into the dragon's claws. After he released the rope from his wrist, he wrapped his hands around the mighty claw and panted. The dragon's grip tightened momentarily, and Sinjin feared his movements had woken the beast. Moments later, though, the dragon's grip relaxed once again, and Sinjin gathered enough courage to look over at Kendra. She was gone.

With his breath stuck in his throat, Sinjin searched for her. Leaning out more than he cared to, his entire body trembled with anxiety and fatigue. He could see nothing in the darkness until a brief clearing in the clouds allowed in the light of the moon, stars, and comets. In the pale blue light, he saw Kendra climbing the dragon's neck, the rope looped over her shoulder and Sinjin's coat over her own. Sinjin shivered. The girl was brave—crazy, true, but brave. She climbed with skill that made Sinjin feel as he always felt around Kendra: inadequate. His breath caught when she reached the base of the dragon's skull. Enormous spikes of jet black bristled around Kendra, yet she was able to traverse the bizarre and dangerous landscape.

When she removed Sinjin's coat from her back, Sinjin couldn't imagine what she was planning, but he had a very bad feeling in his gut. As gently as she could, given the fact that the wind was threatening to send the girl hurtling through the open air, she managed to loop the rope around the dragon's snout and cover one of the dragon's hooded eyes with Sinjin's coat. After securing the coat with the rope, she took off her own cloak. Sinjin was really starting to dislike her idea and would've shouted out if not for fear of waking the dragon while Kendra was standing between its eyes. Other dragons were out there in the darkness, and Sinjin could only guess what chaos a blindfolded dragon would cause.

Once Kendra had her cloak secured over the dragon's other eye, she gave the rope a good yank. As she tied the knot, Sinjin felt the dragon's claw constrict around him, making it difficult for him to breathe and impossible for him to move. His gaze was locked on the place where Kendra crouched. Moving away from the dragon's eyes as the lids began to move under the blindfold, she retreated. Kendra was almost beyond Sinjin's field of view. When the feral dragon eased its grip for an instant, he shifted so he could see more clearly.

"Hold on!" Kendra screamed, and Sinjin did what he could to secure himself in the event the dragon released its grip on him. Kendra knelt behind the dragon's eyes, near the top of its skull, and she appeared to be lifting up on the dragon's scales. When the dragon became fully aware, a lot of things happened at once. The last thing Sinjin saw before the world began to spin was Kendra jamming the lodestone beneath the dragon's scales. Almost immediately, the feral changed course and thrashed its head about. This would have been less concerning were it not for Kendra being atop that head with no rope to secure herself. All the rope she'd had was keeping the blindfold in place.

Sinjin saw another dragon through a quick break in the clouds, and he prayed that the beast did not sense their mount's distress. Still they spun and Sinjin's vision grew darker until he thought he might soon pass out. All he could do was pray that Kendra would find a way to hold on. He might not like the girl, but she'd at least attempted to save him twice, and he certainly didn't want her dead. Though he wasn't certain any of them would survive this.

Deeper into the clouds they dropped, and the dragon now changed direction at random, which only increased Sinjin's disorientation. The changes in air pressure made his head feel as if it might explode, and only the sound of Kendra screaming told him that she was still alive and relatively close by. A moment later, they burst from the clouds into the purple light of a new day.

Waves rushed beneath them, closer than he'd been expecting and offering a cold, silent death. The dragon eased its grip once again as it oriented itself, seemingly using some innate senses to gauge its proximity from the water, a sense not affected by Kendra's lodestone. The beast then let out a terrible roar, one that was answered by a chorus of ferals.

Kendra's plan had failed. The other dragons would soon be there to aid their brethren, and Kendra's efforts would all be for naught. The dragon could not maintain a direct course, but they would still be easy to find, especially if the beast continued to howl its haunting call. Sinjin sighed in acceptance of defeat, knowing what an unenviable fate now awaited him, but then he screamed. To know one's death approaches is one thing; to see it rise up before you is another. Like lumbering giants of stone guarding the coast, mighty bluffs emerged directly in their path.

Even with the random changes in their flight path, Sinjin could see the bluffs getting closer and closer. "Take off the blindfold!" Sinjin screamed. For a moment, there was no sound. Then, to Sinjin's relief, came a stream of curses that would have made a soldier proud.

The calls of the other dragons were getting closer, and Sinjin could hear the panic within those calls. They would not get here soon enough to save their brethren from being dashed to bits against a wall of granite. Kendra made no response, and Sinjin held his breath, waiting for some word, some sound, some change in the dragon's behavior. None came.

It was as if the cliffs drew them closer, just as the lodestone under the dragon's scales would draw bits of metal, as if by magic. Sinjin closed his eyes as cold stone rushed toward them, in that same instant, Kendra let out a strangled cry, and then came a sound like sails in the wind. The dragon vibrated as it let out a startled cry and pulled up as suddenly and violently as it could. Sinjin watched the texture of the rock face flash by and was amazed by the details he noticed in the instants before what would certainly be his death. Nests made from finger-thick twigs housed white birds with sweeping wings that looked too graceful to be real.

The dragon's ascent slowed, the startled feral having only so much momentum, and the beast flapped its wings furiously to clear the tops of the cliffs. There, a wooded plain gave way to rocky and barren inland stretches before a mighty fortress rose from the plains, backed by a range of foreboding mountains. This was an unfriendly place, indeed.

Forced to land, the dragon released its grip on Sinjin, and he went tumbling to the narrow strip of grassland that divided the cliffs from the forest. The impact was jarring, but he felt no pain. The shock of it took his breath, and for a moment, he lay gawking at the dragon and those fast approaching. Instincts screamed for him to run, but he could not leave, not without Kendra. It took a moment for him to locate her. She stood atop the feral's head, holding on to a spiny protuberance that jutted from the leviathan. The dragon shook its head violently, and Kendra could hold on no more. Spinning like a windmill, she flew through the air and struck the ground with force. The grunt that escaped her brought physical pain to Sinjin.

She lay there, amid grasses strewn with stones and gravel, and didn't move. Sinjin knew he should run, knew he should try to get away from the dragons and hide, but he simply could not. He couldn't leave Kendra behind. Still she did not move. The feral dragon spared her not another glance; its eyes were on Sinjin alone, and he could see the surprise in them when he ran toward Kendra and away from the tree line. The other dragons were only moments away, and there would be no place for Sinjin to hide. In that moment, he did not want to take cover. Despite the fear in his belly, he needed to be the kind of man who lived by his convictions, he needed to be the kind of man who could hold his head high and know that his actions had been beyond reproach. He did not necessarily feel the need to be a hero as much as he felt the need to help his friend. It had taken him a while to admit it, but when he finally reached the crux of his decision, he had done it because Kendra *was* his friend. There had been a time when he'd never have thought it possible, but war and dragons and demons had changed his perspective. And if he was honest, he'd admit that there was something else as well, but he was definitely not ready to deal with those feelings yet. When he reached her, she'd already started to come around.

"What're you doing here?" she asked, rubbing her head.

"I came back for you."

"You're a fool!" Kendra said, looking up at the dragon now looming over them both with livid eyes. "Now everything I did was for nothing."

Sinjin felt the sting of her words. He also saw something else in her eyes, and he knew he'd done the right thing, even as waves of fear washed over him in the face of an enraged feral dragon.

Chapter 13
Without communication, we are forever divided.
--Prios

* * *

Cold, gray stone of the northern shores and bluffs came into view, and Catrin felt the full weight of her troubles. She could sense Sinjin, and he was frightened. This, alone, was enough to make her want to leap from her own skin, but she also sensed the Staff of Life and Koe. She couldn't decide if it was better or worse that her staff and Koe were still moving inland and growing more distant whereas Sinjin's movements had slowed. Prios stirred behind her, and she could feel the energy pulsing within him. He was nearly afire with it. Despite their combined rage and desperate need to get to Sinjin, or perhaps it was because of that shared need, she wanted to kiss him.

Ohmahold jutted from the plains, barring access to the mountain passes beyond, an impenetrable fortress that had never been taken. Memories of her time within Ohmahold were vivid and painful, and she could not think of this place without thinking of Mother Gwendolin's death. The fortress now dominated her view, and she could think about little else. She doubted those within the hold had forgotten either. Many of the Cathuran order blamed her for Mother Gwendolin's death since the assassins had been there to kill Catrin. Those within the order who supported Catrin had all fled from Ohmahold in fear of their lives.

There would be no kindness within Ohmahold this time, and enter the hold she would, even if she had to tear down the mountains to get there. Her worsening mood was contagious, and Prios bristled with so much power, it felt as if knives were pressed against her back.

This day will not be forgotten.

It was the first thing Prios had said in quite some time, and Catrin couldn't help but recognize the truth of his words. Kyrien expressed his agreement wordlessly. The keep appeared deserted, but all of them knew it was a ruse. Kyrien sent Catrin and Prios a mental image of demons, dragons, soldiers, ballistae, and catapults.

It wasn't until they were soaring across the plain that Catrin was able to see them. Covered in tarps painted to match the surrounding landscape, an army waited. Thorakis, too, knew this day would be historic, yet he wasn't even present. He cowered within Riverhold, if Catrin was right, and part of her wanted to go attend to him first. By her guess, he would attack Ravenhold and Wolfhold as soon as Catrin attacked Ohmahold. Her cousin, her friends, and her people would die.

No matter what Lissa said, the people of the Greatland were her people, and the people of Mundleboro were especially dear to her. Memories of her grandmother brought tears, and Catrin was conflicted, torn by choices no one should have to make. Tactically, they would be best served by flying to Riverhold and disassembling it and Thorakis along with it. He was the root cause of this war, and he, alone, deserved to pay for it.

Catrin didn't understand what had created the demons and giants, but it seemed obvious to her that they were perversions of nature. The horde below them remained concealed, but Catrin could feel the twisted energy they exuded; the place reeked of foulness. Someone must pay for these crimes against the natural order.

Often Catrin had wondered where the demons and giants had come from along with the soldiers who doused themselves in ash. At times she'd thought they must be coming out of the Westland Wastes, the places now fouled by the Statue of Terhilian that had exploded there. Gholgi were not native to the Westland; they were indigenous to the Firstland, but Catrin had seen no evidence that the twisted and perverted demons and giants had originated from there during the fight for the regent queen. Not knowing gnawed at her, and as the smell of demons grew stronger the closer they came to Ohmahold, it became more difficult for her not to lash out. It was to her advantage, though, to get as close as possible before initiating any attack. So far they were not accosting her, and she could feel Sinjin's presence growing nearer, even if she could sense that he was moving deeper into the hold.

As they crossed the last stretch of land leading up to the rock face, gongs rang out their discordant calls. The clamor arose from the narrow ravine that served as the main entrance to Ohmahold. Catrin didn't have to worry about navigating the gates that guarded the hold. As famously defensible as Ohmahold was, Catrin remembered nothing of the keep that would defend it from above. Kyrien could simply land in the gardens surrounding the inner sanctuary, and Catrin and Prios could take the keep. There would be feral dragons, of course, but Catrin's own determination was bolstered, knowing Prios and Kyrien were equally driven. There would be consequences, and none of them cared.

When the ferals appeared atop the fortifications and nearby mountains, the fighting began. The air rang with the sound of taut ropes releasing their energy, accompanied by thunderous booms and the roars of dragons. Arrows, bolts, and ballista bolts darkened the skies around them. Balls of liquid fire streamed sooty black smoke that clung to the air and soon formed a crisscrossing pattern in the skies above Ohmahold.

It took only an instant for Catrin and Prios to respond even as Kyrien took evasive action. Catrin had fought on Kyrien's back before, but never before had he been forced to evade so many projectiles. He did what he could to warn Catrin and Prios of his sudden moves, afraid one or both of the humans would be thrown off balance or caught by surprise and accidentally unleash one of their potent attacks on him or each other. The thoughts came and went in a flash, and Catrin had no more time to consider the dangers of two powerful people attacking from the back of dragon that was dodging attacks.

Feral dragons leaped from the man-made fortifications and mountain peaks, filling the air above Kyrien. The intent was instantly clear: force them lower and into ballista range. Two black dragons bore dark riders who cast fire from above. Catrin was glad for the time she'd spent atop Kyrien's back before this moment because even with the saddle holding her and Prios in place, Kyrien's movements threatened to unseat them. Catrin's guts churned as Kyrien dipped, dived, and spun. What Catrin liked the least were the times he tucked his wings and shot straight toward the ground. Though it gave them great speed and the ability to evade ferals, it drove Catrin's heart into her throat. Prios gripped her from behind, and neither could launch any attacks while Kyrien dived. When he reached the bottom of his arch, though, Catrin felt herself pressed down into the saddle, her body feeling as if it were made of stone. At times her vision darkened, and she thought she might pass out. When the pressure eased, though, they skimmed along the ground, too low for ballista fire and catapults to target, but low enough to be hit with spears, pikes, and balls of lightning and fire that erupted from the hands of dark-robed men. Catrin targeted these men first.

Bursts of blue fire, filled with geometric patterns, streamed from Catrin's outthrust hands, and Prios sent spheres of twisted lightning into a formation of soldiers with pole arms. The metal-tipped weapons danced with energy, and arcs of power leaped out to grip the armored men and make them dance a pulsing, hypnotic jig before crumpling to the ground.

More attacks came from above, and Catrin craned her neck to see. Attacks of power still came from in front of them, but Catrin knew she could not allow the ferals to come at them from overhead. The dark men on dragonback must have sensed the coming attack, as they all launched attacks at once, showering Kyrien, Catrin, and Prios with fire. Pain erupted along Kyrien's wings, and Catrin could feel his agony as it scorched the skin and threatened to burn through his thick outer hide. Quickly gathering air, Catrin used it to snuff the flames. Prios did what he could to deflect incoming attacks, but Catrin had left their flank exposed, and fire erupted across the saddle. Now it was Catrin and Prios who were afire. A wordless scream rose up from behind Catrin, and Prios's voice was filled with agony.

Trying desperately to get free of the fire, Catrin panicked and lashed out with random bursts of air. She exercised no control over the power, letting it go where it wished. Prios's scream became a strangled cry as her energy doused the flames but nearly launched him out of the saddle. The straps only loosely held him in place, and he had to grab on to Catrin when Kyrien suddenly climbed, thrusting Prios back into the saddle.

Catrin wanted to ask him if he was all right, but she could not catch her breath, and the pain made thought almost impossible. Prios remained silent behind her, only his firm grip on her gave evidence that he was still alive. Catrin could sense him, though; she could feel his energy, just as she could feel Sinjin's energy below them. That was the only thing that kept her going. Kyrien's pain became her pain, and Prios's pain burned into her consciousness, even if he did try to hide it from her, but then she also felt Sinjin's pain. A mother's cry escaped her lips as pain exploded through his body. Over and over, it felt as if his body were being torn apart; then came the sensation of being choked. If Catrin could have breathed, she would have screamed again.

* * *

The spiraling steps seemed to go on forever, winding down the walls of a massive cylinder that dropped away to what might be the very heart of Godsland. Kendra walked behind, chained and shackled, just as he was, but alive nonetheless. Every now and then, she would push him forward and curse him under her breath, as if just to remind him that she was angry with him. Sinjin tried not to care since he'd done what he thought was right, but her persistent anger wore on him, and if she pushed him one more time, he was certain he'd snap.

Two burly men walked in front of him, and he would not want to stumble into either of them. They didn't appear in any way friendly, and they were already struggling under the weight of something Sinjin couldn't quite make out. By the sounds of their grunts and whining, it was heavy. The men who came behind were even more frightening. They spoke in low, deep tones that seemed almost like growls to Sinjin.

One of the men was among the tallest Sinjin had ever seen and lanky as a rail. The other was shorter, stockier, and had a face made for scaring children. It was this man who directed the others, and it was this man Sinjin knew he'd have to watch. Kendra pushed him from behind, and he would've said something, except this time he knew he had slowed down and was in her way. Still, he didn't appreciate some of the things said under her breath.

"Once the deception is cast," the ugly man grunted, "we'll need to move quickly if we're to catch the full moon."

"Shouldn't we just go there now?" the tall man asked.

"No," the ugly man said. "We can go down, but we cannot move beyond the outwardly visible extents of Ohmahold until the deception is complete. And since I don't know exactly where that line is, we're going to stay close to the heart of the hold."

Sinjin did not know what deception they spoke of, but he certainly didn't like the sound of it. From his position, he caught only bits and pieces of the conversation, and he hoped that Kendra was able to catch more of the important details, if she could hear anything over her own curses. Though impressed with her vocabulary, Sinjin hoped she would run out of hurtful things to say about him sometime soon.

After what felt like ages, they reached the bottom of the winding stair, and new torches were lit before they continued into the waiting darkness. Sinjin had heard stories about the tunnels and mines beneath Ohmahold, and the ugly man's comment about the full moon sparked a memory from the tale of his mother's escape from this very place by swimming through daggerfish-infested waters. Sinjin didn't even want to think about it.

"This place will do," the ugly man said, and the two men in front of Sinjin seemed greatly relieved. Immediately they lowered their burden to the floor. It made a muffled clinking sound like a coat of mail, only it appeared to be covered in thick fabric.

Kendra bumped into Sinjin, and he nearly snapped at her, but she spoke under her breath, "Get ready to run." She spoke the words as if they were a curse, and none of the men reacted, seeming engrossed in their own thoughts.

Sinjin had no chance to respond since Kendra did her best to whirl and attacked the men behind her. Limited by the shackles, she was able only to stomp on one man's toes, though she did manage to smash her chains into the other's face.

For a brief instant, Sinjin stood, stunned. He knew he really should run this time. These men would not kill Kendra; he was certain of it. This might be his last chance to escape. Again his mind flashed to the story of his mother and the daggerfish. Pushing back his fear, Sinjin lunged for the guards in front of him, even as they were turning around. Grunts and cries echoed in the tight halls, and Sinjin feared Kendra might convince these men to kill her after all. Sinjin borrowed Kendra's move and stomped on the toes of the guards. One went down in agony, but the other just grinned and looked down at his reinforced boots.

"My mother made me these," the man said just before he wrapped his arms around Sinjin in a bear hug and squeezed.

There was nothing Sinjin could do, he was trapped and could barely move. Kendra still struggled behind him, shaming him, taking on two men when a single man had incapacitated him. It was as humiliating as it was terrifying.

"Can you do nothing right?" she growled at him when she could struggle no more.

Sinjin never got the chance to respond.

"If your mother doesn't kill you, I might," the ugly man said.

Kendra spit at him, but then the sound of gongs filled the hold and filtered down even to the dark tunnel in which they stood. Then there came thunderous booms and the cries of dragons. It sounded as if an army had descended upon Ohmahold--an army or his parents, Sinjin realized. The thought made him feel physically ill. No matter how powerful his parents were, he did not want them to be in danger, especially not because of him. Guilt began to eat at him. If he hadn't allowed himself to be captured, none of this would be happening. His thoughts were cut short when the tall man turned to him with an almost apologetic look in his eyes.

"Now?" he asked the ugly man, who nodded.

"Sorry, kid," was all the tall man said before he punched Sinjin in the face, hard.

Sinjin fell back against the cavern wall and hadn't recovered from the first punch when the second came.

"Stop!" Kendra shouted. "What are you doing? Stop!"

Sinjin wasn't sure who was hitting him, but every new strike dazed him and kept him from properly defending himself. The shackles and chains weighed on him, and he fell to his knees, where a mighty kick drove the wind from his chest and made his ribs hurt terribly.

"You're killing him!" Kendra shrieked. Then she sobbed, "Please stop. Please don't kill him."

Sinjin heard no more as a hand closed over his mouth and nose; he felt a heavy weight, and darkness settled upon him.

* * *

When the pain stopped, Catrin's heart nearly stopped with it. Sinjin was gone. She could no longer sense his presence. Prios stiffened behind her, his grip on her shoulders too tight. Kyrien wept.

Pain no longer registered in Catrin's mind; rage and grief and anguish welled up in her like groundswell and burst forth in the form of words and power--raw, unrestrained, focused, and potent. Catrin's rage found an environment rich with targets, and she attacked with unmitigated fury, sweeping the landscape clean of demons, giants, soldiers, and their monstrous weapons. The dragons must have sensed the change as well as they retreated to the clouds.

Thorakis was not within Ohmahold. Sinjin was no longer within Ohmahold; at least his spirit was no longer there. There was nothing holding them there except anger. And one of the first lessons her father had taught her was that intellect trumped anger. If you were going to fight back, fight back smart and on your terms.

"Let them retreat," Catrin said. "Our battle is no longer here. My son is dead." She choked on the words. "Our son is dead."

Prios wrapped his arms around her, and Kyrien turned for one more pass at the battlefield, taking out his anger on anything that still moved. Catrin made certain that all of the ballistae and catapults were destroyed, and she set fire to supply wagons that had congregated not far from the entrance to Ohmahold.

Then the mighty keep was behind them. A beautiful landscape swept beneath them, seen from a vantage few others would ever experience. Sinjin would never see it. Always Catrin's thoughts returned to Sinjin. If she didn't find something else to focus on, she thought she might explode. Only when she turned to look at Prios did she realize the extent of his wounds. Livid burns covered much of his body, and his clothing was charred. One arm hung limply by his side, and the other he used to staunch the bleeding from a shoulder wound.

Catrin laid her hands on him as gently as she could, and still he flinched at the contact, at the movement of his clothes, at the breath of the wind. Channeling her emotions and needs into singular focus, Catrin fed energy to Prios's spirit. His breathing slowed and became more regular, and though he looked no better on the outside, he let out a deep sigh and slept.

When Catrin ran her eyes over Kyrien, she found him not much better. Kyrien's hide was blistered and blasted away in places, and there were deep gouges in his wing membranes.

I can still fly. I can still fight. I will do so until those responsible are dead.

Those words contained as much vitriol as Catrin had ever heard from Kyrien, and the sound of it frightened her.

We will avenge my kind, and we will avenge your son.

Catrin's loss somehow seemed smaller in the face of that statement--no less painful but smaller. She could not even imagine the extent of Kyrien's pain, though it was clear that he did not begrudge her pain. He made no comparison between the extents of their losses; he simply wanted vengeance for what was lost, for what had been forcibly and intentionally taken from them.

Ignoring his bravado, Catrin drew deeply from the saddle and lent that energy to Kyrien's spirit. She had half expected him to balk, but he received the healing with good grace, and for that Catrin was grateful. Ahead of them, the skies darkened, a storm cloud crowding the horizon. Kyrien flew straight toward it.

* * *

"The Herald is coming, m'lord," Grimwell said, unable to keep the tremor from his voice.

"Good," Thorakis said in a long breath, his eyes distant.

"The men are in place, awaiting your word."

Thorakis looked as if he would speak, his focus suddenly returning, but a black-scaled tail coiled around the base of the basalt throne. This throne was new. The dragons had brought it from where only the gods knew, and ever since, Thorakis had been more and more difficult to reach. The time had come for Grimwell to leave; there was nothing more he could do. His master was lost, and everything they had built was about to come down around them. Seethe was the one truly in control here, Grimwell thought, and that evil beast cared not a whit about what happened to Thorakis or any other human.

"The Herald will be angry," Thorakis said, looking semilucid. "She will come for revenge. She and her tongueless husband will want me to pay. This time there will be no caution, no restraint, and they'll do exactly as I want them to."

"Yes, m'lord," Grimwell said, not knowing what else to say. He felt as if his time were rapidly slipping away. The smell of feral dragons filled his nostrils, and he nearly choked. Not far away, the abominations watched. Grimwell could still not believe such things existed, yet they stood, watching him, as if they knew his treasonous thoughts. Swallowing hard, Grimwell tried to pay attention to what Thorakis was saying.

"The men at the bell are ready?"

"Yes, m'lord," Grimwell said hurriedly. "Good men, all of them. I chose them myself."

Thorakis nodded, looking only half satisfied with the response. "And what of the second phase of our plan, *wizard?* Have the riders been sent?"

"They have, m'lord." *And may the gods have mercy on the people of the Greatland,* Grimwell thought. *May they have the wisdom to accept defeat before they are destroyed.* Though many of the people had treated him as if he were the enemy, Grimwell did not wish all the peoples of the Greatland dead. Yet he'd sent the riders; he'd given the orders. How could he claim anything but responsibility? Again, he hoped the people chose to surrender to the might of the greater force. Perhaps then they would have a chance.

Grimwell had seen the men who bathed in ash, and he knew they outnumbered the conscripted men from the Greatland in Thorakis's armies. For even those conscripted men from the Greatland, Grimwell felt a hint of compassion. They had done only what they thought was best for their people and their families, just as he had. They had been wrong. It would've been better to have starved, but it was too late now. That was the thought that rang most loudly in Grimwell's mind. It was too late.

Chapter 14

Words of disparagement often drown out the sound of praise.
--Master Jarvis, teacher

* * *

The mists of morning hung over the land, blanketing it in white. Hills, houses, and barns poked from the mists, and Kyrien flew down low, weaving between any obstacles that protruded from the fog. Looking behind her, Catrin saw that Prios still slept. It was a blessing since she knew how great his pain must be. Kyrien was awake and alert, and Catrin could sense his pain as well. It mixed with her own and left Catrin's thoughts in a red haze. None of them was in fighting condition, yet none of them would be turned away from this fight.

Nothing was more important to Catrin than finding Thorakis at the earliest possible moment and putting an end to him. Only then would she be able to stop and properly grieve the loss of her son, her home, and the regent dragons. Even the thought of processing so much grief nearly overwhelmed her, and she forced the feelings back down into her gut, all the while knowing she would pay the price later. For that moment, all she wanted was justice. In truth, she knew what she really wanted was revenge, but calling it justice made her feel better.

Before, she'd always found some way to forgive those who'd hurt her, even those who'd taken her mother's life, but what Thorakis and his black army were doing was beyond her ability to forgive. It shamed her, yet she also drew strength from it. Human and fallible, she was no goddess or deity, no matter what power she possessed. In many ways, she was still just a frightened little girl, but not at that moment; fury made her strong.

Kyrien stayed low to the ground, and shouts rose up from around them as they passed. Behind them the mist swirled and parted before slowly drifting back in to cover their path. The land rose up before them, an irregular and angled peak jutting from the mists. The saddle creaked as Kyrien followed the contour higher and higher. More cries echoed from behind them as they could be easily seen against the side of the mountain.

As soon as they crested the peak, Catrin felt her skin crawl; before them lay a sight that inflamed her blood. Dark soldiers, demons, giants, and what looked like normal soldiers clogged the landscape like a black infection. More of the monstrous weapons had been erected here, only these were of a different sort. Catrin was trying to understand the nature of them when a haunting sound cut the air. Ringing a discordant note, what sounded like a giant fire bell rang out in a measured beat. It made Catrin's teeth hurt. Prios stirred behind her, and his grunts made it clear that his pain was as great as she had expected. She wanted to soothe him, but there was no time.

Darkness seemed to spring from everywhere at once.

Dragons dropped from the ubiquitous clouds above. Only a brief stirring of the gray mists served as warning before angry ferals burst from within. The clouds roiled in the aftermath, and the air around them was filled with wings, teeth, and claws. Despite his condition, Prios launched attacks of lightning, fire, and air, though it seemed with little thought or aim. There were so many of the ferals that his attacks struck nonetheless, and Catrin did her best to match his intensity. Her chest swelled with pride at the strength of her husband, and tears refused to remain within her. A price must be paid for their son's death, and the time had come to exact that price. There was no room for restraint or forethought. This was the time to act.

What leaped from her fingers was unlike anything she'd ever experienced. Black flames tipped with orange and blue reeked of her darkest feelings, things she did not want to admit existed within her, yet it poured from her like poison from a festering wound. Only then did she realize she was screaming, and she could feel the satisfying resistance when her attacks struck prey.

Even with her and Prios attacking and Kyrien doing his best to evade incoming attacks, there were too many ferals to avoid. The beasts took advantage of every opening, and Catrin just barely avoided being impaled on a gleaming black claw; Prios was not as fortunate. There came a terrible sound from behind Catrin, a sound she hoped never to hear again, especially from her husband. She wanted to turn and see how badly he was hurt, to lend him energy and heal him as best she could, but there was no time.

Weapons Catrin had seen, and an even larger number that she had not seen, sprang to life and delivered their deadly charges. Some hurled clusters of sharpened saplings that fanned out and filled the air. Others spit fire. Still others hurled smoking clay pots shaped like teardrops. When these struck, they sent flaming pitch in a wide radius. Again, Prios and Kyrien were burned, and this time Catrin knew their pain as she was unable to escape the grip of the sticking pitch, which refused to be put out. Still burning, Catrin cast a spherical barrier around them. It would not keep out the dragons and probably would not deflect projectiles, but it would hold air. Drawing the remaining air within into her palm, she effectively created a vacuum. The flames died immediately, and Catrin's ears popped. Releasing the barrier, the air rushed back in to fill the void with a clap, and Catrin felt as if she were within a giant bell. Her head felt as if it might explode, and she reconsidered the wisdom of that tactic. But it had, at least, put out the flames.

It took several deep breaths for Catrin to regain her senses, and Prios launched attacks from behind her, grunting and panting as he did so, and she knew he was hurt badly. Unable to stand the thought of him in pain, Catrin turned and saw him fighting with everything he had left, which was terrifyingly little. Concern for him was accompanied by pride. She reached out her hands to him, intending to lend him energy, to let him fight, and to bolster his strength.

Her hands never reached him.

In one swift motion, a feral dragon swooped in and snatched Prios from the saddle. A moment later, that dragon was soaring back toward Riverhold, which was now clearly visible in the morning sun. The feral and Prios's silhouette was clearly defined against the towering walls of Riverhold.

Where most keeps had walls protecting them, Riverhold was more wall than keep. From her current vantage, she could not even see an entrance. Yet the dragon was headed straight for the keep, and Kyrien was in fast pursuit. The air tore at Catrin as Kyrien dived, and she thought her ears might explode. Finally she created pressurized pockets of air around her ears and cursed herself for not thinking of it sooner. While it did reduce her hearing, her head no longer felt as if it would split in two.

Lightning enveloped the feral dragon from underneath, and Catrin knew that Prios was fighting for his life. Catrin considered launching attacks of her own, but she held back, knowing that dead, the dragon would surely let Prios fall. Catrin and Kyrien were too far behind, and Prios would be beyond their reach.

Each time Prios attacked, Catrin cried out, exulted that he was still alive, yet wanting him to keep the dragon alive. Given the scope and power of his attacks, he didn't share that desire. The walls of Riverhold rose up before them, the Yan River pouring out of the bottom of the hold creating as formidable a barrier as Catrin had ever seen. One last time Prios attacked, and the dragon looked as if its insides were on fire; it shone from within. The feral released Prios from its grip, and his trajectory would land him in the raging falls that poured from the keep.

Screaming, Catrin hurled ropes of air to catch him, knowing she was already too late. The turbulent air around the falls tossed Prios, and Catrin's ropes of energy were twisted and warped, no longer doing as she wished. Prios fell away from her; she was losing him. Even as he grew smaller, he began to glow from within, and by the time he reached the base of Riverhold, Catrin had to avert her eyes. Perhaps, she thought, he had done that as a kindness to her, not wanting her to witness the moment of his death. In the next instant, Catrin knew it was much more than kindness. This had been Prios's final attack, and the power of it was terrifying. She felt the pressure change first; immediately after came the light--fire--in a racing shock wave.

Kyrien folded his wings and could do little else as the wall of energy threw them backward harder than anything either of them had ever experienced. Darkness crowded Catrin's vision, and only the defensive energy she cast out about herself and Kyrien, albeit late, kept her from passing out. With tremendous effort, Catrin was able to divert much of the energy from Prios's attack around them. She tried hard not to think of it as Prios's final attack, even if she knew it to be true. She could no longer sense him.

Prios was gone.

* * *

Sound came to Sinjin in muffled bursts. Everything hurt and the air he breathed tasted thin and overwarm. Feeling as if he would suffocate, Sinjin forced his aching limbs to respond and pry himself out from under whatever it was that was trying to kill him. From the way he felt, it was succeeding. The weight shifted and light poured in from a lifted corner. Slowly Sinjin remembered that he'd been beaten and shoved under something heavy. With the light came fresh air, and Sinjin felt some relief immediately.

"But you tried to kill him," he heard Kendra say, and he remained very still, not wanting anyone to know he was awake.

"I regret that it was so," came the voice of the tall man. "It was required to maintain the ruse. Had I refused, I would have had to fight these men. That would've ended badly for me."

"Will they die?"

"No," the man said. "They'll sleep until we're well away from here. It's true that some may not wake, and that's something that I'll have on my hands. I regret that it is so, but it is."

"So you want me to help you get 'dead weight' over there to some stone forest, so you can ask what to do next. Have I got it right?"

The man sighed. "I suppose you could put it that way."

"Who's pulling the strings? Tell me," Kendra said, and Sinjin could almost see her standing with her legs slightly apart, her knees bent, ready to fight. It was an oddly alluring vision, and Sinjin struggled to focus.

"As I've already told you, I cannot say. I've sworn an oath."

"Perhaps I should make you swear some new oaths," Kendra said.

"I'm really starting to think unchaining you was a bad idea."

"Tell me," Kendra said with a threat in her voice, and Sinjin thought he heard the man swallow hard. *"Tell me."*

"Lord Jharmin Kyte."

The words fell from the man like an admission of cardinal guilt.

"Wait," Kendra said. "Catrin's cousin's husband?"

"Yes. The same."

"Why?" Kendra asked, no less insistent.

"Why what?"

"Why are you here? Why is the boy under that armor or whatever it is? Why did you betray your brothers? Why should I believe anything you say?"

"It's a long tale, and we need to get away from here." There came a strangled sound, and the tall man continued in a higher pitch. "I'm a spy, sent here by Lord Kyte. Lady Kyte enlisted my help in using the magic of the stone forest."

"Magic. Pah!"

"I swear to you, there is magic there, and I can hear Lord Kyte."

Again there came a strangled sound. "I thought you said Lady Kyte enlisted your help with the stone forest."

"Yes, but she has left Ravenhold—" The man stopped suddenly, as if he had suddenly realized he'd made a very big mistake.

"Go on."

"And . . . and now I talk with Lord Kyte in her stead."

"You're not telling me everything," Kendra said.

"I am. I swear to you that I am."

"I almost believe you," Kendra said. "Get him out from under there before he suffocates."

"No," the man said. Again came the strangled sound. "My orders are to keep him under the blanket until we reach the forest."

"Do I have to explain to you who's giving the orders now?"

"It won't hurt him any."

"I assume you mean it won't hurt him any *more*," Kendra said, the accusation heavy in her words.

"Yes. It won't hurt him any more than he's already hurt."

"Let's see if we can get the little man up, shall we?"

Sinjin bristled at her remark.

"Sinjin," came the man's voice, "can you hear me?"

It took a moment for Sinjin to decide what to say. When he did speak, his face ached and there were shooting pains in his swollen lips. "I can," was all he could say.

"My name is Hand, and I'm sorry I hurt you. It was necessary. I'm in the employ of House Kyte, and Lord Kyte wishes I deliver you to him. Do you capitulate?"

"Take me to him," he managed.

"What is the purpose of the *'blanket'*?" Kendra asked, her voice insistent.

Hand considered for a moment before answering. "It keeps people from sensing his presence."

"People like who?" she persisted.

"People like Thorakis and the monks above and the dragons. Need I go on? If they know he's out from under that blanket, they'll come to find him."

Kendra waved him off. "He can't even stand. How's he going to walk under the weight of that thing?"

Hand again considered his words. Though Sinjin didn't like him, he admitted Hand might be a wise man. "I thought perhaps you would help him."

"*Me?* Why would *I* help *him?*"

"You begged for his life."

The hall was silent for a few moments, and Sinjin wished he could see what was happening.

"Fine."

An instant later, the weight lessened, and Kendra was suddenly under the blanket with him. She was very close, and he could smell her heady scent. He didn't mind the pain as much when she brushed up against him. Then she put his arm over her shoulder and her arm around his waist and tried to lift him from the stone floor. It was awkward. His limbs did not want to obey, and the pain in his ribs was almost unbearable, but they eventually managed to stand. The weight of the blanket was a major hindrance, and Sinjin still felt smothered by it. His legs were unsteady, and he put his other arm around Kendra and grabbed on.

"Watch it, little man," Kendra said, and Sinjin moved his hand up. Despite everything else, he smiled and had to admit that having his arm around her felt good. Perhaps he held on at times a little tighter than needed.

* * *

Fluttering torchlight fell on a silent and unmoving forest, though when Durin shifted his viewpoint, the forest did seem to move. Even frozen in oddly weathered stone, this forest was alive. Durin could feel it, and it made the hair stand on his neck. Chase stood just in front of him, as he always seemed to, and the two of them remained silent, waiting for some sign of real movement within the magnificently carved trees. No sound came. Finding his courage, Durin followed Chase and tried to look wherever Chase wasn't looking, so nothing could sneak up on him. The feeling of some other presence in this place was so strong that Durin could not stop looking for whoever it was that dwelt here. Chase must have felt it as well, for he moved in silence and used hand signals to communicate with Durin.

A sound like the scuffling of boots echoed around them, and Chase turned to Durin with a question in his eyes. Durin just shook his head. He hadn't made the noise. This raised their concern to a new level, and while Chase stood, frozen, listening, Durin couldn't help but run his fingers along the bark of the nearest tree. It felt almost real, and that made the fact that it wasn't even more remarkable. He could almost pretend that he was outside, resting in the shade of an oak grove, and he guessed that was why it existed. The scale of the place spoke of people being trapped underground for untold ages, and memories of the outside world would become precious indeed. It looked to be almost as large as the chamber that contained the God's Eye. Though, in truth, the size was difficult to judge from below the canopy.

"Wait here," Chase said, and he started climbing a nearby tree.

Durin stayed where he was, having visions of branches of stone falling from the tree. Chase moved like the trained soldier he was, and though slow at times, he methodically climbed the stone oak. The branches did not move, and leaves did not stir. The entire experience was wholly unnatural. When Chase finally dropped back to the floor of the cavern, he grunted, and it took him a moment to stand. "There is a clearing ahead. It's a good walk, but I think that'll tell us a good bit more about this place."

"Maybe we should go back," Durin said. "Maybe we should get some reinforcements."

"I didn't see any signs of movement while I was up there, and I think perhaps we were just hearing things. Regardless, it's a long walk back, and I'd like to have a little more information than just the fact that we found a stone forest. Let's go."

Following reluctantly, Durin let Chase lead him into the heart of the forest. Here, the trees bore dark stains, and they were adorned with gray and black lichen.

"Do not touch these trees," Chase whispered.

Durin made no response. He had no desire to lay even a finger on them. Every instinct was telling him to run back the way they had come. He was about to suggest they do just that when the black trees thinned. Looking down, Durin saw that the floor of the chamber here was carved with a flowing pattern, like graceful branches but with no leaves. The pattern grew denser closer to the center of the clearing, where there stood a single massive tree that dwarfed all the rest. From here, Durin could see the vaulted ceiling of the chamber and marveled at the fact that it must have been man made; it was carved to look like wispy clouds, though now they, too, were covered in black and appeared threatening.

The branches of the mighty tree reached out over those that surrounded the clearing, and the air in the shade of this tree vibrated as if it were alive. This stone copse reminded Durin of Catrin's tales about the Grove of the Elders. That was a place that was said to have its own power, a site where the power of the land was closest to the surface. Perhaps this place, too, was similar. Durin had never been to the Grove of the Elders, but he had a picture of it in his mind, a picture that he knew was inaccurate, but he preferred to envision the ancient greatoaks as they were before Catrin destroyed them. Seeing this place somehow made his mental image of these trees even larger. It changed Durin's perception of what was possible. Never before had he realized that mankind could achieve such things. Indeed, he would bet that most of the people of the Godfist would feel the same way. The ancients had bested them in almost every way. Durin was humbled by the experience and wondered if his kind would ever ascend back to such heights.

When Chase finally stepped from the trees and into the open, Durin felt as if there were squirrels in his guts, and his knees trembled. Nothing happened. No attacks came and no sounds broke the silence. Instead, Chase just walked into the clearing and raised his eyes to gaze at the mastery of the ancients. Here their kind had reached some kind of pinnacle, while at the same time, presumably being at an all-time low, since they had been trapped under ground. Durin finally followed when it seemed as if the shadows behind him were moving, and he thought he heard that scuffling sound again.

What amazed him the most about the trees were the details and the durability of what looked delicate and fragile. Leaves with narrow stems hung from slender branches, and it seemed inconceivable that such slight structures could have survived the ages. As they moved closer to the tree, Durin saw that there was more wear on the floor here. The design was still clearly visible, but many of the edges were rounded and worn. And there was a place on the trunk of the tree, at about arm height, where the bark was worn smooth. Durin had visions of people congregating here, and each one stroking the tree in that same place. It came and went in a flash, but he felt a nearly overwhelming urge to place his own hand on that worn spot, to join the exclusive group of people who had done so, to connect with those who had come before, and he was there before he knew it. Without thinking, he placed his hand on the tree. Nearby, he heard Chase hiss.

Durin nearly fainted when the tree spoke.

"Is that you? Are you there?"

Durin slowly took his hand away from the tree and turned with wide eyes to Chase, who looked almost as startled as he. Chase held a finger to his lips and remained still and silent. Durin did his best to follow Chase's example. While it had seemed the tree spoke, it spoke with what sounded like a very human voice, yet no one could be seen.

"Yes. I am here," came another voice, calm and smooth, the sound of nobility.

"I've secured the package and the accessories," came the original voice, which sounded a great deal more stressed.

"Excellent. Bring them to me with the greatest haste."

"I want to know why." This new voice actually sounded familiar and Durin gaped. Again, Chase held his finger to his lips. No answer came.

"Answer me," Kendra said, and Durin had no doubt it was she. She sounded meaner than usual, though, and that was saying something. "If you don't tell me who you are and what you want with Sinjin, your man Hand's name is gonna become an irony. You understand me?"

Durin nearly shouted for joy when he heard Sinjin's name. Still, it didn't sound as if his friend was safe, and Durin did his best to remain quiet. It was difficult considering how many of his questions demanded answers. Where was his friend? And how could they hear those who were presumably so far away? Even the slightest possibility that Sinjin was on the Godfist gave Durin hope.

"With whom do I have the pleasure of negotiating?" the noble voice responded, seemingly unperturbed.

"My name is Kendra Ironfist, and I'm about to start cutting."

"I mean you no harm, Lady Ironfist, and I mean my nephew no harm. I suppose our relationship is a bit more tenuous than that, but with his leave, I would call him nephew. My name is Jharmin Olif Kyte, and I wish to bring you to Wolfhold, so that I can keep you safe until Lady Catrin can come for you."

Nephew? Durin asked himself, but then he remembered the tales of Lady Lissa and Lord Kyte. This was the man who had formed a truce with Catrin that ended an ages-old feud.

"Why should I believe you?"

"I don't see that you have all that much choice," Lord Kyte said. "There's a keep full of people ready to prevent you from escaping the way you came in. Hand knows other ways out of the keep, and provided you don't hurt him, he will show you the way. After that, he'll be able to use my gold to arrange for suitable transportation."

"The blanket is hurting him," Kendra said. "I'm going to take it off of him."

Durin couldn't imagine what she was talking about, but he didn't like the sound of it one bit.

"As soon as you do," Lord Kyte said, "they'll come looking for you, and you can bet they'll find you. The dragons have your scent, boy. I know you can hear me, and I know that if you want to live, you must remain hidden. If not for Thorakis wanting your mother to think you dead, you very well might be."

"My mother thinks I'm dead?" came Sinjin's voice; it sounded thick and heavy, as if he spoke without moving his jaw. The sound of that voice made Durin smile, and some of the guilt lifted from him. It was becoming increasingly difficult to remain silent, but Chase reminded him with a gesture to do just that.

"I regret that it is so," Lord Kyte said. "When you're here and surrounded by friendly stone, we'll remedy that, but it must remain so for now, or you'd be able to hide from no one."

"That figures," Kendra grumbled, and Durin was amazed he could hear her. Whatever magic this was, it was powerful indeed. "If I feel at any time that you've betrayed me, then Hand's life is forfeit. Am I perfectly clear?"

"Perfectly."

The silence grew longer after that, and Durin wondered if they had gone, if he'd lost his chance to talk with Sinjin, to find out where he was and how to help him, and he opened his mouth to speak.

Chase moved to his side, put a hand on his shoulder, and spoke loudly. "Wait. Don't go. You're not alone."

Durin wasn't certain Sinjin or the others could hear him, and he waited in intense anticipation.

Chapter 15

The oceans are the greatest mystery mankind will ever face; those lost may never be found.

--Aerestes, captain of the *Landfinder*

* * *

Walking along the valley floor, Master Edling looked upon what would soon be his. All of it would be his. Everywhere he looked, people were working to clean up the devastation left by the war, and it appeared they were doing an admirable job of it. When he cast his gaze up the valley walls to where the entrance of Dragonhold waited, he saw new stairs leading down to a massive foundation. It appeared as though the girl had some good ideas, but such a massive construction was far beyond what was needed. It would take some time to get things moving in the right direction, but that was a small price to pay, he supposed.

Baker Hollis walked wordlessly beside Master Edling, who found the silence annoying.

"I would've thought you'd be happy," Master Edling said. "Your daughter finally found a way to make you important."

"I am happy," Baker Hollis said, not sounding it. "I'm just a little worried is all."

"Worried? About what?"

"I worry for my daughter," Baker Hollis said. "She's not had an easy life."

"Bah! You worry she'll have more power than you and take revenge for every time you ever disciplined her. But don't worry. I'll assign you as Chancellor of the North to assist with your daughter's rule. As long as you don't do anything stupid, you'll have real power," Master Edling said, wondering if Hollis knew just how lucky he was; after all, few had power handed to them.

When they reached the mighty foundation, Master Edling felt a momentary twinge of jealousy. This was the work of a shrewd and creative mind. Never would he have had the audacity to order something of such magnitude constructed. Master Edling remembered the girl. He'd always assumed she was daft. This and the capture of Dragonhold proved that there was more to Trinda than met the eye. No matter, he thought. There was no reason not to let the girl reinforce the hold's defenses; what Edling wanted was within the hold. He wasn't even certain what it was he sought, but he knew Dragonhold was where he would find it. He'd known it from the time Catrin had declared the place her own, and Master Edling cursed himself for a fool for not having attacked before the girl could establish her stronghold. It had been the fault of those around him--sniveling and weak, all of them. The sight of war had reduced them all to uselessness, and none was willing to risk the people who had survived.

Edling had always figured that fewer people on the Godfist would mean more food for those who remained; after all, they lived on little more than a rock sticking up from the sea. There was little enough to be had, and Master Edling had never been fond of sharing.

The climb up the winding wooden stair was long and arduous, and it left Master Edling wet with sweat. He looked forward to settling into his chambers and having a nice, cool bath. For the moment, he continued to be grudgingly impressed with what Trinda had accomplished. Even the temporary fortifications around the entrance to Dragonhold, which was far above the valley floor, were of higher quality than what had existed before Thorakis's army attacked. But he also knew that mentally challenged people sometimes had remarkable abilities, and he figured Trinda must be one of those cases.

Baker Hollis breathed heavily and constantly wiped the sweat from his brow and eyes.

"Perhaps you shouldn't be so sedentary," Master Edling admonished. "Now you're old and sloppy and weak. It's unbecoming a man of power. I suggest you remedy that situation. Perhaps you should climb these steps every day. Maybe that'll clean you up."

Baker Hollis looked as if he might be ill, and the thought of climbing these steps even a single time clearly did not appeal to him. Not for the first time, Master Edling wished he'd brought along servants. At least then he could have ordered someone to mop the sweat from the baker before the man accidentally came into contact with him. The thought made his skin crawl.

Such was politics, though. Sometimes you had to be friends with those you'd rather see dead. As long as Master Edling got control over Dragonhold, it would all be worthwhile. He would then control every part of the Godfist except what was held by the savages, and Master Edling was pretty sure he didn't want their desert. There was nothing there for him but death, so they could have it until he decided otherwise. The rest would be his before the day was out.

Both men were soaked by the time they reached the top of the stair, and the breeze cooled them as they were escorted inside by a guardsman who didn't appear entirely comfortable with the task.

Master Edling had expected the girl to meet them at the entrance, and the guards looked less friendly than he would have imagined. With every step, he questioned his judgment until he stood before a massive throne. Baker Hollis had not uttered a word, and Master Edling could almost smell his fear. The men escorting them were armed and armored. He considered turning back then, but he chided himself for such cowardice in the face of a little girl sitting atop an oversized throne. Yet when he looked up to the eyes of that woman, still trapped in the body of a little girl, he saw his mistake, and he saw that it was too late. He should have run when he'd had the chance.

* * *

In the silence that hung over the forest of stone, Durin wondered if the others had already gone, but eventually Jharmin Kyte spoke, "Who are you and where are you?" he asked with no warmth in his voice.

"I am Chase Volker, and I am on the Godfist."

"Catrin's cousin?" Jharmin asked.

"The same," Chase said.

"I suppose you already know who I am."

"I do, Lord Kyte. You've been kind to my cousin, and I am grateful for that, but I fear for my nephew's safety."

"With good reason," Jharmin said. "But this conversation is only increasing the danger. My people will bring him to me, and then I'll be in a better position to ensure his safety. As you must have heard, my intention is to keep him safe until Catrin arrives."

"I did hear that. What's the boy's current condition? He didn't sound well when he spoke."

"I'll be all right," Sinjin's voice carried into the stillness, though still sounding as if he were speaking with his mouth full. "They beat me up and covered me in some kind of heavy blanket to make mom think I was dead."

"I'll kill them myself," Chase said, unable to hold back his anger.

"The boy's in good hands now," Jharmin said. "We must let my people do their work. This conversation must end. Come back to this place in one week, and I'll update you on the situation."

"Agreed," Chase said.

"Wait!" Durin said, unable to keep silent any longer. His friend was half a world away, and this might be his last chance to say good-bye.

Chase turned a hard eye on him, but then the look on his face softened.

"You'll come back home when all this is over, won't you, Sinjin?"

"Durin? Is that really you?"

"Idiot," came Kendra's voice.

"It's me, Sinjin," Durin said, ignoring Kendra's remark.

"We have to go. Now!" came Hand's voice.

"I'll come back!" was the last thing Sinjin said before the mighty stone forest fell silent again.

"Well," Chase said. "Now we know why Trinda wanted us to find this place. I'd love to know how she knew it was here, but I doubt she'll ever tell me. I guess we should head back."

Durin wanted to stay, even though Sinjin was gone; this place made him feel closer to his friend, and he wished he could somehow transport himself through the tree to where Sinjin was. The two of them had always been stronger together than apart, and it seemed Sinjin needed him now more than ever before.

It was with a hollow feeling in his gut that Durin finally let Chase lead him away from the stone forest and back toward the main keep.

* * *

A single thought consumed Catrin: No, this could not be happening. Her heart could not cope with such loss, and she thought it might burst. Kyrien, too, wobbled in flight, and the two were clearly in no condition to fly, let alone fight. When her vision refocused, Catrin could see the dragon ore in the saddle around her was now milky white, especially where Prios had been sitting before his . . .

Anguish washed over Catrin again, and she issued a wordless cry filled with vast melancholy. It was drowned out by the sound of Riverhold collapsing. Catrin could not believe her eyes. Kyrien had pulled them up higher, and as he swung back around to face the keep, the upper walls began to crumble. An instant later, one of the footings failed with a massive *thump,* which accelerated the chain reaction Prios's final attack had started.

Pride swelled in Catrin's chest at what he had accomplished, all the while knowing it hadn't been worth it, and she would change it if she could. But she couldn't. It was a strange mixture of pain, regret, resignation, and commitment that rose up in Catrin when she saw a feral dragon perched atop one of the few towering parapets that remained standing while most of the southern face of Riverhold collapsed. The crushing weight destroyed the mountainlike foundations of the hold, and eventually even the parapet on which the dragon perched tumbled away into the rushing fall. Catrin watched, fascinated, as towering stone statues were exposed and went through their final motions before being destroyed by an avalanche of stone.

The feral dragon simply extended its wings and caught the wind, which was quickly filled with dust and debris. It was then that the man riding the dragon was brought into Catrin's view: Thorakis, a brilliant man who'd given himself to the darkness. Beneath him was the darkness itself. It oozed from the feral dragon like a living thing, coiled and ready to strike.

Catrin felt the threat deeply and knew that she and Kyrien were overmatched. Under other circumstances, perhaps they could have been on equal terms, but in their current condition, they would almost certainly perish. It was not only the threat of the dragon and Thorakis; she could sense the presence of potent weapons finely tuned to her that could cut her like no other.

Her connection with the Staff of Life had been forged over time, but the battle of Adderhold had forever linked the two; Catrin's fingers had bitten deeply into the living flesh of the staff. Her defenses against the staff were few and feeble. If Thorakis landed an attack with the staff, Catrin knew it could be deadly. Then there was Koe. Catrin didn't even want to think the name because it gave the carving even more power over her. She had created it, or at least she had released it from within its prison of stone. Koe had been her comfort and security for so long, and now she feared the cat's raw power would reduce them to dust. Though she knew Koe wasn't sentient, the carving had a life its own; if only it had the will to resist Thorakis, but Catrin knew it wasn't so.

She could fully avenge her son and husband only if she survived this encounter, and she tried desperately to arrange her muddled thoughts. Thorakis didn't give her the chance and attacked, even as his keep dropped away into the waters of the Yan River. Massive amounts of water flooded into the aqueducts, which were suddenly and violently relieved of the great stone valves that had previously moderated the flow. The structures that reached out from the keep like the legs of a giant spider swelled with the deluge, and it looked to Catrin as if they would soon fail altogether. She could only hope that the people of the Greatland who lived along those aqueducts were not harmed. Part of her knew that losing the aqueducts would wreak havoc on the farmers who had come to depend on them, but that was not a problem that Catrin could fix or even face at that moment.

It was everything she could do to face the coming onslaught of Thorakis's rage. Prios's attack had destroyed all that Thorakis had wrought, and Catrin knew the resulting rage would be directed at her. His energy radiated and polluted the air; she could taste the madness in it, and it made her want to vomit. In choking, cloying waves, it threatened to relieve her of her own sanity. Kyrien turned away from the crumbling remains of the keep and soared down low over the water of the Yan River, dodging the tips of trees and even shrubs, so low did he fly.

Perhaps he'd hoped to escape the wrath of Thorakis; Catrin didn't know since he hadn't communicated with her in some time. This gave her cause for concern, but she had no chance to ask him if he was all right. Seethe reminded them that he had power of his own, and a river of cold fear washed over them, accompanied by the sound of black wings cutting the air in fast pursuit.

Raw, untempered power radiated from Thorakis, and his first attack was almost the only attack. Red lightning and fire erupted around Catrin and Kyrien before she even knew what was happening. For a terrifying instant, she was afire, but then it was gone. Still, the damage was done. Her ears rang, her clothes smoked, and her exposed flesh stung and burned. She took solace in the fact that she hadn't breathed in while surrounded by flames and did her best to catch her breath.

Though she was weary and injured, she knew it was time to take defensive measures or Thorakis would be the end of them. He wielded her weapons with no restraint, and mixed with his madness, they targeted Catrin's spirit as easily as her physical form. Feeling as if she were slowly fading away, Catrin cast a shield about herself just before the next attack came. Looking strained and fractured, the shield heaved and bucked in the face of that force, and Catrin could feel the staff and Koe in that attack.

A webbing of cracks that covered her shield grew more defined, and even as the massive attack was abating, the shield failed, and Catrin was struck in the face by lightning that arced between her teeth and lit up her face from within. It felt as if she had been kicked in the face, and along with the taste of burned flesh came the coppery taste of blood.

Seethe used his fresh muscles to gain speed, whereas Kyrien had already given his all. Catrin could feel it in his energy and see it in the way he held his head. She couldn't blame him. They had tried to save the regent dragons, they had tried to save her son, and they had failed, and now she had lost Prios as well. There was no more reason to fight it. Death had come for them, and there was nothing they could do to stop it.

The thoughts were familiar enough to Catrin; she had felt the coercion of a feral dragon before, and she knew it for what it was: lies. Drawing a deep breath, she clamped together with her knees, giving Kyrien a signal that the feral would not be able to hear, and hoped against all hope, that Kyrien had simply been playing at being hurt worse than he actually was. Her command was answered in either case, and Catrin had to focus on readying herself to attack. If she could not defend herself, then she would have no choice but to eliminate the threat.

Kyrien soared straight up, his change in direction as abrupt as he could manage. The feral dragon did not fly beneath them as Catrin had hoped, but instead gained on them. Drawing as deeply as she dared, Catrin felt as if the rush of power would slowly but steadily consume her, eating away at her like sand in a wind storm. When the dragon drew close enough that Catrin could almost reach out and touch him, she released her attack, not on Thorakis this time, but on Seethe. She aimed for the dragon's eyes and was rewarded when the beast began shaking its head back and forth and fell behind, steadily losing ground. Catrin, though, had to relent, unable to sustain such a massive attack for any length of time. She felt like a piece of metal that had been heated, and she needed time to cool down, but Seethe was now even angrier than before.

With a terrible bellow, the writhing black mass cut through the air with unbelievable speed, regaining the distance that had been lost and closing fast, and this time Thorakis was ready with an attack. Catrin prepared herself, knowing that she would be unable to defend herself, but Kyrien rolled at the last instant and took the brunt of the attack on his now exposed underbelly. Black smoke rolled around Catrin, as if Kyrien were on fire, and she could hear him straining to breathe. Then they were dropping from the sky so fast that Catrin thought Kyrien might be dead, but he pulled up at the last instant and slowed to skim the surface of the water. They slowed violently when he let his body come fully into contact with the water, and she sensed relief from Kyrien.

Seethe, though, would not be put off, and after executing a wide turn, dropped toward them with terrifying speed. Catrin opened her mouth to scream, but no sound came out. Kyrien leaped from the water with a thrust of his mighty, webbed feet and powerful strokes of his wings, which pushed Catrin down hard into the saddle. With one hand, she cinched the lines that had been loosened when Prios had been ripped from the saddle, and she tried to tighten them, but Kyrien's abrupt evasive maneuvers made it impossible to do anything more than hold on. Thorakis didn't seem to be having any better luck on the pursuing Seethe since no attacks were launched during this mad rush.

In a move that made Catrin's stomach leap, Kyrien suddenly reversed direction. He threw his head back; at one point his head and tail nearly touched, and Seethe flew between Kyrien's head and tail, his massive jaws open and revealing huge, drool-covered teeth that appeared to have much of the beast's last meal stuck between them. The smell of that breath reached Catrin and she gagged. Kyrien, though, moved like a whip and used the tip of his tail to smack Seethe in the face as he soared past.

A range of sensations assaulted Catrin's senses, and her head swam with it. But she was able to sort out bits and pieces from the onslaught. Thorakis was winded, his energy nearly spent. What he had in potency, he lacked in stamina, and that was something Catrin could use to her advantage. Seethe, on the other hand, was lean and strong and showed no signs of fatigue. His jaws alone would be enough to put an end to her and Kyrien, and his equally deadly claws moved like caged lightning.

Kyrien gave an effort born of pure love for Catrin. She could feel him straining beneath her, and she knew that he wouldn't have given such an effort to save himself alone, especially since he blamed himself for the death of his queen and all of his kind. Catrin's heart threatened to break, but life had hardened her and lent her strength. She would not break; she would not relent or be defeated. Her cause was righteous, and she cast aside the restraint that had always underlain her attacks.

Turning to get a good angle on the rapidly approaching Seethe, Kyrien kept their path straight and level. Seethe earned his name as he approached, and it was difficult not to lose courage in the face of such malevolence. Black death stalked her, and she waited until the jaws were nearly upon her, and this time she attacked only one eye, but she attacked it with the full force of her will, no restraint, no holding back. It felt as if chunks of her chest were being pulled out and cast into wind before vaporizing in the path of such massive flow.

The air vibrated and shimmered between Catrin and Seethe. Even when Thorakis leveled another, weaker attack at her, Catrin maintained her assault on the dragon's eye. Smoke poured around it, and the beast roared in pain, even as Catrin cried out from the pain of Thorakis's hit. When flames erupted around Seethe's eye, he turned and dived down low to dunk his head in the waters below. Kyrien took advantage of the respite and gained altitude. Towering plumes of vapor soared above them, and Kyrien aimed for the biggest ones.

Below them, she heard Seethe roar in anger, and she dreaded their next meeting, provided her and Kyrien's wounds didn't kill them first. When the white mists closed around her, though, she knew they had a chance.

Chapter 16

The forces that hold us together can be used to tear us apart.
--Gemino, sorcerer and artist

* * *

"Let me out of here!" Master Edling demanded from behind an iron-shod door.

"I'm afraid I can't do that yet," Baker Hollis said, and Master Edling thought he sounded smug and self-congratulatory.

"If you don't get me out of here, I'll call the liens on your bakery and put you out of business."

Baker Hollis actually chuckled. "I don't really have to worry about that now. Let someone else bake the bread. My daughter is queen."

"You can't really think the people will accept her as their queen, do you? Come on, Hollis, get real. The girl's a freak, and people are afraid of her."

"Even more afraid of her than they *were* of you."

The way he said *were* made the urge to throttle Baker Hollis almost irresistible. If only the man would step a little closer to the bars that allowed the only light into the tiny cell in which Master Edling was being held. The place was dirty and smelled of mud and urine. The mud, he knew was left over from the floods. This would not have been so bad if one of those precious water channels ran through his cell, but they did not. Knowing that the keep was equipped with such amenities only fueled his jealous rage.

A daft child would take it all away from him.

He'd always disliked children, and perhaps this was why. Even if he knew that Trinda was of a woman's age, she still looked like a child, so he assumed she still thought like a child.

"What's it going to take to get me out of here?"

"Nothing beyond your ability to provide," Baker Hollis said, and he stepped a little closer to the bars so he could speak at little more than a whisper.

Just a little closer, and Edling would be able the reach out and choke the traitorous fool. For the moment, Edling let the man speak, letting him lower his guard even further. The rational part of him listened since this was probably the only way he would get out of that cell. That part of him knew he couldn't kill Baker Hollis now. It would have wait until later. He could be patient to a certain extent.

"First, you have to apologize to my daughter in writing."

Master Edling bit back his retort and waited to see what would come next.

"You can do this as part of your relinquishment of power to Queen Trinda. You'll cede to me all lands south of the wall that bears your name and all the way to the sea. You'll deed the Masterhouse, the cold caves, the mills, the mines, all of it. All of this you'll sign with your official seal, and then you'll deliver it to the council at the Masterhouse. You'll assist with a peaceful transfer of power, and then you will be free to select a parcel of land north of the wall on which you can retire. Security forces will be assigned to you to ensure your safety, of course. You've not managed to make many friends along the way."

Master Edling wanted to shout, wanted to scream while wringing the life out of Baker Hollis and his ill-begotten get. To the fires with all of them, he thought. No one could make him do such things; no one could force his hand.

He knew the thoughts were false even as they flashed through his mind. Already part of him had accepted his fate. At least it would get him out of this forsaken place, even if it was only to pick out a larger cell in which to live. In the end, he had to accept the truth in Baker Hollis's words; he'd not made many friends. Removed from power, he'd be lucky to live a month. Trinda's mercy might be the only thing keeping him alive. He would admit it to no one, and he would spend the rest of his days plotting his return to power if that was what it took, but for that moment, he relented and admitted defeat, however humiliating it was to be beaten by a mere girl child. When Baker Hollis moved closer still, Master Edling nearly lost his self-control, his fingers itching for the baker's flesh.

* * *

From out of the morning fog rose Wolfhold. Atop an aged wagon rode a tall man and what looked like two people huddled under a thick blanket. A swayback mare pulled the cart forward at a slow but inexorable pace. It seemed to Sinjin as if they would never get to Wolfhold and he'd never get to see his mother or his homeland again. The world had gone even crazier than it had previously been, and now nothing was certain. Even his relationship with Jharmin Kyte was a mystery. This man was married to Sinjin's mother's cousin--not exactly ties of blood. Not many in the Greatland were likely to find any sympathy for Sinjin, especially if they knew who he was. On the other hand, having him as a prisoner could perhaps give Jharmin power over Sinjin's mother.

More likely, Jharmin's concern for him was genuine, and he did actually have Sinjin's and his mother's best interests at heart. Sinjin felt better when he considered the latter, despite knowing how much Lady Lissa disliked his mother. What if she was also at Wolfhold? Lord Kyte had said that she had left, but he didn't say she wouldn't return. The thought made his guts hurt, but Kendra shifted next to him, and he said nothing when she used his shoulder as a pillow. Initially she'd ridden under the blanket to keep from drawing anyone's notice, but during the night, it had been pleasant to share the warmth with her.

Breathing shallow breaths so as not to wake her, Sinjin watched through the small hole he maintained. He might have to stay under the cursed blanket until they reached Wolfhold, but that did not mean he had to be suffocated or deprived of a little light. Hand had seemed to want to argue but, after a while, had stopped trying to persuade Sinjin to keep the blanket all the way down. If nothing else, he needed to breathe.

Guards lined the roadway that led to a stout drawbridge. A deep channel filled with rushing water ran beneath. Beyond, the keep rose like a towering spire that used a natural formation of stone as its foundation. A thriving community surrounded the inner walls, and rural lands extended from the hold like spokes from the hub of a giant wheel.

As they crossed the bridge, Sinjin couldn't help but wonder if he'd ever leave this place. The wagon wheels found a protruding lip of rock that sent the wagon rocking back and forth. Kendra was thrust closer to him, and he put his arm around her to help support her. The motions of the wagon roused her from her sleep, and she came around slowly. When she realized Sinjin's arm was around her, though, she cast him an accusing glance. After peeking out from under the blanket, Kendra saw that they were nearly there and were now surrounded by Lord Kyte's men.

Lifting the blanket and exposing Sinjin to the light, Kendra shrugged the blanket the rest of the way off.

"Not until we're inside," Hand said, trying to lift the blanket back over her head but failing against its weight. "We don't need everyone to know that you're here."

"If there're just Kyte's men around here, why would anyone else find out?" Kendra said, refusing to rejoin Sinjin under the blanket. In truth, Sinjin was considering shrugging the heavy burden off as well.

"Just as I worked within Ohmahold and yet served Lord Kyte, so do some of those here serve another master. I know not which, but I know they're here nonetheless. Now please get back under the blanket for just a short while longer."

Kendra did as she was asked, but it was clear that she did so grudgingly, and she couldn't seem to resist showing Hand her blade one more time before joining Sinjin.

"Keep your hands where I can see 'em," she said in response to Sinjin's glance.

Watching through the gap Sinjin maintained, they saw hurried preparations being made by people with haggard and worried looks on their faces. Sinjin could feel the dark and tense mood of the place, and the worry in his gut grew more intense. He tried to hide the trembling of his legs from Kendra, but she was so close to him that it was impossible. She looked at him once, an indecipherable expression on her face, but she said nothing.

"Where are you from?" Sinjin finally asked to break the silence. "I mean, before you came to the Godfist?"

"My family was from the Westland," Kendra said after a while, which surprised Sinjin. He hadn't really expected an answer. The truth was that he never really knew what to expect from Kendra. "I never got to see my homeland. By the time I was born, my family had lost everything, our lands were poisoned, and no one and nothing could live there."

Sinjin could hear the pain in her voice as she spoke. He knew that somehow Kendra's life felt incomplete to her because she'd never been to the Westland, and now most of that place was lost to mankind forever, fouled and poisoned by the detonation of a Statue of Terhilian.

"The woman I call my mother and I moved around a lot, and we only stayed as long as the work lasted. I never really knew how long that would be."

Sinjin considered saying something, but this was the most Kendra had ever told him about herself, and he decided to hold his tongue.

"It wasn't so bad," she said with a shrug, as if trying to cast off the mood. "I learned to fight and defend myself. That's more than I can say for most folks, so I suppose I made out all right."

She didn't say any more, and Sinjin concentrated on getting a good look at Wolfhold. A defensible place, he thought, and beautiful. Everywhere he looked there were defensive structures that were also majestic works of art. Perhaps the defensive nature of these features was invisible to the casual eye, but Sinjin's training was not forgotten, and he knew what was coming. He'd been educated more than most on the nature of war and sieges. He'd known all along that Wolfhold would be as safe as its ability to repel armies . . . and dragons. The last bit changed everything, of course, as had proven true for Ohmahold. For all their defensive advantage against traditional armies, a handful of dragons could take this place. An army would not even need to attack the city; they could just surround it and wait for the dragons to drive out those within the keep. Certainly there were places within the spire of stone where the dragons could not themselves go, but their ability to carry troops and place them within the walls was devastating.

Even if Jharmin were able to conceal him at the heart of this mighty keep, he wouldn't be safe, and that haunted Sinjin.

When they approached the keep proper, Sinjin's stomach clenched. Once again the feeling of entering a place he might never leave made him want to scream, to claw his way out from under the blanket and make a break for freedom. Freedom, though, was nowhere to be found. All paths pointed toward his death, and again Sinjin trembled.

"We'll find a way out of this," Kendra said as the shadow of a mighty stone archway enveloped them.

The noises of the outside were almost immediately silenced. Hooves on stone made the only sound, and they echoed sharply. Sinjin wasn't certain he believed Kendra, but he said nothing.

A crowd of people worked in what bordered on chaos within the stable yard where they now found themselves, and there was a sense of deadly urgency in the air. These people knew the storm was coming, and Sinjin got the distinct impression that no one believed what they did would be enough. That was until a man in fine but simple garb walked into the stable yard. Men stepped aside to let him pass. A young man struggled to maintain control of the colt he held. The horse looked to be about two years old and, by the look in his eyes, was about to panic.

The confident man stopped and turned to the young man holding the colt. With quiet calm, he took the lead line out of the young man's hands. The colt continued to prance, sparks flying from his shoes as they struck stone. Other horses were riled by his panic, and the situation threatened to escalate, but the man Sinjin guessed was the stable master reached up and grabbed the colt by the halter and laid a calming hand on the horse's neck. Still the colt danced in a circle. The man just moved with him, sure and steadfast. Slowly the panic receded from the colt's eyes, and he soon stood trembling and blowing but overall unruffled. The man handed the lead line back to the younger man with a soft word then headed toward Hand.

"I didn't think it was possible to cover the distance so quickly," he said.

Hand bowed to him. "I didn't either, my lord. You urged me to make great haste, and I did everything within my power to comply."

"You've done well, Hand. You're a good and loyal man."

"Thank you, my lord. I never meant to deceive you, and I never will again. You've my word. I'm yours, my lord."

"Stand, my friend, I understand that you were trying to serve me and my wife in the best way you could. Now I think the time has come for my nephew to reveal himself."

"The moment he does is the moment the sands begin to fall," Hand said.

"We've made what preparations we can," Lord Kyte said. "My wife is preparing Ravenhold, but we both know it will fall. I wanted the fool woman to stay here, but she's as stubborn as a stone mule. Now the best I can do is to draw the armies here instead. And what better way to do that than to let them know Sinjin is here? Then we'll find out if the legendary defenses of Wolfhold are as impenetrable as the old stories say. The decision is made. Sinjin, you may come out from under that dreadful blanket now. I'm sorry that you've had to endure it this long."

Looking over at Kendra, who had remained concealed along with him, Sinjin felt a long moment's hesitation. Once he came out from under this blanket, if he were to believe what he'd been told, the feral dragons and

Thorakis would know exactly where he was. He had no reason not to believe what he'd been told, and no matter how much he detested being stuck under the blanket, he was afraid. It was an admission that hurt his pride, but that didn't change the truth of it.

Kendra gave him a nod then poked him in the ribs.

Together they moved out from under the blanket. It felt good to have fresh air on his face, but the glory of it was short lived. The reality of what was going on around him was instantly sobering. These were the preparations for war, and Sinjin couldn't help but wonder how many of these people would find their deaths before the winter. That was the problem with understanding sieges; Sinjin knew what horrors to expect.

"I'm Jharmin Olif Kyte, and you're my wife's cousin's son. A tenuous relation, I know, but I nonetheless greet you as family and welcome you to my home. I wish I could greet you under more welcoming circumstances, but it seems the world has come unglued, and we get to have seats close to the action."

Sinjin wasn't certain what to say, and he fumbled for words. "Th—thank you, uh, my lord."

"Please, my boy, call me Uncle Jharmin. I insist! We're family, after all. And we don't get to have family here to visit all that often." His words were spoken more loudly than needed to carry to Sinjin, Hand, and Kendra. "And I'm remiss. I've not made the acquaintance of the lady."

"This is Kendra Ironfist," Sinjin said. "She's my friend." The words came out without much thought.

Kendra made a rude sound in her throat, but Sinjin also caught something else in the look she gave him. He did his best to conceal his smile.

"I welcome you both to Wolfhold. Please, let us retire within. You can refresh yourselves after your journey, and then we can have some time to talk."

Kendra said nothing but she matched Sinjin's stride. The interior architecture of the hold was majestic yet barren of inspiration. The arched entranceways were unadorned, and the vaulted ceilings bore no decorations. The walls, however, were covered in works of art that Sinjin thought somewhat overcompensated for the otherwise bland surroundings. The quality of the works displayed was far beyond anything that Sinjin had seen before, and the sheer number of them kept Sinjin's attention rapt. Jharmin walked ahead of them, and a young man approached at a very fast walk from deeper within the hold. Jharmin stopped to listen to the page's whispered message, and Kendra leaned closer to Sinjin.

"Don't trust anyone," she said. "People are rarely what they seem at first glance, and there are people within these halls who would do you ill."

Sinjin would have liked to scoff at her concerns, but he knew she was right, and that knowing gnawed at him. No one here was familiar, which meant everyone was potentially an enemy, and Sinjin found it exhausting. Hand continued to watch over them, and Sinjin had to wonder even about Hand. The man was a spy. How could he possibly trust a spy? And this spy had beaten Sinjin senseless; that was more difficult to forgive. This man was a professional liar. Sinjin knew he could trust Hand only so far, but he still trusted this man more than he trusted anyone else in this place. Once his captors had been neutralized, Hand had kept them safe. He'd protected them during the harrowing journey from Ohmahold to Wolfhold, and that counted for something.

Even with the warm and personal welcome extended by Jharmin and the insistence that Sinjin call him uncle, Sinjin wasn't certain he could trust Jharmin either. The man's beloved wife despised Catrin and, Sinjin assumed, himself as well. He had to accept the fact that Jharmin could have far different reasons for bringing him to Wolfhold, and he'd need to be careful of everything he said and did.

When presented with food and wine, Sinjin looked to Kendra with doubt in his eyes.

"Don't quite trust your loving uncle?" Kendra teased, but then she grabbed a quartered apple and a flagon of wine. Before Sinjin could say anything, she was washing down some of the apple with wine. "They went through an awful lot of trouble just to poison us, you know," she said with her mouth full.

Blushing, Sinjin grabbed some apple and berries for himself. For the moment, he preferred to forgo the wine. Washbasins and towels were brought to them, and Sinjin wasn't certain what to do. His clothes needed washing--he needed washing--and the rooms to which they'd been brought didn't seem an appropriate place to bathe.

"For you to wash the travels from your face and hands," a young man said in response to Sinjin's confused stare.

"Thank you," he said, and he used a damp corner of a towel to wipe away the grime from his face. He supposed it would have been better to have washed his hands before eating, and he continued to feel out of place and embarrassed by his ignorance. Despite his mother's position, he'd never been considered anything like royalty. Many of the people of his homeland had treated him with respect and kindness, but overall, he was just a regular boy. This place made him feel inadequate and crude.

Kendra didn't appear much more comfortable in these surroundings, and she seemed mortified that the towels had turned dark by the time she finished cleaning her face and hands.

"Now that you've had some refreshment, may we measure you?" the same young man asked Sinjin.

"Measure me?"

"I'm sorry, my lord, but you didn't have any trunks or bags. I assumed you'd need new clothes."

"Oh," Sinjin said, feeling small and uncomfortable. "OK."

Though he'd been measured before, the way the young man deftly tied knots in a length of string to record his measurements amazed Sinjin.

"I'll take you to the baths now," the young man said. "I'll get you something to wear until your new clothes are ready."

"What's your name?" Sinjin asked.

"Munson, my lord."

"My name is Sinjin, and you don't have to call me 'my lord.'"

"Yes, my lord. Thank you, my lord."

Munson proved a competent guide and attendant, and before long, Sinjin was washed, dressed, and somehow feeling even more out of his element. Some things about the hold reminded him of home, yet it wasn't the same. It felt different, smelled different, and he realized, its energy was different, not necessarily better or worse but different. For a moment, Sinjin wondered how Kendra had made out with her attendant, but he heard them before he saw them.

"I look just fine," Kendra said. "I certainly do not need you to brush my hair."

"But, my lady," came the voice of the unfortunate young woman tasked with making Kendra presentable.

Sinjin knew it must be like trying to brush a wild boar. Granted Kendra was a lot prettier but no less dangerous.

When Kendra entered their assigned apartments in a frilly dress, Sinjin had to stifle a laugh, and he wasn't certain he'd managed to entirely keep the smirk from his face. Given the look on her face, it didn't seem anything he said would be appreciated, so he managed somehow to keep his mouth shut. Still she glared at him, and that was when he remembered the grin. Even as he wiped it from his face, she turned her nose into the air and sniffed. So much for self-control, he thought. Long after his grin had faded, though, Sinjin could not stop looking at her.

Chapter 17

Some paths lead only to darkness and must be guarded.
--Brackus, archsorcerer

* * *

Given brief respite, Catrin and Kyrien did what they could to rejuvenate themselves. The clouds had provided cover, and Catrin suspected she and Kyrien were not the only ones nursing their wounds. Sleep alone had been restorative, and the water she gathered from within the clouds had refreshed her, but Catrin longed for something more substantial than jerky to eat. There was little enough of that remaining.

No matter how much she wanted to defeat Thorakis and defend the people of the Greatland, she couldn't do so if her own personal needs weren't attended to. However humbling that may be, it was what maintained her humanity and perhaps her humility.

She didn't think herself better than everyone else, but she did feel capable of making a bigger difference with her actions than most. With that came a huge responsibility. And the people of the Greatland had always been precious to her; they connected her to her mother, and for that, she was grateful. There was precious little of her mother's memory for her to cling to, and that hurt as much as anything else. Kyrien shared her mood, and they said nothing.

In the midmorning light, the land looked like a carpet of green divided by wagon trails and farmsteads. And then there were the aqueducts, which more closely resembled walls dividing the land in more than spirit. This far from the keep, the aqueducts remained undamaged.

When they neared a mighty keep constructed within a towering spire, she saw parts of the aqueduct where the stone walls had fallen away, revealing a chamber within. Pouring from it were steady streams of dark forces. Catrin could only hope that the destruction of Riverhold would keep any more troops from marching through the aqueducts. The possibility that Prios's attack had taken out a large number of dark troops put a sad smile on her face. She'd never wanted to kill anyone, but when people and creatures are determined to take from you everything you hold dear, things change, priorities change, values change or are at least tested.

The dark troops moved south, where a gathering host surrounded Wolfhold, which looked like a pale, dead tree jutting from a festering swamp. Black smoke rose from many cook fires and larger fires whose purposes could only be nefarious by Catrin's estimation. This didn't look like a force that could take this keep through conventional means, save an extended siege meant to starve the occupants out.

Catrin knew, though, that this army had far more devastating weapons:

dragons. The ferals were awesome weapons that could easily tear Wolfhold to pieces. Casting her senses about, Catrin tried to find some sign of the black dragons, but she sensed none. Seethe had been wounded and needed rest as much as they. Catrin had thought for certain that other dragons would've come after her and Kyrien, yet they flew through clear blue skies unaccosted. Kyrien soared higher and gave them a better vantage.

The aqueducts, if repaired in the north, would sustain the armies, but Catrin knew that would require time Thorakis didn't have. Higher Kyrien soared, causing Catrin's ears to pop. Soon she had to open herself to a trickle of power and pressurize the air around her. It came to her more easily now that she'd done it so many times, and she was able to maintain it without thought. Kyrien continued higher then flew east for some time. He said nothing and Catrin asked nothing. She trusted him implicitly, and despite the lack of communication, his determination and purpose were unmistakable.

Some of the lands below seemed familiar to Catrin, though they were difficult to recognize from above. Still, she knew they were above part of Mundleboro, and eventually Ravenhold became visible in the distance. It was a distressing sight, festering as if consumed by plague. An army equal to the size of the one surrounding Wolfhold laid siege to Ravenhold, and here there were dragons, slowly tearing away the hold's defenses. Ballistae and catapults fired from within the walls, but the dragons quickly targeted these, and they were able to bring down only a few of the flying devils before they themselves were destroyed.

Thorakis was here. Now that she was closer, Catrin could sense the staff and Koe, and she knew that there was a hundred times more power here than needed to defeat her. While they remained undetected, Catrin tried to decide what to do. Her family's ancestral home was under attack and would surely be destroyed. Catrin had no warm feelings for her cousin, but neither did she wish to see her dead. Knowing it might mean her death, she decided it was a worthy cause. If the dragons were allowed to raze Ravenhold unchallenged, then surely they would go to Wolfhold next. At least if she were able to reduce the dragons' numbers here, Wolfhold might stand.

No matter what she chose, Ravenhold seemed lost for certain. Much of the outer city and villages burned, though they did appear completely abandoned. Those within would not last long if the dragons continued to peel away their defenses.

There was nothing more to do but let Kyrien know her desires. "Death from above," she shouted, and Kyrien required no further instruction.

Wings folded and torso straight as a pike, Kyrien dived at the cloud of black dragons. The vicious beasts swarmed in the air above Ravenhold, taking turns at the beleaguered defenders. If they sensed Catrin and Kyrien's approach, they gave no indication, and Catrin searched for

Thorakis. Unable to sense his presence, she finally unleashed her attacks on the dragons nearest to her. Kyrien kept their path true, and Catrin attacked with impunity.

Bursts of radiant energy crackled and split the air and exploded with percussive thunder on impact. Again and again, dragons fell to Catrin's attacks, and the thrill of victory ran through her, but surprise was no longer hers, and she was now grossly outnumbered. Among the dragons were those that bore riders, though there were fewer than she'd faced in the past. Catrin took some satisfaction in that, but her time for gloating was short.

Concentrating on those below her, Catrin hadn't paid attention to the skies above her. If she had, she would've seen the dragon coming. Only when the air pressure changed around her did she finally look; it was only to see massive claws descending and wrapping around her. The pain was unbelievable, and she would have screamed if she could get any air back in her chest. The straps that held her to the saddle strained and one snapped, but Kyrien was trying to stay close to the feral and keep Catrin in the saddle. Catrin was being crushed, and only the energy flowing through her kept her from succumbing to the pain and pressure.

Instead, she pulled from deep within herself the will to live and fight. Light flared and Catrin concentrated her attack on a single point where the claw bones came together. Smoke poured from that spot, but nothing else happened. Catrin's vision swam in yellow and brown, but then the pain seemed to hit the dragon all at once, causing it to twitch violently and release Catrin from its grip.

Unable to breathe deeply due to the pain in her ribs, Catrin took in rapid, shallow breaths. Kyrien continued to make evasive maneuvers, and every one revisited the pain in Catrin's ribs. With one hand on her side, Catrin did what she could to direct healing energy to that area. As had been the case for many years, all she had to do was ask her body to heal and direct some of Istra's energy to that purpose. Her subconscious had been silent for more than a decade, and though Catrin sensed the presence and acknowledgment of the need, there was no overt communication. Given Catrin's current predicament, she was grateful. Communicating with her subconscious mind always left her dazed.

Though by no means gone, the pain in Catrin's ribs abated enough for her to let go of them. Breathing was still painful, but it was at least now possible.

The dragons below had been alerted to their presence, and battle was soon joined. Wings, teeth, and claws flashed around them, seemingly coming from every direction at once. Catrin had seen crows harass and chase away hawks by attacking them in mid air, but the violence and speed of these attacks were like nothing Catrin had ever seen elsewhere in nature, except perhaps for daggerfish. The thought was not comforting.

Casting offensive and defensive energy around her in reaction to whatever threat she detected next, Catrin knew she wouldn't be able keep it up for long. After sending a thought to Kyrien, a skill that was becoming easier every day, and making sure the beleaguered regent dragon was prepared for what was about to happen, Catrin reached out to the air and clouds around them. Fire and lightning sailed toward them from the backs of feral dragons, and Catrin used no restraint. She tore the clouds from the sky and compressed them into a raging black mass that surrounded her and Kyrien. She could feel the potent and concentrated energy; her senses were overwhelmed with the taste of copper and the smell of the coming rain.

In that instant, they were the storm; Catrin and Kyrien became the embodied power and primal fury of nature, and they unleashed that potent force on the feral dragons. In a flash of light that spiderwebbed out across the skies, away from Catrin and Kyrien, a thunderclap radiated outward in all directions with such ferocity that it folded up the feral dragons' wings and sent them spinning outward.

If Catrin could've changed it, she would have. As it was, a rain of dragons caused destruction in all directions. There was nothing she could do about it, but that didn't stop her from wishing it were different. Tingling all over, she felt light-headed after the release of so much power. The stones in the saddle were milky white around her, and she worried she would damage the stones and destroy the saddle just as she had Imeteri's fish. She'd have to be very careful about how much energy she drew from the saddle until it had a chance to recharge in the light of Istra and Vestra.

Few dragons had evaded her massive attack, and they congregated around Ravenhold, perhaps knowing Catrin wouldn't release such a devastating attack so close to her ancestral home. Catrin was just glad they thought her capable of launching another attack of that magnitude. The last thing she wanted them to know was that her nose was bleeding and her vision was like looking through water. Her body vibrated and thrummed in the wake of the massive release, and she could barely move.

When she saw Seethe perched upon an upper balcony of Ravenhold, though, she forced her body into action. Kyrien interpreted her thoughts and swooped toward Seethe. Other dragons did their best to intercept Kyrien; he would not be deterred. Claws raked his flesh, and jaws closed around his neck, and still he managed to move them closer to Seethe, who waited expectantly. Thorakis was nowhere to be seen.

A huge black torso slammed against Kyrien's side, and Catrin was trapped between the two dragons from the knee down. The pain was beyond anything she'd experienced before, and she cried out. As if on cue, Thorakis returned to the balcony, smiling and with a dagger at Lissa's throat. Catrin's cousin stood, stoic, no emotion registering on her face, and guilt stabbed at Catrin. Lissa had never liked her and had never been anything but cold to her, but what Thorakis was doing with her now was purely because of Catrin. Otherwise, he'd have no doubt taken her prisoner, but because of her, Thorakis forced Lissa to her knees and looked up at Catrin, making it clear that she was the reason he would slit Lissa's throat.

Seethe raised himself up and partially extended his wings to shelter Thorakis; at the same time, he puffed out his chest and raised a taunting, one-eyed gaze at Kyrien and Catrin. She could feel the boiling rage over the loss of his eye, and Catrin knew the only thing Seethe wanted was to see them dead.

This time it was Kyrien who discarded all restraint. His movements were violent, and Catrin could do nothing but hold on and try to keep from getting crushed. His chest extended, Kyrien slammed into Seethe with every bit of force and speed he could muster. There was a sound like a volcanic explosion followed by a monstrous landslide when the two dragons connected. Seethe's claws were still wrapped around the ornate stone railing that bordered the balcony, and it was torn away on the impact. Bits of stone showered Thorakis and Lissa, and it was not at all certain that the balcony would remain where it was. The jarring force seemed to rattle the foundations of Ravenhold.

Seethe released his hold on the railing, which soared into the town surrounding Ravenhold and tore through a storefront as if it were made of cloth. A cloud of dust and debris erupted from the back of the shop.

Fully extending his wings, Seethe did his best to get away from Kyrien, who had sunk his claws into Seethe's lower torso. The mighty feral dragon let out a high-pitched cry and squirmed in Kyrien's grasp, and Catrin heard a loud crack. The feral dragon's cry became even higher in pitch, and it struggled in a wild frenzy, thrashing back and forth.

When Seethe's tail whipped past and nearly took Catrin's head off, Kyrien released him and pushed off hard. The two dragons flew away in opposite directions, neither looking truly flightworthy. Seethe's wing flaps were jerky and sporadic, but he did manage to remain airborne. He landed back on the balcony, and Catrin saw Thorakis buckled over, and Lissa was retreating into the hold. For once, Catrin cheered for Lissa.

In the next instant, though, everything changed.

It started as a confusing but comforting sensation that grew steadily into wonder and understanding.

Sinjin was alive.

Somehow, beyond all hope, Sinjin was alive! A thrill ran through Catrin that breathed new life and commitment into her. The thought of finding her son gave her strength she never would've thought she possessed. Only in a time of true need did such strength assert itself.

Thorakis abandoned Ravenhold and climbed onto his ailing mount. Seethe looked as if he'd had enough. Missing one eye and with something in his hind quarters broken, it was all the beast could do to get airborne and fly.

Kyrien would have launched into immediate pursuit if not for Catrin's mental request to see her cousin. The more she communicated with Kyrien, the more she realized she didn't have to shout; so connected were their minds that a firm thought was all it took. She didn't see all that was in his mind, and he didn't see all of what was in hers, but when she wanted him to know something, he knew it. The better she got at it, the easier it was to fly since she also now knew how to receive his thoughts without his having to shout, which allowed him to give her fair warning before his more violent moves.

Kyrien landed on the partly ruined balcony, and Catrin waited in the saddle. Moments later, Lady Lissa of Ravenhold emerged from the doorway, looking every inch a queen, save the bruise on her cheek. In her eyes burned a raging fire, but she could not seem to leave that heated gaze on Catrin for long.

"I just wanted to know that you were well, Lady Lissa."

"I am, Lady Catrin. Thank you," the words were said somewhat grudgingly, but Catrin didn't care. It was the most acknowledgment she'd ever received from her cousin, and it was, at least, a sign of progress.

"Does your son live?" Lady Lissa asked, and her concern appeared genuine, which also surprised Catrin.

"Yes," Catrin said with a catch in her voice. "I believe he does."

"Then go to him," Lissa said. "Ravenhold will stand." There were no more words to be spoken between them, and Kyrien waited until only an instant after Lissa disappeared back within the hold before launching into the air. With mighty wing strokes, the last of the regent dragons sent them soaring away, heading in the direction which she now knew would lead her to her son.

Chapter 18

Sometimes, in order to find the light, we must walk through the darkness.
--Gemino, sorcerer and artist

* * *

Wolfhold was surprisingly silent given the size of the army that surrounded it. There were no cries of alarm and no sounds of ballistae or catapults. It was as if the attackers had no intention of taking the keep but would simply wait until the inhabitants all starved to death. The silence drove Sinjin to distraction, and Kendra paced the apartments like a caged beast.

Sometimes she'd disappear into her sleeping chamber, and Sinjin suspected she was pacing in there as well, but most of the time, she walked around the common room and cast dark looks at Sinjin. He wasn't certain what it was that he'd done this time to deserve her ire, but he was pretty sure she'd think of something. It was something of a trend in their relationship. In spite of that, her company was better than being alone. At least her footsteps broke the awful silence.

An unrelenting line of questions competed for his attention and his worry, for that was the only thing he could seem to do: worry. His parents had always been the ones making things happen; Sinjin had spent most of his life trying to stay out of the way. Now, though, he wished he had his parents' ability to actually affect the future. Thinking of them made his chest hurt, and he tried to push them from his thoughts. A dark and foreboding feeling crept over him whenever he thought of them, and he didn't want to look that fear in its ugly face.

Soon his thoughts turned to other worries, such as wondering what would happen if Thorakis suddenly decided to attack Wolfhold. The force gathered could potentially take the keep on their own, but it would be a bloody thing, Sinjin knew. But Thorakis had dragons, and that changed everything.

After a firm knock, Munson entered the apartments.

"Lord Kyte requests your presence, my lord, my lady."

Neither Sinjin nor Kendra made any response beyond a nod. Munson nodded in return and led them through a series of blandly constructed but ornately decorated halls. It was, in some sense, an embarrassment of riches, but it did add an air of age and tradition to the place. Sinjin supposed that Dragonhold was not very well decorated, but the place possessed majesty that overshadowed even the greatest works of art in Lord Kyte's collection.

Thinking of home made Sinjin long for days past, but at least he'd gotten to hear Durin's voice and he knew his friend was all right. That counted for something and boosted his spirits, even as the notion that he might never get to see Durin again threatened to send his mood in the other direction.

Still, he almost managed to smile when entering Lord Kyte's chambers. What lay before him was truly something magnificent. Behind Lord Kyte stood an open-air terrace, and the view beyond would have been breathtaking if not for the dark forces that marred the landscape; even with the army, he could see all the way to the Inland Sea. Within, the walls followed the natural contour of the stone, which ran with rich veins of yellow and brown, and were polished to a liquid sheen. Set into that stone were shelves and nooks filled with books, parchments, and scroll tubes. It was the table at the center of the room that drew Sinjin's attention, though. Hewn from the mountain itself, it was irregular yet orderly and somehow carved into a near exact replica of Wolfhold and the lands surrounding it.

Laid out like pieces of some game of gods and kings were carved wood representations of their enemies. Looking like scars on the land, it was obvious that the representations of the aqueducts were new additions and were clearly meant to be temporary. The quality of the original work was in every way a marvel, and Sinjin felt the irresistible urge to run his hands over the carved, polished, and painted stone. At least, he thought it was painted; when he looked more closely, the color seemed to come from within the stone itself, but he could think of no way that could be possible. It was unlikely he'd ever know for certain, and he let his attention drift to the many wonders adorning the shelves and work surfaces in Lord Kyte's chambers.

"Thank you for coming," Lord Kyte said. Sinjin did what he could not to smirk; it wasn't as if he'd had much choice. "I brought you to Wolfhold because I wanted to be able to protect you, but now I wonder if I made a mistake. If the dragons come, Wolfhold may fall. This place was designed to repel armies, not flying devils. The problem is that I can think of nowhere safer for you to be. Unless you go back under the lodestone blanket, there is really no hold that can protect you."

Sinjin listened with his head bowed.

"I don't mean to frighten you, Nephew," Jharmin said when he recognized Sinjin's discomfit. "But I want you to understand the true magnitude of this situation. You're the best collateral anyone can have when negotiating with your mother. She's the most powerful person in the world, and that makes you the most valuable person in the world."

Kendra snorted and Sinjin squirmed.

"You're not a prisoner here, Nephew. You're free to go any time you choose, and I wanted you to know that."

It seemed a silly thing to say since there was an army surrounding the keep. It wasn't as if he could somehow walk out of Wolfhold and avoid the demons and dragons, but he tried to take it as he assumed it was meant: his uncle was not holding him prisoner. It didn't make him feel any better.

"If I knew a safer place for you, I could get you out of here with no worries from the scum on the plains, but I truly can't think of a safer place. Now that you understand the danger and the situation, do you wish to remain here and have it be known to Thorakis? Or will you go back under the blanket and perhaps try to sneak south?

Sinjin didn't answer.

"I don't envy you the decision, my boy," Jharmin said with a knowing nod. "I made the decision partly for you when I said you could come out from under the blanket. I'm sorry about that. I knew the dragons would take Ravenhold first, and though my wife is difficult at times, I truly love her. I wanted to draw the dragons away from her. I wanted to draw them here, and you were the best way to do that."

"I knew what I was doing when I came out from under the blanket," Sinjin said. "I can't hide for the rest of my life, and I didn't want my mother to believe me dead. There are some things more important than safety."

"Wisely spoken, Nephew."

"What defenses do you have against the dragons?" Sinjin asked.

"That's probably the smartest question you could've asked," Lord Kyte said. "We've pikemen along the parapets, ballistae in concealment within many of the balconies, archers spread throughout, and hot pitch for any who fly in low."

Precious little defense.

Kendra snorted. "We won't last a day."

"I have other methods at my disposal, but they'll only be used as a last resort. I'm not inclined to discuss that at this time, so please do not ask. Just know that Wolfhold is not without teeth."

The way he said it made Sinjin shiver, but all he could do was hope that those teeth were enough to defeat an army of demons, giants, and dragons. It seemed unlikely. Though Sinjin didn't know much about Jharmin, he liked the man. From what he could tell, Jharmin had done things in Sinjin's best interest, and he had no reason to doubt what his uncle said. Thinking of his uncle made him think of Uncle Chase, and he had to wipe away a tear as he pushed the thoughts aside.

In that moment, Sinjin noticed a bit of green flame escaping from Jharmin's clenched fists. Sinjin was just wondering if Jharmin was aware of the flames when the explosions started.

* * *

As soon as Wolfhold came into view, Catrin knew Sinjin was there. She could sense the vibrancy of him, and she knew he was not seriously injured, though it was clear he'd been through an ordeal. The dark forces she'd seen before remained around Wolfhold. The camps were quiet and orderly when Seethe crested the rise and came into view. Once he'd been spotted by the sentries, though, the alarm was raised and the dark forces writhed over the landscape like swarming ants. Giants fanned the flames of oversized bonfires, and firebrands were now making their way to all corners of the encampment.

Before the black smoke even began rising up to meet them, Catrin knew that Thorakis had no intention of mounting a lengthy siege. He would burn them out. Both fates disgusted Catrin, and she did what she could to prepare for the coming fight. In truth, she'd had precious little time to recover from the previous battle, and a voice in her head screamed for retreat.

She needed time to heal, but that would also give Seethe time to heal, and Catrin knew his current wounds were worse than Kyrien's. At great cost, she'd forged an advantage over Thorakis, and she decided nothing would deter her from finishing what she'd started. Kyrien heartily expressed his agreement, and as soon as the torches lit pots of steaming pitch within the demons' camp, Catrin attacked the pots. Bright flashes rose from the shattered pots, and the flames spread outward, engulfing many catapults.

There were too many, though, and the sound of catapult fire was followed by a hissing, whistling sound. Then came the screams. The dark forces attacked with their full might, and more dragons were arriving. Too many, Catrin thought. Kyrien agreed. Not for the first time or the last, Catrin mourned the loss of her lance and sword; it was something that would haunt her.

A single dragon and rider flew toward the Inland Sea, its flight erratic. Catrin watched Thorakis and Seethe go, and she tried to find a way to justify staying, to justify saving Sinjin. The primal need was even more poignant with only the recent knowledge that he was still alive. Every part of her wanted to hold him, to comfort him. But she also knew this could be her last chance to defeat Thorakis. While the advantage was hers, she had to strike. Only when Thorakis was dead could Sinjin ever truly be safe, and that made the decision.

Flying in low, Catrin saw three figures watching from a terrace high above the attacking army, high enough that the entire keep would have to be aflame for the fires to get there. Instantly Catrin knew it was Sinjin, and she could sense Jharmin there as well. As she drew closer, she saw Kendra, and a mixed bag of feelings rushed through her. In the end, though, all that mattered was seeing Sinjin alive and safe--or at least relatively safe.

"Be strong, my son!" Catrin shouted as they flew past, and she could see the look of disappointment and fear on his face. "I cannot let him escape!"

There was no more time to be spared. Already Seethe had put distance between them, and though Kyrien was in better shape than Seethe, it wasn't by much. He would have to give everything he had to catch Seethe, but Catrin knew he would. Wiping the tears from her eyes, Catrin set her sights on Thorakis and exacting the price for all those who'd been lost.

* * *

"No!" Sinjin shouted, and he ran to the edge of the balcony, nearly tumbling over the ledge in his need to stop his mother. Somehow he knew that if he let her leave, it would be the last time he ever saw her, and those words would be the last thing she would ever say to him. The certainty of it felt like an ax in his chest, and he reached his hands out to the retreating forms of Kyrien and his mother. Because of the view, Seethe and Kyrien remained visible for some time, and Sinjin could not pull his gaze away.

"Get back from there!" Lord Kyte scolded, and he pulled Sinjin away from the carved stone railing despite its sturdiness. "You can see just as well from here." Jharmin spoke with a mixture of compassion and firm-handed reprimand.

Flames raced through the air and spread along the outskirts of town and finally to the lower keep itself.

"Lord Kyte," said a hard-looking man in uniform who burst onto the jutting stone balcony, showing none of the awe over the view that Sinjin had experienced. Sinjin pulled his attention away from the shrinking form of Kyrien on the horizon. "We've deployed bucket brigades, and the gray water cisterns are being emptied first."

Jharmin nodded. "Keep the archers and guards pulled back and have them assist with fire control, but the instant those devils come within bow range, I want to rain death on them. Do you understand?"

"Yes, sir. Should we consider more drastic measures, sir? Surely the moors will burn."

"No," Jharmin said, and it was clear that he would speak no more of the matter.

Sinjin wondered what kind of measures the man had been talking about, and he guessed they had something to do with the teeth Jharmin had said Wolfhold possessed.

It seemed only a few breaths between volleys, and Sinjin didn't think the people of Wolfhold would be able to extinguish all the fires that bloomed from the raining hellfire. He felt guilty then for standing so high above it all, watching dark forces set fire to the place while its defenders gave their lives to spare those within. There were men sacrificing themselves for the sakes of their wives, sons, and daughters, for fathers and mothers, for friends, for kin.

A pain swelled in Sinjin's chest, and he found no relief when he looked back to where his mother and Kyrien could still be seen, though they had

344

grown much smaller now, and he knew that if they flew too much farther, they would disappear from view, and perhaps from his life, forever. Nothing could have been more agonizing than knowing his mother was gone, except the feeling of his father's absence. Like a nagging itch, the feeling had grown over time, and now he was almost certain his father was gone. Having just seen his mother and not having seen his father with her only served to solidify what he already felt, though he chided himself that he had an awful lot of premonitions for a man without access to Istra's power. It was a frightening reminder of just how powerless he was. The feelings intensified when he saw the two distant dragons collide.

* * *

Seethe flew in the way a wounded fish swims, and Kyrien's instincts latched on to that. Deep within him, he invoked primal and ancient skills to make speed and close on the wounded beast. Thorakis also did not look well, which led Catrin to believe that she'd made the correct decision, no matter how painful it may have been. She had done the right thing. But still it hurt, and she wanted to inflict that same emotional pain on Thorakis and Seethe. She knew it was impossible; she would have to settle for physical damage.

Like cold air bursting downward from a thunderstorm, Kyrien descended on Seethe. Thorakis was not caught unaware, and with a wild look in his eyes, he held Koe and the Staff of Life above him. Again Catrin felt the guilt that Nat Dersinger had laid upon her soul. She'd allowed one of the most powerful forces in the world to become a tool for the darkness. It was unforgivable.

Returning the staff to the hands of those who would serve the light was a task for Catrin alone, and she would die for that cause, though she wanted desperately to survive and once again hold her son. For too many years, she'd let the power of her position keep her from him, too many herald globes and not enough time playing fitch or strawman as the other boys had with their parents. So many times he had wanted her to play, and so many times she'd allowed the world to take her away. Though she knew she'd been driven by the need to save all those she cared about, that did little to lessen the guilt. Too many of the current circumstances working against her were the result of her own mistakes. That thought was burned into her mind when Thorakis's fire struck.

The pain was worse than what Catrin had felt before, and she did what she could to snuff the flames as quickly as possible. Even with a quick response, the pain and lingering effects were devastating. Now it was Kyrien's flight path that wobbled and strayed, and the two dragons looked as if they might both crash into the waves of the Inland Sea. Catrin could figure no reason for Seethe to come here, and she knew that flying out into the storm-plagued Inland Sea was suicide in their current condition. Even if Kyrien could rest and fly at the same time, Catrin knew storms on the Inland Sea were unpredictable and often formed rapidly.

Unwilling to relent, Kyrien pursued Seethe, and Catrin could feel Thorakis preparing for another attack. It would be the last attack, she knew. There was a certainty that drove her to reckless action. Instead of erecting defenses she knew would not hold, Catrin did something she'd never attempted before.

Reaching out to the staff and Koe, Catrin tried to align herself with their energy, as she'd done so many times before. Even as she did, she found a harmonic resonance in their connection that allowed her to feel the power that coursed through them along with the brute force Thorakis used to control them. He didn't connect with them and draw from them as Catrin did; Thorakis wrung them like a wet towel. She could feel the stress it put on the very structure of these objects that were so sacred to her. The pain of it made her think she might faint, or perhaps it was the thin air around her since she was no longer maintaining the pressure. So much of her energy had been expended that even simple things such as breathing became much more difficult, and her head swam with the slow realization of a fogged mind.

Still, she had made a connection, and though she could draw no energy from them, she felt she could send energy to them. For a moment, she considered flooding them with energy and attempting to overwhelm Thorakis. Perhaps he would burst into flames from the excess, but she knew that she would destroy the staff and Koe in the process, and she looked for another way. She would have to find another solution fast; time was running out. Power gathered within Thorakis, wrenched free from every source available.

Without another thought, Catrin lashed out at the staff, not to destroy it, but using her energy to form a connection between the staff and the base of Seethe's massive skull. Lightning flashed between them, startling Thorakis, who then released the energy he'd accumulated, but it did not obey his intention. Instead, his energy followed the path of least resistance through the staff, which glowed from within. The massive charge was diverted through the staff, along Catrin's tendril of energy, and into Seethe.

The feral's wings twitched violently, and he veered to the right, spiraling toward the water below. Catrin watched him fall, knowing the staff and Koe would be lost. The wounded dragon seemed to be trying to get back over land, to have some chance of landing and surviving, but Catrin knew he would die.

In the end, the mighty feral dragon struck solid ground with fatal force.

* * *

Black smoke curled up from the many fires burning within Wolfhold. At the height where Sinjin stood, it all seemed to congeal into a continuous noxious haze. Still he watched the pair of distant dragons as they struggled. A bright light flashed between the two, and Seethe veered off.

"The whole lower keep is aflame, sir, and they're going to make a run at us with ladders." Sinjin wasn't certain who had spoken, but he didn't turn his head; his mother's fate mattered more than anything at that moment. Even as the cries of "Dragon!" rang through the hold, still he watched, and even after it appeared that Seethe had landed or fallen from the sky, unable to be certain, he watched. Squinting, he ignored the command from Jharmin, telling him to get back inside. Still he watched as a giant shape rose from the waters of the Inland Sea and engulfed the distant silhouette that was Kyrien and his mother.

Sinjin would have continued to watch if rough hands hadn't grabbed him from behind and pulled him away.

"Put me down!" he cried out and struggled against the man who carried him away. He could no longer see what was happening to his mother. He could feel only primal fear after what he'd seen. Nothing could be that big, his brain screamed, but he'd seen it, and there was no other explanation he could come up with. He considered for an instant that it might have been a dragon closer to them, but he'd clearly seen it leave the water, and he knew a monster was attacking his mother. He would have continued to struggle if not for the giant black claws that reached for him amid the flapping of massive wings and the huge jaws closing around them as the man ran for the entrance to Jharmin's chambers. The teeth snapped shut on nothing but air. Though closed, those jaws showed they were far from harmless when they slammed into the entranceway with force that shook the room. Chunks of stone flew across the rooms and demolished whatever was in their path.

In the bustle, the man carrying him stumbled and pushed Sinjin forward. Finally showing his good sense, Sinjin tucked his head and ran, trying to catch up to Jharmin and Kendra and his guards. They were only a few steps ahead of him when the dragon struck again, or perhaps it was another dragon; Sinjin had no way of knowing. Again chunks of stone launched into the air, and one of Jharmin's guards was struck; he went down in a heap. Sinjin paused for a moment in shock, but then he pushed after Jharmin as fast as he could.

The remaining guard urged Jharmin and Kendra to reckless speed, and they were pulling away from Sinjin, but at least he, too, was now beyond the reach of the dragons--he hoped. Somehow he knew the dragons would tear the place apart to root them out if that was what it took. The ferocity of their attacks conveyed such hatred that there could be no other outcome. The ferals would find every last one of them until they were gone from Godsland. Perhaps he should just go back and enjoy a quick end. Why prolong the misery?

It took some time to realize that he was not beyond the reach of the feral. Dark thoughts continued to assert themselves, but Sinjin knew them for what they were, and that made them at least a little easier to resist. It seemed such an insidious and evil power to control the mind of another, to impose the will of one on the many, to remove the ability for an individual to make his own decisions. It was this knowing that bolstered Sinjin's will, and the distance he continued to put between himself and the outside world also seemed to be helping.

Ahead of him, Jharmin and the guard turned, and Sinjin raced along behind them. He thought he heard his uncle's voice shouting his name and saying something else, but he couldn't make out the words over the sound of his feet hitting the stone and the pounding of blood in his ears.

When he made the turn, he found a tight spiral stair that had been cut into the stone. The cylinder was narrow and close, and Sinjin felt confined by the encroaching stone as he climbed. Twice he passed equally narrow landings that opened into larger tunnels that led to only darkness and the unknown. Above him, he could see a dim light and hear the sounds of shuffling boots. Hoping there were no enemies within the hold, Sinjin climbed. When at last he found the dimly lit chamber, he saw Jharmin and his guard struggling to turn an apparatus with long, wooden spokes poking out of it.

"Help us," Jharmin barked as soon as Sinjin entered, and Kendra gave him an exasperated look from another of the spokes. Together they pushed; toward what purpose, Sinjin had no guess, but he wasn't fool enough to stand around, asking questions at a time such as this. Slowly the stone pedestal began to move, and they had it. Movement continued to be slow, but it was steady. As it turned, Sinjin saw for the first time what surrounded them. Giant spheres of stone, as big around as greatoaks, looked as if they were suspended in air. Sinjin could not tell how many there were, but there looked to be many.

With a bone-jarring *thunk,* the wooden shaft in Sinjin's hands vibrated and stopped. It felt as if the entire keep responded to whatever command it was that turning this device had given.

A creaking sound filled the hall, and Jharmin waited with an expectant look on his face. The creaking grew higher in pitch, and there was another bone-rattling *thunk* just before the huge spheres began dropping from sight. The chamber that held the spheres was revealed as more stones dropped, and Sinjin could see that there must be hundreds of them. The keep vibrated and hummed.

Running to where the light streamed in, Jharmin climbed so he could look through a natural break in the stone. Sinjin followed, and no one tried to stop him. When he reached the place where Jharmin now waited in tense anticipation, Sinjin saw what a commanding view the height provided, and he watched in silent awe as the lands around Wolfhold exploded. Some of the spheres erupted from hillsides nearly whole, blasting away whatever had stood there, then rolling and crushing whatever was in their paths; others erupted from under roadways and bridges.

Almost no homes lay in the paths of the crushing, monolithic spheres, and Sinjin knew this must have been by design, though he'd never have guessed it prior to this moment. From the view he'd had when they approached Wolfhold, everything had seemed perfectly normal, not that looking out from under that infernal blanket had given him much of a view.

A cloud of dust clogged the air, and it became difficult to see what was taking place down below. What Sinjin did notice was that many of the demons, giants, and soldiers were crowding onto bits of land that had not been disturbed, only to be annihilated when a stone burst out from underneath them. Some were clever and ran to places where a sphere had already erupted. As the stones continued to drop, Sinjin saw that some followed the same path as stones before, and the black army found that those places weren't safe either.

Dragons continued to fill the air, and Sinjin still had the sense they would tear the stone down around him to get to him, and he suddenly wanted to get away from the opening, remembering how devastating the dragons' attacks had been. But another part of him needed to see this, needed to understand the circumstances in which he found himself. He'd been trained all his life to understand his situation and act accordingly, and all of his training said he needed to find a way out.

* * *

The blackness rose up before them so suddenly that Catrin nearly bit her tongue when Kyrien climbed, thrusting her down into the saddle so hard that her arms were glued to her sides from the force. With a wingspan larger than any dragon Catrin had ever seen, a feral queen rose from the depths and gained the skies. This was a foe like nothing she or Kyrien had ever faced, and she could feel the power of the beast; the air practically crackled with it, and a musky smell that Catrin couldn't identify assaulted her senses. A tingling sensation washed over her, and it took her a moment to realize the feeling was coming from Kyrien. She could not imagine how he could cope with a feral queen after losing his own queen to the ferals; it was cruel irony.

The two dragons flew in near synchronicity, one following wherever the other would choose to flee, so they twisted and spiraled through the air. Catrin knew this battle was one they could not win, especially not in their current condition, and her only thought was to launch a massive attack to buy time for them to take evasive action.

No.

Raw compulsion reeked from Kyrien. His command held her suspended, and she stopped her preparations, trying to understand what it was he wanted from her.

Still they soared higher in the air, and still the feral queen mirrored Kyrien's movements like a deadly dance. Catrin's jaws slammed together from the jarring impact when the two collided. She watched in horror as Kyrien wrapped his neck around that of the feral queen, and she looked back to see their tails twined as well. Kyrien's consciousness was flooded with a red haze of primal need, and locked together, the two dragons dropped from the sky like stones. Watching the water approach with such undeniable certainty, Catrin accepted her fate. After only three more breaths came the darkness.

Epilogue

In shock, Sinjin Volker walked along the corridors of Wolfhold. The news that his mother had been killed by the giant feral dragon did not seem real. He wanted to believe that somehow she would come back, that in some way, all of this was wrong and for naught, but there was a knot in his guts that would not loosen, and his mouth was dry, tasting of ashes. His uncle did not question him, and for once Kendra was silent, which left Sinjin to his own thoughts.

Behind him, men carried the accursed lodestone blanket that would conceal him from the dragons when the time came. He would wait until he had no choice but to go under the blanket before he did so. Memories of his trip to Wolfhold played through his mind; the only good part had been being so close to Kendra. Of course, that was also one of the bad parts.

Sinjin had thought the dark forces might retreat after the deaths of Thorakis and Seethe and the feral queen, but the attacks had only intensified. Wolfhold would fall. Escape seemed the only choice, and Jharmin assured them he could get them out of the hold undetected. But first, they would return to the atrium.

"What kind of diplomat would I be if I had only one spy within Ohmahold?" Jharmin had said, and Sinjin reconsidered everything he knew about politics. "I may be able to get some news from there."

When they reached the grove, Jharmin wasted no time. "Are you there?"

"Yes," came a breathy response. "I'm here, m'lord, but I don't have much time. Things are unfriendly here, and I fear discovery. But I wanted you to know that a ship named the *Dragon's Wing* was seen off the shores of Endland and can be reached by message."

"That's Benjin and Fasha's ship!" Sinjin blurted. At the same instant, he thought he heard something else as well, but whatever it was got lost in a jumble.

Jharmin just gave him a look. "Send a message that a package is on its way to them."

"Yes, sir. Is there anything else, sir? I really must go."

"I want you to be very careful. Let's make it twice the regular interval before our next meeting."

"Yes, m'lord, thank you," the breathy voice said; then she was gone.

Sinjin and the others turned to leave, but then another voice rose from the stillness.

"Sinjin, is that you?" Durin asked, and Sinjin felt tears spring to his eyes.

"Yes, it's me."

"I'm so glad to know you're alive; we've been waiting here for days. I'm sorry for eavesdropping. It was just that the lady said she was in a hurry, and it sounded important, and I didn't want to interrupt."

"It's all right," Sinjin said, "but we don't have much time. How are things under the rule of Queen Trinda?"

A long silence followed.

"I don't think he wants to answer that question right now," Trinda responded.

* * *

Halmsa of the Wind clan was a fool; he just knew it. He'd believed his dreams were real and would lead him to glory. He'd believed that following his dreams would lead him to his destiny. But here he sat, at the top of a mountain, waiting for a dragon that would probably just eat him. He'd been rained on and windblown, and he was bruised and scraped from the climb. No person in his right mind would have climbed to this spot, but it was where his gut had told him to wait. His gut, bah! He was a fool.

Wind gusts grew stronger and threatened to knock him from where he sat on this rocky plain without even the slightest cover available. Waiting for what? The wind made his fingers hurt, and he rubbed them against the chill. Fumbling in the folds of his tribal garb, he pulled out a piece of dried meat, a rare commodity these days.

When he looked back up, however, an enormous feral dragon rested on the rocky plain before him and covered most of it with its bulk. Eyes like vats of ice burned into Halmsa's soul. Part of him wanted to scream, part of him wanted to run, but a bigger part of him wanted to find his destiny, and it was that determination that kept him standing upright in the face of the most frightening creature he'd ever witnessed. This beast could consume him in a single bite with no problem, and he had to cope with that fear.

His legs trembled but he remained standing. The dragon stayed where she was for some time, her gaze never wandering far from Halmsa. There was something new there now. Was it grudging respect? It seemed too much to accept, and Halmsa needed all his concentration to wait where he was. Waves of fear washed over him, and the dragon rose to dominate his vision.

He could feel the beast's breath on his face as that gruesome head drew closer. Though he remained standing, Halmsa closed his eyes. That only made things worse. When he opened them again, the feral queen looked him level in the eye and snorted at him. The force of the air nearly sent him tumbling, and he took a step back to steady himself, but still he did not flee in the face of terror. Halmsa of the Wind clan stood his ground and earned every bit of the respect he would get. In the next instant, the feral queen launched herself into the skies, pummeling him with air and debris, but still he remained upright. Then she was gone, wheeling away and riding the air over the sea, headed somewhere Halmsa could not even imagine.

When his eyes lowered, he saw them, resting on the rocky plain: a clutch of coppery eggs whose surface was crisscrossed with patterns more beautiful than anything else he'd seen in nature. It was only then that he realized his destiny had arrived, and songs would be sung of him.

REGAL

Chapter 1

The word of a fool is only as good as his luck.
--Brother Vaughn, Cathuran monk

* * *

Allette Kilbor didn't fit in. No matter how she tried, she stuck out like a cornstalk in a pasture. It wasn't just her complexion or accent that made her conspicuous; it was the way she moved, the clothes she wore, it was everything about her. In this place, she was an outsider, foreigner, other. That reality kept her on edge at all times, and it was exhausting. There was nowhere for her to go. No place was safe.

Only days before, she'd been swabbing decks, casting lines, and enjoying the camaraderie her father's crew had always shared. Those good people knew that helping each other was also the best way to stay alive. Each of the permanent crew had saved the life of another at some point; it was the way her father selected his crewman. The fact that their lives were often enough in danger to provide a full permanent crew spoke to her father's other side. A cold sweat broke on Allette's brow. It was that other side that had quite possibly gotten him killed, but she tried not to think about that. He'd survived things in the past that had seemed impossible, and she concentrated on saving her own skin. That was what he would have told her to do, and she did her best not to let him down.

The coming sunrise meant scrutiny, and that meant being ready to flee at any moment. There was no way for her to know exactly why her father had been taken, but the vision of him crumbling under the attacks of far larger men and being dragged into a pull cart was etched in stark and painful memory. Tears threatened at the corners of her eyes, and she wiped them away with resentment. This was when the strong got stronger. Her father's words got her moving and she walked toward the shadows beneath the stone archways supporting the spiraling roadway. These places, while patrolled heavily at night, offered some modicum of safety during the daylight. Allette had already seen, though, that it was easy to become trapped here; a single guard could pen her in and call for help. Only the knowledge that she could probably fight her way past a solitary guard kept her moving toward the deepening shadows.

Anger crept out from behind her other emotions, and she wondered once again what her father had been thinking. Coming here had been a mistake, and Allette had known it from the start. She'd begged her father not to make the trip. The cost of the dragon flight alone had required a lien on the *Maker's Mark*. She stood to lose everything: her father, their ship, their crew, everything. The *Maker's Mark* was more than just a ship to Allette; it was her home, her friend, her safe place. Nothing could harm her on the deck of that ship; at least that was what she had always told herself. If only she could get back to Maiden Harbor, then she would find a way to repay the debt. Part of her wanted to think her father would reappear at any time to tell her everything would be all right, but that hope dwindled more every day in his absence.

Getting home seemed impossible. Dragon flights were no cheaper here than they were from the Midlands. Allette was no more accustomed to spending time in the Mids. She'd sailed the waters around the peninsula, but the open seas were her home. The people of the Mids were hearty, rugged people who pulled their livings from an unforgiving land. Here in the Heights, though, there was no soil, only stone. Allette had seen gardens and groves, but those were filled with rich black soil that brought a fortune at market here. Since those in the Heights believed that the soil from the Cloud Forest was cursed, Midland soil was among the most prized and expensive imports. It was one of the primary reasons for trade between the Heights and the Mids. It was heavy and cumbersome, and a dragon loaded with soil rarely carried anything else. Crossing over the Jaga took time, and every trip involved risk. Increased demand had put a strain on the limited number of dragon flights. Rumors said the dragons were being overloaded, and it was only a matter of time until some were lost to the Jaga. The place was wild, unruly, and crawling with darkness. No one with the use of their senses would venture anywhere near that deadly place.

Allette's own flight had been terrifying enough that she suppressed the memory, knowing her only route home was a return flight. She might as well be on the other side of Godsland.

With the morning came the foot traffic and pull carts; the latter seemed one way that Allette might earn her way home, but the thought of how long that might take kept her looking for other options. The fact that all the pull carts were operated by lithe, blond, young men made her wonder if she would ever get these people to accept her. When they had arrived, the looks she'd received had ranged from suspicious to downright hostile. The women here dressed in long robes or flowing skirts. Allette couldn't imagine what she would look like dressed in such frills, and she blushed at the thought. Looking down at her sturdy work clothes, which had been the only kind of clothes she'd ever worn, she thought for an instant of stealing a disguise.

Her father would not like it, but he wasn't there.

Allette wasn't sure what it said about her that almost all of the possible solutions she'd come up with involved stealing something. She was no thief, and she'd worked hard for everything she'd ever had, but here she had nothing. Her father had taken care of their costs, and she had only a single silver coin in her pocket. The problem was that she couldn't even spend that without raising suspicion. She'd tried once, but her clothes and lack of a consort had the merchant asking questions that Allette did not want to answer. Part of her had feared the woman would have the guards out looking for her after she'd run away, but the men on watch continued to look as bored as ever.

Her thoughts turning in circles, Allette came back to the idea of finding the men who had taken her father and spying on them. Perhaps she could steal back whatever it was her father had been selling. The fact that she didn't know what that was bothered her deeply, and had from the start. While others funded dragon flights with voluminous cargo, her father had boarded with no cargo at all. Whatever it was he intended to sell in the Heights, it was small enough to be carried on his person. To that day, Allette could not figure out what it could be. She could imagine nothing so small that could be worth risking everything for, nothing that could be worth her father's life . . . and hers.

Not for the first time, she wished her father had stuck with honest trade. She had no evidence that what he did here was illegal, but his silence on the matter spoke volumes. Most times he gave her more information about their endeavors than she wanted for the sake of her education; she was, after all, supposed to inherit the ship from him in his twilight years. The thought that the *Maker's Mark* might already be hers battered her will, and the fact that she might immediately lose the ship through her inability to repay the debt shamed her. How had she studied all her life and yet somehow remained ignorant? How could she have trained for so long and have no employable skill? These thoughts were not new, but she was coming to realize that it was not a lack of skill or willingness which drove her to stealing; it was prejudice and fear on the part of those within the Heights. They would give her no choice but to become what she very much did not want to be.

Once back aboard the *Maker's Mark* she would make things right.

The grumbling of her stomach reminded her that she'd not eaten in the past day. Hunger was not unfamiliar to her; she knew how to work through it, but there was food aplenty. Had food been scarce, she would not have been so tempted, but all the people here were wealthy. Even those who acted as servants ate better than any ship's captain Allette had ever known. Almost no food grew in this place, and yet it was everywhere. Well-dressed merchants sold every variety of food and spice imaginable. Allette knew what only some of them were. Aboard the *Maker's Mark*, there was little more than salted fish and bitter citrus, things Allette had always loved.

That was when she saw them, stacked to one side and drawing little attention: bitter citrus. Her mouth watering, Allette fingered the silver coin in her pocket. It was of Midland mint, but it should be accepted here, even if under slight protest. Those in the Heights literally looked down on the Mids in almost every way. They were a taller people who lived at higher elevation, and they could fly. The fact still amazed and terrified Allette, and she tried not to think about the very thing she strived for: a flight back to the Midlands. The silver in her pocket wasn't enough to even see a dragon, let alone fly aboard one across the Jaga. The place had been mostly beautiful from above, not that Allette had been able to look down for long. Parts of the place had terrified her, and she had little desire to see it again. Flying, in itself, seemed a completely unnatural thing, but what other choice did she have?

Her mind made up, Allette pulled her hair back, tied it, and tucked it within her shirt. This was something she'd always done when working, knowing that ropes and pulleys were known for grabbing long hair. She also knew that it made her look like a boy. Medrin had always teased her about it. The thought brought a flush to her cheeks, but she shrugged it off and stepped from the shadows, trying to look as if she belonged there.

"Walk as if you know exactly where you are going," her father had always said.

Allette walked with purpose, her eyes thrust downward, hoping to avoid eye contact. Anyone who didn't look at her long enough might just mistake her for a servant boy. The fruit merchant, however, looked her up and down as she approached, no matter how inconspicuous she tried to be. The woman was older and had a hard look about her, but that didn't scare Allette off. She'd known her share of hard women, and most were kind and warm to those who treated them well.

"These are the sweetest," the woman said, gesturing to a pointy orange fruit that looked like the head on Mord's mace.

At least the woman was speaking to her, Allette thought. Pointing to the red and orange citrus, she spoke in a soft voice, deeper than her usual tone, "Six of these, please."

"Those are as bitter as can be," the woman said. "Are you certain those are what you want?"

"Yes," Allette said.

"Suit yourself," the woman said. Her tone was polite enough, but her words had caught the attention of a nearby guard. The man was armed with a studded pike, as all the guards in the Heights were. Such a thing would never have been allowed in the Midlands, where people claimed to be free. Allette knew the truth: only sailors were truly free. The scrutiny of the guard reminded Allette just how tenuous her current situation really was. When she handed the woman the Midland silver, Allette couldn't keep the flush from her face.

"You're a long way from home," the woman said, her voice thick and strange. Allette wasn't certain if the woman was trying the get the guard to keep an eye on her, but the result would be the same. Allette was tempted to flee now since it was obvious the man was taking more than just a passing interest in her presence there. "Here you go. I gave you one of the sweet ones too, just so you can try it."

"Thank you," Allette said, trying to avoid eye contact with the merchant and the guard. The merchant wrapped the fruit in a square of burlap. Pulling up each of the four corners, she tied them into a secure package and handed it to Allette.

Knowing she could not move directly back into the shadows since she was being watched, Allette also didn't want to move any closer to the guard. If he intended to accost her, she wanted as much of a head start as she could get. The longer he watched her, the more convinced she became that he would make his move. That only left moving toward the upper keep, a place where she stuck out even worse. The people in the upper keep made the well-dressed merchants look beggared. Despite those dangers, Allette decided the upper keep was better than almost certain confrontation with the guard.

Trying to look unconcerned, Allette removed one of the bitter citrus from the burlap. Her hands trembled, threatening to give away her anxiety, and she nearly dropped the rest of her fruit while trying to retie the knot. The merchant gave her a dubious look, as if expecting her to complain as soon as she tasted the fruit. Not wanting the attention, Allette walked upward, hugging the inside of the spiral, avoiding the other pedestrians and pull carts.

The first taste she had of the citrus was like being home. It came to her in a refreshing rush, even the bite bringing sweet memory and tears to her eyes. She didn't fight them this time; it was too real and poignant. Somehow she knew her father was gone, the *Maker's Mark* was gone. Her crewmates were lost to her. She was alone.

"It is against the law to discard refuse in the streets," a deep, authoritative voice said from behind her.

Allette turned to find the guard watching. How he had managed to sneak up on her was something of a mystery since she was usually very aware of the space around her, but she supposed distraction had left an opportunity open. Looking down at the sculptured street, she saw a bit of peel.

"I didn't know I dropped it," Allette said, keeping her voice low and deep.

The man just grunted and looked at her as if she were a squirming bug under his thumb.

Allette wasn't going to give him the chance to squash her. Throwing the rest of the fruit at the man, she turned and ran. It gave her a only few steps' advantage over the man; he recovered quickly and used his long legs to outpace her. Only Allette's lithe movements, sudden and seemingly at random, kept the man's hands from closing around some part of her.

People stood shocked and gaping as the two approached, but as the shock wore off, a wide avenue cleared before them.

"Stop her!" the guard behind her yelled. No one stepped in front of Allette, and she put her head down, trying to gain speed while he shouted. At the sound of his feet pounding on the carven stone street, Allette knew she was in trouble, and she turned hard to the right, nearly stopping her forward momentum. To her left was an archway, and despite not knowing where it led, she dashed inside and never looked back. The man's cursing told her all she needed to know: she had achieved a minor advantage.

When she burst into an enormous open area, the first thing Allette saw were men in leather suits, some with long braids in their hair and others with braided beards, all beneath hand-crafted leather helmets and goggles. Allette recognized them as dragon riders and grooms. By then it was already too late. Still at a full run, she could not stop herself when the biggest head she'd ever seen dropped down in front of her. The towering nostril was nearly large enough to sail the *Maker's Mark* through. Still, Allette's momentum carried her forward; that was until the massive dragon snorted. The change in direction was complete and instantaneous. Allette could do nothing but windmill her arms as she flew backward. When her feet touched stone, she was cast onto her backside and her head slammed into the unforgiving stone.

She would have stood and run, but she could not; the leather sole of the guard's boot pressed her face into the cold stone.

Chapter 2

Beware the advice of fools and the mercy of tyrants.
--The Lady Lissa Kyte of Ravenhold

* * *

The shadow of a horse and rider entered the covered entrance to Wolfhold, and the silhouette revealed a long bundle strapped to his back. Sinjin Volker swallowed hard. He knew what the rider bore, and it was all the proof anyone would require that his mother was dead. If she had been alive, she would never have allowed anyone else to get their hands on her staff and Koe, but that was exactly the burden this man bore. Clearly aware of the weight of this parcel, the soldier's shoulders were sagged from fatigue and perhaps something more.

Kendra pressed a little closer to Sinjin without appearing to mean to. Her touch momentarily caused his thoughts to stray, but then he was again reminded of how powerless he was. Two of the most powerful objects in all the lands were about to be delivered to him, and he could do nothing with them. In the hands of his mother, they had been implements of might; in his hands, they were but a walking staff and a carving of a cat, however well crafted they might be, however much potential they might hold. Only to the gifted were the ancient relic and his mother's carving truly useful. Only in their hands could the power be harnessed, focused, and delivered. He was better suited to wielding the belt knife that hung at his waist--a gift from his uncle.

Jharmin stood beside Sinjin, and at his nod, the rider approached Sinjin with the bundle he unstrapped from his back. Going to his knee, albeit slowly and with a groan, the man presented the long bundle to Sinjin. Wrapped in coarse cloth woven of dried reeds, the length and weight of the package gave no question as to the contents. The weight of it surprised Sinjin when he took it from the man.

"Thank you," was all he could say before his voice cracked.

Kendra stepped closer and squeezed his arm. It was odd just how much that gesture helped to keep Sinjin calm. Somehow the contact with her grounded him and allowed the excess energy to flow out from him.

The man stood slowly and, at Jharmin's nod, departed.

"I'm sorry," Jharmin said. "If Lady Lissa were not on her way here, I'd surely go with you. Are you certain you don't wish to wait until she arrives so that we can all go together?"

Sinjin nodded and Kendra squeezed his arm again. For some reason he would never be able to understand, the gesture annoyed him that time. Everything between Kendra and him was complicated, and he never quite knew how to interpret her actions. At times he wanted to think she was there only to support him, but he also knew she had strong opinions about what he should do next, and he couldn't help but wonder if there wasn't some subtle coercion there as well.

"You know you can trust Hand," Jharmin said, "and he'll get you safely to the *Dragon's Wing*."

Again, Sinjin nodded.

"Are you certain you don't want the blanket to conceal you?"

"I'm certain," Sinjin said. "I'm no longer very valuable to the ferals, and they have no way of knowing I have the staff and Koe. I don't think I could stand another journey under that blanket."

"Know that you are always welcome here," Jharmin said, despite all of them knowing that statement was only half true. Jharmin might welcome them, but Sinjin doubted Lady Lissa ever would.

Even as he spoke, the weight in Sinjin's hands became oppressive, weighing down on his soul. Something gnawed at him, demanding he remove the rough cloth and hold the Staff of Life and Koe in his hands, despite knowing the pain it would bring. Somehow he felt he deserved the pain. Why else would he have so much of it? His hands moved without conscious thought, and the cloth of reeds fell away.

Kendra bent down to pick it up. "Maybe you should leave those wrapped up," she said, but then she saw the look on Sinjin's face as he held the staff and Koe, tears streaking down his cheeks, falling to the cold stone, which seemed somehow appropriate. She placed the crude cloth onto the growing stack of items they would take with them. Perhaps Jharmin was normally a generous man, or perhaps he was so in this case out of guilt, but the result was more gifts than they could practically carry.

Sinjin had promised that they would leave Wolfhold as soon as the soldier arrived with the staff and Koe, but he felt reluctant to go. Deep inside, he knew that parting from this place, the last place he'd seen his mother alive, he would be facing a world without her in it. He knew it was ridiculous to think that staying here somehow changed the fact that she was gone, but he also knew that memory would fade, and stepping away from this place was a step farther from that most recent memory.

Men--"good men," Hand had told them--gathered around and stood waiting for the command. Hand looked to Sinjin, who turned his gaze to Kendra; she stood with her arms crossed over her chest and one eyebrow raised. "Could you please help us load the carriage?" Sinjin finally asked, hoping his reluctance wasn't overly obvious. The fact that Kendra rolled her eyes didn't bode well, as few things ever did with her,

Sinjin thought. Either way, the men loaded up the gifts of clothing, food, and coin into the waiting carriage. The horse seemed irritated at having been harnessed for so long without going anywhere. It swatted the air with its tail and made sharp clapping sounds when it stomped on stone.

"Thank you, Uncle Jharmin," Sinjin said. "You have been kind to me."

"I wish I could've done more," Jharmin said, his eyes distant. "Your mother was a good woman."

Sinjin nodded, still not knowing what to say when people said such things. Kendra gave him a firm nod, and Sinjin supposed it was a compliment. Hand held open the door of the carriage, and Kendra seemed to be waiting for him to get in first, which bothered him, but he didn't know why. Instead, he simply climbed into the carriage without another word, the uncomfortable silence lingering, and Kendra climbed in beside him. She wore a sad smile, and the light made her eyes sparkle. It was a rare moment, but it made his mouth go dry. When she grabbed his hand and squeezed it, he nearly leaned over and kissed her; the thought of her punching him in the face intervened. Then the chance was gone as the carriage rolled away from the keep and over a cobbled bridge. The stones made their teeth chatter, and Sinjin almost laughed.

Hand rode alongside and motioned to two of the guards accompanying them to scout ahead, and those men made clicking noises with their tongues and kicked their heels. Soon they outpaced the carriage and four remaining guards who rode in front and behind the carriage. It was an odd feeling to be under guard. Certainly he'd been under his Uncle Chase's watchful eye his entire life, but this was different. Sinjin was very far from home.

"Once you've retaken Dragonhold, things will be much better," Kendra said.

Sinjin didn't respond at first, knowing the words on his tongue would only start an argument. They had an extensive ride ahead of them, and that could make for a very long argument. Sinjin was determined to stave that off for as long as possible. In this case, his silence seemed to have sufficed.

Neither of them wanted to talk about the black armies that still roamed the countryside, albeit in far smaller numbers and without any sense of organization. It didn't seem that the demons and ash men wanted to fight any longer. Jharmin had worried that there were no ship builders among them, so those left behind might be stuck here.

It reminded Sinjin again just how weak he was. There was no guarantee he'd make it back to the Godfist. How could he expect to retake Dragonhold? He had no power. The people were not loyal to him; they had been loyal to his mother. He was just the boy who caused so much trouble in the hold. How could he expect any of those people to fight for him? The people were better off under Trinda's rule than fighting each other over whether she or Sinjin was their ruler. And all of them would face her power. Sinjin had to admit that with his parents and Thorakis gone, Trinda was the most powerful person on all Godsland. Durin had said that she ruled fairly and treated the people well, so there really was no reason for him to depose her. She was, after all, only continuing the work his mother had started and probably more effectively than he ever could.

"Hard roll?" Kendra asked, in her hand a long, slender piece of bread.

Sinjin accepted the roll and tapped it on his tooth; it made a hollow clicking sound. "You didn't get the rolls mixed up with a bag of rocks, did you?"

"They're better with soup," Kendra said. "They keep forever, and if they're all you've got, you get used to them."

That statement rattled Sinjin. He'd never gone hungry an hour in his young life, and even through the trials of the last year, he'd never experienced real hunger. It shamed him. Kendra seemed to sense it, and he could almost feel her anger building.

"Is there anything in there to soften this up with?" he said, partly to break the silence and, he hoped, deflect her anger.

"I've always pegged you as a 'ration the supplies' kind of person, given your heritage," Kendra said, her voice level and even. "Now that you need something to soften your food, let's just have some of everything. Here, here's some apple preserves. Maybe you can soak it in that until it's soft enough for your tender little mouth."

"Are you trying to start a fight?" Sinjin asked against his better judgment.

To his surprise, she smiled. "We've got to pass the time somehow."

* * *

The smell of the sea brought with it both anxiety and anticipation. Kendra had been his only link to his old life, save the thin connection through Jharmin and his brief conversation with Durin. Now he would be reconnected with that life. How would he be welcomed? Would they blame him for his parents' deaths, just as he blamed himself? It was difficult to keep the tears from falling, but he knew how much it bothered Kendra to see him cry. The sight of it compelled her to great lengths to make it stop, which had included everything from yelling, nagging, punching, and tickling; the last hadn't been so bad, but it hardly made up for the rest.

She sat next to him, calm but alert, and definitely not looking at him. He sniffed and wiped away the tears. He'd expected to have to wait for the *Dragon's Wing* to arrive, but the instant the water came into view, so too did the ship. Well-kept sails were furled, and the rich wood of the ship shone lustrous and golden, deeper browns shifting and moving depending on the angle. It was Benjin who saw them first, and he moved silently yet with great speed. Sooner than Sinjin would have guessed possible, the big man was down the gangplank and grabbing him in a mighty hug that lifted him from the ground. His eyes filled with tears when he saw Catrin's staff, but he smiled a sad smile. "Thank the Gods you've been returned to us," he said, and he grabbed Kendra and gave her an equally robust hug.

Blood rushed to her face, and she was momentarily speechless. "My mother--" she began after some thought.

"Did what she did," Benjin said. "And you did what you did. There's a difference. You understand?"

She nodded, and this time tears gathered around her eyes. Sinjin thought about yelling, nagging, punching, or tickling, but his better sense prevailed. He was, after all, rather fond of having teeth.

Hand stood before Sinjin and bowed. "It has been a pleasure to travel with you," the big man said. "I am very sorry, once again, for my original treatment of you."

"I owe you my life," Sinjin said. "You did what you had to do when we first met, and you've done nothing but make up for it ever since. Thank you. And please send my gratitude to my aunt and uncle." He wasn't at all certain how his message would be received by his aunt, but he sent it nonetheless.

Fasha came to them next, and then Gwen and Jessub Tillerman and a man Sinjin didn't recognize. Jealousy stirred in Sinjin when he saw the way Gwen looked at this man. His face flushed when he found that Kendra was staring as well. A jumble of feelings came together and made his stomach hurt. He and Gwen had been close their entire lives, and there had always been something between them, something Sinjin had never been able to figure out. He was reminded of that by the fire in Gwen's eyes when she saw Sinjin standing with Kendra. Though the girls had only barely met before Gwen had left the Godfist aboard the *Dragon's Wing,* their brief meeting had been enough to foster enmity between them, and Sinjin saw that rivalry rising fast.

"I leave you alone for a couple years, and look at what's become of you," Gwen said to Sinjin, ignoring Kendra. "You look a sight."

After a brief hug, Gwen turned to the man. "I don't believe you've met," Gwen said. "Sinjin, this is Pelivor. I believe you know who he is."

"Yes," Sinjin said. "You were friends with my mother."

His use of the word *were* hung between them.

"Come," Benjin said. "We should be on our way. This is not the safest place for us to be; there are black ships patrolling this area."

No more words were spoken as they made their way back to the *Dragon's Wing*.

"Where's my grandfather?"

"No time for questions now," Benjin said. "Get everyone aboard and get ready to set sail. The devils aren't done with us yet."

Sinjin and Kendra moved as quickly as they could to the galley, where they stood in the hatch and watched, feeling helpless. On the horizon were dark ships, and all were pointed toward the *Dragon's Wing*.

"If they've abandoned the assault on the Greatland, why attack us?" Sinjin asked despite the fact that everyone else was rushing around, trying to get the ship ready for departure. The crew moved with speed and grace, and in a short time, the ship was making a wide turn and heading back out to sea. Benjin aimed straight for the ships.

"They need more ships," Kendra said, "and it's far easier to steal a ship than it is to build one." Both fell silent as Gwen moved to the back of the ship where two large wooden tubes had been erected. Sinjin was still trying to figure out what they were when fire and lightning leaped around Gwen's hands.

"Get us out of here," Benjin growled, and Pelivor raised his arms, his right fist clenched and leaking red light.

Sinjin could almost feel the energy radiating from the man, and the air around him shimmered.

Kendra grabbed on to Sinjin when Gwen laid her hands on the wooden tubes and a deep moaning emerged, growing in pitch as the ship lurched forward. Kendra's grip grew tighter, hurting Sinjin's arm, but he could find no words as the ship left the water and turned sharply. Though he'd heard the tales, Sinjin had never thought to see a ship fly, especially not without his mother aboard; the cruel irony of that did not escape him. His mother had been persecuted, and in the end killed because of her power, and yet there were clearly others in the world with similar abilities. How was that fair? He'd learned not to ask why things weren't fair a long time before, but he couldn't help it. Only having Benjin, Fasha, and Gwen back in his life kept his chin up. He couldn't help but smile when he heard Millie cursing from within the galley. "Why can't they tell me when they are going to do things like that?" she grumbled.

Sinjin looked in the galley and saw Morif trying to help Millie clean up the mess. The old soldier gave him a brief wave and a smile that softened his otherwise stone-hard face.

"Is it safe for a person to try to feed the crew now?" Millie asked.

Looking down, Sinjin saw the black ships fading into the distance. Any danger presented from those ships was past, for a time at least. Sinjin knew his world might never again truly be safe. How foolish they had been to have believed the world wouldn't change, that war would not someday come. With a bit of bitterness, he looked back to how his mother had been treated when she'd tried to tell them. And what of Nat Dersinger? Had he not also tried to warn them? Looking back, it was easy to place blame, but he also remembered how he'd felt about it, and it shamed him. He'd been so certain she was wrong, that there would never come a time so terrible that people would have to live underground, yet that time had already come. The world had seemed so permanent as it was; now nothing seemed quite as solid or indestructible. Life was fragile, Sinjin had learned, and so was everything else. All things were just one disaster away from ceasing to exist.

"Come in and sit," Millie said. "Those fools should be done tossing us about now."

"Do you know where my grandfather is?" Sinjin asked.

Millie smiled. "He was his usual stubborn self the last I saw him," she answered, "but he and your great-uncle decided to stay in Endland, just in case Lord Kyte's message was actually a trap. I can't argue that they could have been correct, but they just seemed to enjoy the idea of sneaking around the harbor too much. They were like a couple of children. Kenward and his crew also stayed behind, looking for mischief as well, I'd wager."

"They're good men who risked themselves to make sure Sinjin could be brought home safely," Morif said.

"Home," Sinjin said. Despite having known of Trinda's conquest for some time, Sinjin had still not gotten over it. He'd tried to be her friend, and this was how she returned the favor? She took away the only home he'd ever known.

Millie looked over at him and shook her head, but for once said nothing.

"You've suffered a great loss, lad; that's for certain," Morif said, his voice serious and low. "I know how badly one can hurt, and I want you to know that it's all right. What's over your head isn't what matters. When you're among friends, you're home."

The words didn't make Sinjin feel much better, though he appreciated the sentiment.

"We'll go back for your grandfather and great-uncle," Millie said. "Hopefully they won't be too difficult to find. The black ships are keeping a pretty close watch on all the ports and harbors. We'll need to get in and out as quickly as possible. This ship can do amazing things with those aboard, but she isn't indestructible, something I've been trying to make sure Benjin and Fasha remember. With Gwen and Pelivor aboard, they've gotten cocky, and because of that, they've gotten sloppy. It's going to catch up to all of us eventually."

Morif rolled his eye.

That was enough to make Sinjin smile. Some things would never change.

"Who taught Pelivor and Gwen to fly the ship?"

"Pelivor figured it out on his own but just barely," Millie said. "Or so I've heard--over and over again."

"Kenward?" Sinjin asked.

Millie just snorted and nodded. "You guessed it. Always complains that Pelivor tried to drop them from the sky. The young man seems quite competent to me," she said, and she even blushed a little.

Morif leaned back and laughed. "He hasn't dropped us from the sky yet," he said. "And with Gwen, he can make time like nothing you've ever seen. We're just cruising at the moment. When she's got a mind to, that little girl can send this ship so fast, the wind tries to tear her apart."

"Here," Millie said to Morif. "Put some of this in your mouth and be quiet. You're just going to scare these poor children needlessly."

Despite the humor, Kendra didn't like being referred to as a child any more than Sinjin did. Both let it go since Millie brought more food for them, including thick broth and crusty bread that had little, star-shaped seeds in it.

"It would've had more substance if those fools had given me a little warning."

No one said anything since they had food in their mouths. Sinjin considered this the appropriate response. Millie seemed to as well, and for a brief time was content to watch them all eat. While he picked at his food, his mind wandered, and he tried to understand all that had taken place. It was impossible. He didn't know the source of this evil that attacked the Godfist and the Greatland and now was retreating, if slowly.

"From where do these invaders come?" he asked without meaning to, but no one answered.

Chapter 3

Kindness is one thing of which we should never run out.
--Missa Banks, healer

* * *

Bits of straw clung to Allette's face when she pushed herself up from the crude bench on which she had slept. Running a hand over her cheek, she could feel the indents left by the rough surface on the unsanded wood. Hoping she didn't have any splinters, she ran a hand over her aching head. When her vision finally focused, she drew a sharp breath. She wasn't alone.

A hard-eyed and bearded old man sat across the room, looking at her in a way that made her very uncomfortable. Another man snored on a similar bench and smelled of whiskey. She was trapped in a cell with these men, and she nearly climbed the walls in fear. The reinforced door showed signs of previous escape attempts, its surface pocked and scarred, splinters of wood still hanging. The place had the smell of creosote, and she would bet the door was soaked in it, making the wood caustic to the touch.

"Think you can get out of here, *boy?*" the hard-eyed man said, his calloused hands clenched. And the way he said "boy" gave Allette another start. Did he know she was a girl? The old man looked over at the other, who'd stopped snoring. Allette took the opportunity to check her hair. Some of it had come loose in her sleep, and it must have made her gender obvious to this man. Quickly she tucked it back under her collar. The man turned back to her, aware that the other was still sleeping. He said nothing and instead only grinned at her.

When a loud clang sounded from the heavy cell door, Allette jumped. The door swung inward, and a broad, bald head peeked in. "You there, come with me," he said, pointing to Allette. Then he turned his eyes to the bearded man. "You stay where you are."

Standing slowly and not turning her back on the bearded man, who watched her intently, Allette made her way to the door. The bearded man lunged at her then, and she squealed as she leaped away. The bald man at the door had sweat running down his face from just standing there, and he reacted slowly. Allette was already past him and into the dark hallway before he moved. From within, she heard the bearded man cursing and the sound of the drunken man waking.

The bald man pulled the door shut as quickly as he could and lowered the heavy bar back into place. Afterward, he wiped the sweat from his face and regarded Allette. She hadn't moved. Once she had gained her freedom from the cell and was safely away from that lecherous man, she waited quietly. This man did not look dangerous to her. He was pale and soft, and he jiggled when he moved.

"I am Sensi," he said. "I will represent you. Do you understand?"

Despite being uncertain of exactly what he meant, Allette nodded, her tongue unwilling to speak. This man would know she was a girl, this man who would defend her; at least, that was what she hoped he had meant.

"Follow me. We must speak in private," Sensi said before leading the way through narrow halls.

Natural light did not reach this far into the hold, not that Allette knew just how far in she'd been. The trip into the stone fortress had been a blur, and she remembered little of it. From the bruises she felt, she was almost glad she didn't remember it. Now though, it seemed they were impossibly deep within the hold, and only the light of Sensi's lantern let them see. Deep, cold fear crept into Allette's psyche and shaded her every thought. Waves and storms and darkness at sea she could handle, but to be trapped within cold stone, bereft of light and wind, was too much for her and she trembled.

Looking over at her, Sensi gave a sad but kind smile. "It's not so bad," he said. "Throwing fruit at someone is not the most heinous crime, and dropping a bit of peel is forgivable the first time. And if I wasn't so fat, I'd probably run from Heinlin too. The man is a brute."

Allette said nothing, not wanting to incriminate herself. That didn't seem to dampen Sensi's enthusiasm or optimism. "If you must know," Sensi said, despite the fact that Allette had not asked, "it is quite refreshing to work with a young person; so many of those who end up here know better. But you . . . well . . . I don't know."

Silence was her only response. How could she trust this man? Trust, her father had always told her, must be earned. Still, Sensi had gotten her out of that terrible cell; that counted for something. "I just want to go home."

Sensi stopped for a moment and looked at her. "So you *do* speak. I was beginning to wonder if you were mute. Come inside and we'll talk about 'home.' All right?"

It was only then that Allette saw the doorway. The door was neither plain nor elaborate. It was well made but not pretentious. The rich-grained wood bore no markings or decoration. Sensi opened it and beckoned her inside. At that moment Allette considered running, if only she'd known a way out. They were still deep enough within the mountain that she would need the lantern to light her way, and that would be more difficult than slipping away from the slow-moving man.

There was a difference between being slow and being weak, and Allette wasn't certain she'd be able to wrest the lantern away from the man. If she failed, she would have alienated the one person who seemed willing to help her. Sensi watched her, seemingly aware of the battle that raged within Allette and content to see what she decided. Finally, with a resigned sigh, Allette entered.

The room was better appointed than Allette would have guessed. She'd seen poorer trappings in rooms reserved for honored guests aboard tall ships. The desk was carved of rich, golden wood. Fruits and leaves adorned the legs, and the work surface was polished to a smooth sheen. A leather writing pad covered the center, and there rested quills, ink, and parchment. The clutter was organized, but still Allette couldn't help but wonder how the man kept all those papers straight; just keeping a ship's log had seemed a daunting task to her.

Behind the desk rested a wide chair that looked as if it had been on the wrong end of a pitched battle. The cushion might once have portrayed a scene at court, but now it was faded and stretched. Sensi flopped into the chair with such force that Allette half expected it to collapse, yet it held.

"Sit," Sensi said.

Looking about, Allette saw a smaller chair in the corner. This chair was in far better condition. The scene on its cushion, however, portrayed a man being thrown from a cliff, which was not the most encouraging image. Still, Allette settled herself into the uncomfortable chair.

"Come closer," Sensi said. "We must talk and I do not wish to shout."

Allette leaned forward.

"What's your name, boy?"

"Allette," she said using her natural voice.

Sensi looked up with surprise in his eyes. "Have my eyes grown so old as that?"

"You saw what you expected to see," Allette said before she thought better of it.

"Perhaps I did," Sensi said, eyeing her anew. "From where do you hail?"

"My home is aboard the *Maker's Mark,* and she rests at Maiden Harbor."

A low whistle escaped Sensi's lips. "I suspected you were of Midland birth, but I wasn't expecting it to be the farthest reaches, and aboard a ship at that. How am I to know if even the ship is still there? Ships have been known to sail, you know."

His words caused Allette to flush. The *Maker's Mark* would only sail if her father were aboard or if there had been a mutiny. Her father would not leave the Heights without her, and his crew would never turn on him. The *Maker's Mark* was a ship of reputation and she would remain where she was docked; of that Allette was certain. If her father were dead, though, then what? Gritting her teeth, Allette kept the tears from coming. Show no weakness, her father had taught her.

"Where's your mother?"

"Dead," Allette answered, her voice flat.

Sensi looked apologetic and seemed to wish he'd framed his question differently. "Is your father alive?"

"I don't know," Allette said, a catch in her voice despite her best effort to suppress it. She couldn't help it, though. The thought of her father's being gone was too much for her, and she wanted to cry, wanted to wrap her arms around him and have him sing to her as he'd always done.

"But you came here together?" Sensi asked, his voice betraying annoyance at having to pull the information from her, but he also appeared to empathize with her, and that tempered the heat of his words.

"Yes."

Sensi just looked at her and raised an eyebrow.

"There were men," Allette said. "They hit him. They made him get into a pull cart. I don't know what happened after that."

"That's terrible!" Sensi cried. "No wonder you were lost and frightened."

There were more questions about her father and her past, and Allette did what she could to answer them. Sensi really did seem to have her best interests at heart, and a small glimmer of hope ignited within her. Sensi would help find her father, and everything would go back to normal. She'd had hopes dashed before, and she knew better than to assume things would work out as she hoped. Would this time be different?

"You wait here and I'll go talk to the lord chancellor. I'll get these charges settled, and then we can talk about how to get you home."

Left alone, Allette wondered again if she should run. Sensi came across as well intentioned, but what of the rest? Sensi was, after all, not the lord chancellor. Just the sound of that name invoked visions of haughty disdain. Allette had seen no kindness from those with titles such as that. That was why she and her father preferred to be free people of the seas with no lord but the winds. Her father had given all that up for this trip. *Why?* she asked herself again, but still she could make no sense of his decision. Now he was gone.

When Sensi returned, Allette was searching the back of his

chambers for another lamp; there was none to be found, but her guilt was difficult to hide when he entered. He was not alone. Behind him came a meaty guard, not so unlike the one she'd faced the day before. His eyes held no kindness, and Sensi looked somewhat downcast. Allette knew then that she should have run while she'd had the chance.

"Do not worry, child. Everything will be fine. There is just the matter of a small formality," Sensi said, and his words left Allette chilled. "The lord chancellor does not want to give the appearance of leniency toward Midlanders at a time when he needs the support of the council more than ever. You understand, of course."

Allette did not understand, but she did not give her questions voice. She doubted her words would do anything to improve her circumstances.

"The lord chancellor and I have already agreed that you are innocent of the charges, and we will convey this to the thrower. There is really nothing for you to worry about."

The thrower . . . Allette shuddered. She'd heard the tales of the Heights' justice and how the thrower made the final determination between innocent and guilty. The guilty were thrown from the Heights, and the innocent, allowed to stay. Visions of falling to her death filled Allette's mind and would not relent, making any other thought almost impossible.

"Don't worry," Sensi said as he put a hand on her shoulder and guided her back to the hall. "No one has been thrown from the Heights in decades. You're no Thundegar Rheams, I'll tell you that. That fool left the thrower no other choice."

Again, Allette didn't fully understand what Sensi was talking about, but she understood enough. Still, the way the guard looked at her did anything but bring comfort. Rather than going upward, as Allette had expected, Sensi took them downward. No more was said as they walked, and even the men's gaits became more formal. The guard stood rigid, and his eyes remained straight ahead. At least he no longer glared at her, Allette thought.

After one more turn, natural light shone ahead. Allette had never been so happy to see real sunlight. It felt to her as if she had been imprisoned in stone for weeks. She could not imagine spending the rest of her life in such a place. A small crowd was gathered on an elaborately carved dais; beyond waited a spectacular view. Mists blanketed the forest below, giving them their name: the Cloud Forest. Allette had seen it on their flight in, but this view was like nothing she'd ever witnessed. Wind caressed her face, and she greeted it like an old friend. The sun sent beams of light through fluffy white clouds at much higher elevation. Allette half expected to see dragons in the air, but the skies were otherwise clear. It would have made no difference. Her fate was about to be sealed.

Somehow the cheerful day made it seem as if nothing could go wrong, but Allette had seen that feeling proven false too many times. She could not let down her guard, or it might be the end of her. She wasn't ready for the great beyond; she'd barely figured out what she wanted to be in this life.

The lord chancellor was easy to spot. He was the most finely dressed, and a crowd of lessers hovered around him, waiting on an opportunity to gain his attention. The thrower, too, was easy to pick out. He was perhaps the tallest man Allette had ever seen, and even garbed in heavy robes, the muscles of his shoulders and chest were easily seen. His face was hidden in shadow, and none claimed to know who the thrower really was, but Allette doubted such an enormous man could remain clandestine. It did not matter, neither his name nor his house; all that mattered was that Allette had to face him that day.

The lord chancellor noticed their arrival, and a smile played across his face. Allette could not tell if it was a warm or self-satisfied smile; her gut suggested the latter. The thrower looked threatening even when at ease and Allette once again considered fleeing. The problem was that there were only two places to go: back into the darkness or over the ledge. The darkness terrified her, and if the fall from the ledge did not kill her, then the Cloud Forest certainly would. Prior to their trip, Allette had studied the Heights, and the Cloud Forests were said to be just as deadly as the Jaga, only smaller. If even a few of the creatures she had read about really existed there, then they were truly frightening places indeed. There was no solution to this puzzle. The only way out would be for someone to pay for her dragon flight home, and that didn't seem at all likely.

When the lord chancellor approached, he held his hands cupped before him. Sensi put a hand on her shoulder and guided her forward. Allette kept her eyes downcast and stopped when the lord chancellor stood before her. Sensi's hand remained on her shoulder until the lord chancellor cast him a glance that sent him scrambling backward.

"Now then," said the lord chancellor, his face showing no signs of the warmth his tone implied. Allette looked to his eyes; that was where her father said a man held his intentions. There she saw curiosity; something else lingered behind it, but she could not figure out what it was. "You, young lady, face the lord chancellor's wrath for having assaulted a member of my guard."

Allette said nothing.

"Come with me; let us be apart. Let us enjoy the view."

The lord chancellor drew Allette along and brought her to the very edge of the jutting rock on which they stood. It had been cut, carved, and polished, but rock it would always be. Something in that comforted Allette, and she didn't know why. That comfort did little to quell the unrest in Allette's belly. Her current vantage showed just how deadly the fall could be. A sheer rock face dropped away for a goodly distance, and below that, loose rock formed a slope that disappeared into the mists. It didn't look as if the fall meant certain death, but it did look as if it would guarantee injury. Wandering into the Cloud Forest when injured would mean certain death. If the lord chancellor were looking to soothe her fears, this was a poor place to do it. That reason convinced her his pleasant tone was a ruse.

"There is no one to speak on your behalf and no one for me to grant custody. You put me in a very difficult position But I am not cold of heart. We will go through the exercise with the thrower as a matter of formality, but you have nothing to fear."

Allette maintained her silence, almost certain there would be something more.

"First, though, I've a small thing to ask of you."

Allette looked up, knowing this was his true game but having no idea what to expect. When he opened his cupped palms, her heart nearly stopped.

"Grab hold of this, here, around the handle."

In his hands was a small metal figurine, slender and seemingly frail. The figure was of a woman in a flowing robe, her hands at her sides; one holding what looked like a bolt of lightning, and the other holding something she did not recognize. The metal was cool to the touch and felt good in her hands, even if fear nearly overwhelmed her.

"Yes. Just like that," the lord chancellor said, his cold, blue eyes watching her intently.

Allette almost dropped the figurine when it began to move. Something registered in the lord chancellor's visage, but it was gone in an instant. Allette was left to wonder what it meant when the figurine's arm, the one with the lightning bolt, rotated until the lightning bolt was held above its head. Allette hadn't even noticed the joint required for such movement, which had cleverly been concealed through remarkable craftsmanship.

Taking the figurine back from her, the lord chancellor concealed it within his palms again before turning back to those who waited. "The thrower will decide her fate," he said when he turned around. "Long live the thrower."

"Long live the thrower," echoed those assembled, though they did so with little enthusiasm, as if this were merely the formality Sensi had mentioned. When the lord chancellor turned to the thrower and gave him an almost imperceptible nod, Allette's stomach clenched. If she let that big man get his hands on her, there would be no escape. Still, no other route presented itself, and she found herself standing before the thrower. His face deep in shadow, Allette could glean nothing from him. He might as well have been stone for all the emotion she sensed.

Hands the size of melons descended on her, and meaty fingers gripped her shoulders. Allette was much shorter than this man, and he had to stoop down to grab a hold of her. Still no emotion came from within the dark hood. The thrower began turning them in a circle. Faster and faster they turned; the mountain and the open air flashing by in an alternating pattern that churned Allette's guts. Still, the man's grip remained firm, and still he spun them faster. The force of the spinning motion felt as if it would send Allette soaring into the open air even if the thrower did maintain his grip on her, which he did not.

The release of his grip came suddenly. The darkness of black rock had just flashed by, which meant she would be flying toward the cliff. As soon as his fingers relaxed, Allette acted on instinct, knowing she was about to die. One did not grow up on a ship and not learn self-defense. Allette's subconscious seemed to know then that the thrower would kill her. Instead of fighting their momentum, Allette grabbed the thrower's robes and threw herself at the stone, just before the edge. Her back hit stone and she continued to slide toward the ledge. Curling up beneath the thrower, who was already over leveraged from leaning so far forward, Allette prepared herself for one massive thrust. Planting her feet on the big man's chest and continuing to pull him forward, Allette thrust her legs, despite the man's desperate, last-second appeal. The word *no* was still pouring from him as the thrower sailed over the edge. A moment later, his cry ended abruptly.

Allette turned to see all those behind her stunned. Her hands and legs trembling, she knew she had to think and act fast. She had just killed the thrower, and there would be no forgiveness for her now, if there had ever been any in the first place. The lord chancellor took a step toward her, released from his paralysis sooner than the others as one of the guards stepped toward her as well. Her time had run out.

It was then that she looked at the place where the jutting balcony met with the sheer face, and she saw that the face sloped away and downward at a steep but more manageable angle than from where the thrower had gone. Without another thought, she bolted, using all the speed and agility she possessed, which was considerable. A stone railing surrounded most of the balcony, making it less likely that spectators would join the accused in going over the ledge. Allette planted one arm on the rail and vaulted over, not knowing exactly what awaited her below.

The fall seemed impossibly long, and when her boots finally struck stone, her knees buckled and sent her tumbling forward. Rotating, she came back to her feet on the steep, rocky slope. Her momentum carried her forward, and she danced over the loose stone. There was only so much her dexterity and reflexes could do, and Allette soon found herself tumbling down the slope, her body tucked into a ball in an attempt to minimize the damage. It was too much; she felt as if she would be dashed to bits. Squeezing her eyes shut, she dug deeply into the place from which her strength had always come, the place that had saved her after her mother's death. There she found quiet, peace, and strength; there she was separate from the pain.

When at last she stopped, Allette lay sprawled on stones that dug into her skin. She should be dead, but she was not. The world spun. When finally it slowed enough for her eyes to focus, she saw the lord chancellor, Sensi, and the people of the Heights looking down, and then they drew back and were gone. Allette was alone.

Chapter 4

In the fields of heaven are sown the seeds of stars, and some go astray.
--Brother Milo, Cathuran monk

* * *

When Benjin and Fasha entered the galley, all eyes turned to them. This was their ship, and it went where they wished; it was something Sinjin tried not to forget. These people were all his friends, but they did not always want the same things that he did. Of course, at that moment, he wasn't certain what he wanted. Fingering Koe in his pocket, he let the cool smoothness of it soothe him. The staff lay across his lap, and his other hand stroked its lustrous finish. The items had brought him pain at times, but they also brought solace depending on his state of mind.

"Thank you for feeding our newest crew members," Fasha said, and Benjin smiled, his eyes twinkling with mirth.

"I can't wait to see this one swab the deck," he said, pointing to Kendra.

She just stuck her tongue out at him, though she quickly pulled it back in her mouth when Fasha raised an eyebrow.

"We're a day or so from picking up your grandfather and great-uncle," Benjin said. "After that, it's but a matter of weeks to get back to the Godfist."

Kendra shook her head, as if trying to reconcile the speed and distances involved.

"I know," Benjin said. "I still can't quite believe it myself, and my own daughter making it possible. What will this world bring me next?"

"Bread and stew without most of the vegetables, I'm afraid," Millie said as she handed them steaming bowls and hearty chunks of bread.

Both sat and ate.

"What if Trinda is unwilling to let us return to the Godfist?" Sinjin asked while Benjin blew on his soup.

"Since when do you need Trinda's permission to enter your own home?" Kendra asked, incensed. They'd had these words before.

"I know I've the right to do so, but that doesn't make it the right thing to do."

Benjin nodded and sipped his soup.

"I think the Arghast would accept us," Sinjin continued.

Kendra snorted. "You must retake Dragonhold. It's the only way."

"Trinda controls Dragonhold; I do not," Sinjin said. "Trinda has power; I do not."

"Power is not in the fist of the leader but in the fists that rise to his command!" Kendra said with conviction.

"I don't disagree with the girl on that part," Benjin said. "Though she'll have to concede that a leader must consider the lives that would be lost. If, on the other hand, Trinda would relinquish your grandfather's farm and the cold caves back to their rightful owner, then we would have all we needed."

Kendra made a rude sound in her throat. "How will you ever sleep at night, knowing that her assassins are out there, waiting to kill your family?"

Sinjin had to think a moment before answering. When he drew a breath to speak, Kendra started speaking first.

"You have strength," she said, gripping his shirt and pulling him just a little closer. "You have warriors and scoundrels and you've got me. Did you even consider that?"

Sinjin nodded; he had considered it. He'd lost enough already; he didn't want to lose any more.

"You don't have to go back to the Godfist at all," Fasha said, and Benjin gave her a dark look. It would appear that they'd had these words before. "There are beautiful places we found, perfect places to raise a family, perfect places to disappear."

Kendra didn't appear to have the courage to scoff at Fasha, but she looked like she wanted to. Sinjin took her scowl as a no. After what might have been considered a polite interval, Kendra spoke again. "It's not just the people on this ship who'll follow you," she said. "Most of the people within Dragonhold will rise to your call, but call them you must!" The last was said as if there were no way anyone could argue her point.

A note of sadness colored Sinjin's voice when he responded. "There are some who are loyal--of that there can be no doubt--but I think the number is smaller than you might believe. My mother's ideas were rarely popular, but she had the power and image to make things happen anyway, or at least somewhat. But the average person cares about feeding their family, and war feeds no children."

"Not war," Kendra said. "A coup."

"I don't know," Sinjin said. Then he had to hold on as the ship slowed, gently at first, then abruptly when the ship reentered the water. Before everyone had themselves settled back into their spots, Pelivor walked into the galley, the smile fading from his face when he saw the looks from the others.

"Could you please give us some warning before you do such things?" Millie said, even as she retrieved stew and bread for him. Sinjin just waited for it. "The stew is missing the vegetables because someone was inconsiderate and didn't let the cook know before turning the ship on its side."

"Well, I didn't know," he began, but Millie cut him off with a look. "There were black ships coming, and I didn't turn the ship on its side so much as--" Again, she cut him off with an outraged look, glancing down at her vegetable-stained smock. "I'm sorry," Pelivor said. "I'll warn you next time before I do anything inconsiderate or stupid."

"That's all I'm asking," Millie said, her arms waving in the air.

Morif just shook his head.

She rounded on him. "What are you laughing about?"

Morif just waved his hands in front of him as if to ward off her attack, and he started laughing.

"You big oaf," Millie said with half a smile. "The next time, I'll make you clean up all of it. I'd make you cut up more if we had it, but supplies are hard to keep on a ship. It's just wasteful, I tell you. Disgraceful is what it is."

Morif stood and cleared the bowls, but he walked away shaking his head, and Sinjin thought he saw the big man's shoulders move as he chuckled. Sinjin envied Morif in that moment; his ability to remain happy no matter what others thought of him was something Sinjin could take a lesson from. Though he wasn't certain how he would do it, he vowed to get there someday. In the meantime, he hoped he hadn't made Kendra too angry. That was when it occurred to him that Gwen hadn't joined them.

Since Kendra didn't seem to be enjoying his company, Sinjin took a clean bowl from Morif and filled it with stew. After pulling a sizable chunk of bread from the loaf, he walked toward the hatch, still getting his sea legs and using the staff for support. The flight had been mostly steady and smooth, and it was a sudden and disorienting change. Part of him wanted to get the ship back in the air, but bad weather was coming. Near the stern, he found Gwen, standing with her hands still resting on the wooden tubes. He would have thought she'd want to be away from there, eating or resting, but she seemed content, her eyes closed and her breathing deep. For a moment, he considered leaving her alone since he did not want to interrupt.

"Don't even think about walking away with that food," she said when he started to turn, her eyes still closed, but a small smile on her lips.

"I never could sneak up on you," Sinjin said.

"Still can't," she said, "but since you came bearing food and using the staff, I suppose you weren't trying all that hard."

Sinjin handed her the food. He would ask no questions while she ate, as that would be rude, but he also sensed impatience from her. Still, he waited. Finally she set the bowl aside and just looked at him.

"Were you going to come into the galley and eat with us?" he asked.

The look Gwen gave him in response made it clear he was walking a dangerous path. "I was waiting for *her* to leave."

"Who?" Sinjin asked, immediately wishing he hadn't. By the time the word left his lips, he knew the answer. Now Gwen's face grew sharp and angular, and her eyes danced with fire. That was no twinkle, and Sinjin knew it. "Wait."

"I've had enough waiting," Gwen said, though Sinjin knew it hadn't been his fault that they'd been apart for so long. Always before their relationship had been something of a game between them, just like the enmity was. After a long silence, she said, "I see how she looks at you."

Sinjin could have laughed, but he resisted the urge. There was nothing to be jealous of. He had no chance with Kendra or Gwen; both were impossible relationships. He'd always known, deep down, that Gwen would end up with someone else. Some people lived life; Gwen rode it like a spring colt. Whatever she felt, she felt passionately, and Sinjin always managed to find himself on the wrong end of those passions. His relationship with Kendra was purely circumstantial; she'd been close to him because there had been absolutely no one else to be close to. Part of him knew there were some cracks in his theory, but he was trying very hard not to think about those.

"It's really good to see you again," he finally said, not knowing what else to say. Then he added, "You look nice."

Though she seemed to be trying not to appear swayed by the compliment, Sinjin couldn't help notice her toss her hair. The reason he couldn't help notice was that she'd always been able to do that to him. A toss of her hair, an innocent look, or a twinkle in her eye had always rendered him useless in an argument. If he ever did manage to win, she would cry and get what she wanted anyway. For all these reasons, Sinjin did his best to choose his words carefully, yet the words he spoke slipped out anyway, "I have no home."

There was a catch in his voice when he said it, and he could almost see something inside Gwen change in that moment. There was no more feigned anger or resentment, no more coy interplay; for that moment, he saw his old friend. With tears welling in her eyes, Gwen hugged him, and they both cried. It was at that moment that Kendra emerged from the galley, clearly looking for Sinjin. When she saw him, her face reddened and she turned away as quickly as she could. After a word with Morif, she disappeared into the deckhouse. That was a problem Sinjin would have to solve another time. As it was, Gwen had pulled back, an uncertain look in her eyes.

"I'm sorry," she said.

"Me too."

"Your parents were good people," she said, and Sinjin bit his quivering lip. "And you always have a home with us."

Though he knew it to be true, Sinjin could not imagine himself as a sailor; he'd spent most of his life within walls of stone, and being surrounded by nothing other than air and water seemed unnatural. He would need to find somewhere to call home. It was from the Greatland that they fled, and Sinjin had no desire to ever go back. Dragonhold, the only place he did fit in, was now controlled by someone whom he had barely tolerated. Though he'd been kinder to Trinda than most had, he had hurt her feelings on numerous occasions. It shamed him that it was only after realizing he might actually need her for something that he felt bad for mistreating her. Perhaps he was not as charitable a soul as he'd always liked to think.

Though she remained silent, Sinjin could feel Gwen's eyes on him, and he met her gaze. There was kindness there and vulnerability; that perhaps frightened Sinjin more than anything else.

"Is it hard?" he asked when he could find no other words. "Making the ship fly, that is. Is it difficult?"

Gwen pressed her lips together for a moment, and Sinjin feared he'd upset her, but then she just nodded and smiled. "I don't actually make the ship fly," she said. "Pelivor does that. I just make it go faster. And yes, it's difficult and tiring, but we can do it for long periods of time nonetheless."

"Have you tried to do what Pelivor does?"

"I've tried a number of times," Gwen admitted. "I can affect the movements of the ship, but I've never been able to make her fly. Pelivor was the one who thought of using the thrust tubes, but still he cannot use them for very long. He is better suited to flying, and I am better suited to thrust. Sometimes we play off each other's energy, but the truth is that Pelivor can fly the ship without me as long as there is wind; without him, I wouldn't be able to make much speed with the ship in the water, but I could keep her moving."

"That's amazing," Sinjin said, trying not to reveal that he felt more than a little jealous. He was, after all, powerless. He possessed some of the most potent artifacts in all of Godsland, but he could do nothing with them. That was when he made up his mind and pulled Koe from his pocket. Gwen's eyes were immediately drawn to the carved cat with its aggressive stance. Of course, it was the only dragon ore carving known to exist. "This does me no good. But I bet you could fly the ship using it. Here, take it."

The look of awe on her face soon changed to fear, and she pulled away. "Too much," she said. Sinjin quickly put Koe back in his pocket.

When he looked back to Gwen, there were tears in her eyes. "You have the most precious, beautiful, and dangerous thing in the world, and you want to give it to me."

Sinjin opened his mouth to speak, but Gwen didn't give him the chance. Instead, she grabbed the empty bowl and moved quickly past him and into the galley. Feeling like a fool, Sinjin tried to figure out where he'd gone wrong.

"They're all like that, you know," Benjin said. Sinjin hadn't realized the man had walked up behind him. "They think so much differently from us that they all seem crazy, or you end up feeling like a complete fool. Am I right?"

Sinjin just nodded and Benjin laughed. "I should probably never give advice on women, but you need to start by accepting the fact that you'll never completely understand them; it's against the laws of nature. Haven't you ever wondered why tomcats fight or why stud horses kick trees? Women . . . that's why."

Shaking his head, Sinjin smiled.

"Don't take me wrong, now. I love women and a few of them love me back, but I don't expect I'll ever understand them."

"Thanks, Benjin."

"Don't you worry about it; the girl's always thought highly of you."

The conversation was going in a direction Sinjin wasn't certain he was comfortable with. "Do you know where Kendra went?"

"She's in her bunk. It's right next to yours."

Sinjin was relieved and anxious all at once. Benjin escorted him into the deckhouse and acquainted him with his bunk. It was small but far better than his previous sailing experience had been. Those memories tormented him at times, but he did his best to let the past stay in the past.

Benjin left him to get some rest, but Sinjin knew he wouldn't sleep well if he thought Kendra was angry with him. After a light knock, she said, "Come in."

Sinjin entered with his head bowed, partly to fit through the hatch and partly to avoid making immediate eye contact with Kendra. When he finally did meet her eyes, they looked puffy and red--not a good sign. He tried to remember what Benjin had just taught him, but in that moment, he could find no way in which that information was helpful. It didn't tell him what to say, or how to keep from making mistakes that ended with tears. All Benjin's advice did was to tell him to expect defeat. Grudgingly, he acknowledged that the information wasn't completely useless. At least he could have realistic expectations.

"I hope I didn't upset you," he said.

"You're not the only thing in the world I might be upset about, you know," she said. "Has it occurred to you that I lost my mother just as much as you lost yours?"

"I'm sorry," Sinjin said, feeling genuine regret for not having talked with her about that sooner. Of course she must be feeling the pain of having lost her mother after having been betrayed by her. They didn't know if Khenna was alive or dead, but Sinjin could see why the woman would be lost to Kendra nonetheless. "I know it must sound like I think that everything is about me, but that's not it. It's just that I made Gwen cry, and then I came to see you, and I was feeling pretty thoughtless and stupid--"

"Wait," Kendra said, her voice firm and her anger now clearly directed at him. "You made Gwen cry?"

If Sinjin could have thought of any excuse to leave, he would have, but he was trapped by his own words. How could he have been so foolish as to even mention Gwen's name in this conversation? "Uh . . . well, I, uh. I thought that maybe she could get more use out of Koe than I could, so I was going to give him to her."

The look in Kendra's eyes convinced him to stop talking. "You were just going to give one of the most powerful artifacts in all of Godsland to some girl?"

"She's not just 'some girl,'" Sinjin said, knowing it was a mistake. "I've known her my whole life."

"That's sweet," Kendra said. "There are decidedly less expensive ways to garner the affections of a girl like her. Buy her a good meal and a new dress, and I'll bet she's yours."

Sinjin tried to think of what to say and remembered Benjin's words again. With that in mind, he bowed his head and retreated from Kendra's cabin. From the corner of his vision, he saw a figure move just as the first sheets of rain fell. Knowing Gwen had seen where he'd come from, Sinjin went to his bunk feeling low. He hadn't expected to get much sleep, which was good since something in the cabin next to his kept banging on the wall until the early hours.

Chapter 5

Mistakes are like enemies--easily made but not easily unmade.
--Benjin Hawk

* * *

As the shadows grew long, the mists beneath Allette grew bolder and stalked her. Not much longer and they would claim her. Her doom seemed to wait there and she whimpered. The pain alone brought tears to her eyes, but the fear made them impossible to hold back. After a few testing movements, she found her muscles sore, her skin bruised and a number of scrapes, but no broken bones. A single glance up showed that no one was looking down on her. No one cared. Her father was the only person in this forsaken place that cared for her, and he was gone. Even if he lived, he was lost to her. She was on her own. The Cloud Forest and the Jaga stood between her and the Midlands.

That thought chilled her. She'd flown over the Jaga to get to the Heights, and the memory of it made her skin crawl. What wasn't desolate and barren was verdant swamp, filled with things that crawled and slithered and flew. There were feral dragons there. Allette had not seen any on her flight, and for that she was grateful, but she knew they were there. Deep in the center of the swamps had been a place she'd looked at only once, and the memory still sickened her. Even from the air, she had smelled the stench of it and had been compelled by curiosity to look down. There she had seen a seething pit of wrongness, mottled gray and black, slick with ooze, and from that place crept and crawled unnatural things, things that shouldn't exist.

The jungle surrounding it was surely impassible, and the thought of crossing through that festering swamp stole her breath. There must be another way home, she thought. She was the daughter of sailors, and sailors did not give up when things got hard. They toughened up and survived. Gritting her teeth, Allette pushed herself upright and stood. It took three hops before her right leg would bear her weight, but then the pain became less intense and she was able to stand. Though her bruises ached, the movement helped ease the pain of her stiff muscles, and sweat poured from her. The mists had closed in, and she was bathed in moisture, her clothes almost instantly soaked. Visibility was low and the light from above illuminated the mists, making it even more difficult to see.

Shadows moved within those mists, and there were grunts and whispers. Allette thought that madness might have claimed her when she heard a voice call out her name. It was soft and in the distance. She couldn't be certain, and it troubled her. The mists, her father had said, were actually clouds and could be very dangerous.

Down. That was the only way out. She had to go down.

Slowly and deliberately, she began to move downward, deeper into the mists. It seemed like a journey into insanity. No one would choose to go into those roiling vapors, but Allette had no choice. If she stayed above the clouds, she would die. She would at least have a chance if she made it into the Cloud Forest itself. Certainly there were dangers there, but there was also food. The rumbling of her stomach reminded her that all she'd had to eat was some bitter citrus. At that moment, though, she was worried about becoming food for something else. Not for the first time, she saw shadows moving through the mists, whispering and gibbering as they went, and Allette did not want to know what made such noises, she didn't want to see these beings that seemed to be stalking her.

The stones continued to slope away beneath her feet. Although most were stable, here and there a stone would turn or move, threatening to send her tumbling or twist an ankle. Her progress was fretfully slow, but progress it was, and that pushed her forward. Getting away from the madness and the mists and being able to see at least something of her surroundings was all Allette could think of. Each step brought her closer and was, in itself, a victory. Fear had conquered her in the past, and even she had almost refused to come on this trip to the Heights because of her fear. Now, though, she knew just how right she'd been. She should never have come to this horrible place, and now it would be the death of her. Surely there was no way she'd ever find her way home.

* * *

His lantern dim, Sensi walked the halls like a haunted man. The thrower and a mere child dead--or as good as dead. Even if the girl did survive for a time, the rains would come. There was nothing he could have done differently, he reminded himself. He had done only as his duty required. He hadn't thrown the thrower from the Heights, and he hadn't cast the girl into the Cloud Forest, assuming she survived the initial fall. The memory of it played over and over in his head, his own personal nightmare.

The lord chancellor had said only to prepare a funeral rite for the thrower, and men had already been dispatched to reclaim his body. And what of the child's body? What if they returned with the girl as well? What would he do then?

The questions drove him to walk faster, as if he could run from the feeling of responsibility that would not be deterred. Tears filled his eyes, and he sobbed once before reaching his quarters. He wasn't certain what he would do when the men returned, but for that moment, all he could do was kneel down and beg for forgiveness.

* * *

Beneath the clouds waited what looked like a magical place. And perhaps it was. Her father had always said that magic might be beautiful, but it'll bite you as quick as a snake. That was the way this place felt, as if it were just waiting to show her something beautiful right before eating her. Shivering, Allette stepped from rock onto mossy soil that sank a little beneath her weight. Again she heard whispering in the mists, but this time it had a much more human tone, and she could just make out the words, "Don't know way I come. No one cares. The fool has forgotten about me."

Allette crouched down and moved back toward the concealment of the mists, seeing a distinct form moving through the foliage. The mists concealed her but also blinded her, and she could hear little more than the occasional footfall and what sounded like an animal moving on four legs. Even those sounds faded, and Allette finally allowed herself to move back into the preternatural glow that enveloped the Cloud Forest. This was no place for her, she thought. She belonged on the deck of a ship, not in a jungle. All the things she knew were useless here. It was a realization that crushed her confidence. Before she'd thought herself capable, ready and able to take on any challenge; coming to this place had proven her to be weak and ignorant. Here she was but a child, and there was no one to guide her.

On instinct, she looked for tracks in the rich soil. Her father had always said that a ship's tracks fade quickly, whereas a man's footfall might remain for years. It didn't take long for her to find something. Though not initially obvious, there was something of a trail leading into the jungle. It did not appear heavily used but was just clear enough to allow passage without having to battle the jungle. The plants frightened Allette as much as the wildlife that lurked within the trees and the mosses that covered almost everything else. Moisture clung to her clothing, which steamed, and she tried to remember what it felt like to be dry. Misty rain fell intermittently, and at other times it poured. When the rain stopped for more than a few breaths, Allette looked for more tracks in the soft moss, but the rains had erased most of the evidence. In truth, she wasn't certain she wanted to follow whomever it was who had been within the mists, but she had nowhere else to go, and at least this trail made it easier to move through the forest. It seemed more like a jungle to Allette. She'd always imagined forests as orderly places with long shadows and red leaves carpeting the forest floor.

This place was another thing altogether. Glossy and slick in the constant rain, it was a riot of life, twisting and competing for light. Never before had she thought of plants as competitive, but here they were, the strong smothering the weak and taking the light for themselves. Perhaps plants were not so unlike people after all, she thought. It was then that the forest showed its teeth; finger-length thorns, sharp as cat's claws, hid beneath supple, satiny leaves on a twisted, ropelike vine. It took only an instant for Allette to brush up against the plant and the pain to flare in her side. She took one more startled step but stopped abruptly as the thorns dug deeper. Gasping, she stepped back, and the vine moved with her, causing searing pain as its angle in relation to her body changed. With a slow and deliberate movement, Allette pulled herself away from the vine, which she steadied with both hands. The deep wounds bled freely. Allette took an unsteady step, realizing that she may have reached her end.

It was her father's will that pushed her forward at that moment. He would not give up. He would not just lie down and die. He would fight. He would live! *But he had not,* another voice in her head added. He was dead and she was alone. The thoughts nearly took her to her knees, but she would not let that voice win. Every time she did, it seemed to take a piece of her, and she could not afford to lose any more of herself. This challenge she faced would require everything from her, even the blood that currently dripped past her fingers and onto the moss, leaving a crimson trail. Books had told her that a wounded animal would draw predators, and she tried to push that knowledge from her mind.

Breathing heavily and moving unsteadily, Allette stepped between the gnarled branches of two huge trees whose trunks, a few feet apart, were twisted together several feet up to form something of a grand entranceway. On the other side, things looked different than elsewhere in the forest, and it took her addled mind a moment to register what she saw. It was unlike anything she'd ever heard or dreamed of. This place was made out of plants and trees, but it had been shaped by human hands. Along the borders grew trees that had been woven together to form a massive natural fence. Underneath ran a bubbling stream, its bed covered with rounded rocks free of lichen and moss.

Near the center of the glade stood a house of woven trees. A door made of branches and vines appeared to be the only entrance, and smoke rolled out of a stone chimney. How anyone could have created such a place was beyond her comprehension, and she stood gaping for some time, her mind moving ever slower as the life blood slipped from her body. When the attack came, she didn't even move. Only the sound of an animal running on all fours preceded the attack, and all Allette sensed were claws and teeth accompanied by a terrible howl. It felt as if she'd been hit in the chest with a hammer, and she fell backward onto the thick grasses and moss. Her vision faded as she fell, darkness enveloping her, and the last thing she felt before she succumbed was searing pain.

* * *

A fine wax candle burned on an iron holder. Only the thinnest line of black smoke rose from it, proof of its quality. A pity the holder was so crude, Sensi had always thought; it seemed wrong to foul such fine candles with a crude and wretched holder.

"The world is changing, Sensi," the lord chancellor said. "If we don't change with it, we'll be left behind."

Sensi had heard these words before, but he wasn't so certain. Change seemed the most frightening thing of all to Sensi. He was comfortable and safe. He knew his role in life; he knew his job well. The lord chancellor seemed bent on changing that. It was most uncomfortable, indeed. When the lord chancellor pulled the figurine from within his robes, Sensi got a cold feeling in his stomach. There was already blood on this figurine in his opinion, and it could only lead to more.

"Only a few of these were ever made, and most were destroyed long ago, but the gods have blessed me with this, and I'll not let that gift go unused. If we'd had this twenty years ago," the lord chancellor continued, the figurine inert and lifeless in his hand, unlike when the girl had held it, "we could've avoided all that unpleasantness with Thundegar Rheams."

"How would that have kept him from being thrown from the Heights?" Sensi asked.

"It wouldn't. It would've gotten him thrown sooner, which would have avoided some of the unpleasantness that led up to his being thrown."

"I still don't see how," Sensi started to say, but a look silenced him.

A moment later a knock came at the stout and bolted door. The lord chancellor used this room only for meetings he didn't necessarily want anyone else to know about. Sensi eyed the door with concern and didn't move. The lord chancellor just made a rude sound and opened the door himself, a task that Sensi knew was beneath him. He reminded himself that the lord chancellor could just as easily have him thrown from the Heights; it was a thought he did not relish.

Merini, chief among the lord chancellor's guard, entered the room with a bow to the lord chancellor and a nod to Sensi. He was a thick man wrapped in black hair and looked to Sensi to be as hard as the rock around them.

"My lord," Merini said after the lord chancellor nodded to him, "the protocol for seeking your grace's counsel has been amended per your request. Once you've acknowledged each supplicant, they are to accept the figurine from your hands, turn it about in their hands while keeping eye contact with you, and then return it to you."

"Good," the lord chancellor said, a smile now coming to his face. "And the position of thrower?"

"Has been filled, your grace," Merini said.

Sensi had no doubt the lord chancellor knew exactly who the new thrower would be, but he was not supposed to know, and the game must be played--always the game. Sensi tired of it.

Again, the lord chancellor smiled. "I believe there is a backlog of petitioners waiting for an audience with me. Now I feel inclined to grant some of those audiences. Do I recall Furman Rand and Echter Donds having requests in for additional trading berths?"

Merini nodded.

"Summon them. I wish to hear their petitions personally."

Sensi swallowed hard. Both men had campaigned against the lord chancellor, and he knew now that their fates rested with an ancient figurine.

"And I've been thinking about the members of the old guard. I'd like to check in with each of them, especially Onin. This visit is mandatory; I insist."

* * *

The predator watched her. Allette remained as still as stone. She felt confined, trapped, and she wasn't certain she could stand. Green eyes regarded her with clear intent. Thick brown and black fur reminded Allette of a tabby cat, but this was no house cat. It was the size of a hound with a fluffy tail.

Allette twitched involuntarily, and the cat reacted by crouching down, looking as if it were about to pounce on its prey: Allette. But it didn't pounce; instead, it climbed down from the wood-framed hammock on which it had been resting and lowered itself to the floor, which was where Allette now realized she was lying. There was a blanket beneath her and another folded under her head. A low fire burned nearby; she could smell it and feel the heat.

The cat walked toward her sideways, its back arched and hair raised.

The look in its eyes promised death, and Allette moved her parched lips, her voice coming out harsh and rough, "Nice kitty kitty."

The words had the opposite of the desired effect.

With two hops, the massive cat bounced sideways toward her. Then it was leaping for her face. Allette was so startled that she couldn't even scream. The lithe form slammed onto the floor at Allette's side, and claws whipped out at her, but they did not connect. Instead, they dug into the folded blanket beneath her aching head. After grabbing on to it, the cat wove its head back and forth, its eyes wide and focused. Twice, the cat's mighty back legs kicked the blanket, and Allette felt as if she'd been punched in the face. But then the door swung inward, and a large form filled the doorway.

The cat leaped upright and arched its back again before bouncing once or twice on all four paws, its ears back and eyes wide.

"Quit being a bother, you crazy cat! Off with you!" The man's voice was full of gravel and grit but not malice. The cat let out a trill then leaped back onto the hammock, where it preened. "You're awake, I see."

Allette nodded, unsure what to make of this man. His clothes were ragged and torn, his hair thinning and gray, but his hands looked as if they could crack walnuts.

"They didn't really throw you from the Heights, did they? Was it yesterday?"

Allette just nodded twice, not trusting her voice or this man.

He let out a low whistle. "You're just a child. What have they come to that they are throwing babies from the Heights?"

A flush rose to Allette's cheeks. "I'm no child and they didn't exactly throw me from the Heights."

The man sat back and reappraised her. "Tell me. I must know how you came to be here."

"I don't even know who you are."

Again the man looked her over. "You don't have the look of the Heights about you, but you don't look quite Midlander either. My name may mean nothing to you. I'm Thundegar."

Thundegar. The name tickled at Allette's muddled memory; she knew she'd heard that name before, and that was when she remembered what Sensi had said about the thrower. *"No one has been thrown from the Heights in decades. You're no Thundegar Rheams, I'll tell you that. That fool left the Thrower no other choice."*

Though the old man watched her face, Allette tried not to let on that she knew who he was, though she knew precious little about him beyond the fact that he'd been thrown from the Heights decades before. What crimes had this man committed? she asked herself.

"Please. Tell me how you came to be here."

"I escaped the thrower," she said, fairly certain Thundegar would have similar feelings about the people who'd cast them out but not willing to risk telling him the complete truth. "And then I climbed down."

"Climbed?"

"Fell."

Silence, heavy with tension and doubt, hung between them after that exchange.

"Who died?" Thundegar asked, and Allette felt her stomach churn. Slowly she tried to push herself up. "Not yet. Stay down for now. You had a bad case of cloud rot, and you need food, water, and rest."

As if summoned by his words, a tickle irritated her throat, and she lay back down, coughing, her side aching. Thundegar brought water in a wooden cup that leaked terribly. "I was a metalsmith," Thundegar said when handing her the cup. "I haven't held a hammer in twenty years, and there's no metal here for me to work with, so I'm forced to work with wood. Do you know what it's like to lose your passion, your art?"

There was a faraway look in his eyes, and he no longer seemed to be talking to her. There was an awkward moment when he suddenly recalled she was there.

"I'm sorry. It's been a long time since I've had anyone to talk with except Rastas, and he listens like a rock."

The man's words and manner soothed Allette's fears, and she relaxed, the cool, clear water tasting wonderful.

"You should rest," he said, and he moved toward the door. "Come on, Rastas, you crazy cat."

The feline yawned, stretched, and ignored him.

"You see what I mean?" Thundegar asked and opened the door without waiting for a response.

"The thrower," Allette said before he closed the door behind himself. Thundegar froze and Allette hoped she hadn't made another mistake. "It was the thrower who died."

"How?" Thundegar asked, his emotions unreadable.

Allette sighed. Her life was in this man's hands, and she could not afford for him to think her a murderer, but she no longer wanted to lie to him. "I threw him from the Heights," she said before her courage faded.

Thundegar remained silent for some time.

"He was going to throw me from the Heights, I just knew it," she said, suddenly feeling very vulnerable. This man could seek his own justice if he so chose. "I did the only thing I could think of, I fell on my back and kicked. I didn't know he would go over. I didn't kill him on purpose."

Thundegar stood in the doorway, his body convulsing and twitching. Allette started to push herself up, ready to at least make a feeble attempt at defending herself. But then the sound of Thundegar's laughter reached her.

"You may think me cruel for laughing over the death of a man, but this was a very bad man, and you brought him the justice he for so long deserved. Do not chastise yourself; you didn't kill this man out of malice. You did what you had to do to survive. If I could have, I'd have done it twenty years ago. You succeeded where I failed. You're a treasure indeed. Now, though, you should rest."

"But I killed him," Allette said, suddenly overcome with emotion.

"Yes, you did," Thundegar said, his voice soft, his tone gentle. "If it makes you feel any better, that man tried to kill me and others before me."

"But Sensi said no one had been thrown from the Heights since you."

Thundegar laughed a harsh, bitter laugh. "I assume people learned not to speak out against the corruption and hypocrisy after I was thrown. The thrower was not a man of moral fortitude; he was known for taking bribes. I found this to be true on the day of my trial. I bribed him not to throw me, and he took the money, yet he tossed me from that cliff without a second thought. No. I've no sadness over his death, and neither should you."

"What did you do?" Allette asked, but Thundegar didn't answer; instead he just turned and closed the door.

Chapter 6

In the dawning of a new age, civilization has the opportunity to reinvent itself and equal opportunity to destroy itself.
--Nat Dersinger, prophet

* * *

Clear skies and a favorable wind gave them what must have been record speed. Though the journey had taken weeks, it was but a fraction of the time it would have taken a normal ship. Truly, what Pelivor and Gwen could accomplish was amazing. Under the direction of Fasha, who was as competent a sailor as Sinjin had ever seen, the ship operated smoothly. Benjin oversaw anything not currently under his wife's supervision, and between them, they kept the largely inexperienced crew working safely. In truth, the ship had been constructed to allow just two people to sail her, though she could hold a much larger crew.

Sinjin knew the stories about the ship; it had been carved by his father and Benjin when his mother was pregnant with him. He was grateful to have something he could lay his hands on that was connected to both of them. In many ways, this ship brought him solace; it gave him the connection to his past that he needed while he figured out what he wanted to accomplish with his future. And that was the crux of his problem. He'd not yet figured out exactly what it was he was trying to achieve.

Part of him wanted to disappear, to go to one of the places Benjin talked about and live out his life in peace. It was not what his mother would have done. She would have taken on Trinda. He knew the stories, and he knew his mother had stood up for what she thought was right even before she knew she had power. That was, quite precisely, how she had come to know that she had power. Sinjin had always hoped that some event in his life would trigger power of his own, but he'd never told anyone how much he feared that very same thing. He'd seen the burden power put on those who possessed it and the danger it created for everyone they loved.

Gwen stood at the thrust tubes, Pelivor closer to the prow. Watching the man fly the ship was among the most unusual things Sinjin had ever seen. At times, the lithe but well-muscled man stood with his arms spread out wide, and Sinjin could almost feel the energy cast out to his sides. Now, though, Pelivor had gone to one knee, his other leg shoved out behind him. His arms were still extended, only now they were rotated so his cupped palms faced up. His movements were graceful, and there was a certain beauty to each of the postures. When he rotated his shoulders, Sinjin heard snaps and pops as bones realigned.

"A man can only stand in the same position for so long," Pelivor said when he saw Sinjin watching him.

"I'm just amazed you can keep us in the air while doing . . . whatever it was that you were doing."

"It is an ancient art," Pelivor said. "It is part dance, part fitness and strength, and part fighting technique. You may follow along next time I stretch."

"I don't think I could get myself into those poses," Sinjin said.

"And that is why you need *Keni'ta*. It takes time and commitment, but by working at it every day, you will be able to do as I do. I had trouble at first, just as you."

"Thanks," Sinjin said. The two had not talked much during the trip. Pelivor spent most of his time flying the ship, and Sinjin had never felt comfortable interrupting him. It seemed a great deal safer to let the man concentrate. And when he wasn't flying, Pelivor was usually eating or sleeping. Sinjin knew it was for him that he and the crew did these things and felt unworthy. Even now, as they were approaching the Godfist, he still had no idea what to do. The only thing he could think of was to send a messenger and ask to see Uncle Chase. He had no idea what the relationships were like now, which made things even more difficult. Perhaps it would be better to ask to see Durin; he was certainly a less threatening person than his uncle.

"There is something else I've wanted to talk with you about," Pelivor said, and Sinjin looked up in surprise. Pelivor held out his cupped palm, and inside Sinjin noticed for the first time that it held a translucent sphere. At first he thought it was a herald globe, but there was something different about it. It did not glow, for one thing, but also there seemed to be something inside it. When Pelivor turned his hand to give Sinjin a different angle, he saw there was a black and red spider within the glass.

"What is that?" Sinjin asked.

"I'm not exactly certain," Pelivor said. "Your mother gave it to me. She found it when fighting to save the regent queen. I do know that it can hold a great deal of energy, and that I can draw from this energy over a long period of time. It is one of the reasons I've been able to fly for as long as I have. But now that you are home, I want you to have it."

"No."

"But--"

"No," Sinjin said again. "It would be useless to me, just as Koe and the staff are. I tried to give Koe to Gwen, but she wouldn't take him." A look of surprise crossed Pelivor's face, but he said nothing. "If I keep them, I only endanger myself since those with power will surely want these items for themselves. It would be better if I charged those around me with power to look after these objects and do what good they can with them."

Clearly deep in thought, Pelivor remained silent for a time. Sinjin was continually amazed that the man kept the ship flying while they conversed.

"I will speak to the others about this," Pelivor said.

Sinjin was about to protest when the lookout, Sinjin's grandfather Wendel, shouted out, "Debris!" A moment later, he shouted, "It looks like a log! A big one! More debris! And there's a storm a-comin' fast!"

Though objects in the water were no danger to them, the coming storm was, and Pelivor slowed the ship. Sinjin did something he rarely did; he looked down from the railing. The sensation of height gave him a cold, tingling feeling. Below, he saw the log that his grandfather had spotted, but something about it troubled him. The ends were not rough, and there were no branches. Then waves rolled the log to reveal a hollowed-out underside.

"Man in the water!" Wendel shouted.

Pelivor wasted no time in bringing the ship lower, and Millie shouted curses from the galley. Belatedly, Pelivor said, "Uh, I'm taking us down!"

The cursing from the galley was renewed and increasingly creative.

Sinjin moved away from the rail and helped the crew prepare a boat to be lowered to the water. Pelivor did his best to bring them down gently, but he normally did so over a great distance. He did at least yell before they hit the water. The ship slowed abruptly, shifting anything and everything forward. No matter how well secured the cargo, such abrupt changes in speed shifted the load. The crew moved with extra caution. Pelivor rushed to the railing and was preparing to climb into the rescue boat, but Benjin held him back. Sinjin went over the railing before anyone could protest. Morif joined him and they were lowered into the growing waves.

Sinjin had spent very little of his time at sea in view of the water, and he was amazed by the power of it. In this tiny boat, he was surrounded by deep blue waves that dwarfed him. The *Dragon's Wing* moved up and down independently and occasionally disappeared behind the rolling waves. Sinjin's guts clenched, and he prayed the ship would reappear every time he lost sight of it. All this he felt, while at the same time rowing desperately toward where the man had been spotted in the water.

Moments later Morif cried out, "There!"

Looking to where the old soldier pointed, Sinjin tried to find the man. All he could see was glistening water that lifted them high then sent them falling into the next trough. As they raced down one wave, though, he saw a dark shape in the water. Rowing as hard as they could, Sinjin and Morif did everything they could to get closer, but the wind and waves worked against them.

"Now! Row!" Morif screamed as they crested a towering wave. Just as they pitched forward atop the crest, Sinjin saw the darkened sky, and lightning flashed across the richly woven canvas of thunderheads. Rowing as if all their lives depended on it, the two made progress. When they finally reached the no-longer-struggling form, Sinjin feared they were too late. Grabbing the man, Sinjin pulled him into the boat. Morif used his weight to counter Sinjin's every move, making certain they didn't capsize in the effort to save what appeared to be a dead man.

Once Sinjin and Morif had gotten the man into the boat, he did as his father had taught him and tried to clear the water from the man's lungs and tried blowing air into his mouth while holding his nose. Just as the man coughed and came to, something struck the boat; it was the canoe. Or as Sinjin found out a moment later, it was *a* canoe; several now clogged the water around them. Clinging to one was another man, who shouted. Sinjin had known instantly that the first man was Arghast, and seeing another in the water along with at least three canoes was cause for greater concern.

"More people in the water!" Morif shouted. "Drop all the boats!"

Sinjin looked toward where Morif rowed while pulling as hard as he could on the oars; the waves were more than even the boats could handle. This was what bravery was, he thought, doing the right thing even if it meant risking your life; it terrified him, and he felt like a coward. Part of him wanted to go back to the ship and let those stronger than he rescue the Arghast. Then he saw her, a young, vibrant woman struggling to keep her head above the raging waters. Without thinking, Sinjin dived into the deep blue. In the next moment, he was with her, helping her swim back to the boat, which seemed farther away than it should have been. Morif rowed toward them with little effect, and his shouts were lost to the rushing wind.

A moment later, a boat with Gwen and Kendra aboard crested the nearest wave and raced toward them. Kendra reached out to him while Gwen counterbalanced. Sinjin lifted the Arghast woman to the boat, and Kendra pulled her in. Then Sinjin did his best to get into the boat without capsizing them. Kendra grabbed him by his breeches and yanked. It sent him into the bottom of the boat face-first, and his legs hung awkwardly out of the boat, but he was no longer in immediate danger of drowning.

The girls rowed with more strength than Sinjin would have given them credit for, and that gave him another good reason not to make either of them angry. They soon caught up with Morif, who was trying to teach his barely conscious passenger to row. A goodly distance still separated them from the *Dragon's Wing*, and Sinjin shouted over the wind, "Take me back to Morif! He needs help!"

"Try to remember that before you go in the water next time, you idiot," Kendra said, and for once, Gwen agreed with her. Sinjin instinctively knew this was a very bad sign, but the situation would not allow him to think about it.

As soon as Kendra laid her hands on Morif's boat, Sinjin was moving, trying desperately to switch boats, then realizing just how crazy of an idea that really was. The boats moved independently on the waves, and standing in one was bad enough, but once he had one foot in each boat, he was stuck trying to maintain his shifting footing. The Arghast man he'd saved then returned the favor and pulled him in as he began to fall. Had the man not intervened, Sinjin would most likely have ended up back in the water.

Grabbing an oar, Sinjin rowed with all his might, as did Morif. Rain pelted them and made it difficult to see, but the crew had lit every lantern aboard the ship, it seemed, and it glowed like a beacon of hope. Gwen and Kendra had already made their way back to the ship, and Sinjin saw the shadow of a woman lifted aboard. A smile crossed his face. Whatever else happened that day, he'd saved that woman's life. He supposed he and the Arghast man in the boat with him were even; they had each saved the other. The poor man looked terrified by the raging waves around them. Sinjin shared his concern for their lives, but there was something in the man's face that said his mind was having trouble absorbing newly found truths.

Kendra and Gwen said nothing as they rowed back toward where the others had been found, and Sinjin tried not to think about it. All he could do at that moment was row and hope he could save as many people as possible. There had to be more.

"How many of you are there?" Sinjin shouted while he rowed.

The Arghast man looked at him for a moment as if deep in thought, and he put his arms out wide and said, "Tribe."

Cold realizations washed over Sinjin, adding to the chill of his soaked clothes. An entire tribe was in the water, and the storm was upon them. The instant they reached the loading net, Sinjin helped the tribesman out of the boat and onto the net. Then he shouted up to the deck, "The entire tribe is in the water!"

No words came back immediately, and he and Morif wasted no time in starting back the way they had come. It was difficult to gauge direction in the stormy waves, the *Dragon's Wing* the only reference point they had. The wind was in their faces, and they hadn't made it far before Benjin cried out, "The storm is too much! You'll never make it back!"

Sinjin met Morif's eye. Both nodded and they accepted that possibility. Renewed by the acceptance and driven by sincere desire to save people, Sinjin found strength he hadn't known he possessed. As the wind shifted, there were moments they heard shouting in the distance, but those moments were brief and fleeting, making it nearly impossible to figure out where the sounds were coming from. Lightning illuminated the waters for a moment, and Sinjin thought he saw something in the distance--a patch of water that did not reflect the light. The shouts that came for an instant seemed to confirm that this was the place. Shouting and pointing, Sinjin made sure Morif saw it as well, and the man simply started rowing in that direction. The wind shifted again, now blowing from behind them, for once easing their passage and taking them closer to the place where the water did not reflect.

The shouting and crying grew closer, and they were soon bombarded with floating debris; some small and mostly harmless, but rafts and canoes floated aimlessly around a tight cluster of canoes. The *Dragon's Wing* must have taken advantage of the shift in winds since they suddenly illuminated the area from behind. Now cries could be heard from the ship, and the cries from the Arghast grew in intensity. Sinjin hoped they knew that they were here to save them. That concern grew when Pelivor chose to provide them with light. Fingers of lightning branched out from the *Dragon's Wing* to the clouds and danced there, reaching out like a spiderweb of plasma, not fleeting like natural lightning, but persistent. It danced and morphed, but the light it provided remained constant, making the Arghast easily visible to all.

At the center of the cluster of canoes and rafts was a larger raft, and at its center was a man Sinjin recognized: Halmsa of the Wind clan. Halmsa was guarded by well-muscled men, and those in the boats surrounding him also seemed to be trying to save him. By virtue of Pelivor's lightning, Sinjin saw that Halmsa wore something bulky and heavy, but then his eyes were pulled away when they struck another canoe. A ring of debris stood between them and where the Arghast now clustered together around Halmsa. Sinjin turned to Morif, but the man just shook his head. There was no way for them to safely row their way in. Benjin seemed to agree and brought the *Dragon's Wing* in closer.

"All boats return to the ship!"

With only a short distance to close, Sinjin and Morif made their way quickly back to the *Dragon's Wing*. Hooks were dropped and they were back aboard the ship in the span of only a handful of breaths. It felt surreal and Sinjin had to hang on as the ship pitched beneath him. Gwen and Kendra returned next, and they brought two tribesmen with them. Sinjin was grateful despite feeling inadequate. His gut and conscience churned. He'd obeyed the captain's orders, but he still wanted to help Halmsa and his people. If it hadn't already been apparent that the boats couldn't penetrate the debris field, he might have disobeyed. A third boat returned moments later to Sinjin's surprise; he hadn't realized another boat had actually been launched. This was a night filled with chaos.

Once all crewmembers were back on deck, Benjin barked orders, and people moved. Sinjin was comforted by the fact that the *Dragon's Wing* had been carved from a single greatoak and had perhaps the strongest hull ever built as they unfurled the sails and cut directly into the heart of the Arghast formation. The crew worked as hard as they could to deflect the debris, but it was overall unavoidable. Still, some of the more devastating impacts were averted. Boarding nets were dropped on both sides of the ship. Shouts rose from the Arghast, alarmed at first, but then Halmsa's voice rose above the rest, and his people began moving toward the ship. Some climbed from canoe to canoe; others fell in the water and swam as best they could, their brethren doing what they could to help them from the water.

Slowly but surely, the Arghast began to reach the ship and climb the nets. The men surrounding Halmsa paddled the larger raft toward the ship. The people, no longer obeying Halmsa's order for them to board the ship, now cleared the way so Halmsa's raft could come through safely. The roiling waters continued to claim lives, and no one was unaware of the cost of their actions. These people acted willingly for a leader they loved and also for something else, Sinjin suspected, though he didn't yet know what that motivation might be.

When the raft did meet up with the *Dragon's Wing*, they collided on the waves, sending most of the guards sprawling or into the white-capped water. Halmsa, too, went down, his burden obviously making it difficult for him to move. The remaining guards lifted Halmsa and helped him to the nets. They then climbed on either side of him before pushing him over the rail. A moment later, they followed and looked very uncomfortable with all the eyes upon them. The presence of other Arghast on the ship was met with great joy, though, and tensions were eased. From that moment, the crew and the Arghast worked together to get the rest of the people from the water.

Halmsa stood near the deckhouse, still flanked by guards. Sinjin ran his eyes over the man and nearly fell to the deck when he realized what it was that Halmsa carried. There could be no mistaking it; the burden Halmsa of the Wind Clan bore was a clutch of dragon eggs.

Chapter 7

A persistent idiot can achieve more than a brilliant quitter.
Wendel Volker, horseman

* * *

Struggling to breathe, Allette came awake and nearly choked on a mouthful of tail fur. The weight on her chest was what made her breathing increasingly difficult, and it took her a moment to recover after the cat thrust downward and leaped at something that moved in Allette's periphery, driving all the air from her chest in the process.

"If that cat's just going to sleep on your chest, then maybe you should sleep in the bunk," Thundegar said.

Allette grunted and pushed herself from the hard, stone floor of Thundegar's home. Rastas had already made it clear that the other bunk belonged to him. The cat was a mystery to her. She'd never spent much time around cats, and the creature's behavior baffled her. Why, for instance, would the cat keep her away from the bunk then sleep on her chest? For the moment, she gave up understanding Rastas, who was stalking a small lizard.

Thundegar amazed her. The man claimed no skill in working with wood, but truly he had worked marvels. With very few exceptions, everything in Thundegar's home was alive. Somehow the man had woven trees and plants into a living, breathing structure. Branches held the hammocks, which were supported by a matrix of vines. A similarly constructed chair jutted from one wall, and in front of it was among the only inanimate objects in the dwelling. A rough-edged slab of shale was supported by wooden legs that had obviously been cut, making them stand out in contrast to the living sculpture.

On that slab, which looked heavier than anything Allette could have carried, rested a myriad of implements, tools, and containers, most made of wood. There were a few items, however, that were made of metal, and Allette wondered where Thundegar had gotten them. It didn't seem a very polite question to ask, so she kept it to herself. Beyond the table was the hearth. Made of stones stacked atop one another with layers of what looked like moss and mud in between, it looked sturdy. Nearby rested a stout wooden keg, and atop it was an iron pan. Allette thought she might finally understand the whispering she'd heard in the mists on her first day in the Cloud Forest. Someone in the Heights was helping Thundegar survive.

"You look like you could use something a little more substantial,"

Thundegar said, and he grabbed a rock that had a soft line of rope tied around it from a nearby shelf woven of wood. Allette had not even noticed that one before. "I'll be back in a little while. Stay in here. I won't be long."

"I don't eat meat," Allette said.

Thundegar raised an eyebrow but just put his rock back. "How about fowl?"

Allette shook her head. "Fish?" she asked sheepishly.

"I'll catch 'em but you have to clean and cook 'em."

"Deal," Allette said.

From a darkened corner, Thundegar pulled a slender but flexible rod and a loop of fine fishing wire. There could be no doubt that Thundegar still had friends. A glimmer of hope bloomed in Allette's heart, and she let the momentary optimism pull her from the comfortable bedding. After what seemed like hours, and despite Thundegar's request, she pulled on her boots and shoved the heavy door aside. Bright sunlight hurt her eyes, but the warmth felt good on her skin.

When her vision adjusted and she could see the world Thundegar had created for himself, she found herself awestruck by the beauty of it. Moss-covered stones lined the inside of the woven barrier of trees, creating a sturdy wall nearly as tall as Allette. At one point there was a break in the bottom of the wall that allowed a small creek to enter the glade. Its base was lined with rounded stones, and the water that flowed was clean and clear. There were some very tiny fish that congregated where the water was deepest, but it would take a lot of those to make a meal.

Growing up the rock wall and the trees above were thorny vines, like the one that had bitten into her abdomen. Alongside the mostly leaf-concealed thorns, bright red blossoms appeared at intervals along the vine. Flying insects and tiny birds created a steady traffic flow to and from those and other flowers. It seemed that Thundegar had found a way to make his security fence also serve as a garden. Fruits, berries, melons, and other presumably edible foliage abounded within the woven trees. For a brief time, Allette's world was free of stress, and she actually smiled when she found huckles growing alongside the thorny vine. Careful not to reinjure herself on the hidden thorns, Allette grabbed a handful of berries. It reminded her of a happier time in her life, a time when she and her father had explored uninhabited islands together, uncovering secrets no one had ever seen before.

Walking back toward the stream, Allette finished her berries and bent down to drink, a small smile on her face. That smile vanished when she saw a pair of amber eyes reflected in the water. Black fur, thick and coarse, surrounded those eyes, and when its long mouth opened, the wolf's white teeth stood out in contrast to black gums.

Her breath caught in her chest. Allette could not move, though she did raise her head to look at the wolf directly. Larger by far than any of the dogs Allette had ever seen, though even those had been few, this beast was sprung straight from a nightmare, and Allette went cold. The wolf moved with the quiet confidence of an experienced killer. Allette would make an easy target, and she had absolutely nothing with which to defend herself. Cursing her own stupidity, she thought back to Thundegar's instruction for her to remain inside and wished she'd obeyed.

* * *

Never in the history of the Heights had so many people been thrown; it was unnatural and only the shadow of fear kept the people from objecting. They knew that speaking out would mean their deaths, unless everyone else spoke out with them. Few, it seemed, were willing to take that risk; instead they watched as people they knew, people they cared about, were cast from the Heights for their alleged crimes. Though Sensi knew the first thing the guilty often did was profess their innocence, the sudden and massive increase in accusations, allegations, and verdicts with the highest penalty stank of corruption.

Sensi had held the figurine, and it had not moved, but he knew that his life was in even greater danger than most because he knew what the lord chancellor was doing. In far too many tales, he'd heard what happened to those who knew everything. Part of what made the lord chancellor's purge of the Heights so difficult to ignore was the social standing of those charged with crimes. These were not peasants or simple merchants; the lord chancellor was culling his competition and rivals, and even some who Sensi had thought were his friends. A dirty business this, and one that might be the end of their grand society. Sensi had known it all along; things had been too easy, too comfortable. Such things never lasted, and he'd always known, deep down, that the harsh realities of life would visit themselves upon him and those around him. It was among the reasons he'd always suffered from nerves and a sensitive stomach. What he would do without his remedies shipped in from the Mids, he didn't know, and he shuddered at the thought.

Looking down at his hands, he could almost see the blood. Though he carried but a list of names, he was a part of this, and part of the guilt was his to bear. Some of the people on that list were going to die, and he knew it, and now he supposed they would know it as well. The people were not fools; they knew what was happening no matter what guise the lord chancellor placed on it. The culling violated one of the key tenants of governing, which was not to turn those you govern against you by disregarding their best interest. How the lord chancellor could be ignorant to the damage he was doing, Sensi did not know, but he knew that he, too, would pay the price. The people would not take their anger out on the lord chancellor alone; history told Sensi that a particularly nasty fate awaited him should the people revolt.

After wiping the sweat from his brow, Sensi looked up to see one of Merini's men. "Summon these people," Sensi said, the wavering of his voice giving away his anxiety despite his greatest efforts. The man did not respond or show respect as he did for Merini or the lord chancellor, but he did, at least, do as he was asked.

The walk back to the lord chancellor's audience chambers did little to ease Sensi's mind. Before he was even back in the great hall, he could hear Onin's voice.

"What's the meaning of this? I've served my people, and you have no dominion over me!"

Clearly this was not going to go well. The old guard had always been a problem. They had been loyal to the king, and though the man had dissolved his own monarchy, he had made certain that his guard would remain free men with a status higher than that of even the lord chancellor. It was something that Sensi knew chafed.

"Sir," Merini said, his voice level but laced with malice, "if you'll just follow the protocol, we can all get on with our day. Surely you can't object to--"

"Don't think to tell me what I can and can't object to," Onin said, looking like a relic from the past. He wore layers of pelts and skins, and he kept his long black hair, which was mostly gray, in thick braids with other smaller braids alongside. Large hands were buried in thick leather gloves, and his boots, also of leather and hide and crisscrossed with straps, came up to his knees. "I'll show you what I think of your protocol!"

Stepping into the hall, Sensi bowed to those within. Onin knew him and cast him a disappointed look. Sensi had always tried to protect the old guard, who had saved his parents, but things had changed, and Sensi could no longer offer protection to anyone.

In the end, Merini nodded to his guards, and two strong young men stepped up to Onin, one on each side. The captain of the old guard did not attack or even communicate with these men; he kept his eyes trained on the lord chancellor. One young man grabbed Onin's right arm and forced Onin to extend it. Still the man stared at the lord chancellor. The young man placed the figurine in Onin's hand, but the big man closed his big fist around the object, not allowing the lord chancellor to see if the figurine moved or not, and even more startling, he seemed to be trying to crush the statuette.

The young man now concentrated on trying to get the mysterious object out of Onin's hand, but the big man didn't seem inclined to oblige. After squeezing with all his considerable might, Onin released his grip and let the figurine fall to the polished floor. It fell with a clank but otherwise appeared unharmed.

"I know not what evil this is," Onin said, "but I won't let you soil the land of my father."

The lord chancellor just motioned for his guards to take Onin away.

* * *

Teeth snapped a mere finger's width from Allette's face as a mass of black and brown fur collided with the wolf. Screeching and howling, Rastas climbed onto the wolf's back and raked its eyes. Biting into its neck, Rastas held on until well after the wolf was clear of the glade.

"I thought I told you to stay inside," Thundegar said by way of greeting.

"I'm fine. Thanks for asking," Allette said, but Thundegar just glared at her. "I know. I should've stayed inside."

With a grunt, Thundegar dropped four fish in her lap. It seemed twenty years without human contact had stripped the man of whatever interpersonal skills he may have once possessed. At that moment, though, Allette didn't care. Rastas came bounding back into the glade, and Allette met him with open arms. To her surprise, the cat accepted the hug then bounded off with one of the fish.

One thing Allette wished she still had was a knife, and she wondered how she was going to clean the fish without one. "Do you have a knife?" she asked Thundegar when he came back out of the house.

He walked to where she stood before he answered. "It's sharp," he said. "The handle's a little loose, so be careful. If you only knew what I went through to get that knife."

Allette accepted it with a serious nod. "I understand. I'll be careful."

Thundegar watched her make short work of cleaning the fish. "So you're a fisherman," he said.

"Of sorts," Allette said. "I'm a sailor. Though, sometimes there's little difference."

The two walked back to the house, and Thundegar held the door. Already, the pan rested above the fire, and Thundegar poured a very small amount of oil into it, which soon smoked and popped. A tiny bit of coarse salt and dried herbs and peppers waited on a wooden disk. Allette used these to season the fish under Thundegar's watchful eye.

"I thought there were four fish," he said after a moment.

"There were," Allette said. "Rastas didn't want his cooked."

Thundegar laughed. "He didn't want his first three cooked either." Allette looked surprised at first then cast an accusatory look at the cat, who was now preening in his hammock. "At least he caught the first one himself," Thundegar added.

Cooking without the utensils she was accustomed to took some adjustment, but Thundegar did what he could to help. Still the fish stuck to the pan. Thundegar took two fillets and left the other four for Allette. She finished each in only a few bites, burning the roof of her mouth in her haste. Once the pan cooled, she did what she could to get to the bits still stuck to the pan.

"Wishing you hadn't let that rascal con you out of a fish?"

"It's all right," Allette said. "He earned it."

* * *

Timbers creaked as a still-distant storm drove larger waves into Maiden Harbor, and time was running short. Becker Dan had few options, and all eyes rested on him. "The cap'n should've been back long before now, and I think we all know he ain't comin' today."

A murmur ran through the crew like an ugly undercurrent, one that could pull him under and keep him there. "He ain't comin'," Becker repeated. "I want 'im to just as much as any of you. I'm just being a realist. The slip fees are overdue, we've no more food, and if we stay here, we'll lose the ship. That ain't gonna help the cap'n none. I ain't sayin' we take the ship fer ourselves; I'm just sayin' we should take her off shore, do some fishin', and tie up where we ain't gotta pay."

Another murmur ran through the crew; this one more to Becker's liking, but nothing was certain yet. He'd been on this ship for more than two decades, and he knew this was what the captain would want. Even if his friend was dead, which he suspected, there was the chance his daughter lived, and Becker would do everything within his power to preserve her inheritance. The thoughts nearly brought tears to his eyes, but he would show no weakness before the crew. It was one thing to convince them to take the ship, but it was completely another thing to get them to follow him and continue to be faithful to the rightful captain. He was skating at the edge of mutiny, and he knew it.

"This ship's got history," he continued, "and family, and all of you are part of that family; even those who've not been on the ship all that long are part of that family." There was little response to those words, and they sounded hollow even to Becker. Mate Filps spoke from behind a crowd of men, only his familiar voice letting Becker know who it was. "So we just fish and tie off until the cap'n comes to find us?"

"Yes," Becker said, thankful for Filps.

"And we'll still get paid?" came the voice of one of the newer crew members, who was also concealed behind shipmates.

Filps was a small man and could easily disappear into the crowd, but this man seemed to be hiding toward a purpose. Such cowardice was unbecoming a sailor, and Becker made a mental note to replace the young man, even if it was outside his purview. The circumstances dictated that he take on more power than his position would allow. He'd not declare himself captain of this ship, but he would do what he had to in order to keep her afloat. "If we fish, we can earn money and get paid. It's hard work and we're not set up for large-scale fishing, but it could earn us some coin while we wait for the cap'n to return."

"So let's do what we are set up for, then," Mord said, his deep voice carrying with it the confidence of authority; he'd been on this ship for nearly as long as Becker, though he held the captain in much lower regard. If there was a threat of mutiny, Mord would be at its heart.

"With every operation, we risk losing the ship," Becker said. "That's a risk the cap'n is willing to take but not one that I'm comfortable taking on his behalf."

Mord said no more, but the looks he cast about were cause for concern, and the nods he got in return were even more disconcerting. Becker was amazed at how quickly they could go from a close-knit and functioning crew to the edge of mutiny. If ever there was a time that he'd appreciated the captain, now was the time, and he prayed the man would return no matter how unlikely he knew that to be.

Under the orders of her first mate, the *Maker's Mark* set sail.

* * *

Weaving in and out of the trees, Allette did her best to follow Rastas, but he was too quick; only the fact that he had to stop for frequent breaks allowed her to catch up with the wily beast. Thundegar had sent them out after herbs, which grew in the wild, and Rastas seemed only to want to play. This was Allette's third time away from the glade without Thundegar, and she did not want to disappoint him. Her strength had returned, and now she could be of real use to him. He'd taken care of her, and she felt compelled to repay that debt in one way or another.

A myriad of thoughts bombarded her consciousness, and she

walked without really seeing the world around her. She'd found a semblance of happiness here, but she would not be satisfied until she found her way back to the *Maker's Mark*. She also wanted to know what had happened to her father, but that seemed a far less likely outcome. The men who'd taken her father remained a mystery, but she did know where his cargo had ended up. Though she knew not the figurine's function, the fact that it seemed to have decided her fate gave her no reason to think its purpose noble. It had seemed such an innocent thing the first time she'd seen it, but now she knew that it was much more. One day, she vowed, she would hold that figurine again, no matter what it took. The people of the Heights had taken everything from her, and she would know why.

A gnarled hand reached from the thick growth and wrapped around her wrist, the grip painful. Allette let out a cry and tried to pull away but could not.

"Hold," Thundegar said, and Allette slowly relaxed. "How many times have I told you not to think and walk? Just walk. If you think and walk, you don't heed what your eyes see. What do your eyes see?"

It took Allette a moment to see what he was talking about, but when she did, she was grateful the old man had been there for her. Nearly blending in with the vine around which it was curled, a good sized wood viper watched her from about eye level. Allette might not have walked straight into it, but as Thundegar had told her before, the highly venomous snakes were always prickly and would strike on the slightest provocation.

Rastas appeared on the trail ahead, looking annoyed that Allette had ruined their game.

"How long have you been watching us?" Allette asked, embarrassed.

"The whole time," Thundegar said, and Allette flushed. "You do remember what I sent you after, don't you?"

"Yes, sir," Allette said, and she turned to go, but then she stopped and spun to face him, unable to keep her curiosity under control. "Why do you stay here?" she asked before he could walk away.

"Where would I go?"

There was pain in his words, more pain than Allette had been prepared for, and she asked no more. Instead, she reached down and picked at a nearby cluster of leaves, eyes open and senses engaged. Rastas crouched beside a nearby tree, nearly blending in. Allette gave him a playful look, and he wiggled his rear end before leaping out to get her. When he reached her, the cat sprang into the air and kicked off of her thighs with his powerful hind legs.

Thundegar shook his head. "Crazy cat."

"What kind of cat is he?"

"Cloud cat," he said. "This is the only place they live, and only high up where the clouds are closer. Down lower is the domain of the bigger predators."

"Like wolves."

"Wolves, indeed, and bigger cats and snakes and a host of things you don't want to run into. That's just in the forest; below, in the Jaga, there're more things that'll kill you than those that won't. Up here it's wet, but there is much less chance of being eaten while you sleep."

That thought made Allette shudder.

"That's why I grew the fence. I needed a sturdy, permanent barrier to keep the big predators out. Everything grows fast here, especially if you give it light. It took a lot of work, and I nearly killed myself a half dozen times, but I managed."

"Where did you live while this place grew?"

The silence hung for a while, and Thundegar looked as if he were reliving painful memories. "Here and there," he finally said. "This is far more manageable. And most of the critters respect my boundaries. Rastas can handle small trespassers, and the two of us can handle most others. Sometimes, though, all you can do is hide."

The last part was said in almost a whisper, and it frightened Allette more than anything else.

"If the black dragons ever come, hide in the water," Thundegar blurted a moment later. "Don't try to fight them. Just run. The river is south of here or west. They don't come often, but I wanted to make sure you knew what to do."

"Yes, sir."

"Stop. Dig these two plants up by their roots. Don't break the root."

Allette handed him the brimleaf, as he called it. The plants to which he pointed were unfriendly looking with long, pointy stalks that appeared to have a knife's edge. Wanting to avoid those edges, Allette wrapped her hands around the base.

"That's it," Thundegar said. "Squeeze them together and mind the edges. That's it. Now work it side to side. Easy . . . easy . . ."

It was difficult not to snap at the man while she struggled, but Allette kept her mouth shut and worked the dangerous stalks back and forth. There was a snap that she felt in her hands, and the stalks came free with a suddenness she hadn't been expecting. Thundegar jumped back, making certain to stay clear of the needlelike points.

"Sorry," Allette said, but he said nothing. Setting the first aside, Allette wrapped her hands carefully around the second plant, again being extra careful around the stalks. Visions of the sharp plants severing her flesh kept running through her mind, and she took extra care. After wiggling it back and forth, she felt a similar snap, but this time she was prepared for it, and Thundegar didn't have to take evasive action. Rastas watched from nearby, looking bored.

"Watch," Thundegar said. Using the flat of his palm, he pressed down on the stalks, just above the root. He took out his knife and cut straight down just past his hand. "Up and down," he said. "Side to side is a good way to end up with bloody fingers. Understand?"

Allette nodded and he handed her the knife once he'd finished separating stalk from root. It was tougher cutting than it looked, and Allette grunted with the effort. Normally she would have drawn the knife backward as she cut, but Thundegar's warning was fresh. Soon she had her own root cut free. "That was a lot of work for something that doesn't look very tasty."

"Perhaps," Thundegar said as he turned and moved back toward his home.

His home, not her home. He'd taken her in, but this was not where she belonged. This would never be her home, she told herself. Someday she would make it back to her ship, and her father would be there, and everything would be as it should. It was a meager hope, but it took root and drove her forward.

Rastas bolted past her as they approached the glade and was the first there. He crouched down and moved into the glade as if there could be any manner of predator waiting, and Allette knew it to be true, which made it all the more frightening to watch. But then Rastas was back and bouncing sideways at them with his ears pinned.

"Get in there, you crazy cat," Thundegar said, but Allette knew the man would be lost without his companion. The two of them made an effective team, and she was just there to make things awkward. These two had a rhythm, a routine that worked for them, and she could only imagine how disrupting her presence must be. Not for the first time, she was grateful for Thundegar and Rastas.

"Thank you," she said, a catch in her voice.

"For what?"

"For everything," she said. "For taking care of me when I was sick, and feeding me, and teaching me, everything."

Thundegar just nodded and opened the door to the house. When Allette caught his eye and made it clear she expected an answer, he sighed. "I didn't do anything that any other wouldn't've done in my place."

"You and I both know that's not true," Allette said. "There may be others who would act as you have, and those are good people. You, Thundegar, are a good man."

Thundegar just nodded his head slowly. "Thank you."

After washing the roots, Thundegar put them in a shallow layer of water that boiled in his pan. "A pot would be better," he said, "but we'll eat good anyway. We just have to keep turning these. Slice us up some bulbroot and whickleaf."

Allette did as he asked, trying to fall into a rhythm, to be a functioning part of this household and not just a drag on their resources. If she were to stay here, she would need to find her place. Thundegar knew this, of course, and that was why he'd sent her and Rastas out to forage. She wasn't ready yet, and that was why he had shadowed them. It burned her pride, but she was certainly glad she hadn't been bitten in the face by a wood viper. Thundegar was better off keeping her from getting hurt than trying to nurse her wounds. She flushed deeply with those thoughts.

"This place isn't meant for people," he said, as if reading her mind. "This place belongs to everything else. The Heights and the Midlands might be ruled by men, but the Cloud Forest and the Jaga are ruled by everything else. Those who venture in are as welcome as a roach in the lord chancellor's chambers. Do you understand?"

"Yes," Allette said. "It's like the sea."

Thundegar gave her a confused look.

"People aren't meant to be there, and it's a constant struggle to stay alive. One wrong move, and it's over."

"I think you're starting to get it," Thundegar said. "I built this fortress so that I might have a defensible position, so that I could defend myself from the ceaseless and unpredictable attacks. You saw for yourself; there can be no respite, there can be no rest here. I'm tired."

Guilt rose anew to the fore of Allette's many complex feelings, and she knew she had made things worse for Thundegar. He was stretched to his limit, and she was an even greater burden.

"But with you," Thundegar said, "with you, we have a chance. You and Rastas and I can accomplish more than Rastas and I alone." On his unspoken command, Allette added the ingredients she'd chopped to the pan, and Thundegar sliced the now much softer roots and sprinkled on some seasoning. Then he pulled the pan from the flames and placed it on the slate table. "Here," he said, handing her a pointed wood implement with a slight hook at the sharpened tip. He grabbed another like it and skewered a slice of root that was browned around the edges.

Allette looked for a piece that was cooked about as much, the pan was thick and cooled slowly, and the roots continued to cook even as they ate. Grinning like fools, they devoured the buttery roots, and Allette had to admit that they were well worth the effort, and perhaps even the risk of bloodshed.

With a full belly, Allette moved toward her sleeping spot on the stone floor.

"Sleep in the hammock," Thundegar said. "Rastas won't mind. He sleeps with you anyway, and you're going to need your rest."

"Why is that?" Allette asked with a yawn, wondering what task he would have for her, and looking forward to the challenge.

"Because tomorrow we leave for the Midlands."

Chapter 8

Like rain from a clear blue sky, power can come unexpected.
--Pelivor, flightmaster

* * *

The shining sun belied the struggles of the night before, making them seem as if they were but a dream. The Arghast gathered on the sandy southern shoreline of the Godfist gave evidence enough. Sinjin and the others were saddened by the loss of life, but they took great pride in the Wind clan members they had rescued. The *Dragon's Wing* had never borne such a load, but it was a mostly gratifying haul.

Halmsa of the Wind clan mourned the losses heavily, blaming himself; that much was clear from his posture and expression. The news of the death of Sinjin's parents weighed on the man even further. "You have a very good boat," Halmsa said to Fasha. "Thank you. Our boats were not as good."

An understatement, perhaps.

"Where were you going?" Benjin asked.

"To the land of our fathers," Halmsa said, "to the place of dragons."

Sinjin still couldn't believe it. Halmsa had dragon eggs. They were not as large as Sinjin would have guessed, and he couldn't count how many there were, but it was more than a handful. Dragon eggs. Feral dragon eggs? They had to be, Sinjin realized. The regent queen was dead.

"Where did you get those eggs?" Sinjin asked, and everyone turned to look at him. He'd been silent for much of the journey and had participated little in the discussions on what to do next. He'd been listening and thinking.

"They came to me in a vision," Halmsa said.

"You dreamed and when you awoke, you had dragon eggs?" Sinjin asked, incredulous.

"No," Halmsa said. "They came to me in a vision, on the top of a big rock, so when awake, I climbed the big rock and I waited. They tested my patience, and I nearly left, but she came to me in the night of my despair, all black and cold, and something else. She gave me the eggs, just as the vision promised. Now we must go to the place of dragons, but our boats are not good like yours."

"You got these eggs from a feral dragon?" Sinjin asked.

"Yes," Halmsa said.

Benjin and Fasha both took a step backward.

"No fear," Halmsa said. "These are not feral dragons. These are our children. If I do not fail them, they will rule the skies. It has been foretold. I must not fail our children."

Despite his words, Sinjin and others eyed the dragon eggs with a great deal more anxiety than they had initially.

"What did this dragon look like?" Sinjin asked.

"Big," Halmsa said, and he thought about it for a moment. "Biggest feral I ever saw. Old too. Looked like she'd been in a lot of fights. Wings were ragged and torn. And smart. Looked like she knew things I didn't--many things."

A strange feeling stirred in Sinjin's gut; suspicion, fear, and even a little hope followed. Still, he was far from certain; feral dragons often looked alike, and they were known for their fighting, even among themselves. Any number of feral dragons could fit Halmsa's description, and Sinjin realized that he was pulling hope from little solid proof, but still part of him thought it could be the feral queen that had crashed into the Inland Sea along with Kyrien and his mother. If the feral queen had survived, then there was the chance that Kyrien survived, and perhaps if Kyrien was alive, he would have found a way to save Sinjin's mother . . . perhaps. Either way, Halmsa seemed determined to take his people to the Firstland. At least Sinjin assumed it was the Firstland that the Arghast referred to; again, he lacked sufficient evidence to be certain. He'd always been taught to act only on known facts and not on hearsay and assumptions, but at the moment, he had little besides assumptions.

Since truth wasn't likely to present itself to him of its own volition, he would need to seek it out.

"Could you show them how to build and sail a proper ship?" he asked Benjin.

Benjin looked doubtful and cast a questioning gaze at Wendel.

"I could teach them, given time," Sinjin's grandfather said. "Are your people willing to work and learn?"

"The Dragon clan will do anything to get our children to the place of dragons."

"I thought you were the leader of the Wind clan," Sinjin said.

The assembled Arghast issued a low murmur, and it looked as if some of them were praying.

Then Halmsa spoke. "Do not speak of them, for they are gone. We are the Dragon clan."

Feeling foolish for asking, Sinjin flushed. "I'm sorry," he said.

"No sorry," Halmsa said. "The Dragon clan owes you everything. We will repay you; we will. I give my word as clan chief."

Sinjin's grandfather walked to his side. "This is more about your life than mine, m'boy. I'm an old man, and I've lived a full life. You've everything ahead of you. What is it that you want?"

"Peace," Sinjin said. A long silence followed, and finally Sinjin coughed and gave a different answer. "I'd love to go home, but I don't want to make things worse."

"Perhaps we should send a message to Trinda," Wendel said. "Do you have any concessions you want to request?"

It didn't take long for Sinjin to decide. "Only this," he said, "I want the people to know that I've come back, and anyone who wants to join me should be allowed to do so. If this concession is granted, then I'll not contest Trinda's right to Dragonhold. I'll take my people and go."

Perhaps all those boring lessons his parents had forced on him had done some good after all, he thought, though the bigger part of him wondered what in the world he was doing. He had nowhere to go, nothing to offer anyone except the opportunity to leave the safety of Dragonhold. Still, he knew Durin would come and Uncle Chase. That alone would make his world a better place, and he knew he could count on Uncle Chase to give him good advice. And to have his friend at his side would make everything else easier to bear.

"So it's settled," Benjin said. "Wendel, Jensen, Jessub, and I will disembark with the Arghast near the foothills, where we can get to good wood. Fasha will sail the rest of you to the harbor. Are you sure you don't want to stay with us, Sinjin? It may be safer."

"I don't think Trinda is going to try to kill me," Sinjin said. "And I want to be there when Durin and Uncle Chase come."

"I know they'll come if they're able," Benjin said, and Sinjin's grandfather nodded his head in agreement.

"Don't get yourself set on this working out a certain way," Wendel said. "Chase loves you, and Durin has been your faithful companion. If they don't come, know that there's a reason.

"Yes, sir," Sinjin said.

Tacking into a steady wind, the *Dragon's Wing* sailed along the coast of the Godfist. Benjin and Fasha were unwilling to risk the lives of so many with flight. Pelivor assured him that he and Gwen could fly the ship with the Arghast aboard, at least for a short distance, but Benjin still objected.

"I know how the Arghast are when it comes to flying," Benjin said. "I don't want any of them jumping overboard while we were in the air just to see if they can fly."

Fasha nodded in agreement.

"All this flying has ruined me; I must admit," Benjin said after a time. "Is it me, or does traditional sailing now seem dreadfully slow?"

Fasha gave him a hard look. "Flying the ship is cheating in almost every way. Sailing is still a superior mode of travel. Or perhaps you think you could swim faster?"

Bowing to his wife, Benjin accepted defeat.

* * *

Harborton was a strange mixture of destruction and construction. Blackened and charred buildings stood beside the new, bright and stark. This was what healing looked like, Sinjin admitted, and knowing that Trinda was behind it came as something of a shock. He'd heard that her rule was fair and just, yet he had wondered at her motives. Perhaps she was just lulling everyone until she was ready to reveal her true plans. For the moment, there was nothing for Sinjin to do but wait. He'd watched Pelivor go with a mixture of anxiety and jealousy. Still, it made sense to use him since almost no one on the Godfist knew him, and thus, he had no grudges against him, and he had power a plenty to take care of himself. Sinjin appreciated Pelivor's volunteering to go, but that didn't change the fact that he wished he could have gone himself.

He was home, yet he would not even get to see the place where he grew up, the place that meant everything to him, his mother, his family. His mother had brought life back to Dragonhold; Trinda was little more than an opportunist, and he was nothing more than a coward. A braver man would've gone himself.

Another thing that bothered Sinjin was the act that Trinda had put on during all the time she'd spent within Dragonhold. Always she had played the slow-witted dolt. Always she had used her child's form to make everyone think she was harmless. Now they knew the truth; she was anything but, and she had known all along, of that assumption Sinjin was almost certain. How could she not have known? And even if she hadn't, how could she plan her takeover of Dragonhold so quickly? The thoughts nagged at Sinjin, and he began to pace. He said nothing to those aboard, and people stepped out of his way when he passed, the look on his face making it clear that he didn't want to talk.

The problem of the Arghast came to the fore of his thoughts. He shook his head and mumbled something under his breath. Nothing seemed certain in his world, and he wondered if helping them get to the Firstland, if that was where they were truly destined, was the right thing to do. So much hinged on things his mother had started, things which were now left for him to finish. How a weak and ignorant soul like himself was supposed to carry on the work of the most powerful person in the world was beyond Sinjin's understanding. In that moment, he realized Trinda might have done him a tremendous favor. In her absence, would he have been called upon to lead? He was, after all, the next in the line of succession, if one were to view his as a noble bloodline, but it had never been that way here on the Godfist. Noble bloodlines were the way of the Greatland, and he doubted the people of the Godfist would see it that way. Perhaps having Trinda rule on the Godfist was for the best. From all appearances, she was doing a fine job of it. Seeing his people working together, rebuilding after what had seemed like complete destruction, lightened Sinjin's soul, and he almost smiled. Still, there was a great deal more to be done.

Part of him wanted to stay and help his people, to be an instrument of his nation's rebirth, but not at the cost of peace; always that thought kept him from acting. One friend or countryman dead was too high a price. But that gave him no real option except to leave. Accompanying the Arghast to the Firstland seemed the logical course, but the thought terrified Sinjin. The tales he'd heard of the Firstland involved horrible battles and monsters, and it didn't seem like the kind of place that anyone would go. If he had understood Halmsa correctly, it was the place of dragons that he sought, and that alone gave Sinjin pause. That was the place where the regent dragons had been defeated, where his mother had chosen to go instead of staying and defending Dragonhold. Sinjin still couldn't say exactly how he felt about that.

Not looking where he was going, since people had been moving out of his way almost automatically, it came as something of a shock when he slammed into an unmoving body. The surprise wore off quickly when he saw Kendra. She made no move to get out of his way, and there was no apology in her eyes.

"You look like a worried hen," she said.

"I'm just thinking," Sinjin said.

"Well, stop doing it with that pitiful look on your face. All your pacing is making everyone nervous, including me, so stop it."

"Maybe there's good reason to worry," Sinjin said. "Has it occurred to you that we've no place to go? The dragons may not be attacking now, but what about when they've nursed their wounds and decide to come back even stronger? What then?"

"Then we fight."

Those words defied response, and Sinjin went back to pacing.

"That's not much of an improvement," Kendra said. "Your mood is catching, you know. Now just about everyone aboard is on edge."

"I'm sure they have enough sense to be worried on their own," Sinjin said. "They don't need me to tell them their lives are in danger."

It seemed those words also defied response. Kendra huffed and left him standing there, her scowl chasing away just as many as Sinjin's pacing. Still, he made sure to look up more often so as not to run into anyone else. On one of those occasions, he saw Gwen watching him.

She said nothing when he met her eyes; instead, all she did was cross her arms over her chest and raise one eyebrow. Sinjin wasn't certain what it meant, but he knew it wasn't good. Usually when Gwen crossed her arms like that, he was only a mistake or two away from getting decked.

* * *

When one of the largest carriages on the Godfist appeared on its way to the harbor, four horses pulling it, Sinjin knew Pelivor was returning, and surely he was not alone in a carriage that size. Behind the carriage came a wagon not much smaller, also pulled by a team of four. Sinjin knew that the luxurious ride had been only a part of the journey since much of the way to Dragonhold was not fit for horse or wagon. Still, it made a statement: these people were being treated well.

Pelivor was the first to emerge, an insuppressible smile on his face. Durin came next and ran toward the *Dragon's Wing*. He'd been aboard before, and he wasted no time in getting to Sinjin. With tears in his eyes, Sinjin's friend lifted him from the deck with his embrace and did not put him back down for a long moment. "You're really here! I can't believe you're really here! I thought it was a trick," Durin said, his voice cracking.

"I'm here," Sinjin said. Then he saw his uncle board the ship. "Uncle Chase!" Again, Sinjin's feet left the deck. Chase trembled and shook when he hugged Sinjin, and he didn't know exactly what emotion Uncle Chase was feeling, but it appeared to be all of them at once. Brother Vaughn came a moment later, and Sinjin stuck an arm out to him, though Uncle Chase still held the rest of him tightly. Brother Vaughn joined the embrace, and Uncle Chase shook again. Then he did as Sinjin had always known him to do, he took a deep, if shuddering, breath and steeled himself.

"It's good to see you, boy."

Those words were enough for Sinjin. He knew the pain his uncle felt, and he had no need to make the man relive it. Uncle Chase had always been there for him and had saved his life more than once. Just having him near was a comfort; it went along with the solace he felt in the presence of his grandfather, Benjin, and others. His world was more complete, and he took a moment to be grateful for that. And so it was that he was standing with his eyes closed, tears staining his cheeks, when Kendra stormed up to him. She glared at him for a moment then she burst into tears and hugged him. Stunned, Sinjin just stood there, not even returning the hug. A moment later it was over and she was gone, disappearing into the deckhouse and slamming her cabin door.

419

Shaking his head, Sinjin looked up and found Gwen watching him. This time she raised both eyebrows before she turned and strutted away. He watched with anxiety and a bit of amusement. Why did she feel the need to strut like that? Women were either easier to figure out than he'd been led to believe or they were completely unfathomable. Sinjin suspected the latter, but sometimes he wondered. Thinking about it gave him a headache, so he turned his thoughts to other problems, of which there were certainly plenty. In the end, he focused on the thing that bothered him the most, which was not having a home. Sailors made their homes on ships, but Sinjin didn't feel comfortable at sea. This was not the life he would choose, no matter how much Gwen wished it were so. That thought stung more than a little since it meant they were incompatible. Gwen loved the sea, and Sinjin loved the land. Impossible.

Despite intentionally trying not to think about her, or perhaps because of that, Sinjin's thoughts moved to Kendra. Also impossible--most of the time she hated him. Well, maybe *hate* was not the correct word. She was frequently annoyed by him, and he spent a lot of his time hoping she wasn't angry. Then there were moments such as today when she hugged him; it had felt so right . . . until she had stormed off. What was he supposed to do with that?

Shaking his head, he tried again to think about what to do next. He could leave the decisions to others, but this was his life, and his grandfather had already said he would honor whatever Sinjin chose. To receive that honor, Sinjin knew he needed to make a choice.

The new passengers were getting themselves settled, and Sinjin noticed men unloading the wagon. Bundle after bundle came, and Sinjin couldn't imagine what they might contain.

"Trinda sent a message," Brother Vaughn said when he returned to the deck. "She says she's no thief. Your belongings and those of your mother and father have been delivered."

Sinjin swallowed. Something about other people packing his life into neat little bundles and tossing them out cut more deeply than he would have guessed.

"I'm sorry, my boy," Brother Vaughn said. "There's a bit more. She says you're not welcome on the Godfist since she cannot guarantee your safety. She says she does not want that responsibility, though she's allowed those loyal to you to leave and sent with them provisions to make your journey a pleasant one. Be well and live long. That is her message."

Sinjin's eye twitched. His mind could not reconcile his memory of Trinda and the one they said now ruled within Dragonhold. If she was as powerful and controlled as Durin had told him, then everything he knew about her was a lie. It seemed impossible that she would fabricate an entire life of misery just as a ruse. No. Most of what he knew of her had to be true. That left him to wonder how and why the changes had come about.

"I'm very sorry," Brother Vaughn spoke into the silence, "about everything. Your parents were dear to me, as are you. I'll do everything within my power to help you in whatever you decide to do."

"What *are* you going to do?" Durin asked.

"I have no idea," Sinjin said.

Chapter 9

If you believe you cannot do something, then you are almost certainly correct.
--Nora Trell, captain of the *Trader's Wind*

* * *

After a long night with little real sleep, Allette watched Thundegar prepare to abandon his home. It seemed surreal, and she felt responsible. It was clear he would not have left this place if not for her. He'd spent two decades building his home, and it was among the most marvelous places she'd ever seen. Still, the Cloud Forest was an unfriendly place, and he himself had said it was no place for people. Twice already, she'd tried to talk him out of leaving, but he would hear no argument.

"We shouldn't need large stores of food or water," he said while rummaging through his implements. "If nothing else, your timing is remarkable; you've hit the seasons just right."

"What about this place? What about your home?"

"The forest will reclaim it within a year," he said, not looking up. "This was never my home, just as the Heights were never my home. There are things I love about this place, but there are things I'd sooner never see again."

"But what about Rastas?"

"That crazy cat'll do just fine. He can run, fight, and swim with the best of them. He doesn't like water, but he lives in the Cloud Forest, for Vestra's sake, and he won't drown. And if there's one thing I know for certain about him, it's that he won't be left behind."

As if on cue, Rastas charged back into the house and leaped up onto his hammock to watch. Allette wondered how much the cat understood. His life and Thundegar's were now in even greater peril than they had been, which made her feel terribly guilty.

"I don't see how we can hope to cross the Jaga without flying," she continued, hoping her words would eventually sink in. "Perhaps we should be thinking of how to get on a dragon flight. Having flown over that place, I can't imagine making it on foot."

"We won't have to cross the entire Jaga," Thundegar said," only a piece of it. We can catch a ship from Mesianto Bay. The place is nearly as dangerous as the Jaga, but I have some things that are prized by the Midlanders, and I should be able to get us passage by ship."

For the first time, Allette felt some real enthusiasm for Thundegar's idea. The longing for the sea was deep in her bones, and her excitement was dampened by only her memories of the Jaga. The Cloud Forest had seemed quaint and welcoming by comparison, and the thought of it let the fear take hold.

"As much as I want to return to the seas, we may never make it across the desert, let alone the swamps and forest. How far is Mesianto Bay?"

"It's far," Thundegar said. "But we'll only be walking part of the way. Trust me."

Allette tried to do as he said, but the ease and relative safety of dragon flight was nearly irresistible. "Where did you get your frying pan?"

Thundegar turned and regarded her with a stern eye. "Even if I'll never return to the Heights, there are some things that should not be discussed. That's among them."

"I'm sorry," Allette said. "It's just that there are some things here that I doubt you brought with you, and you said yourself that you had no metal or metal-working tools. So it made sense to me that you must still have friends, and perhaps those friends could find a way to get us on a dragon flight. Imagine how much faster and safer that would be."

"Impossible," Thundegar said, his visage like a thunderhead. "You are just going to have to believe me. Neither of us is going back to the Heights. What we need are weapons, sharp and sturdy while light and flexible. Fortunately I foresaw the need years ago, and I began making these." Tucked into the woven trees and vines were shafts of polished wood. Thundegar pulled them free and handed them to Allette, who piled them to one side. The pile steadily grew.

"Why so many?" Allette asked. "Are you expecting an army?"

"To be honest, I never knew what to expect. Making these kept my hands busy and nimble during the long nights. For most of my life, I had spent my days making things, and that was taken from me. I had to do something with myself."

"They're beautiful," Allette said when she looked at them more closely.

"Find one that suits you and two more. These'll pay part of our passage."

It took Thundegar no time at all to select his staff and a handful more to carry. Most of those he selected were too tall for Allette but bore elaborate carvings that would surely increase the value. Allette wasn't certain how effective they would be as weapons, but they seemed perfectly suitable walking sticks, and the people of the Midlands loved things that were practical yet beautiful.

Running her hands over the smooth and twisted wood, Allette wondered how Thundegar had created such beautiful staves. The first staff she tried supported her weight well and was light enough that it would not be a burden to carry. It still felt a bit long for her, though, and she set it aside. A shorter staff was partially hidden by the longer ones, but Allette pulled it free. With one feint, she knew this was her staff.

"Take it outside and test it a bit," Thundegar said while he did what he could to pack herbs and spices, though his selection of containers was woefully insufficient. Wooden bowls and cups had served well enough here, in his home, but they would do little to keep the precious leaves, roots, and powders safe and dry. The fact that Thundegar had managed to keep anything dry within the Cloud Forest was a testament to his ingenuity.

Once outside, Allette grabbed the staff at its center and twirled it hand over hand. Thundegar watched from the doorway with a smile. "You've handled a staff before," he said.

"I've had weapons training," Allette said. Rastas watched her from the tree line, his tail twitching. "The staff was never my first choice of weapon, but this one feels good in my hands. It has balance and is light enough to keep my movements nimble."

Stepping from the shadows, Thundegar came with his own staff, and he stood in front of Allette. He said nothing, just lunged forward and swung downward at her thigh. Though clearly this was not his full strength, the blow would have given Allette a nasty bruise had she not stepped aside. "Good," he said. "I'm not as fast as I used to be, but perhaps some sparring will loosen these old joints. Just try not to beat me senseless. My body hurts enough on a good day."

Allette smiled and lowered her staff, all thoughts of retaliation fading with his words. Thundegar then went back into the house and returned with two of the staffs that neither of them had selected. "I won't ask you to use your new staff as a shovel," he said, "but we need to dig a hole."

"How big?"

"Big enough," he said. "Just start digging and I'll let you know when to stop."

Allette wondered what it was the man had against giving her a straight answer, but that just seemed to be the way he was. She accepted him in spite of it, but it infuriated her at times. He seemed to like surprising her with things, and she hated surprises. When he started carrying items out of the house and placing them next to her far-too-small hole, she realized she had a lot of digging to do, so her question was answered. After only two more trips, though, Thundegar stopped making the pile bigger and started digging opposite where Allette worked. She'd never minded hard work; it was something she'd always done, but no one liked to work alone, and having Thundegar digging as well made the task go much more quickly. Once the hole was big enough, Thundegar wrapped some of his most precious belongings in a coarse blanket and placed the bundle in the hole. The two of them carried the slate tabletop from the house and put it on top of the bundle before covering it once again with dark, rich soil.

His frying pan wrapped in his bedroll and a pair of staves strapped to his back, he was ready to leave within minutes. For some reason, Allette was having a harder time letting go of the place than Thundegar was.

"Come on, you crazy cat," Thundegar said. "Let's go somewhere dry."

Rastas ran to his side, head-butted his thigh, and rubbed up against him.

"So I guess that's it?"

"That's it," Thundegar said, and the three of them moved into the Cloud Forest with a strange mixture of excitement and foreboding. If they survived this journey, Allette would be returned to her home, but the very real fact that they might not haunted her. The thought of losing Thundegar or Rastas nearly brought her to tears. Thinking of her father was more than she could hold back, and the emotions flowed. She missed him dearly, but lived every day with the pride of all he'd taught her. She was heading back to her world, the place where she knew what she was about and didn't need someone to take care of her. As thankful as she was for Thundegar, she couldn't wait to get back to a place where she was experienced and competent. For at least a little while longer, though, she'd have to rely heavily on her companions. With resolute will, she committed herself to being as valuable to them as they were to her. When the staves strapped to her back almost immediately got caught in the web of vines and branches that lined what could barely be called a trail, she was humbled once again.

"It'll take some getting used to, I know," Thundegar said, "but the lower we go, the less dense the forest will be. And when we reach the desert, we'll have an entirely new set of problems to deal with; getting tangled in the growth won't be one of them."

Allette kept her mouth shut and concentrated on finding a clear path. Thundegar led the way and did his best to clear obstructions and dangers using his staff, but the growth got thicker and more tangled the farther they ventured from the glade. They were moving into land that he'd less often traveled, and with no one to maintain the trails, the jungle encroached. "These paths were clear just a few months ago. It'll get worse before it gets better."

She'd been hoping the jungle would start to thin soon; instead, it became nearly impassable. Rastas expressed his displeasure when the rains came and there was no place dry for him to lie. While Allette and Thundegar hacked their way through the lush vegetation, he lay under broad fronds, looking miserable as water poured over his soft coat in spite of the large leaves. Frustration set in early for Allette, who had trouble believing just how tough the native plants, branches, and vines were. Knowing many of these plants harbored wildlife and just as many bore natural defenses ready to shred skin, slowed progress even further.

"Maybe we should go back," Allette said. "Maybe all this is just a bad idea."

"No," Thundegar said. "I've waited too long already. I'd given up on living because all the other options were just too hard. I gave up on everything, but you remind me what it is to be alive, and now my hands itch for a hammer and my arms for a woman. No. There'll be no going back."

It was then Allette realized that Thundegar was doing more than just leaving his home; thanks to her, he once again wanted to live his life. Feeling much better about herself, Allette took to the vegetation with renewed vigor, and before long they were moving again, albeit slowly. Rastas dragged himself from beneath the fronds and followed, his fur drooping and matted. When he reached her side, the cat shook and sent musky-smelling water in every direction.

"Crazy cat," Allette said and Thundegar smiled.

* * *

"Fishing is a lousy way to run a ship," Mord said.

Becker Dan steeled himself. He'd known his time was running short. There had been no word from the captain or Allette--just thinking the name hurt. Plenty of correspondence had been received from those the captain owed money, amounts far larger than Becker would ever have guessed. He couldn't imagine how the captain could have borrowed so much. What could he have possibly spent such a kingly sum on?

"We either pay the slip fees we owe," Mord continued, "or they're going to stop letting us sell fish in Maiden Harbor."

"If we keep selling fish in Maiden Harbor, the rest of the creditors are likely to try to seize the ship." As much as Becker didn't want to admit it, Mord was right. "Where do you suggest we go?"

A broad smile crossed Mord's face. "Do you remember when that storm pushed us out into the Endless Sea a few years back?"

"I do," Becker said; it had been a harrowing experience. He knew what was coming next.

"You remember those islands we found?" Mord asked, clearly knowing that Becker remembered. All of them had wanted to explore the islands, which had looked like green jewels amid otherwise deep seas. "Maybe it would be good if the *Maker's Mark* disappeared into the Endless Sea, never to be seen or heard from again."

"And what would you name her?" Becker asked, having known Mord's end game for some time.

"Don't care. This ain't personal, Becker. It's business. The way I see it, the cap'n's dead and so's his get. Dead or locked up. Either way, they ain't coming back. We gotta start over, my friend. Would you rather start anew with all the cap'n's debts or start fresh? A new masthead and some paint and all those debts disappear. Besides, you can't tell me you don't want to know what else is on those islands."

Becker knew he wasn't Mord's friend. The man tolerated him only because of the power he wielded, power not gained by tenure or rank, but by friendship and camaraderie with his shipmates--at least most of them. This was the most difficult kind of power to overthrow, and Mord had little choice but to convince Becker to go along with him; without him, he'd lose well more than half the crew's support. Still, Becker knew he needed to watch his back as well as look out for those he held so dear. After all, it was all of their futures at stake. Becker had done the best he could to preserve Allette's inheritance, but the time had come to bow to practicality. The *Maker's Mark* would be no more. The one thing that Mord was right about was Becker's desire to explore those islands. It had seemed the perfect kind of place to hide things, and he'd wondered ever since the day they had discovered them if someone else had found them long ago and what might still be hidden there. It answered all of the desires that had driven him to be a sailor in the first place, to move without boundaries and to explore and find new places and things.

It was with great sorrow that he gave the orders, and many a prayer was said among the crew. These people knew what was happening, and the significance wasn't lost on them. None of them were stupid; the stupid did not survive at sea. The waves were quick to claim those not smart enough to respect her. Becker knew that trying to find those islands in the Endless Sea was risky; after all, it was not named the Endless Sea without reason. With a prayer of his own, he cast a gold ring into the waves, a rich offering from a man who knew he would need the gods' luck to survive.

* * *

The *Dragon's Wing* moved through calm waters by the power of wind and sail alone. Within her deckhouse, most of those aboard gathered; only a couple crewmen were left on deck.

"We can take it back," Chase said. "I know who's loyal to our cause. We could depose Trinda without much bloodshed."

"Her blood being the exception," Sinjin said.

"I'm sorry, Sinjin," Chase said. "If we're to retake the keep, then she cannot be allowed to live. What she did when she took the keep from your mother was an act of war, as is what she's done to Edling, though he deserves everything he gets. That doesn't change the fact that Trinda is a usurper."

"No," Sinjin said. "No one was killed when Trinda took Dragonhold. My mother was gone, and Trinda knew she wasn't coming back." Sinjin had to take a moment to breathe after saying those words. "I don't think she is a usurper, in that instance; she is an opportunist. I'll grant you the point regarding Master Edling, but as you said, he deserved it."

"If we leave Trinda in power, then we cannot stay, at least not without being in rebellion," Chase said. "We do have the Arghast on our side."

"No bloodshed," Sinjin said.

"I agree with the boy," Brother Vaughn said. "Though I detest what Trinda has done, I don't wish her or anyone on the Godfist dead. Despite her short rule, she's been fair and not without compassion. Some people would rally to her. And Catrin is gone." Realizing what he had just said, Brother Vaughn fell silent.

"All right," Chase said, rubbing the dark, stubbly growth on his cheeks. "Where else can we go?"

After a long silence, Benjin finally spoke. "There is a place that we might go. When I was there last, we were ill prepared, but--"

"No," Fasha said. "The shallows are no place for people."

"It wasn't that bad," Benjin said. "And we would be better prepared this time."

"That's where I almost lost you," Fasha said quietly, and no one argued the point. "The Falcon Isles at least have some civilized places," she continued.

"You call that civilized?" Brother Vaughn asked. "That place is crawling with thieves, pirates, and outcasts. And once you leave 'civilization,' you're at the mercy of Nat Dersinger, whose loyalties are as questionable as his sanity."

Fasha raised an eyebrow.

"No offense intended," Brother Vaughn said. "Not all pirates are created equal."

Fasha said nothing, but she no longer looked as if she might loosen his teeth. Sinjin cradled his face in his hands, and no one said anything for a time. All this was simply too much; his mind could not comprehend the enormity of the situation. He had no home. That thought alone made Sinjin want to cry, but that was not what was needed of him and he knew it. Not to mention that Kendra and Gwen were present and he didn't want them to see him cry.

"The Arghast expected my mother to help them," Sinjin said, and Chase made an annoyed sound. "Halmsa has dragon eggs."

"Halmsa's lost his senses," Chase said. "That man is so convinced in the prophecy that he risks everything just to make it come true; that much has already been proven by that suicidal voyage. I thought Kenward was reckless, but Halmsa makes him look staid."

"About Halmsa," Brother Vaughn said, and the gazes that turned to him were not entirely friendly--perhaps rightly so. "I would not tread on this topic if not for its relevance to this decision." The expressions in the room remained unchanged, and Brother Vaughn coughed before continuing. "What has been described as an attack on Kyrien by the feral queen does not sound like an attack to me."

Sinjin tried not to react. Had Brother Vaughn come to the same unlikely conclusion that he had?

"The behavior strikes me as being a great deal more like a mating ritual," Brother Vaughn continued.

Sinjin listened in silence, unwilling to let himself hope. Even if he was right, it didn't explain why his mother and Kyrien had not come back to him. It was that thought which led him to believe that it could still be correct, that is, if Kyrien and his mother had simply perished in the process. Such things were not unheard of in the natural world, and this case was certainly outside the norm.

"You think those eggs are part regent and part feral?" Benjin asked, looking uncomfortable.

"I know it's a stretch," Brother Vaughn said. "But I still think it's possible. I've no reference for the size of feral eggs, but I know from the description Prios gave me, regent eggs are considerably larger."

"If that's the case," Benjin said. "They might not even hatch."

"Absent a dragon queen, they may not hatch even if they are viable," Brother Vaughn said.

"And if these truly are feral eggs, then what?" Benjin asked.

"We'd have to kill them," Sinjin said, and everyone turned to look at him. "Thorakis was lost to a juvenile feral. What would stop the dragons from turning the Arghast against us?" Kendra's expression changed as she watched him. Was that grudging respect he saw there? "Part of me wants to think that the eggs are Kyrien's offspring, but I'm not even certain that changes anything. How can we know that part feral is not worse than full-blooded feral?"

"I don't know for certain," Brother Vaughn said, somehow able to maintain his optimism no matter how slim the chances, "but my gut tells me that those eggs might be our best hope."

"I wish I shared your confidence," Sinjin said, "but either way, I feel that we owe it to my mother and father to see that these dragon eggs don't threaten the world."

"Just remember that not all dragons are evil," Brother Vaughn said, and Sinjin nodded, knowing there was no sense arguing the point.

Either way, he knew he needed to be there if these dragons hatched. Somehow he knew it would be up to him whether these beasts lived or died, and that knowing put a terrible weight on his heart. He cursed himself for feeling the weight of an imagined burden, but it changed nothing. It was almost the same feeling he'd had when he'd woken from a dream where he and Durin had fought, and even though the fight had never taken place, Sinjin had still been angry with Durin. Reason would tell him these feelings made no sense, but his emotions made it clear that they didn't always follow reason. When he looked up and saw Gwen watching him, he suspected she was feeling much the same.

"I'll go with the Arghast," Sinjin said. His statement was greeted with anxious silence. "Trinda did not say that none of you could remain on the Godfist, and for many of you, this is home. I don't wish to take you away from that, especially not for a life of such uncertainty. I can't even say for sure where the Arghast are going. I just know that I have to go with them."

"You're not running off without me again!" Durin shouted, and to make his point, he moved to Sinjin's side and would not let go of his shirt.

Kendra smiled until Sinjin met her eyes; then she frowned. He would never understand her; of that, he was certain.

"All those here are here by choice, are they not?" Brother Vaughn asked.

Sinjin had expected at least a couple of people to cull themselves from his ranks, but all those aboard seemed set on remaining in his company, and he couldn't help but feel blessed, even if he didn't deserve it. These people had been loyal to his mother and somehow that loyalty had transferred to him. It was a strange thing, and he came to see how dynasties might form. Perhaps not all monarchies were built on foundations of blood spilled, but instead from blood inherited. Regardless, he felt responsible for the futures of all these people and came to know some of how his mother must have once felt. She'd been responsible for the future of the entire world. For Sinjin, his responsibilities did not reach so far, yet they felt no less onerous. With this responsibility came an increased sense of urgency.

"Pelivor, Gwen," Sinjin said, and he saw the glint in Kendra's glare. "Would you take us back to the Arghast with all haste?"

"Is there a problem?" Pelivor asked, his concern clear.

"No," Sinjin said. "It's probably silly of me, but now that our course is decided, I find myself ready to get on with the task at hand."

With a nod, Pelivor headed for the prow. Gwen gave him her most winning smile, and drops of liquid fire dripped from her fingers before fizzling out on the floor. Seemingly unaware, Gwen strutted from the room, ignoring the bits of flame and most definitely ignoring Kendra.

Sinjin prepared himself to pay the price for his choices. When he looked up to Kendra, her arms were crossed over her chest. Sinjin sighed. Only the fact Durin was by his side kept him from melancholy.

"C'mon," Durin said. "Let's go somewhere where we can talk-- alone. They don't need us to sail the ship, and you're not going to believe some of what I have to tell you."

Though Durin whispered, others heard his words, though no one tried to dissuade them from leaving the galley. Part of Sinjin wanted to revert into his childhood self and run off with Durin to play, but he'd changed, and now he had responsibilities. In the end, he decided to do as Durin asked, but his reasons were different than they would have once been. For that, he was sorry. Durin might have sensed the change, but it was clear he didn't care.

"I know you probably think I'm being foolish," Durin said almost as soon as they stepped on deck, "but there're things you need to know, and I'm not so sure I trust everyone else on this ship. Don't look at me like that; Kendra's own mother betrayed you."

Sinjin wished he could argue with Durin, but he could not, and his friend knew it.

"Trinda's up to something. She's got her eyes on more than just the Godfist."

"What makes you say that?" Sinjin asked.

"She's building a fleet of ships--big ships."

"The Godfist has always had a large fishing fleet," Sinjin said. "I'm not surprised to hear it's being rebuilt."

"She's building fishing ships too," Durin said. "And those, she's having built in the dry dock in Harborton, unlike the other ships--the warships."

"And where is she building these warships?"

"In the mountains," Durin said, and Sinjin turned to meet his eyes. "At the top of the mountains."

"How does she plan to get them into the water?" Sinjin asked even as Pelivor and Gwen coaxed the *Dragon's Wing* into the air. A cold, sick feeling overcame him. Durin didn't answer and didn't look as if he felt any better about the implications or the sensation of the ship leaving the water. "Is there anything else?"

"By the gods," Durin said. "They're not going to drop us, are they? Are you sure this is safe?"

"You get used to it," Sinjin said.

Durin shook his head, and he looked as if he were doing his best to appear brave. "Trinda has figured out how Dragonhold works."

"What do you mean?"

"The water, the lifts, the stone forest, all of it, somehow she knows how all this stuff works. I don't get it. She always seemed like such a dolt, and now she's figured out the secrets of your mother's ancient underground fortress."

"Will it help the people of the Godfist survive?"

"Yes," Durin said. "I think she's figured out how to have the hold be self-sufficient, though she never says anything about it."

"Good," Sinjin said. "Then it's better that she retain Dragonhold. I've no idea how the hold works, and I lived there my entire life. If she can bring the hold back to its true potential and keep our people safe, then I say we let her do just that."

"It's not all good," Durin said. "She's collecting every herald globe your mother ever made. And she knows how to use them as weapons. And there are other things she knows about in Dragonhold, things she won't talk about to anyone. I bet she wouldn't even admit to knowing about them if she was asked, but I know they exist, and I know she knows. That's one of the reasons I had to come. I wanted to come anyway, but the fact that she was probably going to have me killed was extra motivation."

"You really think she would've had you killed?"

"She told me so herself."

Sinjin's jaw dropped open.

"She didn't use those exact words, but she told me I was free to join you, and that it might be a good idea since she couldn't guarantee my safety. If that wasn't a threat, then I'm an Edling."

His head spinning, Sinjin tried to adjust his perception of reality based on all this new information that conflicted with what he had always believed. Sinjin hesitated. Dragonhold had always seemed like a sleeping giant, but to know that it now lived as it once had, breathing fire and water, Sinjin couldn't help wishing his mother had lived to see it. She had worked for so long to understand the place her father and Benjin had discovered all those years ago, and now that her dreams were coming to fruition, only he remained to witness it. It stung that he didn't get to see it for himself. All his life the people around him had struggled to make a life in that hold, and now someone else had discovered its secrets. Reminded of those who now accompanied him, Sinjin did his best not to feel sorry for himself.

Chapter 10

Each of us has the capacity for greatness, what varies most is the extent of our belief.

--Master Jarvis, teacher

* * *

When at last they reached the lower Cloud Forest, Allette, Thundegar, and Rastas all looked as if they had lost a number of battles, and Allette supposed they had. The Cloud Forest was a worthy adversary, but they had finally won their way free of the thick jungle. What grew at the lower elevations was a great deal sparser in comparison. Here grew majestic hardwoods that cast deep shade beneath a tall canopy. Vines and other creeping vegetation dwindled until the forest was little more than hardwoods, moss, and leaves. Here and there were bushes and other tenacious plants, but traveling through these woods was almost laughably easy. No more did Allette's staves get caught with every other step, and Rastas was having a wonderful time playing in the leaves. When Allette passed between a pair of towering oaks, Rastas jumped out and startled her, then rolled onto his back so she could rub his belly. Soft, light brown, curly hair covered his large but lithe abdomen.

Reaching down, she gave him a good rub, but staying bent over was difficult given her burdens, and she grunted as she straightened. Before she was all the way upright, she froze. Moving between the trees as silently as shadows were wolves. "We have a problem," Allette said. Rastas was on his paws before the words left her lips.

Thundegar crouched down. "Be ready to drop your pack and climb if need be," he said. A low growl came from Rastas, and Allette had never seen the cat look quite so menacing, even when they had first met. This was a real threat, and the cat seemed ready for a fight to the death.

Allette knew wolves could not climb trees, and she knew it would be no problem for her or Rastas to do so, but Thundegar was another matter. He was strong, no doubt, but she'd been with him for weeks, and she'd observed his movements. He had pain he'd never admit, and she thought that perhaps the constant humidity in the upper Cloud Forest had been partially to blame. If they lived long enough for them to get truly warm and dry, she might get the chance to find out. Even with the wolves approaching, the thought of being truly dry was alluring.

"I'll climb when you climb," Allette finally said, and Thundegar made no response. "How far are we from the desert?"

"A mile," Thundegar said. "Perhaps two."

A nearby yip was answered by another even closer, and Allette knew that time had run out. When the first wolf showed itself, it stepped out from behind a cluster of trees and faced Allette. She'd seen this wolf before, and by the way it looked at her, it remembered her as well. Her staff held before her, Allette prepared to fight, though she took a step backward.

"Stop!" Thundegar commanded, and Allette froze. The wolf charged. "Behind you! Blue-faced spider! Attacks anything that touches its web. Duck!"

She barely heard him, yet somehow his words registered. Instead of taking another step back, as her instincts demanded in the face of the bounding mass of muscle and fur that rushed her, she fell onto her back and kicked. It was not so different from when she had thrown the thrower from the Heights, except it felt like the wolf barely touched her, not seeing the web until it was too late. Allette scrambled to her feet and prepared to face more wolves. She heard Thundegar cry out, and she heard Rastas make a sound that she hoped to never hear again. The wolf that had leaped past her, though, was turning and coming back, a look of furious determination on its face, which was partly covered in webbing. Just as Allette squared off and held her staff at ready, she saw a flash of blue moving across the wolf's face and toward its eyes. In the next instant, the wolf issued a high-pitched and strangled cry, whipping its head side to side. The beast charged past Allette and was gone. Another joined it, missing half an ear and leaving a trail of blood behind it.

When Allette turned, she saw Rastas standing over Thundegar, who'd gone down. Two more wolves circled them, nipping and biting at Thundegar, alternating so Rastas could not defend against both of them.

With a cry, Allette charged through the trees and launched herself at the closest wolf. It turned in time to see her boots closing on its face. They collided, and the wolf went down before twisting out from under Allette and charging back into the trees. Rastas was taking parting swipes at the last one, which followed its brethren back into the forest.

Running to Thundegar's side, Allette trembled at the sight of blood. "I gave as good as I got," Thundegar said. "It's not as bad as it probably looks. Help me up."

Doing as he asked, Allette pulled him from the ground. Rastas stalked in a circle around them, his hair standing on end and that menacing growl rumbling in his chest. After he wiped the blood away, a long slash across Thundegar's forehead bled freely.

"Come here," she said, tearing off strips of blanket from her bedroll and securing them around his head. Blood seeped into the cloth, but it kept it out of his eyes, and she hoped it would clot soon. She had no medical kit to stitch with, so it would have to do.

* * *

Standing at the bow, Sinjin watched the shoreline, where the very beginnings of a half dozen ships were beginning to emerge. It was a false sign of progress, Sinjin knew. It would take months for the ships to be ready and seaworthy. There were trees not terribly far from the construction sites, but the trees desirable for building ships grew farther inland. If the Arghast were planning a lengthy sea voyage, they would need sturdy ships capable of surviving storms and high seas. It was no small task to build such ships without the proper tools and skilled workers. Sinjin had his doubts about the Arghast reaching the 'place of dragons,' as Halmsa had called it.

"This isn't going to be any fun, is it?" Durin asked.

Sinjin smiled. It was good to have his friend back. No matter all the other circumstances that weighed on him, having Durin back made it more bearable. "No. I don't suppose it is."

"We might end up wishing we were back carrying water buckets for Miss Mariss," Durin said, and his face contorted with irritation. "And can you believe that all that time we could have just turned the water back on for the entire keep?"

No matter how much he'd grown as the result of all that had happened to him, Sinjin couldn't help but agree with Durin. Knowing all that work had been for nothing made him feel sick inside.

"And do you think anyone will ever thank me for figuring out how to make the keep move? Of course not."

"You did make the discovery by way of laziness," Sinjin said, and Durin punched him just hard enough to make Sinjin shift his weight. When he did, he felt the bulge of Koe, and he pulled the dragon ore carving from his cloak.

"That thing always gives me the crawls," Durin said when looking at Koe.

"I tried to give it to Gwen," Sinjin said.

Durin said nothing; he just raised both eyebrows and waited.

"I thought maybe it would help her when flying the ship."

"How'd that work out for you?"

"Not very good," Sinjin said.

"I didn't think so. You're a smart kid, my friend, but you don't know anything about women."

Considering how things had gone with Kendra afterward, Sinjin couldn't argue Durin's logic, but he said nothing about it, not wanting to admit the changes in his relationship with Kendra. Durin didn't trust her because of what her mother had done, but Sinjin knew her better now. They had been through a lot together, and most of her actions seemed to be in his best interest. Durin would never understand.

Their conversation was cut short when Pelivor lowered the ship back into the water. Shouts and calls came from shore, and Sinjin braced himself as the ship slowed. Durin mumbled something about fair warning while belatedly trying to brace himself. Millie shouted something to the same effect from the galley.

Sinjin, though, took in all the details of what he saw, a knot forming in his gut. There were hundreds of Arghast, which was a blessing and a curse. The larger labor force would make constructing the ships easier, but such numbers also required more ships, which meant a lot more wood. The Arghast, though, had previously gathered enough wood to make their canoes, and a steady stream of fresh-cut timber was traversing the sands. The Arghast horses once again displayed their might as they hauled what looked like locust trees. Knowing how hard locust wood was, Sinjin considered going back to Harborton to request tools from Trinda. Surely Strom could make them the tools they needed. First, though, he would talk with his grandfather.

Not long after the ship settled into the shallows off shore, boats were lowered, and Durin climbed into the same boat as Sinjin, seemingly unwilling to let him out of his sight. He couldn't blame his friend. The world had become a very uncertain place, and he never knew what might come next.

"Six months," Wendel said when they approached. Despite his age, the man remained strong and vital, his skin slick with sweat and browned by the sun. "And that's pushing it. There should be an extra month or two of sea trials before such a voyage, but something tells me there'll be no sea trials. For that reason, I insist the greatest care be taken during construction. Fortunately, the Arghast seem to be listening to good sense. I guess nearly drowning the entire clan has instilled a sense of the risk involved."

Durin gave Wendel a hug, and Sinjin did the same.

"Now you two rascals behave yourselves," Wendel said. "I know how the two of you get when you're together. Now's not the time for any foolishness."

Sinjin flushed, feeling partly angry that his grandfather would scold him so, but mostly because he knew they both deserved it. Old guilt remained, and he realized then that he would need to leave that guilt behind someday. It hung from him like an anchor, impeding any progress he might make, but still he could not absolve himself of the responsibility for the things he'd done. It felt as if he had not yet suffered enough for his missteps, large and small.

Brother Vaughn came to Sinjin's side, fondling some trinket in his palm, and Kenward joined them. Before Wendel spoke again, Kenward looked down at the item that Brother Vaughn was turning over and over in his hand. It appeared to be a small cube of inlaid wood with intricate patterns made up of many colors.

"Where did you get that?" Kenward asked.

"It came from a ship," Brother Vaughn said, his interest clearly piqued, "a very old ship that lies at the bottom of the God's Eye. Do you know what it is? Is it some kind of treasure?"

"I know exactly what it is," Kenward said, "though I've never actually seen one before. I've read a number of descriptions. What you have is treasure of sorts. It's a key."

"A key," Brother Vaughn said in a near whisper while looking at it intently as he rolled it in his palm. The light danced over the surface. "What kind of key is it?"

"It's a very special key," Kenward said, "the kind only the captain of a ship would have. It is a key to the secondhold."

"What's a secondhold?" Sinjin asked.

"The hold is the one everyone knows about," Brother Vaughn said, and Kenward nodded. "The secondhold is the one that no one else is supposed to know exists."

Kenward looked as if he wanted to say more, and Brother Vaughn appeared ready to immediately launch an expedition to the God's Eye, but Wendel cleared his throat. "Halmsa and the remainder of the timber crews should be back in the next few hours," he said. "We should probably figure out exactly what we plan to do before he returns. The man is passionate and strong willed. We need to be decided in our course, of a single mind, and firm in our stance. Do you understand me?"

Sinjin and the others nodded. Benjin and Fasha had joined them and heard enough to express their agreement. The Arghast were a passionate people, and they could easily overpower those not of an accord. In truth, Sinjin felt deeply for these people. Because of their beliefs, they were leaving everything behind, even their prized horses. Sinjin knew the bond between the Arghast and their horses was sacred, and leaving their companions behind must have been heartbreaking. The fact that the horses had returned across the desert after a series of drumbeats and whistles was a testament to their loyalty. These noble beasts who'd been abandoned by those they loved came anyway, and they worked as if it were an honor to do so. It was simply astounding.

"I want to help them, Grandfather," Sinjin said, and no one spoke in opposition. "Without our help, they'll never make it."

"I believe you're correct," Benjin said, and Wendel nodded.

"If we're to remain here for an extended period," Morif said. "Then our position should be more defensible. Trinda has made it clear that we're not welcome here, and I'm not certain the fact that we're building ships will buy us enough time to do what needs doing. The girl could easily perceive the ships as a threat and send her forces here to deal with us."

That was exactly the outcome Sinjin needed to avoid. Though Wendel had wanted them to be of a single mind by the time Halmsa returned, it was not to be. All conversation ceased when a single horse raced along the returning timber route. The burden the rider carried made it clear it was Halmsa who approached. He refused to go anywhere without the eggs, and all those who witnessed his breakneck approach knew something must be terribly wrong, or he would never risk the eggs so. All work stopped and a hush overtook the encampment, save the sound of hammering from a single workman unaware of what approached.

Sinjin was still trying to understand what was going on when Halmsa reined in his horse before the assembled group, dust churning under the hooves of his faithful mount.

"Must go to place of dragons," Halmsa said without dismounting.

These words were nothing new to anyone there, and silence held sway as they waited for Halmsa to elaborate, but he was short of breath.

"Dragons must not hatch here, or all will perish. It has been foretold."

Still Sinjin failed to see what had changed. Perhaps Halmsa had experienced another vision, he thought, and he was about to say something to soothe Halmsa's anxiety, but the man did something unexpected.

He unwrapped the bundle that sat atop his saddle. All those close enough to see watched with a mixture of anticipation and fear. Halmsa said nothing, and though he still found the dragon eggs fascinating to look upon, Sinjin failed to see what good Halmsa hoped to gain from showing them the eggs again. In the next instant, everything changed as one of the eggs moved.

* * *

Martik Tillerman should feel like a fool; he knew he should, yet he didn't. When given the option to go with Sinjin, he had stayed. This place had become his home, and part of him still believed it would go back to being as it was under Catrin's rule--another bit of foolishness. Then had come the orders to build ships designed to carry armies great distances, which was enough cause for alarm. "Build them on plateaus near the peaks," she had said, "or build footings on the upper slopes. You should still be able to build the ships more quickly than if you had to haul the timber to the dry docks."

Having pointed out that it would be impossible to move the ships to the sea once they were constructed, Martik abandoned any argument. The look she'd given him made it clear that she had thought this through. This was cause for even greater concern since it meant she must either believe a mighty flood was coming or she knew of a way to teach hundreds of people to fly ships as Catrin had done; neither seemed at all likely. Yet there he was, placing the finishing touches on massive ships that would never see water in his reasoning. Martik was not a man guided by academics alone, and this was one of those times when his gut, his instinct, his feelings outweighed what his senses and logic otherwise told him. This belief was made easier by the fact that there was no real, lasting harm if he was wrong. At worst, he would have taught a great many people the skill of ship building.

No matter how he justified the continued work, he was still unnerved by the otherwise obvious futility. Did he really need to inspect the sealant again? Would it really matter if those timbers were never beneath the water line? It was tempting to take shortcuts, to be lazy and careless, but those things were not in Martik's nature, and he made sure that even if this was only an instructional exercise, that it be one that taught the people how to do the job correctly. For Martik, there was never a time when that wasn't important. He'd seen people wounded and others killed by carelessness in engineering or execution, and he wanted no more added to the already too high number of casualties.

After another inspection, Martik walked along the footing and examined the braces and stonework. A completed ship would do no one any good if it slid down the mountainside. The foundation had been constructed with care and to support a far greater load than even the massive ship, and there were no signs of stress. Martik nodded his head in satisfaction. Then he stopped and looked north to where the mainmast of the newest ship was being raised into place. That ship would be the last ship, unless Trinda requested more, and it had gone together in record time.

Was it a job well done, or was it a job that had never needed doing in the first place? The question was made more poignant by the knowledge that Wendel Volker was building a fleet on the other side of the Godfist. Had Pelivor told Trinda about the fleet, then she might have never let anyone go, but Martik wished he had been told. Now he knew that he'd been building unusable ships in the mountains while those he cared about built ships in the desert, ships that would sail for somewhere; where he didn't know. It made it all the more difficult to take his work seriously. He could still go and help them; his job was nearly finished here, and they would only be getting started if he had his guess. It was then that he heard a line snap followed by frantic shouting.

Knowing he would be too late to have much effect on the outcome of the accident, he ran as fast as he could.

Chapter 11

Those who seek great power are generally the least suited to have it.
--The Pauper King

* * *

Allette's shoulders ached, and her hands cramped. Descending the mountain with Thundegar had been difficult, but traveling with him through the desert was pure torture. Rastas moved with a determined stride, but Allette could see that it was taking a toll on the animal. Perhaps the only respite provided was the shadow Allette's burden cast. Over their heads, they carried a canoe, a heavy and clumsy canoe.

"I still don't understand why we're carrying this thing across the desert," Allette said.

"Have you ever tried to make a boat out of sand?" Thundegar asked.

Allette didn't respond at first. "I flew over this place, and I don't see how this canoe could possibly be of use. This is craziness."

"You flew over the Jaga once, and you know all its secrets? Be happy for the shade," Thundegar said, again refusing to explain the canoe. It infuriated Allette, but she could get no more from him, and she saved her air. Sweat stung her eyes, and she cursed under her breath. What irritated her most was the fact that they had somehow found the strength to do it, proving her wrong. It had seemed impossible, but Thundegar had insisted they could do it, so they had. Most of the sandy desert was behind them, and ahead lay a dry, cracked landscape. Behind, as if teasing them, the sound of thunder echoed. The rains had come to the Heights days ago, yet none of that precious moisture fell on this parched landscape that so desperately needed it. This added to her frustration as much as anything.

After a bad step, the rough-hewn oar strapped across her shoulders along with her two staves smacked her in the back of the head, and she thought she might scream. Why couldn't it rain here? And why were they still carrying this useless canoe across the desert? Again the land threatened to turn her ankle, and Allette saw that they had reached the ends of the massive expanse of broken land that looked like cracklature. Their progress was slowed further, and now Allette's neck ached from trying to watch her footing.

Looking at Thundegar's back, she asked herself why she was following this crazy old man, asked herself why she didn't just go back and try to sneak her way on to a dragon flight. She'd seen the worst the forest and desert had to offer, and she could go wherever it was she chose. The power of the land spoke to her, and she could sense its awareness of her arrival. Here, where the land was but a husk, she could feel little, but there was nonetheless something there: anticipation. Even with all her complaints, the sight of Thundegar, walking before her in the shade of the canoe yet still wearing that ridiculous hat made her smile. He'd asked if she wanted one, and even offered to show her how to make one for herself, but that had been after he had showed her how to cut the canoe out of a downed tree, and she'd been in no mood for any of his suggestions Why did one need a hat if they were carrying a canoe?

"This'll do just fine," Thundegar said unexpectedly. Groaning as they did, they lowered the canoe to the sun-tortured land. Rastas quickly lay beside it, trying to stay within whatever shade it provided. "Come on, you crazy cat, get in the boat," Thundegar said, and he stretched a blanket over a section of the canoe to provide a meager amount of shade. Rastas did as he was told, which showed Allette just how unhappy the cat really was. The desert was quite obviously a bad place for a cat. All of this contributed to the sour feeling in Allette's gut. What were they doing out here? Adding to her worry, Thundegar unstrapped his oar and staves from his back and climbed into the canoe. With his oar over his knees, he pulled his hat down over his face. "You might as well get some sleep," he said. "You'll need all the energy you can get for later."

Allette grunted. Of course she'd need her energy; she would, after all, have to carry their useless canoe. And how was she to sleep with the sun in her eyes. At that moment, she questioned the wisdom of ignoring Thundegar's lesson in hat making. Now that she had the desire for a hat, she had no raw materials. Glumly she acknowledged that she couldn't make a hat out of sand either. The admission did little to improve her mood. In the end, she settled into the bottom of the boat and squeezed her head under the blanket where Rastas lay. He gave her a dubious look when she first pushed her way into the space he already occupied, but he gave a resigned huff and shifted himself to make room for her. The heat was still unbearable, but at least the sun was out of her eyes and not causing the skin on her face to burn any further. Never would she have guessed just how powerful the sun could be in the desert; it was as if Vestra shone more brightly there and would scald any who chose to defy him.

Thoughts of the gods were not something Allette had ever been comfortable with. Her father had always cast offerings to them into the sea, but that had seemed more ritual than observance. Now she felt the light of the sun god as if it were fire and she reconsidered. What if the gods were real after all? What if the comets were more than just beautiful? She'd always loved to watch them in the skies, and they rewarded her by coming in larger and larger numbers. It was hard to look into the night sky without seeing a comet these days, and Allette pondered the legends of the goddess while trying at the same time to find sleep. Rest was impossible to find, though. She was hot and sweaty and cramped, and even if she'd been comfortable, the flurry of thoughts and emotions that filled her would not be denied. In the quiet of her mind, the thoughts pounded against her resolve, and she nearly cried.

The sun went down of its own accord and mostly unnoticed. Allette had entered a world of half sleep and half worry, and though she was not entirely conscious, she was somehow still aware of her surroundings. Around her came the sound of something that her soul recognized instinctively. Like an old friend, it called to her, softly at first then more loudly. When Allette came awake, she found herself lying supine in the bottom of the canoe, Rastas's rear end pressed against her face, and one of his paws rested on her nose. Above her, the skies were alive with a slight moon, stars, and dozens of comets, casting plenty of light to see by and plenty of light to be reflected by the unexpected miracle around them. Allette watched in awe as water bubbled up from the ground as if by magic. She shifted her eyes over to Thundegar, who still slept. The sound of his snoring was perhaps the only thing that convinced her he was not casting some spell. She'd heard of such things before, but she had never thought to see such a thing for herself. Water sprang from the land, a true treasure indeed.

It took only a few more minutes until the water began to gather around them, and sooner than Allette would have imagined, the canoe began to drift. Even more amazing and terrifying were the other things that now moved in the water. It seemed unfathomable that anything could have been living in that dried-out place, but just as the water had sprung from nowhere, so did life. Thundegar finally came awake when something large slammed into them.

"Oh. Well. It's begun then, has it?" he asked.

"Uh, yeah," Allette said.

"Keep your hands in the boat. Don't touch the water if you don't absolutely have to. These things haven't eaten in months."

That thought struck Allette with terror. She'd always dealt with the fear of drowning at sea; it was what had kept her alive for most of her life. The thought of hungry monsters surrounding her was perhaps the most frightening thing she'd ever experienced. In that instant, she was so grateful for their canoe that she could find no words. Never would she have guessed such a thing was possible. Had they come without a canoe, then they would have already traveled farther, but this lake would have suddenly sprung up around them filled with danger.

"Once it's deeper, it'll be less dangerous, but only by a small margin," Thundegar said. "If you end up in the water, try not to panic. Be sure not to tip the canoe over in your effort to get back in. You understand me?"

"Yes, sir," Allette said.

"The cat needs to stay in the canoe. You hear that, cat? Stay in the boat."

Rastas gave the man a look that said he was no fool. Allette wasn't certain what talking to the cat would accomplish, but he seemed to have no interest in going into the water on his own, and that was enough for her. The growing lake grew deeper by the hour, and Thundegar guided them around areas where the surface churned. This became increasingly difficult as the night wore on, and when the moon reached its zenith, Allette dipped her paddle in the water, uncertain it would come back out. A riot of activity filled the still only waist-deep expanse.

"How did you know?" Allette asked, now in awe of this man who had saved them from near certain death.

"About the water?" he asked, turning to grin at her.

"Yes," she said softly, afraid to let the fish and whatever else was in that muddy slurry know she was there. Long, sleek bodies erupted sporadically from churning water, and she'd no desire to know what those things were.

Thundegar just shrugged. "Happens every year."

Allette flushed. She was a fool. In this place she knew nothing. Here she was but a child, and that shamed her. Always before she'd been strong. Even when she'd failed, she had failed with strength. "I'm sorry I didn't trust you."

Thundegar laughed. "So you've considered what it would be like to be swimming right now?"

"I have."

"I won't belabor the point then," he said, and she silently thanked him for it; she was embarrassed enough. "You see that big comet there, the one with the streaks of red and green in its tail?"

"Yes."

"Just behind its tail there's a star. It used to be brighter, but you can still see it," Thundegar said. "That's what we're aiming for."

"Yes, sir."

"Things are going to change a great deal around here in a hurry. The water is just the beginning."

Allette didn't like the sound of that. She also didn't like knowing just how wrong she had been. It shook her confidence and made her wonder if she could trust her own instincts in the middle of all this land. The water here was a mixed blessing; it gave them an easier route in what Allette now knew was the perfect mode of transportation in this new lake. The nighttime air cooled, and the water seemed to draw the heat out of everything. Allette went from feeling as if she'd been in an oven all day to shivering from the sudden damp cold. Rastas curled up between her legs and shared his warmth with her, which helped. Sudden changes in weather were something Allette clearly understood, and she just did her best to take advantage of the cool. She put her oar back in the water and rowed with renewed vigor.

"Good," Thundegar said. "You're correct to want to cross as swiftly as possible. Things will become more difficult as we go."

The man failed to elaborate on his warnings, which annoyed Allette to a certain extent. There had been no reason to be secretive about the water, and there was no cause to hold back details on how things might become so much more difficult for them in the future. Would it not be better if she were prepared for whatever threat awaited? Part of her wanted to admit that he had taught her a powerful lesson in his secrecy and that perhaps she hadn't yet earned his confidence. Perhaps she was not yet worthy of knowing whatever it was he so obviously held back.

When Vestra announced his coming in the false dawn, Allette saw something she hadn't expected, at least not so soon, yet there it was: a tangled mass of white and green. Floating in gathering clumps were colonies of sprouting greenery. At the first blush of light, the plants seemed to reach for the sun, yearning for the only god that had graced the skies of Godsland for thousands of years. This god they all knew, this god was predictable and reliable. Istra was a fickle goddess, and her light brought with it great uncertainty. Perhaps she had never given the gods true consideration, she thought, and it occurred to her that she would now learn of them whether she wanted to or not. Choice was no longer hers, ignorance no longer an option.

While Thundegar slept, Allette rowed, aiming for a spot in the sky she hoped was where the star had been. She was aided in that by the same thing that concerned her so much now. The bloom had continued to gain momentum as the sun fed the ravenous blanket of greenery. The floating masses grew larger and denser, and the way ahead looked as if it were entirely blocked, and only when she pushed them farther into the growing tangle of new growth was she able to find a way that was clear. Behind her was a trail left in the carpet of green that was straight and narrow, though farther back, nearly out of her vision, she thought she could see the vegetation closing back in.

Still she paddled in a dreamlike state, not quite certain all she was seeing was real. Flowers bloomed and insects danced amid the eruption of life. It assaulted Allette's senses, and she continued to paddle even after Thundegar awoke and could have taken over. Together they made better time, and Allette rowed in a trance. Eventually she felt hands around her wrists. Her arms had stopped moving, perhaps some time ago, she didn't know. Thundegar pried the oar from her hands and laid it in the bottom of the boat. Darkness had come again, and Thundegar bade her to sleep. She was unable to argue.

* * *

Standing at the prow of the *Maker's Mark*, Becker Dan wondered at the course his life had taken and how quickly he might find the end of his days. With no coin and no real plan, the faith his crewman had in him was waning, and it was only a matter of time before Mord made them a better offer. Honor can stand up to greed for only so long, and he had to admit that wanting to get paid for your labors was hardly greed. Still, it felt like a betrayal. The captain must be turning in his grave, if he was truly dead. Becker could find no other explanation that made any sense. From all the evidence he could find, it appeared the captain had gambled in a big way and lost.

This was a big part of Becker's problem. The man they had all looked up to had let them down. At the least, Captain Kilbor had betrayed their trust, and this made it increasingly difficult to muster loyalty. Becker would forever be seen as second to the man who had betrayed them. Most knew Mord was a greedy scoundrel unworthy of complete trust, yet all knew him to be ruthlessly efficient. A man such as Mord could fill your coin purse if you didn't mind his methods. Becker knew he would need to go along with Mord for a time. Eventually he would find a way off the ship. The next time they came even close to civilization, he would leave the *Maker's Mark* behind. The ship had been his home and his life, but if he didn't escape, she would also be the death of him. If the crew decided to follow Mord, then Becker would quickly find himself on the long end of a short plank.

At that moment, though, there was little to do but sail. The familiar rhythm calmed the men and gave Becker a chance to think. Plans formed in his mind, and he contemplated their weaknesses and what he must do to prepare. Of all the seas he'd sailed in his life, these were perhaps the most treacherous. As if to prove his point, he saw the lookout scrambling down the mast from the crow's nest. They had been sailing under an order of silence, and the man was breathing hard by the time he reached where Becker stood. At least the men still came to him, Becker thought. Mord moved to his side, and the lookout addressed him when he spoke. Becker frowned.

"Ship in the distance, due west," he said, "black as night and limping under partial sail."

Making a ship look wounded was an old trick used to draw pirates, and Becker immediately suspected a trick. "It could very well be a trap," he said before Mord could speak. The other man cast him a baleful glare.

"There's always risk," Mord said. "That is why most cowards don't become sailors."

The hook had been baited, but Becker wasn't biting. Fighting with the man would only force the crew to finally decide where their loyalties rested, and Becker wasn't certain how he'd fare.

"Let's see if she can outrun us," Becker said before he lost control completely. "Full sail."

Given a task and the prospect of financial gain, the crew moved with alacrity. Mord muttered something under his breath, and Becker didn't ask him to repeat himself. All he had to do was survive long enough to make his escape. He could no longer trust anyone, and he could tell no one, which pained his noble heart, but those loyal to him would have to forgive him. His departure would send a clear message, and those with good sense would follow. If they were lucky, they might even cross paths again. It was a great big world, though, and Becker thought it might be best for him to get lost in it. A single trip to Maiden Bay and he'd have enough coin to live a comfortable life. He'd known this day would come eventually; he just hadn't known it would come so soon.

"We're making time on them, sir," the lookout called down, freed from the command of silence, and the crew responded with a cheer.

Becker looked at the ship more closely, the details becoming clearer as they gained on the ship. The lookout had been right when he'd said the ship was black as night. The shapes that moved on deck were nearly as dark, and some didn't look human. Becker's blood went cold. Perhaps his chance to escape with his life was already past. The wind shifted and a foul smell reached his nose, making him gag.

"I don't think this is a ship we want to overtake," Becker said, and Mord glared at him. Perhaps the man was blind and unable to smell. "The only thing we'll find on that ship is death."

Mord spit on the deck. "Coward," he said.

The moment had come. The will of the crew would be tested, and Becker knew when it began how it would end.

"Do you want to run away from this wounded ship?" Mord asked his crewmates. "Or do you want to see what's in their hold?" The crew raised a cry after the latter, and Becker was about to open his mouth to speak when Mord gave the order, "Bring us up alongside her!"

In truth, he need not have given the order since their current course would do just that, but the fact that no one questioned his order was of the most significance. The balance of power had shifted aboard the *Maker's Mark,* and Becker Dan's days were numbered. He swallowed hard after acknowledging that the number was far too small. With agonizing steadiness, the *Maker's Mark* closed the gap on the damaged ship. The smell grew stronger, and Becker started to hear complaints from the crew. At least not everyone aboard was a fool.

"Monsters!" the lookout cried.

"Death," Becker said.

"Land!" the lookout called next.

From out of the mists materialized the towering green islands, rounded and worn and covered in vegetation. The other ship was headed straight for the closely packed islands. It looked as if there were winding inlets and sheltered coves all along the vertical shores. Nowhere did he see beaches or gentle slopes; most of what he saw was sheer cliffs. Seabirds crashed into the waters around them, and some swooped across the deck, usually with silvery fish in their beaks. The image of it was burned into Becker's memory.

"Let's burn the foulness from that ship!" Mord shouted. Becker would have objected, but the crew moved to obey his order without question. Pitch, torches, and a small catapult were brought from the hold. Even the small catapult required four men to carry it and just as many to wind and fire it.

The black ship made for all the speed they could muster, now throwing anything they didn't need overboard. It lightened their load and left debris in their wake, but the crew retained their resolve. Then, though, the monsters on deck shed their crude armor and slipped over the side of the ship.

"Get us out of here," Becker shouted before anyone else could react. The crew had seen the same thing he had and they complied. Those at the catapult had loaded a vessel with flaming pitch, and even as the ship began its turn, the catapult fired with a loud thrum. The vessel soared through the air, spitting flame and gouts of black smoke. It struck the black mainsail at mid-sail, and liquid fire poured down the cloth. Though the sails appeared to have been fireproofed with tar, the pitch clung to it and ate its way slowly through. The tar then began itself to burn, slowly and steadily, the growing wind feeding the flames.

A cheer rose up from the crew and ended abruptly as the hull of the *Maker's Mark* thrummed once, twice, then over and over. Cries came from those near the rails, and black claws appeared on the rails not far from Becker. "Repel boarders!" he shouted, and the crew responded with an ordered drill, practiced and skillfully executed. Frightening as the monsters may be, they were not enough to threaten the crew of the *Maker's Mark*. For a moment, Becker dared to hope.

Then he saw a dark-robed figure move to the stern of the black ship and level his arms directly at Becker; at least that was how it felt. He'd feared men before but never like this man. Here was power to corrupt the world. He could feel it; he could smell it. The air was polluted with it, and it smelled like rain. Red lightning leaped from the figure's outstretched robes and struck the mast. The lookout fell screaming to the water. Becker felt as if he'd struck a tree at a full run. Like many around him, he was swept from his feet by the force of the attack.

"Get us out of here!" Mord shrieked.

There was still a chance, Becker knew; the fire had slowed the black ship. If only they could turn aside and distance themselves, then the danger would be greatly reduced. When he was once again able to get his feet underneath him, he stumbled to the wheelhouse and took the wheel himself.

"You're going to have to tack into the wind," Mord yelled.

Becker was trying to do just that when he looked beyond the black ship. The angle at which they viewed the islands had changed, and Becker was able to see within the folds of the landscape a natural harbor sheltered by towering peaks. He saw the scars on the landscape first, places where the forests had been cleared away, leaving little more than stumps as evidence. Below that and along the waterline rested ships, dozens of them, many in various states of repair and perhaps just as many under construction. Turning to look back out to sea, a warning on his lips, he saw another fleet approaching; these ships were larger and of different design, but the threat they posed tipped the scales out of the *Maker's Mark*'s favor. "I had one heck of a good run," Becker said to himself.

"Make speed, man!" Mord called, and Becker just held his course, knowing their fate was already decided.

* * *

With an open palm thrust backward, Thundegar commanded Allette to silence, and for once, she obeyed. He'd been on edge all morning, ever since they had found an existing path to follow. It meandered and did not always take them exactly the way that Thundegar wanted, but it was far easier than fighting through the now-thick vegetation. Still, Allette could tell by his posture that he was worried. Then came a loud snorting sound and a spray of water, followed by deep bellows of rage. Thundegar paddled backward as fast and as hard as he could, and

Allette did the same without knowing what it was they faced. She knew only that they needed to move, and fast. A wall of water helped to carry them away from the thick bushes they had been about to paddle through.

Pushing that wall of water was a massive body that looked black and slick in the water. When a bulbous head suddenly broke the surface, its nostrils as big around as melons and tusklike teeth aiming straight for them, Allette thought they might be done for. An instant before the beast would ram them, the head disappeared back beneath the water, and for a moment, the canoe was lifted out of the water by the bulk of this wild beast trying to squeeze beneath them, but then they were sinking back down into the turbulent wash.

"What was that?" Allette asked, despite Thundegar's request for silence. She was simply unable to keep the words inside of her.

"Swamp pigs," Thundegar said. "One of them can be your best friend out here, but two of them are always trouble."

Before Allette could ask why this beast was their best friend, Thundegar pushed them back into the channel left by the first swamp pig. The massive swine moved through the vegetation with relative ease and cut a channel through the ever-changing landscape. The carpet had now grown so dense that the roots had found fertile soil, and pushing through the growing mass became almost impossible with the canoe. Therefore, they were somewhat at the mercy of the swamp pigs.

"This one is going mostly in the right direction," Thundegar said. "We'll just see how long we can follow behind and make good progress. Keep your eyes open for other swamp pigs. We need to avoid being between them if they decide to charge each other."

Allette did not argue. She remembered the fear of seeing that massive creature headed straight for her. If it hadn't gone under them, then surely they would have been sunk. Looking down, Allette saw Rastas about as unhappy and uncomfortable as she'd ever seen him, and she reached down to give him a pat on the head. He pushed up into the caress but did not insist on more. He seemed satisfied for her to work toward getting him away from this place as quickly as possible.

"Where did those things come from?" Allette asked, certain such massive creatures could not have been lurking under dried mud.

"Deeper in the Jaga, where there is always food," Thundegar said. "These are some of the first to return to the swamps, but there'll be more. All that come will graze well. Soon there will be channels crisscrossing the marsh. As long as we keep going the correct general direction, we'll eventually find what we're looking for."

Allette would've liked to have known exactly what that was, but she was hesitant to question his judgment again. That was a lesson she was supposed to have learned.

Chapter 12

There is magic in art and art in magic; the two cannot be separated.
--Gemino, sorcerer and artist

* * *

The first egg that moved could have been a trick of the light, but the rush of many people breathing in sharply at once told Sinjin that it wasn't so. Still Halmsa did not seem satisfied, and he held forth his precious charge so all those assembled could see. When two eggs moved independently, Sinjin felt something stir within him. It was not terror, and it was not anticipation, and though he could not describe it, he trembled from the powerful mixture of emotions.

"Dragons must not hatch here," Halmsa said again. "No time for big boats. Must make more small boats. Must go now."

"Where is the place of dragons?" Sinjin asked. Those around him waited in silence.

Halmsa closed his eyes and appeared to be listening intently. Then with his right hand, he pointed.

"East and a little south," Kenward said. "The only places in that direction are the Keys of Terhilian and the Firstland beyond that."

"The Firstland was the home of the regent dragons," Sinjin said. "So that makes sense."

"I must get to this place," Halmsa insisted, a look of pure terror on his face. "Must leave now."

"You'll never make it in time," Brother Vaughn said. "It's a voyage of many seasons."

What color that remained in Halmsa's face drained away.

"How long do you think we have?" Sinjin asked.

Halmsa shrugged.

Sinjin turned his questioning gaze to Brother Vaughn.

"Weeks," he said, "at the most."

"There's only one way, then," Sinjin said, and Benjin nodded, as if he'd already reached the same conclusion. "Only the *Dragon's Wing* can get you there in that short a time."

"Even that is a stretch," Benjin said. "Pelivor and Gwen would have to fly us nearly the entire way nonstop. I'm not certain even they can get us there in time, but you'll have a far better chance. And perhaps the deck of my ship isn't the worst place for them to hatch. It's not 'here' after all."

"Must reach place of dragons," Halmsa insisted.

"Then you must leave your tribe behind and travel to the First--er," Benjin stumbled on the words, "the place of dragons aboard the *Dragon's Wing*. My wife and I will do our best to get you there in time."

"No," Halmsa said. "Will not leave tribe."

"We have only the one ship," Sinjin said, hoping Halmsa understood. The man was smarter than anyone else gave him credit for, but still Sinjin knew some of his beliefs were unyielding.

"Dragons must choose," Halmsa said, his words filled with conviction and steadfast belief. "Tribe must be there."

"How many can we fit on the ship?" Sinjin asked.

Benjin frowned. "Any more than fifty people aboard, and we'll be hard pressed, and those fifty will not have a comfortable trip. I'm not certain Pelivor and Gwen can fly us with that much weight on board, and the gods only know what it'll be like when we hit the water again with so much force."

"How many on a skeleton crew?" Brother Vaughn asked.

"Ten," Benjin said. "Two can sail her, but it takes ten to fly her--ten that know what they're doing, that is. With a full ship, I ought to estimate more just to feed so many, but surely some of the Arghast can cook."

By the look on Halmsa's face, he didn't like Benjin's tone. "Forty," he said.

"Thirty-five," Benjin said. "There are some besides my crew who I can't leave behind."

"Thirty-five," Halmsa nodded, his voice heavy with emotion, and for a moment, he hung his head. But then one of the dragon eggs moved. "Thirty-five," he said again, saying it as if it were a curse.

Turning from them, Halmsa gathered his people. When he spoke, Sinjin could not follow his words, but he knew the intent. He could feel the energy; it burned and crawled over his skin. Such anxiety rose from those gathered that Sinjin thought they might suddenly erupt in flames. Sinjin understood when Halmsa said "thirty-five," and the land trembled beneath his feet as the Dragon clan reacted. Shouts of disbelief and dismay rose from the crowd like the raucous calls of flocking birds. There seemed no words, only anger and worry. Then the shouts took on a different tone. As the Dragon clan seemed to accept the number, thus realizing they instead of the dragons must do the choosing, chaos erupted.

When the Dragon clan fought among themselves, it was not like war, where the goal was to kill your opponent. It seemed as if the goal were only to subdue those you fought. Surprisingly, those who had been pinned, knocked down, or otherwise dominated did not rejoin the fray after recovering; instead they moved to one side and watched, heads hung.

At first Sinjin had feared the angry mob would turn on them, but it was as if they did not exist. The Arghast were concerned only about other Arghast. A particularly heated contest approached where Sinjin, his grandfather, and the others stood. In an instant, one of the fighters was thrust between Sinjin and the others. The man turned to face Sinjin with a wild look in his eyes. Drawing back his fist, he looked as if he would knock the head clear from Sinjin's shoulders. Then the man's face registered recognition, and he bowed to Sinjin. One of the men he'd been fighting had also been swinging, and when the first man bowed, the second man's punch passed through empty air and landed squarely on Sinjin's jaw.

Hearing only a ringing sound, Sinjin drifted into darkness.

* * *

Rowing through the growing swamp was becoming increasingly difficult, and Allette wanted nothing more than to get back on solid land. It was an odd yearning for her, but this swamp was nothing like the seas. Given her choice, she'd be back on a ship, but she knew there was a long way left to go before that would happen. Walking would be preferable to blisters on her palms and rear end. Thinking back to the beginning of the journey, she wasn't certain that was entirely true, but it at least seemed better than her current level of discomfort. Thundegar didn't look much better, and Rastas spent most of his time panting.

When the canoe stopped once again with an abrupt thump, Thundegar turned to Allette. "That's about as far as we can row," he said. "We're not far from the jungle, which puts us back on foot."

"Will we cross the entire jungle?" Allette asked, not really wanting an answer.

"Not if we can help it," he said, looking as if he would say no more, as seemed to be his way.

Now that it came time to part with the canoe, Allette was loathe to do so. She thought of securing it to a tree so they could use it again if they came back, but they weren't supposed to be coming back. Doubt crowded her thoughts, and she could not convince herself that they would succeed in this journey--she, an old man, and a cat. What chance did they have in the jungle at the heart of the Jaga?

Even as a sailor, she knew well the barrier the Jaga presented between the Midlands and the Heights. In a constant state of chaos, ruled by dragons and beasts and savage men, it was an impregnable quagmire. If not for the combined might and capabilities of the Midlands and the Heights, then the feral dragons might rule all the land. The ferals had been quiet in recent years, though. Allette remembered from her dragon flight that there had been little worry of attack.

Stepping out of the canoe, she left her oar behind. Happy to have her staff for support and to probe for snakes in the brush, Allette had to acknowledge the fact that she was woefully unprepared for travel through the jungle.

"Hopefully we won't have to travel far through this, but be very alert until we are out of here. This place will kill you as quick as you can blink. Be especially aware of where you put your feet and what is just above eye level. If I tell you to stop, you stop and don't move. You hear me? I don't want any argument out of you."

Allette just nodded. The land she stepped onto was soft and spongy, but it held her weight. Rastas followed, looking very uncertain about this decision. In places where they had to wade through the water farther across than Rastas could jump, Thundegar carried the cat, who complained loudly. Allette began to wonder if Rastas would be able to complete the journey. She wasn't certain she and Thundegar would survive, and it seemed no more likely that the cat would. With a lump in her throat, Allette walked behind the cat, who was currently picking his way around a series of small pools.

Before them, the land once again became dominant, and the water was left behind, save for rivers and streams, which meandered through the thick vegetation, black and glossy against the verdant landscape. Along the shores waited reptilian creatures as long as their canoe had been, and snakes nearly as long sunned nearby. Turtles, crabs, and other life skittered about, providing food for the larger predators. That was no place Allette would have wanted to row, and she was grateful to be on land; she hoped to stay as far from that river as possible. The lush forest surrounding it seemed a far safer place. There was life within those trees, but it was less evident and less immediately threatening.

Thundegar must have agreed since he started moving away from the river. Rastas stayed low to the ground, and a deep growl occasionally escaped him. Allette agreed with his sentiment and hoped for something to save her from this journey. It was a silly hope, but she needed something to hang on to at that moment. Knowing her death could wait behind the next rock or tree frayed her nerves, and her heart beat fast. Thundegar pushed the large, floppy leaves and thorny vines out of the way with his staff, and most times there was nothing there, but other times were different and frightening. Thundegar stopped suddenly, his staff held out at as much length as he could muster and still keep control. Again, the cause was a snake. This one was particularly incensed at their intrusion, and the mostly camouflaged snake struck Thundegar's staff three times before springing from the branch and onto the ground. With a cry, Thundegar leaped backward and slammed his staff downward. Again the snake struck, and Allette tried her best not to imagine what it would feel like to have those venomous fangs sink into her flesh.

Once Thundegar was absolutely certain the snake was gone, Allette stepped forward, Rastas at her side, still growling. Whenever he looked at her, his eyes seem to say that he thought all of this was a very bad idea. She couldn't disagree. They should have stayed. They should turn back. The thoughts were relentless, despite how far they had come. The trees were older, taller, and more widely spaced as they moved inland. The foliage was mostly at the canopy, which was high above them, and much of the forest floor was hidden in shadow. And underneath it all was a scent that pulled at Allette, drew her forward like wind in sails.

Rastas, seemed to feel much more at home and was as happy as she had seen him in days. While Allette avoided the shadows, not knowing what might lurk in the darkness, Rastas had no fear and charged through them as he played. It was good to see the cat running and playing, and it brought a smile to Allette's face. "Crazy cat," she said softly with a chuckle. A moment later, she was glad she hadn't been louder.

A not-too-distant shout split the air, "Black ships on the horizon, sir!"

More shouts echoed through the trees, and the wind shifted, now bringing the scent of the sea strongly to her nostrils. It was then she saw a mast through the trees, and her heart beat faster. Thundegar held out his finger for silence, and Allette rolled her eyes. Crouching down, Thundegar moved toward the shouts, and soon the trees thinned and gave way to a red clay shoreline. Making her way out to sea was a midsized merchant vessel flying no colors. They don't want to be found, she thought.

The ship was tacking hard into the wind, trying desperately to get clear of the small harbor. That was when she saw the black ships. Like a growing stain on the horizon, a massive naval force approached, and it looked as if it were being propelled by some dark god. Thunderheads loomed over and behind the massive armada, and chain-lightning danced between the ships. It made Allette's skin itch, and her breath caught in her throat. They should go back. They should go back now. Turning to Thundegar, the plea on her lips, she saw that he looked equally thunderstruck.

It was obvious that the fleeing ship would be consumed by the approaching darkness, and Allette regretfully let go of the hope she might escape this place by ship. Thundegar had done his best.

Somehow he'd managed to get them to this harbor, and he could not have known that the dark ships would converge on that very place. She'd known of such ships, she'd even seen one or two from a distance. Anyone with good sense wanted nothing to do with those aboard the black ships. Shivering at the memory, Allette knew the evil that approached, and she knew their only choice was to flee.

"We must get back inland now," Thundegar barked, and Allette retreated without answering. Rastas slunk along beside her, his belly nearly rubbing the ground.

The three moved with speed born of terror, and only when a massive shadow passed over them did they stop. Twice more the shadow raced over the foliage, and Allette felt like a mouse hiding from a circling hawk. A feral dragon was up there, watching her, just biding its time before plucking her from where she hid. The urge to run was nearly undeniable; every part of her wanted to run, to get out of the gaze of this predator, but somehow she maintained the will to resist. Only when Thundegar stood from his huddled crouch did Allette even breathe. Never before had she felt such raw terror. Truly the magic of the dragons was all that she had heard, and she hoped never to see one again. She hoped it again for good measure. Then they were off, trying to get as far out in front of the approaching armies as possible. Allette guessed they had only a few hours before many of those ships landed, and she knew her guess was a pretty good one.

Rastas breathed hard beside her, and he often stopped, only to catch up through a burst of speed a moment later. Allette, on the other hand, tried to find her stride, strong and consistent. Thundegar matched her pace, but his breathing was labored, and she worried for him. Sweat poured from both of them, and the landscape took on an otherworldly hue. Allette knew that a normal person would have already succumbed, but somehow she persisted. Even more, the old man nearly matched her pace. They were beyond what Allette would have thought the limits of her own endurance, and it made her feel good. Inside of her that knowledge built, and she moved faster. Purpose fueled the fire, and soon she was outpacing Thundegar, and even Rastas was having trouble keeping up. What was that she saw in the old man's eyes, she wondered. Doubt?

Slowing, Allette initiated a break. This was something Thundegar had always done, but he said nothing at first. "You're strong," he said after catching his breath.

Allette wasn't sure how he could have taken so long to come to that conclusion; she had, after all, carried that canoe across the desert. But then she considered the fact that he meant something entirely different. That thought frightened her, and she turned away, not wanting to continue that line of conversation. Thundegar took the hint and saved his energy. They were going to need it.

* * *

Feeling like something heavy was sitting on his head, Sinjin reached up slowly and touched the puffy skin around his jaw. He sucked air between his teeth in response to the pain and hoped it would go away quickly. Looking around, he saw that he was in his cabin aboard the *Dragon's Wing*. Next, he realized he wasn't alone. Durin was curled up on the floor, fast asleep. The ship didn't creak and groan as Thorakis's ships had; she barely made a sound, which made Durin's snores stand out even more than they otherwise would have.

Unable to get back to sleep, Sinjin was driven by curiosity. The last thing he remembered was someone ducking under a punch. That must have been it, he realized through the pain in his head. It must have been a spectacular punch. Climbing down from his bunk, Sinjin did what he could to keep from waking Durin, but it was impossible. The cabins were small to begin with, and there were simply not enough places for Sinjin to put his feet.

"What are you doing?" Durin finally asked, his voice sounding grumpy and tired.

"I wanted to know what happened, so I was trying to get past you without waking you."

"Nice job you did of it," Durin said. "The Arghast beat each other up until only thirty-five remained, and then we left. You got punched in the face, so you got to avoid all the work of loading supplies and preparing the ship. Happy? Can I go back to sleep now? I worked all day."

"I'm going to take a walk out on deck."

"I wouldn't if I were you," Durin said. "There're too many people on this ship, and everyone onboard is in a mood. If I were you, I'd stay right where you are. Trust me."

Sinjin should have taken his friend's word for it, but still he knew he would not be able to get back to sleep until he understood more of the details of their current situation. Losing the precious hours he'd been unconscious made him feel as if he were no longer in control, not that he felt as if he were in control most of the time. Still, this was worse than usual, and he found himself disoriented; it was as if he'd been knocked from one world and had woken up in another.

"How's your face?" Benjin asked when he saw Sinjin emerge onto the overcrowded deck.

"It aches," Sinjin said, "but it'll be all right. How big was the guy who hit me?"

"As tall as a barn, and nearly as wide," Benjin said with a grin.

"That sounds about right," Sinjin said. "The Arghast who were left behind?"

"A dispirited group, for certain, but we left behind plenty of help to get the ships constructed, trialed, and sailed. The rest will be along when they can. We've more Arghast on board than there are dragon eggs, so Halmsa seems satisfied. Sometimes I wonder about that man's sanity, yet he keeps being proven correct. It's uncanny."

Sinjin couldn't argue that point. Perhaps the things his mother had taught him about prophecies had been wrong. Perhaps Istra's power granted that gift to some, just as it had given his mother great power. And though she hadn't believed them at the time, hadn't even his mother's visions come to fruition? Still, it railed against most of what he'd been taught, and he couldn't convince himself it was true. In the end, he would help Halmsa whether the visions were real or not, and for that reason, he let it go.

Walking to the stern involved pushing his way through a throng of amazed and terrified Arghast. All of them had spent their lives being told that someday some of them would fly, and here they were, soaring above the waves. In truth, Sinjin noted, they were more or less skimming along just above the water. The speed was still impressive, but Sinjin knew the strain on Gwen and Pelivor must be great. He'd caught a glimpse of the man; the silks had been pressed tightly to his skin and clung to him, moist with sweat. The air itself smelled of rain, and whitecaps appeared on the waves below.

Gwen sat, as she always did, between the mighty wooden tubes. People were kept clear of the openings to the tubes, but Sinjin knew he could approach Gwen by staying between them. When he drew near, she looked up with a tired smile.

"How are you faring?" Sinjin asked.

"Not as well as I would like," she admitted. It was a rare moment, and Sinjin recognized it. "It looks like the same holds true for you. Does your jaw hurt?"

"Yeah," Sinjin said. "Is it the weight of all the people onboard that's giving you trouble?"

"Yes," Gwen said. "Pelivor is having trouble maintaining altitude. He could get us higher than we are, but he's afraid he'll drop us, so it's better to be closer to the waves."

"And for you?"

"It's more difficult than when we only have fifteen or twenty people aboard. The harder I push, the harder it feels like the world is pushing back. I can keep us moving faster, but I'm not sure for how long. From what Brother Vaughn was saying, I don't think we're going to make it.

Don't look at me like that; I'm not being pessimistic without good reason. We haven't been in the air all that long, and already I feel as if we've been flying for days."

"I know you said you didn't want to accept Koe as a gift," Sinjin said, fingering the carving in his pocket, careful to avoid the sharp teeth, which had surprised him before by drawing blood.

"No. I still won't accept it," Gwen said, defiant anger flaring in her eyes.

"I don't want to give it to you," Sinjin said, taking a step back in the face of her seemingly unjustified rage. It was even clearer to him then that he would never understand the opposite sex. "I just want to *lend* it to you, not for your sake, but for Halmsa. Look at him; he knows we won't make it at this rate. And I'm completely useless, except perhaps for the fact that I have two of the most powerful objects on all of Godsland. I can't do a blessed thing with either of them, mind you, save maybe keep the dust off of them."

Gwen was smiling now, though the look she gave him said that he'd already made his point and he was pushing his luck.

"I'll want this back when we reach 'the place of dragons,'" Sinjin said, handing Koe to Gwen, keeping the cat's teeth facing his palm. He didn't want to scare her off. The carving could be far more intimidating than its size would imply.

It was with a sense of reverence and awe that Gwen accepted the dragon ore carving from him. It felt strange, seeing it in her hands. Other than himself, his parents had been the only ones he'd ever seen touch the crystalline cat. After gazing at the cat with a sense of quiet disbelief and a hint of fear, Gwen didn't appear to have accessed the power within, but then she closed her eyes and leaned back her head. A glint of light flashed over the surface of the carving, and Gwen's eyes opened wide. She sucked in a deep breath that came back out as a shudder. When her eyes seemed to once again focus, Sinjin watched the concentration take over her face, and the whine of the tubes changed tone. The ship sailed higher from the additional force and Pelivor whistled.

"What's going on back there?" Pelivor called out.

"Just giving Gwen a little assistance," Sinjin shouted.

By the look on Gwen's face, the speed still required a great deal of effort and concentration. Sinjin moved back toward his cabin, a smile on his face. He'd actually done something right; he knew it. And now he needed to do something else. The additional thrust would put even greater strain on Pelivor, and though he had Sinjin's mother's spider stone, Gwen had already said that he was having trouble.

Waking Durin was inevitable, and his friend gave him a very

unfriendly look. "If you weren't my best friend in the whole world, I'd punch you in the shin," Durin said from the floor of the cabin.

"Take the bunk," Sinjin said. "I won't be back for a while. I have some things I need to do."

"Don't rush back," Durin said as he crawled into the bunk, looking as if he'd be back to sleep as soon as his head hit the soft, goose-feather pillow.

Grabbing his mother's staff, Sinjin stepped out of the cabin and closed the hatch. Holding the staff gave him a chill, just as touching Koe did, but for different reasons. Koe was entirely of Kyrien's and his mother's making. Kyrien had converted the noonstone into dragon ore--through what process Sinjin had no idea--and his mother had used her power to carve the otherwise immutable stone. The staff was another thing entirely; this was something that was thousands of years old and had been protected and cherished for generations. Yet it was attached to his mother in ways no one could deny. The grooves in the wood were evidence of her hand digging into the flesh of the staff when defeating a Statue of Terhilian. Then there were the almost indiscernible dimples in the surface of the wood where branches had sprouted and borne seed, seeds that replanted the Grove of the Elders.

Even with such strong ties, Sinjin felt like a thief when he held the staff. It reminded him that his mother was gone and that he was grossly insufficient to carry on her legacy. Still, he did his best and made his way to the steerage, where Pelivor stood. Sinjin could see the beads of sweat on the man's brow and knew that the strain was great.

"I'll not ask you to take this from me," Sinjin said when Pelivor's eyes landed on the staff. There was awe and fear there as well; that made Sinjin feel even more awkward and unworthy of such things. "All I ask is that you use the power this staff holds to get all of us to 'the place of dragons' before Halmsa's eggs start hatching. If not for him, then for me. I don't know what'll happen when those eggs hatch, but I'd rather not be in the air or at sea when we find out."

Pelivor looked as if he would balk, and Sinjin drew a breath to speak before Pelivor could refuse. Before Sinjin could find the words, though, tears ran down Pelivor's face. The man flushed and Sinjin could not fathom the gamut of emotions he was feeling. After a deep breath, Pelivor met Sinjin's eyes with his own, which were puffy and red.

"I loved your mother," Pelivor said suddenly, and the ship dipped. Everyone aboard gasped at the sudden drop, but Pelivor soon regained control.

"As did I and most of those aboard."

"No," Pelivor said. "It's not just that; I was in love with your mother."

Now understanding what Pelivor meant, Sinjin tried to sort out how he felt. Was he flattered on behalf of his mother or jealous on behalf of his father? He found that he was neither. "She was easy to love," Sinjin said.

Pelivor looked heartbroken, but then he smiled. "Yes. You're correct. She was, indeed, easy to love. Then you do not think me a cad?"

"No," Sinjin said. "You were a good and loyal friend to her and my father. To be near my mother was to be affected by her. I could never blame anyone for being attracted to her light."

"She shone brightly," Pelivor said.

"As do you," Sinjin replied, "and these people need you. I can't say exactly why the dragons must be born on the Firstland, but I think that you and Gwen are the only people who can get us there in time. It's too much to ask, and I know it. This can help you, and it cannot help me otherwise. Please."

Tears again filled Pelivor's eyes, but they did not fall, kept back by the force of his will. He smiled as if remembering Catrin, and he accepted the staff with silent reverence. Again, Sinjin watched to see how Pelivor would react to the power. Since he already had the spider stone, Sinjin guessed it would come as less of a shock. Wrapping his fingers around the staff, Pelivor was purposeful in his avoidance of the hand print Catrin had left on it.

"You ready, kid?" Pelivor shouted.

"Yeah, I'm ready," Gwen shouted in response.

"Prepare for speed!" Pelivor shouted.

"It's about time!" Millie called from the galley.

The Arghast assembled on deck looked rightfully terrified, and even Benjin and Fasha looked more than a little uncertain as they battened down everything they could. What experienced crew was on board did what they could to supplement the effort, and Pelivor gave them time to complete their tasks. In the meantime, Sinjin noticed that their flight was a great deal more stable. Pelivor didn't seem to have drawn from the staff yet, but perhaps just having it within his grasp increased his confidence.

After a nod from Fasha, Pelivor closed his eyes and breathed deeply. With the spider stone in one hand and the staff in the other, Pelivor exhaled. With his breath rushed the air, and light flared around Sinjin, causing him to shield his eyes. Lightning crawled over Pelivor's hands and over the staff, dancing and casting fluid shadows. The dragon ore stones mounted in the metal heel flared, and blue plasma pulsed in the shape of a serpent head, the stones serving as the creature's blazing eyes.

Blue-white lines extended out from the mighty serpent on the staff and reached into the skies alongside them. Ropes of light reached forward to latch on to the masthead, which had been carved into a likeness of Kyrien. Suddenly Pelivor's wing structures, something previously only he and Gwen had been able to see, were now laced with fire, and those aboard murmured in fear, especially as the head and neck of the dragon filled in. Sinjin looked back and saw a glittering tail of energy that flowed around and over where Gwen sat. He worried briefly that she would be engulfed by the flow of power, but the energy was translucent and Sinjin could see the wide smile on her face. She was enjoying this!

"By the gods," Pelivor said. "I've felt the power of the staff through contact with your mother, but to hold it in my own hands . . . I could never have imagined such might. When we reach the Firstland you must take it from me. Promise me."

"I promise," Sinjin said, knowing it was a pledge he could only keep if Pelivor truly wanted him to. As if to drive home that point, Pelivor applied his will, and the rigging sung with speed. With the wind in his face, Sinjin wondered at how much his life had changed and steeled himself for whatever might come next.

The *Dragon's Wing* had never looked more like her namesake, and she left a glittering trail in her wake, as if a cloud of fireflies followed her.

Chapter 13

Imagination is not frivolous whimsy; it is the force that drives us to be better than we are.

--Enly Mandone, bard

* * *

Weeks aboard a cramped ship, no matter how fast it traveled, wore on passengers and crew alike. When a dark mass formed on the horizon, there was anticipation and anxiety in equal measure. All knew this was not their final destination, yet it was a glimpse at a foreign land, a land once occupied by their ancestors. Evidence of this was visible some time before the ship approached the Keys of Terhilian. There stood the inspiration for the statues of Terhilian, the Terhilian Lovers. Despite knowing you could not blame the creators of this massive artwork for inspiring devious weapons, the two were now synonymous. The statue of a god and goddess embracing, carved into massive bluffs, also served a practical purpose; it pointed to the Firstland, the place it was believed where mankind had first taken root. The figures did not match the traditional forms of Istra and Vestra, but it was clear these were god and goddess. Sinjin could not figure out why not knowing if the figures were meant to represent Istra and Vestra bothered him so much, but it did. Watching the massive carvings approach, they seemed to look down on him and find him wanting.

Feeling small and powerless, Sinjin was also humbled by the construction of these figures. How powerful had these people been to leave such a massive message for the ages to come. He'd never seen such efforts, save what Thorakis had done, and he hoped the ancients had employed much different methods and thinking. He recognized the fact that Thorakis may have truly had good intentions when he began his work, and perhaps it had only been the presence of the feral dragons that had been his downfall. It seemed peculiar that the dragons used Thorakis as a proxy when they were clearly powerful enough to control the people themselves, but then he realized how much easier it must have been to simply dominate the man to whom most people owed their lives. It was brilliant when he thought about it, and that frightened him even more. Ferals were clever and powerful, and there were feral eggs on this ship.

Worry washed over Sinjin, some of it was his own, but most of it was radiated by those around him. As the statues looked down on them, none seemed immune to the effects. Halmsa was perhaps also responsible; he paced the deck, forcing everyone else to clear out of his way when he reached them. Always he carried the dragon eggs, but no more did he hold out the eggs to those around him, no more did he show the movements of the eggs. This alone gave Sinjin cause for worry and perhaps even for relief. Part of his problem was that he wasn't certain what he wanted to happen, which made it even more difficult to make decisions. Part of him hoped the eggs would never hatch, so he would not have to decide whether the dragons lived or died. It also didn't escape him that he might not be able to kill even a single one if that was the decision he made. How could he ever convince the Arghast that the dragons were evil, and how could he be certain they would be? Another part of him dared for an instant to hope that these dragons would be more like Kyrien. It was a silly hope, and he banished it to the place where all childish things go--not gone but put aside for the reality of adulthood.

When Halmsa passed by where Sinjin stood, Durin came in his wake, moving easily through the crowd.

"Nice trick," Sinjin said.

"I wouldn't stand in that guy's way either," Durin said then looked up. "Vestra's beard! That's just creepy."

It wouldn't be long before the statues would be left behind, but it would not be soon enough for Sinjin. Being in their shadow gave him the crawls, which did nothing to improve his optimism. This did, at least, indicate that they were on the last leg of their journey.

In a rare moment, Halmsa stopped pacing and faced Benjin. "I owe apology."

Benjin did not look as if any apology were required, though there was considerable strain on his face; sailing with this many aboard his ship was plainly stressful.

"I did not believe you when you said place of dragons was too far for small boats, but you were right. We would be dead. We owe you debt."

"It is our honor to bear the Dragon clan to your new home," Benjin said, and Fasha stood behind him, nodding in agreement.

"We won't forget," Halmsa said. It was a simple statement, but there was such weight behind it that Sinjin had no doubt that the Dragon clan would truly never forget, provided they survived.

Sinjin was an optimist by nature, but when he thought about all the things his mother had worked so hard to provide within Dragonhold, he wondered how the Arghast would manage to survive in what could only be called an unforgiving land. People may have once lived on the Firstland, but that had been thousands of years ago, and the wisdom of the ancients had perished with them. Who knew what dangers they would face?

"You worry too much," Durin said; as he did, though, Pelivor and Gwen took them higher and faster now that they were clear of the Keys of Terhilian. Both gripped the railing, and everyone on board did what they could to secure themselves in the fierce wind. Once the speed and altitude leveled off, it was mostly the wind with which they had to contend. Durin looked a little green, and he paled even further. "Good luck," he said and walked swiftly away.

From the opposite direction came Kendra, and the crowd separated before her just as it did before Halmsa, though perhaps for different reasons. The look on the girl's face made it clear she was ready for a fight.

Doing his best to look unconcerned, Sinjin waited. There had been times in his life when he would have yielded to Kendra to avoid confrontation with her, but those days were past. He respected her, and in some ways he owed her, but he would not bow before her; at least that was what he was thinking when she approached.

With her arms crossed over her chest and fire in her eyes, Kendra stopped. She'd been avoiding Sinjin since they left the Godfist. Now, though, she seemed unlikely to grant him the same privilege. She said nothing; she just looked at him with an expression difficult to describe. Somehow she conveyed the sense that she was utterly shocked and deeply hurt by something he'd done. Sadly, he'd seen that look before.

It didn't take long for Sinjin to figure out what it was she was so angry about. "I'm not sorry." Pain and hurt seemed to shift toward smoldering fury. "The extra load is too much for Gwen and Pelivor to handle unaided. I did the only thing I could to change that; I loaned Koe to Gwen and the Staff of Life to Pelivor until this voyage is over."

Kendra did not seem to hear him. "You give to everyone," she said quietly. "Why is it that you never have anything for me?" The last was said with a catch in her voice, which clearly enraged her further.

Stunned, Sinjin stood gaping like an idiot, and Kendra looked as if she would storm away. That, he knew, would be the worst thing he could let happen. He had to keep her there for a moment longer, and in that instant, he let go of his fears. He'd lost his home and most of his family, and it felt for a moment as if he had very little left to lose. Kendra started to turn away from him, but he reached out and grabbed her by the shoulder, turning her back to face him. She seemed surprised by his forcefulness and looked a little confused. The moment would not last, Sinjin knew. Stepping closer, he continued to pull her toward him, and she looked as if she might protest.

Then he kissed her.

It was unlike anything he'd ever experienced. She was soft and warm, and for a moment, she kissed him back. Then, though, she pulled away. No one on deck spoke, and all eyes were on them, including Gwen's; somehow the crowd had parted just enough to allow her an unobstructed view. Kendra looked around and the shock on her face turned back to fury. Sinjin had just been contemplating trying for another kiss when her right uppercut caught him in the chin. Hitting the deck hard, Sinjin would forever associate pain in his head and jaw with the taste of Kendra's kiss on his lips.

* * *

When Allette saw fear in Thundegar's eyes, her own courage fled. Rastas moved alongside her, the hair on his spine standing on end; he pressed up against her leg as if to ask her to protect him. This frightened her almost as much as anything else. Waves of primal fear rained from the skies, along with the compulsion to give up. It was as if the ferals radiated hopelessness, and Allette prayed they would go away. Had she been on a ship, she would have cast an offering to the sea, despite the fact that she'd never believed in such things. As her father had once said, "What harm could it do?"

With his words echoing in her mind, reminding her that he was gone, Allette willed the tears away and pulled several strands of hair from her head and tossed them into the clear waters on the stream where they had stopped. Thundegar filled his water flask and motioned for her to do the same. It seemed like an exercise in futility since they would probably not live long enough to drink it, but she did her best to shake off the melancholy. Some of the feelings were her own and were more than warranted, but part of her knew it was the influence of the dragons that clouded her thoughts with fear.

Moving, taking action, even filling her water flask made her feel the smallest bit better. She would not let the dragons subjugate her will; she would not surrender. Her father had taught her to fight, and that was exactly what she would do. Thundegar, too, seemed to be gathering his strength and will.

"We'll never make it across with the ferals as active as they are, and it would appear they've an army coming ashore as well," Thundegar said in a low voice, barely audible over the bubbling stream.

Allette nodded, not trusting her tongue to speak.

"If we wait for nightfall, we might be able to backtrack without being seen. With any luck, we can walk most of the way back. The grasses will continue to thicken, and though it will take a great deal longer than it took us to get here, I think we'll be able to make it back to the Cloud Forest."

Though the frustration of having to turn back gnawed at her, Allette knew this might be their only hope of survival. No matter what, she did not want to fall into the hands of anyone who'd willingly fight for the ferals. Truly, these must be black-hearted men. No matter how many times she reminded herself of that fact, though, Allette could not help but think about the fact that they could have just stayed in the Cloud Forest. This entire trip, all their struggles and trials, had been for naught; it had been a huge waste of effort, which might now be the end of them.

A low growl from Rastas pulled Allette from her inner torment, and she went cold, her body responding so strongly to the danger that her skin itched. Thundegar reached out a hand to soothe the cat, clearly not wanting anyone or anything to know they were there. Allette moved a step backward into the shadows and tried to make herself as small as possible. Rastas, now silent but still clearly agitated, followed her in the shadows and hid beside her, proving his wisdom. Branches moved nearby, and flashes of movement could be seen through the trees. Thundegar seemed torn between the desire to run and the desire to hide. After a quick glance at Allette and Rastas, he found a shadowy spot alongside a gnarled tree. Bushes grew nearby, and Thundegar brushed up against one, despite his efforts to keep quiet.

The sounds of movement stopped, and Allette held her breath. Whatever lurked amid the trees now knew they were there. Almost instinctively, Allette ran her hand over Rastas's coat, trying to soothe him and hoping he wouldn't give away their position. An instant later, Allette froze. From between a pair of trees, not a handful of paces away, two dark forms emerged from the forest. At first they looked completely black, but as Allette studied them, her body trembling with fear, she saw a spotted pattern of dark orange and black. Liquid green eyes scanned the area, and whiskers twitched with uncertainty. Even these mighty felines seemed unnerved by the presence of the ferals. At almost any other place in the world, these would be alpha predators with no natural enemies save man, but here they were in as much danger as anyone else foolish enough to get caught in feral territory.

Every instinct told Allette that she should run, and it was all she could do to refrain. Reason disagreed with her instincts, and this time she sided with reason. Her father had often said that instincts should rarely be ignored, but Allette was certain she'd be unable to outrun these massive cats. Rastas pressed against her, no less assured; even though these cats might be distant relatives of his, it was clear that he expected no quarter. Given some of the cat fights Allette had witnessed, Rastas was perhaps in greater danger than Allette and Thundegar. Reaching down, Allette once again smoothed the cat's coat. She wasn't certain how much better it made the cat feel, but it made her feel a great deal better.

Stepping to the edge of the stream, the cats drank one at a time, leaving the other to keep watch. In this place, even a drink of water could bring a quick death. Ripples appeared in the deeper, darker water downstream, and both cats moved away from the stream. Not wanting to know what was causing those ripples, Allette trembled. When one of the cats looked directly at the shadows where they hid, Allette held her breath once again. The muscle-bound cat remained intent and met Allette's eyes, leaving no doubt that it had seen her. Rastas growled, despite her soothing, and now both cats were looking directly at her. Visions of a slow death drove away what remained of Allette's courage, and she prepared to run, her instincts quickly overpowering reason. Before she could move, though, the waters exploded with activity. A reptilian creature with massive jaws moved through the water faster than Allette would have thought possible, and it lunged at the big cats. One cat sprang into the air, showing agility that belied its size; the other crouched low and swatted at the reptilian eyes.

Snapping the air with its mighty jaws, the creature tried to grab the cat's legs, but the other cat landed gracefully and attacked from the other side. Convinced this meal wasn't worth the effort or risk, the mighty reptile slid back into the water and disappeared. The fact that so little depth could conceal such a large predator made Allette want to get as far away from the stream as she could. Only moments ago, she and Thundegar had been filling their flasks from that stream, and she doubted the outcome would have been the same if the reptile had attacked them rather than the big cats.

The cats, too, seemed to have decided this place was too dangerous to stay, but one of them looked back and met Allette's eyes one last time before slipping silently back into the trees. She would have breathed a sigh of relief if not for the massive shadow now circling them.

* * *

Seeing the Firstland made a great many things real to Sinjin. His mother had been there twice, and both times she'd nearly been killed. Now he led a group of people completely unprepared to make a new life there. These people had been desert nomads for the gods knew how long, and Sinjin didn't feel all that much more ready than they.

"The city of Ri is the place where the regent dragons lived," Benjin said. "It's also the only place I've any idea of how to get to. I'd suggest starting there."

"Will you come?" Sinjin asked.

Benjin nodded; Fasha glared at him.

"What of the *Dragon's Wing*?" Sinjin asked.

"Fasha can take the *Wing* and see where there are good fishing grounds. The first thing we'll need is a steady supply of food. She won't be able to sail past the Eternal Guardians, so we'll need a clear supply route. There may be fish in the river as well, so it may be that we don't even need to go to sea."

Her glare intensifying, Fasha said nothing, but her look made it clear that she saw right through Benjin's words. He wanted to keep her safe, and she knew it; it clearly did not please her. Fasha was no delicate flower.

"Even that mission will be fraught with peril," Benjin continued. "When Catrin first came here, she was attacked by Gholgi in the wild. If I recall, the creatures nearly sunk the *Slippery Eel*."

Fasha rolled her eyes, obviously unconvinced. Clear blue skies harbored only wisps of clouds, and a warm breeze blew. The black beaches looked peaceful and quiet. Even when they reached the towering stone spires that jutted out into the ocean and sheltered a massive bay, within all seemed tranquil. Here had once rested a Zjhon warship, placed there by a mighty wave thought to have originated from a volcanic eruption in the shallows. The distances seemed inconceivable to Sinjin, having just covered the distance from the Godfist to the Firstland, and he knew the shallows to be nearly as far.

The harbor entrance loomed before them, and Pelivor slowly eased them back toward the placid waters below. Each time he had done so with so many aboard had been a frightening experience, and passengers and crew prepared themselves for the sudden slowing of the ship. Gwen had eased off the thrust, but Pelivor had to maintain enough speed to keep them from simply falling from the sky; it was a fine balance.

"Brace yourselves!" Pelivor cried, the strain clearly audible in his voice even with his augmented power.

The *Dragon's Wing* issued a loud groan when she reentered the water, and the weight of her load shifted forward. The abrupt deceleration and return of the ship's natural motions was sudden and disorienting. Sinjin gripped the rail, waiting for his body and brain to adjust to the ship's movements. The gap in the spires was more than large enough to admit the *Dragon's Wing* into the harbor. He'd heard the story about how his mother and the *Slippery Eel* had entered the harbor airborne, and he couldn't imagine it. Just sailing through it was unnerving. In that moment, Sinjin was glad Kenward had stayed behind. This place held a lot of bad memories for him, and Sinjin didn't want to see any more added to that list.

Fasha was there, though, and it was clear she was reliving memories of her own. She and Benjin had rescued Kenward and his crew from this very place, not to mention the fact that both of them had nearly died the first time Catrin had sailed to the Firstland. Truly, the air around Sinjin was a riot of emotion. Halmsa looked as if he might burst. The eggs had been still for weeks, and he looked as if his will and hope were spent. His people supported him, and that seemed to give him strength, but the man looked older already; truly this burden weighed on him.

Sinjin continued to have mixed feelings. Most of the time, he hoped the eggs would not hatch, but he felt guilty for thinking that. That was not what his mother would have wished, it was not what Halmsa and his people wished, but it was what Sinjin wished. The thought shamed him.

"It won't be much longer," Benjin said to Sinjin. "Once we enter the mouth of the river there, it's not all that far to the Eternal Guardians. Millie is working with Morif to get supplies ready for unloading. We'll just send up prepared food on the first trip. We should be able to get the rest on a second trip, though we'll want to leave a few people behind to keep the wildlife out of our stores."

The reality of what was happening pressed down on Sinjin's shoulders. The Dragon clan was settling here, and since he had nowhere else to go, he supposed he and those loyal to him were as well. Hard days were ahead, and he somehow knew he was grossly unprepared. Even with all of that, there was a sense of excitement, a new beginning, a chance to make things the way he thought they should be. It was then that he saw a massive black shark thrust itself from the water to grab a barking seal. The rest of the seals, which had previously been nearly invisible, now barked, hollered, and backed away from the water. Sinjin's enthusiasm was dampened by the reminder that this was a deadly place, a place of untamed wilderness; the creatures who ruled here were not human.

No more sharks showed themselves, and perhaps that was what made it even more terrifying. Sinjin knew he wasn't alone in moving away from the railing and watching the seas as if the shark might come for him at any moment. The Arghast pressed themselves closer to the deckhouse, and the valley walls seemed to encroach on them. As the sun sank lower in the sky, the shadow grew and the carvings of massive men stood out in exaggerated relief. Such baleful glares the ancients had left to greet them; it did not bode well, and few words were spoken. No matter how much enthusiasm there had been to end the journey, it was impossible not to be daunted in the face of such imposing architecture.

Benjin had been trying to warn the Arghast, via Halmsa, of some of what they would see, but nothing could have prepared them for the sight of the Eternal Guardians. As soon as the ship rounded the last twist in the narrow river valley before the mighty statues, the deck of the *Dragon's Wing* exploded with activity. A great clamor rose and echoed from the valley walls. Sinjin didn't think there was anyone living on the Firstland, but it still seemed to him that a stealthy approach might have been better. As it was, he saw ripples in the water ahead, great V-shaped formations with the tips pointing toward deep water. Sinjin couldn't be certain what kind of creatures these were, but he knew they were big and fast.

"Watch the waterline!" Benjin called out. "There may be unfriendly wildlife. If anything attacks the ship, kill it."

No attacks came but the air was rank with anxiety. Fasha did not take the ship any closer to the Eternal Guardians than she had to, and anchor was dropped.

"Lower half of the boats!" she ordered.

It took a moment for the experienced crew to show the Arghast what must be done. The tribesman, as always, impressed Sinjin. Given the language barrier, it could be easy to dismiss the nomads as unintelligent, but they had proven themselves to be anything but. They were clever, resourceful, and unbelievably self-reliant. Not a single time during the voyage had one of them asked Sinjin for help or even for an explanation of such unfamiliar surroundings.

Gwen stood near the stern, decidedly not looking at Sinjin. He considered asking Durin to talk to Gwen, to give her the chance to return Koe to him without them actually having to talk, but he realized it was a childish thing to do. Still, it was clear she was furious with him; she'd done nothing but glare at him ever since she'd seen him kiss Kendra. What had he been thinking? Now all he'd done was make things worse. Kendra was also avoiding him, though with her, the situation was a bit different; instead of glaring at him, she wouldn't meet his eyes. It was behavior he'd never seen from her before, and he had no idea how to respond.

"You'll never figure her out standing here," Benjin said.

Looking up, Sinjin flushed. Benjin wore a knowing smile. With a nod, Sinjin accepted his fate and stepped toward Gwen. He tried to ignore it when he heard Benjin say, "Of course, you'll never understand her that way either, m'boy, but better to clean the wound than to let it fester."

Gwen looked up as he approached and watched him with an unreadable expression. His steps nearly faltered. His heart raced and his skin felt as if it were on fire. Why did she make him feel this way? And why did he feel so drawn to her when she made him feel such anxiety? His hands reached out involuntarily, wanting to touch her, but she shrank away. Only then did Sinjin realize what he'd done. It wasn't a good start.

"You did it," Sinjin said finally. "You got us here in time."

"Hurray for me," Gwen said, looking at her boots.

"If not for you, we wouldn't have made it. You are . . . amazing."

Gwen harrumphed.

"I just wanted to say thank you--"

"No, you didn't," Gwen interrupted suddenly. "You didn't just want to say thank you, did you? You wanted the cat back."

The words stung Sinjin, mostly because they were true. He lowered his eyes.

Making a rude noise in her throat, Gwen reached into her pocket, pulled out Koe, and thrust the carving at Sinjin. Caught off his guard, he awkwardly accepted it.

"I wouldn't have asked for it back if you hadn't freaked out when I tried to give it to you!" Sinjin said and immediately wished he could take the words back.

Gwen huffed and walked away, disappearing down a hatch and into the hold.

Sinjin tried to accept the fact that he just never knew what to say to Gwen, and whenever he did open his mouth, he'd say something that even he knew was horrible.

Benjin shook his head but said nothing, for which Sinjin was grateful. Walking back to the prow, he searched out Pelivor. This would be a great deal easier, he hoped. Pelivor saw him coming and moved to meet him halfway. The deck was bustling with activity, and it took a concerted effort to get to one another. Bearing the staff, Pelivor looked even more regal than usual, and Sinjin was loathe to ask for it back, especially since it seemed to serve Pelivor so well. Sinjin started to get angry over the situation with Gwen again, but then he forced those feelings back down; Pelivor had certainly done nothing to raise his ire.

"It's been an honor to have use of the staff for this short time," Pelivor said. The gaze he cast over the fine wood and the intricate metal heel, complete with dragon ore in the eyes of the subtle serpent, was covetous.

Again, Sinjin wanted to give the staff to Pelivor, to relieve himself of the burden of caring for it and protecting it. Didn't everyone know he was powerless? How was he to protect such precious artifacts when he had no skill with which to wield them? His questions did not seem to matter, as Pelivor thrust the staff back into his hands.

Once again he possessed the greatest power in the world and could do nothing with it.

Chapter 14

Power in the hands of the meek is no power at all.
--Master Edling

* * *

The journey to Ri was something Sinjin thought might never end. Durin had already made it abundantly clear that he felt the same. In truth, Sinjin felt guilty for grumbling. The Dragon clan issued no such complaints; they saw their future here, and it was worth working hard for. It reminded Sinjin of something his grandfather always said. With that in mind, he shifted the load on his back and used trees along the rain-slicked trail to pull himself up the rise. Always up, Sinjin thought for an instant, then shook it off.

Beside him, Durin slipped and fell. Sinjin reached down and grasped Durin's hand to help him up; it was then that he saw the movement through the thick trees. Along with the movement came the snap of a branch, and Durin turned with wide eyes.

"Did you hear that?"

"I heard it and saw it," Sinjin whispered. Some members of the Dragon clan also whispered and spoke of something in the woods, which struck Sinjin as more of a jungle than forest. The vegetation was thick, and it was truly the Arghast at the front of the line who bore the greatest burden. Though they carried no packs, the ring of their blades split the air whenever they encountered growth too thick to traverse. It was at those times that Sinjin was glad to carry a sack of onions, even if it was a rather large and cumbersome sack.

After that incident, the mood of the group changed, and they climbed with an increased sense of urgency. If they were to face the Gholgi or some other foe, it would be best to do it from high ground. Sinjin knew of one such defensible position, though he also knew what else rested there: the very reason Benjin had not wanted Fasha to come. It was not much longer before the procession came to an abrupt halt. Sinjin thought he saw more movements through the trees, but he could hear little above the murmur that ran through those at the fore. Straining to see, Sinjin cursed; his view was blocked and would remain so for several minutes.

Finally Sinjin heard the words, "The Vale of the Herald." And not long after, he heard, "The place of dragons." It was vindicating to have the Dragon clan confirm that this was indeed the place of dragons, though the entire course of events felt surreal to him. Anxiety returned, full force, when he saw multiple shapes moving through the trees. The shadowy forms did not attack, but it was clear they were monitoring the progress of his party, and it gave him the crawls. Before he could say anything to Durin, the group started moving again, albeit slowly. Each new person who passed the entrance to his mother's vale drew a sharp breath or exclaimed, but all were moved to some reaction. In some ways, Sinjin didn't want to look since it was a window into a dark time for his mother. This land had almost killed her twice, and this place had been among her only salvations. Here, her people had been safe and here alone.

It did not escape Sinjin that this place was very defensible, with high and steep rock walls surrounding the grassy vale; beyond, he knew, was a massive drop overlooking the hollowed-out mountains. He'd heard about all these things, but seeing them was another experience entirely. So many things that had always seemed distant, ethereal, and perhaps even make believe were now in front of him. When he laid eyes on the *Slippery Eel*, the stories struck him over and over, and he found himself gasping for breath. The once beautiful ship told a tale of a nightmare voyage, one that had left her broken, scorched, and bearing massive claw marks. The ship lay on her side, and her masts and rigging were mostly gone. She looked as if she'd been there for ages, yet Sinjin knew better.

Sinjin was glad that Fasha did not have to see this, her brother's ship in such a state of destruction. Yet she wasn't destroyed; she'd continued to provide shelter for her crew even after being rendered unseaworthy. It was clear to Sinjin why his mother had chosen to summon Benjin and Fasha to collect the crew of the *Slippery Eel;* even if the ship could have been fixed, getting her back to the water would have been nearly impossible. Given some of the things he'd seen his parents, Pelivor, and Gwen do, he accepted the fact that there might have been some ways it could happen, but even those seemed perilous.

The people behind him also wanted their chance to see the vale, and Sinjin moved beyond the entrance. Like those before him, he was enthralled by the sight of the vale but had absolutely no intention of setting foot on those hallowed grasses. Sinjin had considered it since it might make him feel closer to his mother, but the *Slippery Eel* demanded his respect, and he chose not to disturb her grave. Behind him, he heard reactions not unlike his own, and he moved forward with grim determination. This was a challenge, indeed, on more levels than he had initially realized.

Beyond lay a nightmarish landscape--the remnants of his mother's and Kyrien's attempt to save the regent dragons. Huge circles of earth looked to have been turned inside out, and a forest appeared to have been yanked from the ground and cast across the expansive valley floor. Rising and disappearing into the mists were mighty peaks like none Sinjin had ever seen. Looking almost like layers of honeycomb stacked on top of one another, the hollow mountains seemed impossible. It looked as if they would collapse under their own weight. Brother Vaughn had once explained to him how miners would leave shafts of the hardest rock in place as supports and take out the softer rock instead. These mountains looked as if that was also the case here, and the structures formed by that hard rock were amazingly intricate and beautiful. As they drew closer, the structures were revealed to be even larger than Sinjin had imagined; the scale of it was difficult to conceive even when standing at the foot of such a mountain.

There was another, less hollowed-out mountain, where there were stairs and much smaller holes cut into the rock face. This, Sinjin knew, was where his mother had faced Archmaster Belegra, and one entranceway in particular stood out from the rest, the rock surrounding it blackened and scorched. Though that mountain seemed a more sensible place to settle, he decided not to offer any argument when Halmsa pointed to this mountain and said, "The place of dragons."

Scaling the rock structures proved easier than Sinjin would have guessed, which was a good thing considering the weight of the packs. He'd considered letting a scouting party go up first, but Halmsa had simply started climbing, and the rest of his tribe followed. What had looked completely smooth from a distance proved to be a scored and pocked surface that clearly had been shaped and formed by massive teeth.

"What do you think is up there?" Durin asked, sounding concerned.

"I don't know," Sinjin said, "but I don't think there will be any dragons there except the ones we brought with us; at least I sure hope not."

"Haven't seen any signs of them, but that doesn't mean they're not here. We should make sure we have an escape route. Maybe we should plan to meet back at--uh--your--uh--mom's vale if things go wrong. That place always kept everyone safe, right?"

Sinjin wasn't so certain it had been the vale that had kept everyone safe; it had been the dragons guarding the vale, and those dragons were now gone. Despite his worry, he kept climbing. The structure he'd been scaling brought him to a flat and level plane. More structures extended upward, some allowing access to higher levels and others branching into a solid stone surface that was presumably the floor of the next level. It amazed Sinjin that such a place could have been constructed or rather carved out of a mountain. The floors were worn smooth in places, and it was clear that there had been many dragons here and for a very long time. Most of the space was open, and in the distance, the stone ended and open air began.

Halmsa did not slow; he moved with a glazed-over look in his eyes, and he quickly found another formation that he could climb even with his delicate and cumbersome burden. It had amazed Sinjin that the man had made the entire climb carrying all the dragon eggs, but the Arghast had been unwilling to let anyone else carry them, saying that if anything happened to any of the eggs he had protected for so long, he would likely kill whoever was responsible. For that reason, he said, it was his burden alone to bear, for he would not risk any of those he held so dear.

It was difficult logic to argue, and Sinjin had given Halmsa an even wider berth to make sure he did not accidentally endanger the eggs. A cold feeling grew in his stomach, knowing he would face Halmsa if he decided the dragons could not be allowed to live. It was suicide, he knew, but he also knew that what had happened to Thorakis could not be allowed to happen again. The Dragon clan was made up of strong, intelligent, and capable people, and he did not want to imagine them under the control of the ferals.

Level after level was rejected by Halmsa, and his people followed without complaint. Durin, on the other hand, was another matter entirely. Though mostly under his breath, Durin continually asked Sinjin why Halmsa insisted on climbing the entire mountain. Surely one of the previous levels would have sufficed, Durin insisted, but he did keep moving, for which Sinjin was grateful. He did not want to have to choose between supporting his friend and doing what he felt bound by duty and responsibility to do. He'd come all this way to make sure the eggs Halmsa bore would not endanger the world, and he intended to do just that, even knowing he was inadequate for the task. If he died trying, then he would have died in a way that would have made his mother proud. That was the only thought that brought him any solace; that, and perhaps the sight of Kendra.

His relationship with her was one he still could not explain, but something had changed. Now when he looked at her, she would blush and turn away. This confused him more than when she had cast him dirty looks and called him names. This somehow felt better but made it no easier to figure out exactly what it was he was supposed to do. His jaw still ached from where she had slugged him, but if he closed his eyes, he could still taste her kiss.

"You're thinking about it again, aren't you?" Durin asked, and Sinjin flushed. "I knew it. I don't get you. That girl has been torturing you for years, and then you up and kiss her, and now here you are, daydreaming about her again. What are you, some kind of idiot? Why would you want to be with a girl who kisses you and then punches you in the lip?"

"I embarrassed her," Sinjin said. "I shouldn't have kissed her like that in front of everyone, and that's why she punched me."

"Unbelievable," Durin said. "I think all the punches you've been taking must've wiggled something in your head loose. You're not thinking straight at all. Gwen was always nice to you, and now she storms away at the mere mention of your name. You screwed up, my friend. Bad."

"I don't know what to do about either of them, and I don't know what I want."

"That's pretty obvious."

Sinjin would have said something sarcastic, but then they reached the seventh level of the hollow mountain. Here were the signs of a massive battle. Little was left besides weapons and bones, but the scale of it was daunting. This was the largest of the open expanses. Here the ceiling was high, and the spires supporting it, megalithic. The supports were also farther apart, leaving large expanses of open space. This was where the regent queen had lived.

Chunks of stone and rubble also littered the otherwise smooth stone floor, much of which was blackened. The air smelled of sulfur and the sea, and at last Halmsa signaled his people to lay down their burdens. Sinjin and Durin did so as well, and Sinjin stretched while Durin complained.

"I'm not sure I agree with Halmsa's tastes," he said.

Sinjin wasn't certain he understood either but was willing to give the man a chance. It was his instincts that had drawn them this far; it seemed a silly time to change that.

Halmsa wandered, still bearing his burden and looking confused. He'd come all this way, and now he seemed lost; it was a cruel fate. Sinjin watched the man intently, leaving Durin behind and following wherever Halmsa wandered. He seemed to have no set destination or even direction, and Sinjin could not understand what guided him, if anything at all.

He had a strange feeling then, like nothing he'd ever felt before. It was as if someone were tugging on his belt knife and the buckle on his pants. Even stranger, Halmsa moved in the same direction Sinjin now felt pulled. Soon he could almost predict Halmsa's movement, and the pulling grew stronger until Sinjin thought his knife might leap from its sheath. Moving his hand to the hilt, he looked around and saw the other Arghast following Halmsa and watching him. Sinjin could see swords tugging on sheaths, and he realized the danger. "Wait!" he said. Halmsa stopped and looked at him without humor. "It's magnetic. Keep swords and knives and other metal objects away from here.

Check your swords."

It seemed the Arghast had already been aware of the tugging, and they moved quickly to lay down their weapons in an orderly fashion, well away from the tugging pull. Sinjin had never felt such massive magnetic force before; he'd seen lodestones at festivals, but those could not compare to this, what must be an enormous lodestone at the heart of this mountain. Could this be what Halmsa felt he needed? Was this what the dragons had dug into the mountain looking for? He doubted he would have answers any time soon, save perhaps one. Halmsa stopped moving and looked as if his burden were being pulled straight down. There he sat and there he laid out the eggs. It was the first time that Sinjin was able to count them--twenty-four in all. Thirty-five Dragon clan members had made the journey; eleven of them would be disappointed. Still, Sinjin felt a sense of accomplishment for what they had done. If not for their intervention, surely Halmsa and the Dragon clan would have perished trying to get there.

It might be more than a year before the rest of the clan arrived, and Sinjin could not imagine what would happen between now and then. The events surrounding him were tenuous and uncertain, and he couldn't even say what the next day would bring. Certainty seemed a thing of the past, and even then it had been an illusion. The eggs surrounding Halmsa moved slowly--not like the jerking motions they had displayed weeks ago, but more of a steady, measured movement that left all of them oriented in the same direction. It was a startling and unsettling thing to watch, and Halmsa seemed as surprised as everyone else, but no one spoke. Even Durin, who had come to see what was happening, kept his mouth shut.

For many long moments, they stood there, waiting for something to happen, but nothing did. The eggs moved no more, and Sinjin began to doubt they ever would again. It shamed him that he felt relief, but he did. That was the only eventuality that would absolve him of the choice, and he prayed for continued silence. It was not to be. One of the metallic-looking eggs moved, and the emotion in the room would not be contained. Collectively, the Dragon clan let out a triumphant roar, but a single wordless look from Halmsa silenced them. This was a time for reverence. This was a time that would be remembered for the rest of eternity. This was the birth of a new age, and Halmsa knew it. Sinjin could feel the conviction that radiated from the man like sunlight from a clear blue sky.

Another long silence held, but this one was less tense. When a different egg moved, those assembled issued a hushed murmur, and Halmsa remained silent, his eyes closed. Sinjin couldn't understand how the man maintained such calm or, for that matter, how the man had done any of the things he'd done. He had acted without fear, driven by belief, and he had survived; it defied logic. Yet here he was, sitting in the place of dragons, surrounded by eggs given to him by the feral queen; surely he had claimed his destiny as none before him. Sinjin was honored to witness such events.

Crack.

That single sound brought every person within the place of dragons, high in the hollow mountain, overlooking the land of their ancestors, to full attention. The covenant would be renewed, and the Dragon clan would become the people their legends said they would be. The thought made Sinjin smile, while those around him pointed to which one of the eggs they thought had made the sound.

Crack, crack.

With that, it became obvious which egg was hatching. It rested very close to Halmsa, and he watched it with wide eyes; even his calm had evaporated. Tense excitement filled the air. Weeks of relentless travel, leaving their homeland, their horses, their lives behind, all of it would have a purpose. The hatching of a single dragon seemed as if it would be enough for them, enough to make all the sacrifice worthwhile. Sinjin wondered how long that sentiment would last. A sick feeling was growing in his gut, and try as he might, he could not banish it.

Through the cracks in the shell, coppery scales moved on something that looked too thin to be a dragon; it was skinny even in snake terms. Then the tip of it emerged. Perhaps that was the tail, Sinjin thought, and everyone around him leaned closer, trying to see every detail, to memorize this most momentous event. Sinjin backed away, the fear in his gut growing. Slipping back even farther, he reached the place where the weapons had been stashed, and there he retrieved his knife. It was sharp and comfortable in his hand, and it should be enough.

Staying toward the back of the group, Sinjin tried to see what was happening. There had been more cracking sounds and excitement building in the crowd, and as people moved, Sinjin was able to see. The top of the shell was nearly gone, and there did not appear to be any space left within the shell. Slowly a black wing unfolded itself, coppery fingers tipped with gleaming black claws giving it structure. A bright green eye regarded the assemblage as the head dislodged itself; a thin, metallic neck supported the narrow, angular head. Next came a body nearly as thin. Two legs followed, tipped with glistening black points that looked ready to rend flesh.

Once the second wing was unfolded, the dragon extended itself and let out a shrill cry. It seemed impossible that a creature now as long as Sinjin's arm and with a wingspan as wide could have fit within the egg;

and the dragon seemed to grow with every breath, as if unfolding itself. Halmsa watched the dragon that was right in front of him, nearly making contact with him. His hands were extended, and he could almost touch the dragon, almost wrap his hands around it. Perhaps he should have waited, or perhaps he should have made some sound, for when the dragon finally realized Halmsa was there, the Arghast did not in any way get the reaction he'd been hoping for.

Shrieking and springing away from Halmsa, the baby dragon reacted as if Halmsa were a predator. Other Arghast reached out to it, and it did not exactly fly, but it did jump and flap its wings and manage to avoid capture. Sinjin watched the whole thing with tense anticipation. He did not raise his hands or reach for the dragon. One hand gripped the hilt of his belt knife, and the other was clenched into a fist, while Sinjin wrestled with this most difficult decision. How could he know if this dragon was evil or just afraid? As he watched it flit away from all those who reached for it, he suspected the latter and began to feel sorry for the poor creature. Surely it was hungry.

No sooner had the thought entered his mind than the dragon suddenly changed direction and flew directly toward Sinjin's unprotected face. His reactions were not quick enough, and black claws flashed toward his eyes; dark, vein-covered wings buffeted him, and even as he reached up, he felt a tail wrap around his throat. What had been a fascinating spectacle had just turned deadly. The scales made a sound like rustling leaves as the tiny dragon used its surprising strength to constrict. Sinjin choked and claws dug into his shoulders. He would have cried out if he could. Reaching up, he tried to pry the tail loose, and the dragon struck like a snake, biting his finger. Perhaps it wasn't so unlike the ferals after all, Sinjin thought, and the dragon pecked him on the head as if to scold him.

His vision swimming, Sinjin could see the Dragon clan watching him in undisguised horror. All their lives they had dreamed of this moment, and he was ruining it for them. It seemed likely at that point that he would die doing it. Already, he could feel his consciousness fading. Doing his best to think calming thoughts, Sinjin thought he felt the dragon's tail loosening just a little. That made it easier for him to breathe and become truly tranquil, and the tail loosened just a little more. Sinjin closed his eyes and let his body go limp, the knife dropped from his hand and slid toward where Halmsa sat.

"It's killing him," Durin shouted, and before Sinjin could wave him off, his friend was trying to pry the dragon loose from Sinjin's neck. Durin cried out as the dragon struck him over and over, but still his friend fought to save him, not knowing he was making the situation far worse.

Terrified, the dragon constricted further. The world grew dark, and Sinjin's ears pounded in the moments before he struck the unforgiving stone.

Chapter 15

Energy and matter are one. We are beings of energy, stardust, and lightning, and we are eternal.

--Brother Milo, Cathuran monk

* * *

The *Maker's Mark* had never run lighter, and Becker knew they had lightened the ship too much; she now sat high in the water, and they had lost vital stores. It would have been better to get rid of some of the ballast bags, which were filled with sand, but people had panicked and had tossed aside anything not nailed down. No matter how much he griped, they had made speed. With the wind at their backs, they had outraced the ships that continued to pursue them.

These ships were slower than the *Maker's Mark*, but Becker couldn't help but feel they could go faster. There seemed no sense of urgency from these ships, and that worried him more than anything. When the Jaga finally came into view, they were too far east for his liking. There was only one serviceable port this far out, and it was not the kind of place Becker wanted to visit. A man was as likely to have his throat cut as to get passage somewhere.

"We've outrun 'em this far," Mord said. "Let's run 'em up the coast and let them deal with the defenses at Maiden Bay."

It didn't sound like a terrible idea until you really thought about it, which Becker did. They had no supplies and would need to stop for fresh water if nothing else. The Jaga west of their current location was far more dense and dangerous. Becker had no desire to seek fresh water in that jungle, and he also didn't want it to be his escape of last resort. The thought of dying there drove him to reckless action. Mord be boiled! "Make for the harbor!"

"What?" Mord shouted, waving his arms, his face turning red. "That's suicide!"

"It's our only chance," Becker said. "I know it." He had nothing to go on but his gut reaction, which as usual disagreed with Mord's. This time Becker was ready to fight about it, and Mord must have seen it in his eyes; he hesitated.

"They'll catch us if we go west," Becker said, "and we'll have nowhere to run but the deep jungle. That place'll eat us all up in a day, if it takes that long. You've seen it, and you've seen what lives in there. You might as well be thrown to the sharks."

Mord glared but said nothing.

"East of here, the bloom is under way. It won't be a pleasant trip by any measure, but then there's at least the chance we could make it to the Heights."

"Through the Jaga and the Cloud Forest?" Mord asked, his voice dripping with derision.

"Given the choice of traveling through the heart of the Jaga or the option to simply skirt the Jaga and climb through a forest, I'll take the latter."

Becker could see that the more experienced members of the crew knew he was right. There were still plenty who would question his judgment and would follow Mord, whether for preference, politics, or simple disagreement with Becker's logic he didn't know. A moment later, it no longer mattered.

From within the Jaga flew a feral dragon. All aboard the *Maker's Mark* looked silently to Becker. Whether it was out of fear or for tactical purpose, he wasn't entirely certain, but he was grateful for it nonetheless. The dragon, it seemed, had something else on its mind; it circled over the shoreline not far away, and Becker pointed to the east with emphasis. His order was obeyed without question. At least he knew that when it came time to act, the crew would still obey.

The dragon dived then and reached out for something. The trees shook and leaves rained, but the dragon came away with empty claws. After two lazy turns, the feral struck again, and this time its prey was flushed onto the open expanse of sand along the shoreline. Now there would be no place to hide. This was made all the more horrifying by Becker's recognition of the dragon's prey. He didn't know who the man was, but he recognized Allette even from a distance. Others aboard did as well, and there could be no doubt; the implications hit Becker hard. The captain had been a good man, but by his reckoning, this could only mean he was dead. By the looks of it, his daughter would be next if they didn't do something.

With a quick look around, Becker gauged the mood of his crew; time was running out, and he had only an instant, but he would not send these men to their deaths against their will. What he saw there convinced him, and he shouted, "To Allette!"

"To Allette!" the crew roared in echo, even Mord, and for the first time in a long time, they worked together as a single cohesive unit. Across the water came a stunned and anguished response. She'd seen them as well and had heard their call. May she take heart from it, Becker prayed, knowing all of them would need a miracle to survive, especially her, the old man, and the cat.

* * *

Seeing the *Maker's Mark* was almost more than Allette could take. The dragon attack had come suddenly and with little warning, and she'd barely had enough time for her brain to register what exactly was happening when she heard her own name being shouted across the water. That was when she had seen the ship she would know anywhere, the ship that had been her home for most of her life. Her heart throbbed with pain, knowing the danger the *Maker's Mark* was in, and that the crew seemed intent on trying to save her from the feral; it was suicide. An anguished cry escaped her lips, and beside her Rastas growled, low and deep.

Thundegar leaned heavily on his staff, having not fared well during their flight from the trees. He didn't look as if he had much left in him, and with the dragon circling above, escape was as likely as being able to put up a good fight. They were doomed.

Looking down at her, the feral made eye contact with her as it turned in a lazy circle. The crew of the *Maker's Mark* made as much noise as they could, trying to distract the terrifying beast, but it was intent. Looking into her eyes, it seemed to read her soul and find it distasteful. Allette didn't care; she just wanted to keep the dragon's attention long enough for the *Maker's Mark* to flee. She wanted nothing more than for the ship and crew to escape. Her life was not worth risking theirs and she knew, deep down, that it was likely they would all die.

With all the courage she could muster, Allette cast her defiance at the feral, and the feeling was almost palpable, as if her anger and determination had made the very air inhospitable. The feral looked down at her with unimaginable fury and issued a roar that rattled Allette's bones.

"Run!" Thundegar urged, but Allette stood her ground a moment longer, not wanting the dragon to attack the *Maker's Mark*. As if reading her mind, the dragon turned on a wingtip, and Allette could almost feel it laughing at her. The cries from the *Maker's Mark* changed then; gone was the blustery bravado, and in its place were the cries of people who saw their deaths approaching fast. The dragon circled the ship three times before it struck. Showing just how intelligent the creatures were, the feral aimed for the base of the mainmast and snapped it off as if it were but a sapling. Allette watched in horror as a man jumped from the crow's nest right before the dragon hurled the mast and rigging away.

"Go!" Thundegar screamed, but Allette couldn't move.

One more time the dragon circled, and it struck again. The crew lashed out with every weapon they could muster, but the feral just ignored them. Swooping in low and with speed, the dragon reached out with its claws and clamped on to the ship, digging into the wood, which groaned and snapped under the intense pressure. Tipping backward, the ship protested loudly as the flying dragon held on and tried to gain altitude. Unable to gain the skies, the feral issued a frustrated cry and gave one final thrust that sent the *Maker's Mark* tumbling forward and capsizing the ship. Three more times the dragon struck the now exposed hull of the ship and made certain she would never sail again. Allette's home was gone, her family dead, everything she'd ever cared about was gone. Rastas leaned against her in sympathy, and she was thankful that Thundegar and the cat remained; at least she had them.

* * *

Pain.
Thought came later along with questions. What happened? Memory was slower to return, and when it did, Sinjin drew a deep breath. His airway was clear. His hand reached instinctively to his throat, and though a little tender, it didn't seem bruised or crushed. Either the dragon had lacked the strength to kill him, or it had chosen not to. With that thought, his vision began to focus, and he saw Durin sleeping on the cold stone nearby, only his cloak for a pillow.

More senses returned and Sinjin smelled fish--raw fish--quite strongly. It offended his already delicate stomach and got him moving, and that's when he felt the weight on his left arm. Looking down, he saw coppery scales coiled there. Sudden fear raised his heart rate, and he must have made some sound, for Durin came awake with a start.

"It's all right," he said, even while rubbing the sleep from his eyes. "The dragon actually likes you. Now that he's fed, he doesn't bite as much, and he hasn't tried to choke you in a while. He's got some pretty sharp teeth, that one."

It was then Sinjin remembered Durin trying to save him. Looking more closely, he saw bandages on Durin's arms and hands. "How badly are you hurt?" he asked.

"It's not that bad. Millie had a fit, though, and had to clean all the cuts and put humrus root on them."

"Did she make you drink it too?"

"You know she did," Durin said. "That stuff tastes like dirty feet."

Sinjin would have laughed, but he was still worried about waking the dragon. Durin had said it liked him, but he still wasn't so sure.

"He likes fish," Durin said. "Well, they all do, I guess."

"All?"

"The rest of the eggs hatched," Durin said. "Benjin convinced the Arghast to follow your lead."

"But I didn't do anything," Sinjin said.

"Exactly," Durin replied. "They were all chasing your dragon around, and you just sat there. The dragon came to you because you were calm."

"And did that work for the Arghast?"

"It did," Durin said, "though the fish didn't hurt either. Benjin also suggested they have fish ready for the hungry hatchlings. They started out with smoked fish, but now some fresh fish is starting to make its way up. For desert people, the Arghast have taken to fishing remarkably well."

Sinjin's dragon shifted and adjusted itself to get more comfortable then gave a great sigh. Hooded eyes twitched and the dragon seemed content.

"You won't believe how much those things can eat," Durin said. "It's only sleeping now because it gorged itself. Two whole fish he ate! I had to cut it up, and I couldn't cut fast enough. I had to let him gnaw on one while I cut the other."

Sinjin noted that Durin assumed the dragon was male, though he had the same sense. There was no outward sign to easily indicate sex, yet Sinjin felt confident that this was a male dragon. If there were a female hatchling, would she be the queen? Could there be more than one? Questions filled Sinjin's mind, and he thought so much uncertainty might relieve him of his sanity.

"Do you think they are like the ferals?" Sinjin asked, knowing there was no way Durin could tell any more than he could. Neither had any point of reference. Perhaps this was exactly how Thorakis had succumbed to the dragons. It may have started innocently at first and grown over time once the bond was formed. This bond was not something of conjecture for Sinjin; already he could feel it. He and this dragon were bonding. Already he felt the need to protect this frail creature that nuzzled his side. Already he knew that he could not kill this dragon; if this were a creature of darkness, then he was lost. Not wanting Durin to know his thoughts, Sinjin said nothing of these feelings.

"The Arghast who weren't chosen have been more gracious than you might guess," Durin said, not noticing what must have shown in Sinjin's eyes. "They've vowed to provide for the 'Drakon,' which is what they call those with dragons."

Drakon--the word raised the hair on Sinjin's neck, and he looked to Durin, who now seemed uncertain.

"They have a name for you now," Durin said after a long pause. Sinjin watched his friend with a strange sense of anticipation. It should not matter what anyone called him since that would in no way change who he was, but still Sinjin felt as if this moment would change things. "They call you Al'Drakon."

The title felt heavy.

"It means 'First Dragon,'" Durin said. "Halmsa said it is the highest honor."

Sinjin let that statement sink in. What had he gotten himself into? He'd come here to help the Arghast and to make sure the dragons did not threaten the world, and now he'd bonded with a dragon and had become something entirely different to these people; he'd become a part of them. In some ways it helped him to feel as if he had purpose and that he belonged, but mostly it made him feel strange and frightened. So much had changed. Once he'd thought he knew what his future held, but now he couldn't imagine what would come next.

"It looks like you're feeling a good bit better," Benjin said from one side, "and you look far better pink than blue."

"I was just telling Al'Drakon about what happened after he swooned," Durin said with a wicked grin.

"I didn't swoon and don't call me Al'Drakon," Sinjin said, and Durin barked a laugh.

"You'd better get used to it," Benjin said. "The Arghast now refer to you exclusively as Al'Drakon, and they say it with a wild look in their eyes."

"But--" Sinjin said and his dragon stirred. All three watched the magnificent little creature as its hooded eyes opened, revealing eyes like sparkling jewels, liquid and looking deep. For the first time, the dragon looked at Sinjin with calm, knowing eyes. Truly he was lost. If killing the dragon was the right thing to do, he no longer possessed the ability to do what was right; that was the thing that worried him most. Still, in the gaze of this wonderful creature, he felt at peace, he felt as if everything would be as it should, even though things in the world were clearly not as they should be.

"What's his name?" Benjin asked quietly, seemingly afraid to frighten the dragon.

"I don't--" Sinjin started to say, but then he knew. The knowing was absolute and left no room for doubt or conjecture. His parents had taught him the power of names, and he knew this was no small thing. "Valterius," Sinjin said, and the named felt good as it left his lips. Valterius closed his eyes slowly and gave a subtle nod then he pressed his forehead against Sinjin's side and nuzzled him.

"Valterius," Benjin said, and the dragon eyed him with a look full of suspicion and doubt. "A powerful name, indeed." At those words, Valterius gave Benjin an even less pronounced nod before hiding his head in Sinjin's armpit. "I'm glad to see you doing well. I suggest you rest a day or two and regain your strength. Millie has some broth heating, and I'm going to go down with the fishing crew and see if I can help them catch more fish. Something tells me that we're going to need a steady supply."

Valterius cooed at those words and continued to nuzzle Sinjin.

Durin shook his head. "I have to admit," he said. "I didn't see this coming."

"Me either," Sinjin said.

Chapter 16

Few things are as dangerous as belief.
--Master Edling

* * *

War was coming. Sensi was a fool. He should've seen this coming. He should have known. Sensi walked faster than he would under any other circumstances. They had been complacent, and now they would all pay the price. Sweat gathered at his brow, and he wiped it away. Entering the Hall of the Forbearers, he ignored the carved representations of the first council; he'd seen them many times before. Only some of those there to represent the Midlands had seen them before, and the others were still a bit wide eyed. The stonework and the way the natural colors within the rock had been highlighted to make them look so real were enough to baffle even the most experienced among them.

At the center of the room was an ancient table made from the cross section of some giant tree, one larger than any known to the lands. This, too, was enough to intimidate and amaze. At one side of the table waited the council and the lord chancellor. They looked as if they were trying to appear nonchalant; they were failing. Sensi knew he was as well. Opposite them sat Lord Bercheron of the Midlands and his sycophants.

Between the groups and clearly not with either group sat Onin. He took up as much space as two other men, and those from the Midlands avoided eye contact with him, which was not so different from those from the Heights. Onin had not officially been invited to this meeting, but he couldn't be kept away; it was within his rights as a member of the old guard. He and his dragon were granted the same rights and access as the current guard, save to the lord chancellor's quarters.

Most of the old guard no longer involved themselves with the business of the realm, but then again, most of the old guard didn't have dragons and didn't still actively fly in defense of the trade routes. Onin was an enigma, as was Jehregard. Neither of them fit in or seemed to want to fit in. They simply were as they were, and no amount of pressure from others was going to change them.

Sensi poured wine for those gathered and drank some from each cup before wiping the rim and handing it to his desired recipient. He started with those from the Mids, and they waited to drink. Next, he served the lord chancellor and the council; they, too, refrained from drinking. Before pouring himself a cup, Sensi poured for Onin and walked around the table to serve him. Before Sensi had even walked away, the big man sniffed the contents of the cup, grunted, and downed it in a single gulp. After slamming the cup down on the table, he dragged his arm across his mouth to wipe away the excess.

The others avoided looking at him even more intensely.

"Would it be so that we met under less dire circumstances," the lord chancellor said. "Your journey's been long. May this wine quench your thirst and wash away the weariness of your travels."

The formal greeting finished, all but Onin drank.

"It's going to take more than that," Onin said, holding his cup out to Sensi and wiggling it just a little.

Sensi had every right to be insulted, but he would leave that to the rest in the room. The air sang with tension, and Sensi had to admit that Onin did serve a purpose at this meeting. He gave the lord chancellor and Lord Bercheron a common adversary, both in the room and in the Jaga. Sensi filled Onin's cup, and the brute downed another cup and grabbed Sensi's arms, guiding him to fill it one more time before he left. "Would anyone else like more wine?" Sensi asked. The fact that no one else had done more than sip the wine only highlighted Onin's behavior.

"The ferals have been fooling us for some time," the lord chancellor continued, ignoring Onin. "We don't know how long, but it appears to have been enough time to amass significant strength."

"How has this activity gone undetected?" Lord Bercheron asked. "You've been flying over the Jaga all this time. How could you have been unaware of this?"

"The state of the black swamp has remained largely the same for years," the lord chancellor said. "We'd see abominations within the swamp and ferals flying low, but we never saw any outside the blackness. We knew the men that lived within the black swamp had a ship or two, but we never saw more than one of them at a time."

"Then where?" Lord Bercheron asked.

"Uninhabited islands," the lord chancellor said, "in the Endless Sea."

Lord Bercheron didn't say anything for a long while, clearly disturbed by the implications. "How many ships and how many . . . troops?"

"We don't know," the lord chancellor said. "We believe we've only seen a part of their overall strength."

"Why don't you send your dragons to investigate?" Lord Bercheron asked.

"The same reason that no one in their right mind sails the Endless Sea: it's too dangerous. Ships and dragons alike tend to disappear within that great expanse. We can't afford to lose dragons. Even flying the trade routes is treacherous. Ferals have been seen flying high, and we'll need all our strength to keep trade open."

"What do you propose?"

"A coordinated strike," the lord chancellor said. "A single, preplanned, and fortified attack with all the supplies and rations needed in place well before the attack starts. Using overwhelming force, we can close the black swamp in a vice."

Lord Bercheron looked as if he liked that plan not at all.

"You haven't the slightest chance of taking that swamp on the ground," Onin said, and Sensi winced.

"On that we agree," Lord Bercheron said.

The lord chancellor looked as if he might burst into flame. "I believe if we come from the air and the ground, we'll have the best chance of solving this problem once and for all. We can set the black swamp ablaze and drive them out. All the ground forces have to do is deal with the filth that crawls out. It should be no more difficult than an afternoon hunt."

Sensi knew the lord chancellor was playing on the Midlands' love of hunting, and he doubted it would be enough.

"There'll be a high price," Lord Bercheron said. "A lord's ransom in blood."

"It will be so either way," Onin said. "They have the strength to defeat us, or they would still be hiding."

"What would you have us do?" the lord chancellor asked Onin, his patience gone. "Lie down and die?"

"I would have you think, and then I would have you fight, but you won't fight. You'll sit up here and sip wine while the people of the Heights and the Midlands die. I would ask you to open your eyes and think, but you won't do it. You're blind."

Sensi wasn't certain Onin was wrong, but he also wasn't certain his input was all that helpful. The others in the room clearly agreed with him on that point.

"Ask yourself why the first time we see more than one of their ships, they're damaged, clearly from battle. Must you not then ask yourself who they fought?"

"You're not going to quote prophecy, are you?" the lord chancellor asked, his voice pained.

"The signs have come," Onin said. "The Herald of Istra will come. And even if you think I'm crazy for heeding the warnings of our forefathers--"he looked around at the lifelike statues of those very people"--then consider the fact that you need to know who they've been fighting, where, and what their strength is. You'll get none of this quickly enough without a dragon."

"If all you were looking for was permission to take your *dragon* and go in search of fairy tales, then you should've just said so," the lord chancellor snapped.

Sensi then saw how clever Onin had been. The lord chancellor did not have the authority to tell Onin where to go, but he did have the right to ground any dragon he felt was unfit for flight. It had happened before when an older dragon's frailties endangered the lives of all those around them, including other dragons. Already there weren't enough dragons to keep up with the trade needs, and too few were the hatchlings. The unspoken fear for all those in the Heights came from the knowledge that the dragons' numbers were dwindling, along with them went the reasons people chose to live in the Heights. They were a dying civilization, even if they didn't want to admit it. Onin's dragon had enough abnormalities that he could have been considered unsafe for flight at hatching, but everyone knew the story of how Onin had saved Jehregard.

"Go," the lord chancellor said. "Take your *dragon* and go. It'll be a pity if you don't make it back."

Onin walked from the room smiling.

* * *

Standing in what was being called the wind channel, Sinjin held onto Valterius, his hands wrapped firmly around the dragon's legs. Never would he have believed how quickly the dragons would grow--or eat, for that matter. Those responsible for catching enough fish to feed all the hungry dragons were hard pressed, but those with dragons were in no position to help. It had become apparent that young dragons required constant care, attention, and feeding. To neglect any of these needs was to be pecked, nudged, nipped, or scolded. The ever-growing creature somehow knew its strength and managed to keep from seriously injuring Sinjin, but that didn't mean he didn't have bruises to show for his missteps.

Benjin had warned that they might not be able to provide sufficient fish for the dragons as the majestic creatures grew. Sinjin worried more about this than anything else, even as Valterius spread his wings and nearly lifted them both from the ground. The steady and predictable wind here made the place ideal for practicing flying, and Valterius seemed to love lifting Sinjin enough to scare him. Part of him wanted to let Valterius go and hope he would come back, but he came from a family of horse trainers, and he'd been warned that he might never see the dragon again if he let him go. It wouldn't be long before he would have no choice but to let the dragon do as it wished. At their current rate of growth, they'd be the size of horses within a week. Valterius continued to fill out, his body no longer thin, yet he flew with ease and confidence.

Again Valterius cried out and lifted Sinjin from the stone. This time he didn't immediately put Sinjin back down, and there was a sick feeling in Sinjin's gut as they soared across the hollow mountain toward open air. Never before had Valterius shown so much strength; Sinjin had underestimated him. Faster they flew, and the time left to make a decision was rapidly running out.

"Sinjin!" Durin's voice called from behind them.

Time ran out.

Trusting his gut and Valterius, Sinjin let go. Hitting the stone, he rolled and skidded to a stop a scant distance from the edge. Valterius moved upward sharply when Sinjin let go, but he quickly corrected and let out a final call before bursting into the skies beyond. Nursing new bruises, Sinjin watched his dragon disappear into the clouds.

* * *

It was with great personal pride and purpose that Onin guided Jehregard away from the Heights, leaving all the land-bound behind. They didn't understand him, and they never would. The lord chancellor thought him daft and had only allowed him to leave in the hopes that he'd never return. Onin had counted on this, and he didn't care how he'd won that victory, only that he got what he needed, which was permission to fly outside the established trade routes. Onin had pushed the limits for as long as the restriction had been put into effect, but he'd never been at much risk of repercussions. The rules were meant to protect the valuable dragons, and Jehregard did not fit that definition for most. For what was to come, though, he would need the support of the council, and this had given him their approval no matter what their motivations.

Though his destination was the Endless Sea, and Onin was more than anxious to begin his search, he couldn't help but do a sweep over the eastern coast of the Jaga. It was beautiful this time of year, at least from above, and he was grateful once again for Jehregard; the two of them had been through more than anyone would ever know. Certainly they had suffered more for the Heights than the lord chancellor ever had, yet most thought him daft or mad. No one spoke of Jehregard within his hearing, at least no one who wanted to remain alive, but he knew the things people said. They'd never know the selfless service his dragon had provided for longer than most of them had been alive, and that was the rub; he was old, outdated, obsolete. There was no more king, and the old guard were little more than decoration; they no longer served any purpose.

Onin had refused to share that fate. He and Jehregard continued to fly flanking maneuvers for the trade flights. Having no official role in the missions left him the latitude to explore along the outer edges of the trade routes. He had seen things there that others would claim were illusions or tricks of the eye, but he'd seen them, and no one had flown as low and close over the black swamp as he and Jehregard. It was not a memory he relished, but at least he understood what they were facing, which was more than he could say for any of those within the Heights. The fools thought their problem was confined to the Jaga, and they were about to find out just how large Godsland really was.

Riding the thermals, Jehregard took them higher, and Onin wrapped his face in furs. The land looked surreal from such height, and he was once again amazed by the majesty of flight. Slapping Jehregard on the neck, Onin knew his mighty friend barely felt it, but it was easier than swinging a hammer at the dragon's rocklike hide.

Looking down, Onin saw a disturbing sight: dozens of feral dragons swarming over the marshes and jungle. It was like looking down on sharks in the water from above, except these dangerous beasts were in the air. Despite the cold, a bead of sweat formed on Onin's brow. He and Jehregard could handle one or two ferals, which was the most that had been seen at one time in years, but now there were dozens. They would tear them apart.

Guiding his dragon out to sea, Onin cursed when he saw the mass of black ships approaching; this was something he'd hoped to be wrong about but he wasn't. War was coming, and the enemy had the upper hand. It was his fault; he should have been more diligent, he should have convinced the rest of the old guard to join him in his quest, but even they thought him mad. For too long they had lived under the mantle of symbolic power, and now they were soft and weak and lazy-- no help to Onin at all--still, he should have tried harder.

When he saw the dark currents, a chill knifed through him. Moving like a single organism, clouds of something dark moved with the currents, riding along with the moving water like a ship sailing downriver. At first he thought it might be schools of fish, possibly a migration, but Jehregard took them lower and it soon became clear that these were large creatures and definitely not fish. Even from high above, something about these beasts seemed wrong. Onin grimaced. It was even worse than he'd thought.

He should go back and warn them, he thought, but then his better sense reminded him that they wouldn't listen; they never listened. Not until it was too late would they act. Even knowing this, Onin cared deeply about the Heights--the people and the dragons. In the end, he did as he'd known he'd do all along.

* * *

Scraped and bruised, Sinjin stepped up to Valterius with mock bravery. Benjin had told him not to flinch, but he couldn't help it; he'd already felt Valterius's displeasure. It was clear now that Valterius and his twenty-three brethren were not feral dragons, nor were they regent dragons; they were also not verdant dragons, which were described as four-legged behemoths. It was generally agreed that these dragons were the offspring of Kyrien and the feral queen, a mixture of feral and regent. Benjin had been the one to suggest that they be called regal dragons, and the name had stuck. Now, though, Valterius didn't seem as much regal as he did dangerous; perhaps it was his feral blood shining through. All Sinjin wanted to do was lay a piece of soft cloth over the dragon's back, but you would think he was trying to kill him. The two were bonded, and it was clear that Sinjin intended him no harm, and still the dragon refused.

When Valterius had returned with his own fish and had come to Sinjin once his belly was full, Sinjin had thought his dragon trained; the next few weeks had proven him wrong. Most of the Drakon had already acclimated their dragons to saddle pads, and some had even managed something akin to a bridle, though no one had attempted to get a dragon to accept a bit. They had all followed his lead thus far. Though having Valterius return from fishing on his own had been a major victory for Sinjin, he still knew he was losing what respect he'd had with regard to training his dragon. The Drakon trained in the same area, and there were no secrets. Successes were celebrated together, and failures were seen by all--especially Sinjin's failures. The last few had been rather spectacular, and he wasn't certain if people were rooting him on or hoping to see how he would fail next. Sinjin just prayed Valterius didn't kill him.

Valterius looked down at Sinjin in a way that dared him to take another step. He was large enough to overwhelm Sinjin and fly away, but that did not appear to be his desire. At the same time, he clearly did not want Sinjin to saddle him. No matter what Sinjin tried to put on Valterius, the dragon would have none of it. This time would be different, he told himself, though he squinted and tensed when he approached. He'd already tried letting Valterius smell the cloth, which had resulted in a sound rebuke, one that had left Sinjin's ears ringing and his ribs hurting. Tucking his wings and twitching his tail, Valterius lowered his head, looking ready to strike.

"Easy," Sinjin said. "Easy there. You know I won't hurt you."

Apparently that matter was still in question since Valterius struck him, closed mouthed, with force that made it feel like a hammer blow. Falling backward, Sinjin tried to catch himself but still he hit the stone hard, driving the wind from his lungs.

"The best ones are always the toughest to break," Benjin said. "If they weren't, you wouldn't appreciate it as much."

Sinjin had heard that before, and it hadn't helped the first time either.

"You're gonna have to blindfold him," Benjin said.

"I don't think that's going to happen," Sinjin said, and Benjin held his tongue. "I need to try something different."

Valterius watched him approach, clearly dubious. Sinjin held nothing in his hands and nothing behind his back; Valterius was far too clever for that. Though clever, he could not speak in Sinjin's mind as Kyrien had with his mother and a few other rather unwilling communicants. In some ways that comforted Sinjin since that made it less likely that regal dragons could control the minds of men, but it also presented Sinjin with his current problem. He was failing to clearly communicate his intentions; it was something his grandfather had taught him and that Benjin echoed, but that didn't make it any easier to accomplish. Steadily he approached, his hands outstretched. His well-muscled side heaving, Valterius watched, his flicking tail indicating his agitation.

Sinjin just remained calm and laid his hands on the dragon's side. Almost instantly Valterius calmed. Unmoving, Sinjin used the physical bond to communicate with the dragon, as his mother had once done with horses. He didn't know if he was doing it correctly, but the fact that Valterius hadn't stepped on him or smacked him with his tail was an encouraging sign. Reaching up, he put his hands higher, and Valterius leaned into him. For a moment, Sinjin worried the dragon might bowl him over, but it remained only a gentle push. Again, he moved his hands higher until his fingers crossed over the ridge of the dragon's back, the scales smooth and cool under his touch.

Hooking his fingers over that ridge, in front of the wing structures, Sinjin pulled gently, applying only slight pressure. Then he pulled again, using greater force. Gradually he built up the amount of force he was using until he was doing pull-ups. With a suddenness that startled all who watched, Sinjin pulled himself up and swung his leg over the dragon's shoulder. Straddling the dragon was surprisingly comfortable, and Sinjin fit well against his dragon; he felt secure and could wrap his hands around Valterius's neck. Pleased with the progress, Sinjin pushed down and raised his right leg to dismount. Valterius had seemed mostly at ease up until that moment, but to this move he objected.

Dropping down and rising back up sharply, Valterius helped Sinjin reseat himself. Then, without warning, he spun and started running. Sinjin wrapped his arms around the dragon's neck and held on as best he could, his perch no longer feeling safe or sturdy. Other dragons reacted to Valterius's calls, and soon all the Drakon had agitated dragons on their hands. Many turned to Sinjin and Valterius with looks of exasperation and irritation, but most just did their best to get out of the way. Sinjin could hear the shouts but could discern nothing.

Once more, he considered leaping from Valterius's back, but the dragon's speed was remarkable and they were nearing the edge. Looking back to when Valterius had first flown on his own, Sinjin once again decided to trust his dragon and abandoned his fear. An instant later, when Valterius leaped into the open air, he reconsidered that decision. Valterius did not soar on outstretched wings as Sinjin had imagined; he trimmed his wings, and they dropped like a stone. Feeling his guts pressing against his chin, Sinjin did what he could to hold on and not faint. The view was incredibly beautiful and yet more terrifying than anything he'd ever seen.

Valterius issued a shrill cry that this time sounded jubilant; he was sharing his favorite thing with Sinjin, and he was doing it his way. The message was clear, and Sinjin wondered at the fact that he understood. It was not what his mother and Kyrien had shared, but it was something, and he latched on to it as hard as he clung to Valterius's neck. He was surprised he wasn't restricting the dragon's breathing with his death grip. It was an awkward moment when he realized that he probably was, and he eased his grip. He received a vague sense of relief in return. It was not a mental image or anything like that; it was more from Valterius's posture and movements. Still they fell, and the wind threatened to tear Sinjin from where he sat. At that moment he would have liked nothing more than a smaller version of his mother's saddle.

Forested foothills raced toward them like a giant hammer ready to smite them. Even in his terror, Sinjin couldn't help but notice the stark contrast between the natural beauty of this place and the vast swaths of land that had been devastated by armies, a monstrous battle, and the death of far too many dragons. Nature would win out in time and reclaim that which marred the landscape, but the history would remain. The place of dragons was not without a painful past. It was a strange thing to think in the moments before certain death, but it kept him from fainting.

At what seemed the last possible moment, Valterius spread his wings, opening them slowly. Sinjin was pressed down hard into the dragon, and the trees whisked beneath them at unbelievable speed. Keeping his head and body low to his dragon's neck, he ducked his head. Tears ran from his eyes from the speed. For a moment, there was a flash of bright white then dark blue; they were over the sea. Sinjin tightened his grip--probably a little too much--and prayed Valterius didn't drop him in the sea. He'd seen the monsters that lurked in those waters, and he wanted nothing to do with swimming in such dangerous seas. All of which assumed he would survive the fall at such speed, which was unlikely.

Sinjin had never considered himself a brave person, but he did his best to overcome his fear. Valterius shifted his course and turned toward where Sinjin could see a dark shape in the water; whatever it was, it was big. Fear continued to build, making him want to squeeze tighter, but he fought the urge, not wanting Valterius to black out. That would be the end of them both, especially with large creatures in the waters around them. Even if they survived the fall, they would likely be eaten, a thought that was almost too much for Sinjin, but he kept his grip loose enough to allow the dragon to breathe.

About when he thought he might be able to identify the type of monster to which Valterius wanted to feed him, the shadowy thing broke apart. It took a moment to register, and Sinjin chided himself for not realizing sooner. When Valterius hit the water, most of the school had dispersed, but one gleaming green, blue, and silver fish lay right in the path of the dragon's claws. The impact jarred Sinjin forward, and he nearly lost his grip. After that, Valterius pumped his wings vigorously to gain altitude, despite the heavy load. The fish was huge, and Sinjin wasn't certain all three of them would gain the air. The seas grew more distant, though, a testament to the dragon's mighty effort, and they were soon sailing on thermals that rose along the strip of sand. Every part of Sinjin tingled, and his arms felt weak. He hoped Valterius wouldn't make any more sudden moves since he wasn't certain he'd be able to hold on.

The dragon seemed a bit smug, and Sinjin sensed something of a rebuke as they returned to the hollow mountain. He hadn't trusted Valterius. He'd expected Valterius to trust him to put a saddle on him, yet he hadn't returned that trust.

"I'm sorry," he said as they glided back into the hold, where a crowd stood watching and waiting. Sinjin could sense the anticipation even from the air. This was a moment that had been foretold. Al'Drakon had flown his dragon. Sinjin hoped this would redeem him in the eyes of the others.

A moment later, the crowd parted, and Valterius landed gracefully. The fish he transferred to his jaws, and he walked to the area designated for him and Sinjin, just as he always did when he returned with a fish. Sinjin remained where he was until Valterius stopped; the dragon then turned and looked at him as if to indicate that he was holding up the meal. The Drakon had gathered round, and Sinjin felt as if he should say something, but the dragon's glare convinced him to dismount first. Pushing down with his hands, Sinjin attempted to swing his right leg over the dragon's back, but he didn't get it clear of the ridge, and he lost his balance. As a result, instead of a graceful dismount, he turned and slid, upside down, to the cold stone.

Looking at the inverted faces watching him, Sinjin had to accept the fact that, in his role as Al'Drakon, he might be something of a disappointment.

Chapter 17

Extreme thoughts yield extreme actions.
--Imeteri, slave

* * *

Standing before Valterius, Sinjin questioned the sanity of trying, once again, to saddle the dragon. Still, he knew they needed the ability to fly together. Though he had never aspired to riding dragons, he knew it was what he must now do. Part of it was the weight of responsibility left behind by his mother, and part of it was to feel closer to her. No matter how much time went by, he missed his parents terribly, feeling the gaping hole inside of him. Working with Valterius eased that weight and gave him the satisfaction that he was, at least, doing something positive, something his parents would've been proud to see him do.

Durin and Benjin stood nearby, ready to help, as always. Kendra also watched from not much farther away but didn't want Sinjin to know she was watching. She had taken on the role of huntress and was revered for her ability to provide skins, meat, and leather. A tannery had sprung into existence on a lower level, and those Dragon clan who were not Drakon worked to provide the materials necessary to construct saddles. It was a more difficult process than Sinjin had initially imagined. He'd always taken for granted the materials available on the Godfist and those skillful hands that turned raw materials into thread, needles, thimbles, candles, and the like. Here, on the Firstland, they had access to only the raw materials with the exception of what they had brought with them. Already he was considering asking Benjin to sail back to the Godfist for supplies and to check on the progress of the ships.

All of these things ran through his mind while he stood with a leather strap in his hands, one that he needed to put over Valterius's now mighty neck. The dragon continued to fill out and ate more than any creature Sinjin had ever seen, but he'd stopped growing longer or his wings wider. Still, he looked at the strap with distaste. Knowing he would need to do something different this time, Sinjin tried to remember all the things Benjin and his grandfather had taught him about horses, but he found nothing in his memory to aid him. It occurred to him then that his mother had taught him some things about animals as well, though seemingly not in as intentional a fashion as the men had taught him about horses. She had told him stories of the things she'd experienced, such as her adventure with Curly the cross-eyed bull, but it was another story that gave him inspiration in the end.

Taking one more step forward, Sinjin saw Valterius adopt a defensive posture, a sure sign that he wanted nothing to do with the strap. Then Sinjin sat on the stone before Valterius, closed his eyes, and held the length of leather. Nothing happened for a long time, and Sinjin was certain that he was, once again, making a complete fool of himself, but he could think of nothing else to do. Around him, the hold was silent save the rush of the wind. Feeling silly and more than a little in jeopardy of being stepped on, Sinjin was about to open his eyes when a puff of warm air hit his hands and the top of his head. Through sheer strength of will, he kept his eyes closed and waited. In his mind, he pictured himself on Valterius's back, a leather saddle beneath him and straps securing him so he didn't have to choke Valterius to stay in place.

There was another long silence, but then there came a muted snuffling sound as Valterius sniffed the strap. The dragon snorted and Sinjin heard the mighty beast recoil. For a moment, he thought he'd failed again, but he remained silent, his eyes closed. He held the strap in the air. In his mind, he pictured them flying together; all he wanted to do was share the skies with his magnificent companion.

It came as a shock when Valterius snorted again and the strap was yanked from Sinjin's hands. Slowly he opened his eyes, hoping he wasn't about to be rebuked. Before him, Valterius stood tall and proud, the leather strap now draped over his withers. Never before had he so resembled the regal name, and he looked as if he wore the strap with great pride, something Sinjin had trouble understanding. He'd tried dozens of times to put something over the dragon's withers, and always he'd been rebuked, but now the dragon beamed with pride. There had been only one difference: Valterius, not Sinjin, had decided, and apparently that made all the difference in the world to the dragon.

In a behavior that Sinjin hadn't seen before, Valterius strutted before the other dragons, many of which already bore trappings of saddles in progress. Sinjin wasn't certain how the other dragons and Drakon would react, but all of them showed Valterius great respect and deference. For the first time, he heard the name Al'Drak whispered then chanted as Valterius stood before the open air, silhouetted before bright blue skies. The dragon spread his wings and gave a triumphant call that was returned by all the dragons. Sinjin knew then that, as Al'Drakon, he did not command reverence and respect, but as Al'Drak, his dragon did. It was a humbling moment, but it taught him something. He and Valterius complemented each other, each strong where the other was weak.

Valterius then resumed a more humble posture and walked back toward Sinjin. He'd once imagined that dragons would walk awkwardly, like many birds, but Valterius moved with fluid grace and economy of movement. When he returned, he bowed his head to Sinjin, who had no idea what to do. Everyone was watching them, yet he did what his heart wanted him to do, he wrapped his arms around the dragon's neck and gave him a hug and a couple of pats on his neck. It was something he'd seen horseman do with their favorite steeds, and it seemed appropriate. Valterius sheltered Sinjin within his wings and arched his neck, his head hovering over Sinjin, daring anyone to threaten him.

When he released his dragon and turned around, Sinjin saw the Drakon approaching. Many of them had made a great deal more progress in making their saddles than Sinjin had, and each of them approached with parts of the saddles they had created for themselves. These items they presented to Valterius by sitting cross-legged and holding their contributions above their heads--they had been watching. The dragon gave each gift equal consideration and inspection, his great waffling sniffs causing some to giggle. To each he gave a gentle nudge of thanks with his forehead; for some the gesture was too much, and they had to be helped away by their brethren. The Drakon paid respect to Sinjin as well, but it was Valterius who commanded that respect. Soon all the components Sinjin needed for his saddle lay before Valterius. By their Arghast heritage, the Drakon were practical people, and once the needed saddle components had been given, people gave other items they thought would be needed for flying. One woman gave a leather water flask with straps to easily bind it in place; another gave a coat made of deer hide, and two men presented supple but warm boots they had crafted together.

It was as strange a feeling as Sinjin had ever felt, as he stood by his dragon's side and watched the Drakon show him their respect. The gifts were generous beyond anything Sinjin had ever received, even if indirectly, given the scarcity. These objects were the things that the Drakon had poured all their resources into creating. These were the hopes and the dreams of the Drakon, the Dragon clan, and perhaps the Arghast collectively. Sinjin couldn't claim to understand the Arghast legends and beliefs, yet he was now deeply entrenched in them. He came to know then how his mother must have once felt. He was part of something over which he had no control and very little understanding, yet his actions would write history. The pressure of it made him tremble.

After the gifts had been given, the Drakon came to Sinjin. He stood before them, humbled and a little shocked. They had all just effectively ignored him in the moments before, but he now realized that they saw things differently. The respect they showed him now made it clear the insult was only perceived; Sinjin reminded himself to be careful of that; he was among a community whose rules he did not know and whose traditions were a mystery to him. If only someone could tell him exactly what it was he was supposed to do. The world was falling apart, and he knew so few of the things needed to make any difference whatsoever, yet here were these people standing before him.

"May we help you assemble your saddle?" Mikala asked, Arakhan at her side.

The two had continued to grow in power and influence, and they wore it well. Sinjin was proud of his mother's choices. Though he missed her dearly, she had, in many ways, made this easier for him. Even if he did still face insurmountable challenges; she'd done what she could. No one could have predicted what the future held, even those who seemed to have some uncanny ability to catch glimpses of the future. Her struggle was over, it seemed, and his had only just begun.

* * *

Numb, Allette followed Thundegar and Rastas in a haze; only the light of comets and the moon shining through the patchwork of clouds lighting their way. Thundegar looked over his shoulder, looking near worn out but still determined. What looked like annoyance crossed his face for an instant, but it was replaced by concern and empathy. "I'm sorry."

Allette said nothing; there were no words. She did meet his eyes, and there was an apology in them.

"Do your best to keep up," he said.

It was pointless, Allette knew, but Thundegar would not give up; he would persist until they died horrible deaths in the swamps and marshes. There was no cover between the jungle and the Cloud Forest, only open expanses of marsh, swamp, and desert, and there would be no place to hide. With ferals in the skies, those were the last places they should go, but still she could find no words. Something inside of her was broken, and she wasn't certain it could ever be mended. The pain was unbearable, and only the need to survive, driven by primal instinct, kept her going. Already the trees were thinning, and the marshes could be seen through the gaps. Despite her thoughts, she continued to follow, unwilling to let Thundegar and Rastas go, yet unable to make them stay.

Not long after the trees were left behind, they found their canoe, which had been mostly claimed by the grasses; even if there had been large enough channels to row through, getting it out intact looked like an impossibility. Thundegar gave her a wistful look and shook his head before moving on. Again she wanted to speak out, to plead with him to stay in the jungle where they at least had some chance, however slim, but still she could not. Tears of frustration flowed freely.

"Are you all right?" Thundegar asked when he next looked back.

Allette shook her head.

"Can you tell me what's wrong?"

Again she shook her head.

Thundegar was about to ask another question, but he went silent when the light around them shifted. He cast his gaze to the skies, and Allette did as well, feeling like a squirrel looking for the hawk. When she saw a dark shape block the light as it moved across the skies, she couldn't help but draw a sharp breath. Waves of fear washed over her, and her strength fled. Thundegar had said that the ferals didn't fly at night and that he, Allette, and Rastas could hide themselves within the grasses during the day. She'd been skeptical of his plan from the beginning, knowing the sands waited beyond, and the thought of being buried in the sand along with the snakes and scorpions frightened her almost as much as the black swamp did. Now knowing the dragons could and did fly at night, the plan seemed hopeless. They'd be lucky to make it back to the trees. She knew they were scant protection, but they were preferable to the wide openness of the marsh.

Silently he pointed back the way they had come, and they moved with all the speed they could muster over the unpredictable and spongy landscape. Thundegar took a bad step and slid up to his knee in mud. Twice he tried to pull himself free, but the quagmire held him fast. Grunting, he tried again, and Rastas huddled nearby, crouched low, his ears folded back. When Allette heard the first growl, she thought it was Rastas, but the cat sat trembling before her and was incapable of issuing a growl as deep as the next one she heard. This one sounded like drums being played in a cave, and she could feel it as well as hear it. Thundegar's movements became more frantic, and Allette reached out to him, trying to help pull him free. There was a long sucking sound, and they both fell backward, Thundegar's bare foot suddenly free of the mud and his boot.

Before either of them could move or react, the big cats struck. Rastas let out a high-pitched howl, and one of the much larger cats squared off with him. More cats came, and Thundegar pushed himself backward with his hands and feet. Allette could not move quickly enough, and a massive paw struck her in the face, the claws only a hair's width from raking her eyes. Sent tumbling backward, Allette was separated from Thundegar and Rastas. She could see their forms struggling in the comet light. Dividing them was the shape of the cat that stalked her. Thundegar screamed and Allette yearned to be by his side, defending him. A moment later Rastas issued a terrifying sound, and Thundegar's cry suddenly rose in pitch and intensity.

The menacing darkness moved closer, crouched low and silent, its muscles bunched and ready to release. Faced with the most difficult and painful decision she'd ever known, Allette shamed herself and the memory of her father and the memory of the *Maker's Mark*. Thundegar was lost and so was Rastas. She could not save them, and she chose instead to save herself. *To be a coward,* part of her screamed. Again, the darkness flying through the skies blotted out the comets and Allette ran. Behind her, she could hear the grasses parting as the land-bound black death descended upon her. Just before she expected to feel the bite of tooth and claw, Allette turned and fell, looking back at the rapidly approaching cat.

For some reason unknown to Allette, the beast slowed and regarded her. There was no friendliness or charity there, only a bit of curiosity. Quivering, Allette stared into the eyes of death and she pleaded. *Not me,* she said with her eyes. *Not me. You don't want to kill me. Not me.*

Another of Thundegar's cries split the air.

Not me.

The cat blinked then slowly turned and walked back toward the others. Allette ran.

* * *

Creating a comfortable space within the hollow mountain, where there was naught but rock and more rock, was a challenging thing indeed. The few items they had brought with them were strewn about with nothing that resembled real order. A small fire circle surrounded by melon-sized rocks was the most organized thing in their camp. It seemed odd to camp within a mountain, but they were far from settled. It would take years to establish the services and materials needed to replicate things they had taken for granted on the Godfist. Here there were no mines, no forges, no mills, no farms, nothing but unfriendly wilderness.

Only the discovery of what people were calling stalk weed gave Durin any hope for establishing some order in the short term. Stalk weed grew in large quantities and was relatively easy to harvest. When mature, the stuff was as big around as Durin's forearm and twice his height. Each stalk was hollow and segmented, forming natural chambers as long as Durin's arm. Beyond the obvious utility for creating containers and vessels, he saw unlimited potential using the stalks as building materials.

After dragging an armload of stalks from the forest to their camp, Durin wiped the sweat from his brow and took a few deep breaths. His back ached but the hard work felt good, and he knew the effort would be worthwhile in the long run. He smiled, remembering how he had gone to such lengths to avoid the work Miss Mariss had assigned him. Now he knew how good it could feel to have worked your hardest and to have something to show at the end of your labors. Sinjin and the other Drakon had their hands full with the dragons, which put even greater burden on everyone else on the Firstland. Those without dragons had little choice but to support themselves and the Drakon at a time when just keeping themselves fed was difficult enough.

For once in his life, Durin applied himself to finding solutions to the problems his people faced. It was strange to him that the Arghast had existed on the Godfist all along, albeit separately, and now he lived among them in a different land and was coming to know them as he never had before. These were good, kind, hardworking people, and they deserved the very best from him. Miss Mariss had deserved the very best as well; it had just taken time for him to realize it.

With so many thoughts and ideas competing for his attention, Durin found he didn't even remember much of the climb back down to the forest. Once there, he didn't simply harvest the stalk weed as other were doing; he explored other parts of the forest where the stalk weed didn't grow. Stalk weed tended to grow in isolated clumps where nothing else grew. Durin had enough stalk to work with and needed something to bind it. Rope was in precious short supply, so he looked for a substitute. Already he'd seen others using thick vines to tie bundles, but those vines were brittle and had seemed more trouble than they were worth. Watchful of his surroundings, he wandered into the forest. Small creatures moved within the underbrush, and not being able to see what they were nearly made him flee, only the fact that whatever it was fled from him kept him moving forward. Sinjin and the others had urged people to forage in pairs, but he'd been paired with Kendra, and she wasn't much for foraging. She'd also made it quite clear that he was not well suited to hunting. In the end, it was easier to just go alone and stay fairly close.

Still, he found himself farther from the base of the mountain than he'd intended, and he froze at the sound of a nearby branch snapping. Pressing himself against a towering oak, he looked around nervously. A shadow detached itself from a nearby tree. Durin was ready to run, but the form was familiar.

"You're gonna get yourself killed coming out this far alone," Kendra said.

"I heard you coming, didn't I?"

"Only because I let you know I was here," she said. "Did you know you have a habit of talking to yourself? It's very informative."

Durin flushed at that comment, trying to remember what he might have said. Odds were that he'd said something uncomplimentary toward Kendra; her looks certainly implied that was the case. "I thought you didn't like foraging."

"I don't," Kendra said. "I'm not foraging. You are. Sneaking up on you is far more fun."

"And so much more useful," Durin said. Kendra just raised an eyebrow. "Why did you even come here? It sure doesn't seem like you want to be here. You could've stayed on the Godfist. In fact, you could've stayed in the Greatland. So why come here? I wonder--"

"Shut up," Kendra said.

Durin was in no mood for her abuse. "No. You mope and complain and whine, and I'm sick of it." He'd half expected to get punched for his words, but all he got was silence in return. When he looked back, she was turning away. Was that a tear he saw on her cheek? She didn't give him the chance to find out as she disappeared into the forest.

"Women," Durin said.

* * *

Watching the Drakon work together to assemble Sinjin's saddle and everything he could possibly need to fly, Sinjin felt unworthy. He'd done nothing to earn such devotion, yet he tried to receive it gracefully. When Mikala insisted on adding a stirrup cup and strap to secure the Staff of Life and another set of straps near the pommel to hold Koe, Sinjin didn't object, despite his misgivings. The additions wouldn't hurt anything, and no one else needed to know how he felt about the staff and Koe; both items seemed to require things from him that he did not possess, especially power. Always they reminded him of what he was not.

There was one thing that he did have now that changed the equation and caused his thoughts to diverge from their familiar tracks. Now he had Valterius and a saddle made with such care, it brought tears to his eyes. He had the power of his mind, and that would have to be enough.

At long last, there was nothing more that could be done to prepare; all that was left was for Valterius to don the saddle. Even though the dragon had accepted the gifts, Sinjin still worried he would refuse. This was far more than a simple leather strap. The dragon's stance was neutral as Sinjin approached, carrying the saddle and dressed in overwarm leathers. Sinjin would have held the saddle over his head and let Valterius try to put it on himself, but it was simply too unwieldy, and there were far too many straps and other bits that needed to be just so. Sinjin was amazed how much the Arghast had picked up on the construction of dragon saddles in such a short time with access to Kyrien and his mother's saddle. The skills they possessed for making horse saddles largely translated, and the craftsmanship was without rival; these were remarkable people, indeed.

Valterius sniffed the saddle and gave a satisfied *woof;* Sinjin thought again of him and Valterius flying together--comfortably. The dragon then presented his withers. It was as clear a message as Sinjin was likely to get, and he wasted no time. Mikala and Arakhan approached Valterius, and he pulled his wings back, presenting his breast to them; it was a sign of implicit trust. The two bowed in deference and helped Sinjin secure the girths and breast collar, which would help keep the saddle from sliding backward.

The bridle worried Sinjin the most, but it had no bit, and he hoped Valterius would not take offense. Standing before him, bridle in hand, Sinjin presented it to his dragon. Valterius eyed the item with suspicion, as if it had changed in nature since he'd accepted the gift. Sniffing tentatively, he gave a snort, and Sinjin wasn't certain he approved. Still, he held out the bridle and moved closer to Valterius's head. To his surprise, the dragon slid its mighty jaws into the leather loop. Sinjin pulled the crownpiece over horned ridges and cinched it snug. Braided reins he pulled back to the saddle, and Valterius lowered himself to allow Sinjin to easily mount.

Durin came with the staff and Koe, and Sinjin secured them out of respect for Mikala.

Durin whispered, "It scares people that you leave these laying around. Do me a favor and just keep them with you. Besides, the staff makes you look more . . .. leaderly, if that's even a word."

Once he was strapped in and secure, Sinjin tested his mobility and smiled; the saddle kept him completely secured and still allowed for a limited amount of movement; perhaps not as much as his mother had enjoyed in her much larger saddle, but she'd also had a much larger dragon. What Sinjin had fit him and Valterius perfectly, and he'd never felt such excitement. He knew what a rush it was to fly, but now he would get to experience it without the constant fear of death. Maybe it was his imagination, but he could almost swear Valterius was laughing at him.

In the next moment, though, the dragon reared up to his full height, not touching the roof of the chamber but close. With his wings extended, he flapped just enough to send swirls of sand and dust into the air. Sinjin felt as if he would fall over backward at first, but the straps held him firmly and he relaxed. All those within the hollow mountain gathered to watch as Valterius walked toward the opening. The dragon took his time and seemed to enjoy the sense of drama he created. Sinjin chuckled that his mighty dragon was also a bit of a show-off. Perhaps Valterius sensed Sinjin's mirth, for he suddenly leaped from the stone and flapped his mighty wings before they had actually reached the edge of the chamber. Roughhewn stone that looked almost smooth from below proved to be jagged and pocked when seen from up close--far too close for Sinjin's liking. Pressing himself down low to the dragon's neck, he could almost hear Valterius laughing. Sinjin reminded himself to be careful of his thoughts around Valterius; the dragon could sense perhaps more of Sinjin's thoughts than he could the dragon's.

All thoughts vanished when the stone surrounding them disappeared, and once again Sinjin knew the exhilaration of flight. This time, Valterius did not head toward the sea; instead, he skimmed the trees and hugged the valleys, allowing Sinjin to get a much better view of the lands surrounding the hollow mountain.

At first, there was the devastation left by the battles, but then they moved into lands untouched by battle or human hands for thousands of years, and still there were traces of that ancient past. Carvings adorned mountainsides and parts of the forest bore symmetrical shapes that resembled the remains of cities and towns. Here and there a mighty statue remained, but few were recognizable beyond vague shapes, the details lost to the ravages of time. Movement within the trees caught Sinjin's attention, and he spotted Gholgi on the hunt, working as a pack to drive their prey, in this case a young buck deer, into a narrow ravine. Valterius swooped in low and gave Sinjin a better look. Though there was resemblance between the Gholgi and the demons, the Gholgi appeared much more natural. The demons were like Gholgi that had been fouled in some way, and the thought made Sinjin's stomach spasm.

Soon, though, the Gholgi were left behind, and rugged coastline came into view. Valterius executed a long sweeping turn that gave Sinjin a view of caves dotting the coast, some partially submerged in water, others higher on the cliff face. Seabirds flocked to these cliffs, and Sinjin ducked as some flew too close. Out to sea, Sinjin spotted the *Dragon's Wing* returning from another fishing foray. He noted that it was far too pretty a ship to be relegated to life as a fishing boat. He was glad the role was only temporary. Eventually the ships from the Godfist would arrive, and those could be converted into fishing vessels, but Sinjin thought they might need to build a ship or two in the meantime toward that purpose.

A storm loomed in the east, and whitecaps dotted the seas. Valterius took them higher, allowing Sinjin to see all of the Firstland at one time. It seemed smaller than he would have thought, but he had no other reference point; he'd never seen any other land from the skies. Still, it gave him the sense that it was half the size of the Godfist--more than large enough for their needs, and though there were Gholgi and other natural predators, the place appeared safe enough.

The people aboard the *Dragon's Wing* shouted and waved as Valterius flew low over the bow. Sinjin could see the shocked faces below and he waved. The look on Gwen's face was something he would never forget; she'd been avoiding him, and she did not appear prepared to believe him a true dragon rider. It was something even Sinjin did not believe of himself, yet there he was; it would appear he did not need to believe he was something to be that very thing. It was a discomforting realization. What else was he that he believed otherwise?

Now that Valterius seemed to have accomplished his goals for this flight, he soared around the Firstland with no apparent destination. Sinjin decided this would be a good time to test the reins. Gently he pulled the dragon's head to one side, and Valterius dipped the respective wingtip, executing a gentle, sweeping turn. Then he pulled back to the other side, and Valterius once again cooperated. Pulling back, he sent the dragon higher, and when he leaned forward, leaving the reins slack, Valterius gently arched into a dive. Trimming his wings, the dragon sent them plummeting toward the cliffs. The longer they dropped, the more concerned Sinjin became, and he started to pull back on the reins; nothing happened. Still they dropped, still Sinjin pulled back, and still nothing happened.

Sinjin began to wonder if something was wrong with Valterius, and as the forested lands atop the cliffs rushed toward them, he closed his eyes and prepared himself for impact. At what seemed the last possible instant, Valterius pulled up, the force pressing down heavily on Sinjin, the tops of trees trembling in the wash of air they left in their wake. The dragon looked back to Sinjin then as if to say, *I am in control. You may express your desire with the reins, but the final decision is mine.*

It was something Sinjin had no choice but to accept. He and Valterius were equals, and if he wanted the dragon to do something, he would just have to find a way to convince him. Dozens of reasons that could be problematic jumped to Sinjin's mind, but what other choice did he have? Even his mother's relationship with Kyrien had been similar: these beasts were not creatures of burden to be used as tools; they were sentient, thinking creatures with the right to decide their own destinies. Sinjin had learned much during this flight, and he returned to the hollow mountain with a renewed sense of purpose.

<u>Chapter 18</u>

You can't make something from nothing because never are you nothing.
--Barabas the druid

* * *

The time had come, Sinjin knew. Either he would lead or he would not, and now was the time he must decide which it would be. Fears and self-doubt told him that he could never lead anyone, let alone the Drakon. There was another part of him, though, the part that had been prepared his entire life to lead. It was the only thing he knew how to do, yet he'd never done it. He'd seen it done well and perhaps not so well, but he'd never believed he would lead, that he would be the one judged by the outcomes of his decisions.

When Valterius alighted once again on the stone of the hollow mountain, those within stopped what they were doing and watched. If he wanted their attention, he had it. A lump formed in his throat, and he had that cold feeling, like right before you did something that could end up being extremely embarrassing. The Drakon, for the most part, were working on replacing the saddle parts they had given to Valterius and Sinjin, and few had more than half a saddle completed. Each person had to learn all the skills required to produce the saddles, and it slowed the process, making it more painful than it needed to be. This was exacerbated by the care they needed to provide for their dragons, not all of whom waited patiently. The Drakon had their hands full, and the sense of urgency that had been haunting Sinjin grew at a greater rate. This felt wrong. He could put no other words or logic to it.

"Hear me, Dragon clan!" he spoke loudly, and near complete silence fell over the hold. "Your generosity has allowed me to receive the greatest gift, for I have flown with Valterius without fear." In a way, it was an admission of weakness, but he hoped those assembled would see it for what it was: a victory for them all.

"Al'Drakon," someone called; Sinjin could not identify who it had been. Another man began chanting the title, and people joined in.

Sinjin held his hands high, asking for silence, and the chant slowly waned. "I feel the need for the saddles will be great and sooner than we may like. We need to make the saddles faster. We don't have time for each of us to learn all the skills required; we need to let people do what they do best."

Stepping forward, Mikala addressed him. "Each of us has wanted to become part of the saddle, to be one with the dragon and the saddle.

512

But you speak of need. We can be faster if you need us, Al'Drakon."

She made it that simple for him. "I need you," he said to Mikala and Halmsa, who had walked to her side to show his support. "I need all of you," he said in a louder voice to all those assembled.

That was all it took. Mikala immediately began coordinating the saddle creation effort. Halmsa spoke with her briefly. Then he and Arakhan began working their way through other parts of the hold.

Leaning back in his saddle, Sinjin took a rare moment to enjoy his victory. It was short lived. Kendra approached and she didn't look happy. Sinjin's victorious feeling evaporated immediately, and he was suddenly back to being an anxious teen about to be embarrassed by a pretty girl. He chided himself for the weakness and did his best to look confident; it wasn't all that hard when sitting atop a dragon. Valterius was growing listless, though, and Sinjin thought it might be time to get the saddle off of him. Unstrapping himself, he swung his leg over Valterius and jumped down, this time clearing the dragon's spinal ridge.

He landed harder than anticipated and stumbled toward Kendra. The expression on her face hadn't changed. Benjin led Valterius back to his stall and began removing his saddle, giving Sinjin a chance to do what he must. He drew a breath.

"Before you say anything," Kendra said, "let me speak."

Words were poised on Sinjin's tongue, but he held them back.

"Your speech was very pretty," she said. "The Dragon clan will follow you. After all, you are Al'Drakon. What you didn't say was that you needed me. Wait. Don't speak yet. Hear me out first."

It was everything Sinjin could do not to at least defend himself. He certainly hadn't meant to exclude anyone.

"I am neither Drakon nor Dragon clan, and I don't belong here. I'm not sure exactly where it is that I do belong, but I know it isn't here. I wish you well, Sinjin Volker, but I must go."

"Go?" Sinjin asked. He knew he should have said something more thoughtful and eloquent, but the word escaped his lips.

"You've found a new future, and I'm happy for you. You have Valterius now; you are Al'Drakon. You can go wherever you choose. I am, again, happy for you. But my future does not involve me staying behind and defending your keep while dutifully waiting for your return."

Sinjin didn't remember asking her to do any such thing, but she had obviously thought this scenario through much more thoroughly than he had, and he really could think of nothing to say in response. "Will you come back?" he asked when nothing else came to mind.

"No," Kendra said, a hint of pain in her eyes. "Good-bye, Sinjin Volker."

"Wait," Sinjin said, his brain finally starting to catch up with what was happening. "Where will you go, and how will you get there?"

"There are supplies you need, and you no longer need a fishing vessel, so Benjin is planning to go back to the Godfist for supplies and to check on the others. I'm going with them, and I'm not coming back. There are questions I need answered, and I'm not going to find those answers here."

"Questions about your mother?" Sinjin asked quietly.

Kendra just nodded, the pain still very evident in her eyes. He didn't want her to go; she was one of the few things in his world that was familiar, and there was more, even if he didn't want to admit it. "You'll always be welcome here," Sinjin said. "If you ever need me, all you need to do is get word to me."

"That should be simple enough," she said. "You only live in the most remote place I've ever seen."

Sinjin laughed a small and sad laugh. "Good-bye, Kendra."

He embraced her and gave her a good squeeze. As he did, he smelled her hair. He wanted to hold her longer, and he would have had she not extricated herself from his arms. He would have said more, but she turned and walked quickly away.

Sinjin looked to Valterius, and despite everything, he laughed when he saw Durin using an awl to scratch right behind where the saddle had rested; Valterius stretched out his neck and had a faraway look in his eyes.

Sinjin saw Benjin approaching from off to his right. He walked slowly toward the older man, meeting him halfway.

"She told you of our plans?"

"Yes," Sinjin said, and he failed to keep the disappointment from his voice.

"It's the sensible thing to do," Benjin said, "and we'll be back."

"Some of you will, at least," Sinjin said, unable to shake the sudden melancholy.

"Don't look at me for advice on women," Benjin said. "That's not my area of expertise."

For some odd reason, that statement made Sinjin feel a great deal better.

"When do you leave?"

"Now," Benjin said. "Fasha has the *Dragon's Wing* ready to sail, her hold filled with cured fish as well as fruits and herbs found along the shoreline. If you don't go too far into the jungle, this really isn't all that bad a place."

His friends were leaving him, and there was nothing he could do to stop it. The truth was that he knew they were right; they did need supplies, tools, materials, and so many other things he'd once taken for granted. And what could he expect from Kendra? He couldn't ask her to stay behind and guard the keep, and now that he thought more on it, what else could he do? There were no more dragons; he'd have given one to her if he could, but he couldn't. He hadn't even planned on having a dragon. Valterius had chosen him, and it bothered him that he felt guilty about it.

"I'll walk down with you," Sinjin said and Benjin nodded. With his staff in hand and Koe in his pocket, Sinjin walked in a daze, his thoughts moving too fast to make sense of them all.

"I'll keep an eye on things here," Durin said when they walked by Valterius's stall. "See you when you get back."

Knowing that Durin, at least, was staying with him made Sinjin feel a little better. Still, worries crowded his mind. He and Benjin descended in near silence. Climbing back down was trickier in places than it had been going up, but he had the benefit of the staff, and he offered it to Benjin after clearing a particularly difficult part of the climb. Benjin accepted it slowly, and there were tears in his eyes when he handed it back. No words were said, but Sinjin did what he could to assist Benjin in other ways after that point.

At the base of the mountain, they rested and drank from a flask Benjin carried.

"I never thought it would turn out like this," Sinjin said.

"Don't feel bad, m'boy," Benjin said. "Most of what I ever thought would happen in this life was wrong. You get used to it."

Though the statement didn't inspire confidence, it did make Sinjin smile, and that was enough to get them moving again. The sun was already starting to sink lower toward the sea, and Sinjin would bet that Fasha was already cursing Benjin for taking so long. When that woman decided it was time to leave, she meant it.

The *Dragon's Wing* sparkled in the light against a backdrop of orange and purple sky; it was a breathtaking sight. She was anchored not far off shore, and a single boat waited on the beach; beside it stood Pelivor. A bit of pain in his chest forced Sinjin to admit that he'd been hoping to see Gwen there, hoping to say something, though he didn't know exactly what. It was not to be. He saw no sign of Kendra, who must have hurried dangerously to get to the shore and onto the ship before Sinjin and Benjin made it to the sea.

"It has been a pleasure to sail with you, and I look forward to our return," Pelivor said. "We'll be back as quickly as the winds allow."

Benjin said no more, and the three of them pushed the boat back into the water. "It doesn't get any easier," Benjin said after climbing into the boat. "Just keep your chin up and do your best. That's really all you can do."

"Would you please tell Gwen that I said good-bye?" Sinjin asked, not wanting to look at Benjin.

The girl's father just nodded and said nothing more.

With that, they set off for the *Dragon's Wing*. Sinjin remained where he was until after the ship gained the skies and disappeared into the horizon.

* * *

Broken.

Allette moved through the jungle like the wounded creature she was. On the outside she was scraped and scratched and bruised, but on the inside she felt the real damage, the wounds that would never heal. Still she moved deeper into the Jaga, knowing it wasn't safe to stop anywhere. She persisted on edible plants that Thundegar had described to her and others she was already familiar with. Seeing huckles growing in a jungle came as something of a shock, but a welcome one. Allette had always known them from growing along the fence lines at her uncle's farm. Though he'd died years before, Allette felt a pang when she remembered the times she'd spent there. Her father and her uncle had been complete opposites--one taking to the land and the other to the sea. Her father had always joked that it could only be expected when a sailor marries a land-bound woman. Her grandmother had always laughed the loudest at that joke.

As she moved through older and more established forest, dark shapes shadowed her. Feeling like a squirrel surrounded by cats, Allette kept moving, her legs fueled by fear. She existed in two different places then. Part of her witnessed the horror around her, smelled the coming foulness, and still found a way to move closer to the Midlands, the only place even remotely like home. The other part of her existed in the memories of her childhood and imaginations of the things to come. The simple vision of sitting before a fire and frying a fresh-caught fish in oil with spices and a cup of mulled wine kept her alive; it kept her moving despite the stark reality of her current situation.

The *Maker's Mark* was gone, she knew, but that did not mean she couldn't sail. No one could take from her the seas, and she would once again be free. The thought of being back on a ship, back in control of her destiny, was even more alluring. For so long now, ever since she'd lost her father, she'd felt like a lost child; it was a feeling she liked not at all, and she vowed to take control of her destiny. No one and nothing would stand before her. She had lost all that was dear to her and had betrayed those she loved at the cost of their lives. Guilt and anguish rolled over her in equal measure, and she fought the effects. It was those thoughts that were the most dangerous; it was those thoughts that would be the end of her. It wasn't her fault. She'd asked for none of this. All she'd done was try to survive. What had she done to deserve such wickedness?

Then came the anger, and it burned within her like a blazing inferno. A growl escaped her throat as she continued at a measured pace. She was strong; Thundegar had said so. Her anger turned on him; he hadn't protected her, none of them had. There was no one left in the world who cared for her, and the part of her that cared for others seemed to die in that moment.

Looking around her, Allette was drawn back into the real world, and what she saw terrified her. She had moved in a trance for so long that she hadn't realized how far into the Jaga she had traveled. Around her shambled looming, upright shapes, moving within a black and slime-covered landscape. Even that which lived seemed to be dying. Allette wasn't certain how such a place could exist or sustain itself, yet here she was.

Beams of sunlight pierced the foliage but were frequently interrupted. Though she wanted to believe it was simply an effect of the wind moving leaves and branches, there was no wind to speak of, and she knew what it really was. The thought of all those feral dragons in the air made her shiver; even a single one was more than she'd ever want to encounter. They were such savage creatures, and though she didn't want to, she could almost relate to them. They existed for only themselves, and anything else that came near them was something to be attacked; what had once seemed evil now seemed like simple survival.

New cuts and gashes crossed her flesh, and she took the time to coat her wounds in mud--anything to hide the smell of blood. Most of her was already covered in the ubiquitous black slime, which helped her blend in with the surroundings. What would have once seemed revolting was now something that might keep her alive. Her perspective had been forever changed, and she would never see things the same, no matter what happened.

Movement.

Allette went rigid beside a twisted vine that almost resembled a tree and remained motionless. Sucking sounds and soft thuds marked the movements around her, and Allette felt she was surrounded. She hadn't rested in hours, and her legs trembled. A soft splash sounded on the other side of the vine where she hid, and Allette sprang away like a rabbit fleeing a fox. The foul creatures might not have been looking for her, but they reacted immediately to her presence. Howls and barks filled the air, and Allette could see the shapes closing in on her. The twisted, bizarre landscape slipped past in a tangled blur accompanied by pain and panic. They were getting closer.

No longer fully obeying her deepest desires, Allette's legs began to give out. She'd run as far and as fast as her body could handle, and both legs felt like old rope. No matter how hard she tried to keep them straight, they simply collapsed under her weight.

Without warning, Allette half ran and half fell into a clearing. The ground beneath her feet changed from slippery muck to moss-covered stone, and the exhausted girl lost her balance. White light flashed around her as she fell; when it cleared, she lay on her back, staring up at blue skies filled with dragons.

The dark shapes that had hounded her now gathered around the clearing, but none would step onto the mossy stone. Not even saplings grew within the near-perfect circle, and no branches encroached overhead. Through breaks in the moss, patches of black stone were visible. It formed a domelike structure with a slightly higher point at the center and a gentle slope outward. Allette pushed herself to her feet and backed toward the center of the clearing.

When she reached the spot, she nearly turned an ankle. At the very center of the grove was a perfectly round shaft that looked to have been bored deep. Allette couldn't see the bottom and had no idea how deep it might go. Curiosity was banished and overwhelmed by fear; the creatures at the edge of the clearing were wrong, distorted, twisted. Each looked very different from the other, the exaggerations of their forms varied and unique, but mostly grotesque. There was no kindness in their eyes, and Allette knew they would have killed her already if not for this place. Something about it kept them back, and she could only hope the spell would last. It didn't.

Stone and jungle alike shook when a full-grown feral dragon dropped into the clearing and cast a baleful glare at Allette. She glared back. Most of her fear had been burned from her, and she no longer had anything to lose. If this was the moment she would die, then she would face death with defiance, no matter how futile the fight. The sound the feral dragon made in its throat was like a roaring river accompanied by a massive rockslide. The power of it made Allette cover her ears in spite of her defiance. Still she stood her ground, and the dragon seemed to find this amusing. Lowering its head closer, it looked at her the way a cat might look at a wounded bird.

"Go away," she said.

The dragon snorted and the buffeting air forced Allette to take an involuntary step backward. The feral seemed pleased with itself but also showed signs of losing patience.

"I said, *go away!*" her voice rang unnaturally loud and seemed to pain the dragon, whose tail twitched now, and fury blazed in its eyes.

Rearing back, the dragon inhaled deeply, the rush of air forcing Allette forward a step. When the dragon had first growled at her was nothing compared to the roar that emerged from it now. So terrible was this call that all the other dragons circled closer, converging on that spot, apparently all wanting to know what could so completely enrage one of their brethren from so deep within their territory. Now instead of one dragon to face, Allette faced all of the dragons. She could not hide, she could not run away.

Still she stood tall, resolute, emboldened by the acceptance of her fate and feeling free for the first time in a long time. This was what she had sought: freedom. Pity it would be so short. That thought almost brought a twisted smile to her lips. The wry look further enraged the feral looming over her, and it no longer seemed to care about intimidating her into submission. Now it just wanted her dead.

The beast stared at her, its reptilian pupils narrowing, and as it drew a deep breath, it also swept its tail through the clearing. Allette never saw it coming and was tossed once again onto her back. Now the dragon stood directly over her, raised up to its full height, its wings partly extended, and its claws tearing into the moss-covered stone. The world trembled beneath the power of this beast, and Allette could feel the thrum of it. One more breath, and it would be done. The last fear within her evaporated like smoke on the wind, just as the rest of the dragons arrived to see her die. She was as of yet unaware that she would disappoint them.

"Obey!" she shouted desperately as the dragon's head snapped downward, her arm reaching toward the sky, toward the comets, toward the goddess she'd always ignored.

The word shook the foundations of the Godsland. Power that had lain hidden, buried beneath a mountain of fear, and building until the pressure was too much, overwhelmed all resistance. Even as the word left her lips, she felt the power of it, tasted the tang of its might, and smelled the fear of all who witnessed her power. Light burst forth from her hand like a gushing fountain. Blasted away by the force of her will, Allette's wounds evaporated and she was remade. The dragon above her was in mid strike, its massive head descending upon her, eyes wide, the whites around them showing. Even if this creature wanted to obey her command, it was too late; there was no way for it to stop mid strike. It was committed and gravity alone would propel the now unstoppable attack; at least it had appeared unstoppable.

When the dragon's mighty bottom jaw struck the fountain of light and what looked like baby stars issuing from Allette's upraised hand, it was tossed backward as if struck by a giant uppercut. The dragon's limp body followed its head and tumbled backward into the black swamp. Above Allette, her energy reached to the sky, now unobstructed--the dragons avoided the column--and it seemed as if she reached out to the comets themselves. Latching on to a large, colorful, and beautiful comet, she drew deeply, and the skies were afire. Bits of colored light leaped away from the towering column of energy and danced through the air. Lightning cleaved the sky, and thunder rumbled a long ominous note.

Light played over the scales of the gathered ferals, and all eyes rested on Allette. Each and every one of them fell to her, overwhelmed by her might. She looked into their minds and was amazed by the sheer capacity, which was now hers to command. These dragons were not brilliant on an individual basis, but they had the ability to share information, and together they were potent. Within them, Allette found their fears and desires; she knew their enemies and took them as her own. Their memories were long, and they recalled well that this world had once belonged to them. Allette soared the skies with them in those days as the experiences flowed over her. She merged with the ferals, and in this way, Allette Kilbor subtly bonded every feral dragon within the Jaga. By the time the creatures realized what was happening, it was too late. She exerted her control. Beneath her power struggled the wills of the feral dragons, and with a single push, she crushed them. Might was hers. They were hers. The world was hers.

Utter disbelief washed through the black dragons, but resistance was gone, obliterated by her will.

Through her domination of the ferals, Allette gained control of the men already loyal to the dragons as well as the abominations that had resulted from the ferals' twisted desire for power and revenge against those who'd vanquished them so long ago. Such hatred and vileness had gone into the perversion of these creatures that Allette wanted to simply rid the world of them. She felt a connection to them, though, through the dragons. What she also knew was that their enemies were massing forces on both sides of the Jaga and preparing for an assault. There was fear, deep and sharp, and not Allette's fear; the ferals had expected to defeat a faraway enemy and use the might of those nations to come back and destroy the people of the Heights and Midlands who had for so long oppressed them.

Violent memories of these battles blasted her psyche, and Allette thrashed side to side from the force of it.

Calm. Allette simply exuded the command, there was no need to communicate, the dragons already knew.

The flock responded to her command with a simple appellation.

Queen.

__Chapter 19__

If you change your perception of reality, you change reality.
--Barabas the druid

* * *

None of the tales about dragons that Sinjin had ever heard mentioned just how much work it took to feed and care for the majestic, if frustrating, creatures. His grandfather had always said that training horses was hours of work and frustration that paid off in just a couple of minutes of exhilaration. Sinjin had never really understood, but working with Valterius enlightened him. The dragon shifted beneath him, and Sinjin cinched one of the straps, which was a little loose. He'd been getting taller, and wider for that matter, and Valterius seemed acutely aware of the extra weight. Whenever Sinjin ate, the dragon watched him as if every pound he gained were an affront. Sinjin had come to understand a bit of his dragon's sense of humor, most of which was at his expense. It was far more frustrating than it was endearing by Sinjin's estimation.

A dark cloud in the water below caught Valterius's eye, and Sinjin saw it shift to bright silver as the fish changed direction. Even knowing it was coming, it was difficult to keep from screaming when Valterius trimmed his wings and sent them racing toward the water below. The wind clawed at his eyes, and he wished he had a pair of goggles like his mother had made. There wasn't much time for him to think about it. Pulling back on the reins, as ineffectual as it may have been, Sinjin tried to convince his dragon to pull up before they struck the water. Valterius knew his business, though, and struck the water a glancing blow while reaching down and grabbing not one, but two gleaming fish from the water.

Show-off, Sinjin thought.

Valterius reeked of mirth. After a few turns on the thermals, they glided back to Windhold. Sinjin thought it a fitting name, and it was a memorial to what had once been the Wind clan. The Arghast had reacted strangely when he first suggested the name, as if he offered them a gift too great and at the same time as if he asked too much of them. It was something he doubted he'd ever understand.

In true Valterius fashion, they entered the hold at high speed. One or two people unlucky enough to have been crossing his path rushed to get out of the way. One Drakon had to dive under his dragon as they passed.

"Sorry!" Sinjin yelled over his shoulder.

Valterius released the fish as they approached the area where the other fish that had been caught that day were stacked. Most of the dragons dropped their fish at the ledge and never entered the keep itself. Valterius, on the other hand, treated it like a game. His aim, this time, was perfect, Sinjin had to admit. The fish bounced once when they hit the stone then slid across the slick area around the fish until meeting up with the rest of the mound, pressed tightly against the pile, one after the other. Had he released them both at the exact same instant, it wouldn't have worked, but the slight delay in between was just enough to keep the two from colliding with each other.

Those cleaning fish knew what to expect, and they ducked down as Valterius passed. As Sinjin had asked them not to, the people cheered Valterius's aim, and the dragon wove his head back and forth, gloating as he burst out the back side of the mountain. Beyond was a sheer face, and again the knowledge it was coming wasn't enough to prepare Sinjin for the force of the sudden change in direction. Valterius reveled in his acrobatics, and Sinjin did his best to hold on.

Their chores were done. They had transported water, game, fruits, nuts, and of course fish. Valterius had done most of the work, but getting the goods prepped for transport wasn't always easy. Those who had spent their time gathering the food didn't take it kindly when what they found was dashed on the rocks. Together they made an efficient and effective team. Valterius seemed not to like the idea of chores any more than Sinjin did, but as long as he was allowed to make games of them, he did not balk at the work.

When they were done working for the day, Sinjin liked to give Valterius the freedom to go where he would. The truth was that Sinjin had little choice in the matter. Valterius had made it very clear that where they went, how fast they went, and the angle of their approach was of his deciding. Sinjin was allowed to make suggestions, but the dragon had the right of refusal. It was another thing that Sinjin would never have imagined. His mother's relationship with Kyrien had been so much different; Kyrien had the ability to speak in people's minds. His mother had known her dragon's thoughts. In comparison, Sinjin was blind.

After a couple of sharp turns, Valterius righted them, and Sinjin was able to think clearly once again. A few turns on the thermals, and they left the world far below. Sinjin had been surprised to find he did his best thinking here. The silence was nearly absolute, and Valterius knew what he was about. Looking out over the sea, Sinjin let the storm of his thoughts settle until he could think about one thing for a time; it was something his mother had taught him. Lost in thought, he barely noticed Valterius cock his head, his interest piqued by something Sinjin also hadn't noticed. He'd been busy wondering if Gwen was still angry with him.

Water rushed beneath them, and Sinjin realized that they were much farther out than they would ordinarily go. In that moment, he recalled the lectures he'd received in the past about going off on adventures and not telling anyone where he was going or when he would return. With that in mind, he used his knees and the lines to guide Valterius back the way they had come; at least that was what he tried to do. Valterius ignored his input and continued on his chosen course: east. These waters were unknown to him, or probably anyone else for that matter, and a knot formed in his gut.

"We should go back," Sinjin said, hoping he could reason with the dragon and feeling silly for doing so. Still, his grandfather said that all horse trainers talked to their horses; even if the dragon didn't understand everything he said, most creatures understand tone and body language. "Think of how everyone will worry if they don't know the fate of Al'Drak."

Valterius just grunted in response and continued on, using tricks to gain speed. The wind made it even more difficult for Sinjin to express himself. At that moment he felt very alone. This dragon could take him anywhere he wanted, and he would be returned to Windhold only if Valterius so chose. It was unnerving. Valterius seemed to find it amusing.

Fluffy white clouds filled the skies ahead, and a trumpeting cry came from within. Sinjin jumped in his saddle as much as the straps allowed, urgently trying to get Valterius to turn around while the dragon took them into the clouds, heading directly for where he thought the sound had come from. Within the cloud, pervasive moisture soaked into everything, and Sinjin was grateful when the air began to clear.

"I knew you would come," said a voice from beside Sinjin, and he nearly leaped from his skin. Beside him and just below them flew a man on top of a wooden and leather structure not unlike a carriage. Beneath that carriage was a patchwork of gray and black squares that looked like stone. Valterius pulled up a little, allowing Sinjin to see what flew beneath them, and what he saw left him speechless. Bigger than even the feral queen and with a head the size of a house, the dragon below had four legs, and its rider was nearly as bizarre as it was. Long gray and white hair formed braids that fell alongside his also braided beard. Thick furs covered a body as wide as it was tall. He looked as if life had taken things from him--many things. Sinjin wasn't certain how he knew it, but he did. "Are you able to speak?"

The accent was thick but Sinjin understood. "I'm sorry. You startled me," he managed.

The big man barked a laugh. "I s'pose finding me next to you would do such a thing."

The wind made it difficult to hear his words and understand the accent. The strange man waved for Sinjin to follow, and he and Valterius did so whether Sinjin wanted to or not. It would seem this was what had gotten his dragon's attention, and Sinjin could only imagine where this man and his dragon had come from. It was a verdant dragon, Sinjin knew; it could be nothing else, though it didn't exactly match the descriptions, which usually said the skin was a dark green color. The only green Sinjin saw on this dragon was moss that was growing between some of the armor plates.

Below, a length of sand bar came into view, and the verdant dragon circled slowly, taking far longer to land than Valterius or any of the other regal dragons would require. The big dragon did eventually land, gingerly and with seeming reluctance. Valterius showed that diplomacy was beyond him, and he made short work of plopping them down on the narrow sand bar. He kept his wings partially extended and wove his head back and forth as if taunting the much larger dragon, who responded with a roar that threatened to deafen him. The mighty beast was impressive, though Sinjin couldn't help but notice that it wasn't entirely symmetrical, and when he looked at the dragon's eyes, he got another shock: One eye was amber and looked similar to Valterius's eyes. The other was ice blue and missing its pupil; the entire eye was streaked with white, looking like a star exploding within a prison of blue stone.

"Well met," the big man said as he walked down his dragon's extended leg and onto the sand.

Valterius fidgeted, making it difficult for Sinjin to get himself unstrapped. His dragon expressed impatience by turning back to him and snapping his jaws. "Just a moment," Sinjin said, but his voice was strained from the effort. Finally the strap came free, and Valterius celebrated by standing to his full height and dumping Sinjin unceremoniously in the sand.

"Sorry," Sinjin said, embarrassed, as he used his staff to push himself back upright.

"Well met!" the man said, a twinkle in his eye. "It took me years to get the dismount right."

"Who are you?" Sinjin asked. "Where did you come from?"

"I am Onin," the man said, "and I would ask the same of you."

"My name is Sinjin, and this is Valterius." At the sound of his name, Valterius bowed his head in greeting to Onin and his dragon; it was far more formal than Sinjin would have expected from his companion.

"And this is Jehregard."

The verdant dragon seemed to move almost in slow motion compared to Valterius, but there was warmth in his reaction, even if the woof he issued sent Sinjin back a step.

"We come from the Heights," Onin said. "The ferals have returned, and it looked like someone dealt them a mighty blow. Do you know of this?"

The ferals. Sinjin swallowed; they had always known that the ferals had come from somewhere, but Onin's words chilled his soul. "It was my mother and the people of the Godfist and the people of the Greatland."

Tears sprung to Onin's eyes. "The gods have given me hope."

"My mother--" Sinjin's words were cut short when an unbelievably massive thump rattled his bones. It felt as if the world had been struck by a comet. Looking over Onin's shoulder, he saw Jehregard silhouetted against a backdrop of roiling light. Reaching into the sky was a column of energy greater than anything the world had ever seen.

"And then they take it away," Onin said after turning to see what had caused Sinjin to gape like a fool. "I must return. I must tell them of you and your mother. If they strike before your forces arrive, we could be doomed. Meet me back here in two days' time. If I do not come, then bring your forces this way." Using the heel of his boot, Onin quickly drew a deep and distinct arrow in the sand: north and east.

"Wait--" Sinjin said, but Onin was already mounting Jehregard.

The mighty dragon spread his wings before Onin was in any way secure, and the persistent wind lifted the leviathan slowly. They hovered there for the span of a breath, and a sudden gust sent them upward. Flapping his wings, Jehregard took them higher, winging their way south and east.

Cursing, Sinjin ran to Valterius, who did not in any way make it easier for him to mount as Jehregard had. They would have to work on that, Sinjin thought, and Valterius harrumphed. It was becoming increasingly clear that Sinjin would have to be more careful of his thoughts around Valterius. He didn't think his dragon could read his mind, but the wily creature seemed very adept at reading Sinjin's posture and body language.

Valterius, in showing that he had, indeed, learned some things from Jehregard, spread his wings and let the wind do the work. Sinjin hadn't even begun to get himself strapped in before Valterius left the sands below. The gusty wind tossed them from side to side, and Sinjin was afraid he would be sent tumbling. Finally he got one strap secured and was working on another while Valterius climbed.

As Sinjin was securing the final strap, Valterius put them into a steep dive that gave them tremendous speed. The wind tearing at Sinjin's face, he kept his eyes closed until they leveled out and slowed to a more reasonable speed. He would have been grateful for the speed, knowing he needed to get back to Windhold and talk with the clan, except for the fact that Valterius was going the wrong way.

Just ahead of them flew Onin and Jehregard, and Valterius was gaining on them. The verdant dragon let out a bellowing roar, and the big man turned to see Sinjin and Valterius overtaking them.

"What are you doing?" the big man shouted.

Sinjin could barely hear the words, and he raised his hands in frustration. After pulling hard on the reins to no effect, he just looked up to Onin with an apology in his eyes.

* * *

It was a long and lonely flight. Onin refused to even look at him, seemingly disgusted by his lack of control over Valterius. Sinjin also got little feedback from his dragon, who was content to fly in near stillness. Jehregard spoke to him through grunts and woofs, turning his head often to gaze at Sinjin, his right eye sparkling like the most precious gem. This seemed to annoy Onin greatly, but Jehregard ignored him, which made Sinjin feel at least a little better.

Gripping the Staff of Life in one hand and Koe in the other, Sinjin wanted for a moment to feel closer to his mother. She would have known what to do; she would have been able to communicate with Valterius. She could do all the things he could not, and he couldn't help but be frustrated by it at that moment. Feeling trapped in the flow of events with no sense of control over his destiny, Sinjin still couldn't help but stare in amazement when the peaks came into view, jutting through low-lying clouds like icebergs in a sea of white.

Not so unlike Windhold, these mountains had been carved and hollowed; only the scale of it dwarfed anything on the Firstland. Also different was the fact that along with large, open spaces common to Windhold and these towering peaks, there were much smaller openings with ornate facades and winding walkways. This was a place where man and dragon truly coexisted. Was this what the future of Windhold would look like? Sinjin asked himself, still in awe of what he beheld.

Never would he have dreamed such a place existed and that there were other dragon riders and verdant dragons. It was almost more than he could absorb. His inner child wanted nothing more than to tell Durin what he had found so they could go exploring. Despite being a childish impulse, it was powerful nonetheless. Sinjin's annoyance with Valterius faded a small amount as he took in the wondrous sights.

Dropping through the first layer of clouds revealed a thriving society. Horses pulled wagons along cobbled paths, and vendors crowded into a colorful market. Soon much larger sections of the mostly hollow mountains became visible. The size of the place made Windhold seem tiny in comparison, and Sinjin wondered, once again, what he'd gotten himself into.

A cry rose up from below him, followed by another. People below stopped what they were doing and pointed at Valterius and Sinjin. Soon many of the openings in the rock faces were filled to capacity with people wanting to see what the fuss was about. More cries echoed through the winding valleys, and Sinjin looked to Onin, who refused to acknowledge him. Jehregard navigated the valleys with ease, despite how close his wingtips came to stone at times. Twice Sinjin thought the massive beast's wings would clip valley walls, but each time the dragon trimmed his wings just enough to avoid contact.

Directly ahead of them was a massive opening that looked as if it could swallow all of Windhold. A man stood at the center of the opening, holding a bright red cloth, which danced and billowed in the wind. Jehregard soared higher, giving himself the room to turn a lazy circle.

Valterius, on the other hand, continued toward the opening. The man with the red cloth pointed and shouted.

"You're not cleared to land!" Onin shouted from above and behind them.

Sinjin threw his hands in the air to indicate that he was not the one in control. Jehregard issued a deep growl of warning, but Valterius ignored the other dragon as well. The man with the cloth was now waving his hands and shouting. Sinjin couldn't hear the words, but he could see fear in the man's eyes. As they drew closer, Sinjin saw more of what lay within the waiting darkness. The stone ahead was clear where the sun struck it, but in the shadows beyond waited a shape so massive that Sinjin couldn't comprehend it, especially when it moved. This dragon made even Jehregard look small. On its back was something that looked like a warship with no masts and with a notched hull that rested on the dragon's spinal ridge, which looked more like a granite outcropping than part of a living creature.

Ladders rested against the sides of the dragon. Men and women scrambled to unload cargo. It was too much for Sinjin's mind to absorb, and all he could do was pull back in futility on the reins. Another roar issued from the dragon within as the people started scrambling to get out of the way. Sinjin could feel the vibrations of that deep, thudding call. Valterius ignored even that and soared over the man with the red cloth. Not taking any chances, the man dived to the stone floor, and they flew over harmlessly.

As if in reproach of all the excitement and concern that he would crash into something, Valterius landed lightly within the hold, though still on the well-lit section of stone and far from coming into contact with any of those who'd panicked. His posture was a clear rebuke, and the massive hall went silent. That was until the mighty verdant dragon lowered its mountainlike head. Its amber eyes were taller than Sinjin, and its head was nearly as wide as Valterius's wingspan. Nostrils large enough to lose a horse in sniffed Valterius then gave a single snort before issuing a deafening roar that echoed far too loudly. Sinjin thought his teeth might fall out.

Valterius turned and looked at Sinjin, his gaze intense and his silent command clear: *Get off.* Sinjin didn't appreciate the tone of the command, but he unbuckled himself anyway. He was going to have some explaining to do, and it would probably be better done when not adragonback. Valterius did not help him dismount, but at least he didn't actively throw Sinjin to the ground. It was an improvement.

People moved silently around him, trying to soothe the big dragon and casting him frightened looks. Once he reached the stone, Sinjin saw a contingent of armed men rushing toward him. Behind them came a group of robed men who walked with unmistakable authority. One man was much heavier than the others and lagged behind, seemingly out of breath. Doing his best to assume a neutral stance, Sinjin laid his staff before him and put his hands out to his sides to indicate that he was unarmed.

Fanning out, the guards drew closer and did not look in any way convinced that Sinjin wasn't dangerous. Valterius helped a bit with that; with a final defiant cry, he puffed out his chest and fanned his wings at the giant verdant dragon. The mighty beast looked offended to the core, but Valterius didn't give him a chance to respond. Instead he spun and leaped into the air. Those who had been behind Valterius jumped out of his way, but Sinjin was not quick enough to avoid his dragon's whipping tail, which caught him in the back of the knees and sent him sprawling to the floor.

Chapter 20
A true hero knows the cost of their actions.
--Catrin Volker, Herald of Istra

* * *

Sinjin had never felt more self-conscious. All eyes in the room rested on him, and none of the looks he received were friendly, even Onin glared at him. It hadn't taken Sinjin long to realize that his association with Onin gained him no favor; and by the looks the man cast him, that association was tenuous at best.

"Why did you come here?" he had asked Sinjin in one of the few moments they had been alone.

"Valterius goes where he will," Sinjin had said. "I cannot force him to do anything or go where he doesn't want to go. Even when we first encountered you, it was of his doing."

This had left the man without words, and he looked at Sinjin as if he were a simpleton.

It wasn't Sinjin's fault. He couldn't communicate with Valterius as his mother had with Kyrien. And even she had not fully controlled her dragon; he, too, had done what he wanted when he wanted. Sinjin had done his very best and anyone who didn't like it would just have to deal with it. With a belly full of anger and defiance, Sinjin felt warm all over; perhaps his face was flushed, but he would not cower before these people.

"And who might you be?" a man in thick, long, white robes asked without preamble. He was trailed by a rotund fellow man who eyed Sinjin up and down.

"My name is Sinjin Volker. And who might you be?"

The fat man drew a sharp breath at Sinjin's words, and the guards shifted nervously.

The man in the white robes seemed nonplussed. "You may call me lord chancellor. I believe you already know Onin, and my distinguished colleague is Sensi." He motioned to the fat man. "Now that introductions are complete, tell me how you've come to be here and how you plan to help us. Onin has been telling tales of your mother defeating a host of ferals. What say you to this?"

Even to Sinjin's ear the claims sounded like too much to believe. "My mother battled the feral dragons after the black armies kidnapped me--"

The looks that passed between Sensi and the lord chancellor gave

Sinjin pause, and he wondered how much he should tell these people, but he had no idea what information might save him and what might send him to his death. He was walking dangerous ground.

"How did she do this?" the lord chancellor asked.

"My mother had great power," Sinjin said, knowing this was the most dangerous ground of all; he had no idea what these people believed, but there was so much similarity in the language they spoke that they might very well have convictions similar to those of the Zjhon. Those in the room with him seemed to be digesting the word *had.*

"Did your mother lose her power?" Sensi asked, earning a glare from the lord chancellor, though the man looked to Sinjin for his answer.

"No," Sinjin said. "She died fighting the feral queen." That statement took the air out of the room. "I have no power. And now I have no dragon either."

"What can you possibly offer to assist us with our fight against the ferals?"

"Absolutely nothing," Sinjin said, unwilling to reveal more.

The lord chancellor nodded and cast Onin a scathing glance. He didn't need to say anything, and he just walked toward the doorway. Before he was out of the room, though, Sensi spoke up, and the lord chancellor stopped. "Where did you get that staff?"

"It belonged to my mother," Sinjin said. "It has no power of its own, but it makes me feel closer to her. It's the only thing of hers that I have left." Sinjin wasn't certain they believed him; the look on the lord chancellor's face spoke loudly of doubt.

"We are at war," Sensi said. "There is no more time for discussion. You have one day to remove yourself from the Heights; if you fail to do so, you will face the thrower. Do you understand?"

"No," Sinjin said.

"Pity," Sensi said as he walked from the room.

* * *

Convincing Onin to take him home was among the most difficult things Sinjin had ever accomplished, and he still wasn't certain he'd managed to persuade the man. At the very least, Onin had allowed him to fly with him. Sitting inside the carriagelike structure atop Jehregard's back was surreal; it provided a very different experience from flying with Valterius. A single strap secured him to the bench where he sat, and Sinjin was amazed at how smoothly Jehregard flew. Valterius frequently tossed Sinjin about in the saddle, seemingly trying to see just how much his body could take, whereas Jehregard floated on the air. Indeed, when they had taken off, all Jehregard had done was spread his wings and through subtle movements of his wings had guided them out into open air without a single flap. Much like the wind channel that was part of what gave Windhold its name, a strong and consistent wind passed through the massive chambers within the Heights.

Once clear of the peaks, Onin used long, flat leather straps he called lines to guide Jehregard out over the cloud-covered forest and on to the barren foothills, which gave way to desert. The massive dragon did exactly as Onin asked without any hesitation. Onin cast Sinjin a look he really didn't appreciate. It wasn't his fault Valterius didn't listen to him. Though he had said almost nothing since he'd agreed to take Sinjin home, he knew that Jehregard would use the hot air over the desert to gain altitude. He also knew from things he'd overheard that dragons were being used to bring soldiers from the Midlands and mass them along the border of the desert, which acted as a formidable barrier between the jungle and the foothills leading up to the Heights. Deep inside, Sinjin knew it would become a battlefield.

They circled higher, somehow avoiding the larger dragons who were also riding the thermals. Sinjin couldn't imagine how they all kept track of each other and avoided collisions. Inland, across the desert, columns of black smoke rose from the swamps--the fires of war. Sinjin knew all too well that the world could be a cold, hard place, and he steeled himself for what was to come. Onin had never said how soon he would take Sinjin home, and he guided Jehregard out over the desert. Taking them lower, he gained speed, and the marshes soon rushed beneath them; they crawled with life. Soldiers bathed in ash and demons marched toward the desert in disarray. There was no order or regimentation, only a seething mass of pain and wrongness headed toward the Heights. Feral dragons flew low over the Jaga, carrying what looked like giant crates made from the twisted vines that populated the black swamp. The dragons brought the crates low over the marshes and dropped them; without landing, flapping hard, the ferals returned to the skies.

Sinjin saw the crates fly open and out poured more troops. The ferals were amassing their forces, and they were doing it far more quickly than anyone would ever have imagined.

"I cannot leave," Onin said. "There is no time."

"It's all right," Sinjin said. "I want to help."

"Good," Onin said, and he took them back toward the front lines. More verdant dragons delivered Midlands troops, but it was clear it wouldn't be enough. They would be overrun within a day. Slowing, Jehregard brought them in over the sands where other dragons were unloading.

"Get out," Onin said.

"What?"

"Get out," Onin repeated. "You want to help, then get out and fight."

Jehregard skimmed just above the sands, only having a short distance left before he would have to take them higher to avoid a huge verdant unloading up ahead.

"Go!" Onin bellowed.

Sinjin undid the strap securing himself and opened the hatch. He looked out over Jehregard's wing, and the speed of the sand slipping beneath them was daunting. Sinjin was seriously considering just clinging on to Jehregard or climbing back onto the bench when a large boot found itself on his bottom. In the next instant, he tumbled across Jehregard's wing and into the open air. His scream lasted only a second and ended with a resounding thump.

* * *

Orange light surrounded Sinjin when he came awake with a start. He was in a rectangular tent reeking of herbs and backlit by the waning sun. He lay on even ground covered by only a blanket. In his pocket, he could feel Koe pressing against him. It was probably not coincidence that the contact was accompanied by sharp pain. Slowly he reached out, searching for the staff.

"It's here," a soft voice said, and Sinjin turned to see a young woman sitting cross-legged and watching him. The staff rested on the blankets next to her. "Does your head hurt?" she asked.

"Not much," Sinjin said.

"Is your vision blurry?"

"A little," he admitted.

"You need rest," she said with a sad smile. "You're very lucky, and so is your cat." She pointed at the pocket that held the carving. "No one will take anything from you," she said in response to his expression.

"I'm sorry," was all Sinjin's muddled mind could think to say. She smiled that sad smile again and moved to the tent flap.

"Rest," she said. "I'll bring you some water in a few minutes."

Sinjin leaned back, but his head never hit the rolled blanket beneath it. A sudden clamor erupted outside and through the entire encampment. Unable to remain where he was, Sinjin crawled to the tent flap and looked outside. At first he could find no reason for the sudden alarm. Soldiers milled in confusion, but many were arming themselves, and Sinjin knew the fight must have arrived and apparently sooner than expected.

Another uproar suddenly split the air, and this one had a note of amazement and confusion. Pushing himself slowly upright, Sinjin waited for the dizziness to pass. A moment later, he nearly fell over backward. The *Dragon's Wing* raced across the desert, leaving a swirling cloud of dust in its wake. Directly above the ship flew Valterius, and behind him came the rest of the flock. The crew of the *Dragon's Wing* and the Drakon had come to save him. He'd never felt so grateful and so terrified all at the same time. They should not be there. War was upon them, and now everything Sinjin cared about was in its path, and it was all his fault. The weight of responsibility was his as a leader, but this wasn't the same. If he'd only done something differently, then they wouldn't have risked everything to come here looking for him.

Doing his best to wave and jump up and down without falling over, Sinjin somehow managed to get the attention of those aboard the *Dragon's Wing.*

"There!" Brother Vaughn's voice carried across the tension-filled air.

Valterius saw him then and swooped in front of the *Dragon's Wing.* Soldiers from the Midlands lined up with long spears, ready to hold off a charge.

"They're on our side!" Sinjin cried out desperately. "Don't attack!" His words were heard, but the men held their ground, and Sinjin ran screaming toward the lines, ready to tear the spears from the men's hands. "Those are my people!"

The shrill note in Sinjin's voice cut through the din, and someone cried out, "Hold your formation! Lower your weapons! Allow them to approach. If they make an aggressive move, leave none alive."

Sinjin's heart was on the verge of breaking as the *Dragon's Wing* gradually lowered and slowed until she skimmed the sands; then she slowed abruptly and jerked to a stop. Valterius flew ahead and landed in front of Sinjin, using his wings to shield Sinjin, daring anyone to threaten him. Where had this sentiment been when the dragon had left him there? Sinjin wondered. At least his mount had returned for him and with help.

The Drakon landed behind Valterius and assumed defensive postures.

"Please remain calm," Sinjin said. "These are my people, and they mean you no harm. They have simply come to get me because my dragon left me here." He cast a reproachful look at Valterius, who didn't even have the decency to look apologetic. Sinjin turned to the Drakon. "These people have treated me fairly, and they've battled the ferals for years. We share a common foe; we share a common cause, and I will stand with them." He knew he gave those from the Heights more credit than they deserved, but it would serve none of them to fight among themselves with the ferals preparing their attack.

Looking out to the desert, Sinjin saw black dragons there, bringing troops ever closer. These troops were far ahead of the others, but they were safe. Even if an attack were launched against them, they would have sufficient time to fall back to the main force. If no attack came, then the ferals had established a forward presence. It was a brilliant tactic, and one Sinjin could think of no defense against, and those facts frightened him terribly.

* * *

Feeling tingly all over, Sinjin strapped himself into the saddle and looked around. It could not truly be real. He could not really be on some previously unknown continent about to fight ferals adragonback. Around him could not truly be the Drakon, and surely the *Dragon's Wing* did not rest on her side in the middle of the desert.

The air grew chilly, and the skies were clear, allowing the full moon and the comets to cast the world in a mystical hue. Nothing seemed real to Sinjin's eye. He had to be dreaming. Gwen watched him from nearby, her right leg fidgeting, as it always did when she was nervous, and flames dripped from her fingers. She hadn't said anything to him, but she did surprise him with a quick hug--too quick--before he mounted. Complicated thoughts ran through Sinjin's mind, but he had to push them aside. The dragon riders from the Heights were about to mount the first assault, and the Drakon would fly in support, though he knew there wasn't a great deal they could do. Each had been armed with a sword and a lance, even though they all knew engaging ferals in midair would mean a quick death.

Pelivor stood not far from Gwen, talking with Brother Vaughn, who was doing his best to coordinate with the men from the Heights and from the Midlands. It was chaotic but both groups knew they needed allies. They were still outmatched, but at least the outsider had brought some power to the fight. Sinjin wasn't yet convinced how much help the Drakon would be. They had never flown in battle; most had only a few hours in the saddle, and Sinjin cursed himself for not preparing them better. There simply hadn't been enough time. The events of the world raged around him, and he seemed to have precious little control over the course of events.

Lights moved through the sky as the verdant dragons approached bearing fire and pitch, a dangerous combination. In each claw the dragons held huge cisterns filled with burning pitch, and the wooden structures on their backs, the things they called tierre, were lit up from within.

Valterius sprang into the air, which caused a minor uproar among the troops. Regal dragons were nimble and quick in comparison to their formidable cousins. The Drakon followed closely. Sinjin found the front of the formation to be just about the loneliest place in the world. With Valterius beneath him, he could never be alone, and even if the dragon tested his patience with alarming regularity, he could no longer imagine his life without him. They were a unit, even if a dysfunctional one.

Valterius took them higher. Ferals flew low over their soldiers, while others continued to bring more men and demons. From above, they looked like swarming insects, and Sinjin knew these bore a far more potent sting. The first of the verdants swooped in without a sound save the roar of the wind over its wings and the fanned flames. Sinjin could only imagine how hot those flaming cisterns must be, but the verdants showed their strength. Time seemed to slow as the first verdant released its grip on a cistern, which slowly tumbled away before striking the sands and erupting into flame. Screams rose from the flames, and those who were not on fire were illuminated brightly. The verdant released the second cistern and it struck a feral on its way down, raining fire across a wide expanse. Black smoke now clogged the air over the sands. The instant the verdant released the second cistern, the ferals below attacked as one.

That was when Sinjin saw the feral queen. Though not as large as a verdant, or even the smaller verdant Jehregard, the feral queen radiated fear. Flying at the fullest of her abilities, the queen came. Atop her back sat a wisp of a girl with dark hair streaming behind her. She didn't even look to be strapped in. With a flick of her hand, she cast red lightning and fire at the lead verdant. Those within the tierre hurled flaming clay pots at the ferals, and one struck the feral queen at about the same time the girl's fire struck the tierre. A thunderous boom sounded, and droplets of fire were cast high and far, like one of Brother Milo's fireworks.

More verdants released their cisterns, illuminating the clouds of smoke from below and casting huge shadows that danced and writhed. The black army advanced, and screams rose up from behind Sinjin as the ferals attacked from the rear, using the night skies to their advantage and sneaking in low over the Cloud Forest. More ferals attacked the verdants from above. The verdants did what they could to defend themselves, but the girl riding the feral queen used her power to turn their own weapons against them, sending dragons crashing to the sands in flames. Regal dragons were not immune to the danger, and Sinjin felt the pain as if it were his own when he saw Drakon struck down. The world was in chaos, and all Sinjin could do at that moment was hold on. Valterius made a series of sudden and violent maneuvers, and Sinjin would have protested if he could have spoken, but then he saw the feral bearing down on them, eyes locked on Valterius's neck.

Sinjin used the staff and the stirrups to help him endure the forces applied by such sudden changes in direction. Something crashed into them, and Sinjin saw Halmsa thrusting his lance into the breast of a feral dragon. Such strength! The lance was torn from the man's hand as the feral flashed by, but the sound of the dragon striking sand that followed was unmistakable. The jolt had shifted his grip on the staff, and he loosened his hold on it enough to slide his hand back up. In that same instant, Valterius veered sideways. Sinjin's grip closed around the staff at the same moment he saw the reason for the evasive action. The feral queen was bearing down on them, and the girl drew back her balled fist, which leaked fire.

Sinjin's fingers landed in the impressions left by his mother's grip; a cold, tingling feeling made the hair on his arm stand, and his own muscles tightened. His fingers clenched of their own volition and no matter how hard his mind tried to release the staff, his hand would not obey. He could feel his mother then, as if she were there with him, as if she had prepared this moment just for him. It was an odd feeling to have, but that was how he felt. Power surged through him, and he felt as if part of him were being washed away, like a dead shell being blasted away. Suddenly he could smell more acutely, and his vision focused on things he shouldn't be able to see. Even his thoughts raced so quickly that the world moved slowly.

The girl mouthed some words as she approached, and Sinjin could feel the compulsion to let down his guard, to accept his coming death, to make it quick and painless. It would be a gift. That was when he felt his mother's presence more strongly than ever before, more strongly even than when she had been alive. He channeled her energy, her love, her care, and he focused it into single-minded intent. To his utter amazement, a blast of crystalline light shimmered and raced from his outstretched hand. With blinding brightness it illuminated the shock on the girl's face, and it struck before she could release her own attack. With such force that Sinjin thought he might have killed her, the girl was blasted from the back of the dragon and disappeared into a column of smoke.

The feral queen continued forward, and the impact jarred Sinjin so hard, he thought he might have broken his jaw. Valterius spun three times before righting himself, and Sinjin could feel and taste the blood on his cheek. Looking down, he tried to find the girl, and it didn't take long to locate her. He'd expected to see her broken form lying still, but instead she was rimmed with fire and leading a far more organized charge against those from the Midlands. Verdants continued to rain fire on the black armies, but those weapons were too dangerous to use anywhere close to the fighting. It would do no good for those from the Heights to kill those from the Midlands; the two had been aligned for hundreds of years, even if Sinjin had heard hints of ongoing tension between the two. It would appear, at least, that they could work together when threatened by a common foe.

Valterius took them higher and did his best to disengage from the conflict; it was apparent to Sinjin that his mount was shaken. Below them, the battle played out, and Sinjin was horrified by what he saw. From his vantage, it was clear they had no chance. Casualties were already starting to mount, and they had no reserves, no reinforcements, no second chances. No matter how much he wanted it, there was no way to go back, no way for his loved ones to escape.

A deep grunt of exertion was the only warning Sinjin received before the feral queen swept into his vision from his periphery. Still gripping the staff, Sinjin waited until he could see the queen's pupils then he exerted his will. The power still flowed through him, but even so, he'd had doubts. But the staff rewarded him by issuing another blast of crystallized light that sent rainbows in all directions. This one struck the feral queen on the bridge of her long snout. Lightning crawled over the dragon's face, eyes, and nostrils. Her head smoking, the feral queen dropped away.

Sinjin would have urged Valterius to go after the queen, but he could feel the irregularity of their flight. Valterius was hurt. Sinjin let the lines go slack, and Valterius circled lower, landing behind the *Dragon's Wing,* where Pelivor and Gwen were rallying the crew. Pelivor unleashed devastating attacks, and Sinjin thought of Koe. Reaching his hand into his pocket, he pulled the carved cat free, and he could feel the vast store of energy trapped within, just waiting for his will to release it. The rush of it made Sinjin's body vibrate, and he began to go numb from it. In the span of the next breath, he had to react or die. The feral queen came in low and quiet, her claws extended toward Sinjin and Valterius. He didn't have time to think, and energy simply leaped from the staff toward the approaching dragon.

Koe thrummed in Sinjin's hand, and the staff focused the combined energy. Lightning struck the feral queen again in the face, and as soon as it connected, the line of liquid plasma pulsed and grew brighter as more and more energy flowed between them. The massive dragon's skull lit up from within, and Sinjin could see the underlying bone structure. It lasted only a moment, but the outline of it was burned into Sinjin's vision and would not go away. The feral queen could withstand no more and crashed into the trees in the distance; the sound of the snapping timber was horrific.

It was a hollow victory, Sinjin knew. The feral queen had not been in charge of this army; it was the wisp of a girl. Sinjin thought of Trinda and knew better than to underestimate the childlike. When his dragon responded to his input and came in for a very awkward landing, Sinjin's concern grew. Running his hands over Valterius, his fingers found a jagged rib and another that caused the dragon to flinch. The saddle was making it worse, by the looks of it, and Sinjin didn't hesitate. He put Koe back in his pocket, drew his belt knife, and cut the saddle free. Unrestricted, Valterius gave him a trembling woof of thanks and took back to the air. Sinjin could only hope he found safety there.

Chapter 21

Rare moments exist where the actions of one forever change the world.
--Imeteri, slave

* * *

Bright light on the horizon caused a momentary distraction, and Sinjin gulped in as much air as he could. The end was near, and this might be what finished them. He knew not what horror approached, but he could do nothing to stop it. No matter how much power the staff contained, his body could take only so much. A vast well of power remained available to him, yet he felt that he would simply burn into a wisp of smoke if he let any more of that power flow through him. His hands trembled, and his knees felt weak. Only the sight of his friends fighting for their lives kept him upright. Benjin was under pressure from three demons, and Gwen was cut off from him, unable to protect her father's back as she had been. Pelivor was at his own end from the effort of keeping the ferals at a distance; Sinjin had no idea how the man was still standing after releasing far more power than Sinjin had.

The light drew closer, and he could see that there were clusters of light, many of them, and that light cast shadows over hulking wooden forms: ships. At the bow of one ship stood a diminutive form in a deep red dress, her blonde hair flowing behind her, and as always, a dour expression on her face. Much of the blinding light coursed from her outstretched fingers and formed a web between the flying ships. Sinjin heard the dark armies could do such things, but never would he have guessed that Trinda could as well. She landed her flat-bottomed ship within a few feet of the *Dragon's Wing.*

From the deck of another ship came a different hue. Standing at the prow were Jharmin Kyte and Lady Lissa. He had never seen the lady before, but he knew her instantly; the resemblance to his mother was painful to witness. Sinjin's grip tightened on the staff even knowing he couldn't use it. The greenish tint came from the flames that danced around Jharmin, who used strategic attacks of green and orange fire to clear a perimeter around the ships, while Trinda plucked ferals from the skies with incredible accuracy. The tide of the battle had changed already, and when the sides of the ships dropped open, a flood of people from the Godfist and the Greatland alike charged out in precise order, rank and file.

The first group that emerged carried shields, save a few among them with long pikes. They established themselves along the perimeter

Jharmin had created. Half went to their knees, and the other half stood behind them, forming a dense matrix of shields. Already the attacks from Trinda and Jharmin were slowing, but the line was established and more soldiers charged out. Each of these carried a bow over a shoulder and ran with cupped hands--hands that leaked blinding light. Kneeling down behind those with shields, the first rank uncapped their hands and set glowing orbs onto the sand. After cocking the odd-looking crossbows they carried, they loaded what Sinjin now recognized as herald globes. His mother had created them as a way to provide light within Dragonhold and as a way to grow food, and now they were poised to act as tools of war. Sinjin couldn't help but hope they were potent weapons in spite of his mother's original intentions.

Looking down on him, Trinda gave him a wry smile. "I told you that you'd need something from me someday, and even though you weren't always nice to me, I won't make you ask." She raised her voice to her troops. "Fire!"

On her command, the first volley was released, and dozens of bright lights flashed overhead, further illuminating the battlefield. The ferals, demons, and soldiers had been driven back, and the dark-haired girl was at the heart of the seething mass. Each herald globe struck with concussive force that made the ground tremble. Sand and whatever else within close proximity was thrown into the air and it rained down for long moments after each attack. Those under Trinda's command were calm and efficient, and rather than a hurried and haphazard process of reloading or rotating, the shields parted and a wave of runners sprinted onto the battlefield, looking for the globes. Despite being made mostly of glass, they all rested, unharmed, at the center of circles of destruction.

Every globe was retrieved in the lull after the attack; the runners did nothing else. With speed and efficiency, they were back within the shelter of the shields before the remaining demons and soldiers regained their senses. From the ships charged a new volley, and that alone might be enough to secure an unlikely victory. Sinjin had no time to react to the fact that he recognized Kendra within the ranks of the runners; how she had come to be there was a mystery, but he had no time for conjecture.

By the time the crossbows were loaded, the dark-haired girl had regained her feet and stood at the center of the destruction. Her armies were in tatters, and already many of her dragons were dead; she was defeated, yet she didn't look the part. Defiant, she strutted forward, her arm raised and her fist extended. A fierce wind blew back the smoke and cleared the air, making the girl easy to see. She was plainly dressed in what looked more like boy's clothes, and it was clear that she'd been through a great deal. Sinjin wondered what could have led her to such a place, but she would accept no empathy from him, that was clear. Within her eyes raged a maddened fire that spoke of unyielding conviction, and few things were as dangerous as unyielding conviction.

"I will not let you beat me!" the girl shouted through her tears.

Sinjin wanted to console this girl, wanted her to understand that they were not enemies. He could see in her face and posture that her heart was broken, and despite his greatest desire, there was nothing he could do to fix it.

Then she did the most terrible thing imaginable. She reached into the land and turned it into a weapon. It was not the soil she called upon, but everything that lived within. And she did not ask these creatures for their service; she yanked them from where they hid and hurled them over the row of shields. Snakes, lizards, scorpions, stinging insects, spiders, mites, and a host of others lashed out at whatever was nearby. Screams erupted from within the ranks. This girl was subverting nature itself. Sinjin realized how great the extent when he saw wolves loping from the trees. They would be beset from both sides.

Trinda also saw the attacks coming, and Sinjin could see the word forming on her lips. He wanted to shout, to tell her no, but he was too late. "Fire!" she shouted.

The second volley raced toward where the girl stood tall. Sinjin watched the fiery globes race toward her before slowing. They were doomed; the girl would use their own potent attack against them. Something happened then that defied explanation. A dark shape burst from the tree line, driven by the wolves and other animals sent to attack the combined forces gathered there. Low and sleek, this shape continued, avoiding man and wolf and heading straight for the girl. She still held the globes in the air over her head, and she looked as if she would lob them back at any moment until she saw the shape approaching. For an instant Sinjin thought the girl would blast the poor creature out of existence, but something changed in her expression. Was that recognition?

The shape slowed then and approached the girl with its trembling body hugging the ground. What Sinjin saw was a sizable but terrified cat. The girl stood motionless, caught between two worlds, caught between two selves; Sinjin could see the struggle on her face. The herald globes slowly drifted down and gently came to rest in the sand around her, illuminating her and the cat for all to see. Tears fell to the sand. After closing the last distance between them, the cat tentatively head-butted her leg.

A mournful wail formed on the girl's lips, and it cast a spell of silence on the rest of the world. Regret, remorse, pain, and longing all mixed together and brought tears to all who heard it. The cat stood on its hind legs and pressed its head into her hand, and she scratched behind its ears as if by reflex. Movement in Sinjin's periphery caught his attention. An old man limped out of the trees. The wolves and other creatures were already dispersing and paid him no mind, nor he they. He limped slowly but with single-minded purpose onto the battlefield and toward the girl and the cat.

"What kind of trouble have you gotten yourself into?" he asked.

The girl turned upon hearing the words and sobbed when she saw him. "I'm sorry. I'm so sorry!"

The man looked as if he would say something more, but the girl didn't give him a chance; instead, she reached down and picked up the cat before turning and running back into the desert, back toward the jungle, and Sinjin could not believe his eyes.

The old man turned to him and shook his head. "I do believe that girl just stole my cat."

Epilogue

Beneath the Terhilian Lovers met the Council of the Known Lands, a newly formed body meant to foster peace in the world. Sinjin looked at those around the huge table, which had been flown in for the occasion, and he could imagine no more unlikely allies.

"The girl's a good kid," Thundegar Rheams said during his testimony. "She lost everything she had, and I think she just snapped. That cat gave her something to hold on to, something to believe in. Before anyone goes in there after her, I'd ask you to think about that." The conviction in his words spoke as strongly as the tears rimming his eyes.

"I make a motion to declare peace with Allette Kilbor," Jharmin Kyte said, "until such a time as she initiates hostile action."

"I second the motion," Trinda Hollis, the child queen, said. Afterward she cast Sinjin a look that said, *I, too, deserve forgiveness.*"

She had a point. Sinjin gave her a smile and a nod.

"All in favor say aye," the lord chancellor said.

The provisions had been mostly agreed upon months prior to the meeting, but it was a relief to have them formalized.

"Within my power as lord chancellor of the Heights," he continued, "I do commit all resources, including our dragons and their riders, to the defense and support of the Council of the Known Lands, which shall meet here biannually to reconfirm this commitment."

Sinjin tried to imagine what the world look like now that they were all connected and could communicate with each other. Already trade relationships were forming, and there was talk of a common message delivery system. Change was a certainty.

"As lord of Wolfhold, I, Jharmin Kyte, do commit all my resources and power to the cause of the Council of the Known Lands."

Sinjin smiled; his uncle wasn't one to overburden a subject.

"I, Trinda Hollis, guardian of Dragonhold, do commit all my resources toward the defense and support of the council, but I must retain the sovereignty of my hold, for that is my charge. I welcome trade but I must reserve the right to refuse entrance in the absence of sufficient cause."

Sinjin tried to forgive her, but she had certainly duped him, and he couldn't help the sting. And now she would risk the treaty by denying him access to her hold.

"We've all heard the argument," Nat Dersinger said, not sounding much happier than when he'd committed his resources to the cause. "I personally object, but I'll not stand in the way of a vote."

"I make the motion to grant the lady the right to sovereignty unless this body deems necessary," Sinjin said, surprising even himself.

Trinda cast him a hurt look.

"I second the motion," Lissa Kyte said. Sinjin tried not to stare at her. They still hadn't officially met, which was no accident.

The Midlands and Madra of Far Massing committed themselves without qualification, and Sinjin knew this was the beginning of a new age. Kendra sat beside him, but he tried not to look at her either. One wrong move could get him decked, and that wasn't the image he wanted to project to the council. She was a fiery woman, of that there could be no doubt. Her appearance on the battlefield had been a complete shock, and though Sinjin was sorry to hear of her mother's demise, he was grateful it had allowed her to come back to him.

Never would he have guessed that she would bond with the second clutch. This was in ways even more of an honor than being in the first clutch. What Kendra and her clutchmates had were proof that regal dragons were a viable species and could reproduce on their own. There had been much worry that regal eggs would be sterile, but Gerhonda, Kendra's dragon, had proven them all wrong when she hatched.

Sinjin smiled at the memory of telling her how he had bonded Valterius and the look on her face when the same thing worked for her. Seeing Kendra with her dragon never ceased to put a smile on Sinjin's face; passion and life had returned to her eyes.

"In the massive power granted to me as someone cast into the Cloud Forest to die, I, Thundegar Rheams, do commit my considerable resources to the Council of the Known Lands. Oh, and if you do happen to run across the girl, tell her I'd appreciate having my cat back. I rather liked that cat."

* * *

Life at Windhold suited Sinjin, and he began to feel more at peace. There were questions that might never be answered, but he accepted some of the mystery. Rebuilding their lives, fortifying Windhold, and maintaining their newly established responsibilities were challenges that kept him busy and kept his mind from darker thoughts. Still some things nagged at him; he could go all day and not think about the past, but as he laid himself down for sleep at night, those fears and memories visited themselves upon him.

On this day he needed to deliver a message to Nat Dersinger. A distasteful task, perhaps, but the time alone with Valterius was worth it. Flying had become more and more natural to Sinjin, and he found that he no longer minded the sudden movements. Just like his grandfather had told him about horses, you could usually see the next move coming if you watched the body language; it had just taken a while for Sinjin to learn the language. Now he could lean in to turns and work with his dragon instead of responding after the fact.

Valterius had been unusually placid for this entire day, and Sinjin wondered if perhaps his dragon was simply happy to be with him as well. It seemed less likely when Valterius flew over the Falcon Isles and never slowed, ignoring Sinjin's request to land and do what they had come there for--at least what *he* had come there for. His dragon, it seemed, had other ideas. Knowing how much work awaited him at Windhold, Sinjin couldn't hide his annoyance. Valterius ignored him.

The longer they flew, the more concerned Sinjin became. Surely he could trust Valterius by now, but Kendra would worry if he didn't return when he'd said he would, and that was a sure way to get decked. Still Valterius flew and Sinjin let his anxieties go. Somehow, no matter what, everything would be all right. That feeling lasted until Sinjin saw a spire of black stone rising from deep water. There was nothing else for leagues in any direction, and he knew this must be where Valterius wanted to go. The place looked ancient, and he could see no doorways, windows, or other openings. Valterius circled over the ominous spire, and there appeared to be no way to get in from the top either. Crying out, Valterius continued to circle.

For a long moment, nothing happened. Then the seas around the spire started to roil. Some force sent water flying away from the stone tower, and a gap opened in the waves. Deeper the gap grew as more and more water was cast aside, revealing a gaping hole in the side of the black keep. Sinjin wanted nothing to do with that quick route to death, but Valterius was making the decisions, and he trimmed his wings, sending them into a steep dive, as he seemed to do any time Sinjin opened his mouth to object.

The waves continued to yield to the unknown force, and Valterius swooped into the darkness. Once within, he immediately changed direction and shot straight up. Not terribly far above, he alighted on a stone roost that seemed to have been custom made for just such a purpose. Water rushed back in to fill the keep below them, and Sinjin knew the keep was sealed along with his fate. There would be no escape unless whatever it was that had let him in decided to also let him go.

Valterius turned his head and looked at Sinjin as if to say, *Get off.* Sinjin had seen that look before. After unbuckling himself, Sinjin slid down to the stone and took a moment to stretch his sore legs and back. He often told Valterius that dragons made lousy furniture. The regal dragon looked at him as if her were daft then pushed him toward the massive stair leading from the chamber.

Realizing there was no sense in delaying the inevitable, Sinjin climbed the wide stair, feeling insignificant amid the scale of the architecture. He couldn't help but wonder how and why anyone would have constructed such a place, and who or what might live there. After crossing what seemed a too-large landing, Sinjin saw something very unexpected. Plush carpets lined the wide halls, and row after row of shelves held books of all description. An oversized fire filled a gaping hearth, and elaborately carved sofas and chairs awaited nearby where the air was just the right temperature.

Trees grew amid the carpeted halls, and freshly fallen fruit lay uneaten. Light filtered down from above, and Sinjin wondered what could be the source. He'd seen no openings in the roof of the place, yet it felt like the light of the sun on his face. Another staircase spiraled up from that room, and Sinjin was shocked to see a mighty stag standing on the masterfully cut stairs. Part of him wanted to see where the stairs led, but something pulled him forward; perhaps it was the sound of running water. Regardless, he found himself moving in that direction.

Around a bend he found the source of the sound; within a chamber whose ceiling was lined with moss-covered stone was what looked like a wading pool, like someplace one might expect to see a fountain. There was no fountain, but there was a figure sitting there with its back to Sinjin. He approached slowly, despite knowing that he had been allowed to enter by whomever this was.

Then the figure stood and turned and pulled back the hood of her robes. Clear, translucent hair fell alongside a beautiful face, one that Sinjin could never forget.

"I'm sorry," Catrin said.

Sinjin was dumfounded and stood in mute shock.

"I'm sorry you grieved for me. It was the only way I believed I could save you. Only by making the ferals believe I was dead could I give you a chance at life, and look at what you've done for yourself!"

Sinjin tried for a moment to understand how she could know what he had or hadn't done.

"Please, sit with me."

Doing as his mother asked, Sinjin tried to figure out if he was livid, grateful, happy, or all those feelings at once.

"I've done what I can to help you and to nudge events in the right direction."

Even that justification fell flat.

"Kyrien knew of this place," his mother continued. "It was among the only places where the ferals wouldn't be able to find me. Fortunately, it's a well-kept secret."

"Getting in and out is no treat," Sinjin grumbled and Catrin laughed. Hearing that laugh lightened his soul, and he couldn't stay angry with her for long. Doing what he should have done the instant he saw her, Sinjin wrapped her in an embrace and refused to let go. "Don't *ever* do that to me again," he said, giving her an extra squeeze. He noticed when she sat that she favored her right leg.

"It only hurts when it's wet outside," she said in response to his look, and he couldn't help but laugh.

After sitting back down beside the pool, Sinjin noticed for the first time the tree that grew closest to the pool, it was little more than a sapling, but it bore two deep green leaves encase in crystals.

"A gift," his mother said.

It was then that Sinjin really looked at the pool. What had looked like a simple fish pond changed as he gazed within. He began to think of Dragonhold, and within the fountain, the Godfist came into view. It was unmistakable from above. A glance at his mother revealed her grin. "It's one of the seven great magics of the last age," she said.

"Seven magics?"

"This is the Well of Sight," his mother said, and just hearing her voice restored him. "The Staff of Life is another, and the Statues of Terhilian are considered one. The Keystones you've seen as well; they allow communication over great distances."

"That's only four," Sinjin said, and his mother nodded.

"Some mysteries, my son, still remain."

The story continues in the *Artifacts of Power* trilogy.

About the Author

Born in Salem, New Jersey, Brian spent much of his childhood on the family farm, where his family raised and trained Standardbred racehorses. Brian lives with his wife, Tracey, in the foothills of the Blue Ridge Mountains.

More information at BrianRathbone.com

9 781945 465079